READER'S DIGEST
BOOKS

With the exception of actual personages identified as such, the characters and incidents in the fictional selections in this volume are entirely the product of the authors' imaginations and have no relation to any person or event in real life.

www.readersdigest.co.uk

The Reader's Digest Association Limited 11 Westferry Circus Canary Wharf London E14 4HE

For information as to ownership of copyright in the material of this book, and acknowledgments, see last page.

Printed in France
ISBN 0 276 42989 3

READER'S DIGEST BOOKS

Selected and condensed by Reader's Digest

THE READER'S DIGEST ASSOCIATION LIMITED, LONDON

CONTENTS

THE MURDER ARTIST page 9

John Case

Alex Callahan is visiting a fairground with his six-year-old identical twins when the unthinkable happens—they disappear into thin air. After a frantic search he calls the police, but it soon becomes clear that if Alex wants to find his sons he will have to hunt for them himself. A gripping thriller that takes readers into the fascinating and strange worlds of magic and voodoo, where nothing is quite what it seems.

PUBLISHED BY HEINEMANN

START FROM HERE page 165

Sean French

Mark Foll has no career, no steady partner, no goals in life—just a dull job in insurance. One day, feeling bored, he decides to stick his neck out and ask for work that is 'more fun'. The result? He's despatched to Suffolk with a colleague to report on the progress of a local campaign against a waste-disposal company suspected of causing cancer. Suddenly, for the first time in his life, Mark is forced to decide what he really stands for.

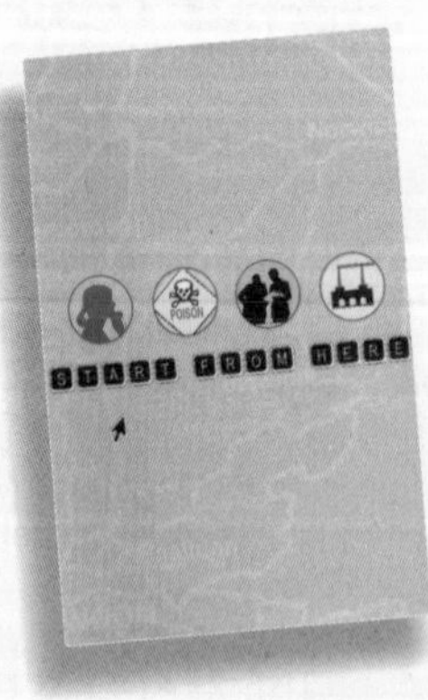

PUBLISHED BY PICADOR

AT RISK page 295

Stella Rimington

When the intelligence services learn that a terrorist strike is planned against a UK target, MI5's Liz Carlyle is asked to find out who's behind it and what, or who, is the target. Her investigations take her to the Norfolk coast, where pieces of the puzzle start to come together . . . In her debut spy novel, the former Director-General of MI5 draws on her own first-hand knowledge of the British intelligence community.

PUBLISHED BY HUTCHINSON

THE No.1 LADIES' DETECTIVE AGENCY page 437

Alexander McCall Smith

If your husband goes missing or you're the victim of fraud, and you live near Gabarone, you need to find Mma Ramotswe, owner of Botswana's first female detective agency. With her special blend of down-to-earth wisdom and insight, this lady delivers results every time. Alexander McCall Smith's award-winning best seller offers a glimpse into a world where courtesy and old-fashioned values still reign.

PUBLISHED BY POLYGON

THE MURDER ARTIST

JOHN CASE

One minute they're there,
the next they're gone.

In a heartbeat, Alex Callahan's life is changed for ever as he realises that his six-year-old sons, Kevin and Sean, are missing.

CHAPTER ONE

Five hours of sleep. I rub my eyes, head out front, and bend down to extract my rolled-up copy of the *Washington Post* from beneath an azalea bush. I never know where I'm going to find the thing; whoever pitches it never got past T-ball.

'Good morning! Beautiful day in the neighbourhood.' It's Yasmin Siegel, my eightysomething neighbour from across the street, with her black Lab, Cookie.

'I guess.' I slide the paper out from its plastic sleeve.

'Seriously, Alex, a day like *this* in Washington, DC!' She shakes her head in disbelief. 'It's a gift. End of May? You can get some real stinkers. You enjoy it, you and those boys.'

'I was hoping for rain,' I tell her, looking up at the blue sky.

'Ri-ight,' Yasmin chuckles. 'O-*kay*, Cookie. I get the message.' She gives me a jaunty wave and heads toward the park.

Actually, I *was* hoping for rain. I check the weather map on the back of the Metro section, just in case. No. No rapidly moving front, no storm pelting towards DC from Canada. A beautiful day.

In the house, I set up the coffee machine. While I wait for it to do its thing, I put out bowls and spoons for the boys, pour two glasses of orange juice, and get the box of Cheerios down from the cabinet.

The problem with the beautiful day is that I've got work to do, last-minute cuts on a piece scheduled to air tonight. But I promised the boys—my six-year-old twins—that every Saturday they could pick out some kind of excursion. And they're dead set on this Renaissance

Faire, which is way out past Annapolis. The drive alone will take more than an hour each way. It'll kill the whole day.

And since this is the boys' first visit since Christmas—and only their second visit since Liz and I separated—this is the first of these excursions. No way I can bail.

I tell myself there's nothing for it. I need to make the cuts in time to drop off the file at the station on our way out of town.

The boys and I are doing great so far—although after only six days, I'm already wiped out. This would make Liz happy, both the sleep deprivation and the fact that after less than a week I'm already falling behind at work. She built in the time crunch when she set up the conditions for the visit. She wouldn't let me take the boys on a trip, for instance. 'How can I compete,' she said, 'if every time they're with you, it's a vacation?' (I took the kids skiing in Utah during my allotted four days at Christmas.)

What Liz wants is a month of 'regular life,' as she puts it. She works full-time at the Children's Museum in Portland, Maine. She wants me to experience the reality, 24/7, of having kids and a job, wants me to hassle with car pools, laundry, bedtimes, picky eating habits, friends. If there's any chance for a reconciliation, being a single parent for a month will force me to put family first.

Instead of work. In the station's official bio, I'm the guy who 'goes after the toughest stories in the hardest places'. This has won me several awards, but it's beginning to look as if it might cost me my marriage. And my family. I was in Moscow when the twins took their first steps, in Kosovo when Kev broke his arm, in Mazar-al-Sharif on their first day of kindergarten.

'You'll probably see more of the boys this month than you have for the past two years,' Liz said. 'Maybe you'll even like it.'

Coffee's ready. I splash some milk into it.

The thing is I *do* like having them around, even with the hassles. Turns out, that routine stuff is when you really get to know your kids. I forgot how much fun they are, their bursts of insight, the earnest concentration they bring to certain tasks. How much I missed them.

This Renaissance thing, though—I'm *not* looking forward to that. I'm guessing it will be a hokey and overpriced tour through what amounts to a faux Elizabethan amusement park. Costumed knights and ladies. Jousts and faked swordplay. Jugglers and magicians. Not my kind of thing. Not at all. I tried to promote a baseball game, a trip to the zoo, a movie and pizza—but the boys have been relentless about the festival ever since they caught the ad on TV.

It all seems kind of lame to me, and I made the mistake of saying that to Liz last night on the phone—looking for a little good-natured mutual grumbling about parenthood.

What I got instead was a lecture. Didn't I get it that what parents enjoy is their *kids*' enjoyment? 'And here I was going to compliment you on finding something that fitted in so well with their after-school enrichment programme,' Liz said. 'I should have known.' She explained that the boys have been up to their ears in Arthurian lore.

This had gone right by me; although once Liz mentioned it, I realised the kids had been rattling on about the Round Table. And they'd spent hours in the backyard duelling with plastic swords.

OK, so I demonstrated a lack of curiosity about the plastic swords—is that so bad? Or is Liz right and I'm the most self-absorbed parent on the planet?

I drop down into the chair in front of the iMac in my study. I tap a key and wait for the screen to shimmer out of sleep mode. My segment—'Afghan Wedding'—was all wrapped and ready until nine last night, when I got the word that the addition of some promotional clips meant I had to cut another two minutes. I made the logical cuts last night, but I still need to lose forty-four seconds.

Originally 'Afghan Wedding' was part of an hour-long special about Afghanistan, pegged around a Donald Rumsfeld visit to that beleaguered country. I got a nice long interview with him about the postwar recovery. And then there was a pastiche of feel-good stuff about life in liberated Kabul and Kandahar. Capped off with the wedding: Afghan couple celebrates long-postponed nuptials.

The wedding was to take place in a village near Kandahar. A safe zone, or so we were told. The crew and I got there with our equipment. The wedding got started on time. And then the happy occasion turned into a nightmare when the crew of an off-course US F-16 seeking a rumoured Taliban conclave misread the wedding tableau on the ground. Four killed, fifteen wounded.

The segment was removed from the hour-long progress report about Afghanistan. Now the wedding footage was going to be part of an ambitious show about collateral damage.

I cue up my segment on the iMac.

'Dad, can we eat breakfast in the TV room and watch cartoons?'

I jump. Liz took off with the kids more than six months ago and one week into their visit, I'm still not used to the way they just *materialise.* 'Jeez, I gotta put bells on you guys.'

Kevin laughs. Sean says, 'Can we?'

I shrug. 'Why not?'

Kevin asks, 'When are we going to the Renaissance festival?'

'I'm thinking . . . noon.'

'No way!' Kev complains. 'We'll miss the whole thing.'

'Kevin,' his brother tells him, 'it doesn't even *start* till eleven. And it goes on till seven.' Then, because he's just learned to tell time, Sean adds: 'p.m.'

Kevin gives his brother a look. 'No kidding, p.m.' He turns to me. 'You promise? Noon?'

I pretend to think about it. 'Nahhhh, I can't *promise.*'

The two of them moan in chorus: '*Daaaaad.*'

At least they know, after a week, when I'm kidding. The first couple of days, worried looks flashed from one to the other. To say they'd forgotten my sense of humour understates it: they'd forgotten what I'm like—a depressing reminder that six months had been just about long enough to turn me into a stranger to my sons.

When the kids are gone, I cue up the bits of footage I picked out last night for possible cuts. I lean back to watch. And I decide that maybe the dark-man sequence has to go. It's thirty-eight seconds long and if I can live without it, I'm just about home free.

The dark man is one of the bride's brothers. The ceremony is over and he's holding his weapon in one outstretched hand. With a loopy grin on his face, he squeezes off a few rounds in sheer jubilation. Just as the camera closes on the man's gleeful face, the whole screen jumps. That jolt was, in fact, the impact of the first bomb from the F-16. The man hurtles through the air. Then he's propped up against a rock, powdered in dust, eyes dazed, blood seeping from an ear. Then the camera shifts to the bride staring at the face of her fatally wounded groom. I wind it back, check the frame counter. The sequence is good, but it's peripheral. I tap a few keys and it's gone.

I tinker with a cut I made last night and I shave off the remaining few seconds I need. I freeze the screen when the kids come in to remind me that it's time to go. '*Past* time to go,' Kev says. 'Almost twelve thirty.'

'Let's go-ohhhh!'

'Let's be off,' Kevin says in a funny, stilted voice—a *knightly* voice, I realise.

'Yes! Your loyal servants Sean and Kevin beg thee!'

Suddenly, I'm engulfed by the two of them: the towheaded Lord Kevin and his mirror image, Sir Sean. They tug at my sleeves.

With a sigh, I reach for the mouse. 'OK.'

'Who's that?' Sean asks, pointing at the monitor.

I paused on a frame that shows the groom's face, his eyes wild, his face obscured by a skein of blood.

'Just a guy,' I tell him. I right click and cut the frames.

'What's the matter with him?' Kevin asks as the haunted and battered face of the wounded groom disappears from the screen.

I click through the shutdown procedure, then pop out the disk. 'He was scared,' I say.

'Why?'

'Because he was in a war, and he was hurt and that's . . . scary.'

Sean bursts for the door, but Kevin stays where he is, big blue eyes locked on me. 'Is that man going to die?'

I hesitate. Finally, I say, 'Yeah.'

'Dad? Were you there . . . with that man?'

'Yes.'

'Couldn't you help him?'

I take a breath. 'No. No one could help him.'

Kevin nods, but after a moment, he says, 'Daddy? I don't think the man wanted someone to take his picture.'

I get down on my haunches, so that I'm at his level. 'Sometimes if you show a terrible thing—like war—then people can see how terrible it is and that can help stop it. I think the man—'

'What are you guys doin', anyway?' Sean blasts into the room.

'Yeah.' Kevin hurls himself into his brother's wake. 'Let's go!'

I'm grateful for the interruption, not at all sure I buy my own rap. It's a fine line. What's hard-hitting, unblinking coverage? And what's exploitation? Sometimes I can't help feeling guilty. The deal is that I make a living from suffering and death; hell, I even win awards for it.

'*Daaaaaad!*' the boys yell from the front room. 'Let's go!'

KEVIN AND SEAN are on their best behaviour at the station, where I turn over the segment to one of the techs. Back in the car, they point out the monuments as we head out of town.

'Lincoln Memorial.'

'Big French fry!' they yell. This bit of enshrined toddler wit celebrates Sean's keen observation, at age two, of the similarity between the shape of the fast-food staple and the Washington Monument. It never fails to trigger a cascade of cackles.

'Are we almost there?' Kevin asks. And laughs. 'It's *a joke*—get it? Because: *we just left!*'

An hour-and-a-half later, we *are* there. I park the Jeep amid thousands of other cars baking in an open field in tiny Cromwell, Maryland. The boys are excited, running ahead towards a pair of crenellated plywood towers. Banners flutter from the ramparts on either side of a lowered drawbridge across a 'moat'. The three of us join a stream of families ready to cross the bridge into another world.

'One lord, two squires, is it?' the costumed woman at the gate asks, taking my credit card. 'On Her Majesty's royal Visa.'

And then we're in. Suddenly, it's 400 years ago. Wood-chip paths wind through a forested Elizabethan settlement of shops, food stalls and open-air amphitheatres. The boys dash this way and that from a falconer to a man selling armour to a group singing madrigals. Their excitement is contagious and before long, I realise that I'm having a good time. The place is interesting, half amusement park, half time machine. And educational, too. Liz would approve. And she's right: it's great to be with the kids when they're having such a ball.

Liz, sweet Liz. She should be here; she'd love it. For a moment, my longing for her nags at me. She left only after a series of failed promises about how I was going to change my workaholic ways, but I still felt blindsided by her departure. I knew she was right, that's the thing . . . but I just never quite got around to making the changes I promised to make. And then she and the boys were gone, leaving a hole in my life the size of the Grand Canyon.

I cast the thought out of my mind. 'Let's go get some food,' I say.

The three of us spend the afternoon wandering from surprise to delight. Kevin and Sean gasp at a sword swallower, a sweaty man in a leather vest who leans back and gulps down the blade of an outrageously large scimitar. They can't decide whether they're impressed or grossed out. A street magician tears up a card picked by an onlooker, does some elaborate shuffling of the deck, then plucks the magically restored card out of a woman's hair. Kevin gapes at Sean. 'How did he *do* that?'

We watch as fairgoers try their luck at climbing the Jacob's ladder. No one makes it more than two rungs up the wobbly affair before a failure of balance causes the contraption to pivot. Dumped hard, challengers land on a pile of hay, laughing in surprise. It's a buck a pop, and even though the twins are athletic for their age, it's clear they don't have a prayer. Still, they want to try it, and I give in.

They both get to the third rung before they lose it and they both beg me to let them go again. 'One more time,' I say, and they get back in line. Kevin wipes out immediately, but Sean actually negotiates the swaying rope loops and makes it to the top. The crowd, which has seen every contestant defeated, goes crazy. Kevin is a little jealous but happy for his brother and proud, too. 'Way to go!'

We move on. All three of us try our hand at juggling and archery (without much success), and we make messy brass rubbings of knights in chain mail.

'Let's go to the joust next good sir!' Sean bellows.

And so we're off to the *pièce de résistance* of the waning afternoon. The boys have been hectoring me for the last hour about it, Kevin checking the time every ten minutes. The jousting match is scheduled for four thirty. As we turn down a lane and enter the amphitheatre, I can see there's already a big crowd gathered; we have to sit quite a way back from the action. The seats consist of bales of hay, arrayed on shallow concentric tiers surrounding the arena.

The joust involves four knights, decked out in armour. As they prance around the ring on their horses, presenters dressed as squires work up support for the different contestants. Each part of the arena sports pennants of a different colour—red, green, white, black—and these match the colours worn by the knights and mounts.

We sit in the green zone. Each squire rouses support in his section by cuing the crowd for cheers and leading it in taunts. As part of the buildup, young well-wishers for each knight are summoned to the fence surrounding the ring.

The boys clamour to join 'the Green Machine', a band of children assembling to cheer the Green Knight. I hesitate. Liz would never let them. She knows she's overprotective—she even worries about it. 'I know it might make them feel insecure,' she admits. 'I'm sending the message that the world is full of danger.'

'*Daaaaad, please.*'

Down in front, the green squire is handing out emerald pennants and green balloons to the Green Machine kids. I tell myself this is exactly the kind of thing they *should* be allowed to do. I'm right here, after all. I'll be able to see them. What could happen?

I give in and watch their blond heads bob down the aisle as they make their way towards the fence to join the throng of children. The squire hands each of them a green pennant. Then the joust begins. When the riders come together, the clash is loud and violent. A roar goes up from across the arena as the Red Knight tumbles from his mount and goes sprawling. The White Knight plants a kiss on his lance and raises it into the air. I check for the kids and spot them towards the right of the cheering section. Along with some other children, they're petting a little dog. Even the dog is in costume, wearing an Elizabethan thing—a ruff—around its neck.

All eyes return to the arena as a trumpet heralds the next match. Green and black charge towards each other. After a tremendous collision, the Black Knight crashes to the turf. Even I have to admit it's exciting. I turn to see how the boys are liking it. My eyes go to the fence where the Green Machine is gathered, but I can't find Kev and Sean in the crowd. Not at first, anyway.

And then: I really can't see them.

Getting to my feet, I crane for a better view. But the boys—they just aren't there. A sizzle of panic surges through my chest.

As the victorious knights prepare for the final joust, I work my way through the crowd. *'Kevin?'* I raise my voice so that I'm shouting louder than the cheering. Arriving at the fence as the Green Knight charges towards his opponent, I realise I'm more terrified than I've ever been in a war zone. *'Sean?'* I'm shouting at the top of my lungs. I scan the mob, searching for blond hair, a yellow T-shirt. I can't see them. Kids begin to disperse, skipping back towards their parents.

After a minute, I return to the hay bale approximately where we were sitting. I fasten my eyes on the dissolving crowd, willing it to reveal my sons, but after a few minutes, I'm alone.

It's five twenty-two in the afternoon, and the twins are gone. *Gone*.

I sit there hoping the boys have gone to the rest room and will soon be back, but I have a terrible feeling in my chest. I know they wouldn't have gone. Not without telling me.

For a few minutes I can't bring myself to leave the jousting area. It's where I last saw them, where they would come back to—if they'd just wandered off. The moment I walk away, I'll be admitting that my sons are really gone, that something terrible is happening, something that requires the police. Several minutes tick by while I'm paralysed in this fog of superstition.

What bubbles up through me as I break my inaction and rise to my feet is a rush of sheer terror. Within ten seconds I'm running full out, so recklessly that the meandering crowd parts for me in alarm.

It takes a while to find someone from the fair's security staff.

'Prithee, stranger—'

'I can't find my kids.' The edge in my voice dissolves the centuries. Suddenly, it's 2003.

'Happens all the time,' the guy tells me. 'People get distracted. A juggler comes along . . . It's easy to lose track.'

'I didn't lose track,' I insist. 'We were watching the joust . . .'

Everyone's sympathetic. Announcements go out over the PA system, informing 'Prince Kevin and Lord Sean' that their father is lost. Would the lads be good enough to make their presence known at any of the booths?

I wait, telling myself the boys will be along any minute. But even as I try to reassure myself, I don't really believe it.

CHAPTER TWO

I sit marooned on a bench outside the building that houses Her Majesty's Headquarters. There's nothing medieval about the interior. The section devoted to security and Lost and Found is crowded with desks, computers, an elaborate communication system.

A grey-haired man pokes his head out of the door. His name is Gary Prebble, chief of security for the fair. He wears a blue uniform, badge on the chest pocket, equipment belt with truncheon, walkie-talkie. A rent-a-cop, in other words, who works weekends at the fair.

'When kids go AWOL,' he told me, 'which they do all the time, we put out the word, and then wait for 'em to turn up. They *always* turn up.' He advised me to 'stay put'. 'When folks get separated, it's best if one party remains in a fixed location.'

That was ten minutes ago.

I do my best to believe that any second, some helpful adult will come around the corner with Kev and Sean in tow. But after a while, there's no way I can just sit there any longer.

'Look,' I tell Prebble, 'if they show up—'

'They will, Mr Callahan. You want to go looking for them? You go right ahead. When they show up, we'll call you over the PA system and we'll keep them here. I can promise you that.'

It's a relief to be in motion. Doing something is better than just waiting. First I head to the Jeep, figuring that maybe when we got separated, the boys thought of going to the car. Is this what they'd do? It seems logical to me, but I've spent so little time with them in the past half year, I'm not sure how they'd act. Anyway, I can get my cellphone. They know the number. Maybe they called.

I lope through the acres of gleaming cars and finally locate the Jeep. The boys are not there. I didn't expect them to be, not really, but I'm still disappointed. I open the door and grab my cellphone with a brief surge of hope that I'll find a message. But there's nothing. I call the machine at home. Nothing there either.

I trot back to the gate, re-enter the fairground and begin my search. I plan to be methodical, to check every stall, concession and shop. As I go round, I call out the boys' names. The tone of desperation startles those around me; they look wary and alarmed.

I start to stop people at random: 'I'm looking for twins?! . . . Twin boys, have you seen them? Six-year-old boys, blond hair.'

After about forty-five minutes, I've covered most of the fairground. Some people remember seeing the boys, but when pressed, many of these recollections are from much earlier in the day and others are so vague as to be useless. Some people seem to produce memories of the boys for my benefit. I look so distraught that they want to help. Then comes the PA announcement informing the crowd that the fair is scheduled to close in thirty minutes. Almost immediately, people begin streaming towards the exits.

I head for the fair's headquarters.

What I want is for Gary Prebble to throw a wall around the place.

'We can't do that,' he says. 'Can you imagine the panic if we try to pen all these people in? Besides, the fair is enclosed, except for staff. Everybody has to go in and out through one entrance. In fact, why don't you and I head there?'

GARY PREBBLE AND I stand on the bridge that crosses the moat, scanning the exiting crowd. 'One way in, one way out,' he tells me. 'On the way in everybody pays, and on the way out, visitors are funnelled straight to the parking lot so they can't intrude on the privacy of the performers and artisans who live on the premises.'

'They live here?'

'Oh, some of 'em, sure. Out back, they got Winnies and campers. There's fairs like this all around the country. Some of these folk, they just travel from one to the other. And that's their life.'

I focus on the approaching crowd, my heart picking up a hopeful beat every time my eyes catch on a couple of blond kids—or even one. But each time, the hope lasts only a few seconds, fading as their features are clarified by proximity. Not Kevin. Not Sean.

The crowd is noticeably thinner when Prebble's walkie-talkie crackles. I can see from his face that it isn't news about the boys.

'Before we left headquarters,' he tells me with a somewhat pained look, 'I had Mike call Anne Arundel County to alert them we might have a situation here. They'll be here any time now.'

Five minutes later, the exodus is down to just a few stragglers. Inside the fairground, cleanup crews begin to collect trash and litter. People in shops near the entrance stow their wares for the night.

A squad car, blue and red lights flashing, threads its way through the stream of exiting cars and pulls up outside the entrance gate.

Detective Shoffler is a big guy, ruddy-faced. He's fifty, maybe a little older, and overweight. Despite his rumpled khakis and a blue blazer that's seen better days, he gives an impression of authority.

Officer Christiansen is a skinny guy with a buzz-cut, buckteeth and a high-pitched voice. He wears a brown uniform.

Shoffler's hand is big, the skin rough, and he does not release my hand immediately. 'Mr Callahan,' he says, and fixes me with a gaze so piercing that it feels to me as if I'm being scanned by a biometric device. Then he releases the hand, and points an accusing finger at Prebble. 'Gary, you shoulda called me sooner. You know better. How long these boys been missing? More than two hours?' Shoffler heaves a sigh. 'All right. What you got in the way of a crew today?'

'Me plus four,' Prebble says.

Shoffler makes a face. 'Get 'em down here.'

Prebble nods.

'I'm gonna get K-9,' Shoffler says, snapping a cellphone off his belt. He turns to Christiansen. 'In the meantime, we're gonna seal this place up.'

YOU'D THINK this burst of activity would make me feel better, but I'm paralysed by fear. I think of the Ramirez boys, Californian twins murdered a few years back. I think of all the less famous missing children whose faces haunt the world from milk cartons and post-office walls.

The fear must show on my face because Detective Shoffler reaches out reassuringly and grips my upper arm with one of his big hands.

'Kids hide,' he says. 'That's the thing. They get lost, they get scared, and usually what they do is hide. They might even think you're gonna be mad at them, you know? Because you couldn't find them? So we're going to take a long hard look at the fairground. The dogs might help, that's why I summoned K-9. OK?'

'Right,' I say. 'I understand.'

He frowns. 'You look familiar. You a lawyer or something?'

'Reporter. Fox.'

'Right,' Shoffler says in an automatic way, but then he actually remembers. '*Right.* OK.' He pulls a small spiral-bound notebook out of his blazer pocket and opens it. 'Now, your boys. They're what?—six years old, Gary tells me.'

'Kevin and Sean Callahan,' I tell him.

'Birth date?'

'January 4, 1997.'

'Describe them.'

'They're, I don't know, up to here.' I hold my hand out at their approximate height. 'Blue eyes, blond hair—'

'What kinda blond?' the detective wants to know. 'Dirty blond like yours or more like platinum?'

'Almost white.'

'Any distinguishing characteristics, scars, anything like that?'

'Well, their front teeth are only halfway in.'

'Good,' the detective says, as he writes this down, as if the state of the boys' dentition is a really useful bit of information.

This strikes me as nuts, given the one truly unusual fact about Kevin and Sean.

'They're identical twins,' I say. My nerves have notched up the volume and this comes out too loud. I take a breath. 'You know that, right?'

'Right, but see, they might get separated. They dress alike?'

'No.'

'So tell me what they were wearing. Kevin first.'

'Yellow T-shirt with a whale on it, jeans, white Nikes.'

'And Sean?'

'Cargo pants, blue T-shirt, black shoes with white stripes.'

Shoffler takes it down then turns to Gary Prebble. 'You got a list of fair employees, who's working where and what hours? I'll need that. Let's talk about how best to search the grounds.'

The two men walk over to a large wall map and discuss how to deploy the available manpower. 'When you search the residential area,' Shoffler says, 'ask permission to look inside campers and Winnies. But don't push it. Just keep track of the hesitant ones because that might mean coming back with a warrant.'

'Do you think?' I blurt out, 'I mean—'

Shoffler gives me a look. 'I don't think anything, Mr Callahan. I really don't. It's just—we have procedures, you understand?'

I nod, but I'm losing my mind. *Warrants.*

Shoffler turns back to Prebble. 'Take down everybody's name, note whether you took a look inside. Ask about folks who might not be on the fair's official list of employees. If this turns out to be an abduction, we need to ID potential witnesses.'

Although I've thought of this—of course I've thought of it—I'm still hanging on to the idea that the boys are lost. The word *abduction* crashes through my head like a bullet.

Once Shoffler has dispatched the search crew, he lowers himself onto the bench outside fair headquarters. He pats the seat next to him. 'Now you tell me about it,' he says to me, 'your whole time here at the fair. Everything you can remember.' He pulls a small tape recorder out of his pocket. 'Myself, I'm partial to handwritten notes, but if you don't mind, I'll record what you say, too.'

'Why would I mind?'

Shoffler shrugs, turns on the machine, then speaks into it. 'Saturday, May thirty-one, two thousand three.' A glance at his watch. 'The time is seven thirty-two p.m. I am detective Ray Shoffler, responding to a two-four-two at the Renaissance Faire in Cromwell, Maryland. I am speaking to Alexander Callahan, the father of the missing boys, Sean and Kevin Callahan, who are six-year-old identical twins. By the way, Mr Callahan, your wife know about this yet?'

Jesus. Liz. 'She's in Maine,' I tell him. 'We're separated.'

The detective hitches his head to the side with a little frown, as if this is not what he wanted to hear.

'And where do you live? You local?' he asks.

'DC.' I give him the address. 'The boys are with me for their summer visit.'

'OK,' Shoffler says. 'Start with where you were when you last saw your boys, and then let's go through the day—how you got here, and everything you did within the fairground proper. Let's get this down while it's fresh in your mind.'

'We were at the joust,' I say. 'The boys went up to cheer for the Green Knight . . .'

Once I've recounted this part, I attempt to reconstruct the day. The red diode on the tape recorder glows, I talk, Shoffler listens.

THE FAIR is for the most part deserted now, the booths shuttered and padlocked. Shoffler and I head towards the jousting arena. The detective stops everyone we meet. He asks each of them if they remember seeing a set of twins. No? What about me? No.

We've been through about a dozen such encounters when Shoffler stops walking, cocks his head, and looks at me.

'What?'

He shakes his head. 'I'm just surprised nobody remembers them, that's all. I mean—identical twins.'

The remark skitters past me like a mouse in the walls.

At the arena, Shoffler follows me as I walk through the hay bales. I describe—for what must be the fourth or fifth time now—exactly what happened. Shoffler flicks back through his notebook and checks something. 'So the last time you saw them, they were down at the ringside, cheering for the Green Knight.'

I close my eyes, concentrate. 'No,' I say. 'That's not right. Last time I saw them was right before the final joust. They were in a crowd of other kids, petting a dog.'

'A dog? What kind of dog?'

'Skinny dog. Like a greyhound, but smaller.'

'Whippet?' Shoffler asks.

'Right. It had a thing around its neck—you know, a collar. A ruffled white collar.'

'You mean—like out of Shakespeare? A ruff?'

'That's right. A ruff. In fact'—the image jumps into my mind—'the guy was wearing one too.'

'What guy?'

'There was a tall guy with the dog.'

'Huh.' Shoffler says. 'So you took your eyes off the kids to watch the joust and then the next time you looked, they're gone.'

'Right,' I say, with a trap-door feeling in my chest, as if I'm on a plane that's suddenly dropped twenty thousand feet.

As we approach the ring, I see that someone's inside the arena: a skinny guy in a faded red T-shirt. He's raking up horse manure.

He answers Shoffler's questions politely. 'Allen Babcock,' he says in a British accent. 'I'm the head groom, take care of the horses and all that. Mind if I ask what's this about?'

'We've got a couple of young boys missing. Twins.'

Babcock shakes his head. 'Sorry. I'm not out front much. A few fans find their way back to the entrance chutes, but not many. No twins. Not today. I'd remember.'

'Entrance chutes? So where exactly are you during these events?' Shoffler asks.

'Have a look.'

We follow Babcock through the arena and out of a gate to the staging area. Two metal chutes, consisting of lengths of tubular metal fence chained together, lead to two wooden corrals.

'In one chute,' Babcock says, 'out the other. The horses can be a bit headstrong, so I'm back here, helping with them, and getting the knights on and off their mounts.'

'What happens afterwards? You trailer the horses away until the next day or the next weekend?'

'No, we stay right out back here.'

We follow Babcock towards a six-foot-high perimeter fence.

'This fence enclose the entire fairground?' Shoffler asks.

'Right.' The groom unlocks a padlock and pulls open a gate.

As soon as we walk through it into the area outside the fence, I feel panic. There's a whole wide world out here. If Kevin and Sean are not in the fairground they could be anywhere.

'Horses and tack in there,' Babcock says, nodding towards a white clapboard barn. 'Humanfolk in the caravan.' He gestures towards a large Winnebago.

Beyond the barn, a field enclosed with white four-board fencing leads back towards dense woodland.

We're on our way back into the jousting arena when I see it, near one of the chutes: a small white Nike shoe with a blue swoosh on it.

The sight of it stops me cold. Shoffler and Babcock are through the gate and into the arena before the detective notices I'm no longer with them. 'Mr Callahan?'

I beckon, unable to speak. I stare at the shoe. It's just sitting there, in the dirt, as if someone just stepped out of it.

'That looks just like one of Kevin's shoes,' I say.

'What?'

'Right there. That shoe.' I point to it, a small white shoe with a smear of mud on its laces. 'My son Kevin has shoes like that.'

I lean forward, as if to pick it up, but Shoffler stops me.

'Wait a minute,' the detective says. 'Don't touch it.'

Ten minutes later, Christiansen arrives and the shoe ends up with its own little fence of traffic cones and yellow police tape. Christiansen will await the arrival of the evidence technician.

'Now, let's take it from the top, from when you got here,' Shoffler says. 'What time was that? What'd the clerk look like?'

I pull my wallet out of my back pocket. 'I should have the receipt. Two eighteen,' I tell Shoffler, reading the time stamp.

The detective has his notebook out again. 'And the person who sold it to you?' he says, without looking up.

The question bothers me. It's like the detective is checking on me. I answer the question. 'Thirtysomething female, eyebrows plucked almost to oblivion.' The woman's voice comes back to me: *One lord, two squires, is it? On Her Majesty's royal Visa.*

Shoffler eyes the wallet. 'You have a photo of the boys in there?'

'Yeah. I do.'

'I might send one of the detectives back to the station with a photo. Put us a step ahead. We can prepare to distribute to the surrounding jurisdictions. And to the media.'

'This is almost a year old,' I tell Shoffler, sliding the snapshot out of its transparent plastic compartment.

Half an hour later, after I've refined my account of the day, Shoffler's satisfied. He switches off the tape recorder, pulls out his cellphone and takes a few steps away from me. I can still hear what he says. He's summoning everybody to headquarters.

'I think while we've still got some light,' Shoffler is saying into his phone, 'we'd better expand the search into the woods.'

SUDDENLY IT'S NIGHT. A crescent moon, startling in its clarity, hangs in the inky, star-strewn sky. I pull my cellphone out and call voicemail at home—for about the tenth time. Nothing's changed, no messages.

Shoffler wouldn't let me go out with the initial search teams. Everyone offers the same advice: the best thing I can do is wait. It's my sons who are missing, yet I'm supposed to sit and watch, a spectator at my own disaster.

When yet another squad car arrives with four more uniformed men (and more on the way), Shoffler organises teams. Food has appeared from somewhere. Pizzas, cans of Pepsi, big Thermos dispensers of coffee. Someone's pinned a topographical map to the wall and marked it into a grid. The first search party departs in a welter of raspy walkie-talkie communication, and then the second. As the third assembles to watch Shoffler delineate their area on the map, I find myself on my feet. 'I'm going.'

Shoffler hesitates. 'If we find them,' he starts, 'it's possible . . .'

His voice trails away, but I can read his mind: *It's possible they won't be alive.* I nod to show I understand.

We walk through a densely wooded area in a ragged line, each person separated from the next by the prescribed double arm's length distance of six feet. Flashlights burrow into the darkness, probing and tunnelling in well-defined cylinders of light. The search party makes a huge amount of noise as it crashes along, each man or woman yelling, 'Sean! Kevin!'

Above, a helicopter contributes even more noise as it makes methodical sweeps over the fairground.

We trudge and grope and clamber our way through terrain that's not only rugged and full of unexpected and hidden ravines, but choked with brambles and vines. Within ten minutes, my legs and arms are torn up from the thorns, and my face is bleeding.

I sink into a kind of trance, focused only as far as the end of my beam of light, which I swing from side to side, making certain to cover every inch of my patch of terrain. The boys are so small, really. When I check on them, asleep in their beds, I'm shocked sometimes by how small they are—considering the space they take up in my life. If they were covered with leaves . . . it would be so easy to miss them. I blink my eyes, close my mind to the thought. But I can't keep it from the terrible notions that float into it.

When Shoffler orders the team to return 'to base', not a single member of the unit wants to do it. But they surrender grudgingly to Shoffler's insistence. Replacements are standing by. Exhaustion causes mistakes. 'And besides,' Shoffler says, 'I need to discuss something with Mr Callahan.'

Fairground headquarters is a mess, overflowing with foam cups, pizza boxes, water bottles.

I wait for the promised discussion but Shoffler slings an arm around my shoulder and tells me it's time to go home. I sputter my objection.

Shoffler shakes his head. 'If this *is* an abduction, and there's a call, they're not going to leave a message on your voicemail. They're gonna want to talk to you. We'd like to install a trace on your phone, and that'll go much faster if you're there. Otherwise, we got to get a form signed, get it to these guys, get 'em keys, it's a whole rigmarole. If you're there, it's done inside a coupla hours.'

'OK.'

'Second thing is you can't have all these people, helicopters'—he makes a sweeping gesture—'and keep it secret. Point is, this is gonna make the early news in some form, and then, by the regular morning news . . .' He shakes his head. 'Well, you would know.'

'Right,' I say. And of course Shoffler *is* right. I should have thought about this, but didn't. Not until this moment.

'And that's all to the good,' Shoffler is saying. 'It's time to enlist the public's help. And the media, they will do that for you. They will get the word out.' He stops talking and waits for me to say something, but I don't see what he is after. 'You probably got people,' the detective finally says, 'that shouldn't hear about this on the TV.'

I'm going to have to tell Liz. I stare at my feet.

'I think you should go home. Chris here,' Shoffler continues, with a nod towards Officer Christiansen, 'he'll go with you.'

'I'll be all right,' I say.

Shoffler ignores me and nods at Christiansen, then walks us towards the entrance gate. 'You got juice in your cellphone?' he asks Christiansen, who lifts the phone from his holster and checks.

'I'm all set.'

Outside, it's quiet. We walk through the small cluster of cars and squad cars parked near the entrance gate. After Shoffler heads back to the fairground, Christiansen walks beside me, talking in nervous bursts about 'a kidnap case I worked on couple of years back. They found the kid in Florida,' he says. 'Boyfriend's backyard.'

On the long walk to the car, the notion that Shoffler sent the officer with me out of some kind of compassion dissolves into a darker truth. I realise this as I fumble in my pocket for the keys and press the button on the remote. The door locks pop. 'That's what they say, y'know,' Christiansen rambles on. 'Nine times out of ten, it's someone who knows the kid. Nine times outta ten, it's a parent.'

Here's the truth: Christiansen isn't babysitting. I'm a suspect.

I can't bring myself to get into the car. Going home without the boys is . . . *wrong.* It feels like a signal of defeat, as if I'm giving up on them. Then a sudden effervescence of hope bubbles up in my brain and I can't get into the car fast enough.

Christiansen slides into the passenger seat, and by the time I've flipped on the lights and made it from the parking lot to the gravel drive, an entire, hopeful scenario has constructed itself in my head. Maybe the boys got disorientated . . . When the joust was over, it was chaotic . . . If they couldn't find me, maybe they met someone from the neighbourhood. Who drove the boys *home*.

Now that I'm on the road I have an irrational need to get back to the house. Tagging home base. I'll be safe. The kids will be safe. Somehow it's in my head that the kids will be there, waiting for me.

'You better slow it down,' Christiansen whines.

I glance at the speedometer. I'm doing eighty.

I slow to seventy-five, and then my cellphone rings and I hit the brakes, fishtailing onto the shoulder in a spray of gravel. I fumble for the phone. 'Hello? *Hello!*' I'm yelling. But no one's there.

'Sir? Who is it?' Christiansen bleats, but I shove my hand towards the cop to shut him up. I don't hang up because I realise it's not quite silence I'm hearing. It's breathing. Someone breathing.

'Who is this?' I ask, trying to control my voice. 'Who *is* it?'

And then a candle of relief explodes in my chest as Kevin's voice flutters into my ear, tremulous and tentative: 'Daddy?'

CHAPTER THREE

Then a *click*, and the candle goes out as suddenly as it flared. 'Kevin? *Kevin?!*' I stare at the tiny glowing rectangle of the phone's LCD screen. Like most cellphones, mine displays the numbers of incoming calls. But this can't be right. It's the number at the house, my own home phone number. Does this mean—my heart does a somersault—that the boys are at home? I don't see how it's possible, in that case, that no one bothered to call me during the eleven hours they've been missing, but still, I go nova with happiness.

My cellphone must have cut out on Kevin's call. It happens all the time. The signal is strong now, though, so I press the 2 key, which automatically calls the house.

The phone rings four times, then I hear my own voice. 'You've reached Alex Callahan. I can't come to the phone right now . . . '

I hang up. The phone has call waiting, so if you're on the line and you don't cut over to the new call, the machine picks up. The boys must be calling at the same time I'm calling the house. I wait, try again, get the machine again, in the meantime explaining to Christiansen what I'm doing—and that it was Kevin who called.

After the fourth try, I give up. Why doesn't anyone answer? I press the tab for *time of call*. The time tag pops up: 4.42 a.m.

'Mr Callahan,' Christiansen says, 'you sure that was one of your kids?'

'Yes, I'm sure,' I say, voice shaky with emotion. 'It was Kevin.'

'What did he say? What happened to them?' Christiansen asks.

I'm pulling back onto the road and don't answer. I can't get Kevin's voice out of my head. *Daddy*.

I try home again. The machine picks up and I hear my voice again and the beep. 'Kev? Sean? If you're somehow there by yourselves, pick up the phone, OK, guys. It's Dad. Just pick up the phone.'

Nothing. I call my next-door neighbour, Fred Billingsley. He's efficient and reliable.

'Sir,' Christiansen says, 'I need to report to Detective Shoffler. Can you tell me—'

Fred is more than surprised to hear from me at this hour. 'Alex? What time is it?' His voice is alarmed. 'Is there a problem?'

I explain the situation, tell Fred where to find the key for the front door. Fred promises to go right over; he'll call me back on my cellphone in a few minutes.

I'm on the Beltway by the time Fred gets back to me. 'No one here,' he tells me. 'You sure they called from here?'

I say my cellphone listed the call as originating from home, but maybe there's some mistake. I thank him profusely and hang up.

I have it in my mind that the kids are in the house, hiding from Fred. For no particular reason besides the man's stiff formality, they've always been afraid of 'Mr B'.

Christiansen reports to Shoffler, and they're still talking when I pull into the driveway. And then I'm out of the car, running towards the house. I yank open the screen door, turn the dead bolt, and then I'm inside, charging from room to room at warp speed, yelling the boys' names, my eyes practically strip-searching the rooms. I check their bedroom last. Some demented optimist inside me continues to hold out hope that somehow I'll find them here, asleep in their beds.

But their room is deserted. A void.

With Christiansen trailing behind, I'm on my way out of the bedroom when my eyes catch on something I never noticed before. It's some kind of little rabbit, perched on the double dresser. It's on

Sean's side, which, unlike Kevin's half, is almost free of clutter—or I never would have noticed it. Up close, I see that it's origami. The little figure is maybe four inches tall, folded out of brown paper. This is not some simple cartoon rendition of an animal. It's sleek and sophisticated, more like a piece of miniature sculpture.

And when I pick it up, it feels weird. It's not made out of paper, but some kind of animal's skin. Which spooks me, somehow.

Was this always here? I don't think so. I would have noticed it.

But maybe not, I think, setting the figure back on the dresser. After all, did I notice the boys' obsession with knights? There's no way Kevin or Sean made this thing. Their mother, maybe.

The thought of Liz hits me like wind shear.

Ohmygod. I've gotta call her. . . .

SHE GETS IN LATE that same morning, stumbling out of the secure area at National Airport, her good looks strained by tears. After a stiff embrace, I introduce her to Christiansen.

Christiansen is here as a courtesy, to—as Shoffler put it—'help escort Mrs Callahan to your house.'

I told the detective to forget it when he first put forward this idea, but he talked me around, noting that uniformed policemen can really help get you through a media crowd. 'A guy in uniform can be all business; he can be rude to reporters—and it just looks like he's doing his job. The squad car, the uniform—they'll help.'

'Oh,' Liz says, her eyes widening at the sight of the policeman. She thinks he is here in some official capacity, to deliver bad news.

'Ma'am,' he mutters, tilting forward in a kind of bow.

She waits, frozen, and when it becomes clear that Christiansen is not going to say anything else, she collapses into me, her face hot and damp against my shoulder. 'Oh, Alex,' she says, weeping. Then she steps back, bats her face to dry her tears and starts off towards the baggage claim area, moving so fast I almost have to run to keep up.

The phone call to tell her what had happened was a nightmare, but this—this is so much worse. Instead of Liz arriving to the reunion I've been imagining—the jumping, excited boys and their beaming please-come-back-to-me-I've-changed father—this is how the love of my life re-enters my world. She stands not twelve inches from me, enclosed within a force field of grief and anger.

Of course, as I struggled to explain on the telephone what had happened, she did everything she could to reassure me it wasn't my fault, that I shouldn't think that way, that she doesn't blame me.

But of course it's a lie. How can she not blame me?

'That's mine,' she says, in a tight little voice. Her hand jerks up almost mechanically and points towards a green suitcase.

I don't recognise the suitcase. The sight of it—bright lime green with leather trim—makes me sad. It's one more thing that seems to emphasise the divergence of our lives. I wrestle it off the belt and carry it. If hefting its weight is not exactly a pleasure, it offers—like meeting the plane—a respite from my sense of uselessness.

Already, it's clear that as the machinery of disaster gains momentum, I am more and more peripheral to the effort. I've given my account of what happened a half dozen times and tracked down the most recent photos of the boys. I've called the neighbours to see if anyone spotted anything at the house—a car, the boys, anything. I've given consents: the phone may be tapped, phone records accessed, house searched.

In fact, I'm irritated that they haven't searched the house yet. I don't understand what's taking so long, as I complained to Shoffler over the phone right before I left for the airport. 'Kevin was here,' I told the detective. 'He called from this telephone. He didn't get here on his own, that's for sure—which means that the kidnapper was here. You should be crawling all over this place.'

Shoffler tells me to relax. When there are jurisdictional issues—they have to liaise with DC Metro—it takes a little while to get the wheels rolling.

I've surrendered my cellphone to a female communications technician dispatched by Shoffler. The two of us went through the call lists, so I could identify the phone numbers, both of incoming and outgoing calls. I recognised all of the numbers. She affixed an evidence number to my Nokia and gave me a receipt for it and a clone—a phone with the same number in case a repeat call comes in from Kevin or Sean. Or from someone with a ransom demand.

I also talk to a kind woman named Shelley at the Center for Missing and Exploited Children. I scan a photo of the boys into the computer so that the organisation might begin its national poster campaign. Another woman—Shelley's superior—is supposed to call later to discuss other options and to offer advice.

We glide along on the moving sidewalk towards the parking garage. Behind me, Christiansen jingles the keys in his pocket. In front of me stands Liz, rigid with the effort of suppressing her terror.

WHEN CHRISTIANSEN eventually turns the corner towards our house, Liz gasps. The little knot of reporters that began gathering early this morning has ballooned into a crowd. There are light towers, cables snaking across the lawns, camera and sound crews. As the crowd catches sight of the squad car, there's a rush for position.

I feel dread, a weird sense of exposure. I've been part of scenes like this plenty of times, one more reporter in the press-conference crush, or in a mob waiting to waylay some key figure in a story. I think—too late—that I should have warned Liz. The story is going to be the top of the news. The fact that I'm in the business, that I appear on TV, that I am (as Liz and I used to joke) 'a third-string celebrity', will just stoke what is going to be a firestorm of coverage.

Liz cringes against me as the crowd begins to engulf the car. She's weeping against me, really losing it.

'It's all right,' I murmur. She takes deep breaths, trying to compose herself. 'Just get us into the house,' I tell Christiansen. 'Walk fast, no eye contact, don't talk to anybody.'

And that's what we do. We somehow get through the blizzard of flashes, the cacophony of shouted questions and comments.

Making it inside and closing the door on the madness feels like a victory, but the sense of triumph lasts only seconds. Liz looks at me, her eyes wet. 'Alex,' she starts, but then she just stands there.

'Liz—'

'Alex!' she shrieks. She pummels my chest with her fist. *'Where are they? You have to find them!'*

WE SIT in the kitchen. 'So there's no news . . .' she starts and then her voice fades.

'I'll call Shoffler—the detective. I told him we'd check in after we got back from the airport.' I head for the phone.

But Shoffler is in conference. I leave a message, then make Liz some tea. She sits like a rag doll, slumped and loose-limbed.

'Did you call your parents?' she asks in a listless voice.

'They're on their way.'

'My mom . . . broke down,' Liz says. 'She's in the hospital.'

'Oh, Liz . . .'

'She's all right, just—you know, she's sedated.'

'I'm sorry.'

'I begged my dad to stay with her, but he's coming. I couldn't stop him.' She rests her elbows on the table, holds her face in her hands.

'We'll find them,' I hear myself say. She draws a deep, jittery breath, lifts her face up towards me. She searches my face, but whatever she sees doesn't reassure her. She lowers her head to the table, rests it on her crossed arms, and begins to sob.

LIZ IS in the shower when the call comes from Claire Carosella.

'I'm returning your call,' the efficient voice says. 'I'm with the Center for Missing and Exploited Children.'

'Right. They mentioned that you'd call.'

'At the Center,' she begins, 'we realise parents don't know what to do when this sort of thing happens, so . . . someone like me usually calls to offer advice.'

'Right,' I say, not knowing where this woman is going. Advice?

'First things first,' she says. 'The media. They'll drive you crazy, but they're your biggest ally. As soon as possible, you and your wife should go on the air and plead for the children's return.'

'My wife—she's really . . . '

'I'm sure she's a mess. Believe me, I know . . . ' A pause. 'But you've got to do it. It humanises you as victims, both to the viewing public and to the abductor. Lots of these guys watch, you know.'

'Isn't there a chance that they get a kick out of the media coverage?'

'Yes. That's one of the negatives.' A weary sigh. 'But on balance, going on the air is more plus than minus. It can really help the investigation. And these guys—sometimes they just can't resist calling in. They might say something that gives the police a lead.'

'OK,' I tell her. 'We'll do it.'

'And just . . . speak from the heart. Don't try to write out a speech and read it. It's better if you . . . if you just do it. The more emotional, the better. Incidentally, do mention them by name. "Kevin and Sean." Not "my sons" or "my children."'

'Right. OK.'

Her final advice is unsettling. 'I feel I'd be remiss if I didn't mention this,' she says, and then hesitates. 'Some families hire public- relations advisers. I know it sounds strange, but it can be a huge plus to have someone to interface with the media. They can also help maximise your exposure. If the case drags on—they can keep it in the news.'

'I don't think . . . '

'Look, I only mention it, because it's something to consider. If you decide to go that way, I can give you a list of firms.'

I thank her, but when I hang up, I feel as if I've stepped through a looking glass. My children are missing and they want me to do stand-ups and get a PR rep?

SHOFFLER CALLS to tell us that there's no news from the search parties, but that the switchboard is swamped with volunteers. The plan is to broaden the search.

'Great,' I say. If my voice lacks enthusiasm, it's because when I try to remember an instance of one of these big efforts actually locating the target of the search, I can't think of a single one.

'We're canvassing people who work at the festival, looking for anyone saw your boys yesterday. So far, we're not getting very far.'

'Oh?' This from Liz on the extension in the kitchen. 'That's strange. Everybody notices the boys.'

It's true. Identical twins hold a universal fascination.

'Probably haven't talked to the right folks yet,' Shoffler says. 'I'll be by sometime today.'

I hang up as Liz's father plunges through the front door. 'They're like a pack of vultures. Where's my daughter?'

She comes through the door from the kitchen, gives a little cry, and then he takes her clumsily into his arms, patting at her shoulder. 'Liz,' he says, 'it'll be all right. You'll see.'

After a minute, they separate and he extends his hand to me. 'Alex,' he says. 'Hell of a thing.'

'Thanks for coming, Jack.' It's an effort to address my father-in-law by his first name. What comes naturally is 'Mr Taggart'. Jack is a high-school principal in Rockland, Maine. He's conditioned to expect deference from anyone younger than he is.

'Marguerite—this thing was just too much for her,' my father-in-law says. He shakes his head. 'High-strung, but—' he claps his hands together, 'she'll be fine.'

Liz may have wanted her dad to stay with her mother, but I can see that she's buoyed by Jack's presence. Jack Taggart is one of those supremely self-confident men who believes he can do anything. This clearly includes finding his grandchildren.

My own parents are scheduled to arrive in about an hour. I'd pick them up at the airport, but Shoffler and the search unit are due to come by and I don't want to leave Liz here to deal with them.

When Dad calls from baggage claim, I suggest he tell the cab to come the back way. 'I'll unlock the gate.'

'Okey-doke. Hey, I see the bags. We'll be there in a jiffy,' he says.

The plan doesn't work. My parents' arrival is heralded by a stampede from the front of the house to the end of the block and then down the alley and into our backyard. Jack and I rush out the back door, finding my mother engulfed by reporters and microphones. A few feet from the gate, Dad, grim-faced and tight-lipped, is trying to get through the crowd with the suitcases.

'Good Lord,' my mother says once we're inside the house. Dad gives me a slap on the back, but he looks terrible. 'We'll find them,' he says firmly, but his voice is tinny and unsubstantial.

LATER THAT afternoon, Liz and I stand just outside the front door, elevated a few steps above a forest of microphones, a sea of cameras. Liz flinches from the noise and dazzle.

'I'm Alex Callahan,' I begin. I plead with whoever has taken Kevin and Sean to return them, I plead with the public to be our eyes and ears, to call the hotline with any information. I realise too late that I should have insisted Liz do most of the talking. Even to me my voice sounds polished and composed—my on-camera voice. I'm left with the perception of having given a performance, and not a particularly good one.

Liz makes up for it. She can hardly manage a sentence without breaking down, but she goes on anyway, a forced march of bravery so moving I spot tears in the eyes of some of the female reporters. At the end, she speaks directly to the boys. 'Kevin? Sean? If you're watching . . . hang in there guys. We love you. Daddy and I . . . we just love you . . . so much. And we're going to find you! Wherever you are. I promise! You just . . . hang on.'

She can't go on. She sags against me, and I realise after a moment that I'm actually holding her up. Reporters continue to shout questions as I half drag my wife back in through the door to our home.

SOMEHOW WE GET THROUGH the day, a maelstrom of emotion, interrupted by what seems like hundreds of telephone calls.

I speak to Shoffler half a dozen times, but there's nothing new except his change of schedule; instead of 'sometime today', he'll come by 'sometime tonight'.

I speak several times to my assistant Krista at the station—which, she tells me breathlessly, has pledged ten grand to a reward fund. The boys' pictures, an announcement of the reward and the hotline number will be shown at the top of every hour.

At five o'clock I realise that the boys have been missing for twenty-four hours.

SLEEPING ARRANGEMENTS. I've been awake for so long, I'm approaching an altered state of consciousness. Liz bustles around, making up the sleep-sofa in the study for her father, changing the sheets in the master bedroom, which she has assigned to my folks. I trail her, carrying towels and sheets. It's her intention to sleep in the boys' room, but she stops in the doorway, frozen. 'I can't . . . I can't sleep in here,' she says. She begins to sob and I put my arm around her shoulder, but she stiffens under my touch, pulls away, composes herself. 'I'll take the futon in the family room,' she announces. 'You get the living-room couch.'

She heads into the bathroom. I follow, with the towels. She stands in front of the vanity unit. 'What's with these dimes?' she asks.

On the upper edge of the backsplash rests a row of Liberty head dimes. Seven of them, precisely aligned.

'I don't know,' I say.

'Do these belong to the boys? Did they start a collection?'

'I don't think so.'

But the ambiguity is only notional. I've never seen the dimes before—and I would have seen them. It's my habit to stand and watch Kev and Sean brush their teeth, to make sure they stay at it for more than two seconds. No way I would not have noticed a line of coins on the sink. They seem like some kind of crazy sign or message.

'Someone put them there,' I tell Liz.

'Who? What?'

'The kidnapper. Come here for a sec,' I say, pulling her towards the boys' bedroom. 'I want you to take a look at something.' I point out the little origami rabbit on the dresser. 'Does this belong to Kevin or Sean? Because I never noticed it before.'

'No,' Liz says. 'I never saw it before.' She looks at me. 'Alex, that rabbit. The dimes. What does it mean?'

'I don't know.'

WHEN I HEAR the loud rap at the door and my father and the detective arrive, I'm in the family room down on my hands and knees, trying to get the rickety futon frame to fold down.

'How you holding up?' Shoffler asks me.

I manage a shrug. Shoffler himself looks terrible. His weary eyes make it clear he needs sleep.

'Bob—do I have that right?' Shoffler says, looking at my father.

'Yes, you do. Robert J. Callahan.'

'You mind calling the others to come in here?'

A gush of fear blooms in my chest. 'You have . . . news?'

Shoffler shakes his head, and bends to help me, yanking on one of the futon frame's recalcitrant legs. The whole thing unfolds with a crash. 'There you go,' he says.

Once Liz and the others are in the room and seated, Shoffler gives us an update. The search in the woods outside the fairground proceeds, he tells us. The hotline is swamped with calls, but it's going 'to take time to sort things out'. The questioning of fair employees, he says, 'is slow, but it's coming along'.

Shoffler manages to charm and reassure Liz and my mother and to impress Jack and my father. He has a knack for listening that would put most reporters to shame. 'You folks have any questions?'

'There's been no ransom call,' my dad says with a worried glance my way. 'Isn't that, I mean—why do you think that is?'

'Well, it's early days,' Shoffler tells him, 'but I don't expect you're going to get one.'

'*No?* But, but—why not?' Jack demands.

Shoffler sighs. 'First off, if you're after money, why take *two* kids? It's not like it's a bake sale, if you see what I mean.'

'I'm not sure that I do,' Jack says.

'Two kids'd be twice the trouble, but they wouldn't get you twice the payoff. Desperate parents—my opinion is they'd cough up just as much for one child as for two. And then—' he hesitates '—fact is, there's plenty of rich folk in the world. I think somebody with a profit motive would go for parents with . . . ah . . . greater resources than Alex and Liz. Unless—' he looks inquiringly from Jack to my father to my mother '—the boys' grandparents . . . ?'

'I'm a high-school principal,' Jack says. 'Maybe Bob here is one of those secret millionaires next door.' He looks at my father.

'No,' my father says. 'I'm not saying we—' he looks at my mother '—couldn't come up with a good piece of change if we liquidated everything. Which we would do, of course, but it would take time.'

'Well,' Shoffler says, 'you see what I mean.'

'What about a non-monetary reason?' my father asks.

Shoffler frowns. 'Such as?'

'My son, the kinds of stories he does—' A glance my way. 'He makes enemies.'

I hadn't thought of this. The idea that whoever took the boys did so because of me—it's sickening. But maybe . . .

'My father's right,' I tell Shoffler. 'I didn't think of it.'

'Well,' Shoffler says. 'If you can come up with anybody who might take a grudge that far . . . '

I promise to take a look at my files, after which Shoffler looks at each of us in turn. No one seems to have anything else to say.

Jack gives in to a mighty yawn. 'Excuse me.' He stands up. 'Well, thank you very much.'

'Actually,' Shoffler says, 'I know it's late, but we'd like to conduct the search now.'

'The search?' Liz asks. 'What search?'

'The search of the residence,' Shoffler says. 'Your husband and I have talked about it. He thinks the kidnapper was here. That maybe we'll find something. Anyway, it's routine.'

'I don't *think* he was here,' I correct Shoffler. 'He *was* here.'

'Did you tell them about the dimes?' Liz says. 'And that rabbit?'

'What's this?' Shoffler asks.

When I explain, he pulls out a notebook, makes a notation. 'We'll take those into evidence.' He continues, 'We'd like to get started. You'll all have to remain in this room until we're done with the rest of the house. Then we'll finish up here. And we could cross something else off the list. Get everybody's fingerprints.'

'What?' Jack says.

'Strictly routine, Mr Taggart. We need the prints of the people who have been in the house, so we can exclude them.'

'Why can't this be done tomorrow?' Jack asks, his arm around Liz's shoulder. 'My daughter is exhausted.'

Shoffler wags his head. 'I know. It's very late. But I'm sure you understand that if there is any evidence here, anything that might provide a lead, we want to know about it right away. Plus the crime team's here, outside . . . You mind if we get started?'

LISTENING TO THE EVIDENCE team pawing through my family's belongings makes me feel as if I'm under attack, my territory violated. I hate the sound of their footsteps, the murmur of voices, the occasional spurt of laughter. It bothers me so much that I lift the TV remote from the end table, press the power button.

A mistake. I've caught the start of the ten o'clock news. There's a collective intake of breath as a photo of the boys flashes on the screen, the announcer saying: 'No news in the case of the missing Callahan twins . . . '

'Oh, God,' Liz says, as I punch the television off.

It's almost a relief when a jittery redhead with bad skin and green fingernails arrives to take our fingerprints.

Shortly after she finishes, Shoffler shows up. 'Can I have a word with you, Alex? With you and Mrs Callahan?'

There's something about the look on Shoffler's face that freezes my heart. And the latex gloves he's wearing provide a chilling, clinical note. I stand up fast. 'What is it?'

Liz is grey. We follow Shoffler upstairs into my study, where a uniformed officer, also gloved, sits on the corner of my desk holding a clipboard. Shoffler introduces the man as Officer David Ebinger and explains that it's the custom, post-O. J. Simpson, to have a single officer handle evidence, from tagging and bagging, to checking it in and out of the evidence room, to introducing it in court. 'We have to establish chain of custody,' he says, in a matter-of-fact way.

We nod. We understand.

And then Shoffler closes the door. 'We found something,' he says.

On my desk sits a brown cardboard box about the size of a shoe box. Shoffler, using the eraser end of a pencil, extracts from the box a crumpled and badly stained piece of clothing. Once he's got the whole thing clear of the box, I see what it is: a yellow T-shirt. The stain is reddish brown and I know instantly that it's blood.

Liz moans. I put my arm around her. Shoffler is trying to gently shake out the piece of cloth suspended from his pencil. Finally the folds of fabric in one part of the T-shirt lose their adhesion, and suddenly I can see what the bunched folds hid—a cartoonish drawing of a fish tail which I know to be that of a whale, the interior of which I know is printed with the word NANTUCKET. I don't need to see any more.

'That's Kevin's,' I say. 'Sean has a green one.' I can't take my eyes of the shirt. Liz is shivering in my arms. 'Where did you find it?' I hear myself ask.

'Could you confirm the identity of the shirt, Mrs Callahan?' Shoffler asks.

Liz lifts her head, takes a look. She manages a few choppy nods.

Shoffler manoeuvres the shirt back into the box. 'There's one more thing,' he says. 'Would you follow me?'

Shoffler leads, Ebinger follows in our wake. We enter the boys' room. I can hardly breathe.

Shoffler levers open the door of the closet with his pencil. 'Can you explain this?' he asks, pointing to the top shelf. There is a small glass mixing bowl full of a clear liquid.

'What is it?' Liz asks. 'Is it water?'

'We're not certain yet, but if you can tell us what it's for, that would help.'

Liz frowns and looks at me, but all I can do is shrug. I have no idea what a bowl of liquid is doing on the top shelf of the boys' closet.

'We'll take a sample of the liquid and fingerprint the bowl. Is it your bowl, by the way?' He looks from me to Liz.

'I don't know,' I say. 'I guess so.'

'I don't recognise it,' Liz says.

'Huh. Well, Dave is going to deal with this,' Shoffler says, nodding towards the closet, 'and the crew can take on the family room. You can have the run of the rest of the house now.'

'The shirt,' Liz squeaks, 'does that—?'

'Sorry,' Shoffler says, retreating into formality, 'the shirt is evidence, and questions about it will have to wait. We'll send it to the lab and then I'll be in a better position to discuss it.'

He's moving towards the door now, walking past Liz and me. We pause before returning to the family room, so that the two policemen coming out of my study can get to the front door. Each of them carries a large cardboard box sealed with evidence tape.

'What's that? What are you taking?' I ask.

'I think it's your computer,' Liz says.

'My computer?'

'Relax, Alex,' Shoffler says. 'It's routine. The kidnapper was here, right? Naturally we have to remove some items to examine them. Officer Ebinger will give you a search warrant inventory when we're finished, and you should look that over.' He then asks, 'Alex, would you be willing to take a polygraph test?'

'What?'

I say *what,* but I heard him. I also know what it means. Murder is often a family affair. I can hear Officer Christiansen's voice during our walk back to the Jeep outside the festival gates. *'Nine times out of ten, it's a parent.'*

Asking me to take a polygraph means that the shirt—or maybe they've found something else in the house—makes them think I might be involved in the boys' disappearance. Anger bubbles up in me. 'I'll take the test,' I say, 'but it's a waste of time. You know Kevin called me from here. Your guy—Christiansen— he was in the car.'

'Look,' Shoffler says, 'the phone call? You say that was your kid—but no one else can confirm that. It could have been anyone. Even if the call did come from here. . . ' He stops and shakes his head. I know what he's thinking and the word explodes in my brain: *accomplice*.

'It's just like that shoe you spotted out by the fence. You know?' Shoffler says.

'What shoe?' Liz asks in a panicky voice. 'There's a shoe?'

'We found a child's shoe at the fairground,' Shoffler says. 'According to your husband, it belongs to one of your boys.'

'Kevin,' I say. 'One of Kevin's Nikes.'

'You can understand why we'd like you to take a test,' Shoffler says in what I guess is meant to be a soothing voice, 'because . . . the thing is, what we've got, it's all . . . ' He doesn't say it, but I get the message. I could have put the shoe there, outside the jousting ring, then pointed it out to Shoffler. An accomplice could have made the phone call from this house to my cellphone. There's been no ransom note, no telephone call. There's no outside corroboration for my story. It all begins and ends with me.

'Somebody had to see us there,' I say. 'I mean—it's crazy. Thousands of people saw us.'

'As for the fair visitors,' Shoffler says in a conciliatory tone, 'I'm sure you're right. We got plenty of volunteers claiming to remember you. But of course the thing's been all over the tube. Most of the folks who have come forward weren't even there during the right stretch of time. Now, I'm sure we'll eventually find plenty of reliable witnesses who saw you and your sons and can confirm the time frame. But until we do, my advice is—take the test.'

'Of course I'll take the test,' I say.

'Good,' the detective says. 'I'll schedule it.'

My parents and Jack have materialised in the hall.

'What's this about a test?' Jack asks.

'They want Alex to take a polygraph,' Liz blurts out.

'A lie detector test?' my father says to Shoffler. 'What the hell is that supposed to mean?'

'It's routine,' he says. 'Exclusionary. Like the fingerprints.'

'Uh-huh,' my father says. 'Look, Detective Shoffler, be frank with me: do we need a lawyer here?'

'If your son wants—'

'No,' I say, interrupting the detective. 'I don't need a lawyer.'

'I'll set it up for the morning,' Shoffler says.

I'm sinking. Subconsciously I've invested more in believing that the authorities will track down whoever took my sons, will find Kevin and Sean and bring them home, than I realised. I put faith in their professionalism and energy, in their manpower and resources, in evidence technicians and databases. But if the request that I take a polygraph means they think I played some active role in my sons' disappearance, then there's no hope. The authorities are so far off the track that I may as well put my faith in the yellow ribbons neighbours have begun to string around the trees up and down the street.

CHAPTER FOUR

The polygraph test is scheduled for eleven that morning. Despite my innocence, I can't help worrying. How can a machine designed to measure galvanic response distinguish kinds of stress? How can a mechanical device separate anxiety about telling lies from anxiety about taking the test, about being falsely accused, about the fate of my missing children?

Every time the phone rings—which is once every five minutes—we wait, suspended between hope and fear. We're relieved when the call offers no information about the boys, when it's just another call from the media or the police or a friend. The cliché turns out to be true. No news is good news. A reprieve.

Then it's time. Christiansen arrives with a fellow officer to escort me to the squad car. Although I'm not in handcuffs, 'escorting' doesn't begin to describe how I'm hustled down the steps and propelled through the shouting, strobe-dappled crowd. By the time we get to the car, I'm blind from the dazzle.

Christiansen pushes me inside. I'm being transported to the Park Street station for the polygraph. DC is involved now because there are 'jurisdictional questions to be resolved, dependent on the location and the nature of the crime'. This is the way Shoffler explained it at this morning's press conference. Like most authorities, he didn't explain further. I got it, though—along with millions of Americans who watched various 'experts' deconstruct Shoffler's statement. It comes down to this.

Scenario 1: I murdered my kids at home, disposed of their bodies, then drove sixty miles to Cromwell, Maryland. I then wandered around the fairground for a couple of hours to establish my alibi before reporting the kids missing. Jurisdiction: DC.

Scenario 2: I murdered my kids in Maryland, somewhere near the Renaissance Faire. Jurisdiction: Anne Arundel County.

Scenario 3: The boys were kidnapped from the Renaissance Faire (this has now been referred to by at least one broadcaster as 'the father's version of events'). Jurisdiction: Anne Arundel County in conjunction with the FBI.

THE POLICE STATION has a kind of played-out atmosphere which, against all odds, calms me down. It's so different from the adrenalised energy at home. I get the sense that most of the people who work there see so much barbarity on a regular basis that it's blunted their emotional response. No matter how unthinkable a crime—even the murder of children—there's a precedent, a process, a number for it in the criminal code.

Just like when I was getting fingerprinted, I feel trapped. Just being asked to take a polygraph counts against me. I won't fail the test, but as someone who's covered a lot of court cases, I know it's possible the result will be 'inconclusive'.

The test is a form of pressure, pure and simple. You have a suspect, you squeeze him, make him nervous in every possible way. That's what Shoffler wants: to squeeze me.

The technician squirts gel onto the sensors and attaches them to my skin. The gel is very cold.

The polygraph man asks me routine questions ('Is your name Alex?' 'Is the shirt you are wearing blue?') before moving on to the heart of the matter ('Did you kill Sean and Kevin Callahan?' 'Do you know the whereabouts of Sean and Kevin?').

And then it's over. I'm handed a foil-wrapped, moisturised wipe to remove any residue of gel from my skin. I roll down my sleeves expecting to return to the squad car and be driven home. Instead, Shoffler materialises, with a young African-American man he introduces as Detective Price. We go to Price's cubicle.

'Tell me something, Alex,' Shoffler asks, 'you mind going through your story one more time?'

I shrug. I don't see the point, but why not? 'Fine.'

'Thing is, Detective Price has some special training in . . . ah . . . questioning people. What I hear is he's got a real gift for tickling the memory bank. What I hope is maybe you'll come up with something that will help us find your sons.'

'Some kind of lead,' Price says. 'That's what we all want.'

This is bull and all three of us know it. Shoffler's looking for inconsistencies in my story. Which means that's what he thinks it is—a *story.* 'Whatever you want,' I say.

Detective Price sits across from me, straddling a chair. 'You must be sick of this,' he says.

It's just me and him in the room. Shoffler is probably behind the long mirror against the opposite wall.

We start by going through my account of Saturday one more time, in great detail. Then we move on to my finances.

'It's tough, isn't it, running two separate households on more or less the same income?'

I admit that it's a strain, financially, but tell Price that Liz and I are getting by.

'I understand you were late with your support payments twice.'

I nod. 'That's true. But it wasn't because of the money. I was abroad. On assignment. You can check with the station.'

'Abroad,' Price says. His face twitches when he repeats the word, as if he just got a whiff of something unpleasant. 'I see. Your house—that's a pricey neighbourhood, isn't it? If you don't work things out with Liz, you're going to have to sell, right?'

I suddenly get angry. 'What are you saying? You think I killed my kids because I don't want to move out of Cleveland Park?'

He makes a conciliatory gesture. 'OK, new subject. Did the boys have insurance? Some policy out there?'

'Insurance? You mean medical insurance?'

Price shakes his head. 'I mean life insurance.'

'Life insurance? They're six years old!'

Then I get it, and my voice, angry and too loud, shows it. 'Now you're suggesting I killed my kids for insurance!? What—and after a decent interval, I'm going to cash in and move to Brazil! Are you out of your mind?'

'No one's suggesting anything of the sort,' Price says calmly.

'We're just talking about the pressures you're under. Personally, I think it's far more likely that you simply lost your temper, the way you did just now, and it went a little further than you intended . . .'

'*Look*,' I say, my voice shaking. 'I didn't kill my children.'

'Mr Callahan, maybe we should take a break here. Maybe you *should* consult an attorney.'

'I don't need a break and I don't need a fucking attorney.'

'Did Detective Shoffler tell you that someone saw you in the parking lot, opening your car after you reported the boys missing?'

'I was checking to see if the boys went to the car when they couldn't find me.'

It goes on like this. One hour, two hours, three, four. We're into hour five, when Price suggests we go over the whole story again.

We do. Price has a powerful charm and he uses it to persuade me that he wants to be my friend, he really does. And the way to get in tight with my new friend is to tell him what he wants to hear. And what he wants to hear—not that he'd hold it against me—is that I did it. I lost it, we all do, it's the human condition.

As the hours slide by, I begin to slip into a dangerous apathy. I want to stop talking. I want to sleep.

We're going over the journey through the fairground yet again when someone raps on the door. Detective Price frowns, says 'Excuse me one moment,' gets up, opens the door a crack, conducts a brief conversation with someone. Although this discussion is conducted at the volume of a whisper, I can tell it's an argument.

Then Price comes back and launches into a whole new line of questioning, one that baffles me. 'What is your religion, Alex?'

'I'm not very religious. I'm sort of a lapsed Catholic.'

There are questions about what I think about animal sacrifice, my spiritual convictions, my opinion on religions such as Wicca.

'Look,' I say finally, 'where are we going with this? I don't understand the relevance.'

'It's not idle curiosity,' he says. 'I can assure you of that.'

And looking at him, at the professionally disappointed expression on his face, I finally realise that no amount of cooperation on my part is going to exonerate me. Price is interested only in answers that point towards my guilt.

And since I'm not guilty, there's no reason to sit here and endure this. I tell him I want to go home.

'You refuse to submit to further questioning.'

'I don't see the point.'

'You refuse. Is that what you're telling me?'

I decide to oblige him. What can it matter? 'Yes,' I say. 'I refuse.'

Price gets up. He leaves me alone in the room.

A RAP on the door jolts me out of a half-sleep. It's Shoffler, not Price. 'Let's go,' he says. I know right away that something's happened. His attitude towards me has changed, but in a way I can't read. I follow him out to his car, a big white Ford, a Crown Victoria. It's daytime—morning. I spent the night in the interrogation room.

It scares me when Shoffler holds open the door for me. Why is he suddenly solicitous of my feelings? *Because: he feels sorry for me.*

When he gets in and fastens his seat belt, I brace myself, rigid against the expected sombre tone, the terrible news.

'The test came back,' Shoffler says, shaking his head.

'What?' This is not what I'm expecting, and my relief is immediate and profound. 'You mean the polygraph test?'

'No,' Shoffler says. 'No—the lab test on the T-shirt.'

'And . . . what?'

'Chicken blood,' he says, with a quick look my way.

'Chicken blood!' I repeat, elated. The blood was not human blood. It wasn't my *kid's* blood.

I realise now what Jason Price was getting at with his questions about religion and animal sacrifice. My elation fades.

'Look,' Shoffler says, 'we pretty much, well, we also came up with some solid witnesses who saw you at the fair with the boys. The guy who runs the Jacob's ladder—he remembered your boys real well. Told us one of the kids climbed the ladder like a monkey.'

'He just sort of came out of the woodwork?'

'Had Sunday and Monday off, so we didn't get to him until this morning. And then after we questioned him, we wanted to check him out. Make sure he doesn't know you.' A sigh. 'Actually, we got a number of fair employees who saw you and the kids. Anyway, what gets you off the hook is we got your afternoon pieced together now from stand-up witness to stand-up witness, got you covered from the time you dropped off the tape at the TV station with the kids in tow to the time you showed up at security saying the kids were missing. So, looks like I owe you an apology, Alex.'

We're sitting at a light. My euphoria lasts about as long as it takes for the lights to turn. Yes, it feels good that I'm no longer a suspect.

But the kids are still gone, so it's still the same nightmare.

'I'm sorry about the polygraph test,' Shoffler continues, 'and that whole routine with Price. I apologise. I really do.'

'You thought I did it. In the meantime, whoever took my kids has all the time in the world . . . ' I rant on until it seems pointless to continue. Outside the window a couple of little kids holding balloons from the zoo walk past with their mother. *If only we'd gone to the zoo.* I try to suppress these useless excursions into rearranging the past, but they pop up at least a hundred times a day. I press my eyes shut.

After a while, Shoffler says, 'This man with the dog, at the joust. Got a couple of witnesses claim they saw him with your boys.'

My heart goes cold. 'You think that's the guy?'

'Well, we don't want to get ahead of ourselves. The tall man, the dog with the ruff—all that was in the news, so we take everything with a grain of salt. Lucky for us, somehow it never got into the news what kind of dog it was—so that gives us a kinda litmus test for the witnesses. We know it was a whippet, so if they saw a man with a German shepherd or a dachshund . . .'

'Right.'

'I was gonna ask you about what kinda look you got at the guy. You remember his face?'

I hesitate. 'I don't know. I didn't really pay attention. I noticed his costume, and the dog. I thought he worked for the fair.'

'I'd like to put you with a sketch artist, see what you come up with.'

IN THE NEXT TWO DAYS, energetic friends and neighbours rally around. Now that I'm no longer a suspect, the floodgates are open again. The household is inundated with food—casseroles, cookies, salads, enormous baskets stuffed with every imaginable edible.

The police established a hotline and although they discourage the idea of a second one, a tag team of neighbours can't be stopped. Jack organises the volunteers who run this 'totline.' Unlike the official hotline, this one promises a reward plus confidentiality.

A trio of Liz's old running buddies organises the printing and distribution of thousands of fliers. The boys' faces are on every conceivable storefront and bus shelter, each flier with its little fringe of tear-offs printed with the hotline number.

I work with a police artist named Marijke Wilcke, trying to dredge up the image of the man with the dog. Since I just caught a glimpse of the guy, I'm not optimistic.

We have trouble right away, trying to establish the shape of the man's face. The fact that he was wearing a ruff, too, creates problems, not only because it makes it hard for me to determine the length of his face, but also because it obscures the conjunction of neck and shoulder and his jawline. The neatly trimmed goatee and moustache don't help, either. Despite Marijke's skill at translating my vague impressions onto the page, the result is generic.

Shoffler stops by to take a look.

'What do you think?' Marijke asks.

'Looks like they're all on the same bus.'

'What?' I ask.

'Marijke and Larry—he's another sketch artist—they been through this with three other eyewitnesses who saw this guy with your kids.' To Marijke he says, 'Go on. Give him the tour.'

She brings up in sequence five versions of the man with the dog, all of which prominently feature the goatee and sharply trimmed mustache. Apart from that, the sketches vary. 'Facial hair,' Marijke sighs, 'especially when it is trimmed into geometric shapes and clean lines—it's just so dramatic it makes the other features fade. It's what you remember. Maybe it's even pasted on.'

THE OFFICIAL POSITION shifts. With the boys stipulated as the victims of a kidnapping, an FBI agent is assigned to the case. Shoffler tells me ahead of time that Judy Jones is very young but very smart. 'A rookie, but a real firecracker.'

We gather in the family room. Shoffler introduces her while Liz sits next to me and holds my hand, although there's nothing intimate about this. We're like two strangers at the site of a disaster. Liz and I present a united front in public. But except for moments when she breaks down and needs a shoulder to cry on, she's formal and distant.

'The depth of the Bureau's involvement varies,' Judy Jones says. 'Since we are satisfied with police conduct of the investigation, our role will be limited to support.'

'How can you be satisfied with the police conduct?' Jack asks. 'They thought Alex was the guy and while they're putting him through the wringer, the real guy's making tracks.'

'I understand your feelings. But you have to understand that there's nothing in the conduct of the case that warrants criticism. As soon as he was summoned, Detective Shoffler took steps to secure the scene. He immediately launched a vigorous search. He and his team have questioned a large number of witnesses, some of them more than once. He's pursued the case by the book, and that includes—' she glances my way and offers a tiny sympathetic grimace '—suspecting and questioning Mr Callahan.'

'How's that?' Jack says, his face red with belligerence. 'The police waste their time with Alex here, and boom—no one's even looking for my grandsons. Everyone thinks they're dead.'

'In the field of criminal justice,' Jones says, 'we are all to a certain extent students of history. In suspecting Mr Callahan, Detective Shoffler was going with history. The truth is that most child abductions and murders are committed by parents—especially when those parents are separated.'

I change the subject and ask, 'What about the T-shirt? Do you have any theories about that?'

She glances at Detective Shoffler. 'There's nothing in the database. Maybe some kind of animal sacrifice. We're looking into that.'

Shoffler grimaces. 'What I think is maybe the T-shirt was just to throw off pursuit. Until that lab test came back, it was natural to focus certain resources on Alex.' He wags his head sadly. 'I think the T-shirt was deliberate and it worked like a charm.'

Liz groans and her head droops.

'Detective Shoffler asked me to pick up a couple of threads in the investigation,' Jones tells us. 'First, the dimes. The lab checked them for prints to no avail. And that folded rabbit—I've looked into that.'

'Really—what did you find out?' I ask.

She shrugs. 'Not much. We ran it by an origami expert. He said it was cleverly constructed and of high-intermediate level, but that's about all he could tell us.'

'What about the material?' Liz asks. 'That skin or whatever it is.'

'Apparently it does feel like skin. It's called elephant hide. But in fact it's a special kind of paper used in origami. Very commonly available and pretty much the paper of choice at a certain level. I'm afraid tracking the source of it doesn't look promising.'

Liz looks as if she's going to start crying.

'The other area Detective Shoffler has asked me to pursue,' Jones says, 'is the question of Mr Callahan's possible enemies. I've got a copy of the list Mr Callahan supplied, and when we're done here—' she shifts her gaze to me '—I'd like to go over it.'

'What if it's because they're *twins*,' my mother blurts out. 'I keep thinking about that Nazi doctor . . . his experiments.' She presses her hand to her mouth. 'I'm sorry.' She looks at Liz and me.

Some modern-day Mengele. I can't handle it.

'I checked on twins,' Judy Jones tells us, 'and I can tell you that in the past twenty years, there are very few cases of twins being kidnapped. None at all that seem relevant to this case.'

'What about those boys out in LA? Some kind of Hispanic name . . . .' This from Jack.

'The Ramirez twins,' I say. 'Police caught the kidnapper with the bodies of the boys,' I tell them. 'Then he committed suicide.'

'That's about as closed as a case can get,' Jones says. 'So . . .'

TEN DAYS after the disappearance, Shoffler stops by again. Everyone else is busy so we talk alone.

First he tells me he's getting a lot more information about the man with the dog. 'What we're getting is that this guy had kids around him all the time. It's the dog, right? It's very cute. It works like a magnet for this guy. A kid magnet.'

'That's what I saw—a bunch of kids petting this dog.'

'We got some confirmation from one of the ticket sellers at the gate. He remembers the boys leaving with a man and a dog.'

'Really? Where's this ticket seller been?'

'He's kind of a reluctant witness. Has a rap sheet. He wasn't volunteering to come forward. But we got to him the second time around. This time we ask did he see a tall man with a dog and two kids *leaving* the park. Well, this kid, basically a law-abiding citizen except he likes to smoke pot, you know—he worries about it. Would keeping his mouth shut be lying? Would that be a parole violation? So, he comes forward.'

'Huh.'

'I was sceptical, too. So anyway, here's what the guy tells me. He doesn't really remember the twins, just two kids about the same size. What he remembers is that the group struck him as weird.'

'The group?'

'The two kids, the man, the dog. I ask what does he mean. Weird how? And what he tells me is he noticed that the man was in costume, the *dog* was in costume—but the kids were not. That didn't make sense to him. When he said that, it rang true, you know? It's not the kind of thing you'd make up. Plus, he nailed the dog.'

'Said it was a whippet?'

Shoffler pulls out his notebook, puts on his glasses. He's very attached to his notebooks and he writes everything down. Sometimes he'll refer to notes several times in the course of a conversation.

Now he finds what he's looking for. 'Yeah, here it is. I ask him what kind of dog the tall guy has, and he tells me it's "one of those fast dogs. Like a greyhound, but not as big."'

'There you go.'

'So then I ask him what the owner was wearing. And he says: "I told you—a costume." The guy's getting real tired of me,' the detective says, 'but I press him. Can he be more specific? Well, the tall man wasn't a king. He wasn't a knight. The guy didn't know *what* he was. His costume had this ruff, same crazy neckwear as the dog. And then he tells me the guy wore tights and he had a *flute.*' Shoffler looks up at me over his reading glasses. 'I say, hold it—he had a *flute?* Cause I got that from one other source, but I didn't make much of it. The kid brightens, like he's just had a realisation. "The guy wore this jacket, four different colours. And the flute. That's what he was supposed to be: the Pied Piper."'

Shoffler closes his notebook. He looks pleased with himself, but I feel a skitter of dread down the back of my neck. How did that fairy tale go? The way I remember it, the piper got rid of the village's rats, but the town wouldn't pay up. He piped a tune and all the children followed him. And then—didn't the children disappear?

CHAPTER FIVE

I always know how long it's been since the boys disappeared. I don't have to do the maths. Today, as I drive my parents to the airport, it's been thirty-one days, eight hours and a bit.

I suggested they go home (as Jack did a week ago) and it didn't take much to get past their token resistance.

As the days roll by, the media hoopla fades. Kevin and Sean are relegated to the occasional news update. The calls and emails, volunteers and donations fall off too. Meanwhile, the police are doing 'everything we can'—which isn't much.

The situation between Liz and me continues to deteriorate. During the first few days after the boys were abducted, what happened was so terrible, we took some comfort in our common loss. That's long gone, replaced at first by formality then something less friendly. When our eyes meet, hers skid away from mine. Behind it all is the undeniable fact that at rock bottom, she blames me. As the agent who could have prevented the catastrophe, I am slowly becoming—in the heart and mind of my wife—its cause.

We attend a fundraiser sponsored by the Center for Missing and Exploited Children. It seemed impossible to refuse but the event is tough to stomach. Liz and I sit at the dais, along with other celebrities of misfortune. Some of the parents wear laminated photographs of their children pinned to their chests—a heartbreaking gallery of winsome smiles and sparkling eyes. The main speech is delivered by a single mother named Melinda, who tells the harrowing tale of her eight-year-old daughter's abduction and murder.

After the public departs, there's a prayer circle for parents and relatives of the missing. We sit on folding chairs, holding hands, and take turns reciting aloud the details of our personal catastrophes.

I walk out when I realise that most of those in the circle are in fact grieving. Like the parents and spouses of missing-in-action victims lost in Vietnam, they no longer seek their 'loved ones'. What they're after is 'closure'. In other words: the remains. Evidence of death.

'I can't stay here,' I whisper in my wife's ear. 'They think their kids are dead.' When I stand up to leave, she comes with me, but not because she wants to.

Her eyes are hard and unforgiving. 'Who do you think you are, Alex—judging them about how they were handling their loss?'

'They think their kids are dead. I don't.'

Liz bursts into tears.

That night, she announces, 'I'm going back to Maine.'

The next day, she's gone.

ALTHOUGH MY BOSS told me from the moment he heard about the boys that I could forget about work for 'as long as it takes', last week I got an email asking me to 'clarify' my plans. We were closing in on the 'month-mark', the message pointed out. Either I should come back soon, at least on a part-time basis, or I should request formal leave of absence.

Almost everyone agrees that returning to work is 'the best thing'. The basis for this conclusion is some sketchy notion of work as distracting and therefore therapeutic. It boils down to this: if I'm too busy to think about my sons, I'll be less depressed. I doubt it.

Getting up, getting dressed, the familiar commute—it seems so strange to resume this routine. And the station itself feels foreign. TV stations are crazy places, everyone rushing towards or recovering from a deadline. Me? I feel inert and idle amid the hive of activity. Voices lower when I walk by, glances slide away, no one knows what to say to me or how to act in my presence.

The day after I return to work, Shoffler drops by at the house. He arrives with a six-pack of Sierra Nevada and a huge soggy pizza. 'Health food,' he says, with his stuttery laugh.

I'm glad to see him. In fact, I can't think of anyone else I'd rather see at my door—except my sons. For openers, Shoffler is just about the only person in the world who's always ready to talk about the one thing of actual interest to me. Besides, he's cynical, funny and, I've come to realise, very smart. We usually end up going over and over the busted leads to see if there's something we missed.

The case file, he tells me, is seven binders thick. Each case, he's explained, starts with a single three-inch loose-leaf binder. The binders—which Shoffler has allowed me to look at—contain copies of every piece of paper generated by the investigation: report, witness statement, interview, crime-scene photo, forensics tests, search warrant, search warrant inventory, evidence receipt, and so on.

We eat the pizza, watch a baseball game, and shoot the breeze for a while before he gets around to the reason for his visit.

'I hate to tell you this, Alex,' he starts, then stops. At the look on my face, he pushes his hand towards me. 'Don't worry. It's not about the boys. It's about . . . me: I've been taken off the case.'

'What?' Shoffler is known as a bulldog, who never lets go, who sacrificed two marriages to work, who spends any spare moment pounding away at his cold cases. 'What do you mean? Why?'

A big sigh. 'It's not just you. All my cases are being reassigned. There's this new thing been in the works since 9/11 and it's finally happening: Metro Area Counter-Terrorism Unit. Officers from every jurisdiction. I'm the guy from Anne Arundel. I'm sorry.'

I say nothing. It's a real blow.

'Your case has been handed over to a young detective named Muriel Petrich. I may be a bulldog, but she's as smart as they get. And ambitious. That's a good combo.'

'Right.'

'Look, I know . . .' He shakes his head. 'You can count on me to keep my hand in, right? And call me anytime, any reason. You get an idea, a lead, whatever, I'll do what I can. But give Petrich a chance.'

'Right.' I can't keep the bitterness out of my voice. I feel Kevin and Sean are being abandoned.

That night I come to a decision. Going back to work, stumbling through the hours in a preoccupied fog—I can't do that.

I'm going to find my sons.

WHEN I TURN in my resignation, everyone tries to talk me out of quitting. I should give it more time, etc. I guess they think I'll fall apart entirely without the structure of work. And, in fact, I'm not sure what I'm going to do about money. Technically, according to the terms of our separation agreement, I can't even take a leave of absence because it diminishes my ability to provide support for Liz. I'll have to hit on my father for a loan. I've got a couple of friends good for a few grand. I'll beg. Borrow. Whatever it takes.

Everyone tells me I'm making a mistake. What can I do that hasn't already been done? What goes unsaid is that most of them think I'm chasing smoke, that my children are dead and that I should face that likelihood—while not abandoning hope, of course. Miracles do happen.

Even Shoffler tries to dissuade me. 'Alex,' he says on the phone. 'Don't do it. I've seen it before, and it's nothing but heartbreak. You do this and you're gonna burn yourself out—emotionally *and* financially.'

'So what?'

The detective sighs. 'I know what you're thinking—that you're gonna bring more energy to the search than any professionals could and so you'll succeed where the rest of us have failed. You think just because you *care* more, you'll find your boys. What I'm saying—'

'I will find them,' I interrupt. 'Or I'll find out what happened to them. If it burns up all my resources, if it burns me out—so be it.'

Shoffler lets out a long sigh.

In the background, I can hear people talking, phones ringing, the clacking of computer keyboards. 'Well,' Shoffler says finally in a weary voice, 'keep in touch.'

IN MANY WAYS, I'm much better equipped for the task of searching for my sons than most parents would be. I'm a reporter: finding out things is what I *do*.

I go over it all again. Starting with the Piper. I still think of him that way, despite Shoffler's caution about the costume being a disguise.

Since I don't know enough about him to have a real image of him, I concentrate on what I do know.

He's a man who lives somewhere, who buys groceries, drives a car, wears a particular kind of socks . . . and he kidnapped my sons. And he had a reason for it.

MOTIVE, I write at the top of my yellow pad.

Profit? The absence of a ransom note seems to rule that out.

Retaliation? Did someone abduct the boys in retaliation against me, for some story I did? True, my work put me in contact with some bad people, but Shoffler looked into this angle and ended up discounting it.

Sexual predator? I don't really buy it. Why grab two kids—which would only make the abduction more difficult. And then—why return them to the house? Sexual predators are impulsive and opportunistic. Or so they say. Going back to the house, leaving mementos—that was premeditated. Not a classic pattern.

Kiddie porn? Cute blond twins. Were they abducted by a ring to make a film or procured for sale to someone with a twin thing? Shoffler looked into this, but it didn't go anywhere.

Medical experiment? Shoffler rejected the Dr Mengele theory.

I sit for a long time trying to think of other possibilities. It's conceivable the boys were abducted by someone desperate for children. I mull this over, the idea of an obsessed wannabe parent. Whoever it was, he'd have to be a total recluse, living outside of society—because there's been no credible sighting of the boys since the day they were abducted. And what about the dimes? The T-shirt? The phone call?

I take a deep breath. Beneath the list of motives, I write a second word: CLUES.

Origami rabbit
Chicken blood
Row of dimes

The abductor's mementos. FBI agent Judy Jones established that the rabbit was folded of standard material, bore no fingerprints, was of high-intermediate difficulty. And that was about it. Still, the Piper left the thing on the dresser. Why?

The chicken blood. It was possible that the T-shirt was a ruse to focus suspicion on me, but that was only an assumption. The chicken blood might have some other meaning.

The dimes. The lab checked them for prints. There was also an attempt to source them—the FBI looked into mint marks and the dates of the coins—but 'Liberty head' dimes were minted for almost thirty years and there are millions of them out there.

There are other clues. For instance, the dog. Then there's the Piper himself—his costume. Was that just a disguise, or did it have meaning? And what about the costume—where do you go for Piper gear? Did Shoffler check that out? If, so what did he find out?

Under CLUES, I add:

Whippet
Piper costume
Ruff

I need a look at Shoffler's files. Muriel Petrich's files. I pick up the phone and call Petrich. She's not in. I leave a message.

UNTIL PETRICH gets back to me, I hit the Internet. I've been to a lot of the sites dealing with abducted children; maybe there's something I've missed, some angle I've overlooked. I'm engulfed by the faces of the vanished—including the smiling faces of Kevin and Sean.

I correct myself. No one 'vanishes'. The man who went to the Renaissance Faire dressed up as the Pied Piper is the one who ripped my sons out of my life . . . and into his world. And I'm going to find out who he is and why he did it.

On an impulse, I plug *twins* into the search field of Google along with a couple of other key words: *abduction, missing, children.*

Google kicks out more than a hundred thousand sites.

I specify *missing twins.* Still more than thirty-three thousand listings. Virtually all of the stories are about Kevin and Sean.

I log on to LexisNexis, using my password from the station. I enter the search terms *missing twins* and restrict the search to news stories published before the date of the boys' abduction.

The list gives more than a thousand stories, but once I get into it, I see that in real terms there are only three stories about abducted twins.

The Ramirez boys. The press raised this case within hours of the story about Kevin and Sean breaking because the similarities were so striking. A couple of years ago, Julio and Wilson Ramirez were abducted from a gymnastics class in West LA. Not only were the Ramirez boys identical twins, but at the time they were abducted they were seven years old—almost the same age as Kevin and Sean. Three months after they disappeared, the killer was apprehended at a cabin in the mountains not far from Big Sur. The bodies of the dead boys were found at the cabin—one in his refrigerator, neatly packaged like cuts of beef, the other suspended in a well shaft. The killer, Charley Vermillion, was taken into custody. He turned out to be a sexual psychopath who'd been released from a loony bin about a month prior to the boys' disappearance. Vermillion was cuffed and slapped into a squad car. But before the squad car made it to the local lockup, he was dead, having chewed a cyanide capsule he'd taped under the collar of his shirt. So the Ramirez case was closed, and with the perp dead, there wasn't any way it could be relevant to my boys. Thank God.

The second story involves the Gabler twins. This is a false hit, though, because the Gablers were women—and Vegas showgirls, at that. The story showed up in my search because one of my search terms was *children* and the newspapers reported that the Gablers had appeared in a musical revue called *Children of the Future*. They disappeared about three years ago and turned up a month later, their decomposing bodies found by a hiker in a 'rugged area' twenty miles outside Vegas. It's hard to see how they could possibly have any connection to my boys.

Which leaves the Sandling twins: Chandler and Connor. I'm familiar with this one, too—the one with a happy ending. The way I remember the case, the mother was implicated in the abduction of her kids—although never prosecuted.

Because of the mother's alleged involvement, I never really focused on the case. I'm willing to take a second look now, because it's just occurred to me: who else do I know who is wrongly suspected of being involved in the disappearance of his children?

I take a look. Unlike myself, Emma Sandling was not an upstanding member of the community, but a heroin addict who'd been through countless rehab programmes; she wasn't much of a mother. Then there was the 'live-in boyfriend', plus the fact that at the time of the abduction, Sandling and her two sons were living in a tent in a state park near Corvallis, Oregon.

The boyfriend was a drifter, Dalt Trueblood. It turned out he was a parole violator. When the boys disappeared, Trueblood did, too, and until he turned up a few weeks later in Portland, it was not unreasonable to think that the Sandling boys might be with him.

Between her addicted past, her lifestyle and the missing boyfriend, suspicions settled on Sandling. The idea seemed to be that she and Trueblood were in collusion. As for Trueblood, when the police arrested him in Portland and questioned him, he said he fled because the kidnapping 'spooked' him.

The circumstances of the kidnapping were simple enough: Sandling took her boys to the McDonald's in Corvallis, intending to treat them to a Happy Meal. She left them in the ball pit while she went to get the food. No other kids—or adults—were in the play area. When Sandling came back with the food, the kids were gone.

Unfortunately for Sandling, the adults and staff in the restaurant remembered seeing her, but none of them saw her children. It didn't help Sandling's case that at the time she reported her sons missing, she was known to leave her sons for hours at a time in the public library while she worked cleaning houses.

What followed was predictable: an explosion of recriminations within the Oregon child-protective bureaucracy and a police investigation with a tight focus on Emma Sandling. She was not charged but held 'for questioning' for thirty-two hours.

The boys showed up eight weeks later at a shopping mall near Eureka, California. According to a story in the *Sacramento Bee*, the boys had been riding in a small motor home for 'a long time' when the driver stopped for gas. It was the kind of RV—a truck and trailer, really—where the driver's cab is separated from the passenger compartment. The boys waited for the driver to let them out, but he didn't come. They banged on the side of the trailer and yelled, then one of them threw himself at the door and, to their surprise, it fell open.

They climbed out. One boy wanted to find the driver and get money for ice cream. But the other boy had come to doubt the story their abductor told them. He wanted to telephone their mom's best friend, Phoebe. So he and his brother ran towards a shopping plaza, and went inside. They went into a gift shop to ask if they could use the phone to make a collect call. The clerk recognised them and called the police.

By the time a squad car came to the scene, the RV was gone.

In the aftermath, press coverage of the happy reunion of Sandling with her sons was muted. There was cynical speculation about how that RV door 'fell open', about Sandling's successful efforts (enlisting a helpful lawyer to work pro bono) to protect the boys from aggressive interrogation by the authorities. Despite a wave of testimonials from employers, personnel at the school the boys attended, and friends about how Sandling had turned her life around, it took months for her to regain custody of her sons.

I expand my search and pull down everything I can about the Sandling case. The parallels—six-year-old twin boys kidnapped from a public place—are so striking I can't stop reading the clips. Maybe there's something I overlooked when I bought into the assumption that Sandling's sketchy personal history meant she'd rigged the kidnapping of her own sons. Reading through it all, it seems that what Sandling said happened did, in fact, happen. Trueblood had an alibi. No other accomplice surfaced. Sandling never changed her story.

I spend the next two hours talking to the police stations in Corvallis and Eureka. When I introduce myself and explain my area of interest—the Sandling case—I get stonewalled.

Using names published in the newspaper accounts of the kidnapping, I hunt down the telephone numbers of Emma Sandling's social workers, her lawyer and anyone else whose name I can prise out of the media coverage. I reach about half of them and I get the same reaction. They don't know where she is. They can't help me.

'So what's up?' Shoffler says.

'The Sandling twins.'

I catch the hesitation in his voice. 'So—what about them?'

'The more I read the more it sounds like Kevin and Sean. The parallels are compelling. I can't understand why you and Judy Jones dismissed the case as irrelevant.'

'We checked into it, Alex. You got the ages of the boys and the fact they're twins. That's it. There was a thorough investigation. But the mother . . . she wasn't exactly a pillar of the community, wasn't cooperative and afterwards she made herself scarce. She *said* it was to protect the boys, but she won't talk. And yet there's no perpetrator, no charges, no trial. The consensus was that she had a hand in it.'

'I don't think so. The more I look at it, the more I get this creepy feeling that whoever took the Sandling kids is the same guy who took mine. They got away, so he took my kids to *replace them*.'

'Huh.' A pause. 'A "creepy feeling"?'

'I'm looking at this thing and it sounds so much like my boys. I figure I'll take a closer look. But I *can't*, because for one thing, Emma Sandling's gone. She's fallen off the face of the earth. Then I talk to the cops out there in Oregon. Well, no, that's not accurate. I'm talking *at* the cops out there in Oregon. They flat out won't talk to me. They give me some bull about "privacy issues".'

'So this is why you called me.' He lets out a sigh.

'Yeah, I thought you might be able to talk to them.'

'I'm sorry, Alex. I can't help you. My hands are tied.'

'We're talking about my *sons.* Ray, you can't—'

But the detective is no longer on the line.

TWO HOURS LATER, I'm outside Shoffler's house in Greenbelt, Maryland, waiting in the car for him to show up, listening to the radio and periodically cranking up the air when it gets too hot.

I'm jolted out of a doze by a deep metallic concussion that seems to take place inside my skull. The sound is actually a rap on my car door. I open my eyes to see Shoffler looming next to my window. He's not happy to see me. Half in shadow, illuminated by the sickly green of the streetlight, he looks terrible, and so exhausted that my eyes flick to the dashboard clock. It is 3.32 a.m.

Shoffler scowls at me. 'Go home, Alex.'

'No, I need to talk to you.'

He pivots on his heel and moves towards the front door; he's inside before I can get out of the car. My impulse is to lean on the horn, force him to deal with me. But, remembering the look on his face, I decide against it. If I lean on the horn and get in Shoffler's face, I won't get anywhere. He might even have me arrested.

I move my car two blocks away and set the alarm on my cellphone to wake me at six. The detective won't catch me dozing again.

When he comes out of the door at 7.44, he looks surprisingly jaunty for a man who got four hours of sleep. And then he sees me, as I step out from behind his Crown Vic.

His shoulders drop. 'Jesus, Alex.' He wags his head. 'Get in.'

It's already hot outside, the sun a white blur behind the dull haze of sky. The interior of the car is stifling.

He backs out of the driveway and before long we're on Route 95.

'Where are we going?'

'I got a meeting,' he says. 'On the Hill.'

Shoffler plunges in and out of dense traffic, his driving so fearless and aggressive I have to work not to push my feet against the floor.

'Look,' he says after a while, 'I'm not really pissed at you.'

'You're not?'

'You know why? Because you're right. Jones and I—we did see the parallels. Jones gets on the horn to Corvallis. And what happened? Were they helpful? No. They more or less told us to get lost.'

'She's the FBI and they blow her off?'

'They're polite, but yes they blow her off. Here's the deal: Emma Sandling has some issues with the way her boys' case was handled. She's suing the police out there. Now, the cops don't trust Sandling. They still think she was *involved.* So why—ask yourself—would Sandling be anxious to talk to anybody connected to law enforcement? Anyway, when Jones called, she got nowhere. Sandling won't talk, the cops won't talk, the lawyers won't talk. We asked.'

'Did Sandling know about Kevin and Sean?'

Shoffler just looks at me. 'The thing is, your boys' kidnapping brought the whole thing back. It terrified her.'

'How do you know?'

'We had a conference call: me, Jones, Sandling and her lawyers. We laid on the guilt as thick as we could. Here were two boys in peril, her boys might have information helpful in the investigation, how could she as a mother . . . blah blah blah.'

'And?

'Nothing. We did not get to first base. Wherever she's living now, no one knows who she is. And she wants to keep it that way. She's worried about some kind of leak, that her boys' case will end up all over the news again, that they'll be outed in their new place. Maybe the perp will come back for another round. Sandling is not interested. She won't say boo.'

I just sit there, in a funk of anger and impotence. I'm pissed at Sandling, the cops, everybody. And what's worse, I'm sick at heart.

'I can do two things for you,' Shoffler says. 'First—and I doubt this will do you a lot of good—I can get you a copy of the sketch. The one they did working with the Sandling kids. Jones got that out of them. I wasn't supposed to make a copy, but I did. Second thing, Sandling's maiden name is Whalen.'

'You think that's the name she's using?'

'I wouldn't know,' Shoffler says, flashing me a grin. 'I was constrained from pursuing the matter.'

WHEN I open the door the next morning to go out for the paper, there's a manila envelope inside the screen door. I'm not expecting much, but I'm still disappointed when I see the sketch. The face is expressionless, as real faces never are. I take the sketch to my study and line it up with the sketches Marijke made, one from my glimpse of the Piper, the others produced by sessions with other eyewitnesses. There's something about the eyes, maybe, that looks the same from sketch to sketch. But apart from that . . . The faces gaze down on me, inscrutable, almost mocking: *You don't know who I am.*

On the advice of several friends, I call an investigative agency who put me on to their best missing-person investigator—a woman named Mary McCafferty. 'Finding her shouldn't be a problem,' she tells me. 'She may not have had an address, living in a park, but she apparently had a library card. There will be school records, grocery shopper cards. Believe me, unless you really work at it, you're in a thousand databases these days. If she's using her maiden name, it's a piece of cake. I might have something by tomorrow. Email OK?'

'Email's fine.'

'We're all set.' She hesitates. 'But mine's the easy part. *You* still have to get her to talk to you.'

CHAPTER SIX

McCafferty comes through. Emma Sandling née Whalen lives in Florida. The next morning, I'm on a flight to Daytona Beach.

Then I'm coasting along Highway A-1-A, a sun-bleached strip flanked on both sides by fast-food outlets, motels, miniature golf courses and the occasional wind-lashed palm. Every once in a while, between the hotels and condos on the ocean side, I catch a glimpse of why all this exists: white sand and the hard glitter of the Atlantic.

After several miles, I spot the landmark I've been looking for, the huge sprawl of the Adam's Mark Hotel. My room at the Drop Anchor Inn is a block away on the other, less desirable side of the road. When I step out of my rented Hyundai Sonata, heat radiates from the pavement, so dense and humid and hot it's like an assault.

Emma Sandling, now Susie Whalen, works near here, right on the beach. She operates a concession stand called the Beach Bunny, a couple of hundred yards from the Adam's Mark. She's also a part-time student at the Daytona Beach Community College. Her boys attend a string of free vacation Bible schools. Whalen drives a red

'84 Subaru with Save-the-Manatee plates. She and the boys live in a tiny rental apartment in Port Orange. All as per an email from McCafferty, who billed me for just two hours.

My plan is to go to the Beach Bunny, rent a chair and umbrella, buy a tube of sunscreen, and chat Emma Sandling up. I'm good at this kind of thing; most reporters are.

I PAY for a day ticket, put the receipt on the dashboard, and turn my car onto the beach, falling in line behind a black Explorer. We roll along the sand at ten miles per hour. To my left is the white beach, the forest of umbrellas, towels and people, the expanse of ocean and sky. I spot the van where Emma Sandling works. It's under a huge inflated rabbit—dressed in a bikini.

And then I'm past the van, my first glimpse of Emma Sandling that of a figure inside the service window, counting out change. She's a small woman with coppery hair pulled back in a ponytail. She wears pink shorts and a white halter top. About a hundred yards from the Beach Bunny, I nose the Sonata into a space between a white pickup and a rusting Blazer and approach the van.

'Help you?' She has an engaging smile. Dimples.

'Just a bottle of water.'

'Sure thing. The small one or the one-litre size?'

'I'll take the litre.'

'That's good,' she says. 'It's hot. You want to stay hydrated.'

She puts the change on the counter, looking past me to the woman next in line.

I find an open spot on the uncrowded beach, stretch out my towel on the hard sand, and watch the waves roll in. I sit there with the sun beating down on my back and the image of Emma Sandling in my mind. My skin feels too hot, and when I close my eyes, there's a sort of thudding in my head. By the time I get back to the car, there is this single depressing thought: *It won't work.* Sure, I can get close to Emma Sandling, maybe even make friends with her. But what about when I get around to the subject at hand? When her new friend starts talking about the abduction of her sons—an incident she's gone to such lengths to bury in the past? There's only one thing to do: throw myself on her mercy.

Thanks to McCafferty's email, I know Emma's schedule. She'll close the Beach Bunny at five, then drive to Ormond Beach to pick up the boys from Bible school. Some fast food, I'd guess, and then she'll drop the kids at the baby sitter's in Port Orange. Leaving just enough time to get to her seven o'clock class at the Daytona Beach Community College. That goes on until nine-thirty, after which she picks up the kids and heads home. If I can find her car in the parking lot at the community college, I'll wait for her there.

AT NINE-FIFTEEN, I drive into the college's parking lot and find Emma's red Subaru with the Save-the-Manatee plates. I park a few spaces away and get out of the car. I feel conspicuous just standing there, so I gravitate towards a small strip of vegetation that separates the parking lot from a service road and wait. I'm edgy and restless. It's dark now.

Five minutes later, I see Emma, hurrying in my direction. It occurs to me it might seem creepy, the way I'm standing in the bushes, so I walk to my car and open the hood. Instantly this seems like a mistake.

She has her keys out and she cuts a wary glance my way before opening her door.

I feel paralysed.

She rolls down the window and turns on the ignition. By the time I can get myself to move, she's fastening her seatbelt. Finally I approach her, holding my hand up. 'Excuse me?' I say.

'I'm sorry, but I'm really in a hurry.'

'Wait,' I blurt out. 'We have a tragedy in common. I'm Alex Callahan. My sons Kevin and Sean have been abducted. Your tragedy's over, Emma, but mine is ongoing. I need your help.'

My rehearsed words sound strange, even to me. Emma frowns. It's the sound of her name, I think, that does it. The name she doesn't use any more. I see the realisation hit, recognition followed by horror. Then she's gone, driving away in a pebbly screech.

I blew it. The air presses in on me, heavy and dense.

I'm still standing in the the same place when she comes back.

She stops her car, opens the door. Light spills out and she sits there in its illumination. 'Look—I'm sorry. I didn't feel good about it—me being the one person who could really sympathise with you but instead I did everything I could to keep you away . . . And when I saw about your boys on the television—oh God.' She takes a juddery breath. 'I knew it was him, I just knew it. And . . . ' Her voice is falling apart now. 'I thought . . . *good*, now he won't come back. He's got what he wants.' She chokes in a sob. 'I'm sorry.'

'Hey,' I start, 'that's OK. I under—'

'No, it's not,' she says. 'I'm so ashamed of myself. The thing is, when the kids showed up in Eureka—you'd think everybody would be sooooo happy. But they weren't, not really. The happy ending was good for forty-eight hours. After that, they wanted to get back to tragedy. It was so hard. They just would not leave the little guys alone. They kept picking away at them. And then they took them away from me. I'm still afraid they'll find some way to take them away.'

'I understand.'

'See, they still don't believe I'm innocent. They just wouldn't believe the truth—that Dalt just *left*, just spooked when I called from the police station and told him what happened. He'd had a kind of messy past; he spent some time in prison. So they were always thinking they'd find the kids buried somewhere.'

'Look, I have a lot of sympathy for you. But the reason I came looking for you is because I'm desperate. I think whoever took your sons has my sons now.'

She looks away from me, and when she looks back, I see that she's crying. She holds her face in her hands. 'I know.'

'Will you talk to me? Just tell me about it.'

'I don't know what I can tell you that's going to help, but . . . ' She shrugs, then looks at her watch. 'The baby sitter's going to be worried. Why don't you come to the Bunny tomorrow?'

I don't know why, but I play innocent. 'The Bunny?'

'I saw you there—you bought a bottle of water.' She taps her temple. 'Too bad I didn't see the guy who took the kids. I never forget a face.'

I HELP EMMA during the times when she gets slammed with customers—handing her cans of soda, restocking the back-up cooler. We talk during the slow periods. By midmorning, we've each recited our basic stories. To me, there's little question that the man who abducted her sons is the same man I think of as the Piper. But there's no real detail, let alone evidence, to link the two cases.

We compare notes on what it was like to be suspected of responsibility for the disappearance of our own children.

'With me, you can figure it would happen,' she tells me. 'I mean, I'm a junkie—clean for three years now, but so what?' She shrugs. 'They thought I was trying to get money. But with you? I don't get it.'

'My wife and I were separated. Anyway, the Piper—he made it happen. He left this bloody T-shirt in the closet and for a couple of days, anyway, they thought I killed the kids. And a bowl of water—that was part of it, too. I don't know what they thought—I was keeping the boys locked up in the closet?' I shake my head.

'What bowl of water?'

'There was a bowl of water up on the shelf in the closet in the kids' room. Way up high. I don't know what it was doing there.'

There's no way to miss the sense of alarm coming off Emma Sandling. 'It really is him,' she gasps.

'What do you mean?'

'What about dimes? Was there a row of dimes?'

'Yes. They were lined up on the bathroom sink. How . . . '

Emma puts a hand on my arm. 'There was a row of dimes down the middle of Connor's sleeping bag. I thought Con did it himself. But then Amalia—she lived in the tent next door—she took one look at those dimes and freaked out. She noticed the water, too—a bowl up on this little shelf I had, rigged to the side of the tent.'

'Why did she freak out? What does it mean?'

'Well, that's what I wanted to know, but Amalia—first she tells me not to touch anything. Don't touch the water, she says, don't move the coins. And she is serious about this, like it's life and death. She tries to explain it to me, but she's hysterical and her English isn't all that good. What I get out of it is that it's some kind of voodoo thing. Did I say she's from Haiti?'

There's a lightness in my chest. 'You still in touch with her?'

'Never saw her again. Right about then is when the cops came. They started questioning all the people in the park. Amalia and her guy Bertrand—they were illegals. They sure didn't want to talk to the police. Amalia just clammed up. When the police came back to her about those dimes, because I mentioned it—and this was, like, a week later—Amalia and Bertie were long gone.'

'So you never found out what she was talking about?'

'Well, I found out it was some kind of curse—which I'd already figured from the way Amalia acted. But that was about it.'

'She told you not to move them, not to even touch them?' I ask.

'Right.'

'The police seized the bowl of water from my house. And the dimes. As evidence.'

'Oh, me too.'

I take over the window while she goes outside to sign out two beach umbrellas. I sell two ice-cream sandwiches.

'Emma?'

'Please try to call me Susie.'

'I'm sorry. Susie? Can I talk to the boys?'

'Oh, Jeez,' she says. 'I knew it would get down to this.'

'I just think maybe there's something—I don't even know what—but something they know that might help me.'

She sighs. 'I just don't want to *revive* it all. What if they tell you something and you want to tell the police? And then they question them again—and it leaks out. I don't want to move and have to start all over.' When Emma looks at me, I see the glitter of tears.

'I guess I shouldn't ask.'

'How can you not ask?' she says. She balls up her hands and rubs at her eyes with her knuckles, like a child. Compassion finally overwhelms her instinct for self-preservation. 'OK,' she says, pressing her eyes shut, as if she doesn't want to witness her own assent.

EMMA SETS the ground rules. I will call the boys by their Florida names (Kai and Brandon). I won't press them too hard if they don't seem to want to answer. The session can last only fifteen minutes and whatever they say is for me only.

We meet the following night. My first sight of Kai and Brandon almost takes my breath away. It's not that they look like my boys. They don't. But they share the habits of twinship, the way they look at each other, play off each other, finish each other's sentences.

I'm braced for a horror story, but what they tell me is almost reassuring. 'Where were you?' I ask them, first of all.

'It was a big house.' Brandon looks at his brother, who nods. 'A humongous lawn. Lotsa trees. Like in a forest.'

'Were there other people there—mowing the lawn or doing the chores—or just the man who took you at the McDonald's?'

'Just him. I mean there were other people sometimes, but we couldn't meet them. We had to stay in the big room. Doc told us.'

Doc. I didn't like the sound of that. Doctor Mengele. Papa Doc.

'But we didn't have to be quiet or nothing.'

'Or anything,' Emma corrects.

'Why couldn't you meet anyone?'

''Cause they might tell, and then Mommy—' he shoots a look at Emma '—might get into trouble and we'd never see her again.'

'When the man approached them,' Emma explains, 'he told them that he was a friend of mine, that I had to go back into treatment—'

'Doc told us she had a relapse,' Brandon says.

'He told the guys it would break my heart to say goodbye,' Emma explains. 'He told them I'd come for them as soon as I was better. But if anyone *knew* they were staying with him, he wasn't authorised—so they'd have to go into foster care and child services would never let them live with me.'

'Ever again,' Kai says earnestly. 'That's what he told us.'

'Now we have a code,' Brandon elaborates, 'so we know if it's true from Mommy or not.'

'Don't tell him!' Kai warns.

Brandon turns to me with an apologetic smile. 'We can't tell anyone or someone might find out and then they could trick us.'

'That's a good plan.' I say. 'So what did you do all day?'

'Mostly we did training.'

'Training?' I look from one to the other. 'Like what?'

'Exercises,' Kai says. 'Push-ups, sit-ups, gymnastics—'

'We did gymnastics a lot,' Brandon says. 'You know, somersaults and stuff.'

'We climbed up ropes, too,' Kai says, with some animation. 'Right to the ceiling. We did that *a lot.*'

'So this was in a gym in this big house?' I ask.

'Yeah—it was a giant room in the basement.'

'So, did this man . . . did he . . . *do* anything to you?'

Brandon shakes his head. 'He didn't hurt us. He *liked* us.'

'He liked you. So . . . was he . . . *friendly*?' I ask.

'Nah,' Kai says, 'he was just . . . ' He looks at his brother, but Brandon shrugs. Neither one of them seems able to characterise their captor's manner. 'He was just kind of regular,' Kai says finally. 'Mostly he left us alone, except when we were training.'

'So what made you stop trusting him?' I ask. 'At the mall.'

'I don't know,' Kai says, frowning. 'He just—I don't know.'

The fact that their captor didn't exploit the boys is a huge relief, but I can't get any kind of fix on his intentions towards them.

I'm trying to think of what else to ask when Kai volunteers something. 'Sometimes he did tricks for us, remember, Bran?'

'Tricks?' Emma frowns. This seems to be new to her.

'Yeah, with cards.' Brandon says. 'You know—*magic* tricks.'

Emma taps her watch and the reminder propels me into the kind of question I never ask as a reporter—an open question.

'Can you think of anything else about the house, the man or . . .

I don't know . . . anything that happened while you were there?'

Brandon turns to Kai. 'Did we ever say about the dogs?'

'Dogs?' I ask.

'Skinny ones,' Brandon says. 'You could see the bones. But they weren't hungry. He said they were supposed to be like that.'

I thank Emma at the door so profusely that she's almost embarrassed. 'I hope it helped,' she says. 'I hope you find them.'

I can hear the boys in the room behind us, and the sound of their voices sets off a throb of loss. It's with some effort that I turn away from her door. Yes, I've confirmed my guess that the abductor of the Sandling boys is the same man who took my sons, but where does it get me? Am I any closer to finding them?

BACK IN DC, I consult my notebooks and throw myself into the pursuit of my 'leads', such as they are.

The dimes. If Emma's friend Amalia was correct about the connection with voodoo, I know where to start. One of the producers at the station—Scott—did a piece about voodoo last year. He was somewhere down in Florida, where there's a significant Haitian population.

'Hey, Alex! Miss you, man. How's it going?'

'I'm hanging in.'

'If I can do anything, you—'

'That's why I called. Remember that piece on voodoo? I have a question. Thought you could tell me where to go with it.'

'A voodoo question? Sure. If I can't answer, I'll know where to point you.'

'The person who took the kids brought them back to the house and he left some things behind. I'm not sure the police ever released any of this.'

'*Voodoo* mementos?'

'Some of them. I think so, anyway. There was a row of coins. And a bowl of water, placed up high.'

'You know—that reminds me of this case at a nursing home in Cocoa Beach. The union was trying to reorganise some of the help in a series of nursing homes down in that area. In one of them, the management retaliated by leaving voodoo . . . *messages*, I guess you'd call them . . . all over the facility. The janitorial staff was mostly Haitian, right? And these warnings, or whatever they were, took the form of patterns of coins and bowls of water in weird places. The management was charged with unfair labour practices—intimidating the work force, you know? Because those coins—they were curses. And those bowls of water—those were for the spirits to drink—implying that there were spirits *around*. Thirsty ones.'

'No kidding.'

'The coins in your house—were they winged Liberty dimes—with the wings sort of coming out of Liberty's head?'

'How did you know?'

'Because those dimes are the coin of the realm in voodoo. I couldn't squeeze any of this into the programme, but it was fascinating stuff. First off, because of those little wings, most people call the things Mercury dimes. And Mercury was the Roman god of messages, of games of chance and sleight of hand. The god of magic. The way that fits is that Haitians believe some of the *houngans* have supernatural power—can do magic, in other words.'

'What's a *houngan*?'

'That's a priest, a voodoo priest. Getting back to those Mercury dimes, the voodoo equivalent of Mercury is called Legba.'

'The voodoo equivalent? There's an equivalent?'

'Voodoo's a very syncretic religion. It just appropriates bits and pieces from everywhere. Probably why it's still rolling on. So Legba, he's also related to St Peter—guardian of the gates, right? He's all about access and thresholds. I guess the Mercury dime can go either way luckwise, because people down in Louisiana and Florida wear the things around their necks on chains. Supposed to attract money.'

'Really.'

'Plus the dimes are used in mojo bags.'

'Mojo bags?'

'Don't knock it. I got one made up when I did the story and maybe it's coincidence, but my life's been *happening* ever since. So for a mojo bag, you need a Mercury dime. You need a couple of roots—the *houngans,* they decide what kind—and some sugar; you wrap it all up in a two-dollar bill; you wrap *that* up in a red flannel bag; you tie it all tight. Then to get your mojo *workin',* as it were, you have to anoint the bag with the menstrual blood or urine of the woman you love. That part was a little tricky with Christine.'

'I'll bet.'

We talk a little longer, and in case I need to know more about voodoo, he gives me the name of an academic at Florida State.

Next I compile a list of medieval festivals.

The first site Google kicks out—a Directorie of Faires—turns out to be a huge help. It features an extensive list of events: *Faires, Festivals, Re-enactments, Pageants, Jousts* and so on. Apart from 209 'major events', it lists the artists and companies that drive these festivals, a mind-blowing catalogue that encompasses everything from 'birds of prey demonstrations' to fire-eaters and 'baudy' comics.

Using the directory as a guide, my routine is to spend a few hours every day on the telephone with people who run the events. When I tell them what happened to my sons, most agree to post a Wanted poster in employee areas.

I create the poster myself. Under the classic banner WANTED, it displays an array of sketches of the Piper (including the one created by the police artist who worked with the Sandling twins). Beneath the sketches is a brief description of the abduction of my sons, the circumstances and date, along with what's known of the Piper's physique, costume and dog. Finally, there's contact information and the promise of a reward.

I send several packets a day—a cover letter and several copies of the poster. I log the mailings into my computer, so I can track follow-up calls and emails, responses, and the actions taken.

I follow a similar path in the canine realm, hoping I can get to the Piper via his dog. I'm shocked when I find more than 200 websites devoted to whippets. There are more whippet breeders, whippet clubs and whippet fanciers than I've ever imagined. The woman at Whippet World promises to put a link to my poster on her website and to send me a list of groups and breeders.

The Elizabethan neck ornament known as the ruff provides another avenue for research. The market for ruffs extends beyond Renaissance festivals to drama companies, minstrels, troubadours, jesters, choirs and circuses. You can buy them by mail, over the Internet, or at the festivals themselves. I make a few calls a day, but what looked like a narrow and promising angle now looks like it could consume months of my time.

I feel overwhelmed, daunted, depressed. This is obviously the kind of manpower-intensive activity the police should do. Should have done. In my opinion.

I SPEND HOURS a day, grinding away at my lists, working the telephone. Days pass when I hardly go outside. I'm living on pizza and bagels and beer. The house is a wreck. My clothes are loose and the face in the mirror is haggard and grey. I work with a kind of mindless determination, but once in a while, a bleak mood settles over me and I admit to myself that none of this work seems likely to get me one step closer to Kevin and Sean. The day comes when I allow myself to think about what it would be like to just . . . give up.

And that's worse—the chasm of emptiness—much worse than the feeling that I'm mining blind veins. Maybe the work I'm doing is useless, but I'm doing *something.* I keep at it, working with the despairing energy of an underprepared student cramming for finals.

Because I can't shake off the feeling that time is running out.

'YOU LOOK like shit.'

Shoffler. It's Saturday night and the detective has dropped by unannounced with a six-pack of Sierra Nevada.

'Hey.' I hold open the door.

He screws up his face at the state of the living room and follows me into the kitchen, which earns another frown.

Shoffler pulls out two beers, then sticks the pack in the fridge. He twists off the caps, hands me one of the beers, then plonks himself down at the table. 'Cheers,' he says.

I reciprocate. 'What's up? How's the new gig?'

He makes a face. 'Essentially it's an exercise in crowd control.' He tells me that if there's a terrorist incident in DC, my best bet is to steal a canoe or rowboat. 'Paddle out on the Potomac.'

'You call that an evacuation plan?'

'Don't get me started. What's up with you?'

We've talked on the phone a couple of times since my trip to Florida, so he knows all about my meeting with Emma Sandling. 'Come to headquarters,' I tell him.

We migrate to my study, and I give him a quick tour through my lists, the stacks of Wanted posters, my online pursuits. He nods.

We head back towards the kitchen where Shoffler ambles to the refrigerator. 'Another beer?'

'Why not?'

He sits back down at the table. 'What you're doing—it's like digging to China with a teaspoon. You know that, right?'

I shrug. 'Thanks for the concern.'

'Yeah, well, I feel like I owe you. I never should have bit on that T-shirt.' A frown of self-disgust takes over his face for a moment. 'He suckered us.'

'So this is . . . what? Some kind of damage control?' I'm sorry as soon as this comes out of my mouth. I know he's here out of simple human concern. 'That was out of line, Ray. I'm sorry . . .'

He pushes my apology away. 'I consider you a friend, Alex. I came here as a friend. And that stuff you're doing—who knows? Maybe you'll get something. But in all my years, I have never seen that kind of legwork pay off. Ever.'

'I can't just sit here.'

'You been keeping notebooks, writing stuff down?'

'I'm your disciple there. I'm on number five.'

'Tell you what. You go out and get a pizza, and some more beer wouldn't hurt. And while you're doing that, let me take a look.'

I shrug. 'OK.'

When I get back, we have to clear space on the table for the pizza. Shoffler tucks a napkin into his collar, separates a slice of pizza and more or less inhales it. 'Damn,' he says, taking a long pull of beer. 'Burned the roof of my mouth. I always do—I missed that lesson on delayed gratification.' He taps notebook number three. 'Here's what I'd go after,' he says. 'The Gabler twins.'

'The showgirls?'

'Showtwins. You went as far as you could with the Sandling boys, so next, I'd say check out Carla and Clara.'

'But, they're women. Adults. *Showgirls*. I don't see how—'

'Think outside the box a minute,' Shoffler says. 'I'm going through your notebooks and what I see is *twins* who disappeared. Just like the Sandlings. Just like yours.'

'Except they didn't come back.'

'Right, right, right. They were killed, so you don't want to think there's a connection. But what I'm saying is that there's a parallel. So maybe you should check it out. Go out there.'

'To Vegas? Why?'

'Look at it this way—your instinct to follow up on the Sandlings was right, OK? *Twins*.'

'But they were the same age, they were kids . . . '

'You're making assumptions. You're thinking it's about kids, and maybe it is. But you shouldn't assume that. What if it's about *twins*? You gotta have an open mind.'

'I don't know.'

'So what—you think it's a waste of time,' Shoffler says. 'Like you've got something better to do?' He picks up the notebooks and holds them aloft. 'I looked through these. I gave them a good hard read. And the only thing that stuck out was the Gablers. That's the only unturned stone.'

'This is . . . I mean, is this a *hunch*?'

'Don't underestimate it.'

I shrug. 'If you think it's worth a shot.'

'Anyway, Vegas is cheap this time of year,' Shoffler says. 'And I'm wired into the homicide squad there. A friend of mine—Mike Goldstein—he'll get you the file on the Gabler girls.'

CHAPTER SEVEN

Vegas. I've never been to Vegas before. But like everyone, I guess, I had a full-blown notion of the place—equal parts glitz and sleaze. As it turns out, my mental Vegas pales before the real thing.

The initial mile out of the Avis lot from McCarran Airport is sleazy, torn up and disreputable. Tired motels and seedy casinos vie for space with down-at-heel wedding chapels and commercial enterprises.

Then I hit the first big hotel-casino, the sheathed-in-gold Mandalay Bay. It's bigger than any structure in the DC area except maybe the Pentagon. And it's the first of many of these monsters. Each hotel is like a separate theme park, a huge, lavish stage set. Lights, billboards, crowds. It's Times Square on steroids.

But I'm not staying in one of these nouveau palaces. Priceline found me a bargain at the Tropicana. It's still huge, but compared to the new places it seems almost petite. I drive around to the self-park lot, go into the hotel, and check in at the registration desk.

'WELCOME to the Big Sleazy,' Mike Goldstein says when I get him on the phone. 'I pulled the files on the Gabler case. Got some time at three if you're not tapped out from your flight.'

I tell him I'll be there.

'Folks expect we're right near the Strip or in old Vegas, but we're way out of town, in the burbs. It's a thirty-minute drive, depending on traffic,' he tells me and he gives directions.

At two fifty, after driving through miles and miles of subdivisions and strip malls, I turn into what looks like a suburban office park. I spot a clutch of white vans marked CRIME SCENE, and a set of doors identified as CRIMINALISTICS, and I figure I'm in the right area.

In the Las Vegas PD reception area, two women tap away on computers. One woman asks my business, then buzzes Goldstein and tells me to wait.

Goldstein is a tall, handsome man in his early fifties, with silver hair and jet-black eyebrows. We shake hands, and he delivers what amounts to a testimonial to Ray Shoffler. 'Ray's ears must be burning,' Goldstein concludes, 'but I kid you not, the guy is really something. Ray cracked a case for me one time strictly on a hunch.'

'I'm here on one of his hunches.'

'There you go. Hey, Cindy,' he calls out. 'Open Sesame.'

I follow him through a metal gate that swings open with an electronic growl. We make our way through a warren of offices, edging past a crew working with a huge camera, photographing a piece of paper. 'Cold case,' Goldstein says. 'They're assembling documents. You gotta preserve the original—so they have to be photographed. The deal is we just elected a new sheriff and one of his campaign promises was to go after the cold cases.'

'Like the Gablers?'

He shrugs. 'I don't know. They're kind of an orphan case.'

We arrive at a conference room. Goldstein gestures towards one of the dozen chairs arrayed around a wooden table.

'So the Gablers . . . what, do you mean they're orphans?' I ask.

He slaps his hands down on the two binders on the table. 'They're orphans two times over—their folks got killed in a car crash down around Searchlight. The girls were seventeen.'

'That's terrible.'

'And their *case* is orphaned, too. The way it works is, every detective *owns* his cases and they're always his. The guy who ran the Gabler investigation was Jerry Olmstead. Anyway, Jerry had high blood pressure, the wife was antsy. So he retired. A month later—his ticker goes off.' He shrugs. 'With Jerry gone, the Gabler case has no built-in advocate. And the Gabler case has another strike against it.'

'What's that?'

'No one's beating the drums. Sometimes you have a murder and ten years later Mom or Dad is still making it their business to follow up with us. But the Gabler girls? No one making noise at all. Sort of the opposite.'

'What do you mean?'

'The murder was so . . . grotesque. These girls, they worked just two blocks from the Strip. And the Strip—that's our bread and butter. Horrific unsolved crimes are not the publicity you want.' Goldstein frowns. 'So anyway, the case kinda faded away.'

'So it's OK if I look at the files?'

He holds out his hands and rolls them open in the direction of the binders. 'All yours. Not that there's a lot in there. I mean—no one reported these girls missing for more than two weeks.'

'Jeez.'

'Well, you know, it's *Vegas*. New people pouring in all the time. Other people pouring out. Even after Clara and Carla's room-mate gets around to wondering if something happened to them, it's another week before there's any evidence of foul play. In the meantime, the trail's gettin' *way* cold. I mean—two weeks is a lifetime.'

'This evidence,' I say. 'You're talking about when the hiker found them?'

'Right. *That* poor s.o.b. He had to be hospitalised! They had to helicopter him out of there. But he didn't *find* them. Not exactly. He just found half of Clara. The bottom half.'

AFTER AN HOUR and a half with the files, I don't know much more about the murders than I did from the news stories.

The last time anyone saw them, the Gablers were working the topless show at the Blue Parrot. The personnel director at the Parrot, one Clay Riggins, left three messages on the twins' voicemail—and then gave up. The messages provided the police with a probable date for the girls' disappearance. And no, Riggins didn't call the police, figuring the girls just left town or got a better gig somewhere else.

Tammy Yagoda, a twenty-three-year-old showgirl at the Sands, had been the Gablers' room-mate. She was the one who reported them missing. She hadn't seen them for two weeks—and that time frame meshed in nicely with the date of their first no-show at the Parrot. Tammy told the police that the last time she saw them, the twins were fine. The thing was, Tammy had just moved in with a new boyfriend, Jaime, so it wasn't until she went back to the apartment to get some clothes that she realised something was wrong. The stench from the litter box hit her as soon as she opened the door. Romulus and Remus, the two Burmese cats who belonged to the Gablers, were ravenous. Yagoda reported that the twins never would have left them like that. So she knew something was wrong.

She was right about that.

Red Rock Canyon is a popular tourist site about twenty miles from Vegas. A well-marked thirteen-mile scenic drive leads the visitor through the Mojave Desert landscape, dramatic rock formations forming a backdrop for native fauna and flora. It's a haven for hordes of hikers, mountain bikers and rock climbers.

Josh Gromelski, hiking in an isolated area behind Icebox Canyon, had entered an area around it, which led to a much smaller canyon known as Conjure Canyon. He nearly tumbled to his death after picking a handhold that, when he pulled himself up, brought him about four feet from the torso and legs of what turned out to be Clara Gabler. Gromelski had a GPS system and a cellphone in his backpack. He lasted just long enough to call in his gruesome discovery before going into shock.

I can see why. The crime scene photos are stomach turning. Despite the damage done by predators, the lower half of Clara Gabler did not deteriorate much in the dry Mojave air. The shapely legs are encased in fishnet stockings, the feet are still shod in patent-leather sandals with four-inch heels. Gold-sequinned fabric—shredded and twisted at the waistline—covers Clara's lower trunk.

It didn't take long to find the other half of Clara once the police went looking. It was twenty yards away, wedged into a crevice, apparently dragged there by coyotes. This was the half with a face.

Carla was found about fifty yards away, face-down in a little gully. She was shot, execution style, behind the right ear. The crime-scene photograph shows Carla in her costume: fishnet stockings, high-heeled sandals, gold sequinned panties, jewel-encrusted bra. Livor mortis, predator damage, and the exit wound made by a .38 calibre bullet made her face unrecognisable.

The autopsy report notes that Clara was cut in half by a saw powerful enough to slice through her spinal column. But it's even worse than that. According to the medical examiner, *injury to subject's trunk occurred premortem.* The cause of death was exsanguination.

The language of the report fails to blunt its meaning. Clara was alive when she was cut in half. The murder was an act of sadism. But not the result of a sex crime. Neither woman had been molested.

The former room-mate, Tammy Yagoda, made the formal identification of the girls. For the record she stated that when the Gabler twins were alive, she could tell Clara from Carla with ease, through mannerisms and figures of speech. But now . . . Distinguishing identification was eventually made through dental records.

The reports also make it clear that the Gabler girls were not killed elsewhere and then dumped in Conjure Canyon. They were killed not far from where they were found.

I go through the binders again, taking notes. And when I'm done, I feel sick. And it looks as if I've wasted my time. This can't have anything to do with my kids.

Still, I'm in Vegas and I know that when I get back, Shoffler's going to ask me—did I do this, did I do that? Did I interview Tammy Yagoda, go to the Blue Parrot, find out where the costumes came from? And so on.

Goldstein nods his head when I tell him this. 'You should speak to Barry Chisworth. He's the medical examiner worked the case. Bright guy. Probably noticed stuff that didn't make it into print.'

'Like what?'

Goldstein shrugs. 'Who knows? A guess at the weapon, a hunch about the murderer—but nothing really substantiated by evidence. Guessing is not part of the ME's job, and they don't speculate on paper for good reason: anything they put down has a good chance of ending up in court. But they *do* have opinions. You get a good ME, like Chisworth, he might pass on his take on this thing.'

I write down Chisworth's name and phone number.

'But you can cross off the costumes,' Goldstein says. 'I can tell you where they came from—the Parrot.'

'So why the costumes? Why were they wearing them?'

'They were probably on their way to work. Apparently they liked to dress at home. Didn't like the dressing-room scene at the Parrot.' Goldstein's digital watch emits a chirp. 'I gotta go.'

He sticks out his hand. I thank him for his help.

'My pleasure. And if there's anything else—just call me.'

BACK IN MY ROOM at the Tropicana, I flesh out the notes I took at the police department and then make a to-do list:

1. The Blue Parrot/Riggins
2. Yagoda (room-mate)
3. The ME: Barry Chisworth

Two young women, identical twins, dressed in provocative costumes. One butchered, one assassinated. Shoffler may be famous for his hunches, but he's got to be wrong this time. This doesn't have anything to do with my kids. It *can't*.

THE BLUE PARROT is only a couple of blocks off the Strip, but it's several steps down from the splendour of the big casinos. A few non-functioning tubes in the gigantic sign give the neon parrot a dishevelled look, as if it's moulting.

At 6 p.m., the place seems tired and dingy, only a couple of its tables going, stage curtains drawn, the place mostly empty. A fatigued woman in a cheetah-print micro-dress shows me into the boss's office. Clay Riggins, fifty, bald, has seen better days himself. He's on the phone, a Diet Dr Pepper in his hand. He raises it by way of hello and continues his conversation.

I stand there for more than five minutes before Riggins finally hangs up. 'Sorry 'bout that,' he says. 'So you're here about the Gabler sisters.'

'Right.'

'Well, I don't mind talkin' to you, but I hardly knew these girls.'

'They worked for you for eight months,' I point out.

'Yeah, but plenty of people work for me. I didn't really know the two of them. They came out in their costumes, took their tops off along with a dozen other girls, and no—they weren't very good at it. They had the twin thing going for them, and that was about it.'

'So what did you think when they didn't show up for work?'

'Now, that,' he says, as if this never occurred to him before, 'was not like them. Dependable—yeah, I give 'em that. Never missed a single day of work.'

'Didn't you think something might be wrong?'

'Nah—this is *Vegas*. I thought they went home. Took a job in Wal-Mart or Dairy Queen. I thought they were like a lot of girls come here—hoping to meet Prince Charming. I thought maybe they figured out it wasn't going to happen and decided to bag it. That's what I thought.' He drains his Dr Pepper. 'But maybe not.'

'What do you mean?'

'Tammy? Their room-mate—she's the one brought them to me. A good kid, Tammy. Works at the Sands now. Anyway, the twins told her they had an audition, thought they had a line on a new job.'

I sit up straight. This is new. 'What audition? Where?'

Riggins shrugs. 'I don't think Tammy said.'

TAMMY YAGODA lives with her fiancé, Jaime, in a new condo five miles out of town. The living room contains a huge television and an overstuffed couch.

'We just moved in,' she apologises. 'Good thing we're minimalists—right, honey?' She gives Jaime a megawatt smile and asks him to get me a chair.

Jaime brings in a beat-up, straight-backed chair from the dining alcove. The two of them twine together on the couch as we talk.

'I still can't believe it,' Tammy tells me, her features clouding. 'They were such sweetiepies, really nice girls. It was so horrible.'

'How were they nice?'

'In just about every way,' Tammy says. 'Do anything for you. Plus—' she looks at Jaime '—they were, you know, a little *naive.* I lived with them for almost a year and maybe they each had a couple of dates. They weren't virgins, but they were like—they had to be in love to have sex with someone, you know? They hated doing the topless thing.'

'No old boyfriends, no stalkers they were worried about, no admirers, no one romancing either one of them?'

'I met Jaime a couple of weeks before they went missing and it was—' she looks at her fiancé '—it was love at first sight. So maybe they met someone in that two weeks, 'cause I was *busy*.' A chuckle from Jaime. 'But far as I know, there was no one.'

'How about a guy with a dog? You ever see anyone like that?'

'No. Clara was afraid of dogs. They were cat people.'

I ask Tammy's opinion: what does she think happened to them?

Tammy shivers. 'I don't know. Some psycho. I mean, what else? It has to be. Someone who followed them from the Parrot. Found out where they lived. Stalked them.'

'Clay Riggins mentioned some kind of audition,' I tell her. 'You know anything about that?'

'Yeah! They were so stoked about that. They worked their butts off—speech classes, dance, Pilates, got their teeth whitened. And it looked like it was all about to pay off. And then . . .'

'What kind of audition was it? I mean, what was it for?'

Tammy shrugs. 'Some kind of magic show.'

'A magic show? You know anything else about it?'

Tammy shakes her head. 'This is like two days after I met Jaime. Clara told me about it when I called to tell her where I was—because I knew they'd worry. She said she thought they really had a shot. She was excited, but . . . I was on my cell, at work. I didn't get any details.' She sees the look on my face and says, 'Oh, Lord. And them in their little costumes. You think it was this audition, don't you? That some crazeball *lured* them, used their hopes and dreams to suck them in, had them put on their costumes, speak their lines, go through their routines, and then . . . like he had them *try out* for their own murder.' She sucks in her breath. 'That's dark. Downright *evil*.'

When the skin on the back of my neck stops crawling, I thank Jaime and Tammy for their time.

In the car, I think Tammy is probably right. The Gablers auditioned for their murderer.

BACK AT THE TROPICANA, I have two messages. The first is from Liz. 'Alex, what are you doing in *Las Vegas*?' Her voice is shrill and disapproving. Then she's all business. 'Please give me a call.'

The second is from Barry Chisworth, the medical examiner. He says he'll be happy to talk to me and leaves a string of numbers.

Liz is not easy to talk to these days. She can't get past focusing all her negative feelings on me. She feels guilty for letting the boys come to stay with me and indulges in endless versions of what-if.

I force myself to call.

When she answers her voice is tremulous. 'What are you *doing* in Las Vegas, Alex? Are you *gambling*?'

'I'm following a lead that Shoffler suggested.'

'What lead?'

My mind spins. I'm not going to tell her anything about the Gabler twins, that's for sure. I doubt the connection anyway, and what happened to the women is too gruesome to raise with Liz. 'A bad lead. It didn't go anywhere.'

'Well, you shouldn't be in Vegas. You should be canvassing the houses near the fairground. That's the most likely—'

'Liz. The police checked those homes. Over and over.'

Her voice is shrill, out of control as we go on for a while. 'I'm still expecting my spousal support. Whether you have a job or not. I'm not supporting trips to Las Vegas. I mean it, Alex: the cheque better be on time.'

I tell myself this sour woman isn't really Liz. She doesn't want to feel the loss and terror, so she's sticking with anger.

I wish I could say something to comfort and buoy her up, something to give her hope. But the descent of my wife into this petty bitterness makes me so sad I'm afraid if I open my mouth I might break down. I hang up.

AT HIS SUGGESTION, I meet Barry Chisworth at Rumjungle, an elaborate bar-restaurant in the Mandalay Bay Hotel. Sheets of water cascade down the walls. Flames dance from an open pit. A safari fantasy, I guess. Chisworth is a stocky guy in his fifties with the overdeveloped shoulders of a weightlifter. 'Try a mojito,' he suggests, holding up a tall glass. 'Hemingway's fave.'

'Why not?' I say.

'Two more of these bad boys,' he tells the bartender, and then turns back to me. 'So, you want to know about the Gabler girls.' He leans forward. 'I want to make it clear that I won't go on the record. Whatever I say—it's strictly background.'

'You got it.'

The waiter serves up the two mojitos and Chisworth pushes his glass towards mine. 'Cheers. You know,' he says, 'I always figured the guy who did those two girls was more than a one-shot wonder, so to speak. You find anything yet?'

'My interest is more specific.' I explain who I am.

He does a double take. 'I thought you looked familiar. Well, for what it's worth a couple of things bugged me. You've got this girl. Cut in two. Now, animals had been at her wounds for two weeks so that wiped out establishing what kind of implement was used to sever her torso. You can conclude it was something sharp, probably metallic, but that's about it. On the stand, you can only present evidence and conclusions. And while I couldn't testify to this, I'd say beyond *my* reasonable doubt that Clara Gabler was cut in two by a power rotary blade—a sweep from left to right across the torso.'

'And saws like this . . . you could buy them?'

'Oh, sure. You could get it at Home Depot. But the thing is, to use a big table saw like that in the wilderness, you'd need a generator. And a platform to work on. And you'd have to get all that gear up there, way up past Icebox Canyon. A good off-road vehicle like a Land Rover, and you could do it. We found lots of tracks. But why bother schlepping a rotary saw and a generator and some kind of table up there? I just couldn't get my head around it.' He takes a sip of his mojito. 'Whoever murdered the Gablers is obviously a whack job, so I guess there's no reason the method should make sense. You read the autopsy report? You know Clara was alive when this took place?'

I nod.

'There were traces of sawdust on her body. Pine dust.'

'A coffin?'

'It's possible. But here's what I really thought was weird: you get this massive injury to Clara Gabler, who was alive at the time it was inflicted. Yet I found no sign of restraint. And no visible damage from a struggle to get free, no defensive wounds at all. Nothing.'

'And that means, what? Drugs?'

'That's what I thought, but I found nothing. Zip. The woman is cut in half, but she's not restrained. You tell me—how do you pull that off? Just lay down there, honey. This won't hurt a bit.'

Something dark begins to crawl around in the back of my mind, but whatever it is, I can't get a fix on it. 'How about the other Gabler—the one who was shot?'

'She was executed,' Chisworth says. 'Prone, on the ground, face down. One shot, back of the head. That got me, too, to tell you the truth.'

'What do you mean?'

'The comparison. Clara's death involves a lot of trouble and hassle. Dragging a lot of equipment to an inconvenient spot. With her twin, it's just the opposite. No muss, no fuss. Why?'

And that's when it hits me. Where were the Gablers found?

Conjure Canyon.

What were the Gabler girls auditioning for?

A magic act.

They were on stage. That's why they were wearing their costumes. It was a *performance.* During which Clara Gabler was sawn in half. The blood seeping out of the box was real, the screams not the work of an actress but cries of pain and terror. Sawing a lady in half. And then the real live girl emerges, her two halves magically reunited. Only in this case the trick was: there was no trick. There was a double. A twin.

I remember the Sandling twins telling me their captor did tricks for them. What kind of tricks? *Magic tricks.*

Card tricks. Sawing a lady in half.

Twins in the first case, twins in the second.

The link is tenuous on the surface, but in my heart I know that Shoffler's hunch was correct. There is a connection between the Gablers and the Sandlings and my sons, and the link is *magic.*

For the first time since the boys disappeared, I have an inkling of what might be in store for them and it drops me into despair.

My sons are the raw material for a murder artist.

CHAPTER EIGHT

While I'm in Vegas, I decide I should try to determine if the Piper worked here as a magician and follow whatever local leads I have. Turns out, if it's about magic, Vegas is the place to be. After three days, I've seen more doves and lighted candles disappear than I can count. I've witnessed feats of mind reading, miraculous escapes, levitations and dozens of transformations. Any number of times, I've seen leggy beauties disappear, after which they step out, preening and smiling, from impossible and unexpected locations.

After the shows, there are opportunities to buy merchandise. Shops sell mementos along with standard tricks and magic kits, and books about magic. It's in these shops that I show my sketches of the Piper to clerks and cashiers, but no one can put a name to him.

I'm getting myself a beer before the Lance Burton show when a bear of a man approaches me. 'Boyd Veranek,' he says, 'with a V. Pleased to meet you. Watch this.'

I get it. The guy's going to do a magic trick. He cups his huge hands together and pulls them slowly apart. In between his palms, a paper rose hovers and trembles in midair. He plucks it out of the air, and with a little bow, presents it to me.

'You just made this . . . here? That's pretty good.'

Veranek smiles. 'I saw you at Showgirls of Magic, saw you at Penn and Teller. Figured you're a fellow illusionist. Am I right?'

I tell him that I'm a private investigator, looking into a murder.

'A murder?' Veranek squints at me, as if he's not sure whether I'm joking or not. 'And all of these magic shows fit into this investigation . . . how? If you don't mind my asking.'

'I think the killer is a magician.'

'Oh, boy. There goes the neighbourhood. A professional?'

'Don't know. But I have some sketches. Mind taking a look?'

'By all means.' He squints, studies the sketches, shakes his head. 'The murder was here? In Vegas?'

'Nearby. It was about three years ago. Showgirls murdered out in Red Rock Canyon. You might have heard of it.'

Veranek frowns. 'You really want to know about magic—you ought to talk to Karl Kavanaugh.'

'Who is he?'

'He's a magician, although he doesn't perform much any more. He works for David Copperfield—who has a museum of magic here. But the point is Karl knows everything about magic—A to Z. He's a magician's magician. Might even recognise your guy.'

'You have his number?'

'I don't. Not on me. He's probably in the book—Karl with a *K*, Kavanaugh, also with a *K*.'

'OK, thanks a lot.'

KARL KAVANAUGH *is* in the book. I arrange to meet him the next morning. He suggests the Peppermill on the upper Strip.

The restaurant occupies a low, seventies shingled building. Inside, blue velvet banquettes are shaded by faux cherry trees.

Kavanaugh waits for me just inside the entrance, a tall, graceful man in his sixties, in a blue suit. A young woman escorts us to a table. Kavanaugh has lemonade. I sip a cup of coffee.

'Do you perform here in Vegas?' I ask him.

'No. I'm retired, more or less. I came here—well, I came here because I was following the craft.'

'What do you mean?'

'Well, some industries stay put, geographically speaking,' Kavanaugh says, 'but magic keeps changing its capital. And right now it's here in Vegas.'

'And before?'

'At the turn of the century, it was New York, which makes sense. The stages were there, theatrical agents, gossip columnists, magic shops, vaudeville. Not to mention the big audiences. Remember, movies didn't exist yet, so live entertainment was the *only* entertainment. So you'd get someone like Houdini, he'd draw huge crowds. But then the movies really started to come on, and vaudeville died out. And a lot of magic acts went down with the ship. So the epicentre of magic relocated to Chicago. This was in the twenties, and Chicago was where all the rail lines met, the home away from home for fleets of travelling salesmen. Magicians got a kind of second wind working trade shows—still probably the biggest employers of magicians.'

'Trade shows? You're kidding.'

'Oh, no. Because trade shows are essentially *live entertainment*. Say you're trying to attract attention to your booth . . . Nothing like a magician. People *will* stop and watch.'

'Where do magicians work these days—besides Vegas and trade shows?'

'Cruise ships. Birthday parties, bar mitzvahs, adult residences.'

I start taking notes. There must be associations for cruise ships, for trade shows. I could paper them all with the Piper sketch.

'And Renaissance festivals,' Karl adds. 'Pretty popular.'

Renaissance festivals. It's one of those moments when the past crashes in on me. My head fills with vignettes of the day at the fair: the look on Sean's face as he bore down on his brass rubbing, Kevin's slightly alarmed expression as he stared at the falcon perched on the leather-gloved arm of its handler . . .

I concentrate on writing in my notebook. Karl must see something in my face, because he asks if I'm OK. I mutter about jet lag and the moment passes and he's talking again about magic's geographical journey. 'So, magicians congregated in Chicago for a while, say 1930 to 1962, then the scene moved to LA.'

'Why LA?'

Karl shrugs. 'A well-known magician bought an old mansion there and opened a club. Called it the Magic Castle. Eventually, the Castle drew more and more magicians out to the West Coast. And LA became the new epicentre of magic. Then in eighty-five or so, when Vegas started to take off, magic relocated here.'

'Why Vegas?'

'Because magic is at its best live and in person, and the oddity of Vegas is that it's the one place in the country where stage acts flourish. Not just theatre but music, dancing, stand-up . . . and magic. People can't gamble all the time. They pay to see live shows because that's what you *do* in Vegas. You take in a show. And magic is popular because it works so well on stage.' He leans towards me with a shy smile. 'In fact, I have a theory about it.'

I make a gesture. 'Please.'

'We're all so jaded by filmed special effects that almost nothing can really startle us any more. We look at some stunt or effect that was actually quite difficult to pull off—but it doesn't blow our minds. Not any more. We don't even care how it's done.'

'It was done with computers, with stuntmen, whatever.'

'Exactly. That's why magic doesn't play well on television, because *anything* can be done on film. I mean in a way, what is a movie but an extended magic effect? But when you see something in real time, with your own eyes, you still trust your senses. So even the simplest trick provokes amazement. Magic is still *magic* in other words, when people see it up close. It still gets that response every magician is after: "How'd you *do* that?" And by the way—I never tell.'

'Never?'

'Almost never. It's too disappointing. Some *very* complex devices and mechanisms enable certain magical illusions, don't get me wrong. Once, magicians were on the cutting edge of technology and mechanical invention. So I don't want to minimise the role of ingenious devices. But pretty often the secret is something simple, even crude. Some wax, a string, a magnet. You hate to pull the curtains aside like that. That's not why people come to magic shows.'

'Why *do* they come?'

'They come to be deceived, to be fooled, to be amazed. That's where the pleasure is—not in finding out that something astounding was enabled by a secret latch or a mirror. The pleasure comes in not being able to figure out how it happened.'

'OK . . .'

'Now, someone like Houdini, a real showman, he used to press the point. Before one of his escapes, he'd insist on being examined naked—usually by the police—to prove he literally had nothing up his sleeve. Fortunately, this was in the days before the cavity search.'

'You mean—'

'Yup. Something up his keister. That's the suspicion—although this is not to disparage Houdini. He was an astonishing athlete and he trained like hell. For instance, he had this one effect where he was cuffed and wrapped in padlocked chains and then lowered into cold water—icy water, mind you. Now, sure—he had to have some kind of file or pick to get those locks open. But still—he's upside down in thirty-five-degree water with his hands and feet cuffed, and wrapped in heavy padlocked chains. And he still has to spring all those locks. Years before, he'd practised holding his breath until he could do it for three and a half minutes. Amazing. And to get ready for these cold-water escapes, he trained by sitting in a tubful of ice cubes every night for weeks until his body could tolerate the shock.

'That kid David Blaine recently did something of the sort. Encased himself in ice for several days—actually an endurance feat more than anything else. That kind of thing also has a long and honoured tradition in magic. Being buried alive. In fact, all kinds of physical feats used to be part of the magic shows. Water spouting. Stone eating.

Walking on coals. Interesting to see Blaine revive that aspect. You should check him out—he had a few TV shows. *Street Magic* was the first, I think. Very impressive.'

'But . . . you said it yourself. Magic doesn't play on the screen.'

'Blaine did something really innovative: he concentrated on the audience. He shows himself doing the effects for small groups—one, three, four people, that's all. And watching their response is fascinating. They go nuts, absolutely crazy, they are *transported*. They literally can't believe their eyes. It's wonderful stuff. Some of them actually cover their eyes, as if they can't trust themselves to look at the world any more.' Kavanaugh sighs. 'I could go on all day. So maybe you should tell me what you really want to know.'

I tell him I'm investigating the murders of the Gabler twins, and that I think the murderer may have been a magician.

He steeples his hands and rests his chin on the point. 'I remember the case. Dreadful. The lady sawn in half. But what makes you think a magician was responsible?'

I tell him what I've learned and show him the poster with the sketches of the Piper. His face contorts. 'Mind if I keep this?'

'No problem.'

He folds the poster precisely in half, then folds it again and slips it into his pocket. 'I'm not sure I agree with you, but if it is a magician, you'll find there are certain characteristics many of us share. Would that kind of thing be helpful to you?'

'Please.'

'Well, most magicians take up the art as children. It takes a long time to develop the dexterity a magician needs. And many tricks take a *really serious* amount of practice. So much practice that an adult would just give up. But kids—they'll put in that time.'

'Are there any tricks that use kids as their . . . subjects?'

'Well, at kids' birthday parties, sure. But if you mean the magician's assistant—the assistant is almost invariably a young woman, the better to inject a little sex appeal into a show. In the past, children were very commonly used as assistants. And they would perform all the roles that women do today—I mean they'd be levitated, locked in cabinets, or put into urns or baskets, then transported to distant spots or transformed into animals and back again.'

'Anything else about magicians I should know?'

'Well, actually, I've been thinking about *your* fellow. If he is a magician, I'd say he's a student of the art, aware of the history.'

'Why do you say that?'

'Well . . . just what he did, with those girls. I mean, dismemberment and restoration have been part of the magician's stock-in-trade for centuries, but nowadays you only see antiseptic tricks. You might see paper, or money, or rope torn or cut into pieces. That's enough for today's audiences. But there was a time when people enjoyed dismemberment tricks. In India it used to be popular for conjurers to rip apart birds. They would show the blood, might even dip stones into it. Then once the bird was restored to life, they'd sell the stones as lucky amulets, imbued with the life force.'

'Wait a minute—you don't mean it was real blood?'

'Oh, yes. Dismemberment and restoration to wholeness and life—it's the power of life and death, isn't it? Magicians didn't start as mere entertainers, you see. They used to fill a more elevated role in societies. Today's magician was yesterday's priest or shaman. Religion and magic have always been mixed up together. That's because magic explores that region between the natural and the supernatural, between life and death, between reality and illusion.'

'And you think the man I'm looking for—if he's a magician—he might be aware of this aspect of magic.'

'I think he might be a student of magic's history, yes. The dismemberment of that girl is what makes me think so. The trick with the bird I was talking about . . . Here's how it works. There's a traditional magic device called a dove pan—it has a hidden compartment for a secret load. So at the beginning of the trick, the magician opens one compartment and out comes a bird. Fluttering and so on. A little business with the bird and then the magician tears it apart. The audience is encouraged to handle the dead bird.'

'*Actually* tears it apart?'

A shrug. 'Or cuts it apart. A bird would be sacrificed, in any case. Usually a white dove if the magician could afford it because blood shows up so well against the white feathers. It's very dramatic.'

'And then?' I feel light-headed.

'The magician closes the pan. He exhorts the spectators to focus their own energy on restoring the bird to life. Then a big show of concentration, a few magic words, and . . . presto! The magician opens the pan—this time exposing the hidden compartment—and out comes the live bird, fluttering with life.'

Kavanaugh misinterprets the look of horror on my face. He thinks I'm confused. He thinks I don't get it.

'It's just like those girls killed up in Red Rock, you see? One is sacrificed, then the other is produced, vibrant with life. That's the second desirable thing about white doves: they all look the same. From the point of view of the audience, two white doves are identical. They're *all* twins, you might say.'

A rush of pressure. I'm standing in the path of a freight train, but I can't move. *They're all twins. They're all twins.*

WHEN I GET BACK to the hotel I put in a call to Shoffler to get his advice. But it turns out he's in France for some kind of security conference. I leave a message, then call Muriel Petrich, the police detective who inherited the case. She listens to me talk about my breakthrough and promises that the police will contact every magician's association and trade-show booking agency with the Piper's sketches and so on. But I can tell from the way she's talking to me that that my case has slipped down on her list of priorities.

My plane home is a red-eye. I get in at dawn. The drive home soothes me. The green trees and grass seem jungle lush after my sojourn in the desert.

The house has that stale, uninhabited smell. Liz used to light candles when we returned from vacation. I consider giving her a call, but what would I say? Now that I'm home, the connections between the Gablers, the Sandlings and my boys don't seem so solid.

MURDERED TWINS. I spend a few hours online, trying different search engines to see what turns up.

The only other murder of twins—apart from the Gablers—was the one in southern California. I remember it from my early forays online: the Ramirez twins, Wilson and Julio. I never paid much attention to the case despite the fact that the victims were seven-year-old twins. The perpetrator was dead.

But I can hear Shoffler telling me not to make assumptions. And Harry Goldstein explaining how certain facts or insights never make it into police reports, let alone the news. Maybe there was an accomplice in the Ramirez case—a suspect whose name hadn't surfaced. Maybe the police didn't have enough to charge him, and now he's back.

At first, it's not promising. The killer, Charley Vermillion, had been released from the Port Sulfur Forensic Facility, an asylum for the criminally insane in Louisiana, weeks before the Ramirez boys went missing.

Ten minutes later, I'm talking to Harvey Morris, a detective in Big Sur who worked the case.

'Wasn't much work to it,' he tells me. 'We got a tip and we went where the informant pointed. And there was Charley with a fridge full of body parts. He surrendered without a fuss, just seemed confused. He's in the squad, we've secured the crime scene, and we're ready to go to the station. All of sudden he starts making these noises like he's strangling. I think he's having a heart attack or something. He turns red, bright cherry red. Starts convulsing. We call an ambulance, and give him CPR, but he croaks.'

'When did you find out he'd poisoned himself?'

'Not until the next day. We didn't see him take the pill. I thought a stroke or something—what do I know? But the medico guessed cyanide and the autopsy confirmed it. That and a load of valium. No wonder he was no trouble. Forensics found tape residue on the underside of his shirt collar.' He pauses. 'So you got questions?'

'I was wondering about the Ramirez boys' cause of death.'

'The one we found in the freezer? Loss of blood. Apparently, he was stabbed dozens of times. I mean, the kid was a pincushion. There's a technical term for it—'

'Exsanguination.'

'Bingo. Bled to death.'

'And the second boy? The one they found in the well?'

'He was shot in the head. Single shot. Thirty-eight calibre.'

Just like the Gablers. One dismembered, one shot in the head.

'This tip you got?' I ask. 'The one that led you to Vermillion's cabin. Didn't you wonder about that?'

'Oh, sure we did. We tried to run it down, but Vermillion's only out of the bin a short while and it's not like he's got a lot of friends and acquaintances we can question. We figured a drifter.'

'You're probably right,' I say. I thank Morris and hang up.

But he isn't right. He's dead wrong.

Whoever killed the Ramirez boys also killed the Gabler twins—and that was not Charley Vermillion. It couldn't have been because Vermillion was dead when the Gabler murders took place.

So whoever killed the Ramirez twins is the monster who kidnapped the Sandling boys. Provided the anonymous tip-off about Vermillion. And abducted my sons.

I CAN'T just show up at the Port Sulfur Forensic Facility. If I waltz in there asking questions about 'Cannibal' Charley Vermillion, I won't get past the door.

Even if the hospital did everything by the book, when an institution for the criminally insane releases an inmate who then goes out and butchers a couple of kids, there are consequences. And, in fact, heads did roll. But the top guy—Peyton Anderton—managed to hold on to his job. Meanwhile a ten-million-dollar civil suit brought against the institution by the parents of the Ramirez twins is still winding its way through the courts, virtually guaranteeing everyone's silence. I'd guess that no one's talking to anyone.

I decide to call Anderton. I'll tell him I'm with a Fox news programme and pitch a story that he'll want to see on television. Like how difficult and dangerous his job is. How forensic facilities need more funding. Better facilities. More staff. That ought to get me through the door.

So I call him. He's a little wary, but he's flattered by the attention. He says, 'Looks like I have a window Thursday afternoon. If you can be here at three o'clock?'

'I can do that.'

THE WOMAN at the Alamo counter at the New Orleans airport is friendly, asks where I'm headed, do I need directions?

'Port Sulfur.'

'Where?'

'Plaquemines Parish.'

She slides my licence and credit card back to me, pulls out a map and marks the route with a green pen. I scoop up the keys.

An hour later, I'm past the sprawl of New Orleans, driving down a new four-lane highway through undeveloped countryside. There's not much to see. On the river side, the levee blocks any view, and as far as I can tell, the Gulf side is just flat country. I know that there are oil rigs out there, but all I can see is low-lying trees, reedy vegetation and some small towns. The names are a trip in themselves: Pointe A La Hache, Diamond, Happy Jack, Magnolia.

And then I'm there: Port Sulfur. I read in a guidebook that the town got its name from a sulphur mine out in the salt marsh.

I follow the directions, then see the small sign for the Port Sulfur Forensic Facility and turn up a long drive. The hospital is an ugly rectangle of yellow brick surrounded by a fence strung with barbed wire.

The man inside the guardhouse slides open his window, then asks my business. I tell him my name and he studies his clipboard, finds what he's looking for, then fills out two bright orange visitor's passes. 'Clip one on your shirt,' he tells me, 'and place the other on your dashboard. Turn them both in when you leave.' He raises the gate and retreats to the comfort of his air-conditioned cubicle.

I know from Dr Peyton Anderton's CV that he is forty-three years old. He wears a seersucker suit and a bright smile.

'Mr Callahan!' he says, shaking my hand with an enthusiastic grip. 'Glad you found us.'

His office is in a big room with high ceilings and generous windows, and a set of beautiful wood-and-glass display cases lines the walls. 'Some of the artwork,' Anderton says, following my gaze, 'created by the patients. We've had some talented folks here.'

We sit in a pair of easy chairs, drinking iced tea and talking about the challenges the work force faces in this facility.

After we've been shooting the breeze for fifteen minutes or so, I ask, 'Do you find the work gratifying?'

'Not really,' he says with a sigh. 'Most of our patients fall into two categories. Many are here for pre-trial evaluations—to see if they're capable of standing trial. The rest are insanity acquitees.' I must look puzzled because he explains, 'Not guilty by reason of insanity. The point is, our patients are here to be treated, not punished. And we *do* treat them. So long as patients are monitored and taking their medication, they're not a threat to themselves or anyone else. But when they're released—and we *have* to release many of them at some point—we have no means of keeping track of them.'

'When you say you "have" to release them—'

'The courts have held that unless we have clear and convincing evidence that someone is mentally ill and dangerous to himself or others, we can't keep him here. He can be antisocial and capable of all kinds of things, but if he isn't crazy, he gets a bus ticket. Even when it's against our better judgment. We have no choice.'

I smile encouragingly, wondering how I'm going to bring up Charley Vermillion without putting a bullet in the conversation. I decide to take a flier. 'It's like that guy a few years back.'

Anderton laughs. 'Which guy? This happens every month.'

'The one who killed those little boys out west.'

Anderton sags and lets his head droop. 'Charley Vermillion. You see? We could turn every patient into a Nobel prize winner and we'd still have Charley Vermillion thrown in our faces. He's exactly what I'm talking about.'

'What do you mean?'

'He had a personality disorder that was chronic and probably incurable. He was a violent paedophile. And that made him a danger to the community. No question about it. But here, in the context of this facility, with the right medication, he was a model patient.'

'So you felt he could be trusted?'

'In the context of this facility? Absolutely.'

'So how did he get here?'

Anderton frowns, trying to remember. 'Attacked a child. I think it was in a rest room. As I recall, the boy's father intervened and Charley cut him up pretty bad with a knife.'

'And he was acquitted?'

'Drug-induced psychosis.'

'So he got off.'

'Well . . . he spent nineteen years at this address, so I wouldn't say he "got off". But the point is we didn't have a choice. Charley was disturbed, and he could be violent if he didn't take his meds. But he knew right from wrong when he walked out this door.'

'It took *nineteen years* to decide that?'

Anderton shrugs. 'He petitioned for release. Someone put a bug in his ear. Probably another patient.'

'Any idea who?'

Anderton frowns, and instantly seems on guard. The question was too specific. 'I'm really not at liberty to talk about individual cases,' he says in a stiff voice.

'I'm sorry, of course you can't. I understand. It's just a pretty dramatic example of what can happen—'

'There are patient confidentiality issues.'

'Yes, but in this case Vermillion is dead, isn't he?'

A mistake. I regret it instantly. I try to change the subject, ask about Anderton's training, his prior experience, but he is now on guard. He stands up, looks at his watch. The interview is over.

I'm getting to my feet and following Anderton towards the door. And then I see something in the display case along the wall—and the hairs stand up on the back of my neck.

Inside the case, among the sculptures, weavings and pottery made by the patients as a part of their therapy, is a set of origami figures. A rhino, an elephant, a lion . . . and a duplicate of the rabbit I found on

Sean's dresser. In front of the origami figures is a little paper label, like a place card at a table: 1995.

I can't speak. There's a hammer in my chest. Finally, I hear myself say. 'Who made these origami figures? Was it Vermillion?'

'Oh, no. Charley wasn't interested in art.' He hesitates and now his voice is suspicious. 'Why do you ask?'

I can't take my eyes off the rabbit. And I'm not sure what to do. Anderton is wrapped in his bureaucratic armour now. If I tell him the truth, will he identify the patient who folded the rabbit?

'Dr Anderton, I have to confess something to you . . .'

I know after thirty seconds that it's a mistake. Anderton is less interested in what I'm telling him than he is angry at my deception. I plead for the name of the inmate who created the origami menagerie. I explain about finding the rabbit on my son's dresser. I spell out my theory that Vermillion was not the killer of the Ramirez twins, that the man who folded the rabbit was the real murderer.

He shakes his head. 'That sounds like a wild theory to me,' he says. 'I mean, these showgirls and all? I don't know how you can make all these connections.'

I tell him if my boys die, he has blood on his hands.

But Anderton won't budge. He cites patient confidentiality.

'Just tell me one thing,' I plead. 'Whoever it was, he's not still in custody, is he? How long was he here? When was he released?'

'That's three things.'

I say nothing.

'No,' he tells me. 'The inmate in question is not in custody. Came to us in 1983. Released in 1996.'

'What did he do? What was he in here for? What's his name?'

Dr Anderton wags his head sadly. 'I'm sorry, Mr Callahan.'

I want to throw him into the display cases and then ransack his office. But I get control of myself. 'Thanks for your help,' I tell him.

IN THE PORT SULFUR library I log onto the Internet with my laptop and book a bargain room at the Crescent City Omni. I also email Muriel Petrich to request that photos of the origami rabbit be scanned and emailed to me. Before the library closes, I establish that the Plaquemines Parish seat is in Pointe A La Hache. Which is across the river. That's where the courthouse is, and that's likely where the petition for Charley Vermillion's release was filed.

When I ask a kid how to get to Pointe A la Hache, he tells me there's a free ferry that goes across the river every half hour. I can catch it a few miles north. Look for the signs.

I sit in my car and I realise there's no point in making the crossing today. It's too late. The courthouse will be closed. I drive back to New Orleans and check into the Omni.

IN THE MORNING, I grab some free coffee from the lobby, plug in my laptop and check my email. Petrich came through with the pictures. Even in two dimensions, the rabbit is impressive and powerful. I made no mistake—it's identical to the one in the display case in Anderton's office. At nine, when the hotel's 'office suite' is available to guests, I print out a few copies of the photo of the rabbit.

In the car, I look at the map. Plaquemines Parish is a peninsula divided by the Mississippi River. The courthouse in Pointe A La Hache is on the west bank. I plan to go there, looking for the petition for release that freed Charley Vermillion.

My guidebook confirms what the kid in the Port Sulfur library told me: ferryboats run back and forth across the river. I head for the one that crosses from Belle Chasse to Dalcour.

I'm lucky, catching the ferry five minutes before it leaves. The river is wide, the water a turbulent roil of chop and current. The ferryboat's powerful engines muscle their way towards the far shore.

In twenty-four minutes, I arrive in Pointe A la Hache. It's not hard to find the courthouse, which is the largest structure I've seen in Plaquemines. But it's a burned-out shell, surrounded by crime-scene tape. A construction trailer sits to the side. A rap on the door summons a red-faced man in a battered yellow hard hat.

'What happened to the courthouse?' I ask.

'Burned down,' he says.

'When did *that* happen?'

'January twelve 2003.'

'What a shame.' The sight of the fine old building depresses me. 'Where are the records now? Did they survive?'

'Shame and a half is what it was,' Hardhat says. 'Stood more'n one hundred years. Lasted through I don't know how many hurricanes. And then—' He snaps his fingers. 'Gone. Nature couldn't destroy the place, but man could. And did.'

'You mean it was arson?'

'Right,' he says. 'The Bureau of Alcohol, Tobacco and Firearms found accelerant residue. Big time.'

Arson. 'But why?'

He wags his head. 'They's a hundred years of history in them files. Least there *was*. Some say that's it, some old record somebody wanted permanently lost.'

'But there must be electronic records.'

He laughs. 'For the past few years, they is. But for the other ninety-five or whatever. Nossir. Those records is solid gone.'

Maybe I can find out the name of Vermillion's lawyer. The case is recent enough to fall within 'the past few years.' I ask, 'So where do they conduct court business now?'

'Temporary courthouse. Bunch of trailers over there in Belle Chasse,' he says with a chuckle. 'It's more *convenient*, you see, for the *interim*. Lawyers and judges don't got to hassle with the ferry and all.'

I FIND the temporary courthouse in Belle Chasse—a half-dozen trailers in the parking lot of an abandoned shopping centre. Each trailer bears an identifying sign. When I find the one housing records, the clerk of court tells me I'm out of luck. All the files pertaining to the Port Sulfur Forensic Facility were destroyed in the fire.

'I was told there were computer records for the last few years. I'm just trying to get the name of a lawyer connected to a case.'

She's a white-haired woman with bright brown eyes and an ironic smile. 'Supposed to be electronic back-up, but it never took. We got four months of records and that's it. You might find something about your case in the newspaper, though. The *Peninsula Gazette* right here in Belle Chasse is the paper of record.'

I mull over the dates as I follow the clerk's directions to the *Gazette*'s office. The Ramirez twins were abducted in May 2001, two weeks following Vermillion's release from Port Sulfur. The petition for release would be earlier, maybe a lot earlier. I can start in late April and work my way back.

But not right now, it seems. As I approach the newspaper office, a young girl with dark spiky hair is locking the door. She's wearing a halter top, cut-off jeans and flip-flops.

'Will you open again this afternoon?'

The girl sizes me up. 'Why? You want to place an ad?'

I explain that I want to look through the morgue.

'Excuse me?'

'I mean the old newspaper files.'

'Ohhhhh. Yeah, I knew that. I heard my daddy say that one time.

He's not here. He's fishing. So what are you looking for?'

'I'm looking for a notice of suit. The courthouse records were destroyed in the fire, so this is my only hope.'

'Huh. The *Peninsula Gazette* is your only hope? I wish Daddy *was* here.' She smiles at me. A surprisingly sweet and shy smile. 'I'm Jezebel,' she says. 'Jezebel Henton.'

'Alex Callahan.'

She shakes the keys. 'Well, Mr Callahan—I *could* let you in. Of course, I'd have to stay with you. How long is this going to take?'

I shrug. 'It could take a while.'

She twists a ring on her pinky. 'Well, since I have to sit there, I think it's only fair if you pay for my time, don't you?'

'I guess so.'

'So you pay me ten dollars an hour,' Jezebel says. 'Plus, I'll help you look. I'm experienced—so that's why I'm worth ten bucks an hour. I've done courthouse searches for Pinky Streiber.'

'Who's Pinky Streiber?'

'He's a private investigator. You've never heard of him?'

'No.'

'He's legendary,' she insists, sticking out her hand. 'Deal?'

She takes me upstairs. I explain what I'm looking for. 'What I really need is the name of Charley Vermillion's lawyer. I'd like to talk to him . . . or her.'

'Right away I can save you some time,' she says. 'The paper only publishes arrests and suits once a week. Wednesday.'

Jezebel finds it at 3.48. 'Binnnnnnnn-go!' she shouts. 'Am I good or am I good? January 9th, 2000. Charles Jimmie Vermillion vs Port Sulfur Forensic Facility, et al., filed by Francis—'

'What's it say?'

'Filed by Francis Bergeron,' she says. 'Frankie Bergeron. I hope you don't need to talk to him real bad.'

'Why?'

'He's dead. Car crash. Over by Des Allemands. Single car accident. Went flying into the bayou. Hey—what's the matter?'

I shake my head. 'Every time I think I'm getting somewhere, I hit a dead end. Maybe Bergeron's firm would have records. Do you know who he worked for?'

'Lacey and Bergeron here in Belle Chasse. You could call Mr Lacey. I'll get you his telephone number. Don't call him after three. He drinks a little.' She twirls a Rolodex file and then writes a number on a Post-it and hands it to me. Then she locks up, and I fork over thirty-five bucks.

'I almost feel bad about taking this,' she says.

'Deal's a deal. Thanks for the help.'

She pushes the money into the back of her jeans, then sticks out her hand. 'Well, then, good luck, Mr Callahan. Maybe things will turn around. Pinky says they always do in an investigation if you just keep pounding it.'

'I hope he's right.'

CHAPTER NINE

In the morning, I put in a call to William Lacey, formerly the partner of Francis Bergeron. He tells me that his partner's work on behalf of Charley Vermillion was pro bono. I ask him if I could take a look at the case file.

'I turned Frank's files over to the district attorney,' he says. 'You aware there's a suit pending over Vermillion's release?'

'The parents of the Ramirez boys.'

'Bingo.'

'So the district attorney is . . . where? Belle Chase?'

'Now he is, sure. But my understanding is Frank's files went up in the fire. It's right after the parish court took custody of those files that the place burned down.'

THAT LEAVES the rabbit. I stare at the image on my computer screen. Shoffler looked into it and I did, too. At the time it represented only one of several leads. Now it's all that's left. When I go online and type in *origami rabbit,* into the Google bar, Google kicks out thousands of listings. I slog through them for an hour and a half, but I find nothing that looks like the rabbit I found in the boys' bedroom. However, I learn that the origami world is very chummy and active on the Web. Maybe the origami cybercommunity can tell me more about my rabbit. Judging from the menagerie in Anderton's display case, the Piper wasn't a novice. Maybe he had access to a computer at Port Sulfur. Maybe he communicated with people in the subculture.

I compose an email requesting help in identifying the rabbit in the attached file and send it out to two dozen website addresses.

After about an hour, I already have eight responses to my email plea. One of them (folderman@netzero.com) recognises the rabbit as the winner of a competition at the Prospect Hill branch of the Philadelphia Public Library.

> The Prospect Hill Origami Society sponsors an annual competition, posing a different figure challenge each year. The rabbit in the photo you're circulating was the grand champion in 1995, and we were all irritated when the creator was identified only by his first name. No address. Clearly the guy was a spectacular talent and some of us wanted to communicate with him, but there was no information about how to do so. Get in touch with George Esterhazy—he's the president emeritus of the group. Cheers, I hope this helps.

Folderman appends Esterhazy's phone number and email address. I shoot him a fervent thank-you, then send my original email to Esterhazy along with a copy of folderman's message.

A few minutes later, I call Esterhazy. He might be one of those guys who checks his email once a week.

'Esterhazy,' the reedy voice says.

'Mr Esterhazy, my name is Alex Callahan. I don't know if you've had a chance—'

'Yes. I got your email. And of *course* I remember that brilliant little rabbit. Byron B. Very frustrating.'

'Byron B.? What do you mean?'

'That was his name—all the name we ever got.'

'Excuse me, but how was the rabbit submitted, if you didn't know the identity of the person who made it?'

'Turned out the fellow who sent the piece was an occupational therapist at the . . . wait, I'll remember.'

'Port Sulfur Forensic Facility in Louisiana?'

'Yes! A madhouse! We might have been permitted to communicate with this Byron B. fellow except that by the time the competition was judged and we were ready to inform the winners and announce results, he'd been released. And our attempts to persuade the institution to pass on the news of victory and the small cash award were very firmly rebuffed.' A sigh. 'So that was it.'

I'm so excited I barely thank the man before I hang up.

Byron B. might not be much, but it's something. The facility in Port

Sulfur is an institution for the criminally insane. Which is to say that whoever Byron B. is, he screwed up badly and in a very public way—otherwise he wouldn't have been in that particular bin for so many years. And he hadn't checked in of his own volition. Which meant that somewhere in Louisiana, there was a court order committing a man named Byron, last name initial B., to the Port Sulfur Forensic Facility. Thanks to Dr Anderton, I know the year: 1983.

Ordinarily, I might not select a private investigator on the advice of a thirteen-year-old girl, but nothing about my life is ordinary any more. Jezebel Henton is happy to give me Pinky Streiber's name and his number, which she apparently knows by heart.

'Thanks, Jez.'

'One thing about Pink maybe you should know . . .' She hesitates.

'What's that?'

'Just 'cause it kinda startles people. See, Pinky—the reason that's his nickname? He's an albino.'

I meet Pinky Streiber at his office in the French Quarter. It has to be one of the hippest waiting rooms I've ever been in. Jazz on the sound system. Paintings, antique furniture and a scatter of big plants. Tall ceilings and rotating fans. Pinky Streiber is doing all right.

Five minutes later, he's shaking my hand and leading me to his dimly lit inner sanctum. He sits behind a slab of polished wood, which has nothing on it but a red telephone. I sit on a red leather chair. Streiber wears sunglasses and his skin is dead white. There's a familiar smell in the air, but I can't quite identify it.

'Sunscreen,' Streiber says, as if he's read my mind. 'I'm drenched in it. That's what you smell. Coppertone Sport 48. And I apologise for the sunglasses, but I only take 'em off at night.'

After he understands the task, Pinky says, 'Well, it's labour-intensive, but even so, it's just legwork. How big is your budget?'

I shrug. 'Don't hold back. Whatever it takes.'

'I'll give you a break, seeing as how this ain't exactly a run-o'-the-mill divorce case, but I'll still need a retainer, let's say five hundred dollars. And just so you know, I don't do courthouse searches myself. I've built up a kind of motley crew of paralegals, retired folks, teenagers and the chronically underemployed. You say go, I'll turn 'em loose on this and they will hit every single courthouse in Louisiana until they find that commitment order.'

'Great.'

'Ohhhhh-kay. So it's Byron B. Commitment order to the Port

Sulfur Forensic Facility. Entered the system in 1983.' He writes this down. 'You know when he got out?'

'Ninety-six.'

'OK, then, that's all I need.'

'I might as well help,' I tell him. 'If there's somewhere you don't have enough bodies, I know how to search records.'

'Dynamite. You just earned yourself a stint in St John the Baptist Parish. Parish seat's in LaPlace. It's not far from here.'

DAYS IN THE LaPlace courthouse, nights in the local Comfort Inn. Poring over the records, I drink gallons of coffee. The third day, I'm on my way back to the motel when my cellphone rings.

It's Pinky. 'You in your car?'

'Yes.'

'Pull over.'

'What?'

'I'm excited and chagrined and a little disappointed, my man,' Pinky says, with a little bray of a laugh. 'This search coulda really helped out with the unemployment statistics here in Louisiana. Deal is, I hired a woman to work St Mary's Parish. She's visiting her sister in Houston until today, but she's worth waiting for because this lady is real smart. Schoolteacher. Anyway, the assignment from me is waiting on her fax machine when she gets home. She calls me right off. Turns out, she knew the sumbitch. "Byron B.," she says to me. "Pinky, you can only be talkin' 'bout Byron Boudreaux."'

'You're kidding.'

'"Oh?" sez me,' Pinky continues. '"I think so," she says. "See, I grew up in Morgan City and right across the river they had this crazy kid name of Byron Boudreaux, who did some terrible stuff. I remember when they put that boy away because we all slept a little better. And it had to be round 1983 or so." So how about that?'

I don't say a thing. *Byron Boudreaux.* Having a name for the man who abducted my sons has in some way given focus to my torment and, for the moment, I'm so inundated with emotion, I can hardly see.

'Alex? You there?'

'Yeah,' I manage. 'Good work.'

'Blind fool luck is what,' Pinky says. 'By the way, Miss Vicky went ahead and put in for that commitment order because there might be other information on there of use to us. But it's gonna take a couple days to get our hands on it. You gonna get yourself over here?'

'TELL YOU WHAT,' Pinky says, once I'm settled into the leather chair in his office. He's given me a map of Louisiana, the route to Morgan City marked on it, and an index card listing the various telephone numbers of Miss Victoria Sims. 'Why don't I come along?'

'Well, I—'

'Cajun folks is friendly but they can be a little twitchy towards outsiders. And, truth be told, Morgan City can be a kind of rough-and-tumble place.'

'Well . . .'

'You thinking about the money, don't think no more. It's on the *château*, so to speak.'

'Well, that's—'

'Hold the applause. I been thinking about those two little boys of yours. 'Bout time for the Pinkster to do a little pro bono *travail*.'

'I appreciate it.'

'Forget it,' Pinky says. 'I need to get out of the office, pleasant as it is. And I know some boys out that way might prove helpful.'

We head out into the sunset in Pinky's car, a new silver BMW. It's about a ninety-mile drive from New Orleans to Morgan City—where Pinky's secretary has booked rooms for us at the Holiday Inn. Despite the darkness, the way the lights are strung along river banks, clustered on shores, absent in large black expanses, conveys the constant presence of water.

THE NEXT DAY, Vicky Sims meets us for the buffet breakfast at the Holiday Inn. She's about thirty, with bad skin and a sweet, soft voice. 'I located the case file at the courthouse in Franklin,' she tells us, 'after I talked to you, Pinky. It's in the public record, so there's no problem with getting it, although some of the medical opinion leading to commitment is likely to be under seal. I did my best to hurry 'em up, but it's going to take a couple days to retrieve and copy.'

'Why don't we just start with what you remember your own self about Mr Byron Boudreaux,' Pinky says. 'Then Alex and I plan to go talk to people mighta known the guy.'

Vicky smiles. 'I don't know as I can help you all that much with Byron. He lived in Berwick—across the river, so I didn't really know him. Just knew about him. Good-lookin' boy, and really smart. He was the kind of kid could turn out to be a great man, or could turn out to be as crazy as a bedbug. Which was the way Byron went. He had quite a following during his preaching days.'

'He was a preacher?' I ask.

'Oh, yes, people came from all over to see him. As I recall, he took up preaching after his little brother drowned.' She frowns. 'I didn't live here when that happened, but there were rumours.'

'Like what?' Pinky asks.

'Like it wasn't an accident. Like maybe Byron drowned his baby brother. But I can't really remember whether people had suspicions at the time, or if it just came up later, after he killed his father.'

'Is that what he did?' I ask. 'He killed his father?'

'Now, this I do remember very well. And that's what sent him away to the asylum. He murdered his crippled daddy.'

'You're kidding,' I say, although nothing this monster did would surprise me.

'I'm not. Byron was seventeen, and they were planning to try him as an adult. Then he was found incompetent, twisted as a corkscrew.'

Pinky drains his coffee. 'His father was crippled?'

'Claude, Byron's daddy, worked out on the rigs for Anadarko,' Vicky says. 'Had some kind of accident and surgery. He was on the mend, but he was still in a wheelchair at the time of the murder—which seemed to make it even more terrible.'

'What'd he do—shoot his old man?' Pinky asks.

'Oh, nothin' that normal,' Vicky says. 'Poisoned him in some sneaky way—through his *skin,* I think it was. Can that be right?'

'Transdermal,' Pinky says. 'How'd he get caught?'

'I don't know as I ever knew that. It never did come to trial. But since it was *poison*—there was no question it was premeditated.'

'He pled insanity,' I say.

'Right. The lawyers said he was crazy, that he heard voices, that his daddy abused him from when he was a little guy.' Vicky sprinkles salt on her grits. 'There'll be more about it in the court records. Or in the paper—the *New Iberian* might be your best bet. I know the editor, Max Maldonado. You want his phone number?'

We call from my hotel room, with Pinky on the extension. I explain who I am and what I want, and Maldonado says he's on a deadline but he was a reporter back then and, of course, he remembers the Boudreaux case. He'll call me in the afternoon. I'm agreeing to that when Pinky weighs in. 'Shame on you, Max. Start talking right this minute. Surely you can spare five minutes of your invaluable time for two missing bambinos. Come on now.'

'Am I talking to the whitest private investigator in Louisiana?'

Maldonado says. 'Shoot, Pink, why didn't you say it's you?'

'I'm testing your moral compass, Max.' He lets out a rumble of laughter at the protesting hoot from Maldonado. 'All we want is a heads-up on this fellow, somethin' to go on.'

'My moral compass? Well, all right. I'll try to swing it around your way, Pink. Byron Boudreaux—why am I not surprised we didn't hear the last of him?' A sigh. 'I can give you five minutes now, all the time you want later tonight.'

'Great.'

'Let's see. Byron's family lived over towards Berwick in a trailer park called Meadowlands. Marie, Byron's mother—she was a fine woman by all accounts. Claude—he was a good man, too, is what I hear, hard worker. Imagine being poisoned by your own son. That boy was just plain *rotten* through and through. Most folks didn't believe that crap about Claude abusing the boy.'

'Where do we find Meadowlands?' Pinky asks.

'You get on across the bridge to Berwick, go along about . . . maybe half a mile. You won't have any trouble finding it.'

'Does Boudreaux still have family there?' I ask.

'I don't think so,' Maldonado says. 'Daddy died from the poisoning, mom died a few years beforehand. And—hang on.'

We hear a bunch of shouting in the background.

'Sounds like you gotta go,' Pinky says.

'I can meet you later tonight—after we get this baby to bed.'

'Buy you dinner,' Pinky suggests.

'Deal,' Maldonado says.

WE CROSS the expanse of the Atchafalaya River on the Huey P. Long bridge, and find Meadowlands within ten minutes. Despite the bucolic name, there's nothing resembling a meadow in sight. The complex consists of two dozen trailers, most of which have obviously been there for decades. Ragged front yards hold plastic chairs, more seating in the form of inverted white buckets, kids' bicycles, toys of all sorts, plastic wading pools, boat trailers, discarded tyres.

Pinky rolls down the road and pulls up in front of trailer number 14. The BMW gleams on the rutted dirt like an alien spaceship.

I rap on the door. A grey-haired woman with her hair in pink foam curlers calls over from the porch of the trailer next door. 'They ain't home. Help you with somethin'?'

'We're looking—' I start, but Pinky takes over.

'How're you doing today, ma'am?' he says.

'You selling something, sugar? 'Cause I don't have a dime. I got time, though, so y'all can practise on me if you want.'

'We're not selling anything,' Pinky says. 'We're—'

'Pardon me but are you a *albino*?'

I start to say something, offended on Pinky's behalf, but he just laughs. 'Yes, I am. I'm a genetic oddity standing right here in your front yard. I know it can throw people off their normal manners at first, just like someone with a deformity. In a funny kind of way, I think it's a form of racism. Now, who would believe that here in Louisiana there'd be such a thing as being too white?' He smiles.

'Why don't you and your friend come on up here out of the sun, and tell me what brings you to Meadowlands?' the woman asks.

'Up here' is a rickety deck made out of plywood and elevated on cinder blocks. Metal folding chairs comprise the deck furniture.

'I'm Pinky Streiber,' Pinky says. 'And this is Alex Callahan.'

'I'm Dora Garrity,' the woman says, then turns towards me. 'I seen you on TV.' And then, the light really dawns. 'Ohmygod, you the daddy of them two little tykes.'

'We think Byron Boudreaux might be the one took those boys,' Pinky says.

Dora's hand flies up and covers her mouth. 'That boy,' she says, after lighting a cigarette, and exhaling a long stream of smoke. 'That boy was born bad. Bad to the bone.'

'Do you know where he is? Where any of his family is?'

She shakes her head. 'Sorry, sugar. I can't help you there. I haven't seen him since they took him away. His folks're dead. I didn't even know he was out of the asylum.'

'What about the people who live there now? Are they related?'

'No. Claude and Marie, they didn't own the home. It's a rental, you understand. So there's been a whole string of folk in there.'

'What about friends?' I ask. 'Did Byron have friends here?'

'He had no friends. No friends at all. Time he killed Claude, he was spending most of his time hangin' with some witch doctor.'

'*Witch* doctor?'

'What I heard.' She seems to bristle at my scepticism.

Pinky asks, 'You know this witch doctor? Know his name?'

Dora looks offended. 'Nossir, I do not.'

'But you did know Byron?' I manage.

'Honey, he lived right next door. Your home is a trailer, you spend a lot of time outdoors. I been living here for more than thirty years. And, believe it or not, that's not even the record.' A smoker's laugh, half cough. 'Old Ralph Guidry been here even longer.'

'Can you tell us anything else about Byron?'

'Lemme see. Byron was one of two children. At least he was for a while. When Byron was ten and his brother, Joe, was four, Byron saw—some say he *watched*—Joe drown in the municipal pool.'

Pinky looks at me. 'This is what Vicky was talking about. His brother drowned in front of him? That's terrible. Did he try to save him?'

'Well, that's the thing. Everyone agreed it was a tragedy, but some wondered if it wasn't something even worse. On account of it happened at night, when Byron and his kid brother snuck out of the house. Anyway, they were marauding around the neighbourhood. Byron had a bright idea and helped his little brother climb over the fence around the pool, which was closed, of course. According to what Byron said, the two of them were horsing around when Joe slipped and fell into the deep end. Since neither of the boys knew how to swim, that was it. Byron couldn't save his brother.'

'So people actually thought Byron drowned his brother?'

'They were suspicious. See, there was this aluminium pole with a net attached that they used to remove debris from the pool. When the police and Fire and Rescue arrived, it was lying there. Dry as a bone. Hadn't been touched. Byron was bone dry, too, and there was no water around the side of the pool. It didn't look like Byron so much as went to the edge of the pool and stuck his hands in. Why didn't he use the pole?'

'I don't know,' I say. 'It's a big jump from that to think the kid murdered his brother. Maybe he just froze. It happens.'

'That's what Byron told the police,' Dora says.

'You'd think at ten years old, you'd get the benefit of the doubt.'

'Oh, but even then, that kid kinda scared people. And it wasn't just that. There was a witness, a waitress coming home that evening. She walked past the pool and said she saw Byron sitting at the end of the diving board looking down into the water. There wasn't anyone else around. The scene was as quiet as a photograph. So where was little Joe? "In the bathroom", is what Byron said. But that was a lie, 'cause the doors were locked. What we all thought was that little boy's down in the water and Byron's up there on the diving board looking down on him. 'Bout creeps you out, you know? But it never did amount to nothing. The death was ruled an accident.'

Dora rises to her feet with a soft grunt. 'Why don't we go down the way 'n' see Old Ralph? Together we'll remember more. He knew the family real well. Worked with Claude—that's Byron's daddy.'

She asks us to wait and comes back out, five minutes later, hair still in curlers, but wearing a gleaming pair of running shoes.

'Should we walk?' Pinky asks, looking at the shoes.

'Hell, no,' Dora says. 'I want a ride in that car.'

RALPH INSISTS on making iced tea. He distributes the glasses, then excuses himself to 'fetch something'. We wait in the living room and Ralph comes back with a couple of photo albums. 'I had the camera bug in those days,' he says, leafing through one album, until he finds the page he's looking for.

'Here,' he says, and we lean in, looking at a three-by-five snapshot. 'That's Claude.' Ralph points to a handsome man with long side-burns, seated on a park bench. 'And that's Marie.' He indicates the demure-looking woman next to Claude. Her head is turned, and she gazes fondly at the well-scrubbed little boy next to her.

'And that there is Byron,' Dora says. 'This was before little Joe came along. Oh, how she doted on that boy, Marie did. Wasn't nothin' that boy wants, she doesn't get for him. Every toy and game, every bicycle. Guitar. Trampoline.'

Ralph finds another snapshot, taken a couple of years later. Byron is seven or so. Dressed in a suit, top hat and a cape, he's got a curly moustache penciled onto his upper lip. Behind him is a handmade banner: BYRON THE GREAT.

I remember what Karl Kavanaugh said about magicians starting as kids. The photograph gives me chills.

'Oh, the magic shows!' Dora says. 'I plain forgot about that. Byron would sell tickets for a quarter. We'd watch the show on folding chairs that Byron set up outside the trailer.'

'He got pretty good at it, too,' Ralph says. 'He had this one trick—he'd put a few feathers and scraps of grass in a pan, say some abracadabra stuff, and next time he opens the pan a bird flies out. I looked at the pan, too. No place to put a live bird in there.'

A dove pan, I think, remembering Kavanaugh's description.

'I heard something about Byron being a boy preacher,' Pinky says.

'My goodness, yes,' Dora says. 'After little Joe died, Byron *really* got religion. He caught the preaching bug. And was even getting a reputation as a healer, right Ralph?'

'Absolutely,' Ralph says. 'Folks said he had a calling. It was bullshit of course. But he had quite a following. He was quite the little showman. Then that thing with the puppy happened and—' He turns to Dora. 'Didn't they bounce him out of the church?'

'What "thing with the puppy"?' Pinky asks.

Ralph lets out a sigh, rocks back in his chair. 'It's Christmas time. And maybe this is hindsight, but what folks say now is that Byron was getting a little scary. You just plain didn't want to be around the boy. He's what?' He turns to Dora. 'Fourteen?'

Dora nods. 'And the boy next door,' she says with a shudder, 'gets a puppy for Christmas.'

'Now remember how Dora said Byron got *everything* he ever wanted?' Ralph asks.

Pinky and I nod.

'There's one exception,' Ralph tells us. 'Marie—she's got the asthma, bad, and she can't have no animals. So Byron couldn't have no puppy or kitten, not even a hamster.'

'What happened is this,' Dora says. 'Little Emory Boberg, the kid next door on the other side, gets a puppy for Christmas. And he's out walking this little pup past Byron's trailer, and Byron asks can he play with it. Emory doesn't want to, but he's scared of Byron, so he hands him the leash. Byron sent Emory to the 7-Eleven to get Slurpees for the both of them. As soon as Emory's out of sight, Byron digs a hole in the yard and *buries* the puppy up to its neck. Byron tried to explain this later—some lame story about how the pup keeps slippin' his collar and puttin' him in the ground is Byron's way of keeping him from runnin' off. While Byron does his chores. Like anyone believes Marie really told him to mow the lawn—it's *December.* Anyways, he gets the power mower from the shed and begins to cut the lawn.' Dora puts her head in her hands as if she can't stand the memory. 'I'm down here when Emory comes back and lets out this horrible scream. And me and whoever else is around, we come running.'

'He mowed the dog's *head* off?' I ask.

'So, Emory's mother calls the police', Ralph says. 'And they come. And no one's buying it when Byron insists it was just an accident.'

'He was charged with malicious mischief,' Dora adds.

'And what happened to him?' I ask.

'Nothing. He got off with counselling.'

'Word got out,' Ralph says. 'The Boudreaux boy ain't right. Got a screw loose. Parents told their kids to stay away from him. The church wouldn't let him preach no more.'

'Byron dropped out of school,' Dora says. 'And that's when he started hanging out in Morgan City with that witch doctor.'

Pinky asks, 'You got a name for this guy?'

'I already told you,' Dora replies. 'How would I know something like that?'

'I think I know who it is,' Ralph says, 'but I don't know his name. You go down to Morgan City and you ask and somebody will tell you where to find him. He's world-famous, that fella.'

'Just . . . uh . . . ask for "the witch doctor"?' Pinky says.

'Well,' Ralph says. 'They don't exactly call themselves witch doctors. They got some voodoo name for it. *Higgan? Hungin?*'

'*Houngan,*' Pinky says.

'That's the one. And see, there's more than one o' these guys over there in the city. Ask for the one with no upper lip.'

'Get outta here,' Pinky says.

'Swear to God,' Ralph tells him. 'I seen him. I don't know the actual cause of the injury. What *he* says is a zombie got pissed at him and bit it off.'

PINKY AND I catch lunch at Katy's, a ramshackle place that offers sandwiches and drinks.

'Now, that's a *good* po'boy,' Pinky says, taking a swig of Coke to wash down the last bite. 'Good as the food is in N'Awlins, it's gettin' hard to find a top-drawer po'boy. My personal theory is you got to get out into the countryside, because the places in town change the grease too often. What you think, Arthur?'

Arthur is the man behind the counter, apparently an old friend of Pinky's. Arthur's dark face opens in a gap-toothed smile. 'This a genuine compliment or you sayin' my grease got whiskers?'

'No, I mean it,' Pinky insists. 'It's like aged beef. Young oil's got no bouquet. It's just neutral. Doesn't add a thing.'

'*Ça s'adonne. Comme ça se fait ici?*'

The two go back and forth in a patois I can't understand, and then Pinky says, 'My friend here, man stole his chirren.'

'No!' Arthur looks at me with a shocked expression.

'Little boys, friend. Not but six years old. My friend breaking his head and heart tryin' to find them. Afraid they goin' to come to harm, you know. Looking for the man who took them. The path takes him to Berwick, where the man we lookin' for lived.'

'You hunt this man?'

'That's right. *Boute à boute.* He's a crazy man, name of Byron Boudreaux, and we hear he took up with a *houngan* round Morgan City a few years back. All we know about the *houngan:* he missin' his upper lip.'

'No top lip?' Arthur says. 'I heard of this man. He's famous.'

'What's his name?' I ask.

'Diment. Doctor Aristide Diment. Big *bizango.*'

'What's a *bizango*?' I ask.

'Diment's a voodoo priest, yes?' Arthur says. 'The *bizango,* that's kind of his congregation only they be real close, like a family. You got the sickness or problem in your life, you go to the *houngan.* The *houngan* know how to please the *loa,* the beings who rule the spirit world, how to make the mojo—keep your marriage strong or get your business goin'. Some of them know the dark ways, too, serve with both the hands. Doctor Diment—he one of these.'

'"Serve with both the hands"?'

'That means the priest is a sorcerer,' Pinky says. 'Got supernatural powers. Worship with one hand, do magic with the other.'

I nod. 'So Diment is a magician. Now I understand Boudreaux's interest.' I turn to Arthur. 'You know where we can find Diment?'

'He live near the cemetery in Morgan City. They's a place down there, Lasseigne's, little corner store. You ask the man in there, Felix. Tell him I sent you. He know where to find Maître Diment.'

'Thanks, Arthur,' Pinky says.

'Yes,' I add, shaking the man's hand. 'Thank you very much.'

'*Pas de quoi. Bonne chance.* I hope you find your chirren.'

FELIX IS a small coffee-coloured man. He and Pinky talk in an impenetrable Creole patois. Felix draws a crude map. And then we're back in the BMW, driving past a bank thermometer that reads 101. I wonder if that's the temperature *and* the humidity.

'That thing about the lip,' Pinky says. 'If you don't happen to believe in zombies, they's another explanation. Seen it before. That kind of mutilation can happen when a fellow gets caught fooling around with somebody's daughter or wife. Father, husband—he mess up the man's face, make him ugly so women stay away.'

'Well, at least that's straightforward.'

Pinky turns a corner and pulls up in front of a liquor store. 'Felix said we should take a present to Diment. He says the doctor has a fondness for rum.'

And then we're on our way again until Pinky stops at a crossroads and consults the map.

'Let's see,' Pinky says. 'I think here's where we go to the right.'

A few more turns and we're on a dirt road. After a mile or so, we pull up in front of a nondescript concrete building. The front yard is dirt with a few patches of weeds and tyre ruts full of standing water. The building would look like a storage shed, except for the 'door', which consists of strings of plastic beads.

'This is it,' Pinky says. '*Chez* Diment.'

We step out into the sledgehammer heat. There's no place to knock on a beaded door, so Pinky pushes the beads aside and sticks his head in. 'Hello?'

'Come in then,' a voice calls from some distance.

It's dark inside and even hotter than it was outside. Stifling. In the moments it takes my eyes to adjust, I become aware of sounds in the room, laboured breathing, snuffling and coughing. Then the dozen or so humps on the floor resolve themselves into people.

'I heard about this,' Pinky says. 'It's a clinic. A voodoo hospital.'

'This way,' a voice calls from the back of the room. I follow Pinky through the corridor between the patients. We pass into a separate room, illuminated by a string of Christmas lights and three votive candles. Facing me is an altar crowded with objects: a baby's rattle, statues draped in beads, bottles holding liquids, crosses, a painted skull, a small soccer ball, plastic dolls, a photograph of J. F. K.

There are five folding chairs in the room and on one of them is Doctor Diment. His teeth and eyes seem to glow in the dark. The missing lip is unnerving because all his upper teeth are visible, like the teeth of a skull. 'Welcome,' he says, in a rich voice. 'The white man, and the not-so-white man.' He chuckles.

'Pinky Streiber,' Pinky says. 'And this is Alex Callahan.'

'Sit and tell me what Doctor Diment can do for you,' Diment says.

I hand him the bottle of rum, and he says, 'Thank you. Appreciate it. Which one of you need the doctor's help, you?'

I wipe my forehead. Sweat begins to trickle down my back. I nod. 'I'm interested in Byron Boudreaux. They say he was a friend of yours. I'm trying to find him.'

'By-ron,' Diment says with a sigh. 'He's not having any friends. Let's have a drink.' He twists off the cap of the rum bottle and takes a long swig, then passes it to me. I don't really want to drink from the bottle. But somehow, I know I have to. I take a long slug. The rum burns, all the way down. Pinky declines.

I can see the doctor better now that my eyes have adjusted. What I see is a very thin man wearing a dirty white tank undershirt, a pair of ripped khaki shorts and an old pair of flip-flops.

'What's your interest in Byron?' he asks.

'I think he's kidnapped my sons, my two boys. I think he plans to kill them. I need your help.'

'I tell you this much,' Diment says. 'Byron, he comes to me after he killed that little dog. You hear about that?'

'Yeah.'

'Wouldn't no one talk to him after that. The parents, they tell their children stay away. Then Byron find me one night. He do errands for me, clean the clinic. In return he wants to learn what I know. The ways of the world.' Diment takes another hit of rum and holds the bottle towards me. I have another slug.

'Then what?' I ask.

'Then nothing,' Diment announces. 'I can't tell you any more.'

'But you haven't told me *anything.* Do you know where he is?'

Diment shakes his head. 'Byron is part of the *bizango.* We're a closed circle. I tell you more about him, I break the faith.'

Pinky lists reasons why Diment should help us, including money. I plead with the doctor. But Diment is resolute. He'll say no more.

'There's gotta be a way around this,' Pinky suggests.

'One way,' Diment tell us. 'If the man here wants to learn more, he'll have to become a part of the *bizango*. Then, we have no secrets from each other.'

'Fine,' I say. 'Where do I sign up?'

Diment laughs. 'It's not that easy. There's a ceremony. Initiation.'

'Whatever it takes.'

'Some people uncomfortable with it,' Diment tells me. 'Because you have to have faith—in me, the *bizango.* Then you'll be born again in *vaudoo.* And a part of us.'

'I have to "have faith"?'

'You don't have to believe any particular thing,' Diment says. 'It's like getting on the airplane. You put yourself in the hands of the pilot. You put yourself in his trust. You don't understand what keeps the plane up in the sky, but still you get on, buckle up and trust that you goin' to end up where you want to go. It's like that. You trust us.'

'I don't know,' Pinky says. 'I've heard these things can be dangerous.'

'Is this the only way you'll tell me more about Byron?' I ask.

'That is true,' Diment says, nodding.

'Then let's go. Count me in.'

'Come back at midnight.'

'Tonight?'

Diment nods and then gets up and heads for the door. As we weave a path through the poor souls hunkered down in the heat and darkness, he asks, 'What size you wear?'

'What *size?*'

'Yes!' He seems annoyed. 'What size do you wear?'

'Forty-two regular,' I tell him.

'Ahhhh,' Diment says. 'That's perfect.' He pulls the beads aside.

Pinky and I step through into the front yard, and the beads fall closed behind us with a kind of liquid rustle.

'Whoa,' Pinky says, once we're back inside the car. 'I'm not sure I'd be keeping any future appointments with Doctor D there.'

'What was that question about my *size?'*

'I doubt he's gonna kill you for your Gap khakis, but who knows?' Pinky says as we lurch forward. 'The guy looks like a death's head! Don't that *worry* you, pardner?'

'Yeah,' I say. But the truth is, it's hard for me to work up any fear about Doctor Diment. I'm all played out on the fear front.'

'You're not really going there?'

I shrug. 'I'm thinking about it.'

All the way back to the Holiday Inn, Pinky tries to talk me out of it. 'It's crazy! You don't know this guy or what crazy thing he might do. And voodoo—it's nothing you want to mess with. It's all blood and drugs and stuff. I say let's see what Maldonado says. Look, you can always go back to this guy if you have to.'

'Yeah, we'll see,' I tell Pinky.

Pinky has a phone service called OnStar, which he calls his 'travelling concierge'. On the way to the Holiday Inn, he punches it on, secures Max Maldonado's number, and then instructs the machine to call the reporter.

'Hey!' Maldonado's voice booms from the dashboard. 'Good news, Pink. I called up the doctor who admitted Claude Boudreaux when the ambulance brought him in. Sam Harami. If not for Sam, Byron would have got away with murder.'

'You saying what, Max?'

'I'm saying this is the guy who figured out old Claude had been poisoned. And he's ready to join us for dinner if you're buying.'

'My pleasure,' Pinky tells him.

While they go back and forth, figuring out where to meet for dinner, I'm thinking about how I'm going to get out to Diment's later tonight. I think of the dimes, the bowls of water left to me by Boudreaux. Somehow I know that if I'm going to find him, the man with the death's-head face will be the one to point the way.

CHAPTER TEN

We're to meet Max at Prideaux's Eat Place, an upscale restaurant in the countryside by New Iberia, a pretty town a few miles from Morgan City.

We're escorted to a table, where a small grey-haired man bounces out of his seat at our approach. This is Maldonado, 'seventy-five years young' as he later puts it.

'Pinky!' he says, with an enthusiastic pump of the hand. 'It's been way too long, baby.'

Pinky introduces us.

'Pleased to meetcha, pleased to meetcha. And this quiet fella here—' he indicates a black-haired Asian man to his left '—this is Sam Harami.' Harami raises his glass in acknowledgment.

'Would you like a drink?' the waitress asks.

'Absolutely,' Pinky tells her. He orders a Jack on the rocks. I ask for a beer.

'So . . . Byron Boudreaux,' Maldonado says. 'Remember when that s.o.b. got out, Sam?'

Harami nods. 'That guy scared me,' he says, his voice a strange combination of Deep South and Far East. 'And I don't scare easy.'

'He did come right back to Morgan City, soon as he got out. That had us worried,' Maldonado says. 'But he didn't stay long. Spent a week with that witch doctor, and that was it. Haven't heard a peep about him since.'

After we've ordered dinner, I ask, 'What can you tell me about Boudreaux that might help me track him down?'

'Well, he never came across my watch,' Maldonado says, 'until that thing with the puppy. You know what I'm talking about?'

'Yeah,' I say. 'We heard from people at the trailer park.'

'Well, it turned that boy into a pariah. And the next thing was his mother, Marie, died. Got ovarian cancer. Byron was fifteen years old. Some people thought maybe that's what sent him over the edge—when Marie passed. Anyway, a few months after she died, Claude gets hurt in an oil-rig accident. He's gonna be in a wheelchair for months. When he gets out of the hospital, Byron's the one who's goin' to "take care" of him.' The reporter makes quotation marks in the air.

The waitress arrives with gumbo and oysters, and the food silences us for a while. Finally, Maldonado picks up the thread of the story. 'Anyway, here's old Claude, slowly making progress after this operation. Then, for no apparent reason, he gets real sick one afternoon.'

'At this time, I am admitting doctor at the ER in New Iberia,' Harami says. 'It's my residency, you know. My English not so good now, but then? Very bad. And Claude—the man can hardly talk by the time he gets to the hospital. But he has friend with him, Boot. So Boot, he tell me what happens. They watch the television together, drinking beer. All of a sudden Claude tell his friend the room is . . . turning?' Harami makes a circular motion in the air.

'Spinning, Sam.'

'Ah, right. *Spinning.* Claude, he feels light-headed.' Harami points to his head. 'But then he start screaming. He telling Boot that his mouth numb, stomach hurt. Boot—he call 911.'

'They come in record time!' Max says. 'And they get to the hospital pretty quick, too.'

'This right,' Harami says. 'They get here very fast. Otherwise, Claude would be DOA and I never figure out what happen to him. Anyway, they get here and I can't understand what Claude saying, because by this time, he talks in a mumble. But between Boot and the paramedics they tell me what happen. First, Claude dizzy and light-headed, then his lips and tongue numb. Boot say Claude happy for short time, then gloomy. Then Claude vomits in ambulance. In ER, he tell me he feeling stiffer and stiffer by the minute.'

The waitress arrives with our entrées.

'Oh, boy,' says Maldonado, 'they know how to do crawfish *étouffée* here.' He digs in.

Harami lets his Laotian catfish special sit for a minute. 'I'm native of Japan,' he tells us. 'And I am—' he hits his forehead '—my mind blown away by my patient, Claude Boudreaux. I tell myself: "It can't be." I go over list of symptoms again. By now Claude finding it hard to move, hard to breathe. I order him intubated. I order his stomach pumped. I start intravenous rehydration. But it does not work. Two more hour, he is dead.'

'Here's the thing,' Maldonado says. 'On the death certificate, Doc writes: "Respiratory arrest—fugu poisoning".'

'*Fugu poisoning?*' Pinky sputters. 'Isn't that what you get from eating some kind of fish in Japan?'

Harami nods, taking a bite of his dinner.

'That was a corker,' Maldonado says with glee. 'This is a death that normally befalls only Japanese gourmands practising a form of culinary Russian roulette. Every year, fifty or so Japanese diners crash into their plates, struck down while indulging in the delicious taste of the puffer fish, fugu sashimi. It's a highly prized delicacy, but the one serious drawback is that its skin and liver are highly toxic.'

'You rely on the chef skill,' Harami says. 'But sometimes . . .'

'All it takes is a little nick of one of these no-no regions by a sushi chef's knife to deliver a lethal dose of tetrodotoxin poison,' Maldonado says. 'Most doctors in Louisiana would not have recognised the symptoms. But Sam, he's *sure.*'

Harami nods. 'I *know* I'm right. I never doubt, even when autopsy shows deceased stomach contents not contain puffer fish. No seafood at all. They want me change death certificate, but they can't tell me what make Claude stop breathing.'

'So they do a test,' Maldonado says, 'just to shut Sam up. Gas chromatograph. And, sure enough, old Claude's bloodstream was *saturated* with tetrodotoxin.'

'But none in his stomach,' I say.

'The police were baffled,' Maldonado says. 'How can you get fugu poisoning without eating fish? Were there other sources of the toxin?'

'I don't know this answer,' Harami says. 'So the ME refer the question to the Centers for Disease Control in Atlanta.'

'They get on it,' Maldonado says. 'How did the poison get into his bloodstream? Was it something he inhaled? Maybe so. Because we do find a source for the stuff. Turns out tetrodotoxin powder is used in voodoo rituals. Zombie dust.'

'So we think we got something now,' Harami says. 'ME does more tests. But no—Boudreaux's nasal passages and respiratory system show no trace of toxin. None.' His hands fly up. 'A real mystery. Finally we do another gas chromatography test. Focus on victim's bloodstream. This time we get answer. In addition to tetrodotoxin, Boudreaux's blood contained traces of latex and dimethylsulphoxide.' He smiles. '"Ahhhh," we say.'

Pinky and I look at each other.

'DMSO,' Maldonado says. 'It's a solvent. Byron mixed DMSO with tetrodotoxin and smeared it on the tyres of his daddy's wheelchair. So old Claude, he rolls from room to room and this lethal cocktail passes directly from the tyres into his bloodstream.'

'A transdermal delivery system,' Harami says.

'From there, it didn't take long to figure out that Byron was the one who did it,' Maldonado says. 'Everybody knew he's hanging out with that voodoo witch doctor. That's where he got the poison. And he ordered the DMSO mail order, through some weightlifter catalogue. Didn't even try to cover his tracks. But why would he? He was *sooo* unlucky. If any other doctor in Louisiana had been on duty in the emergency room . . .'

'His goose cooked,' Harami says, with a laugh. 'I cook it. That's why I'm nervous when they release him. Why release this man? Someone like that—kill his father, so sneaky, so clever—he not get better.' He looks at me with an expression of commiseration. 'I am sorry. I hope you find your sons.' He lowers his eyes from mine. He does not look hopeful.

On the drive back to Morgan City, Pinky's OnStar phone rings. The system is hands-free and broadcasts over the car's sound system.

'Mr Streiber?'

'Jez—is that you? The fair lady of Plaquemines? I've got Alex Callahan in the car with me, so don't talk dirty.'

'Hello, Mr Callahan. Matter of fact, I'm calling about you.'

'Hello, Jezebel. What's this about?'

'Mr Streiber asked me to look and see if I could find the discharge order concerning Byron Boudreaux. 'Course, I couldn't. It went up in flames when the courthouse burned down. But I found the next best thing—a psychiatric nurse who worked out at the asylum. Worked there eight of the years Byron was there.'

'Jezebel, you are a wonder,' Pinky says.

'Oh, yikes, it wasn't *hard*,' Jezebel says. 'I just asked my daddy and he asked his girlfriend and she asked her stylist.'

'So who is she? You got her number?'

'Well, that's the thing. She's a little bit afraid of Byron. So I'm not supposed to disclose her name. I promised.'

'Jezebel—'

'I won't tell you, so you might as well save it. Anyway, you interested in what I found out? Or not?'

'We want to know,' I say.

'Here's the deal. Byron was a busy little bee while he was at Port Sulfur.' Her voice changes and it's obvious that she's reading from notes. 'First thing, he earned his GED at eighteen. Six years later, he earned a bachelor's degree in psychology—this is all by correspondence courses. Two years after that, he got his master's. He led a Bible study class at Port Sulfur. Byron also had a lot of hobbies; the therapists are big on that. One was origami. And he learned to be a magician, although my source said he already knew how to do lots of card tricks and stuff when he came in. Apparently, he just spent hours and hours practising. Everyone there agreed he was good. Anyway, Byron petitioned for release, starting the first year he was in care, but he didn't get anywhere until ninety-four. That's the first time the release committee really considered his case. Even though he did kill his own father, there were files about the abuse Byron's supposed to have suffered at the hands of his daddy when he was a kid. They didn't really believe that, but . . .'

'With the man dead, they couldn't entirely discount it, either,' Pinky puts in.

'Right. In ninety-six, his case comes up again and they decided Byron was sane, or sane enough anyway, and not a danger to himself or the community, that it was time to let him go.'

'What changed their minds?'

'Time,' Jezebel says. 'It had just been so long. Plus he was a juvenile when he was committed, and he'd done so well with his studies and all.'

'Did Byron have any friends inside? Any special friends?' I ask.

'I knew you'd ask that,' Jezebel says. 'You want to know if Charley Vermillion was a special friend of Byron? And the answer is Byron did spend time with Charley. Charley was in Byron's Bible study class. And it was a close-knit group, according to my source. Byron was some kind of nuthouse lawyer, helped them file petitions and all. You're breaking up. Whereabouts are you?'

'Near Houma,' Pinky says.

'I can't hear you. Call me tomorrow or something.' She hangs up.

'That young lady is dynamite,' Pinky says. He makes a right turn. 'Between Max and Sam and Jez, we learned a lot today.'

'Yeah.'

'Why are you so quiet? You're not thinking of going out to that witch doctor's tonight, are you? Don't be foolish, pardner. I mean it's one thing to throw caution to the winds, and go all out looking for your boys. But it's another thing to head to a shack in the swamp to spend the night with some guy who ain't got no lip. And the only thing you know about him is he was the only friend Byron had, and the likely source of the poison that killed Claude.'

We roll on in silence for some time. I don't say anything.

'I'm going with you then.' Pinky says finally.

'I think it's better if you don't. That way, if I don't come back, you can—'

'Call the po-lice?'

'I just have a feeling Diment might have some idea where Byron is and that he might help me. I don't know.'

'How you plannin' to get there? You even remember how to go?'

'I was thinking a cab. And maybe you could draw me a map.'

'I'll draw you a map. But forget the cab. I'll give you my car.'

'I can't take your car. What about you?'

'I'll be asleep. I'll have me some breakfast right at the Holiday Inn. Read the paper. You don't call or show up by noon or so, I'll sound the alarm. Anyway, call it an insurance policy.'

'What do you mean?'

'First of all, it's easy to track the car. OnStar has this GPS system. Second thing is that the po-lice might not jump into action if some guy from Washington DC gets himself lost in the swamp.' He glances at me. 'But a sixty-thousand-dollar vehicle? Something like that goes missing, you see some action then, all right.'

THE CAR'S LIGHTS tunnel into the night, illuminating unmarked roads that seem indistinguishable to me. I get lost a couple of times, despite Pinky's painstakingly drawn map. I left plenty of spare time, though, and even with wrong turns I arrive at Diment's place fifteen minutes before midnight.

I step out of the car into the warm night. A sibilant insect hum rises up around me. The BMW's lights stay on for a few moments, illuminating with brutal clarity the dark concrete-block structure before me.

It looks like a great place to get killed.

The car gives a little click and the lights fade. I step forward and rap on the siding next to the door. No sooner have I touched the house than the beads are pulled open with a clatter. It's as if the two men were standing just inside, waiting. They smile.

'Welcome, welcome,' one of them says. He's a skinny man, with a fuzz of greying hair. He's so thin he looks skeletal. 'Come in.'

'I'm here to see—'

'The *houngan* not here,' the second man says. He's a big dark-skinned man, at least six-five, two-fifty, and while the skinny man scared me, I find this big man reassuring. 'But first you have to get dressed,' he says in his booming baritone.

'I *am* dressed,' I tell them.

But, no. They tell me they have something special for me to wear. I follow the two of them, tiptoeing past the patients lying in a row against the wall.

'In here,' the big man says, opening a door. I'm being shown into a john. 'You change. We'll wait outside.' He closes the door.

My new outfit is hanging on the back of the bathroom door: a white tuxedo with a red carnation in the lapel. Now I understand the question about my size. Still, it's not reassuring. A white tuxedo . . .?

I'm drenched in sweat; it's coming off me in sheets. And suddenly, I have all kinds of questions: Why do I have to change clothes? Just what is 'an initiation ceremony'? And how can I join something if I don't know what I'm joining? Diment said I had to enter into the evening with trust. How can I put my trust in Diment? I don't even know him.

And why midnight?

Some not helpful portion of my brain chimes in: *It's the witching hour*. I fight off a reflex surge of claustrophobia and try to calm down, but it's hard. I'm breathing too fast, and a voice inside my head is screeching: *What are you doing?* I take several deep breaths. *You came to him,* I tell myself. *You sought out Diment, not the other way round. You asked for his help.*

I put on the tuxedo and the crimson cummerbund. Not surprisingly, it's a perfect fit. I put my clothes on the hangers and put my shoes back on. Then I rap on the door.

It's pulled open. The skinny man cocks his head and contemplates me. 'Aw*right,*' he says, with a cackle. 'My man! You look good.'

The big man reaches into his pocket and pulls out a bottle. 'Close your eyes,' he says. Before I can protest, he's spraying me head to toe with insect repellent.

We pick our way through the clinic again, single file, the big guy leading, and we go outside. The big guy has a Maglite, but the light it casts is a watery yellow disk that doesn't do much to illuminate our way. We're trudging along a narrow dirt path through a vine-tangled wood. The trees are spooky, shrouded with Spanish moss. The insect hum rises up around us.

'Where are we going?' I ask.

'To the place,' the big man says. 'Don't worry, we'll be there soon.'

After a few more minutes, I smell wood smoke and hear the murmur of voices. We emerge into a clearing where Diment and a dozen others, men and women, sit around a fire. A couple of bottles of what looks like rum are going around the circle.

Seeing me, Diment gets to his feet. The rest of the *bizango* follows suit. Diment embraces me, then holds me at arm's length. 'Damn, you look fine.' He smiles, teeth gleaming. Everyone embraces me in turn, introducing themselves and offering a formal welcome.

My heart feels unsteady in my chest, and over and over again I hear that little voice saying: *What are you doing?*

After all the hugs and bows, my legs feel shaky. I'm more than happy to sit down next to Diment, as I'm invited to do. The rum goes around in both directions and I drink as much as I can. Finally, Diment raises his hand, and everyone falls quiet. He turns to me and puts a hand on my arm. 'Alex, are you ready?'

I nod. What I'm thinking is: *Let's get this over with.*

'Bon!' The big man distributes torches. The members of the *bizango* dip the torches into the fire, and we're on the move again, heading even deeper into the swamp. The insects roar and I'm grateful for the repellent which keeps them at bay.

I follow Diment into a clearing. A crude wooden cross stands waist-high, stuck into the ground. A few feet away is a freshly dug grave, and next to that, a pine casket.

It takes me a second to grasp what I'm seeing, and when I do, I take a reflexive step back. Everyone laughs.

Diment faces me. His bizarre smile is anything but reassuring. 'Have faith, my friend. Don't worry. We dig you up quick!'

'Quick!' I say. 'You mean, like, right away, or—'

Diment laughs, throwing his head back. 'No. See, you spend the night, restin' underground. We be up here, makin' music. With the *loa*.

When the sun comes up, your brothers and sisters here get you out.'

I take a deep breath and stare at the coffin. I think about the ME out in Vegas speculating that Clara Gabler had been in a pine box, maybe a coffin, but that she seems to have waited for her fate willingly, without struggle. 'I don't think I can do this,' I say.

The jolly look evaporates from Diment's face. Suddenly, he looks grim with disappointment. 'Then I can't help you,' he says.

I fumble for the words. 'What I'm being asked to do,' I say. My mouth is so dry, I can hardly speak. 'Will it be worth it?'

'That up to you,' Diment says to me. His face is stone. His eyes glint in the torchlight. He looks angry. Around us, the others murmur.

'No,' I tell him. 'It's not up to me. It's up to you. Can you tell me how to find Boudreaux?'

Diment shakes his head. 'You out of turn, son. That a question for *after.* First you prove your trust.' His eyes are fastened on me. 'If you trust me, I help you.'

I don't know why, but I believe him.

A drumbeat starts up. I keep my eyes on my feet as I walk over towards the casket. And then, before I can change my mind, I climb into the box. The whole crowd leans over me. I can see the big man, bending to lift the wooden cover. I close my eyes. *I'm crazy.*

A clear soprano sings 'Amazing Grace'. Panic rolls through me. Isn't that for funerals? And then I think: This *is* a funeral. *They're burying me.*

'Trust me,' Diment says, then the lid clatters into place.

I keep my eyes shut tight. Suddenly, I can feel my breath against the wood, and my heart vaults into my throat. *Maybe they're going to let me out now,* I think for one glorious moment. *Maybe all I had to do was prove I'd do it, and then . . .*

But no. That hope evaporates and it's all that I can do to stop myself from panicking and hurling myself against the wood as they begin to nail the top of the casket into place. It's so loud, each blow of the hammer a deafening concussion. The nailing starts at my head and goes down to my feet and then back up towards my head.

And although I really can't stand it, somehow I endure the noise. When it stops, I find to my shock that I am praying.

The casket shakes and there's a smell of plastic as a pipe is fitted into a hole in the casket, just above my face. I never noticed the hole. Slightly cooler air drifts through it. With some effort, I raise my head up and fasten my lips around the pipe and draw in air.

I feel the casket sway as it's lifted into the air. I can hear voices, a shout. And then the coffin is lowered. With a couple of feet left, they let go. Newtonian forces prevail. I slam into the top of the coffin, my nose crashes into the breathing tube hard enough to make me cry out. I have a terrible fear that I've dislodged the tube. I squirm up, to see if my lips can reach it. *Yes.*

And then a shovelful of dirt crashes onto the wood.

Then another, and another.

Then . . . nothing. Just the darkness.

I'M NOT SURE if I'm asleep or in a trance when I first hear the sound. It's a muffled scraping noise, one that means nothing to me, that seems to exist in a separate universe.

The sound goes on and on. It comes to absorb my attention. After a while it seems to me that it is inside my own head.

It's not until a shovel hits the wood that the sound represents an event in time. It's the sound of a metal implement striking the wooden object in which I am encased. The realisation propels me out of my trance. *I am buried alive and someone is digging me out.*

I try to shout—wanting to offer some sign that the effort is worth it, that whoever my rescuer might be, there's a person down here. I want to shout out: *I'm alive. I'm here. Don't give up.*

What emerges is not a shout, not even a scream. It's more like a moan, so low-pitched I doubt anyone could hear it. As they work on my exhumation, I wonder how long I was under.

While I was buried, I lost my bearings in time and space. At first, I counted my breaths in cycles of one hundred, but eventually, I lost track. I went insane for a time, screaming and trying to claw my way out, which left my fingers raw and bleeding. I used the pain to keep my spirits up. As long as it hurts, I told myself, I'm alive.

I felt regret about it: disappearing. It would be tough on my parents and Liz. My main concern was for the boys, because I considered myself their last chance. Everyone else had given them up for dead. By thinking of Sean and Kevin, by recounting every memory of them, I was able to keep my head together for some time. And I had a vision of them, which, I was persuaded, was true.

Somehow my mind slipped the temporal-spatial chains and delivered me to a room I'd never seen before. The boys were asleep in wooden bunk beds. They slept under burgundy-coloured fleece blankets, Sean on the lower bunk, Kevin on top. Kevin stirred and turned over from one side to the other. His mouth was open and I could see that his two new front teeth, which had just begun to emerge from his gums when the boys arrived from Maine, were almost fully in now. The edges had a vaguely scalloped appearance, and the teeth looked too big for his face, as such teeth do. Then the vision vanished and I was back in the dark.

And then I passed beyond regret, into a new arena, where I was beyond any interest in myself. This is the way I think I survived. I gave up. In a way, it was a relief to give up. To stop counting, to stop thinking of Sean and Kev, to stop hoping. To stop thinking at all.

The screech of the nails being pried off is the loveliest music I've ever heard. When the lid comes off, I'm blinded by the light and my eyes slam reflexively shut. Hands grasp my arms and sit me up.

Someone holds a paper cup of water to my lips and I gulp a few sips, a messy process.

'That's OK,' says a voice I recognise as Diment's. 'You be all right. Didn't I tell you, man? You jez have to trust. Body don't like bein' pinned down like that, that's all. But you be all right. Just take it easy. Let the world welcome you back, brother. You reborn.'

Strong hands under my arms lift me to my feet.

'Open your eyes, Alex. Jest a little, tha's right.'

The world is bleached out, like an overexposed photo, but I can see enough to step over the side of the coffin onto the dusty earth.

Liberated from the coffin, I am drenched in sheer wonderment. The humid air against my skin, the sun, the trees rustling in the breeze, the dirt . . . I tremble with delight. I even start to cry.

'Oh, yes! Now he see!'

The members of the *bizango* are gathering flags and drums, and stuffing bottles and plastic plates and cups into trash bags. Some of their faces are smeary with white powder. They look worn out, as if the night was a difficult one for them, too.

I'M OUTSIDE Diment's place, sitting on a disintegrating rattan chair on a little concrete patio. I'm back in my own clothes, and I put in a call to Pinky from the BMW's phone to let him know I'm all right. I take heart from that strange vision of the boys in their bunk beds, which somehow, to me, means they are alive.

'You know why I help you?' Diment asks when he joins me. The old man looks tired, his colour bad, his rheumy eyes exhausted.

'No.'

'Twins. You seek your boys and they are twins. It is for this. Otherwise, I am an old man who does not like to miss his sleep. Twins are very special in *vaudoo.* Above every other *loa*—which be the spirits in charge of the whole world, the living and the dead—above all of them, is the *Marassa*, the twins. They make the rain fall, they make the herbs that heal the sick. The two in one—they symbolise the harmony of the world as it should be, the balance of the earth and the sky, the fire and the water, the living and the dead.'

'The twins.'

'So it is,' Diment says in his mellifluous voice. 'In *vaudoo*—twin children in a family, this a thing of great importance. They are a reminder of the mystery. You must have ceremony for them. In their honour. This you must do if you find your sons, yes? You must promise me. Every once a year. Christmas, this one possible day, but the celebration must be apart from the Christmas celebration. January fourth, that a second appropriate day. The third one is the Easter eve, the day before the Christian Easter. If you not have ceremony for the twins, it bring unhappy days.'

'We always celebrate. Their birthday is January fourth,' I say.

This stuns him. 'You are sent to me. So I may serve the *Marassa*.' He closes his eyes, mumbles, crosses himself. When he opens his eyes, he looks so tired I ask him if he wants to rest for a while.

'No, no, no, no. I tell you now what I know about Byron. I might know one or two thing. We can hope it will help you.'

We're interrupted by a woman arriving, holding a white rooster in her arms. Diment gets up to inspect the bird. 'It's good,' Diment says, and instructs the woman to put the chicken into one of the pens to the right of where we're sitting. The bird goes inside in a flurry of squawks and feathers.

'She bring for the sacrifice,' Diment says, when the woman leaves.

My mind vaults to the chicken blood on Kevin's shirt, the one the police found in the house. 'You're going to *sacrifice* it?'

Diment nods. 'You don't like this.'

I shake my head as if to dismiss the idea, but he's right.

'Sacrifice the core to all worship, go way back. The god or the gods create the entire world and give you life in it. To honour the god, you perform the ritual, you give him back one of his creatures, you give the life of the thing back to nourish him.'

'I understand the idea, but—'

Diment makes a harsh and dismissive gesture, then puts his hand on my arm. 'Let me ask you one thing: you a Christian man?'

'Sort of.'

'The Christian faith built on sacrifice, you understand, yes? God ask Abraham sacrifice his son Isaac, then God relent. He take a lamb, instead. He take a *lamb* instead of Isaac. He take a life. No, he not require the son of *Abraham,* but God require this of *himself*. He *sacrifice* his only son, let him die on the cross. And Jesus, he know ahead of time. Don't he say at the Last Supper, "This is my body, this is my blood"? The communion—it's about sacrifice.'

'You're right,' I tell him. 'You're absolutely right. But—'

'You think to kill the chicken—this somehow backward, yes? How you respect life if you don't respect death? You live in your head. Alex, you must also live in your body.' Diment thumps his chest. 'You must learn to live in here.'

'I live in my body.'

'No. Three hours out of the ground and already you back up here.' He touches his head and sighs, a deep, fatigued sound.

'I think maybe Byron still practises sacrifice,' I tell him. 'He left one of the boys' T-shirts at my house, soaked in blood. It made the police think I'd killed my sons.'

'Byron—he like to kill things. He like the owl or the panther. He hunts, he spill blood for his own self, to slake his own thirst. I try to teach him how to use that, but . . .' Diment shakes his head.

'What do you mean?'

'That dog. Byron come my way, about that time. I tell him that dog was a waste. I tell him, "You piss away your power, boy, you got nothin' left." He ask, what power is that? So I tell him, "The power you get when creatures be dyin". The power of the sacrifice, yes?'

'And what did Byron say?'

Diment shrugs. 'He asked me to teach him about magic.'

'Like card tricks?'

Diment shakes his head. 'No, no, no. He already know that kind of thing. He wanted to know about the Mysteries. He wanted to know about the sacrifice, what we call the "real magic".'

'Like what? What did you teach him?'

'I teach him the *loa,* the signs and the meanings, the sacrifice, the dance, everything to bring the power of the other world into this world. How to help the spirit move on when somebody die. How every spirit have a place in this world. I teach Byron everything I know. I teach him the herbs and leaves. And he use that to kill.'

'His father.'

'Yes. I teach him the ways. But he not really learn. He use everything only for Byron. That not the way. He pretend to learn. But he stay the same. The same Byron.' I see tears in Diment's eyes. 'He come by here when he gets out, you know that?'

'From Port Sulfur?'

'Yes. After those many years I hope . . . he's changed. But—' He shakes his head. 'He the same Byron, only stronger. I am happy when he go away again.' Abruptly, Diment stands up. 'You come.'

I follow him inside, into the room with the altar. He plucks a postcard from the array of objects and hands it to me. 'You look.'

It seems to be no more than a smear of colours. I have to stare at it for three or four minutes before it gives up its secret. Concealed within a field of blood-red blobs is a pair of clownlike faces. A printed note identifies the painting as *The Marassa* by Petit Jean, Port au Prince, Haiti, 1964.

'The twins,' Diment replies. 'You see? And look what Byron say.'

In the message box is a handwritten note: *Finished with the Castle. Doing real magic now.*

'What's "real magic"? What does he mean?' I ask.

'The twins,' Diment says. 'They guard the gates to *les Mystères*. Without them, you can't do real magic.'

'But what is real magic?'

The old man ignores me. He taps the postmark with his finger:

Aug. 10, 2000 Point Arena, CA

'For *vaudoo* people, August 10th a most important day. Sacred to the *Marassa*. This is why Byron sends the card that day. You might say—' Diment smiles his terrifying smile '—this is our *vaudoo* Easter.'

'You think Byron lives there? Point Arena?'

'I don't know. This is the last card I get from him.'

Three years ago. I'm not exactly hot on his heels.

I look at the signature, which is a scrawl. I squint, but there's no way it looks anything like *Byron*.

Diment looks over my shoulder. 'The name? That's "Maître Carrefour". Byron used it when he worked as a magician on the stage.'

'*Worked.* But not any more? Why not?'

'You saw the postcard. He says he's doing real magic, now.'

'But what does that mean?'

Diment inclines his head, frowns. 'What it means is you make the world do your bidding, with the help of the spirit. You come to be one with them, they work with you, you make thing happen. That what it mean to me. With Byron, I don't know.'

'This thing about a castle . . .'

Diment shrugs. 'I don't know what he means wi' that, either.'

'And *Carrefour*?'

'Ah, yes. That I can tell you. Maître Carrefour is like . . . you would say a patron saint,' the old man tells me.

'Of what?'

Diment looks at me. 'Sorcery,' he says.

I CATCH UP with Pinky in the Holiday Inn's breakfast room. He's drinking coffee and looking at a copy of *USA Today*.

As I slide into the seat across from him, he says, 'You don't look half bad for someone got hisself buried alive. What was *that* like?'

'Dark.'

Pinky lets out a peal of laughter that makes everyone in the room look our way. He ends up wheezing for breath. 'I bet,' he says finally. A sigh. 'Well, I hope you found out something useful.'

I shrug. 'Diment doesn't know where Byron is.'

'Doesn't know? Or wouldn't tell?'

'I don't think he knows. I think he wants to help. He told me a couple of things. After Byron got out of the bin, he worked as a magician under the name Maître Carrefour.'

Pinky nods and pulls out an index card from his pocket. '*Carrefour*, huh? We can put out a search for that. There's got to be magicians' societies, associations, booking agents. Anything else?'

'Byron's retired—he's not performing any more. Last Diment heard, Byron said he was doing "real magic".' I bracket the phrase in the air with my index fingers.

'And what the hell is that?'

'Diment couldn't really explain it or maybe I couldn't understand it. Byron went through the process of becoming a *houngan*—you know, a voodoo priest.'

'Huh. Thinka that. What else you got?'

'Byron sent postcards to Diment, the last one three years ago from Point Arena, California.'

Pinky frowns. 'So this is it?' he says. 'Maître Carrefour. Real magic. A postmark on a three-year-old card.' He looks at me. 'For someone spent the night in a coffin, you didn't get much, buddy.'

On the drive back to New Orleans, Pinky tries to soften his take on things. 'We may get something out of the Carrefour thing. One thing you got going for you is that you know a lot about Byron, including his name, but he doesn't know he's even on your radar screen. Maybe he lives in this Point Arena. What'd it say on the postcard, anyway? Besides this stuff about *real* magic?'

'It said: "Finished with the castle. Doing real magic now."'

'Huh,' Pinky says. 'A castle. In California.'

It comes to me like a bubble rising to the surface: Karl Kavanaugh sitting across from me in a restaurant in Vegas talking about the history of magic and how the centre of magic relocated from Chicago to LA. There was a club in LA. The Magic Castle.

'KARL. It's Alex Callahan.'

'Yeah, sure. How you doing? You back in town?'

'No. I'm in New Orleans. I'm just . . . following up on something.'

'With the Gabler murders?'

'Right. Remember when you were telling me about the Magic Castle? Is that still in business?'

'Very much so. They have shows every weekend, different stages going simultaneously. If you want to attend, I could sponsor you.'

'Is that necessary?'

'Well, it's a *club.* You have to be a member or the guest of a member. Or belong to the Society of American Magicians.'

'I don't know about attending a show, but thanks for the offer. The thing is, the guy I'm looking for, he might have worked there.'

'*Really*. Got a name?'

'Maître Carrefour. His real name is Boudreaux.'

'Carrefour. Boudreaux. Hmmmm.' A pause. 'No bells ringing, but that doesn't mean anything. I don't get over there much any more.'

'Do you know someone at the Castle I could talk to?'

'Sure. John DeLand, the curator, he'd be your best bet.'

He gives me the number, then offers to call DeLand on my behalf. 'Magicians can be a little . . . cliquish. There's a tendency to circle the wagons when someone starts asking questions about one of our own. If you'd like, I could grease the tracks . . . ?'

I'M IN a cubicle in the back of Pinky's office in the French Quarter, checking my email, when Kavanaugh gets back to me.

'John DeLand will be more than happy to talk to you, Alex. He remembers Carrefour, who worked at the Castle for a few years.'

'Great. Thanks!'

A pause. 'I don't know what your budget is, but if funds allow, it might be worth your while to go out to LA.'

I'd been thinking exactly the same thing.

CHAPTER ELEVEN

The Magic Castle is a mouldering Victorian mansion in the hills above Hollywood. And John DeLand looks right at home in it. His hair is white and wispy, his eyes pale blue and sharp. Half-glasses perch on his long nose. He's dressed in a black suit with an old-fashioned cut and a waistcoat with a fob watch. The only anomalous note is a big blue digital watch with a velcro strap on his left wrist.

He meets me downstairs and takes me up a winding staircase. 'I've got about an hour,' he tells me, 'before I've got an appointment with the periodontist. He's promised to scour my gums into submission.'

His office is straight out of Dickens: a cavernous space furnished with heavy Victorian antiques. It's cluttered, every surface covered: books, globes, crystal balls, cards, skulls, plants. Antique posters advertising various magic acts and magicians hang from every available patch of wall. Cats repose on the windowsill.

DeLand gestures me towards a heavy carved wooden chair.

He moves behind his huge black desk, picking up a long-haired black cat from his chair before he sits down. 'So you're here about Carrefour. And your interest, Karl tells me, is a murder case?'

'That's right. A series of murders.'

He sits back and regards me with pale blue eyes. 'Oh dear. And you're . . . what? A police detective? I only ask because we magicians are a kind of . . . a brotherhood, I'd guess you'd say. If I'm to contribute to your effort to find Carrefour, I'd like to know exactly how your inquiries brought you to the Magic Castle.'

'I'm not with the police,' I start. 'My interest is personal.' As I tell him the compressed version of my story, Deland's detached smile fades into a look of alarm.

'How terrible,' he says, in a shaky voice. 'I'm so very sorry. Of course I'll help you in any way I can.' He picks up a black telephone. 'Starting with the Society of Magicians. Carrefour was a member, as well as being a member of the Castle. He'll have paid dues and literature will have been sent to him—the bookkeepers ought to have an address and telephone number.'

When he's finished giving instructions over the phone, he replaces the handset. 'Now, what can I tell you?'

'Why don't you talk about what you remember about Carrefour?'

'I'm not certain how he came to perform here,' DeLand starts. 'Could be he came, reputation in hand, already booked for a night or two. Or maybe he just came to a show, and went on from there. We have something like five thousand members. And if a magician's in town and wants to check out the competition, maybe pick up a new wrinkle for an effect, he comes to the Castle. Before the show—say, in the bar, or waiting in line for a performance—people take advantage of those times to perform. Show their stuff.'

'So it's like an audition?'

'It can be. It's one way to get your foot in the door. Maybe a scheduled performer falls ill and a slot opens up. The visiting magician might get a chance to fill in. After that, who knows?'

'So Carrefour ended up as a regular.'

'Yes. He's quite a gifted performer, brilliant stage presence. And, at first, very much in the tradition here of classical magic. But, as time went on, he revamped his act. He began performing tricks from earlier centuries, particularly from the Indian tradition. Amazing stuff, but . . .'

'What?'

'Tastes have changed in what people want to see on stage. His new act wasn't very popular. People don't want to be terrified any more. Amazed, baffled, delighted—but not horrified or scared out of their wits. People have lost their appetite for gore, and Carrefour's act was . . . well, it was quite gory, actually.'

'But he was allowed to continue?'

'Before he revamped his act, he was very popular. So even when he redid his act, there was some carry-over. He was a tremendous performer. And there was a lot of support for what he was doing within the ranks of the Castle. Part of the Castle's *raison d'être*, if you will, is to preserve the history of magic as an art form. So it was nice to see some of these effects revived, if only as historical curiosities. One of his standbys was the basket trick. Do you know it?'

I shake my head.

'Well, it's quite in the old tradition of putting the magician's assistant in peril. You might see something stagy and antiseptic these days along that line: knives thrown around the pretty assistant, or the lady sawn in half. No real sense of danger, though. This was not the case with the older tricks. The danger was emphasised.'

'I see.'

'For tricks of the vintage Carrefour was working in, the magician would have had a child assist him. Often it was his son—we didn't get to the pretty girls until later. One of the assistant's jobs is to serve as an agent of misdirection. You want the audience to look away from whatever you're doing, so the magician might toss a ball, say, to the assistant. The eyes will follow the ball—it's instinctive.'

'I see what you mean.'

'A child has wonderful attributes as an assistant. He's small and can fit into smaller spaces. Plus, he wears a mantle of innocence, so the audience never thinks of a child as in on the deception. You can't employ children now because of legal constraints, so Carrefour did the next best thing. He employed a young man—quite slight and youthful in appearance, but actually of legal age.'

'Interesting. So, how did the act go?'

'In the basket trick the boy blunders during an earlier part of the show, does something clumsy with one of the props or acts defiantly. He's forced into the basket as a punishment by the master, while the magician carries on with the rest of his act. But the boy won't shut up. He keeps whining. Finally, the magician loses his temper. He's in the midst of some effect requiring swords and he impulsively picks one up and thrusts it into the basket. The boy cries out, but this just enrages the magician further. With bloodcurdling screams emerging from the basket, the magician thrusts more swords into it, crisscrossing them in such a way that it seems no one inside could survive. The screams weaken, turn into moans, and then finally, there's silence. The audience is nervous. The magician heaves a sigh of relief and returns to his act, materialising rabbits, joining and separating rings, doing other tricks.

'The audience becomes concerned at the appearance of a pool of blood gathering beneath the basket. At their shouts, the magician stops what he's doing and crosses to the basket and sees the pool of blood. He yanks off the top of the basket and he's overcome with remorse. It takes a good actor to pull this off, mind you, but

Carrefour *is* a good actor. He begins the process of removing the swords, gingerly, with much wincing. Then the magician exhorts the audience to help him bring the assistant back to life.'

The skin on my neck begins to crawl. I'm thinking of the detective from Big Sur, talking about the Ramirez twins. He told me that one of them had been stabbed dozens of times, *like a pincushion*.

'You all right?' DeLand asks.

'Go ahead,' I manage.

'The thing about the basket trick—the swords are real, the thrusts hard. The trick works because the assistant has rehearsed how to squeeze his body here and there in sequence, so he's never touched. You can see why children are not permitted to perform such tricks nowadays. Like many old tricks, the basket trick *can* go wrong.'

I'm only half-listening as DeLand goes on. Boudreaux performed the sawing-the-lady-in-half illusion with the Gabler twins, the basket trick with the Ramirez twins. But what the Sandling boys told me didn't sound like preparation for either of these tricks.

DeLand continues. 'The grief-stricken magician pleads with the audience to bring the boy back to life, and does some chanting to concentrate his power. Finally, the magician is ready, he removes the top from the basket and *voilà!*—the boy climbs out, good as new.'

'Why didn't people like Carrefour's basket trick?'

'Carrefour's rage, the blood, the screams—it was all too *real*. He scared people. Of course he did have his admirers.'

'What admirers?'

DeLand frowns. 'Let me think. I remember a little Thai fellow and there was a sheik . . . This was years ago and I don't remember names. Oh, except one: *Mertz*. I almost forgot Mertz—and he was Carrefour's biggest fan. I don't think he ever missed a night when Carrefour was on. And they usually left together, after the show. I only noticed because they were quite the odd couple.'

'What do you mean?'

'Carrefour, you know, he's a tall fellow and quite striking to look at. Mertz, on the other hand, is short and powerfully built, bald as an egg and almost as wide as he is tall. Rich as hell. Drove a Rolls.'

'Was Mertz a member of the Castle?'

'I don't know. I can check. He didn't perform. Certainly, he was a regular. And he was quite serious about magic. He is French or something. Maybe Belgian.'

'How was he . . . serious about magic?'

'He collected rare books on the subject. Mostly about the old Indian rope trick. We talked about it a couple of times.

'The rope trick?'

'Ah, yes,' DeLand says. 'The legendary Indian rope trick. Marco Polo mentioned it in his journal in the thirteenth century, but it's thought to be much older than that. Originated in China, probably, then brought to India on the Silk Road.' The watch on his wrist emits a series of beeps. A sigh. 'I have to go. My periodontist beckons.' DeLand stands. 'Why don't you come back tonight? You can take in a show. I'll be back here in time to put together whatever info we have in the archives about Carrefour. Mertz, too, if we've got anything.' I follow him down the stairs. 'And there's a fellow who knew Carrefour—he's on stage tonight: Kelly Mason. You might want to talk to him. He probably knew Mertz as well, because they shared an interest in the rope trick—Mason's written several articles about it, and I believe Mertz allowed him access to his collection. So he might know where Mertz is, and then if you find Mertz . . .'

'Right,' I tell him. 'I really appreciate your help. Information about Carrefour and Mertz and any addresses you might have—that would be great. And I'd be interested to talk to Kelly Mason.'

'Happy to help,' DeLand says as I follow him outside. 'I'll arrange a ticket for you. You can pick it up at the box office.'

'What time?'

'Shall we say eight? I'll meet you at the bar.'

'Fine.'

'I should warn you,' DeLand says. 'There's a dress code. Suit and tie.'

I'm thinking about Mertz as I drive back towards my hotel, thinking about the whole idea of Boudreaux having *fans*.

And then it hits me. Of course Boudreaux has fans, and not just for performances at the Magic Castle. I remember the medical examiner in Vegas telling me he thought Clara Gabler's body had been severed by a table saw. Barry Chisworth speculated about how hard it would have been to transport the table saw, a platform to hold it, and a power source to run it, all the way up to Conjure Canyon. The ME had been baffled. Why would anyone bother? Even when I puzzled it out—that the murderer went to all that trouble because the Gablers were killed in the course of a performance—I never gave a thought to a key element of any performance.

The audience.

Byron Boudreaux may have stopped performing magic in public.

But he didn't stop performing. There would have been an audience to see Clara Gabler sawn in half. A circle of spectators to witness the murders of Julio and Wilson Ramirez. Just as there will be an audience to witness the spectacle when he murders my sons.

It must be that these hideous inversions of standard magic tricks are what Byron meant on his postcard to Diment, what he meant by the phrase, *real magic*.

Do the members of this audience know that the illusions are not illusions? That lives are sacrificed in the course of the show? I think they do. I think they *must*. I think that's the point.

Mertz. What had DeLand said about him? He was French or something and rich and he collected books about the rope trick.

The rope trick. What I know about the rope trick could be written on the back of a postage stamp: *It's something they used to do in India. They threw a rope into the air, and it hung there. Then they climbed it or something.*

I have a terrible sequence of thoughts. Mertz is Boudreaux's biggest fan. Mertz is obsessed with the rope trick. And what did the Sandling boys tell me about what they did before they escaped? They exercised. For hours, every day. They . . . climbed . . . ropes.

I GET to my hotel. I check in, throw my stuff down, and take a look in the phone book under *Magic*. I find two listings for bookstores specialising in books about magic and the occult.

The closest one is on Hollywood Boulevard. It's small and crammed floor to ceiling with old books. That old-book smell, an amalgam of disintegrating paper and mould, pervades the air. A man sits at a desk. He's young, with long dark hair, wire-rimmed glasses, a gold hoop in one earlobe. 'Help you with something?'

'I'm looking for a book about the rope trick.'

'I think I can find something.' I follow him down a narrow aisle and watch him ascend a library ladder. He comes down with a paperback encased in a plastic sleeve. 'This is a compilation of famous effects in the history of magic. It has a nice little chapter on the rope trick.' He smiles. 'Anything else?'

'One more thing. I'm looking for a guy who used to work at the Magic Castle? His stage name was Maître Carrefour.'

'No.' He shakes his head. 'I don't think so.'

'Or a guy named Mertz? European guy, maybe French. Collects books about the rope trick.'

'Sorry.' (Is it my imagination or does he answer too quickly?) 'But I'm just the hired help. It's my uncle's shop.'

'I guess just the book then,' I tell him.

He goes to the till, rings it up, then slides it into a paper bag.

I SIT ON THE BED in my hotel room and read about the rope trick. The chapter begins by describing how old the trick is. Sacred Buddhist texts mention it as one of the entertainments performed in a (failed) attempt to raise a smile from the young prince who later became the Buddha—a boy who never smiled in his entire life. The trick became so famous during the time of the British Raj that in 1875, a magician's society in London offered a huge award to anyone who could perform the trick before an audience.

There's a long sequence about the trick's parallels with Hindu cosmogony, and also with the English folk tale, 'Jack and the Beanstalk'. And finally, I come to an excerpt from the 1898 edition of the *Lahore Civil and Military Gazette:*

> The conjuror took a large ball of rope, and after having attached one of the ends of the rope to his sack, which was lying on the ground, hurled the ball into the air with all his might. (In many versions, the ball repeatedly thumps back down to the ground before the conjuror succeeds.) Instead of falling back to the ground, the ball continued slowly to ascend, unrolling the while until it disappeared high into the clouds. A large portion of its length remained rigid.
>
> The magician ordered his son, who was his assistant, to climb the rope. Seizing the rope in his hands, the little boy climbed . . . with the agility of a monkey. He grew smaller and smaller until he disappeared into the clouds. The conjuror then ceased to occupy himself with the rope and did several minor tricks. After a little while he told the audience that he required the services of his son and called up to him to climb down. The voice of the little boy replied from above that he did not want to come down. The magician became angry and ordered his son to descend under penalty of death. Having again received a negative answer, the man, furious, took a large knife in his teeth and climbed up the rope and disappeared . . . in the clouds.
>
> Suddenly a cry rang out, and to the horror of the spectators, drops of blood began to fall from the place where the magician

had disappeared into the sky. Then the little boy fell to earth, cut into pieces. First his legs, then his body, then his head. As soon as the boy's head touched the ground, the magician slid down the rope with his knife stuck in his belt.

Without undue haste the magician then picked up the parts of the child's body and put them under a piece of cloth atop a basket . . . He gathered together his magician's paraphernalia often muttering magic incantations, drew aside the cloth from the basket and the boy emerged . . . perfectly intact.

A subsequent essay explains how the trick was thought to have been accomplished. It was always performed in rugged terrain, with a braided catgut cord or cable strung between two promontories. Platforms were thought to be erected on either side from which unseen assistants, waiting above in the mist and out of sight, could pull on the cross support and thus hold the rope rigid. When the rope was thrown, its weighted end would loop around the cable. The assistant would walk out and secure it. The trick was always performed at dusk or dawn and in a location where fog was common, so as to obscure the area where the rope, and then the child, and later the magician, disappeared. If nature didn't cooperate by producing fog or mist, braziers were employed.

As to the rest of it, opinions varied. Some thought the parts of the child were pieces of a dismembered monkey, shaved of fur, the face smeared with blood and obscured by a turban. Some thought the pieces thrown down were a parts of a wax effigy, ingeniously identical to the child assistant. In these cases, the child was thought to descend the rope hidden in the magician's loose robes.

One historian held forth on the origins of magic, in 'the tabernacles of ancient religions'. These were faiths in which sacrifice, even human sacrifice, were commonplace, part of the liturgy. According to this historian, the 'magic' that we see on stage is a re-enactment of these ancient religious rites. As to the rope trick, in the course of its performance a boy dies and is later restored to life. Accordingly, it represents the most profound of these sacred re-enactments.

And then the expert drily opined that the reason no one in London, in 1875, accepted Lord Northbrook's challenge—the offer of ten thousand pounds to anyone who could perform the rope trick—was that the 'key ingredient to the trick is a set of identical twins, and such are hard to come by. The secret is, of course, quite simple: one twin is sacrificed in the course of the proceedings.'

I knew . . . of course I knew. I'd figured it out long ago. Clara Gabler was killed on stage. Carla was produced, alive and whole. And when the performance was over, Carla was disposed of with one efficient shot. Ditto the Ramirez twins. After these performances, the surviving twin became redundant, a nuisance and a danger. In the case of the Ramirez twins, Byron Boudreaux had planned it well. He'd undoubtedly helped Charley Vermillion petition his way out of Port Sulfur, and then set him up to take the fall for the murder of the Ramirez boys. I'm sure Boudreaux located the cabin near Big Sur, then provisioned it for Vermillion. After the performance in which the Ramirez boys were killed, Boudreaux provided the cyanide capsule for Charley. Who knows what he told him it was. And then he tipped off the police.

I sit there, my heart thudding with dread. *I've got to find them.*

I plug *Mertz* into the Anywho website and come up with half a dozen listings in the LA area. But after checking them out, it's clear none of them are the man I'm looking for.

I call the private investigator, Mary McCafferty, and ask for her advice. She found Emma Sandling; maybe she can locate Mertz.

McCafferty's sorry, she's heading out for a wedding, but gives me the name and phone number of an 'information broker' in LA.

I contact him and set up a meeting for the next morning.

And then it's time to put on a clean shirt and tie and go back to the Magic Castle. I'm anxious to see DeLand and Kelly Mason, the magician who knew both Carrefour and Mertz.

THE SKY is full of clouds, and the Castle, a brooding structure, has a menacing look as I drive up the hill. But, up close, it has well-tended landscaping, well-dressed guests and valet parking. I retrieve my ticket from the box office, where I'm pointed in the direction of an ornate door and told what to do. Which is to speak the words 'open, sesame' to the red-eyed owl perched in the centre of the door. The door swings open.

The whole place is like that—hokey and charming, just the thing for an offbeat date or an adventurous evening with one's mother. I make my way to the crowded bar, where I find a tiny table against the back wall. True to DeLand's promise, I see half a dozen guys doing card tricks. In the ten minutes before DeLand arrives, it becomes clear to me that at least half of the people around me are magicians.

DeLand speaks to some of them before he reaches me. Finally, he sits down and slides a manila envelope my way.

'I don't know that this will be much help to you. There's an address and a telephone number for Carrefour, and a tax ID number—although not a social security number. It's all probably useless, I realise. But I also checked on Mertz. He was an associate member of the Castle. Lived in Beverly Hills. The address is in there.'

After we chat for a few minutes, DeLand tells me that I can catch Kelly Mason's show at nine and then talk to him afterwards.

DeLand gets to his feet and we say goodbye, and then I head for a quiet area to call in the addresses and phone numbers in the packet to the information broker. Although I somehow doubt that Carrefour left a forwarding address.

'HE SCARED ME.'

I'm talking to Kelly Mason, in his tiny dressing room, after the show. 'Carrefour?'

'No. His act was a little gruesome, but he seemed a good enough guy. Luc Mertz—he's the one who scared me. His mansion—'

'You went there?'

'Yeah. He invited me. A Spanish-style place in Beverly Hills. But—I don't know. We had this interest in common, but I couldn't talk to him. Maybe it was the language thing. Or maybe it was the income disparity. He had stuff . . . I couldn't believe it. As a scholar, it was really a privilege to see some of the old posters and documents, and he was quite generous about letting me photograph them, even publish them. But the whole time I was there, I felt uncomfortable . . .'

I'M TIRED by the time I get back to my hotel, and when I get through the door, I find that someone's been there before me. The lamp and telephone are gone from the end table next to the bed, replaced by a display of Mercury dimes arranged in the shape of a cross. Above the top of the cross is something utterly unexpected—a sugary white marshmallow bird, an Easter-time confection. And a cross.

I don't get it, at first. And then I do. Diment's ugly face flashes in front of me. He's pointing to the postmark on the card from Point Arena. *For vaudoo people, August 10th a most important day. Sacred to the Marassa. This is why Byron sends the card that day. You might say . . . this is our vaudoo Easter.*'

So now I know: who, what, when, why, and how. Byron Boudreaux is Who, and what he's going to do, what he wants to do, is the boys—my boys—one with a knife, the other with a gun. Today is August 6. It will happen four days from now in a performance of 'real magic' that amounts to a kind of religious ceremony.

I just don't know where.

THERE ARE DOZENS of ways Boudreaux could have learned I was on to him, but the fact that he knew where I was staying narrows the field of potential sources to people in LA because no one else knows I'm here. Maybe it was the kid at the bookstore, or one of the magicians I spoke to at the Castle.

In some ways his intrusion is good news. It means that he's breaking cover. It means he wants to play. Maybe he'll slip up and I'll find him. But I can't just sit around and wait for Byron and Mertz to come after me.

Four days.

In the morning, I have an appointment with the information broker. I park near his office in a down-at-heels neighbourhood near Mann's Chinese Theater.

'Got your phone call.' The broker shakes his head. 'Carrefour was a complete dead end. Sublet everything, leased his car. The tax ID was a fake, checked back to some retiree in Iowa. Your guy was a ghost. Had every document you need to survive in the information age, but none of it was legit. I checked the Boudreaux name, too. Got nothing. As for this guy Mertz, I did a little better.'

'The house in Beverly Hills?'

'A nice place. Mertz was renting it, but he left last year.'

'Is there a forwarding address?'

'PO box. But he closed that six months ago.'

I wasn't really expecting much, but even so, it's another dead end. And it's almost more than I can stand. I can't afford any more cul-de-sacs; I can't spare a minute. I reach for my wallet to settle up with the broker, then head back to my car.

I want to check my messages at the hotel, maybe give Shoffler a call. See if he has any advice.

I unlock the car. There's a brochure on my seat. At first I just pick it up and put on the dashboard, but then it comes to me: *I locked the car*.

On the front of the brochure are the words: HOLLYWOOD FOREVER, and a photo of an obelisk near a lake and four oval cameos of old movie stars. (I recognise Rudolph Valentino and Jayne Mansfield.)

I unfold the brochure and find that the interior is a map of a cemetery. Not far from the entrance, two little stickers have been pasted: twin golden angels, side by side.

My hands are shaking and my head screams with unanswerable questions. A map of a *cemetery*? Does this mean my boys are dead?

I start the car and hang a U-turn, earning long bleats of displeasure from several drivers. I know about this cemetery. I know where it is—down Santa Monica in a gritty Russian neighbourhood near Plummer Park.

Sure enough, soon I'm passing storefronts with Cyrillic lettering. Stopped at a light, I roll down my window and call out to a pedestrian. 'Excuse me? Can you tell me where the cemetery is—you know, Hollywood Forever?'

The man turns to me, smiles. 'Sure, buddy,' he says, his voice thick with a Russian accent. 'Ten blocks down on your right. You'll see it.'

We once did some footage in this part of LA and, as I recall, Hollywood Forever is still a working cemetery—one of its specialities being filmed tributes, archived on site and available for viewing, so that after visiting the earthly remains, family and friends can also watch films starring the deceased.

I drive in through the gates. It's clear from the Russian and Latino graves that the changing demographics of the neighbourhood are represented here. When I seem to be in the area marked by the angels, I park by the side of the road and get out of my car.

Nestled against a stone wall are the graves of children. Displays of toys, bronzed baby shoes, photographs, statuary of angels, heartbreaking testimonials of love and loss, crowd every tiny gravesite. I stumble past them, searching for I don't know what, until I reach the end of the row. And there—on a bare patch of earth, two plastic horses ridden by two plastic knights face each other, lances drawn. Looking on are two identical blond-haired Fisher-Price figures, their painted faces locked in perpetual grins.

For a moment, I'm paralysed and then I'm running towards my car. It takes me a while, but eventually I persuade a woman who works at the cemetery administration building to accompany me back to the children's graves. We ride in her car, a sombre black Mercedes. She is so used to talking to the distraught that my agitation doesn't seem to faze her. Periodically, she places a reassuring hand on my arm.

At the site where the plastic knights face off, she uses her cellphone to call the administrative centre. Then—while fixing me with sympathetic eyes—she recites the number of the plot and its coordinates. 'Call me back with the status on this, OK? I'd like to know identity of the interred—date of interment, responsible party, whatever you've got. Great.'

We stand there, waiting. 'There's supposed to be a stone,' she tells me. 'But sometimes that takes a while.'

I can't say a word. To her credit, she gives my arm a squeeze and lets it go at that. We wait. She seems to be studying the cloud patterns. I can't take my eyes off the plastic knights, the Fisher-Price figures, the raw earth.

Her phone rings, a discreet chirp. She turns away from me as she talks. 'No?' she says in a hushed voice. 'You're kidding. Oh, God, people are something, huh?'

She puts the phone back in the holster on her hip and looks at me with a frown. 'This is somebody's idea of a bad joke,' she says, bending down to scoop up the toys from the dirt. 'There's no one buried here. This is one of six plots that we've taken off the market. We're putting in a fountain here, for the little folks area.' She puts her hand on my arm. 'Look, it's a big place, it's easy to get confused. This isn't the only location where children are buried. If there's someone in particular you're looking for, you should go to the graves registration office. OK? I'll give you a ride.'

She starts to walk off towards the car and I fall in step next to her. We both hear it at the same time: the crystalline notes of a flute. It's a haunting and beautiful sound.

'Isn't that pretty,' she says as we turn in unison to look for the source of the music. 'I didn't know there were any ceremonies this morning.'

And then I see him—leaning casually against a gravestone not thirty feet from me. He's wearing khakis, a white shirt. He holds the flute to his lips.

'Hey!' the woman protests as I take off after him, but I'm gone, running between gravestones, crashing past startled cemetery visitors. And I'm gaining on him. He's heading towards a small lake, the grounds around it beautifully landscaped and interspersed with family mausoleums. The area provides so many places to hide that I lose him a couple of times—but each time he pipes a tune and then emerges from behind a tree or gravestone.

My lungs are burning, my quadriceps screaming by the time I see him run onto a little causeway that leads to an island in the middle of the lake. I accelerate: it's a dead end for him. I can practically feel it, his body under me when I launch myself and take him down.

We're running alongside the large mausoleum on the island and I'm so close that I can see what brand of shoe he's wearing—Nikes. He reaches the end of the structure and turns the corner. I'm seconds behind him, and yet when I turn . . . impossibly, he's not there.

He's vanished.

I CAN'T believe my eyes and yet . . . he's gone. I spend the next forty-five minutes searching—for him at first, and then for how he did it. But I find nothing.

I approach other visitors. Many of them saw the Piper, heard his flute, even saw me chasing him—but no one saw where he went. No one saw him disappear.

How did he do it? I can't find anything—*anything*—that would have enabled him to vanish like that. But he's a magician, after all. Given a day or a week, maybe I could figure out how he did it, but I don't have time. I'm still shaking my head when I reach the car.

I'm stuck in traffic when I get an idea. Maybe I can make Mertz come to me.

I catch John DeLand on my cellphone just as he's leaving the Castle. 'A quick question.'

'Sure.'

'This guy Mertz—he collects stuff about the rope trick. Is there a particular book he'd want?'

'Something he'd really covet as a collector? Let me think.' He thinks for a minute, but then shakes his head. 'You know, I really should ask Kelly. Hang on. Let me see if I can get him on the other line.'

DeLand puts the question to Kelly Mason. Then he says, 'Can you spell that? OK. Thanks, Kelly.'

DeLand comes back to me. 'There is something, but Kelly says to warn you—he's never seen a copy. *The Autobiographical Memoirs of the Emperor Jahangueir.*' He hands me his note. 'The book was written in the seventeenth century, but the edition Mertz is after is a translation by an Englishman, name of David Price. Published in 1829. According to Kelly, it contains one of the most complete descriptions of the rope trick that has ever been reported.'

'How much would something like that go for?'

He thinks for a moment. 'Rough guess? Hmmmmm. It's rare, but there's not that much market. Something of that vintage? I should think Mertz might pay five thousand for it and be happy with that.'

'I owe you a drink.'

'I see where you're going, Alex. Be careful.'

IT TAKES ME half an hour to establish an email account at Yahoo under a name I pick out of the phone book, Daniel Helwig. I execute a Google search to come up with a list of dealers who specialise in rare books about magic, then fire off an email to the group.

Using the pseudonym, I offer a first edition of the *Jahangueir* for five thousand dollars, but note that the book will only be available for two days. After that, 'Daniel' writes, he'll be leaving for an extended stay abroad.

And now there's really nothing for me to do but bide my time—and check and recheck my email messages, waiting for a response. It's a long night.

I finally get a bite the next day. A dealer in San Francisco has a client who is interested. Depending on the book's condition, cost is not an issue.

I reply with an email of my own, seeking the client's name and address: *I can send the book for his examination. He could have it by tomorrow morning.*

But the dealer is unwilling to give up the information, undoubtedly fearing he'll lose his commission on the book: *If you'll send the book to me, I can show it to my client in the afternoon.*

But it's impossible. There *is* no book. Nor, for that matter, is there any guarantee that the prospective buyer is Luc Mertz. Even so, it's the only lead—and the only plan—that I have.

I call the information broker. The dealer—qjwynn@coastal.com—must have contacted his client after learning of the book's supposed availability. So they must have spoken to one another.

The broker confirms that he can find out who the dealer called the day before—but not until the end of the phone company's billing cycle. 'Until they collate the data, I can't get at it,' he says.

Frustrated, I telephone a friend who knows a lot about databases. Chaz designs simulations—war games—for the Pentagon. But it turns out he doesn't have a clue as to how I can get a list of the dealer's phone calls. 'And, anyway,' he says, 'how do you know he phoned him? Maybe he sent him an email.'

Good point. 'So how do I get into his email?'

Chaz thinks about it. 'You know his user ID?'

'Yeah.'

'Then all you need is his password.'

'And how do I get that?'

'Depends. If he's got an email programme that lets him use unencrypted passwords, you could download an automated dictionary word list and let it roll. But that could take you days.' Chaz pauses. 'Of course, you could try to guess it. What's he do for a living?'

'He's a bookseller. Mostly books about magic.'

'Try *Houdini.* Words like that.'

And so I do. I try the names of magicians mentioned in the books I've read about magic.

Zilch. I try a different tack:

abracadabra
opensesame
sesame
hocuspocus
pocushocus

Immediately, the page opens. Going to the dealer's inbox, I see a dozen emails from the day before. Among them is one from *lxmertz@sequoia.net.*

I'm interested, of course, but I'll have to see the book first. Are you sure the offer is genuine?

I read it, and I read it again. But that's it. There's nothing more to be got from it. Switching from the bookdealer's account to *sequoia.net,* I try to crack Mertz's password—but it's no use.

Then it occurs to me: *sequoia.net* is a business address of some kind. Using the Anywho search engine, I take a look: first for *Sequoia Net* and then for *Sequoia Networks,* and so on, down the list of generic corporate names. And there it is:

Sequoia Solutions, Ltd.
11224 Fish Rock Rd.
Suite 210
Anchor Bay, CA

I search for MapQuest and ask for driving directions and a map. Anchor Bay is only a few miles from Point Arena—where Byron's postcard to Diment was mailed. Eureka, where the Sandling boys escaped at the shopping mall, isn't that far, either. Perhaps Byron and the Sandling boys were headed for Mertz's at the time.

It's possible the connections I'm making are hopeful and tenuous. Maybe it's all smoke, as Shoffler would say.

But I don't think so.

It's 545 miles from LA to Anchor Bay—about an eight-hour drive. I should fly to San Francisco and drive from there. I slam everything into my suitcase and check out.

An hour and a half later, I'm flying north.

CHAPTER TWELVE

By the time I cross the Golden Gate Bridge, after a slow crawl in a rental car from the airport, it's almost five. The address I found online, with its suite number, is certainly an office and not where Mertz lives. Still, I head straight for Anchor Bay. It's not a metropolis. If Mertz lives nearby, maybe somebody will know it.

I'm getting close when I put in a call to Shoffler. 'So how was France?' I say when he answers.

'Great beer. Unbelievable.' A pause. 'Alex, where the hell are you? You sound like you're on the moon.'

'I'm in northern California. The coast above San Francisco.'

'Why? What you got?'

'I think my boys are here, near Anchor Bay. About forty miles south of Mendocino.'

He heaves a long sigh. 'You better tell me about it. What makes you think your boys are there?'

I hesitate. 'It's a long story, and there's no way I can get through it on this cellphone. Bottom line, I know who grabbed them.'

'You *do?!*'

'His name is Byron Boudreaux, and if something happens to me, Ray, you've got to promise me you'll go after him. He's got a rich patron named Mertz. Luc Mertz.' I spell it.

Shoffler heaves another sigh. 'You know, for me to play back-up, I really need to know the story, Alex.'

The telephone crackles and hums. 'If something happens to me,' I tell Shoffler, 'get in touch with a PI named Pinky Streiber in New Orleans. He can tell you all about it.'

'I don't like the sound of this, Alex. Hold off a day or two. I know a couple of guys in San Francisco. Let me network a little.'

As I make the turn to head for the coast, I realise I'm wasting my time. Law enforcement isn't going to help me. Everything is circumstantial. Paper rabbits and voodoo burials, postmarks and the rope trick. And the connection to Mertz is even dicier. No judge is going to authorise a search warrant based on what I've got.

'Pinky Streiber,' I tell Shoffler. 'Decatur Street, New Orleans. You writing this down?'

'I'm telling you, Alex, hold off on this. I can—'

I press the button to cut him off.

I FIND the Sequoia Solutions address with no problem. It's in a faux-Western wooden structure with dozens of small offices. It's almost ten, and everyone's long gone with the exception of the tired-looking man in Coastal Chiropractics.

He opens the door cautiously and peers at me. 'Help you?'

'You know the guy in number two-ten, down the hall? Sequoia Solutions. Guy named Mertz?'

He wags his head. 'No. I don't even think I've ever seen anybody in that office,' he tells me. 'Sorry.'

I ask him for the number of the rental agency, which he gives me. They'll have a lease, more information about Mertz. I'll get in touch with them tomorrow. In the meantime, I need a room.

This turns out to be a problem. It's August, there are not that many places to stay, and they're all booked solid. I strike out in Anchor Bay. I head north towards Point Arena, and I strike out there, too. Everywhere I go, I ask about Mertz. No one's heard of him.

It's almost eleven by the time I find a vacancy at the Breakers Inn in Gualala, a town south of Anchor Bay. Mine is a big room, with a balcony facing the sea, the kid at the desk tells me. He takes my card and runs it through his machine.

'You know a local guy named Mertz?' I ask him. 'Short guy, bald, lots of money. Has a place around here.'

'Sorry, man. I'm just here for the surf.'

'You know anyone who might know?' I ask.

He thinks about it. 'The little grocery store—right next door. That's open till midnight. Local people work there. And there's a couple of restaurants in town. Try the Cliff House.'

I thank him and he hands me my room key.

AT THE GROCERY STORE, the woman working the register is young and huge, at least six feet two, two hundred and fifty. With her round, cherubic face, she looks like a giant baby.

I put my bottle of water on the conveyor belt. 'I'm looking for somebody,' I tell her. 'Maybe you know him?'

She scans the water. 'Dollar twelve,' she says.

'Guy named Luc Mertz. He's—'

'A damn frog is what he is,' the cashier snarls. 'Tells me no, he ain't a frog, he's *Belgian.* Same difference. They hate our guts, too. Some kind of *allies,* huh?'

She knows him. I'm stunned. I feel the unfamiliar radiance of luck. 'He live around here?'

'Hell, yes. I worked a party down there one time, bartending. Big place, down by Sea Ranch. Got some frogoid name.' She concentrates, her face contorted. 'Mystère!' she says like a quiz-show contestant. 'You know, it's like frog for *mystery.*'

She puts my water in a plastic bag, hands it to me.

'Where's Sea Ranch?' I ask her.

'You don't know where *Sea Ranch* is?' She rolls her eyes. 'It's probably the biggest development between here and San Francisco. You go south on 101. You can't miss it. It's a million acres or something. Got a rental office, lodge and restaurant. A few miles past the end of Sea Ranch, there's a little road on the right called Estate Road. You go down that and at the end, you get to Mystère. Iron gates with a big *M* in the middle. Guardhouse and all.'

I CROSS the county line, leaving Mendocino County and entering Sonoma County.

Ten minutes later, I'm past the Sea Ranch, and I'm on Estate Road. It's dark, and as I drive past Mertz's estate, all I can really see is the guardhouse and the general lay of the land. A series of rolling hills fall away towards the sea. The moon slides out from under a cloud and illuminates a boulder-strewn patch of ocean.

The estate is huge, its borders protected by the sea and by an iron fence whose verticals end in sharp points. Every twenty yards or so, red diodes mark the location of surveillance cameras.

Somewhere down there is a house. And somewhere in that house are my boys.

I roll along at a crawl beside the iron fence, tempted to climb it right now, but I am deterred by the cameras. The road comes to an end in a gravel cul-de-sac on the edge of a cliff. I can see the property line clearly. The fence turns the corner and extends a hundred feet or so along the flat area at the top of the cliff. Then, as the land abruptly falls away into a rocky crevasse, the border of Mystère is demarcated by a nine-foot-tall fence of barbed wire that stretches down into the sea. Even here, in terrain that would challenge a rock climber, surveillance cameras sit atop metal stanchions supporting the barbed wire, every twenty yards or so as far as I can see down towards the ocean. I hope I've managed to stay beyond their reach.

I swing around and head back towards the highway.

A half-dozen ideas on how I might get into this fortress flicker through my mind—disabling the guard, climbing the metal fence, renting a small boat and arriving by sea, cutting through the barbed wire, posing as a delivery person—but I reject each one. They share the same risk. If I go in now and I get caught, I don't think Boudreaux would hesitate to kill me. He'd tuck me away somewhere until the performance was over, and then I'd be disposed of, along with the bodies of my sons.

I believe, from what I read about the rope trick, that the performance will occur in the early morning of August 10, before the fog burns off. It's August 9.

I SPEND the morning at the county clerk's office in Santa Rosa, sitting at a computer looking at a plan that covers the area of coastline I'm interested in. The property belonging to Sequoia Solutions comprises 521 acres, with almost a mile of coastal frontage. I note that the house and outbuildings are set quite a way back from the ocean. The huge parcel belonging to the Sea Ranch lies directly to the north of Mertz's place.

I ask the clerk if there's a store in town that sells outdoor equipment. She directs me to one in a mall on the outskirts of town.

I go there and buy hiking boots, socks, a backpack, a fleece jacket, and a Maglite flashlight. The big flashlight is heavy. But as a beat cop in DC once pointed out to me, there's a reason cops favour Maglites. They're better than truncheons.

It's only seventy miles from Santa Rosa to Gualala, but the road is full of twists and turns—and speed zones. It takes me more than two hours to get back to the coast. I head straight for the Sea Ranch rental office.

The blonde woman at the desk doesn't seem to read my impatience. When I'm ready to take an available oceanfront condo on the southern fringe of the Sea Ranch property, she wants to show me all the other alternatives.

'No, really, the Housel Hut, that's perfect.'

'It's three hundred twenty-nine dollars a night, minimum two-night stay. Actually, it's booked on Monday, so I could only—'

'Two nights is all the time I have. That's perfect.'

I put it on my Visa. She gives me maps of the compound, passes to various facilities, a tag for my car, and finally, the keys.

It's five-twenty by the time I park behind the condo. I go inside only for a minute, long enough to grab a bottle of water from the complimentary basket. I put the water, my wallet, the Maglite, my cellphone and my fleece jacket in the backpack. At the last minute, I rummage through the kitchen drawers, and find a stash of ziplock bags. I put the cellphone inside one, my wallet in another.

And then I head for the beach that abuts the land belonging to Luc Mertz. On my way, I pass a silver-haired couple, as fit-looking as nineteen-year-olds. They wave and stride on.

It's a wild landscape. For centuries, the surf has thrashed against the stone, leaving an archipelago of pinnacles. They look like minarets, sculpted by the water. Standing among them is the occasional monolithic boulder and a scatter of rounded rocks, like giant bowling balls. The water thrashes wildly amidst all this.

The high-tide line is clear, marked by a dark irregular line of seaweed, driftwood and other detritus. Looking inland, the dramatic rock formations continue 200 yards or more up into the hillside, where they end in a craggy cliff-face, above which glows the bright green of rolling meadowland.

Then I glimpse it, running through the meadowland—the glint of razor wire that identifies the property line between Sea Ranch and Mystère. The tide is low, and I'm careful as I approach to stay out of view of Mertz's surveillance cameras. The fence continues down into the rocky area, but stops a few feet short of the high-tide mark.

I have to admit that when I saw 'beach' on the plan of Sea Ranch, I was thinking of sand, not rock. I'm wearing khaki pants and I picked out the fleece jacket for its beige colour, wanting to minimise my visibility. Wrong choice. There's not much sand here. Just rock, and where the rock is wet, it's almost black.

There are two ways to go. One is to wait for night and try to creep into Mystère. But I'd have to do it here, through the rocks, and the landscape is so rugged that would be almost impossible.

The other choice is to go out into the water and try to climb from rock to rock until I'm far enough beyond the reach of the cameras. Such CCTV cameras normally don't have much depth of field. Then I'd traverse until it seemed safe to head in towards the shore.

My watch reads six-thirty-five. When does it get dark? Eight-thirty? At best, I've got a couple of hours of light left.

I can't climb in the area close to shore because I'll be visible to the cameras. This means I have to get out past the surf break, which is wildly irregular, given all the rocks.

I see that I'm going to get wet. The water is cold, very cold. I test it with my hand and try to guess. Fifty? Cold enough that after thirty seconds of immersion, my hand is numb. So cold that I should have a wet suit. Climbing shoes. Gloves. Picks and ropes.

I try to plan a route from rock to rock that will take me out beyond the surf. I pull the hood on, tighten the closure, shove my trouser ends into my socks, put my head down, and go.

At first it's not too bad. The rocks are so craggy that I don't have any trouble finding footholds. But then I come to a spot where there's no way to avoid going into the water without retracing my steps and losing maybe half an hour. I go in up to my hips, holding the backpack to my chest. It's a clumsy process, thrashing through cold water. By the time I'm on the rocks again, my legs are numb.

I did a good bit of rock climbing before the boys were born. I liked the precision and focus it required. This is different. For one thing, I never climbed wet rock. For another, I'm not really *climbing* to a summit. I'm climbing up and down only enough to traverse a lot of rugged terrain. And unlike with recreational climbing, I'm in a hurry.

Still, I'm getting there. Before I left the Sea Ranch beach, I picked out the tallest pair of rock formations within the boundaries of Mystère. It's hard to be sure, but it seems to me—sighting towards the two spires—that I've traversed far enough inside the fence line to turn back towards shore.

I'm slowly making my way through the surf break, when it happens: a little jump from one rock to the next—an easy jump. But the rock is wet and I land wrong and my ankle turns and the next thing I know, I'm in the water.

To say it takes my breath away doesn't begin to describe it. Not only does the cold water squeeze out the air from my lungs—the lungs themselves don't work at all. The moment I fell happened to be in the lull, just before the wave breaks and crashes. That was a piece of luck, and at first I think it's going to be all right. But before I make it to a good place to hang on, a wave crashes down on me.

I try to grab onto a rock, scrabbling my fingernails for purchase. I've got it, until the water begins to recede. There's a tremendous sucking sound, a clatter and rush of gravel, and my grip on the rock is torn away. A second later, I'm slammed against rock.

Now for the first time, things begin to feel out of control. I can't breathe, and I feel a burning sensation in my leg. I think I may have slashed my left calf. I know that if I don't get out of the water right now, before another wave tags me, I'm not going to make it.

Something propels me. The thought of Sean and Kevin and what awaits them . . . The thought of my broken body in the surf . . . I climb the rock face like Spider-man, high enough to reach an outcrop I can wrap my arms and legs around. The wave hits, but I don't think a bomb could have dislodged me.

I'm in bad shape as I close in on the shoreline. The light is fading, it's getting colder, my ankle and my calf hurt, and I'm shivering uncontrollably. I move forward slowly, from one rock to the next, looking for the red eyes of surveillance cameras. I see nothing. And then, at last, I'm back on dry land.

I find a sheltered spot and drink some of the water in my backpack. I take my boots off, dump the water out of them, squeeze out the woollen socks. My ankle is the size of a small grapefruit. I put it all back on, lacing up the boot as tight as I can. I look at the gash on my calf. It doesn't look so bad.

I take off my fleece, my sweater, my T-shirt. Wring them out, put them back on. I still can't stop shaking.

The flashlight doesn't work, but I decide to keep it anyway. It's the only weapon I have. I take a look at the cellphone, but no: There's water inside the ziplock bag. It's toast too.

I feel like I need a forklift to get to my feet, but I manage to push myself up. I have to find the site of the performance.

Amidst the rocks and in the dusk, I can't get a sight line on the two rock spires I'd picked out before. I was sure that these would provide the setting for tomorrow's performance, but as I stumble around in the warren of rock formations, doubt suffuses me. Wasn't I just here? Maybe I should just go for the house.

And then I find it. The theatre takes my breath away.

A flattened gravel stage is defined by huge concrete urns overflowing with flowers. In this spectacular location, a tiny amphitheatre has been fashioned. Three semicircles of polished granite are stepped back into the natural rise of the land. To the right of the stage a latticed screen, draped with vines and flowers, conceals several padlocked chests— and, under a large canvas tarp, an enormous basket.

I'd like to look around some more, but I've already abandoned the idea of waylaying the party on the way to prepare for the morning's entertainment. Boudreaux may have an assistant, maybe two. I'd be outnumbered, and except for the Maglite, unarmed.

My only chance is isolation and surprise. With the light almost gone, there's no time to do anything but ascend one of the spires before full dark. They are tall, more than sixty feet high. They're not identical formations, but similar. The distance between them is a little more than a hundred yards. Thick at the base, the towers taper irregularly towards the tops, which even now are hidden in mist.

Ordinarily, the formation wouldn't present a challenge to a climber of modest ability, but I'm so tired that the climb proves very difficult. Above me, the moon scuds along beneath thick clouds.

About halfway up, I come very close to my physical limit and almost . . . almost let go. That scares me and I proceed slowly, resting every few feet. Finally, I find what I knew must be there: a wooden platform. I pull myself onto it and collapse.

No more than four-feet square, the platform might as well be a palace as far as I'm concerned. It is such a relief not to have to maintain a grip and support my weight. There's really not much light, but my eyes have adjusted to the darkness. I can see that two cables cross to the opposite spire. But there is no platform on the opposite side— at least I can't see one. I practically weep with thanks that I picked the right tower to climb.

One cable extends beneath my platform, the other some four feet above me. The one beneath me is attached by a kind of flywheel-and-winch contraption. The one above has several levers and gears and some kind of bulky power source bolted into the rock.

Dangling several feet down from the cable beneath my platform, hanging into the chasm between the spires, are several dark loops. Suspended from the cable above me is a contraption that seems to have a wide 'mouth' consisting of triangular metal teeth, like a giant version of the constricting jaw into which you insert drill bits.

It takes me a few minutes to figure out how it all must work. The magician throws the rope until it catches one of the dangling loops— which must be covered with Velcro. At that point, a remote control device, or maybe radio signals, bring the device on the second cable into play, guiding it into position and lowering it until it bites the loose end of the rope. The mechanism is then withdrawn vertically and winched tight until the rope is held taut.

At first I think—with horror at the risk of it—that Sean or Kevin, whoever has the job of climbing the rope, must walk on the cable to the safety of the platform. But no. A loop of rope waits, hooked to a brass fitting on the cable above me. Anyone climbing the vertical rope can slip a leg into the loop and pull himself over to the platform.

I sit on the platform. I'm still wet and the effect of evaporation makes me even colder. I concentrate on conserving warmth. It seems impossible that I might fall asleep, but just in case, I set the alarm on my watch for five a.m. I hunch my knees to my chest, tighten my hood, lock my arms across my chest, and settle down to wait.

I WAKE with a gasp at the sound of my beeping watch. It's still dark, and so foggy I can't see farther than a few feet. I drink the last of my water. I feel as if I'm a hundred years old; every part of my body hurts. I wait for my eyes to adjust. I try to stretch out.

Half an hour later, the sky begins to brighten. Behind the platform, on the opposite side of the rock, is a small ledge, almost a niche. It's eighteen inches deep, but the rock face hangs over it. The only way I could fit into the space would be to crouch. I reject it.

I climb the spire, looking for a place to hide. I find one without too much trouble, fifteen feet above the platform, a spot I can wedge into. I can see the platform and the cables, the centre of the chasm. But no one can see me.

I look at my watch every few minutes. After an hour passes, I'm worried. The cold is getting to me. I bite down on the fleece to keep my teeth from chattering.

And then, at last, I hear the scrape of shoes on rock. I hear the voices of two men, one speaking in an odd cadence that suggests a foreign language. And then—tears crash into my eyes—interspersed between the low voices of the men, I hear the high, sweet voices of children. Sean laughs—his characteristic high-pitched chuckle, a laugh totally unlike Kevin's raucous guffaw. My heart lifts.

I hear their voices, but I can't understand what they're saying. There is the sound of padlocked chests being opened, the moving and dragging of heavy objects. Obviously, they are making preparations for the performance. Someone begins to whistle.

I work to keep within myself. Ordinarily, I'm good at waiting. It's something that comes with spending a lot of time in airports. But now, the immobility is almost too much. I consider making my way down the rock, taking them on. But no. My chances on the ground—two of them and one of me—are terrible. I'm only going to get one shot and it's got to be up here.

TWENTY MINUTES LATER, I hear music from down below. Drums and a sitar. Not long afterward, the guests arrive and the clink of glasses and the murmur of conversation float up to me.

Then the show begins. I can hear Boudreaux's banter as he performs different effects, and occasionally, Kevin's voice—or is it Sean's?—in counterpoint. From the audience: bursts of applause and exclamations of astonishment. The Piper, performing his tricks.

And then it happens. The Piper heaves the rope up. 'Get up there!' he commands. The rope plops to the ground. 'I don't know what's wrong,' he says. 'The heavens are defying me.'

A sprinkle of laughter.

'I'll have to really *concentrate*.'

Again, the rope slaps back down onto the gravel.

Another try. And then the end of the rope comes into view, ascending through the mist. And he gets it—the rope catches. The audience cheers, and I move down to the lower platform.

The mechanism goes into action, catches the rope in its jaws. Instantly, the pulleys and winches begin do their job, tightening the rope from both directions until it's taut.

'Let's just see if it's really up there,' the Piper says. The rope shakes—he's testing it to make sure it won't fall out of the sky.

'Why don't you climb it? See what's up there?' the Piper suggests to my son.

'I don't know,' Kevin replies. 'It's *high*.'

'You'll do as you're told,' The Piper tells him.

'Oh, all right.'

A big round of applause as the boy starts up the rope.

The Piper continues to talk, but I'm not listening. I watch the rhythm of the rope and then I see it—Kevin's blond hair shining as he comes up out of the fog.

He's dressed in a loincloth, with a sash across his chest. He's concentrating so intently that he doesn't look towards the platform until he's very nearly to the top. When he sees me—finger to my lips, head moving side to side in warning—there is total astonishment in his eyes. I'm afraid, for one terrible moment, that he'll fall.

He fits himself into the sling with practised ease, and then pulls himself towards me.

Then he's on the platform. I have my arms open to embrace him, but he's wearing a lavaliere mike, clipped to his sash. I unclip it, fold it into the hem of my fleece jacket, squeeze it into my fist.

'Dad,' Kevin says in a whisper, his face a mix of delight and perplexity, 'what are you doing here?'

I don't know what to say.

He continues in a whisper. 'He said we wouldn't see you till Christmas. He said they came to get you at the joust, the station did, that you had to go on 'signment, that he would take us home until Mommy got there. And he *did* take us home, but only for a while. And we tried to call you—he said you were on your way to the airport. *I* tried to call you, and you said hello, but we got cutted off. Then he told us you got in a car accident and you were very hurt, that Mommy had to take care of you and she couldn't take care of us, that—' His voice trails away, and his face begins to collapse.

On some level, he must have understood that he was a captive. But he's held himself together all these weeks, fitting in with what he's been told, accepting the strange life he and his brother have been leading. But underneath, he must have wondered a million things.

Now he's my little boy again and he starts to cry.

At last he comes into my arms and I hold him.

It's not possible, really, to describe how this moment feels, the ineffable sweetness of reunion as I hold my son in my arms.

But it doesn't last. I push him away, hold him at arm's length. '*Kevin,* listen to me. What are you supposed to do now?'

'Nothing. Oh, I have to slide this back.' He flicks his wrist and sends the sling back to the middle. 'Then I just wait.'

'How long?'

He shrugs. 'Until he calls up to me.'

'Look, Kev.' I put a hand on his shoulder. 'You have to understand that I wasn't in an accident. Mr Boudreaux lied to you.'

'Who?'

'Mr Carrefour?'

'*Doctor* Carrefour,' he corrects me. *'Doc.'*

'OK. Well, whoever he is, he *kidnapped* you. I wasn't hurt or sick. Mom and I have been out of our minds searching for you.'

'But he *said* we were helping, he said we . . .' His voice is querulous now, unsure. He starts to cry again.

'Kevin.' I pause, shut my eyes. 'He's planning to kill you—it's part of his magic, part of the show. And then he'll kill Sean, too.'

'But *why?*'

I shake my head. 'You have to help me now.'

'Dad? Is it going to be OK?'

'Absolutely. But you have to listen to me. You have to do exactly what you're supposed to do. And then, when he comes up the rope—I want you to hide.' I take his hand, pull him around, show him the tiny niche behind the platform.

'What if I fall? Dad—I might fall.'

'You won't fall. You have great balance.'

The Piper's voice rises up to us. 'What do you see up there, boy?'

'*Kev*—you can do it. There's plenty of room. Look, I'm going to give you my backpack. I need you to keep it safe.' I give him the backpack, more to give him a task than anything else, although I take the Maglite first, and stick it in my waistband.

The Piper's voice again. 'I *said* what do you see up there, boy?'

I open my fist, unfurl the mike from the fleece, pin it to Kevin's sash. 'Tell him,' I whisper.

'Sky,' Kevin says, his voice trembling.

A laugh from below.

'What else?'

'Clouds.' He still sounds as if he's about to cry.

'I need you back down here now.' The voice is matter-of-fact.

'But I like it up here. I don't feel like coming down.'

They go back and forth, the Piper growing more irritated.

I have to leave Kevin, climb up the rock.

'If you don't get down here this minute,' the Piper says, his voice stern now, 'I'm going have to come up and get you.'

'Go ahead,' Kevin says. 'Try it, old man. I bet you can't even climb the rope.'

I'm now wedged into my old perch above the platform. Kevin looks up at me. I motion for him—time to hide.

The rope begins to twitch back and forth as the Piper ascends.

And then I see him, his brown glossy hair coming up through the mist. Like Kevin, he's dressed as a fakir, and like Kevin, he's intent on the climb. He holds a knife with a curved blade between his teeth.

Cautiously, I begin to make my way down towards him.

Once he's reached the sling and put an arm through it, he looks at the platform. And frowns. I can read his mind: *Where's Kevin?*

He pulls himself onto the platform, and removes the knife from his mouth. 'Where are you, lad?' he calls out, still in character. 'Come on now, I've had it with you. I'm serious!'

Laughter wells up from below.

The magician gets to his feet and begins to turn.

I'm not a fighter. It's not that I run away from confrontation, physical fights just never came up much. Where I grew up, nobody got into fights. It wasn't hip, it wasn't something you did. I never took karate or boxing lessons. In other words, nothing about my background has prepared me for what I'm about to do.

And yet I come down off that rock like a raptor.

Before the man even knows I'm there, I've hit him so hard with the Maglite that I can hear the bone splinter in the back of his head. Suddenly, there's blood everywhere—on me, on the rocks, *on him.*

He's staggered, but he doesn't go down. He makes a wounded sound that's picked up by the mike, and then he turns, knife in hand. I could swear he's smiling. He slashes at me with a sidearm motion, laying open the sleeve of my jacket and the arm beneath.

Boudreaux takes a swipe at my throat. Incredibly the world has gone silent—or almost silent. I can hear the surf crashing and the hushed expectancy of the audience beneath the fog.

I block the swipe of the knife with the flashlight. The edge of the blade skitters along the Maglite's shaft, slices into my fingers, and sends a spray of blood into my eyes.

Boudreaux takes a step back, and gathers himself. For a moment, he stands there, panting and swaying, the knife hanging down at his side. It's almost as if he's about to collapse, but then he lunges towards me with a roar, slashing wildly at the air, feral and insane.

From behind me, I hear a gasp from Kevin, half-whimper, half-scream. The sound electrifies me. I throw myself at the magician, and we go to the platform in a tangle of blood, growls and groans.

Incredibly, I'm on top, with my forearm across his throat, and my right hand pinning his wrist to the ground. He makes a feeble effort to hit me with his other hand, but he hasn't any strength left. His muscles relax, and his eyes soften. 'Now what?' he asks.

With my heart slamming against my chest, it takes more than a moment to get my breath. When I'm able to stand, I do and, reaching down, grab Boudreaux by the hair, and pull him to his feet.

He's leering. 'How do you think you're going to get me down?'

'That's the easy part.' And with that, I grab him by the scruff of the neck, spin him around, and, with a shove, send him off the edge of the spire towards his fan club sixty feet below.

It's chaos down in the amphitheatre, everybody screaming. Kevin crawls out from the little niche towards me, terrified and sobbing.

I know we have to act quickly. I don't know what makes me think that the boys who were to be the centrepiece of the show have, for the moment, been forgotten, but I am hoping that's the case. Sean himself might have wondered what was going on and emerged from his hiding place to find out. But I don't think so. I think he's in the basket, waiting for his cue. 'Kevin,' I say, 'we have to get Sean.'

His eyes are huge. 'Dad, you're bleeding.'

'It's OK.'

Together, we scramble down the rock face. Halfway down, we come out of the mist and I tell him to stop for a moment. 'We have to be careful. Stay to the side near the ocean, so they don't see us.'

'OK.'

Kevin climbs down, surefooted and agile as a monkey. He actually has to wait for me from time to time. I'm the one having trouble. The arm Boudreaux cut is weak. My hand is a mess. The blood is slippery. Even so, we're on the ground in less than five minutes.

I have to rest, lean against the rock. From the amphitheatre come the sounds of disagreement. Not too many voices. Obviously, some of the guests have decided to leave.

'*What* a disappointment,' a female voice says.

'A different *dénouement* is all,' says a British man. 'Equally dramatic in its way.'

'We're not going to call 911,' an accented voice says. 'I won't have them crawling all over the place.'

'There's a back way,' Kevin tells me. 'I can sneak in. I can talk to Sean. He'll hear me through the basket.'

I follow my son as we creep along towards the back of the stage. From our vantage point, I can see the little gathering of guests. The basket is at centre stage, terribly exposed.

Before I can stop Kevin, he's gone. I see him approach the basket, I see the basket quiver slightly. I can't believe Sean can get out of it without being seen.

It comes to me: *misdirection.* Just as I see the top of the basket tremble, I hurl the Maglite to the right, throwing it as far as I can. It cartwheels through the air, end over end, and lands with a huge percussive clang against the rocks.

All heads turn towards the sound as Sean scrambles out. I see the little group in the theatre begin to move slowly towards the point of impact, as the boys dash towards me.

IT COULDN'T BE more than a half-mile walk from the amphitheatre to the Sea Ranch beach. We don't have to go out into the water. It's a simple walk along the hardened sand, amid the rocks. I know that sooner or later someone will come after us and I do my best to hurry. It seems to take forever before I see that string of razor wire demarcating the property line between Mystère and the Sea Ranch.

A silver-haired couple—the same one?—walks the rocky beach. I turn towards them, one boy on each arm. They're tugging me along now, I'm moving so slowly. Then I just can't manage another step.

'It's going to be OK,' I tell the boys, trying to get my feet moving. 'It's going to be OK.' I stumble and fall.

Kevin takes off like a shot, and I see the three figures, the elegant couple bending slightly to catch my son's words. Kevin points—they look our way. Sean holds my hand in a ferocious grip.

Kevin and the couple are running now, and I see that the man has a cellphone to his ear.

My eyes close.

'*Dad,*' Kevin says.

'Sea Ranch,' the man is saying into the phone. 'Down on the beach.' And then, 'Meg, I'm going to get the Jeep.'

'Oh, my God,' the woman says. She wraps something around my injured hand. 'You boys, you press down on this. OK?'

'Yes.'

'Keep up the pressure boys, that's great.'

'Is he going to be all right?' Kevin asks, his voice trembling.

'Yes,' the woman says in a confident voice. 'Everything's going to be just fine.'

And somehow, although I suspect she's said this just to calm the boys, I know she's right.

JOHN CASE

John Case is the pseudonym of husband-and-wife writing team Jim and Carolyn Hougan. He is a an award-winning investigative reporter and the author of several nonfiction books; she is a writer with three published novels to her name. They began to work together several years ago when they were faced with a tight deadline for the book that eventually became *The Genesis Code*. In a week or so the two of them had brainstormed an outline. Carolyn then wrote the first draft, Jim did the rewriting and polishing, and Carolyn made final changes. This collaboration was so successful that they decided to work in the same way on their subsequent books, *The First Horseman* and *The Murder Artist,* taking the pseudonym John Case from Carolyn's grandfather who was also a writer.

The inspiration for *The Murder Artist* came from an incident that occurred when the Hougans' children were aged seven and ten and the family were visiting a Renaissance Faire, similar to the one described in the book. 'I still don't know how we became separated, but it happened. I'll never forget the terror I felt,' says Carolyn. 'We found them fifteen minutes later—an eternity for any parent. The nightmare that Alex, the hero in our book, enters when he doesn't find his children was, happily for us, unknown terrain.'

The couple enjoy travelling together for the purpose of research. 'It's important to us that the narrative plays out against a background that feels real,' Carolyn explains. 'We usually plan a trip to the places where the book is set, even if we've been there before. Often we see the place through the eyes of the character we're writing about. And we always take lots of notes and photographs, and collect maps and cocktail napkins and anything else that smacks of "place".'

When it came to writing about voodoo—a key element in *The Murder Artist*—Jim drew on an experience he'd had a few years earlier as a reporter. He and a photographer had been sent to Port-au-Prince in Haiti, to visit a clinic run by a voodoo 'priest'. 'We got there about one in the morning,' Jim relates, 'and I remember the unease I felt as the taxi drove off and left us. The priest—in fact a witch doctor—was missing his upper lip, which gave him a rather startling smile. His explanation that a zombie had bitten off his lip did not make me feel any more comfortable. And there we were, in a stifling shack in the middle of nowhere . . . After a brief interview, the *houngan*, or priest, offered to bury us alive—no charge—explaining that it would bring us good luck! We politely declined.'

Start from here

Sean French

If only life came with a road map, a few warning signs to let you know when the hard decisions are about to crop up, or when a major crossroads is looming.

But it doesn't work like that. All you can do is start from here, wherever you happen to be, armed with the little you do know.

All I can say is that this isn't the way it was meant to be. This wasn't the plan. I know that it isn't the best moment to assess my life—lying awake at four with a warm, scarred body lying next to me, breathing in and out, in and out. I sometimes lean over to check, the way mothers are supposed to with a new baby, worried that the breathing may have stopped.

The birds wake me in the morning. I thought the dawn chorus was a figure of speech, but I've discovered that out here it really exists. A mob of whistles, hoots, screeches until the sun comes up.

At four in the morning you shouldn't think about your life. Do anything else instead. Get up. Have a bath. Go for a walk. They say the dawn is beautiful out here.

That's the other point. If this wasn't the plan, then what was the plan? Where was I meant to be? Anywhere but here. What was I meant to do? Anything but this. I think about the past because if I can put it all together, maybe I will understand why I'm lying in the bed I'm lying in, why I'm lying next to the person I'm lying next to.

So at four in the morning I remember it all over again. That's a problem as well. I'm tired, so tired. It's dawn and I feel I am the only person in the world who is awake.

Sometimes when I'm telling myself the story of my life—silently, inside my head, so I don't wake her—I feel that I wasn't in the story I thought I was in. But it could be that if I had *been in the story I thought I was, then I might not have ended up here. And it's where I want to be, I think. Which is a good thing, because from any other point of view, it looks remarkably like a fuck-up.*

In the dark I think of other things. I think of the future, and that can make me cry. I try to keep to the past. The past is difficult enough.

1

You don't know it, but you may have talked to me. That time the phone rang while you were watching TV or pouring a mug of tea. You answered. A voice asked for you by name. Because the companies buy these lists. That time you filled out a form because you had a chance of winning a car. That time you sent off two tokens for a free oven glove decorated with a scene from *The Lord of the Rings*. You forgot all about it but your name and address and financial details were filed and became a commodity to be sold on until it appeared on my screen as one of the three or four hundred names I had to throughput during every eight-hour day.

Yes? you said, caught by surprise. I informed you that I worked for a company that was conducting market research in your area and could you spare a couple of minutes to answer some questions. Maybe you said that you didn't have time because your child was in the bath. Then I asked what would be a convenient time. At that point you might just have slammed the phone down. That was the response I liked most. I just clicked the No Further Action icon. Another one down. As if I cared.

If you did agree to help with our market research, I asked you if you would be interested in a free quotation for double glazing. If you said you were interested, what I really felt like saying was, If you want double glazing, do you really think that you're going to get the best deal from someone who just rings you at random? But I only felt that the first few times. After that you were just a number on a screen. And I was just one of three hundred people in headsets in a giant warehouse in Hendon or the Isle of Dogs.

It might not have been double glazing. It might have been a cable connection or it's even possible that you called me to arrange your mobile-phone agreement. The terminals had a small mirror attached and we were instructed to smile before the next call. Customers can always hear on the phone when a person's smiling, we were told. Hello, I'm Mark, thank you for calling whatever cowboy outfit I was working for at the time. What can I do for you?

It was the shittiest job of all the jobs you could imagine that weren't actually dangerous. But there were compensations. You didn't have to get up early or stay late. There was nothing difficult. It was in London. The pay was crap but at five seventy-five an hour times eight hours times five days times the two weeks of a contract, that added up to four hundred and sixty pounds. It was a nice chunk of money to get in your hand.

To be honest, though, I've got to admit that I'm a bit like those lazy bastards who are not entirely against the idea of getting double glazing. What they're against is the idea of arranging double glazing for themselves. They'll sit at home and if they never get the double glazing, then there's all that money saved. If somebody rings and suggests a free quote, then that's good too. All right, so they haven't gone round the superstores and compared the different brands, but what's to compare? Don't they all keep the draughts out?

The point I am making is that I'm passive. There was a Chinese saying somebody told me once: if you sit by the river for long enough, the body of your enemy will float by. The basic meaning is that things will sort themselves out in the end. If you chill in your armchair for long enough, someone will phone you and offer you double glazing.

AT THE END of a day of being glued to a headset, everybody was just too shagged out to do anything and we all crawled away like victims of a disaster. But every so often we'd all go to the pub and one of the managers might buy you a drink and you were supposed to fall down on your knees in gratitude. This particular time we were in a pub and I was talking to one of the managers, a gentleman called Selim. His official designation was Operational Systems Manager. As befitted his standing, he wore a grey suit and a sober tie. The rest of us were in track suits, jeans, combat gear, everything you could think of.

He looked around the pub, which was crammed with the human debris of our shift, and shook his head. 'What a shower,' he muttered.

I just grunted and sipped my beer. I had my own thoughts on the subject, but I wasn't going to share them with Selim.

'You're one of the better ones,' he said.

'That's not saying much. This isn't exactly the most motivated workforce of all time.'

'They do what we ask. But you do a bit better. Your figures aren't bad.'

'It's all just chance. It just depends which names you get. Skill doesn't come into it.'

'You're too good for this job,' he said.

'I'm not.' I suddenly had this horrible feeling that he was going to offer me a proper job at CC5 Ltd, which was the name of the organisation I was working for that fortnight. The idea was completely grotesque. I hurried to correct him. 'If you think I ought to stay on at CC5, I'd better tell you . . .'

'No, no,' said Selim. 'I didn't mean that at all. I was just thinking that you ought to be thinking about a career. I mean this . . .' He looked around with an expression of distaste. 'You might as well be flipping burgers. You should think of the future. You can't build a career in this place. These call centres are going to be finished in a few years. They'll all be in India where they're a tenth of the price.'

I took another sip of my beer and looked over Selim's shoulder. There was an interesting-looking girl who worked three screens to the left and two down from me. Once or twice we'd caught each other's glances, raised eyebrows at each other to show how we were united in despising CC5 and everything it stood for, and I wanted to grab a word with her before she left the pub.

'I've never really given much thought to my career,' I said.

'You should,' said Selim. 'How old are you, Mark?'

'Twenty-six.'

He gave a sharp intake of breath. 'It may seem fun now, but it won't seem so much fun when you're thirty.'

'It's not that much fun now.'

'Of course not,' said Selim.

I was halfway down my beer and I should say straight away that I've not got much of a head for alcohol, and I get very speedily disinhibited. I suddenly felt pissed off. 'For example,' I said. 'Have you ever looked at this whatever it is we work in? I can't believe it was ever meant to be an office.'

'It was originally designed as a storage facility.'

'A storage facility, right. Well, it's a dump. Has CC5 ever thought of making it a moderately bearable place to work in?'

'What for?' said Selim. 'If an office is too pleasant, then people get attached to it. They want to stay. If they stay, you have to give them holidays and pay their pension. That's not what CC5 is there to do.'

I drained my beer. 'This is starting to sound a bit too much like a committee meeting,' I said. 'Much as I'd like to stay and discuss company policy, there's someone I need to—'

'I've got a friend over at Wortley,' Selim said suddenly.

'What's that?'

'It's an insurance company. I've a friend who works there. Human resources. I put people in touch with him.'

'Sorry, Selim, I'm not interested.'

He took a card from the top pocket of his suit and handed it to me. 'Don't be an idiot, Mark. You'll be doing much the same work you're doing here and you'll be paid twice as much. And there are probably pot plants in the office. It's a good company.'

I sighed and took the card. He gave me a fatherly pat on my shoulder and moved across the room to some other poor sod.

I did go over to the girl, my dear neighbour at CC5. She was even better looking without her telephonic apparatus wrapped around her head. She was called Julia and she let me buy her a drink. I talked to her about the awfulness of the CC5 office and she said it wasn't worse than the last few places she worked in. I asked where she lived. She said Harlesden. I said I lived in Balham. She said they were a long way apart. She was already calculating how long it would take for her to get from my place to her place. That was an especially good sign. I asked her what sort of things she got up to after work. She finished her large gin and tonic and said that unfortunately she had to rush because she was meeting her boyfriend.

There ought to be a rule that people should have to wear the information on their lapel badge to save wasting time. Julia Whatever, Call Operator, Has Boyfriend.

So I drew a blank there. But I did phone Selim's friend. He invited me to come over on the Monday my contract ended.

I turned up at a huge modern building by London Wall, expecting it to be an aimless sort of chat, but Selim's mate, Phil, gave me a form to fill out and a personality test. Half an hour later I had a job in the claims department of Wortley Insurance Ltd.

YOU STILL might have talked to me but this time it was definitely *you* who wanted something from *me*. The back wall of your house had fallen down. Your husband had tripped on the stairs and he was in a coma. You'd had a head-on collision in Reading, and the car wouldn't move. It was pretty depressing, if you stopped to think about it. Every call was the worst day of someone's year or of their life. I then spoke to you in a calm voice. There was a procedure. I would find an approved garage and they would come and get your car and give you another one and life would go on.

Selim was right. It was better. There weren't just pot plants. There was a fluffy brown carpet and a coffee machine in the corner. There were posters on the wall of families, of houses, of cars. Mike, the Resource Supervisor, pointed them out to me. Look at them, Mark, he told me. They're what we're about.

There were only 120 of us in the room now, so we were a bit less like a termite colony and more like some slightly higher form of life. Rodents, maybe. There was a bit of a view, although because I was new I didn't get one of the good terminals by the window. But there was light, real light from the sun, and that reached me even in the middle of the office.

The most obvious difference was that we had to wear suits. When Mike told me this the first time we met, I made a token protest. 'We're on the phone all day,' I said. 'It wouldn't make any difference if we were naked. They wouldn't know.'

The problem with dealing with Mike is that he had a procedure, a line for everything. 'But *you* would know,' he said. 'When you're on our time, you're representing Wortley Insurance. For the customer, you are the voice of Wortley. And I believe that deep down, the customer knows if you're dressed for business.'

'I was just asking,' I said. 'I don't mind wearing a suit.'

And my starting salary at Wortley was almost twice what I'd been earning before, basically for doing the same job. Easier, if anything, because I wasn't trying to hassle people about things they weren't interested in and I didn't have to meet some ridiculous throughput target day after day. A guy two rows along told me about a studio flat over between Camden Town and King's Cross, so I was able to move out of my hole in Balham. It was great. After a fortnight I could do the job in my sleep and I was back to sitting on the bank of the river, waiting for a body to float by.

Telephone sweatshops are a good place for meeting women. For a start, women make up about two-thirds of the staff. Two rows to my right and one back was Sonia. Like every woman in the room, she wore a suit with a skirt, and she had her hair tied back tightly in a bun, and wore black stockings. She had light-brown hair and pale skin and blushed easily. I saw this the first time that I caught her eye. She had a soft voice, so most of the time I couldn't hear her talking on the phone. But one day Chas, who occupied the terminal on what you might call the hypotenuse between us, was out of the office, and Sonia got into a long and involved conversation. I quickly gathered that she was dealing with a householder who was having a major raw-sewage problem. There were new carpets and there was furniture and a dog and raw sewage everywhere. Sonia was trying to take down the details, but the customer was apparently in a confused state and Sonia kept having to read passages back over the phone. Apparently the customer was deaf or it was a bad line and Sonia was having to virtually shout about spreading brown stains, putrescence and unidentified objects floating through the door.

She was looking round guiltily and I caught her eye and smiled. She looked away.

Our exchange of glances gave me an opening line. The next day, in the cafeteria I saw her sitting at a table with a friend, and came across.

'Hi,' I said. 'We're almost neighbours.'

'Oh, yes,' she said.

'I really like it when you talk dirty.'

She looked startled. 'What are you talking about?'

Like virtually all classic opening lines, it was a complete disaster. I had to embark on a ridiculously laborious explanation of how I'd overheard her conversation about the sewage. But at least we were talking and, painfully, I managed to steer the conversation into another direction and then we were away.

THE POINT about the body in the river is that it's not entirely about sitting on the bank and doing nothing. Lots of strange things drift down rivers, and you have to recognise the body when it floats past. For me that moment came four or five weeks later. It was a rainy Sunday morning and I was lying in the bed of my flat with Sonia Vaughan. She was pale all over, as if she'd never been out into the sun. There was something very slightly creepy about her skin. I thought of baby mice when they are just born and haven't opened their eyes and have no fur. But even now in the closing stages of our relationship—she didn't know that they were the closing stages, by the way—even now I loved stroking that impossibly smooth, soft skin.

The original plan had been that we would get up and go to the market but the rain was splattering on the window, so I got up and made some coffee and toast and brought it back to bed where she was lying half asleep.

'Mmmm,' she said, biting off a piece of toast. 'That's nice of you.'

We sipped coffee in silence for a moment. I looked round and caught Sonia looking at me.

'What's that?' I said.

'What?'

'You were looking at me with a suspicious expression.'

'I was thinking about you.'

I wasn't sure I liked the sound of that. 'What were you thinking?'

'I was thinking about you, what you ought to do. I mean at work.'

'Is there something I'm doing wrong?'

'Not really, but that's not what you want to be doing: sitting at a desk handling claims all day.'

'What's wrong with it?'

'Aren't you ambitious?'

'No. I'm happy with what I'm doing. The job is a doss and I get well paid.'

'You should go and see someone. In management. Go and tell them you want to do something better.'

I thought for a moment. This wasn't what I'd planned at all.

I took the mugs and plates over to the sink. Then I came back to the bed and she pulled my dressing gown off me, giggling because the cord had become all tangled. She ran her hands down my chest.

'So you reckon I should talk to Mike?' I said.

'What? Oh, that? No, don't bother with him. He's got no power. He just wants to keep the phones working.' She took my hand firmly. 'Look. Show some initiative. Find someone in management who's got some power and go and bang on their door.'

'What? Really?'

'Try it. Either they'll kick you out and forget about you or they might be impressed. Oh, there's one other thing.'

'What's that?'

'I think I'm falling in love with you.'

It took me a bit of time to make sense of what she'd said. My brain was still expecting careers advice. When my brain finally did compute, it said to itself: Oh, shit. *I* said nothing.

'I can't believe it's a big shock. We've been together enough.'

I had to say something. 'I wanted to talk about that,' I said. 'I've noticed the stuff in the bathroom. Your knickers in the drawer.'

'Is there a problem?' she said.

'We should have talked about it,' I said. 'It's like you're secretly moving in. Suddenly you'll be there.'

'And wouldn't *that* be awful,' she said. She gave a huge gulp and I saw that her eyes were glistening.

Quite suddenly she threw the cover back and got out of the bed. I looked at her pale, slim body and it took a serious effort not to stop her and say it was all right.

'It'll only take a few minutes to get it all,' she said. I watched her put on her jeans and a T-shirt and a pullover. Then she was in the bathroom, rattling things loudly as they were thrown into a plastic shopping bag.

She came back into the room. 'I think that's everything.' She stopped, searching for words. 'You . . .' I thought she was going to say something rude but she didn't. 'I'm sorry,' she said. 'It was probably my fault. I was probably pushing too hard. I always seem to, I . . .' She choked and wasn't able to say anything.

She looked so sad and lovely and I wanted to say something of comfort, but mainly, of course, I wanted her to go. I managed a sort of shrug and she went.

THE EIGHTH FLOOR smelled of money. Everything was better than on the second floor. Things you wouldn't think could be better. Better door handles and magazine racks. There weren't normal offices either. The minions were dotted around in a semi-open-plan way, but the executives were around the edge in offices with glass walls. You'd have to go to the executive washroom to pick your nose. It would probably be worth it, though.

I walked around the perimeter trying to look as if I knew where I was going. I came to the door I was looking for. Darryl Wingate. Divisional Manager—Underwriting. This was one of the good offices, on the corner, wall-to-wall windows. It was such a good office that there was a sort of pre-office you had to go through to get to it, a filter, to filter out people like me. A very neatly dressed woman was sitting at a desk. Wingate's secretary. She wore a patterned scarf fastened around her neck with a little gold clasp.

'Hello, can I help you?'

'I'm Mark Foll,' I said. 'I'd like to see Mr Wingate.'

'Have you got an appointment?'

She knew I didn't have an appointment. She had the appointment book. She *was* the appointment book.

'I work downstairs. I just wanted to have a quick word with Mr Wingate. It'll only take a minute.'

'Mr Wingate is in a meeting.'

'I'll wait and then it'll just take a minute.'

'Mr Wingate is leaving for another meeting straight afterwards.'

'I could talk to him very briefly just between the two meetings.'

'That's quite impossible. Really, what is it you want, Mr Foll?'

My palms were starting to sweat and I had an impulse to leg it back down to the second floor. But it had taken me days and days of steeling myself to get this far. I had to stick it out. On the other hand, I'd told the floor supervisor downstairs that I was going to the toilet. There was a limit to how long I could be gone.

Then the inner door opened and two people stepped out. The first was a woman who looked about my own age, maybe even younger. She wore a dark suit with a skirt and black shoes, but her hair wasn't tied back in any way. It was blonde and she wore glasses, the narrow kind, without any frames.

Behind her was the man I took to be Wingate. He was older, with greying hair and a greying face. His jacket was off and his shirt was striped, like a pyjama jacket. It shimmered painfully. No tie in the world would have gone with that. His didn't. It just floated in front of it in a hopeful sort of way.

'So is it daughter's day?' I said.

He looked round and noticed me. 'What?' he said.

That was meant to be an ice-breaker, and we were meant to then go on and discuss my future career prospects. But there was an awesome silence. I clearly had to expand on my comment. 'You know, daughter's day,' I said. 'When I was at school, they had a day every year when fathers brought their daughters to work with them. Kind of to encourage them.'

Wingate and the woman looked at each other in disbelief.

'Who are you?' Wingate asked.

'Foll,' I said. 'Mark Foll. I work in claims. On the phones.'

'You're on the wrong floor,' Wingate said. 'You need to take the lift back to the second floor.'

'No, no,' I said. 'I wanted to see you. I want to talk to you.'

'What about?'

'I thought maybe when you two are all done, we could talk.'

'Can I introduce you to Donna Kiely?'

'Hi, Donna.' I held my hand out. She didn't take it.

'She's our general manager.'

'That sounds important.'

'Important?' said Wingate. He'd gone a bit red in the face. 'What did you say your name was?'

'Foll,' I said. 'Mark Foll. Claims Department.'

'Wait there,' he said and retreated into his office. This was a bit awkward, just me and Donna and Wingate's grumpy assistant standing in an office without much to say to each other.

Fortunately Wingate came back in. 'I just phoned Claims. The supervisor told me you'd gone to the toilet.'

'Yes, that's right. You see, I wanted to come and see you. But if I did it out of hours, you wouldn't be here. If I did it in office hours, I'd have to explain why I was coming to see you.'

'And why are you coming to see me?'

'I want to have a more interesting job.'

When I had gone over this scene in my mind, I had imagined various kinds of reaction and I'd planned responses accordingly. But I didn't expect what happened. There was an explosion next to me. Donna was laughing.

'Are you for real?' she said finally.

'What?'

'Did the guys in the office hire you? Are you suddenly going to start singing or take your clothes off?'

'No,' I said. My cheeks were starting to feel hot.

'This is the way you apply for a promotion, is it?'

'I want to do something different.'

There was a silence. I could see Wingate's jaw flexing. 'How long have you worked here?'

'Just over two months.'

He gave something between a snort and a sigh. 'Have you thought of talking to your supervisor?'

'What can he do?'

'He's your bloody boss.' He glanced across at Donna. 'Sorry. Shall I sack him or just chuck him out of the window?'

'Look, I was just asking.'

Glances were exchanged. I saw Donna nod at Wingate. 'Talk to him,' she said. 'It took some nerve to come up here.'

'Fine,' said Wingate. 'Fine. Come on through.' He looked at Donna. 'Shall I catch you later?'

'I'll sit in, if that's all right. I don't want to miss this.'

'Fine, fine, let's have everybody in. Margaret?' His assistant looked round. 'Could you call down to Claims? They may think that Mr Foll is having some sort of medical emergency. Tell them he's here.'

We processed through. It was great. It felt like I'd won something.

I sat in a chair that directly faced Wingate's desk. Donna sat on the sofa by the wall, out of my eye line.

Wingate picked up a pen and tapped it on a notepad. 'So?' he said. 'What have you to say?'

'I deal with claims over the phone. You know, little crashes, fires, things spilled on carpets. Not factories being burned down, nothing big like that. But talking to these people, it's obvious that about a quarter of the claims are pretty dodgy and about half of those are bloody dodgy.'

'That's no problem,' said Wingate. 'If a claim is false, we don't pay out on it.'

'It is a problem. I mean, I can't tell over the phone that they've deliberately tipped the coffee over an old rug or that a bike that they say has been lifted from the shed was actually given to their nephew for Christmas. I'd have to go there and look. What I'm saying is that I could guarantee to save this company more than my yearly salary. I can absolutely guarantee that five, ten per cent of claims would just collapse if I put my head round the door.'

Wingate looked amused. 'I'm sure you would, Mark. I'm sure you know that this is an idea that's occurred to people before. We have claims assessors who do exactly that.'

'Yes, but I'm talking about the claims I deal with over the phone. Nobody checks those.'

'I don't want to get bogged down in a discussion about procedure, Mark, but I assume that your supervisor selects some of the claims for further assessment.'

'I'm sure there are other things I could do,' I said.

Wingate put some very severe-looking steel-framed glasses on and looked at me over them. 'What sort of qualifications have you got?'

'The usual, a degree. Business Studies.'

'Where?'

'You wouldn't have heard of it.'

'Try me.'

'Cleoford University.'

'Cleoford?'

'It's in Shropshire. It's not very good. But look, Mr Wingate, this business is about what you know.'

'Mr Foll, I think that the first thing you should be aware of is that Wortley Insurance Ltd has one duty above all. Do you know what that is?'

I felt like I was trapped in a nightmarish, unending exam. But I knew this one.

'To sell insurance.'

'No, it is not. Our main duty is to maximise shareholder value. Nothing else matters. I don't know what I'm doing here having this conversation. I was going to say that we do have a career path in this department, with mentoring and in-house training and CII but I would literally stake the life of my children on a guess that you have no idea what that stands for.'

'Something insurance,' I said.

'Brilliant,' he said. 'Mr Foll, do you know anything at all about insurance?'

'I'm sorry,' I said. 'And I know I'm not an accountancy expert. Basically I'm just sick of talking on the phone all day. I wanted to have more fun.'

'Fun?'

'It should be fun. Well, it should, shouldn't it? Miss Kiely, do you have fun?'

Donna had surprisingly large breasts for such a slim woman. Large eyes as well, behind those rather snazzy glasses. It made her expressions very appealing, even when they were disapproving ones. She bit her lip. 'Yes, Mark,' she said. 'I think I have fun. What about you, Darryl? Do you have fun?'

'Some of the time,' he said, not looking as if he meant it.

'It should be exciting,' I said, feeling that things were finally going my way. 'Because what we're doing is calculating that, on the whole, the risk people are facing isn't as serious as they think. So they are paying us just a bit too much money to be safe, and we make a profit.'

There was a pause now. Wingate was screwing his face up in concentration. 'No,' he said. 'That's not true. What we're doing is spreading risk. Everybody benefits from this. Look, it's . . . well, look, I'll tell him the pig story.' He looked at Donna. 'You know the pig story?' She rolled her eyes. Clearly she knew the pig story. 'There were eleven men and they each owned a pig. One of the pigs suddenly died. The man couldn't afford the ninety pounds to buy a new pig so he gave it all up and got a job somewhere else. So the remaining ten men went to see a wise man. They told him about the dead pig and they were worried it could happen to any of them, so what could they do? He asked if they could afford ten pounds for a new pig. They said yes, so he made the following proposal: "All right, each give me ten pounds. If one of your pigs dies in the next year, I'll buy a new pig." They all said yes to that. In the next year one of the pigs did die. So the wise man bought a new pig to replace it. That man had a nice new pig for his ten pounds. The wise man had made a profit of ten pounds. So nobody suffered. Except for the pig.'

'And the other men who paid their ten pounds and didn't get anything for it.'

'They got peace of mind.'

'What if two pigs had died? Did the wise man have enough money for that?'

'That was his risk.'

'What if there had been an outbreak of swine fever and they all died? He wouldn't have looked so wise then.'

'It's just a story. That's not really the point.'

'I hope he checked up on the pig. The man might have been tempted to sell the pig, slaughter it and then get the insurance as well. If the man were really wise, he'd insist on getting the dead pig.'

'Shall we leave the pig story?' Wingate looked over at Donna. 'I'm sorry.'

Donna smiled. 'Why don't you send him out with Giles?'

'Giles?' said Wingate. 'Are you sure?'

'It would get Mark out of the office. If that's what he wants.'

'Great,' I said. 'That's great. Who's Giles?'

Wingate held up his hands. 'All right, all right,' he said. 'I'll phone him. Go back downstairs. We'll be in touch.'

'Thank you,' I said. 'That's so great. That's fantastic. Thank you so much.'

'Just go,' he said.

Donna and I stepped out into the corridor.

This was just so my lucky day, I couldn't stop myself. 'Thanks so much, Miss Kiely,' I said. 'I'm really grateful.'

'Good,' she said, and turned away.

'By the way . . .'

'Yes.'

'I wondered if we could maybe meet for a drink. You know, to talk about it. You could tell me about things. Maybe.'

To do her credit, she didn't flinch. She didn't change expression at all. 'Are you insane? Are you hitting on me? After that?'

'It was just a drink.'

'I'll tell you what,' she said. 'Maybe you could baby-sit for me and I could go out for a drink with my husband. It's *Ms* Kiely, by the way.'

And she was gone. She was ten times more beautiful, even, than she'd been back there in Wingate's office.

When I came back to the sweatshop on the second floor, I sat down at my terminal, put my headset on, took the first call and, in the best way, I felt a little drunk and I could see that everybody else was stone cold boring sober. Suddenly the job was fun because I knew that in a week's time I'd be gone.

At the end of the day I finished just a little bit early so that I could see Sonia on the way out.

I caught her by the arm. 'I did what you said. I went to see Darryl Wingate. And this woman, Donna, was there. She's very high up.'

'What did they say?'

'It was great. It worked out really well. They've arranged this other job for me. I'm going out on the road with someone.'

'That's great, Mark. I'm really happy for you.'

She turned and left me there. Her manner had gone all the way back to the way it was at that first meeting in the cafeteria. A bit more disdainful, perhaps. For some reason I hadn't noticed before what a striking face she had, like a smoothly sanded mask made out of white clay. Funny that, with all the time we had spent naked together. In fact we had spent almost all our relationship in bed. During that fairly short period we'd sometimes vaguely planned to go out to a club or a movie but it always seemed simpler to miss out the middle bit and go straight to bed. That's what I should have said to Sonia when she said she loved me. That's one of my problems. I'm always either blurting out the thing I shouldn't have said or else about three days later suddenly remembering what I really meant to say. It's just that Sonia threw me when she talked about loving me. I thought she was going to say that we should go away for the weekend or that I should meet some of her friends. Love was something else altogether.

What I would have said if I'd had about an hour of preparation is that we couldn't say we loved each other because we'd never had a conversation. That sounds stupid but I think it's almost completely true. Looking back I was unable to remember a single thing she'd said. I don't mean a single clever or funny or emotional thing, I mean a single thing. I should have said: How can we be in love when we've never talked? Except that might have seemed crueller than saying nothing. I don't know. I don't know about these things. It generally seems to work out fairly badly either way.

Anyway, who knows what we would have found out if we had really talked? Maybe she would have turned out to be incredibly boring or she would have started telling long, unfunny jokes.

On my last Friday afternoon I was on the phone as usual settling a complicated motor claim.

As I was winding it all up and replacing the receiver, I saw that Mike the supervisor was standing over me.

'Congratulations on your change of job,' he said.

'Thanks, Mike.'

'Why didn't you tell me about it?'

It was a bit sad, really. Mike wanted to know why I hadn't told him that I wasn't happy in the department. We could have discussed it and sorted the problems out. He went on to tell me that it didn't make him look good, someone from his department going over his head and saying they weren't happy.

I couldn't take all this suffering and guilt. First there was Sonia and now I had rejected Mike's little kingdom and undermined him in the hierarchy. 'I'm tired of just hearing voices on the phone,' I said. 'I want to go out into the world and actually meet some people.'

'We'll see,' said Mike, sounding angry and sarcastic. 'Customers have only had to hear your voice up to now. We'll see what happens when they have to see your ugly mug as well.' With that he was going to march off but then he stopped. 'I forgot. You report to Giles Buckland on Monday morning. Eight-thirty. Third floor.'

'Wanker,' I said. But very much under my breath and when he was about ten yards away with his back to me. You never know who can lip-read.

2

One of the things about these offices with glass walls is that it presumably provides some incentive to keep them tidy. But this hadn't worked with Giles Buckland. His office was staggering. I didn't even think of going inside, because I couldn't see any floor. Where a floor should have been, it looked like a model of downtown

Hong Kong constructed out of piles of books and files and envelopes.

'You're admiring my office,' a voice said behind me.

I looked round and saw a man who looked about forty, carrying a shoulder bag under his arm. He was wearing a dark-blue suit and a tie, but it looked as if he had made an effort not to. The tie was pulled down loosely and, although the man was quite big, the suit was bigger. He had a big face as well. Everything about Giles Buckland—because it was obviously him—was large.

'Dr Foll, I presume.'

'What? I'm not a doctor.'

'I do not love thee, Dr Foll. The reason why I cannot . . .' He paused. 'I'll have to think about that one. You were looking at my office. You think it's the most disorganised room you've ever seen.'

'I don't know about *ever*,' I said cautiously.

'Did you know that some people say that bebop was invented by jazzmen who wanted a kind of music that white musicians couldn't steal? That's like my office. They can't interfere with my work if they can't get into my office.'

'Who's "they"?'

'I don't know. Them. The suits. But there is a way in. Look.'

It was actually pretty impressive. With a sort of balletic delicacy Buckland tiptoed through the chaos and reached his desk without toppling a single pile.

He turned around and leaned back on his desk. 'This all looks disordered but it is actually an organic arrangement. I can put my finger on any document within seconds.'

He rummaged around and grabbed what looked like a small desk diary. Then he tiptoed back across his office. 'I'm Giles Buckland,' he said, holding out his hand. 'Have you brought sandwiches?'

'No. Nobody said.'

'Oh,' he said.

'I guess I can buy some.'

'Maybe,' Giles said. 'It depends where we end up.'

Giles sounded mysterious but it wasn't as if we were going up the Amazon. We weren't going to a world without sandwich bars.

He looked at me with narrowed, suspicious eyes. 'I wonder why they sent you to me. Did you do something wrong?'

'No.'

'I'm not a mentor, you see. They sent one person before. It didn't work out. After a week he asked to be moved. He was an ambitious man, I think. He kept talking about the fast track.' Giles suddenly looked cheerful. 'I don't think he thought this was the fast track.'

'I said I wanted to have fun.'

'Fun?' said Giles, now looking very thoughtful. Almost tragic. 'You're going to see life at its very worst. Widows, fires, atrocious crimes, floods, infestations. I can't promise you fun.'

'I didn't really mean fun. I wanted to get out and meet people.'

'All right. We'll pop up the corridor and collect the claims files and then we'll go out and meet some people.'

Giles eventually led me down to the car park where we got into his incredibly smart silver executive-style BMW which was completely at odds with his office and everything about him.

He seemed puzzled by it himself. 'They give me a new one every year. We're the interface between Wortley and the general public. Did they tell you that? We're the policy holders' friends.' He fastened the top button of his shirt and then pulled up his tie. It was a slight improvement. 'Get in, get in.'

Giles was a better driver than I had expected. It's just that he seemed to have so much else on his mind. At first he seemed preoccupied by the idea that he had to teach me something, so at odd intervals he would insert a random fact about insurance assessment.

'You see,' he said suddenly, 'it's not just a matter of the claim itself. We have to make a judgment about the level of insurance. If the property or whatever is underinsured, then we scale down the compensation accordingly.'

'What if it's overinsured?' I asked.

'Same thing,' Giles said. 'Unless it's a valued policy allowing for insuring above the value. But we won't see that in the sort of place we're visiting together. I'd just warn you that this is all going to be routine. I'm a bit worried about what you said about wanting fun.'

'But as I said . . .'

'Actually, it has got more fun recently. Ever watch TV in the day, Mark?'

'Not so much.'

'About every second commercial shows a man in a suit promising they can get money for you if you've stubbed your toe in the last five years. Consequently, I can promise you you'll spend about half of your time on the phone to Islington Council telling them to fix a cracked paving stone in Upper Street. How's your numeracy?

'I got a maths GCSE.'

'GCSE? That's after my time. Means nothing to me. What's a quarter of a fifth?'

'What? Er . . . a twentieth, isn't it?'

'Excellent. What about maps?'

'My geography was weak.'

'There's a street map in the glove compartment. We've got to get to Portondown Road. It's somewhere along here.'

We pulled up outside a terraced house on the corner of Portondown Road. 'The files are in the back,' said Giles. 'Reach them over, will you? We're starting with something simple.'

PAULA RENTON WAS a large harassed-looking woman, with long, curly brown hair.

'I'm sorry,' she said, 'I really didn't expect anybody actually to come round about this. It was just a coat.'

'It's a formality,' said Giles. 'For claims above a certain amount we like to do it in person. It's old-fashioned, I suppose. We'll only be a minute.'

'Come through. I'm sorry, we're in the middle of breakfast. It's complete chaos.'

We followed her into the kitchen, where two very small children were at the table tipping food over themselves. Paula Renton ran around pushing chairs under the table, wiping faces, clearing away dishes.

'It was the most stupid thing,' she said. 'I was just going out and Chloe was sick absolutely everywhere, including the coat, which needless to say is the only good bit of clothing I've got.'

The boy was rubbing yoghurt in a circle on the table with the palm of his hand.

'Jack! Stop that! Anyway, I put the coat in a binbag. I was going to take it to be cleaned. And the childminder thought it was rubbish and put it outside and the bin men took it before I realised. So . . . I know four hundred pounds is a lot. It's certainly a lot to me at the moment.'

'Don't worry . . .' Giles paused because there was the sound of the front door opening.

Paula looked confused. 'Who's . . .? Oh, she must be early.'

A young woman walked confidently into the kitchen. 'Hi, Paula.'

'This is Sally,' said Paula. 'She looks after the children. These two men are here about the coat.'

'Oh, that,' said Sally, laughing. 'I'm sure you've heard it was completely my fault. Well, my boyfriend's . . .'

'It's all right, Sally,' said Paula weakly.

'Your boyfriend's?' asked Giles.

'That's right. I was just dropping them off at the station and that's where Chloe was sick on Paula's coat. So we shoved it in a bag and I took it back to my flat and I was going to sort out the cleaning while Paula was away. And then Guy, my boyfriend, put the bag outside with the bins downstairs. It was really bad luck because our bin men only come about once every two weeks. But by the time I ran down after it, they'd whipped it. Beautiful coat as well, beautiful. So, Paula, shall I get on with things?'

'Sure, Sally,' said Paula quietly.

We stood in silence while Paula helped Sally to hustle the stained and sticky children out of the kitchen.

Giles looked over at me. 'Can I have the file, please?' he asked. He turned to Paula. 'You know that this is a household policy?'

Paula had gone fiercely red. She was blinking quickly. 'I didn't . . .' she said. 'I wasn't sure.'

He handed her the form, with a pen. 'If you'll just sign this release revoking the claim.'

She signed it. 'There,' she said. 'I'm sorry. I don't know what to say.'

Back in the car, Giles asked me to check the next address.

'That was a bit unfair,' I said. 'What did it matter which bloody doorstep the binbag was left on?'

'It matters because it was excluded by her household contents policy. She knew that. That's why she lied about it.'

'Didn't you feel sorry for her? She obviously didn't have much money.'

'She was perpetrating a fraud. Now read the map.'

The next case was fairly similar except the house in Highbury was about fifty times as big. Mrs Furneau was a very elegant woman who clearly didn't spend much of her life chasing after small children. She made us tea and then sat down with us in the upstairs living room. The downstairs room was uninhabitable.

'It was the silliest thing,' she said. 'I was fiddling with the radiator, and suddenly water was spraying everywhere. Honestly, it was like something out of a Keystone Kops film. So I rang up this wonderful man, Jimmy, who does all of that sort of stuff for us. He was pretty quick, but it still took him about fifteen minutes to get here and it was all just ruined. The really silly thing is that Jimmy arrived and just did a little twist on the pipe and it all stopped straight away. I feel awful, because we only had carpets put in there a couple of months ago.'

'Not to worry, Mrs Furneau,' said Giles in his warmest manner. 'At least it will make the costs easy to establish.'

'Yes. I hope so,' said Mrs Furneau. 'I dug out the receipts. Here they are.' She passed over a sheaf of them. Giles glanced at them and passed them to me. The figures almost made my eyes water. Now she was going to spend that sum all over again. Or rather, Wortley Insurance was.

'If you could arrange for an estimate, Mrs Furneau and then phone me, I'll send young Mark here along and he can take down the details. Would that be all right?' He handed his card over to her.

'Yes, of course. You've both been so kind. Do you think it could all be settled quite quickly? I was so hoping the carpet could be replaced before the boys are back from school.'

I couldn't stop myself from blurting out, 'You mean this afternoon?'

'No, no,' she said. 'They come back at Easter.'

'I'm sure that will be no problem, Mrs Furneau,' said Giles, glancing at me. I couldn't tell whether his look was one of anger or deeply subdued amusement.

'IS THERE A PENALTY for being an upper-class idiot?' I said after we had left Mrs Furneau.

'Not unless it's in the policy,' said Giles, inspecting his lunch, which was elaborately arranged in a Tupperware box. Although it was only March, it was warm and sunny and we were sitting on a bench in Highbury Fields. I'm not really much of a lunch person. I had bought one banana from a rack outside a shop.

'Don't you feel that it's unfair?' I said.

'What? Life?'

'That Mrs Furneau. She was pissing around with the radiator valve and then couldn't switch it off. It was completely her fault. And there are parts of England where you can buy a house for what Mrs Furneau spent on carpeting one floor. Then that really poor and very nice woman lost her coat and didn't get compensated at all.'

'I checked through the policies over the weekend and it may be that Mrs Furneau was stupid, but she's insured against being stupid.'

Giles was eating avocado, feta cheese and sun-dried tomato with great relish. 'Do you know what you are, Mark?'

'No, what?'

'A philosopher. Do you believe in God, Mark?'

'I don't know,' I said. 'I'm not sure. A sort of God, maybe.'

'I wonder what God thinks of Mrs Renton and Mrs Furneau? Perhaps he believes that we should have given our shareholders' money to alleviate Mrs Renton's relatively straitened circumstances. Or perhaps he is preparing rewards for her in eternity. On the other hand, he might be preparing to consign her to eternal damnation for being a liar and criminal. What do you think, Mark?'

'I wish we'd given her the money for her coat.'

'You see, I'm not a philosopher, Mark. I'm not even a businessman.'

'What are you, then?'

'I'm not sure. But when I was your age I was a scientist.'

'What sort?'

'Oh, I don't know, biology, zoology, that sort of thing.'

'Why did you change?'

'Got tired of it, I think. But I'm still a sort of scientist, in a way. I like gambling. Do you like gambling, Mark?'

'I used to play a bit of poker at uni.'

'Dangerous game, poker. Too dangerous for me. Too much psychology. Blackjack's my game. I'll tell you about blackjack some time. But what I was starting to say is that we're gambling with our customers, Mark. We're betting against them. Betting a small amount of money that something won't happen. If it does happen, we have to pay them a large amount of money. But if you lose, you don't try and change the rules, and you don't whine about it. Now, this afternoon we should be seeing something that will probably be more to your taste. Also I'll be able to introduce you to one of our loss adjusters.' He looked at his watch. 'He'll be there already.'

'You seem very different when you're with those women from the way you are the rest of the time.'

'Oh, dear. Really? You mean, fawning, obsequious, oily, that sort of thing?'

'No. Just different.'

He gave a sad-sounding sigh. 'Customers. That's what we're supposed to call them now, isn't it? When we're with customers I sometimes feel like a drunk man pretending to be sober.'

I wasn't so sure about that. I thought that Giles Buckland was a bit more of a businessman than he let on.

We drove down the Balls Pond Road towards Hackney, to the

mews street that ran along the back of Cheston High Street. Giles explained to me that there had been a fire in a fabric shop that had also burned down a storeroom at the back. There had been moderate damage to the interior of the shop but the storeroom and its contents had been totally destroyed.

As we got out of the car, we were met by two men in suits. Giles introduced me to Pete Stenecki, the loss adjuster. Stenecki was tall, dark-skinned, with hair cut right to the scalp. He introduced us to a paunchy, double-chinned man called Matt Fender who told us that he was chairman of the holding company.

Fender seemed quite cheerful. He took us through the rubble and the charred beams as if he was rather proud of it all. 'It's a bloody mess, that's what it is,' he said. 'Mind yourselves.' This last was as he stepped over a black oily puddle. 'The shop's not too bad. The fire started at the back and mainly burned itself out there.'

He led us through into the shop.

'Most of the damage was done by the firemen with their silly hoses and their axes. It's mainly a paint job through here.'

'What did you have in the storeroom?'

Matt Fender looked as if he had sucked deeply on a lemon. 'Oh dear,' he said. 'That was not good. Bloody awful luck. A whole lot of deliveries had come in from all over the place. You know, ready for the spring collections. The whole lot up in smoke.'

Giles looked around the shop. 'How did the fire start?'

Fender gave an eloquent shrug, proclaiming innocent bafflement. 'There's always boxes and packing cases out the back. Sometimes people sleep rough out there. They might have made a fire, and the whole lot went up. Or it may have been kids.'

'Yes,' said Giles reflectively. 'Will you give us a moment, Mr Fender?'

'Take as much time as you want, gents.'

We walked out of the front of the shop onto the High Street.

'It's a right old bit of dodginess,' said Pete Stenecki.

'What's he asking for?' said Giles.

'Twenty-five for rebuilding the storeroom, another twenty for the contents.'

Giles gave a short laugh. 'What do you think, Mark?'

'It's classic, isn't it?' I said. 'You're having a few cash-flow problems, so you shift your dresses out of the warehouse, knock them down for cash. Then torch the warehouse, get the insurance for the building and the dresses you've already sold, and you're laughing.'

I saw that Giles and Pete were both smiling.

'Well, that's Nipper of the Yard's theory. What do you think, Pete?'

'I talked to the police and the fire investigator yesterday afternoon. It's just like Mr Fender said. The boxes behind the warehouse were set alight. But no traces of fuel or wood shavings.' Giles sniffed and Pete continued. 'There was a pile of cardboard with a few wooden crates mixed in. You didn't need to be in the boy scouts to get a fire going. That cuts both ways, obviously. Some winos might have made a fire to keep themselves warm. Got out of control.'

'Have you seen invoices for the dresses?'

Pete gave a sour smile. 'I've seen invoices. But who knows what invoices they are? This company's broken up into so many pieces it's almost impossible to work out what's what.'

'What were the figures again?'

'Twenty-five and twenty.'

There was a long pause. Giles was frowning, deep in thought. It was a couple of minutes before he spoke. 'Wait here,' he said.

He walked back into the shop. The two of us watched as he talked to Matt Fender.

He came back. 'Thirteen and seven,' he said, as he joined us.

'What? Just like that?' said Pete.

'Yes, yes, otherwise it'll go on for ever. Bring the papers into me and I'll sign off on them. Then I'll cancel the policy.'

Pete left us and Giles took several very deep breaths.

'Are you all right?' I said.

'What's the next file?'

'Something about a greenhouse.'

I HAD PLANS for the flat. It was not on the face of it an impressive place to live and it was never going to be a place to invite six people back to, but I could imagine it as perfect to bring one person back to. A good scrub down would be a start. A vacuuming would be better than nothing. Put the torn lampshade and the browny-green curtains and the ancient carpet in a skip and replace them with bright new things in pastel colours and it would be quite a dinky little top-floor flat.

I never even got around to the vacuuming. Worse than that. Hanging over the sofa, there was an awful old picture that looked as if it had been knitted of a boat sailing into a sunset. The very first moment I walked into the room, I was irritated not just by the badness of the painting but the fact that it was hung very slightly askew. All I needed to do was to pull a chair over, stand on it and straighten the picture. Then that little bit of my life, at least, would have been sorted. But I never did. I never seemed to have the time.

I should explain a few things. I'm not the sort of person to hang around the office. I mean, if work was enjoyable, they wouldn't call it work, would they? The idea of a career at Wortley was a joke, as far as I was concerned. My plan was to work for a year or two, build up a stash of money, then throw in the job and go abroad until it was spent. I certainly didn't want to hang around the Wortley office. The problem was that Giles Buckland was a weird sort of teacher. He hardly ever explained anything. I just had to pick it up as I went along. I noticed that he never looked at the files, even though we had to bring them along. He'd always read through them before and he remembered all the details. So after a couple of days I thought I'd have to do something about it.

Usually after we'd been out, I'd have stuff to finish up back at the office, phoning surveyors and loss adjustors and checking appointments. That took me through till seven or eight. Then I'd get hold of the claims forms and photocopy them, call up the policies they referred to and print them out. I'd take all that home with me and grab a pizza and a few cans of beer and read through them, get them in my head for the next day. And reading through an insurance policy isn't like looking at the sports pages. I don't mean that it's technical. It's just that everything hinges on a particular word, or a thing that is disallowed or whatever. I was never done before midnight.

I'm not quite sure why I did it. It just made more sense when I was standing there next to the broken window or burned-down shed or whatever. It's like looking at a forest. Whenever I've looked at a forest, I've always thought it would be more interesting if I knew what kind of trees they were.

A couple of days after I'd started going through the policies, Giles asked me some renewal date and I told him without opening the file. He gave me a funny look, took the file himself and looked at it. He just gave a grunt. No wink. No pat on the back.

He didn't really respond to what I said either. He'd quite often ask me what I thought, and I'd say something. Sometimes he would just carry on as if I hadn't said anything at all.

It didn't bother me. What I liked about it was travelling into weird bits of London I'd never thought about: industrial estates, lock-ups, mansions, Underground stations, ruins, hospitals. We'd sit there while women cried, and we'd meet plump men in suits who'd start making demands and threaten us with lawyers. A lot of the time Giles would have a cheque in his inside pocket. We'd have a few words, the client would sign along the dotted line, we'd hand the cheque over and be on our way. Another time a lorry driver had fallen asleep on the motorway and there was a massive pile-up and fourteen people were killed. For that one we went to a preliminary meeting with about five different insurance companies. And that was just about the procedure for appointing engineers.

Only a couple of visits really stick in my mind. One time we were in Hampstead, to see a wife about her husband's life policy. He'd just died of a brain haemorrhage.

Giles stopped on the front steps. 'Did you read the policy?'

'Yes.'

'Did you think there was anything funny about it?'

I didn't answer straight away. If Giles was asking that, he must be suspicious. But I couldn't think of anything. 'It's just a completely standard life policy. Nothing else.'

'Really?' he said. 'Oh well.' He looked up at the tall house with a gloomy expression. 'I hate these ones.'

When she spoke Isabel Fry's voice trembled. Her features were blurry. I think she'd been crying just before we arrived. She asked us to sit down and she talked.

'They said it could be years,' she said. 'The specialist said that people sometimes went quickly but it wasn't very likely. The average was three or four years and some people were alive for seven years or even longer. That seems so far off. And it's stupid, but you start thinking that maybe they'll find a cure by that time. They're doing so much research, aren't they? The treatment was going to start next week. Then last Sunday he started having a fit. All of a sudden he just went quiet. I dialled 999 but they were so long getting here. They couldn't revive him.'

'I'm terribly sorry,' said Giles. 'I'm sure they did the best that they could.' Then he turned to me and asked, 'Mark, can I have the file?'

I passed it across. He laid it on a coffee table in front of him and opened it. 'And now,' he said. 'We have your husband's policy. Assigned to you.'

'Yes,' she said faintly. 'I didn't know anything about it. Our solicitor rang yesterday and told me about it. I didn't know.'

Giles adjusted the document carefully, as if it was really important that it lined up perfectly with the edges of the red cardboard file.

'I'm very sorry, Mrs Fry,' he said. 'But would it be all right if I used your bathroom?'

I tried not to let it show on my face how startled I was. It was a totally bizarre and insensitive time to suddenly go off for a piss.

'No, of course. There's one at the top of the stairs.'

Giles got up and left. It was especially embarrassing because I was then left alone with Mrs Fry. I consider myself quite good at keeping a conversation going, but this was beyond me. First I said how sorry I was about her loss. She said thank you and that was it. I guess that she thought that if she was going to give a grief-stricken monologue, she ought to give it to the organ grinder rather than to his monkey. I just kept a feeling of concern on my face until it started to hurt.

Giles was a long time. I began to think that he must have amoebic dysentery. Finally, I heard him coming down the stairs. He sat down and started talking as if he hadn't been away. 'Normally we wouldn't trouble you at this time,' he said. 'But we have certain guidelines. One of them, obviously, is if a life policy-holder dies shortly after the commencement of a contract.' He picked up the paper. 'And your husband took out this policy only recently—last November.'

'I didn't know that,' she said.

'This is painful, Mrs Fry, but we have to assess whether any pertinent information may have been withheld when the policy was signed.'

There was a silence that was even worse than the one when Giles had been out of the room. I saw her jaw muscle flex.

'Are you saying that my husband was a liar? He died very quickly after being diagnosed with a brain tumour. I cannot believe that you've come here two days after his death accusing him of deception.'

Still looking puzzled, Giles reached into his left jacket pocket and took something out. It was a plastic pill container.

She looked at it. 'What's this?'

'It's dexamethasone,' said Giles. 'It's a steroid that's used for reducing the swelling around brain tumours. It has your husband's name on it.' He gave it to me. 'What's the date on it, Mark?'

I looked at it. 'The third of November.'

Isabel Fry's face was chalk-white, her eyes flickering this way and that. 'He took a medical,' she said. 'He told me you made him have a medical. They didn't find anything.'

'They didn't find anything, because the routine medical doesn't include a CAT scan. I'd like you to save us all trouble and embarrassment. Please. I have a release form I would like you to sign.'

Isabel Fry stood up. 'I can't believe it,' she said. 'You were rummaging in our medicine cabinet.'

'I apologise, Mrs Fry. It wasn't ideal behaviour, but I . . . I wanted to bring this to a close without involving doctors and the hospital authorities.'

'Get out of my house. Now. This moment. You two *disgusting* men. I am going to call the police, and I'm going to call my lawyer . . . I will see you both in court.'

We were hustled out onto the front steps and the door slammed behind us. We walked down onto the pavement.

'That was better than I expected,' said Giles.

'Better?' I said. 'How the hell can that be better?'

'I thought that maybe she didn't know anything about it, but she did. That's the way some people react when they're in the wrong. They shout and bluster and get angry and self-righteous. It would have been much worse if she'd just been quiet and sad.'

When we came back to the office at the end of the day, there was a hand-delivered message waiting from Mr J., Mrs Fry's legal representative. He said that if we would forward the release form to him, it would be signed and returned.

ANOTHER JOB I particularly remember from that time was a burglary at Dalby Douncy Pountain, an advertising agency in Clerkenwell, housed in a bright, shiny new building of metal and glass.

At reception there was a beautiful girl with short, blonde hair that made her look like an elf. She looked at us expectantly—we could have been two more detectives—but when Giles said we were from Wortley Insurance, you could see the interest drain out of her face. I felt like I should have a card printed and I'd hand it out whenever I saw that expression. It would say: 'This isn't really me. I'm disguised as an insurance man but in real life I'm completely different.' She just told us to take a seat.

Minutes later a man came through. You could tell that he worked in an advertising agency because of his suit. It was green, the kind of green you have on snooker tables. It was an amusing suit, but the joke would wear off.

He was called Jem and he took us upstairs to see the damage. I expected to find lots of men in white coats sprinkling chalk dust on window sills but there was just one bored-looking man in an ordinary suit like ours. He was Detective Constable Maguire.

'This is our design and layout section,' said Jem.

'Did they take them all?' asked Giles.

'On this floor,' said Jem.

'What about the floors below?'

'The fire doors are locked and alarmed.'

'So how did they get in?'

'They came up the back fire escape,' said Maguire. 'In and out in a few minutes. They must have had a van in the alley behind. There's a gang been doing this over the last couple of years. They hit offices where there are high-end machines, rip them out of the wall and they're gone.'

I could see that there was plaster on the floor and exposed wires where they'd been pulled away.

'They've done the same thing in Covent Garden,' continued Maguire. 'They did one in Waterloo. Another in Shoreditch.'

'It doesn't sound as if you're hot on their trail,' I said.

I thought I'd put my foot in it but Maguire looked unconcerned. 'It's not my case,' he said. 'I'm just standing in for someone.'

'So what's the damage?' said Giles.

Jem had a piece of paper ready in his hand. 'We've drawn up an inventory of what's missing,' he said.

This was a scene I'd got used to. There'd been a burglary and nobody cared. Maguire didn't care because it wasn't his case. Dalby Douncy Pountain didn't care because they were going to get a set of nice new computers. Wortley Insurance didn't care because this was in line with a projected payout rate.

Giles nodded at me. 'Give it to him.'

Jem handed me the typed list.

'So it was just the ones in here?' said Giles, as if it hadn't been made tediously clear.

'That's right,' said Jem. 'Here and in the annexes at the end.'

Giles started walking around the office. He wandered to the window and looked out. I assumed that he would be recommending stringent changes to the rear access. What he called the stable-door bit of the job. I started to wander around as well, doing my impersonation of the very professional insurance investigator.

I walked over to the annexe. There were two small spaces with lockable doors screened off from the rest of the office. The connecting cables were hanging off the desk. I started walking back towards Giles, and then I stopped. Something was buzzing in my head. I looked over at the mess, the plaster on the floor, the ripped-out sockets in the wall. Then I walked back to the annexe. I stood there looking at the cables. One of them was neatly coiled. The list that Jem had given me showed twenty-two computers and four printers. Two of the computers were identified as coming from these two offices.

I walked across to where Jem was standing. 'Who installs your computers?' I asked.

'A company called Byte Part.'

'Right,' I said, smiling. 'That fire door you mentioned. Where is it?'

He pointed. 'Over there.'

'I'll just take a look.'

I walked across and pushed it open. I wasn't interested in the fire exits. But I wanted to have a bit of fun. I walked down some concrete steps and pushed open the first door I came to. I was in a virtual carbon copy of the floor above. I smiled at a girl sitting at a desk close to me. 'Hi,' I said. 'I'm from Byte Part. I do your computers. Do you know where the new computers are?'

'Over there, in the corner.'

'Cheers,' I said.

There they were, crammed on a table, waiting to be put somewhere. I checked the serial numbers. They were the same as those on my list. I had to stop myself grinning like an idiot.

When I came back through the fire door, Giles walked up to me, looking irritated. 'Where the hell have you been?'

In a low voice I explained what I'd done. 'So you can cross two of the computers off the list.'

A smile spread across Giles's face. 'The greedy little bastards. I don't believe it,' he said, then caught my eye. 'By which I mean that I do.' He turned round. 'You.'

'Jem,' said Jem.

'Jem,' said Giles. 'Do Dalby and the rest actually exist?'

'Of course,' said Jem indignantly.

'Then get one of them up here. Now.'

Jem scuttled away.

'What are you going to do?' I asked.

'I'm voiding the contract. We're not paying them a penny.'

'What about the computers that really were stolen?'

'Doesn't matter.'

Helena Douncy swished into the room in a beautiful black suit. It didn't disarm Giles at all. I was really impressed. He got very angry indeed while staying amazingly quiet. At first Helena Douncy said it couldn't be true. Then Giles offered to march her downstairs to check for herself. Then she said there must be some sort of mix-up. Giles then said that if she said one more word he would call Detective Constable Maguire over and there would be two investigations instead of one. She didn't say anything for a while.

'There were only two,' she said.

Giles's eyes were locked on Helena Douncy's face but his next words were addressed to me. 'Mr Foll. Will you note that Ms Douncy stated that there were only two computers in her company's fraudulent insurance claim.'

'Fraudulent?'

'I'm voiding the insurance contract.'

'What? The whole thing? I'm going to have to talk to our lawyers about this.'

'That's no problem,' Giles said. 'We'll expect to hear from them by the close of business tomorrow or we'll call in the police.'

Giles didn't say anything more to me until we were back walking along the Clerkenwell Road.

'That wasn't bad, Mark,' he said.

It was the nicest thing he'd ever said to me.

3

At the end of the next day, at almost seven, I was back at the office going through some forms when I felt a tap on my shoulder. It was a woman I'd never seen.

'Are you Mark Foll?'

'Yes.'

'Ms Kiely would like to see you. Come with me, please.'

We went up in the lift. I asked her what it was about but she just shrugged. She took me through a series of doors that ended in a large office with Donna Kiely sitting at a desk at the far end. The windows went from the floor to the ceiling. It was spectacular.

'Ms Kiely, I'm sorry about, you know, that thing, when we last met. At the end of when we met. That last thing.'

'You know, I actually gave you some credit for it as an attempt to pull something out of the ashes of disaster.'

'Right. So is that it?' I started to turn back towards the door to escape.

'I just got off the phone with Gil Pountain. As in Dalby Douncy Pountain. He was grovelling to me for a solid twenty minutes. There'll also be a humble letter to Giles and one for you as well. You should frame it.'

'Right. So has the contract been—what was it?—voided?'

'No,' she said. 'That was what the grovelling was about. They've cancelled the claim, made a payment to cover our expenses and promised to improve their security arrangements. In return, we'll maintain the cover.'

'Does Giles know?'

'I've only just sorted it out. I'll tell him tomorrow. That was a good call, Mark.'

'I couldn't believe it,' I said. 'I mean, if someone had just taken the bloody computers home nobody would ever have known.'

'If they'd done that, they would have been admitting to themselves that they had something to hide. They saw it as just like helping yourself to a couple of pens from the stationery cupboard. Mark, are you busy? Have you got to get somewhere?'

I thought for a mad moment that now she was going to ask me out for a drink. As a sort of reward. 'No,' I said.

'There's someone I want you to meet.'

We got into a different lift from the one I'd come up in. It was a sort of superlift. The buttons were gold-coloured and the numbers were carved in a curly shape. It was wood-panelled.

'We're going to meet our CEO,' she said. 'Walter Broberg.'

We were met at the lift door and led into an office that was about three times the size of Donna Kiely's. At the far end, a man—Broberg—was standing silhouetted against the lights of the city outside the window. He was talking on a cordless phone. The room was lit in zones, so whole areas seemed dark or blurred. Several small spotlights lit up a sculpture—it looked like a deformed hourglass carved out of rough granite and left unfinished. Other spotlights shone on paintings on the wall and on a bookcase. I felt ill at ease. There was a bit of a feeling of a visit to the headmaster about it.

Broberg snapped his phone shut and moved towards us, into the light. He had milky blue eyes, greying hair drawn back quite casually over his head, and he was well over six feet tall. I was interested in the details. When you're at the top, what do you do to distinguish yourself from those who are nearly at the top? His jacket was off. He wore a striped shirt and a blue satin tie, grey trousers, black shoes. Maybe it was the kind of outfit that was so expensive that it didn't need to try. Maybe it was just ordinary. I couldn't tell. As he came closer, I saw that his lined face was creased in mild amusement.

'Walt,' said Donna. 'This is Mark Foll.'

He held out his hand. 'Good to make your acquaintance, Mark. Donna told me about that DDP thing yesterday. That was a good catch.' The accent had a bit of mid-Atlantic about it.

'Thank you, Mr Broberg.'

'Did you smooth it out, Donna?'

'Yes, it was no problem.'

'Good.' Broberg walked over to his desk and picked up a piece of paper. 'Cleoford? That's where you went to?'

'That's right.'

'Never heard of it. I never went to university at all. I did all sorts of things. I worked on farms, then I trained as a chef. Hardest I ever worked in my life. Chopping the carrots at eight in the morning and I was still there at midnight scrubbing the stoves down. Then I worked as a salesman. In fact I sold stoves, funnily enough, door to door . . .'

'Then what?' said Donna, in a flirtatious tone.

He ignored her question. That's one of the things about being in charge. You don't have to answer questions, if you don't want to.

'So what do you think of Wortley, Mark?'

I looked across at Donna Kiely. I didn't know why I had been dragged up there to be asked the sort of stupid question your uncle asks you when he can't think of anything to say.

'I've been out of the office mainly,' I said. 'It's been interesting.'

'I sometimes think I should get out a bit more,' said Broberg. 'What do you make of Giles Buckland?'

Broberg had an unnerving technique. He would wander around the office, talking virtually at random, like some old man blabbering away. Then suddenly he would ask a question and look at you with a piercing expression and you'd feel you'd been put on the spot in a way you didn't quite understand.

'Giles is not exactly like everybody else,' I said. 'But Ms Kiely told me Giles told her about that thing at DDP. He didn't have to do that. Lots of people would just have not got around to mentioning it and the credit for it would sort have stuck to them.'

'Hmm, interesting.' said Broberg not sounding as if it was all that interesting. 'This DDP business. What did you think of it?'

'Obviously it's not right to claim for things you've still got. A bit pathetic as well, this big rich company, all of them in their lovely suits, lugging computers downstairs. They could have been charged with fraud.'

'But we didn't call in the police. In the end we didn't even cancel the contract. What do you think of that?'

I felt that Broberg was jabbing at me, tempting me to say something. I shrugged. 'Ms Kiely said they rang up and grovelled over the phone. If they said they were sorry and promised not to do it again, I guess that's enough.'

'Are you married, Mark?'

That piercing look again. What was *that* about?

'I'm sorry,' I said. 'I don't really think . . .'

'I don't mean to be intrusive,' Broberg said. 'Well, I *do*, but it's for a reason. I was chatting to Donna. We were wondering if you and Buckland'd be interested in doing some work for us. But it's not in London. You'd need to go away for a bit.'

'What is it?'

Broberg put his hands in his pocket and wandered across the office, all casual and ruminative again. 'Nothing much,' he said. 'We've got a meeting tomorrow. Ten-thirty. I'd like you to be there, Mark.'

'We've got some visits . . .'

'Put them off,' said Donna sharply.

'Sure,' I said.

'And you'll get Buckland,' Broberg said to Donna.

'Yes, Walt.'

Broberg's attention was now apparently focused on one of his paintings. We started to leave but then Broberg nodded at me. 'Can you stay for a moment, Mark?'

Donna left, a bit reluctantly. She probably thought Broberg was going to ask me what I thought of *her*. Broberg didn't look at me. His attention was focused on one of his paintings.

'Donna told me that you said you wanted to do something fun. It's not often that I hear people wanting to come into insurance for the fun. We should have you stuffed. We should have you stuffed and mounted and put on display in the foyer.' An answer didn't seem called for. Broberg had the way of thinking aloud of someone who knew that people wouldn't interrupt him or tell him he was talking rubbish or just walk away from him.

'"Fun",' he went on. 'I was struck by that word. And intrigued. Because I think the exact opposite. Life used to be very interesting. Hundreds of years ago. If you took a thousand merchants, in a particular few years, a few of them would be completely wiped out. Not by the market, but because their boat was wrecked or their warehouse burned down. If you had a boat coming from Constantinople full of silk and spices, you were tossing a coin. If it arrived you were rich, if it didn't you and your family were sitting in the mud with a begging bowl. You put your entire life on the line. So you'll try anything that's going. You'll pray, you'll throw bones, you'll see patterns in the sky, whatever. Because all that matters is that boat. But with a thousand boats or ten thousand boats or a hundred thousand boats, now we've got something. Because then if six per cent of boats sank two years ago and five per cent sank last year and seven per cent sank this year, then if you insure the merchant's cargo in return for ten per cent of what you'll pay him if it's lost, then his life stops being interesting. He knows where he'll be in six months' time. You hear what I'm saying? No God, no fate. Art and religion become things you do in the evening and at weekends. I'll tell you, Mark, I'm glad to have you aboard. See you in the morning.'

THE PHONE RANG in my flat at six-thirty the next morning. I picked the receiver up and groaned something.

'Mark? It's Giles. Are you up?'

'I am now.'

'What's happening? Donna Kiely rang me late last night. There's a meeting. What the hell's going on? They went behind our backs on the DDP case. Are we out?'

I told him about the previous evening, and what Broberg had said.

'He asked what you thought about me? What was that for?'

'I don't know.'

'It's a trap,' said Giles. 'I don't trust them. Be careful what you say. When you go in there, look on the table. If there's a cheque lying there, that means you're being fired. That's your severance pay. Admit nothing. If they can prove gross negligence, you won't even get the cheque.'

THERE WASN'T A CHEQUE on the table. There was coffee on it, in silver pots. There were two kinds of mineral water. The table was about twenty-five yards long and made out of something dark and heavy and expensive. When Donna Kiely brought Giles and me in, there were two people already sitting at the far end. Donna had told us about them on the way up.

'They're Ross Cowan and Vicki Hargest. They're both vice presidents. Ross is an actuary. That's basically statistics and strategy. Vicki's risk management. They're big wheels in the company.'

Vicki introduced us all, then made us sit at the end of the table with the others. She was the most intelligent-looking woman I'd ever seen. She had these round glasses with frames made out of what looked like thin copper wire. She even had intelligent-looking hair, fiercely curled. I wondered if she had sex intelligently and was lost in that train of thought when I saw there were two more people in the room. Walter Broberg was murmuring to a man whose immaculately groomed hair and clothes and skin showed that he was even more senior.

Broberg introduced him as Fergus Nielsen from the Horton Group, Wortley's parent company.

'It's good to be here,' Nielsen said in an affable tone. 'I just came over to be a fly on the wall. You just go right ahead.'

But when someone's flown over from the States in one of the company's Gulfstreams just to be at your meeting, it's like a ten-ton fly sitting in the middle of the table. Giles started nervously lighting a cigarette and then Nielsen wondered aloud whether there wasn't a no-smoking policy in the building and Giles virtually ate it in his rush to get it out of sight. Broberg nodded at a woman in a black dress with a white pinafore and she poured us both coffee.

'Giles, Mark,' said Broberg. 'We want you to go up to a village called Marston Green for us. It's in Norfolk.'

Giles stopped looking nervous and looked puzzled instead. 'What for?'

'Vicki, can you give them the short version?'

Vicki Hargest took her glasses off and placed them on the table. Her brown eyes looked larger without her glasses on.

'Marston Green is a village near the Norfolk coast. Over the past few years there have been reports of illness scattered over the area. In the local press an action group has described it as an epidemic. It has also been called a cluster. The illnesses cover a whole range of conditions from respiratory illnesses and skin complaints to certain cancers.

There have been reported cases of childhood leukaemia, of multiple myeloma, lymphoma, as well as breast cancer. Obviously these illnesses occur across the country. The question is whether there is a concentration in the area of Marston Green. Whether there is a pattern.'

'What's our exposure?' asked Giles, sipping at his coffee.

Vicki Hargest leaned back in her chair. 'Four miles north-west of Marston Green is an industrial site operated by a company called Marshco. In 1999, we took over their public liability insurance contract. They are a waste-management company and they operate an incinerator on the Marston Green site and an adjoining landfill operation. There have been accusations about levels of dioxin emissions. There have also been claims about leakage into groundwater and into the River Teel, which flows beside the Marshco complex and through Marston Green. These have been denied by the company.'

'Truthfully?' asked Giles.

'There is much about this situation that is complicated and unclear,' Vicki said. 'We're here to talk about ways forward and there are a lot of variables. It would be realistic to assume that new information about Marshco's operating practices will emerge. There is nothing sinister about that. They are involved in a large-scale waste processing.'

'Are Marshco being sued?' asked Giles.

'No. But there have been protests. And a so-called action committee has been formed. There are rumours of a TV documentary.'

There were some mutterings around the table.

I started to feel a twitching in my stomach. This sounded big.

Fergus Nielsen leaned forward. 'What is the very worst that could happen? Ballpark figure.'

Ross Cowan coughed. 'If what we mean is, what is worst for Wortley Insurance shareholders, the worst would be if this case came to court and it was established, one, that acts or omissions of Marshco had caused lots of people to be made ill and die and, two, that Marshco had behaved recklessly. If this were established it would be a question of hundreds of millions of pounds.'

'That's a lot to prove, though,' said Nielsen.

Vicki Hargest nodded. 'I'm a very long way away from being convinced that we've even got a case to answer. On the other hand, we're not sure how this case is going to develop. We don't know what the campaigners have.'

Now Broberg spoke: 'That's where you two come in.' He meant me and Giles. 'We'd like you to go up there.'

'The best thing,' Cowan added, 'would be to prove that Marshco's processes are not causing the illnesses. That's difficult. But we could prove that something else is causing the illnesses, or is a factor. We could demonstrate that another form of contamination was possible. If nothing else we—or you two—could kick a little dust around.'

'This is good,' said Nielsen. 'I like the sound of this.'

'The question is,' said Giles, 'whether this is a type-one error or a type-two error.'

This was a typical Giles pronouncement in that it resulted in an embarrassed silence.

'What the hell are they?' said Nielsen.

'A type-one error is seeing patterns that aren't there,' said Giles. 'A type-two error is not seeing patterns that are there.'

That cast a bit of a pall over the conversation. I think people were trying to work out in their minds which was which. And then, I don't know what made me do it, but I spoke for the first time since I'd said, yes, I wanted milk in my coffee. 'There is one other thing we might do, while we're up there. We might find out that Marshco *were* responsible for the illnesses.'

Another long silence. I thought to myself: What did you say that for?

'That's true,' said Nielsen in a quiet voice. 'And if that is so, Mark, we would certainly like to be the first to know. But a thing like that is hard to prove.'

'Why us?' said Giles.

'What?' said Broberg.

'Ms Hargest has a whole department of risk assessors. We've got lawyers. Why are you sending claims investigators?'

Broberg gave a shrug. 'Good question,' he said. 'What we're not doing is sending down people to negotiate with the different parties on behalf of Wortley Insurance. Because nothing has crystallised. So far as we and Marshco are concerned, there's nothing to investigate. It's just a few people sounding off. So it'll all be nice and casual. We just want you to go there, get to know people, get a feel for the place. Have fun. That's what you want, isn't it, Mark? I'll tell you where you can start.' Broberg had been fingering a piece of paper. Now he slid it along to Giles. Giles looked at it and then passed it to me. 'There we are. Document One for your file.'

It was the sort of handbill you might get for a school fête or a car-boot sale. 'The Marston Green Cluster' was written in large letters. And underneath: *The Marshco Incinerator has been poisoning our neighbourhood for years. People are dying and it is time to act. Residents interested in forming an action committee are asked to attend a meeting in the Village Hall.*

'So there you are,' said Broberg. 'Go and get to know them.'

Giles was silent and glowering as we made our way back down in the lift to his office. We reached it and he pushed the door shut behind us. 'So what do you think?' he said.

'Can you get away?' I said. 'Is that all right with your wife?'

He gave a sarcastic laugh. 'That's the least of my problems. But what do you make of it? What do you think they're playing at?'

'I don't think they're playing at anything in particular.'

'They're setting us up. If we achieve something, then they'll take it over, the way they always do. But if anything goes wrong, we'll be the ones who are hung out to dry. They don't care about us.'

'I don't think so, Giles. I think the main thing is that we're cheap and they can send us up there with nothing much to lose.'

'No,' said Giles. 'There's a plan. There's always a plan. Oh, and something else. Can you come to supper? With me and Susan, my wife. Tomorrow. It would be good.'

Oh fuck, I thought.

'That would be great,' I said. 'Thanks.'

SUSAN, GILES and their two children lived in a small house in a terrace of small houses. The internal walls had been knocked down so that the ground floor was one medium-sized room rather than about three mouse-sized rooms. There was no hallway. I stepped straight off the street and bumped into a sofa.

While Susan was getting a jug for the bunch of flowers I'd brought, I saw that it had company. All around the room were small vases and pots with feeble stalks projecting out of them. I knew that one of the signs of being grown up was to have indoor plants, the sort you have in offices, with huge creepy plasticky dark-green leaves. These were just shoots, dotted around.

'You're puzzled,' said Giles, appearing in the doorway from the kitchen. He was in off-duty dress of T-shirt and very faded jeans. 'You're wondering what it is, all this horticulture.'

'I don't really know much about it,' I said, meaning I didn't care much about it.

'Guess what they are, though,' he insisted. 'You want a beer?' He had two bottles in his hand and he handed me one. 'Look more closely.'

I bent down and made the effort. 'They look like pips,' I said. 'Pips and stones. Is that a peach stone?'

Giles took a gulp from his beer. 'Probably. There are peach plants, grapes, nectarines, apples, pears, avocados, almost anything you can think of. It's not me, it's Susan. Every single grape pip, every avocado stone that enters these premises is put in water, and some of them sprout and some of them don't. The ones that don't go into the bin and are replaced by the stones or pips from whatever plums or apples we've eaten that day.'

Susan came back into the room with my flowers in a plastic measuring jug and put them on the table. She noticed that I was looking at her plants. 'The ones that do well,' she said, 'I'll take outside and put in pots.'

'Will you get peaches and avocados?' I said.

'No,' said Giles, so firmly that there didn't seem anything else to say.

There was a silence and I looked at Susan in her black trousers and floppy purple sweater. Whenever I meet a couple, I compare them, see which one is better looking. At first glance, I thought that he had done a bit better than she had. She had a face that was all angles, cheekbones and chin, but it looked softer because of her curly dark hair and her large brown eyes. Those eyes were shiny, dark-ringed, the aftermath of something. I wondered if there had been an argument before I arrived.

While Giles and I were talking she went back and forth to the kitchen with dishes, bottles, glasses. She opened two bottles of Bulgarian wine, and ladled soup into three bowls. Giles started eating without apparently noticing, as if it was something that had always been there in front of him. Susan poured about a third as much for her as for me and just dipped her spoon in an exploratory way. I tried to think of something to say.

'Do you work?'

'I'm a social worker.'

'Nice,' I said.

'What do you mean?' she said with a frown.

I was fully aware that it had been an inane comment, but I thought it was mean of her to make a big deal of it. I just mumbled something about helping people. Susan didn't reply.

'How are you feeling?' Giles asked. 'About going up to sniff around in this village.'

'I'm rather looking forward to it. What about you?'

Giles scraped the remainder out of the soup bowl. He took a sip of wine as Susan collected up the bowls and took them off to the kitchen. 'When I want to know how I feel,' he said, 'I observe my own behaviour, just in the way I would look at someone else's behaviour. Does that sound strange?'

'I don't see the point.'

'So what do *you* do?'

'If someone asks how I feel, I look at how I feel and tell them. When you asked me how I felt, I thought for about one second and then told you.'

'You mean, you noted some sensations in your brain and then decided what sort of feelings they were.'

'I know how I feel, Giles. It's not a difficult thing to find out.'

Giles looked dissatisfied, as if he had an itch down at that awkward spot in the lower part of your back and knew he couldn't reach it. 'Imagine a frozen pond,' he said. 'You ask a woman if the ice is safe to skate on and she says yes. But then you notice that she's keeping her own children away from the ice.'

'She's just lying about what she really thinks.'

'Lying?' said Giles. 'If she was a politician, she would say it was a matter of privacy and personal choice. "Why should I sacrifice my children to my personal views?"'

'You've lost me a bit,' I said.

Susan returned with a large piece of fish in a yellowy sauce on a platter. 'Why does the villain in your little parable happen to be a woman?' she asked.

'That's irrelevant.'

Susan cut the fish deftly and arranged it onto three plates. Then she heaped broccoli, green beans and potatoes around the fish.

'You might make the same observation of yourself,' Giles said. 'Someone might ask you how you are, and you say, "Fine." You might even think you really are happy. Then you look at your own behaviour. You discover that you find it hard to get out of bed in the morning, you get into trivial arguments, you leave your food unfinished, and you realise that you're depressed.'

'The reason that you leave your food unfinished,' said Susan, 'is that you talk all the time.'

'I was giving an example.'

I noticed that Susan wasn't eating her food at all, just rearranging it on the plate in a way that mimicked all the processes of eating except for the bit where the food is put in the mouth. She looked at me. 'Do you know why Giles went into insurance?' she said.

'No,' I said.

There was something wrong with the evening. It was like having dinner in some Viking household where there's a man of the household and a guest comes to dinner and the two of them talk and the wife stands in the corner and only comes forward to pour a jug of mead or whatever it is that Vikings drank. Susan was sitting at the table but she might as well not have been. It was all about Giles and me. Even when Susan spoke, it was to get Giles to say something to me or me to ask Giles something. None of it was about her.

He spoke dismissively. 'The story of why I came to work for Wortley is not why we're here this evening.'

Susan took a deep gulp of wine. 'Giles was an evolutionary geneticist,' she said. 'Doing research in a laboratory outside Cambridge. And now he's going door to door checking stains in carpets. Surely that's a story worth hearing.'

'It's not much of a story,' Giles said.

'It's a great story,' said Susan, looking at me. 'I bet that Mark would like to hear it.'

Maybe this was not a good area to stray into. 'There'll be plenty of time for that,' I said. 'In the long evenings up in East Anglia. I'm not at all clear what you were on about—that pond and the ice—but if what you're saying is that you don't want to go, Giles, you don't have to. You've got a family. I don't care where I am.'

'So what are your thoughts, Mark?' said Giles.

That was the problem. Giles's answers to me never quite seemed to follow on from what I'd said.

'You mean Marshco, the whole thing? It's going to be interesting,' I said. 'But I'm not sure why they're sending us. I mean, why *us*.'

'That's the whole point,' said Giles, emptying more wine into his glass. He was becoming expansive. 'With this cancer stuff, who's going to prove that there is a connection? Or that there isn't?'

'You're the biologist,' I said.

He snorted into his wine. 'It's not my field,' he said. 'Look. The point is . . .' His brow was furrowed as if the point was eluding him. 'It's like gambling. The point about gambling is not who plays beautifully. It's about who walks away with the most money at the end. That's all that Wortley care about. We can collate statistics and argue with Green activists, but Wortley want to get out of there having maximised their shareholder value. They'll want a deal, and they haven't sent us up there as deal-makers. We've got no kind of brief, so we've got to make our own and I'll tell you what it is.' He waggled a trembly finger at me. 'We'll go there, compile a brief report, get out.'

I took a small sip of my wine. I was taking about a quarter of a sip for every eight sips he took. 'Giles,' I said. 'If you want, I could go ahead, get things ready, find somewhere to stay.'

Giles shook his head. 'No, not at all.'

'That's a good idea,' Susan said.

'I'll find out who's who and make some basic arrangements. Then after a couple of days you can come up and we can get to work.'

There was a silence. I wondered if the argument had been about Giles going away.

'We could talk about that,' Susan said.

'It's fine by me,' I said. 'Just let me know.'

'Giles said he thought you were a good thing,' said Susan. 'You know why it was that he gave up research?'

'Susan . . .' He made an attempt to stop her.

'He got depressed by it.'

'That's not true,' said Giles.

'Not true?'

'Not true. That's what you said at the time. And I said then, as I'm saying now: not true.'

'I'm sorry, Giles,' she said. 'I'm just following the example of your pond story. When asked if you were depressed, you said no, you were fine. But for me that was just another one of your symptoms. You were unable to get out of bed in the morning, you couldn't sleep. You started drinking more heavily.'

'I could argue with those points one by one, except it would bore Mark.' He turned to me. 'It generally needs to be explained to people who blunder into our little psychodrama that my wife has a theory not only that I need therapy but that it ought to be conducted in public. As it happens, the reason that I went into insurance was not because of depression. It was because of my aunt.'

'Your aunt?' said Susan, looking baffled.

'Auntie Frankie. She was the cleverest person I've ever met. She was a mathematician. She did secret stuff in the war, but her real work was with an insurance company. She was an actuary, like Ross

Cowan. I was amazed by that, using figures and formulas to tell you how many people were going to die in car crashes next year, applying mathematics to people falling off ladders and going through windscreens. So when I wanted a change, insurance seemed a good idea.'

'Which is why you now spend your time checking up on broken washing machines.' Susan gave Giles a sarcastic look. 'I don't remember you talking about Aunt Frankie at the time.'

I wondered if Susan would dare to carry on. She was looking at me as if she expected me to prompt her by asking more questions about Giles's psychological condition.

'It's late,' I said, making that strange sort of symbolic preliminary movement out of my chair to signal that my departure was imminent. 'I've got to get across London.'

'Make your escape while you can, Mark,' said Giles. 'The laser beam of my wife's analytic attention hasn't moved on to you yet. Soon it'll be your turn to be interrogated about your parents and your childhood.'

'It's not very interesting,' I said.

'Ah,' said Giles. 'That'll be Susan's starting point, your strange evasiveness.'

'We'll do it next time,' said Susan, standing up. That meant that my symbolic movement had to turn into a real one. Sometimes you have to fight your way out of people's houses. Oh, please, have some coffee. Have a third portion of cake. But Susan seemed happy for me to go. At the door I kissed her on both cheeks and said thank you and how wonderful the food was. A minute later I was walking towards Kilburn High Road, feeling relieved.

4

Marston Green's website invited tourists to visit the village and see the tenth-century church with its unusual rood screen. There was the Guildhall and there was a cross in the High Street which marked the spot where the Catholic martyr John Cornysshe was burned at the stake. I wondered what Cornysshe would have thought about his execution being used to entice people to Marston Green to eat cream teas. I sat in the Wortley office and read about the bus service (four a day, fewer at weekends) and felt even gloomier.

The site gave the phone number of a tourist office. I rang and spoke to a very nice woman called Jo and told her I was looking for somewhere to stay that wasn't a hotel. The thought of spending weeks scraping butter out of little foil wrappers and making coffee with a kettle in the room gave me acute suicidal impulses.

That wasn't a problem, said Jo. She knew of some holiday cottages, well, chalets really, that had been refurbished, just off the High Street. Within two minutes I was talking to Geoff Otley, landlord of the Four Feathers Tavern and owner of the chalets, and within five I had made an open-ended booking of two of them. Two. That was very important. If I was going to be spending days in the countryside, I didn't want to see Giles's face over the breakfast table.

I would go up ahead and get some basic information. Giles would follow a couple of days later. We would cobble together a report and get the hell back to London. We had a brief meeting with Donna Kiely before we left.

'No heroics,' she said. 'This is a preliminary fact-finding visit. Don't provoke anything. Don't try and solve the problem on our behalf. You have no authority to speak on behalf of Wortley or Marshco, or to enter into any agreement of any kind.'

'And if we're caught,' I said, 'you'll deny all knowledge of us.'

'What?' said Donna.

'It sounds like a spy film,' I said. 'We're being sent on a hopeless mission.'

'I think it's more like one of those science-fiction stories,' said Giles. 'We're being sent in a time machine into the distant past. I mean, going into the English countryside *is* like travelling to the distant past. And our prime directive is that we mustn't interfere with history while we're there or else we'll come back to London and discover that electricity hasn't been invented.'

Donna left a long pause. 'Are we done?' she said finally.

'No,' I said. Giles looked at me and mouthed an urgent no, but it was too late. 'Donna, what is it that you *really* want?'

Donna looked thoughtful. 'We want a resolution we can all feel good about,' she said finally. 'But what we want mostly is for nothing to happen. That's how insurance companies earn their money. From nothing happening.'

I wanted to ask who 'we' was, but Giles must have noticed a dangerous gleam in my eye because he hustled me out of the door.

I ARRIVED AT THE STATION in Worsham, a town dominated by a sugar-beet factory, and a taxi took me through a council estate and along country lanes to Marston Green and the Four Feathers. I found Geoff Otley, tall and pale with curly dark hair, in an office round the back. He took me to the chalets, which had been made from an old stable yard. Each one was given a horse-type name—Blackie, Dobbin and so forth. I was put in Clover. The chalet was neat and simple inside. I had a bedroom, a living room, a little kitchen in the corner, a dining table, everything.

I met Geoff for a pint of Suffolk bitter as soon as the pub opened that evening, thinking that he could fill me in on the anti-Marshco campaign. He'd never heard of it.

'I know about the Marshco plant,' he said. 'A lot of the employees drink here. Now if you want to hear about a campaign, I'll tell you about the one to stop the airfield. Total failure. Later in the summer you won't be able to move for parachutists landing on your head. I'm surprised the villagers have got the stomach for another fight.'

I'VE ALWAYS DISLIKED the countryside but previously I'd only disliked it from a distance. My reasons were vague and underinformed. What I disliked mainly about it was that it wasn't London. There wasn't enough in it and what there was was too scattered.

But you have to spend a lot of time in the countryside to hate it properly. My authentic loathing began only after I found myself with a spare hour before the inaugural gathering of the Marston Green Cluster Action Group, or whatever it was going to be called. I decided to do that thing that people do in the country: go for a walk.

The previous day I'd stood with Geoff and looked up at the fields that sloped up and away to one side of the town. I'd thought there was mainly wheat and corn and sheep in the countryside, but the two giant fields were beautiful. One of them was full of yellow flowers so bright that it was hard to look at them. The other field was a much more delicate blue, like a blue cloud hovering just above the ground.

'Is that lavender?' I said.

Geoff shook his head. 'That's linseed. The other's rape.'

'That's a really terrible name,' I said.

'You wait till you cop a whiff of it.'

So on that May afternoon I walked along the lane that led up and between the two fields.

I saw a ripple of wind across the rape field and then the smell hit me in waves. At first it was just the basic nice smell you get from a bunch of flowers, but there was more to it than that. I've never suffered from hay fever at all, but when I felt that breath of the rape flowers in my nostrils and my throat, I knew what hay fever must be about. There was an almost undetectable scratchiness, like tiny razor-sharp hairs being dragged through my throat and lungs.

And there was the smell. A bit difficult to place, but it wasn't nice. It was a little bit like puke, but there was also just a whiff of dog shit. And once I'd noticed the under-smell, the flowery over-smell started to seem sickly and made me want to gag.

I wended my way along the road and left the rape behind me. There was a field of grass, then a pair of semi-detached houses that looked as if they had been lifted by helicopter out of a street in Croydon and dropped here. I heard a moo and saw that there was a farm ahead. I don't want to go on about smells too much, but the smell from this farm was staggering. There were some cows in the field on the far side, with matted muddy coats and snotty noses. In the main yard, there was a line of pigsties. I couldn't be exactly sure which one the smell came from, but I would have bet on the pigs.

I guess you don't have particularly high expectations of a place where pigs live. Hence the saying, this looks like a pigsty. But this pigsty really did look like a pigsty, even for a pigsty. It looked like the pigs had built and maintained it themselves.

The smell was so rank that I didn't want to get too close but the yard really was worth looking at. I thought of the sort of books you'd read as a toddler with pictures of Things You Find in a Farmyard. This muddy, smelly yard was full of things you wouldn't expect to find in a farmyard. There were piles of wooden pallets. Some of them had been broken up and I could see that here and there they had been used for reconstructing parts of the wall in the wooden shelter, where I could glimpse various tools. There were piles of bricks and breeze blocks, a stack of railway sleepers, a couple of plastic buckets, heavily stained with white paint. There were blue plastic barrels that had been jaggedly cut in half. There were also various mysterious parts of machines, dark red with rust.

The strangest things—torn bits of plastic sheeting, lengths of inner tubing, half-door frames—had been incorporated into various structures. It was almost an advertisement for recycling, except that it was also the best advertisement in the world for throwing things away, for burying them, or, best of all, for burning them, in places like the Marshco incinerator just a few miles up the road.

I heard a yelping and a dog skidded round a corner. It ran towards me, all teeth and dripping tongue, and flapped around as if there was an invisible barrier about a yard away, and barked at me.

I heard an angry muttering and a man appeared. He was wearing rubber boots, green canvas trousers, a ribbed grey sweater and, oddly, a white shirt and tie.

'Oy, Stiff,' he said, or something like it. 'What yer doing?'

That last bit was addressed to me, not the dog.

'I'm going for a walk,' I said. 'I was wondering if there was circular walk.' He looked blank. 'So that I could carry on and go in a curve that would bring me back into the village.'

He still looked blank and said nothing.

'I need to get back to Marston Green and I know what you're going to say,' I said. 'You're going to say, if I were you, I wouldn't start from here. Because that's what people say when you ask them the way. But obviously I've got to start from here. Because here is where I am.'

If I had been anywhere but there I would have started a conversation about how this was the story of my life. You've got to take responsibility, you take the decisions, but you don't take them in circumstances of your own making. I would like someone to explain this contradiction, but it was typical that the thought had entered my mind as I was talking to a man who didn't seem to be able to direct me to a village that he lived next to. I felt that he belonged in London. In the middle of the city he could have walked along the street with strange parcels, he could have talked to himself on park benches, he could have rummaged in litter bins and stolen supermarket trolleys.

'So anyway,' I said, 'I'll carry on to try and find that circular route. If that's all right with your dog.'

The man nodded, then grunted something at his dog.

I set off again. Just around the corner there was a wooden footpath sign pointing across a field. I was now walking across the slope to the west of Marston Green and it gave me a nice view of the village, freakishly clear on this late spring evening. There was the church, of course, and a patch of green in front of it, and there was a line of half-timbered houses along the main street. There were a couple of pubs, a small hotel and some shops. I could see the tiny school with its playground, a field with a fence around it. Next to the field was the village hall, where the meeting was due to start—I looked at my watch—in just over twenty minutes' time. Looking slightly away from the centre of the village there were other houses, a farmhouse, a manor house, groups of cottages with thatched roofs.

At either end of the village, a couple of factories had come and gone, leaving rusting hulks of warehouses. There were also three new housing estates, and to the right of one of the defunct factories a fourth one was clearly marked out. Clearly there were still a few people willing to move into this contaminated area. The newest estate, on the eastern edge of the town, was the most obviously prosperous. These people didn't work at Marshco. They drove to work in Bury St Edmunds or even up to Norwich. If it wasn't for them, the village would have died. Geoff Otley had told me that there were fifty-two children in the village school. Before the last estate had been built, it had been forty-two.

It was time to get to the meeting. I walked across the field and found myself, with relief, in a lane that led back down into the village.

THE GOOD THING about lying in the dark thinking about how I got here—or there, from your point of view, because I'm here and you're there—is that it's like watching my life on video. Sometimes I play one bit over and over again, trying to work it out. Other times I just fast-forward until I get to the bit I'm interested in. The problem with real life, with things like the meeting of the Marston Green Cluster Campaign, is that it proceeds at the same pace as the parts of your life that you're interested in.

I suppose that most meetings are the same the whole world over. You get fantastically excited about something and you believe you can change history and then someone says, Yes, I agree, let's form a committee. And before you know where you are, you're appointing auditors and arguing about whether you've got a quorum. As people started to make their way onto the stage of Marston Green village hall, I could guess who the 'someone' was: the florid-faced, bald, middle-aged man, wearing a blazer and a striped tie who introduced himself as Charles Deane, the chairman of the campaign group. He said he just had a few things to say, and then there was about forty-five minutes of procedure. That's another problem. The fact that almost all meetings are boring doesn't necessarily mean they aren't important. You fall asleep and suddenly Stalin has been elected chairman of the party. But I couldn't see any immediate threat to Wortley as they proceeded to 'we must appoint auditors and committee members'.

While the discussions droned on, I distracted myself by looking at the other two people on the platform. The first was a man who must have been in his mid-thirties. He was more casually dressed than Charles Deane, in red canvas shoes, grey chinos, a faded blue shirt and a brown jacket. He had close-cropped hair, which was receding drastically. Beside him was a woman who may have been a touch younger, around thirty. She was tall, very slim and the effect of that was emphasised by her hair, cut spikily short and tufted up. She was wearing a blue velvet suit with a white T-shirt underneath, and white tennis shoes.

After what seemed like nine hours, Charles Deane said that without further ado he would ask for brief reports from Mr Kevin Seeger and Miss Hannah Mahoney. 'Kevin and Hannah have been busy on the ground, on our behalf, as you all know. I've asked them to give us a brief summary of how things stand. Kevin?'

Kevin stood up. He was holding a single sheet of paper. That was a good sign.

'Hi,' he said. 'Glad to see so many of you here. Obviously, the big question we face is how to go forward. What we urgently need is good-quality data. As you know, I'm dealing more with the environmental aspect, so I've requested information both from Marshco themselves and from various local and central government bodies. Marshco, needless to say, have not been very forthcoming.' There was a murmur of laughter. 'Their reply basically deflected all my enquiries, and referred me to the inspectors. The letter mainly talks about the proposed substantial expansion of the whole incineration and landfill operation. We've all known about these plans for a long time because of the coverage in the local press. But let everybody be very clear: we're not facing a company that's on the defensive here. They are planning aggressive expansion and their letter's all about economic opportunities. They talk about a hundred new jobs in the expanded facility.'

A hand had been raised in the audience. A man stood up.

'Do jobs come before people's lives?' he asked, and there was a ripple of applause.

'That's what we're here to find out,' said Kevin. 'It's my view that we're not really going to get very far approaching Marshco directly. So I've been putting out feelers in different directions. Most notably at the Physical Science Department at the university in Worsham. All that's very much at an early stage.'

Feelers. Early stage. That meant he hadn't achieved anything.

He looked at his piece of paper with a furrowed brow, as if there should have been more on it. 'I think that's about it. So I'll pass you on to Hannah. Thanks very much.'

He shuffled awkwardly back towards his chair.

Hannah Mahoney stood up and walked to the far right of the stage to what looked like a painter's easel with a large blank card on it. She dragged it out so it was almost in the centre of the stage and started talking. Her style was passionate, earnest, humourless. Not that a talk about an epidemic of cancer should be mixed with jokes, but still. She talked about the difficulties in defining clusters.

'Our situation is like smoking and cancer fifty years ago. When the first research was being done, the researchers had no knowledge of the science mechanisms involved. Instead they just collected the figures, put them together and through the power of statistics showed without a shadow of a doubt that tobacco was responsible.'

It was difficult to be neutral about Hannah Mahoney. You'd either become a disciple or be irritated beyond belief. Maybe it was the fervency of her tone. In the earlier part of the meeting, the audience had been bustling and fidgeting and murmuring among themselves. But now there was a stillness and a concentration across the hall.

'Although this will sound impersonal,' she continued, 'this is about you and me. About our children. One of our ways forward is to collect the figures and make them compelling, just as the researchers into tobacco and cancer did in the 1940s and 1950s.'

It was indeed all about connecting. If they could associate their cluster in people's minds with tobacco and asbestosis, their battle would be won. The strategy of Marshco and Wortley would be to break the connection and make them seem like cranks and fanatics. Then I caught myself. What was I doing? I wasn't a Wortley shareholder. I was a long way down the feeding chain. I was the one who had been sent ahead of the person who was being sent ahead. I put my feet up on the empty chair in front of me and settled back to enjoy the show.

'What I've been concentrating on,' said Hannah Mahoney, 'is building up a picture of the people who are affected. This isn't the easiest business. I can't just walk into the medical centre and read through the medical records. I started just by asking everybody I knew. As we've progressed, we've got a bit more professional, developing a questionnaire that we can circulate. What we're going to be interested in is the sort of pattern that emerges. There won't be a single killer detail. It doesn't work like that. Imagine dots on a piece of paper. Individually they mean nothing. But as more and more are put on the paper, a picture takes shape, like a body appearing out of a mist. That's what we're doing.

'You've probably been wondering what I've got on my easel here. What I've done is to take the significant illnesses I've found in this area and mark them on a map. Just to be safe, I've eliminated any illness suffered by anyone resident in the area for less than five years. The effects on new arrivals will only show up in ten, fifteen, twenty years. All I've been able to do is to deal with the people I know about, whose histories I'm fairly secure about. The markers on the map I'm going to show you represent, in many cases, unusual forms of cancer. Apart from more familiar kinds, we have liver cancer, various forms of leukaemia, myeloma, sarcomas of the soft tissues, thyroid cancer, lymphomas and a few very rare examples. So here it is.'

She stepped forward and lifted the card. There was an audible gasp in the room.

The map looked as if it had measles. There were clumps of different round stickers, black, red and yellow.

I tried to make a rough count but it was difficult to identify the individual blobs from where I sat. It was clear that there was a large number. Maybe forty. In this village. Suddenly I felt nervous about being here alone. Giles should be here.

Hannah Mahoney sat down and immediately there was a babble of questions and comments from the audience. This was Charles Deane's moment. He stepped forward, holding his hands up, calming people down. He looked at his watch and said that there was a lot for everybody to digest. He fully appreciated that there were many issues to discuss. Rather than continue the meeting any further, he was going to propose that another meeting be held a week today. Was that generally agreed? There were shouts of agreement. Passed *nem con*, he said. Another meeting. He was a happy man.

Mainly people drifted away, still in animated conversation. But some others drifted to the front and I followed them. I saw people talking to Hannah Mahoney; at least a couple of them seemed to know the names of other sick people. More stickers for her chart. I quickly tried to tot up the number of stickers. Suddenly I became aware of a presence behind me and looked round. It was Hannah Mahoney herself. I felt unnerved to have her full attention.

'We haven't met,' she said.

'My name's Mark. Mark Foll.'

'Do you live here?'

I took a deep breath. I'd talked to Giles and we'd agreed that there was going to be no cloak and dagger about our presence in Marston Green. We had nothing to hide, he said. We weren't attempting to sabotage the campaign. We were checking things out. So there was to be no deception. We were to be completely open.

'I live in London,' I said. 'I work in a very junior capacity for Wortley Insurance. They're Marshco's insurance company.'

Before my eyes Hannah Mahoney's friendliness drained from her face and was replaced by suspicion. 'You're a spy from Marshco.'

'I've never had any dealings with anyone from Marshco. I just came up to have a look and see what's happening.'

Hannah's expression hardened still further. 'To see what's happening, eh? You were examining my map. What's your particular field of expertise? Epidemiology?'

'No. I'm a claims investigator. A pretty low-grade one.'

'That's interesting. Is a claim imminent? Are Marshco trying to assess how much they can pay us off with?'

We were getting into very dodgy territory.

'It's nothing like that,' I said. 'The people at Wortley heard about your campaign and they sent me down to have a look.'

'And we're supposed to be grateful for the attention, are we?' Hannah said, sounding angry now. 'Would you like the medical files so you can get some paid medical expert to tear them apart? Or would you like to meet the dying people and con them into signing some sort of release?'

There was an awkward pause. I was going to say, in some sort of high dudgeon, that I didn't do that sort of thing, but then I remembered that I did do that sort of thing.

Hannah's expression softened very slightly. 'Put yourself in my position,' she said. 'What can you do us except harm? What you should do is talk to Kevin. He's the walking encyclopedia on what Marshco have been up to. Hey, Kevin.'

Kevin was much friendlier. He seemed eager to do anything he could for me. I almost felt like telling him not to be so trusting. He suggested a proper meeting.

'I teach at the comp over in Melwarth. Tomorrow I'll be back around five. That sound all right?'

I DIDN'T WANT to be just the guy who had booked the room for Giles. I wanted to be able to tell him something useful. Kevin Seeger seemed perfect for this. The campaign was his hobby, he knew the science of it and also he was a teacher, so he was used to dealing with the ignorant.

He lived in one of the new developments, an enclave called 'Hawthorns' that twisted and curved off the High Street on top of what, ten years ago, must have been a green field.

When his wife, Pam, opened the front door to me, she said in a tone that managed to be at the same time amused, slightly contemptuous and a touch resentful that Kevin was in his study. It was clear she thought that the study ought to be used as a second bedroom for one of the children and in any case Kevin ought to get his arse out of it occasionally and help her with the housework, since she had a job as well. That's the wonderful thing about marriage. You can convey so much in shorthand. When you're single everything takes so long.

I liked Pam, though. She was pretty and tired and slightly sarcastic, and was wearing a red T-shirt that didn't quite reach the waistband of her jeans. I didn't go straight up to Kevin. There didn't seem to be any rush. Maybe I was adjusting to their slower country ways. I went through to the kitchen and she made us some tea. She talked about how she worked in an old people's home but that she was training to be a dental hygienist. It was a growing profession, she said. There was going to be a big demand for dental hygienists.

There was a rumble and thumping from the stairs and Kevin appeared in the doorway.

'Mark,' he said. 'I didn't know you were here.'

'I was on my way up.'

Kevin led me upstairs to the study, which was stuffed to the ceiling with material to do with Marshco and environmental cancer and waste management. There were three filing cabinets and bundles of material on every surface.

'The whole story is in here,' he said. 'It's just a matter of knowing how to find it.' He tapped one of the filing cabinets gently, as if it was the bonnet of a classic car. 'You know, I like being a teacher. But at the level I teach, I'm just passing on a pre-packaged body of pretty basic knowledge. What I've always wanted is to do some really startling original research. So anyway, what do you want to know?'

'I want the story,' I said.

'It's long.'

'I'm in the middle of the countryside,' I said. 'I've got nothing but time.'

Kevin sat me down on his chair, while he paced up and down, apparently collecting his thoughts. 'People have always been concerned about the Marshco complex,' he said. 'We all produce tons of rubbish but we don't like to think of how it's got rid of. A lot of people have vaguely Green ideas about recycling. As far as I'm concerned, recycling is largely bullshit. You know all those bottles you take to the bottle bank? All those newspapers you bundle up? In terms of resource management, you'd be better off burying it in a big hole.'

This was my kind of Green activist. One who didn't believe in doing anything.

'But whatever our point of view,' he continued, 'none of us likes having a rubbish dump in our backyard. Marshco was sprung on Marston Green back in the fifties, without any real consultation. They bought a small dump and gradually expanded it, buying land whenever they could. Over the years there have been rumours of shoddy practice, and there was a prosecution in the eighties for dumping unauthorised waste on the site. When I arrived here a few years ago, I knew about the facility but didn't think much about it. Then I started to hear about the cluster of illnesses in the area. Fiona Jopling, our Green candidate, was the first to make the connection between Marshco and the sickness. A lovely woman, Fiona, but mad as a hatter. She'd done a bit of work on dioxins, in an amateurish sort of way. She showed it to me and I had a look at it to humour her and then I suddenly realised that she had something. A group of us in Marston Green became interested. Some of them have looked at it more from the illness end, like Hannah Mahoney. Me, I'm a scientist and I've done the industrial chemistry.' He gestured around the room. 'It's not a small job. Now, you really want to hear all this?'

'If it's all right with you.'

'I should start by making a very simple point. Industrialists and politicians love incinerators. They take large, bulky, messy rubbish and make it small and neat. But it's not magic. All the process does is effect a chemical transformation. Sometimes a technician at an incinerator will go to a public meeting and produce a plastic box containing eight pounds of ash. He'll say that this is the product of a hundred pounds of garbage. The ash can be buried in a tiny landfill and that's that. To which the simple answer is that another ninety-two pounds has been pumped into the air.'

'Yuck,' I said.

'Exactly. The rearranged molecules of the rubbish can cause all sorts of problems. The buried ash can contaminate the groundwater. And obviously the fumes can do all sorts of harm.'

'Can't they filter the smoke?' I asked.

'Sure,' said Kevin. 'But this doesn't solve the problem. It just rearranges it. The better the filters in the incinerator, the more toxic the ash that remains. There's no way round the law of conservation of matter. During the incineration process, carbon and chlorine atoms rearrange themselves to create molecules of dioxins, and the relatively similar molecules of furans. There are many types of dioxin and furans molecules, but they share some crucial characteristics. . .'

I was starting to feel lost. I wondered if Kevin was lost as well, in a way. I knew too little. He knew too much. While saying something, he was always aware of something else that needed mentioning in order to explain it and sometimes he never got back to the thing he'd started with. Every so often he would rifle through a filing cabinet in search of a particular figure. The narrative then was disrupted even further because it was slightly recast in the order in which he had discovered certain pieces of information. Because this wasn't just the story of a polluting company or of people with cancer. It was the story of a schoolteacher making something of his life.

At one point, I did make an attempt at keeping up by asking a question. 'An enzyme?' I said in a slightly non-questioning way, as if it had only just slipped my mind and I just needed prompting. He paused and, I thought, looked slightly alarmed. It was as if Einstein had been giving someone a highly advanced description of the theory of relativity and had been suddenly interrupted with the question: 'By the way, that word "multiplied", what exactly does it mean?'

Kevin thought for a moment. 'An enzyme is a complex protein,' he said, 'produced by living cells. It promotes specific biochemical reactions without undergoing change itself. The point in this context is that the dioxin molecules are exceptionally stable and can't be broken down by the enzymes.'

'Right,' I said, nodding. That hadn't helped at all. As his dioxin narrative washed over me, with little whirlpools and rapids and tributaries here and there, I began to think about what it must be like to drown. You'd struggle and struggle for breath, and it would get more and more tiring. Maybe the effort would suddenly be too much, but then there would be the relief as you slipped under the water and descended into darkness. That's what it was like, me and Kevin in his study full of papers and filing cabinets. With a feeling of calm, I gave up any attempt to follow what he was saying.

He must have noticed something was wrong. 'Is this too technical?' he said.

For about a quarter of a second, I thought of saying, no, please go on, we're just getting to the good bit. Then I said, 'I'm sorry, Kevin, but you've lost me.'

'At what point?'

'I'm too lost even to know.'

He looked crestfallen. 'Should I go over it again?'

'It's not you,' I said. 'It's me. I should have explained in advance that I'm an ignoramus. My colleague, more specifically my boss, is arriving tomorrow and apart from being generally more intelligent than I am he's a trained scientist. I'll put you two together and you'll be talking the same language. The only thing I'd say in my defence is that at some point you're going to have to tell your story to an idiot like me—a lawyer or someone from an insurance company—and those sorts of people didn't study anything except Latin at school. You're going to have to come up with a simpler version.'

'You're probably right,' he said. 'But I sometimes wonder if you can reduce real science to the sort of evidence you can present in a courtroom.' His expression turned serious. 'Maybe we'll lose,' he said. 'But the fact will remain that I will be on the right side and you'll be on the wrong side.'

'I'm not on any side,' I said. 'I'm too low grade.'

'You can't hide behind that,' he said.

When he said that, I was sure he was wrong. The way I saw it, I wanted to observe the different sides in Marston Green, and I had the idea I could somehow remain impartial while doing it.

He walked me down to the front door. We shook hands.

It was such a relief to get outside again. It was a warm, bright evening, with only streaks of cloud in the sky and birds circling, far, far up. There was a light wind blowing that must—if I had understood at least part of Kevin's talk correctly—have contained an unhealthy dose of dioxins and furans from the Marshco plant.

As I entered the High Street I saw Hannah Mahoney coming towards me. She was wearing tight jeans that came halfway down her calves and a white sweater with green and blue hoops, and she was accompanied by a small boy. She didn't recognise me at first because

I was walking with the evening sun behind me, so I could watch her in conversation with the boy, who had a small ball that he was throwing up and catching, not very expertly. Once it bobbled out into the road and she ventured out into the dangerous flow of traffic to retrieve it. That was what they really should have protested about. All day and all night heavy lorries drove along the narrow High Street, travelling to and from the container ports further down south.

Hannah recognised me when we were just a few yards apart. 'Oh?' she said. 'It's er . . .'

'Mark,' I said. 'Mark Foll. We talked at the meeting.'

I felt a bit awkward. She was the most impressive person involved in the campaign and I hadn't made the most brilliant impression when we met.

'Is that your little brother?'

She looked puzzled. 'Are you joking? He's my son.'

'I was just being nice.'

A sarcastic expression came over her face. 'Oh, I get it. That's a really suave line.'

'It's not a line,' I said.

'This is Bruce.'

'Hello,' I said. Bruce didn't seem aware of my existence. He was trying to pull a thread out of his tennis ball. I turned back to Hannah. 'I've just been at Kevin's. I got the talk. Well, some of it. It was a bit tricky to follow.'

'So what did you expect?' she said. 'Did you think you could just breeze in and learn everything you needed to know about this complicated and controversial subject in an evening?'

'Do *you* understand all the science?'

'I know what I need to know.'

'All right,' I said, thinking desperately. 'What's the difference between a dioxin and a, er, furans?'

She gave a sour laugh. 'I'm not going to stand in the street and answer a half-arsed pub quiz by someone from an insurance company.'

'I'm not "from an insurance company".'

'Aren't you?'

'As it happens I am, sure, but you make it sound as if that's all I am.'

Bruce was tugging at her sleeve.

'I'd better go.'

'Hannah, do you think Kevin is going to convince anybody?'

'It's not a question of convincing anybody. Kevin is assembling data. It needs to be scientifically robust.'

'I wonder if anyone apart from Kevin will ever look at it.'

'There's a lot of it, admittedly,' said Hannah.

'From your point of view it needs to be simple,' I said. 'Are these dioxins or whatever they are dangerous? Are they causing the illness? Those are simple questions. I assume it will be Marshco's aim to drown everybody in data, not yours.'

Hannah looked at me more keenly. 'Whose side are you on, Mark?'

'I'm just having fun in the country.'

Her face hardened again. 'There are people dying in this village.'

Fuck. Wrong direction. 'Sorry. Anyway, don't judge anything by me. My boss is coming tomorrow. He's clever. He's a scientist.'

'So you're just the pretty face of the company,' she said, and then stopped herself, looking embarrassed. 'I mean the *public* face of the company.' Bruce's tugging was now impossible to resist. 'See you.'

I was left wondering if there was anyone I'd met in Marston Green in front of whom I hadn't made a fool of myself. Geoff Otley, maybe. And that pig farmer.

5

The next evening, Giles's BMW purred into the parking bay outside the Four Feathers. When he got out of the car, I saw he was wearing jeans, a checked shirt and scuffed brown shoes.

'You'll see that I'm dressed for the country,' he said. 'No gentleman wears brown shoes in London. That's what they always used to say.' He opened the rear door and took out a leather hold-all and a bright new pair of Wellington boots. 'I should probably have brought a tweed jacket and a cravat,' he said. 'For sherry with the vicar.'

'I'm not sure if there is a vicar,' I said.

I took him over to Dobbin, his chalet, and he seemed moderately satisfied. I filled him in on what I'd seen at the meeting and then I walked him over to Kevin Seeger's house.

I had intended to escape but Pam made tea for me and I stood and talked to her in the kitchen. I asked her if she knew Hannah Mahoney.

'She's Daniel's teacher. That's our nine-year-old. She's been away, but people think she's very good.'

'What does her husband do?'

'She's not married,' said Pam. 'I've never seen her with anyone.'

I'd got through a couple of mugs of tea before Kevin and Giles came down the stairs. Giles had a grimly polite smile as he said goodbye and I led him back to the Four Feathers. I promised that I would do a supermarket shop but suggested that in the meantime we could try Geoff's food.

Giles ordered cod and chips and I ordered a steak and kidney pie and a salad and two pints of beer.

When Giles's fish arrived, he cheered up very slightly. 'Like being a bachelor again,' he said. He picked at his food with his fork and took a taste. 'I was about to do my rant about shameful food in English pubs,' he said. 'But this isn't bad.'

'I talked to Geoff about it. A van comes from the coast every morning. His wife, Jan, sometimes does the fish Thai style.'

'At least it's fresh. A few years ago, I went for a walk with Sue, in the days when I still went for walks with Sue, and . . .'

'Giles,' I said. 'I don't want to intrude, but is everything all right? With you. With you and Sue. Generally.'

Giles looked puzzled, as if the thought had never occurred to him before. 'I'll give you the short answer,' he said. 'You know how when you buy a suit that doesn't quite fit and you tell yourself you'll get it altered and it'll be fine. Then about a year later you trip over it because the trouser legs keep dragging over your heel and you think, oh fuck, I never got around to it, and at that point you can either decide to put up with the trouser legs dragging or you can get rid of the suit?'

'Why not get it altered?'

'It's too late. By that time the fabric has faded and you can't get the creases out any more.'

'I'm not sure about that. I found this suit a few months ago that I hadn't worn for over a year. I took it to this little guy round the corner and he did the most amazing job on it.'

'This isn't a conversation about tailoring, Mark,' Giles said.

'I know that,' I said. 'I was just trying to say that there are different options.'

'To get away from the fucking suit for a moment,' said Giles, 'we did this walk on the Kent coast. It was real Dickens country, lobster pots and barges and old oyster beds. A very cold, sunny afternoon. We walked along the sand and arrived at an old pub on the edge of a promontory. It was called something like the Smuggler's Arms. We sat on the decking outside and we ordered fish. We could almost have leaned over from our table and lifted the fish out of the water. And I saw the woman behind the bar open a fridge, tear open two plastic bags and put them in the microwave and that was our fish and chips. It was a formative moment in creating my attitude to England and the English countryside. Unfair and irrelevant, of course, since this is really quite good. On the other hand, I don't know what it is with the Thai thing. They ought to rediscover their heritage. Beef and oyster pie. Chitterlings. How's your pie?'

'Great,' I said. 'Very traditional. So how was Kevin?'

'I'm a biologist, so it wasn't exactly my field.'

'But you know what an enzyme is,' I said.

'Yeah, I heard about you and enzymes,' said Giles. 'By the way, what did you think of Mrs Seeger?'

'You mean Pam?'

'It's Pam now, is it? I could see she had her eye on you.'

'Don't be daft, Giles,' I said. 'She's married.'

'What does that matter? Meeting someone like Mrs Seeger plays a bit to the fantasies I have about provincial life. People think it's all very respectable and prim out here, but it's the opposite. All wife-swapping and adultery.'

'Where do you get this information from?'

'You read about it. Hasn't it occurred to you that here we are, two men, away from home, in a strange place, amusing, intelligent, not unattractive . . . For example, look at those two young women over there.' Two admittedly good-looking women, around twenty, one blonde, one brown-haired, were indeed sitting at the far end of the bar. 'If we were real men, we'd be wandering over there and buying them a drink.'

This was becoming ridiculous. 'Giles, Mrs Seeger just saw me as this lonely, slightly pathetic person stuck out on his own in a new place. And thought I'd like a cup of tea.'

'That's one way of putting it,' he said.

Giles seemed like a man who didn't spend very much of his life in pubs and now that he was in one he was going to talk in the way he assumed that men are supposed to.

'You were going to tell me about your meeting with Kevin,' I said.

'Oh, that,' he said reluctantly. 'It's funny about men, isn't it? Some of them build conservatories and some of them construct cathedrals out of matches and Kevin has spent two and half years of evenings and weekends doing an unofficial doctorate in solid-waste incineration. And you know the funny thing? He's never actually seen an incinerator. You'd think he might have wandered around at an open day and had a look, but they probably don't have open days at incinerators. If Marshco had any sense at all, they'd give old Kev a ring and invite him for a wander around the plant with their technical director. Kevin would see these strange furnaces that he's been fantasising about at night and see that it's a pretty ordinary industrial complex which could probably do with a tweak here and there. And he'd go away satisfied.'

'Yes, but is he right? Are these dioxins in the air giving people cancer?'

Giles pushed his plate aside. 'I'm not sure. There seems to be general agreement that if you take a lump of it and shove it up a guinea pig's arse then the outlook isn't too good, but beyond that, there's been a debate.'

'Isn't there a way of knowing, one way or the other? I mean of proving that there is a connection. Or that there isn't.'

'Oh, I see. You've got this confused with pure mathematics. Almost every other kind of science is basically a mess. What you have is a whole lot of different data, some of it contradictory, some of it dodgy, most of it controversial. Also you've got different *kinds* of data, some of which are more relevant than others. What you try to do is to put it together in a way that makes some kind of sense.'

'So what are we actually going to do?'

We had our coffee now and Giles drained his cup. 'In the medium term,' he said, 'my plan is that we do almost nothing. We prepare an interim report. "Interim" means that we do it quickly and don't come to any conclusions. Since this is a really amazing opportunity for us both to fuck up and get fired, the real task is to get back to London without anyone realising we've been away. However, the one thing Donna told me we really have to do is to look at the Marshco site. You know, due diligence and all that. So we're going there at noon tomorrow. Are you up for that?'

'Great,' I said. 'Not that I think I'm going to be able to look at an incinerator and spot a dodgy valve or whatever.'

Giles laughed, which was a welcome change. 'It's never like that.

And now I'm going to bed, and we're going to leave those lovely young women over there without talking to them.'

'What's the big deal?' I said. 'If you want to talk to them, let's go over and talk to them.'

'Are you serious?'

'Sure.'

'No, it would be gross. Don't women have a right to sit and talk in a public place without being hit on by two predatory men? Anyway, I'm physically and psychologically incapable. I've had girlfriends and relationships of different kinds and not a single one of them came about because I walked up to someone I didn't know.'

'How did you meet them, then?'

'I worked with them. Or they were friends of friends. There was always a way I got to know them that had nothing sexual about it, and then that came as a bonus. I've always felt sorry for attractive women being looked at and hassled. I thought they could do without me on their back as well.'

'Rubbish,' I said. 'That's just an excuse. Have I told you about my sister?'

'No,' said Giles. 'I thought you were an orphan left on a doorstep.'

'I remember when she was fifteen and I was fourteen she said I should ask some girl out. She was called Fiona Seaton and she had hair that was so blonde you could almost see it in the dark. I said absolutely no way, she'll just laugh. Val said she's not a different species from you. She's just a girl, she's a bit shy, she doesn't have a boyfriend but she'd like one, and it's not a big deal. When she said that, it was like a window opened.'

'So did you ask her out?'

'Yes. It turned out that she already had a boyfriend. But it didn't matter. I'd done the difficult bit. Then I asked Samantha Mitton out and she said yes. And so I'm going to go over to those women at the bar to talk to them.'

Giles held up his arm. 'And then there's point two.' He looked embarrassed now. 'I'm married. I suppose I could put a sticking plaster over my wedding ring, but instead I'm now going to my bed in a place I can't quite believe is called "Dobbin". I'll see you at breakfast,' he said and then left the room.

I looked across at the two young women sitting at the bar. One of them—the blonde one—caught my eye and then said something to her companion and laughed. I stood up and walked over to them. They turned round and looked at me with an expression of surprise.

'Hi,' I said. 'I'm in Marston Green for my work. I'm doing some research and I need to talk to some typical residents of the village. Would it be all right if I asked you some questions?'

'Like what?' said the blonde one.

'Is it all right if I sit down?' I said. They shrugged. 'Can I get you a drink? Don't worry. It all goes on expenses.'

They both ordered Bacardi Breezers and I had a bottle of cold beer.

The blonde one was called Sandy Yates and the brown-haired one was called Linda Perry. They were both catering students over at Worsham but they lived in Marston Green with their parents.

I explained that I was in Marston Green doing research about the Marshco incinerator.

'My dad works there,' said Sandy.

'That's interesting,' I said. 'What does he do?'

She shrugged. 'I don't know,' she said. 'But he's an engineer.'

'What I really want to know is what *you* think about it.'

It turned out they didn't think all that much about it, really. I asked if they had heard about people getting ill in the village. They looked at each other.

'There's always people getting ill,' said Sandy. 'But it doesn't have to do with anything.'

Did they like living in Marston Green? That made them laugh.

'It's a right old dump,' said Linda. 'There's sod all to do. You should see it on a Saturday night in the summer. The kids just hang about the bus shelter. They come up from Hyland and Worsham to deal. You know, drugs.'

'Yeah,' I said. 'I knew what you were talking about.'

I'm only twenty-six. They were talking to me as if I was their geography teacher.

They looked at each other. Linda said she had to go. She said she had to meet her boyfriend. Sandy stayed where she was. Linda raised an eyebrow, suspiciously, and left us.

I bought Sandy another Bacardi Breezer and a beer for myself. Now that Linda had gone, Sandy turned and looked me directly in the eyes. She smiled. She was wearing more make-up than her pretty, rounded, pink face needed, and a tight red T-shirt with puffed-up, very short sleeves. I asked her why she was living at home with her parents. She said that if she left home she'd probably get settled and she didn't want to get settled around Marston Green. Her plan was to finish her course and then get a job in London.

'So what is it you're doing up here?'

'I told you,' I said. 'There are people getting ill in Marston Green. Some people say it's because of the incinerator plant. We're here to see if there's anything in it. We're the insurance company.'

She took a sip from her drink and looked mischievous. 'I've always thought that insurance was boring. It's just stuff you don't want to know about filling in forms and people knocking at the door trying to sell you life policies.'

'I don't do that sort of thing. I'm a claims investigator.'

'What's that?'

'It's hard to say,' I said. 'It's a bit like a private detective. There's a lot of money involved in insurance, and some people fake fires or burglaries or accidents. If there's a claim that looks suspicious, then we go in and investigate it.'

Her eyes widened. 'Is that ever dangerous?'

I gave a shrug. 'You need to develop a feel for situations,' I said. 'An instinct.'

'What do you feel about Marston Green?'

'We've only just got started.'

'My dad thinks the protests are stupid. Maybe you should talk to him.'

'Maybe I will. We're going up to the plant tomorrow.'

'He's called Steven Yates. Steve, people call him.'

'I'll look out for him.'

It was eleven o'clock and Geoff was starting to clear up. Everybody else had gone.

'So where are you staying?' she said.

'In one of the chalets out the back.'

'Those stables? Can I come and have a look?'

'Sure,' I said.

We walked out of the pub the back way. I opened the door of Clover and we stepped inside.

'There we are,' I said, as I put the light on and closed the door behind us. 'A beautiful work of conversion.'

Often at this moment there is awkwardness. But Sandy moved herself against me and looked up so it was really only giving in to gravity when I let my face down on hers and kissed her. I thought: how good not to be married, like Giles. How good to be out here in the country, away from everything.

I HADN'T CLOSED the curtains and we were both woken before five the next morning by the sun through the window, hot on us on the bed.

'Mark,' she said. 'Have you got a girlfriend? In London.'

'No,' I said.

'Are you looking for one?'

Everything had seemed simple the previous night, and in the bright morning light it seemed even clearer.

'No, I'm not,' I said.

'Oh,' she said. 'Right.' She got out of bed, walked naked across the room into the toilet then came back into the bedroom and started to pick up her clothes. For some reason this made me feel sad, the sight of her looking around on the floor for socks and knickers. She pulled her clothes on, not looking at me. She looked lovelier than she had the night before, the sun making her features look sculpted.

When she was done, she came and sat on the bed by me. 'We could have done stuff, while you were here.'

'I'm going to be busy,' I said.

'Yeah,' she said.

And with that she was gone.

GILES SMILED cheerfully as I got into the car. 'So did you go over and talk to those two girls?'

'Yes, I did.'

'How did it go?'

'Fine.'

'How long did you talk for?'

'Quite a long time. One of them, Linda, the brown-haired one, had to go.'

'So you talked to the blonde.'

'That's right. Her dad works at the incinerator.'

'Really?' said Giles. He didn't sound particularly interested. 'But what I want to know is what you actually did.'

I gave a casual jerk of my shoulders that was meant to show that we ought to get on with our work.

'Oh, no,' he said. 'You didn't?' He looked across at me. 'You did. You bloody did. Oh, no. While I was lying miserably in bed counting sheep and thinking about dioxins. What was it like?'

'Giles, I'm not going to say anything.'

'You've got to tell me. I exist in a state of sexual deprivation. Even hearing about it would be something.'

'You're married.'

He banged the steering wheel with his hands. 'All right. Just one question. I just want to know, just in case—God forbid—Susan should be run over by a truck and I should find myself a single man again, what was the magic first sentence?'

'I just went over and said something stupid like, I was working in the area and wanted to ask them some questions about it.'

'Is that it?' said Giles. 'I could have thought of that. Does that one always work for you?'

'I don't have a line. They wanted to talk. I talked to them.'

'So you're saying that the best line is the line that doesn't seem like a line.'

'No. I'm saying that there's no such thing as a line.'

'That's quite Zen. The only line is not to have a line.'

'Maybe the line is not to want to have sex with women. It's wanting to talk to them.'

'You mean as a way of having sex with them?'

I looked at my watch. 'I think we've reached a dead end,' I said.

'An interesting dead end, though,' said Giles. 'To be resumed. I suppose we'd better get going.'

We drove a few miles out of Marston Green and turned off down a side road. We drove along a perimeter fence for more than half a mile before we got to the main gate. In fact, there were two sets of gates, one for cars and the other for the trucks that were driving in and out.

We gave our names at the first gate and were told to go to the car park at Block D. Two men were waiting for us there. Paul Creek was the technical services manager—basically the manager of the whole operation—a tall, broad-shouldered man with greying hair, neatly parted. Graham Bittles was the operational manager, heavy set, with large, rough hands. Creek welcomed us and said that we could go in for a coffee and then we could get the tour.

They led us up the stairs of a modern office block to a bare room. There was a Thermos flask of coffee, a jug of milk and a tin of biscuits on a table. Creek collected cups from a sideboard and served us all. I chose a chair that looked out of the window over what was unquestionably a rubbish dump. A flock of seagulls scattered whenever a lorry came near.

'That's the biggest rubbish dump I've ever seen,' I said.

Paul Creek smiled. 'We've got seventy acres of landfill operative on this site at the moment. And as you know, we hope that that's only the beginning. Now, gents, I just wanted to say that we're delighted to have you here, and you have completely open access. We'd say you could wander off where you want, but frankly we've got some nasty stuff around and most of it won't make sense to you without having someone like Graham here with you. Is that all right?'

'That's fine,' said Giles. I could already see that his manner was completely different from what it had been in the car. 'I know you've talked to our head office. I'm sure Donna Kiely told you that this should all be routine. I don't want you to see us as inspectors. We're on your side and what we don't want is any surprises. If there is something dodgy you know of, some problem you had that is now solved, then please let us know.'

Creek and Bittles looked puzzled.

'I don't know what to say, Giles,' said Creek. 'We're in waste management. We deal with hazardous materials and there are constant technical challenges. But we're all genuinely baffled by these protests in Marston Green. When Graham takes you round, he'll show you how refined our incinerating process has become. One of the major problems the world faces is what to do with rubbish, and I think we're dealing with it in a more responsible—dare I say Greener—way than almost anyone else in western Europe.'

It was very unfair, but I was becoming very slightly irritated by Paul Creek. I felt he was trying to sell me something.

'So why don't we have the guided tour?' said Giles.

'Lovely,' said Creek, looking a little dissatisfied. We probably hadn't reached the end of the talk he had prepared. 'We'll go down.'

On the way down, we were given pristine orange overalls, which we put on over our clothes, and yellow hardhats.

In the car park a minibus with a driver was waiting. We got in and set off, driving along past the stinking, rotting remains of the last few weeks' chuck-outs from quite a slab of south-east England. Paul Creek was looking at it with a sort of fascination.

'I love rubbish. I always have. I like making fires at home. We spend weeks piling up branches and old cardboard boxes at the end of the garden. I pretend it's for the children but really it's for me. I love it when the first crackles turn into an inferno. And I love reusing anything that can possibly be reused. I regard it as a personal defeat to throw a household item away. It drives my wife up the wall. But my real hobby is composting. Do you compost?'

I said no. Giles didn't speak. He was looking out of the window.

'It's one of the great pleasures of life,' Creek went on. 'Within a few months you can turn your old teabags and grass and eggshells into a loamy chocolatey compost that you almost want to eat. Here we are.'

We pulled up at an industrial building. It was huge, like an ocean liner. From the top rose a huge metal container and a tall chimney, also of metal. At the far end, forklift trucks and lorries and vans were driving in and out. Fifty feet above there was a crane moving on rails.

'Hats on,' said Graham Bittles.

He was different from his colleague. Paul Creek seemed like the sort of person you'd find running a stall at a trade fair. He'd give you a T-shirt and a pen and you'd try and swat him off like a fly. Graham Bittles was more like a man just doing a job.

'This is the basic incinerator facility,' he said.

Giles whispered in my ear. 'Do you ever notice that everything in the world has become a facility. It can't just be a plain old incinerator.'

Graham didn't hear him and continued with his explanation. 'That there at the end is the storage. We can keep three days' supply of solid waste. You see the bridge crane? That lifts the waste into the feed hopper. Hang on a second.'

He walked across to say something to a man operating a hoist. Just a few yards away two men were struggling with the hydraulic lift behind the cab of a lorry. I wandered over.

'How you doing?' I said. They looked round and nodded at me. 'I'm just getting the guided tour. We're doing some enquiries into pollution.'

One of them laughed. 'Pollution?' he said. 'In this place? It's all fucking pollution, mate.'

'Either of you know Steve Yates?'

'Steve,' said the man. 'He works the cabs. You want to see him?'

'No, I'll see him sooner or later,' I said. 'He's sort of a friend of a friend.' I noticed that Bittles was back. 'I'll see you.'

Bittles took us up some steel steps and through a door. We were in a large corridor. Above us it looked as if railway transport cars were suspended upside down.

'Right above these,' Bittles said, 'is the combustion chamber and these are the ash-removal containers. The solid waste is fed in at one end and it's inclined down into the combustion chambers, then into the subsidence chamber—the dust collector—and then finally into the stacks.'

Paul Creek was hovering eagerly. 'But, Graham, tell them how the process has been improved. We've got to make it clear that it's not just a bonfire we're talking about.'

'Right,' said Graham. 'People might think that an incinerator is like a furnace in a crematorium. You shove whatever it is in the furnace and it burns and the smoke goes up the chimney and you shovel out the ash. But if you do that with these quantities of solid waste, then the ash clogs up the machine and the chimney fills up and then there's the pollution. So a new model we have here removes the ash. It burns the exit gases and at the same time there's the wet scrubbers that remove the fly ash from the exit gases. So what goes up the stack is almost nothing.'

Giles got into an intent conversation with Bittles about a piece of machinery called an inclined rotary kiln and I drifted away. I walked along the corridor and out of an open door that led back out into the sunshine. The smell was appalling. After a while the others followed.

Creek was talking urgently. 'But the really good thing is that the next stage—and this is part of the proposed expansion—is to use the exit gases to generate electricity. We'll be less and less polluting, we'll be creating energy out of what just went up the chimney. And there's jobs as well. We'll be employing almost two hundred more people. Who could possibly object to that?'

'Have you never thought of reaching out a bit to the local community?' said Giles. 'Open days. Parties of schoolchildren. Inviting your critics over to discuss their concerns.'

Creek shook his head. 'There are health and safety issues,' he said. 'You're an insurance man. Could we get insurance for a party of toddlers running around here?'

'You can get insurance for anything,' Giles said.

Suddenly Creek looked serious. 'We've got a business to run. We're not a theme park. This protest is crap. It's a few people with a grievance. What we need is for them to go away. As you said, you're on our side. Can't you make that happen?'

As we drove away, Giles was looking cheerful again. 'Interesting problem, incineration. They've made some imaginative advances. Didn't you like all those machines, that activity?'

'I had a problem with the smell.'

'That's not them,' said Giles. 'They're not manufacturing the rubbish. We are.'

'So are you letting them off the hook?'

'I don't know if they're even on a hook. But that's not our business. We'll sniff around a bit and then head back to London. Nice place, though, the waste facility.'

And so we drove back to Marston Green, with the smell following us downwind and Giles talking about it with more enthusiasm than I'd ever heard from him.

I TRIED to look up Hannah Mahoney's phone number but it wasn't in the book. I walked out into the High Street, noticed the post van parked outside the village shop and walked in to find Dave the postman drinking a mug of tea with the woman behind the counter. See that? Dave the postman. In my entire life I'd never known the name of a postman before. Now I regularly talked to Dave in the morning, even though I'd only had two letters from Wortley while I'd been in Marston Green.

I told Dave that I had something I wanted to drop off at Hannah Mahoney's. Could he tell me where she lived?

'No problem,' he said. He even drew me a map.

It was half-past four, school would be finished, so I walked along the High Street and turned right up a narrow lane. There was a line of cottages, and the third was where Hannah Mahoney lived. It was whitewashed stone with a thatched roof. I knocked at the door. She opened it and looked puzzled, and not especially pleased. I was getting used to the slightly sarcastic expression that she reserved especially for me. She was wearing jeans and a man's shirt, with the sleeves rolled up to just below her elbow.

'Sorry for just appearing on your doorstep,' I said. 'I just want to ask you something.'

She gave a sigh. 'What?'

'My boss, Giles Buckland, has arrived.'

'Yes, I heard.'

'Anyway, we went up to the site and looked around.'

'What did you think?'

'I don't know,' I said. 'I don't think I could tell a good rubbish dump from a bad one. In any case, it only gives us a partial view of what's happening. I was wondering if I could come here with Giles and we could have a proper talk.'

'How can I do my cause anything but harm by talking to you and your boss about it? What your company wants is for this campaign to go away. Why should I clue you in on what I'm up to?'

'I've talked to Kevin and I've looked at the incinerator and I've heard their spiel, and the only really impressive thing I've seen so far is your map. I don't know much about your campaign and I've got no authority here at all. All I can say is that if there's anybody who can lean on Marshco, it's Wortley.'

She looked undecided, which was better.

'I can send Giles on his own,' I said. 'If you prefer.'

'I can look after myself,' she said. 'Even if I'm outnumbered.' A smile appeared on her face. 'Sandy's pissed off with you.'

For a moment I was completely baffled. 'What?'

'Her sister works part time at the school. So what is this? A sort of Club Med holiday? You think you're in Ibiza?'

I took a deep breath, conscious that my face had gone deep crimson.

'Sandy seemed very nice,' I said. 'I don't want to say anything.'

'There aren't many young women in Marston Green. You should be careful with them. I don't mind you and Giles coming. Come at seven. Bruce will have eaten and be pretty much ready for bed.'

WHEN WE arrived back at seven, Bruce was running around the living room. This was a perilous thing to do because the whole ground floor was polished boards with rugs dotted around. Whenever Bruce's feet hit a rug, the rug followed him. Giles and I sat awkwardly clutching mugs of coffee. Hannah was clearing the supper things away and wiping surfaces.

Suddenly Bruce halted in front of us and said: 'How many ears does Davy Crockett have?'

'Two?' said Giles in mock puzzlement.

'Three,' said Bruce. 'A left ear, a right ear and a wild frontier. Wassa wild frontier?'

'That's a hard one,' said Giles. 'A frontier is a border between two countries. There was a frontier between the cowboy country and the Indian country. Davy Crockett used to fight against the Indians a lot. So there's a song that calls him "King of the Wild Frontier".'

'And now it's time for bed,' Hannah said. 'Say good night, Bruce.'

She took him by the hand and led him up the narrow staircase.

I stood up and looked around the room. There weren't many things in it, apart from quite a lot of paperbacks on a shelf. I was hoping there would be some photographs but there was just one, Hannah with longer hair and a much younger Bruce on a beach in bright sunshine. I wondered who the photographer was. I picked it up and looked more closely.

'She's not married,' I said. 'No sign of a man anywhere around in the house, that I can see. I wonder if she's gay.'

'Why don't you ask me?' Hannah said.

I put the picture back with amazing control. It would have been quite possible for me to have dropped it and then the situation would have been just a little bit worse.

'Maybe you can tell from the decoration of my house,' Hannah said. 'Is it basically heterosexual, or is there a touch of dyke-ishness about it?'

'I'm trying to think of something to say,' I said.

'Mark is normally good at thinking of things to say,' Giles said. 'With women.'

'Thanks, Giles.'

'I've heard,' said Hannah. 'Now maybe we should get a move on.' Giles and I were sitting on the sofa. She pulled a hard-backed chair over and sat on it. 'You'll understand that I'm going to be a bit cautious talking to you. Anything I show will reveal a strength or a weakness in our case, and either way that will help you and harm our campaign.'

Giles rubbed his face. 'In an ideal world, what is it you want?'

'We're not in an ideal world,' said Hannah. 'We're in a messy, contradictory world. What do we want? We're trying to formulate that at the moment. I don't speak for the victims, but I suppose it will include a proper inquiry into the damage done by that incinerator, a discovery of where the responsibility lies, reform so it can't happen again, and some kind of compensation. But nobody believes that compensation will come in time for the majority of them. I think what most of them want is for someone to stand up and say: "It was our fault and we're sorry."'

There was a silence. Hannah's face had gone very pale, with just pricks of red around her cheekbones. Her dark eyes showed fiercely against her pale skin. 'More coffee?' she asked.

'Yes, thanks, that would be good,' said Giles and I just nodded. Giles asked where the lavatory was and Hannah pointed to a door at the far end of the house from the kitchen. They returned at the same moment, Giles looking ill at ease and sombre.

'I can't do much to dispel your worries about us,' he said. 'Obviously we haven't come to town to help your campaign. All

I can say is that we're not here to campaign against you. We're not here to have any influence of any kind. Could you tell us what you've been doing?'

She filled our coffee mugs. 'Mark must have told you. I've been gathering information about illnesses in this area. Then I've put them on a map to see if there is a pattern.'

'There's a problem with that . . .' Giles began.

'There are lots of problems,' she said. 'One is that it's hard to see a pattern if it's only in one place. And if the dioxins emitted from the incinerator are causing the cancers, then it's crucial that we research all areas downwind of the plant. So I've been extending my search into similar-sized communities that are further away and in other directions. We've sent out questionnaires in five other communities, in what is basically a continuous strip running north-east from here.'

'What's your response rate?' asked Giles.

'We only sent them out a few weeks ago, but it seems to be quite high, and about the same level in each community.'

'And then?'

'The plan is to plot it on the map, the way I did for Marston Green, and then maybe a compelling pattern will emerge.'

'Could I have a copy of the chart you made of the Marston Green illness?'

'Sorry,' said Hannah. 'One of the promises I've made to people who've responded is that their anonymity will be protected. In the end, I would like to make the information public. But I've got to think of how best to do it.'

'You showed it at a public meeting.'

'I know. I thought it was important for people to have a look at what we were talking about. But I was careful to keep it anonymous.'

'Can I at least have a look?'

She looked thoughtful. 'Why not?'

She got up and left the room and returned with her large piece of card. She propped it up on the edge of the sofa.

Giles looked at it in silence, his eyes screwed up. 'And these are . . . what?'

'Leukaemias, multiple myeloma, lymphomas, lung cancer, breast cancer, bone cancer, bowel cancer. A range.'

'Mark was right,' Giles said. 'That's startling. You've done a remarkable job, Hannah. It's the most interesting thing I've seen since I got here.'

'What about Kevin?' said Hannah. 'What about that mass of information he's gathered?'

'I don't know.' Giles rubbed his face with his hands again as if it was all too much for him. 'I think Mark told you that I was a sort of scientist, years ago. When I started out I used to think that when we did science we were finding out about reality. What I came to see is that it was nothing like that. What we were doing, in effect, was building bridges and sometimes the bridges stay up and you can use them, and sometimes the bridge falls over and you assume something must have been wrong so you build the next bridge in a different way. Kevin's trying to find out how the world works. Maybe he's right, maybe he's wrong. But you've given us figures we can work with. That's what I like about your map.' He looked directly at Hannah. 'Would it be possible to meet any of the victims?'

Hannah looked startled by this. 'What for?' she said.

'We want to gauge the feelings of people in the village.'

Hannah looked uncomfortable. 'I'll have to think about that. These people are in a very vulnerable state.'

'We're aware of that.'

'And I'm worried about them being picked off individually.'

'Hannah, I can promise you that we're not empowered in any way to negotiate with anybody on behalf of Marshco or the insurers.'

She stared at him. 'Then what is the point of you being here at all?' she said. 'You come in here and you're being all sensitive and "I feel your pain", and as soon as anything actually arises, then you're sorry but you're not empowered.'

There was a pause. I certainly wasn't going to say anything. Hannah scared me. I'd never met a woman who scared me like that before.

'I'd never say anything as crass as "I feel your pain". If you think about it, how could we possibly arrive and start negotiating? What meaning would that have for anybody?'

'You're probably right,' she said. 'I'm oversensitive on the subject.'

'We'll go,' said Giles, and she ushered us over to the door. She opened it for us, showing another golden evening outside.

'So you think I'm gay, do you?'

'I hope not,' I said.

'What?' she said. 'What do you mean?'

My mind went horribly blank. Worse than blank. It was a black hole which sucked up words and thoughts and obliterated them. 'Er, well, you've got a child.'

That was a stupid start.

'A child? Oh, I see.'

'But obviously,' I added, 'I hope you're happy whatever you are.'

She closed the door without saying anything more.

GILES AND I sat in the garden behind the Four Feathers with our beer and our sandwiches. I hadn't got to the supermarket yet, so we were still depending on Geoff Otley.

The garden looked out on a scrubby piece of field behind the pub. Bunches of gnats, blurred like smoke, were caught in the evening sun. Swallows were swooping and circling, feeding on the insects. For me it wasn't a peaceful, rural scene. The swallows were like fighters, F16s coming in low. A magpie sat on a fence pole and then I saw that the swallows were attacking it at high speed, diving and then curving away, missing it by a couple of inches. The magpie flapped noisily away.

Giles took a sip of his beer. 'Your lines are getting worse.'

'What do you mean?'

' "I hope you're happy, whatever you are." Even I could do better than that.'

I took a bite of my sandwich. Good, strong cheese with pickle, a doorstop-size hunk of fresh white bread.

'For a start, Giles, it's not a line. I don't have lines. And secondly we were there interviewing her about people dying of cancer.'

'It's the best way of meeting women,' Giles said. 'When your mind is meant to be on other things. What do you think of her?'

This wasn't the conversation I'd thought we were going to be having. 'What do I think of her? I don't think that our meeting went particularly well.'

'I think she's wonderful,' said Giles. 'She's really my type. Intelligent, forceful, beautiful.'

'She's not *that* beautiful,' I said.

'Not beautiful?' said Giles. 'Who's beautiful? Oh, you mean your floozy, Sandy?'

'Will you stop it with Sandy, for fuck's sake? But yes, Sandy is more obviously pretty, I guess.'

Giles took a gulp of beer and gave a little burp. 'This is what I like,' he said. 'We're sitting in a pub sizing up women. This is what men ought to be doing. You know, I'm genuinely impressed by Hannah, by that map. Information like that is hard to get. I hope it's as reliable as she says it is, but that can be checked in due course. She's got breast cancer, you know.'

I almost felt as if I were going to tip over and fall. I had to grip the table. 'How do you know?'

'There were bottles of tamoxifen in her bathroom. You have to take it for several years after certain forms of cancer treatment.'

'Giles, you've got to stop doing this. You can't keep rooting around in people's bathrooms. It's not right.'

He took another sip of beer. 'I wasn't rooting around. I asked if I could use the lavatory. The bottles were in the open. I can't force myself not to see what's in front of my eyes. In any case, our knowing doesn't do her any harm.'

'That's not true, because now you'll judge her in a certain way. You'll see her campaign differently. Now we know that she's doing it on her own behalf.'

'You want another beer, Mark?'

'Yes,' I said. 'I'd like to stick my head in one.'

Giles went into the pub and I went over our meeting with Hannah again, remembering one bad thing after another. I tried to remember our exact words when we'd talked about wanting to meet some victims. Had either of us made any light-hearted comments about them? I couldn't remember, but I couldn't be sure. Giles came back with two large glasses, and two packets of crisps held in his teeth. He leaned forward and deposited them on the table.

I took a deep drink. 'Do you never feel guilty about spying on people?'

Giles calmly opened a bag of salt and vinegar crisps and put a couple in his mouth, crunching them obnoxiously loudly. 'I thought we could have these for pudding,' he said. 'We should take advantage of not having anyone around to tell us what to do.' He sounded like a six-year-old whose mother had left the room. 'You mean, do I feel guilty about looking at people, making judgments about them? What else is one meant to do with people? Anyway, you're wrong. I don't think worse of Hannah Mahoney. I think better of her. What impresses me is that she doesn't talk about herself. It would have been so easy for her to take on the moral authority of the victim. She didn't say a word about it. Amazing. If it were me, I'd be obsessed with it every second of the day. You know, Mark, that a cancer cell is so small that you can hardly see it under a microscope. If you had a single cancer cell and it grew by dividing in half once a month, how long would it be before you had a two-kilogram tumour which your body couldn't tolerate?'

'I don't know. Twenty-five years?'

'When we get back to London, if we ever do, I'm going to get Wortley to send you on a maths course. People like you, Mark, walk around in a fog of bemusement. All because you don't understand the way large numbers work. The answer is less than three and a half years.'

'Oh.'

'Where was I?' said Giles. 'Oh, yes. Then I'd be obsessed with death. Sometimes I look at photographs that were taken before I was born and I get a little jab of horror because that's a hint of what being dead will be like. Not being there. And in fact, being dead after you die is very slightly worse than being dead before you are born. Before you were born you were dead for a finite amount of time. When you die, you really could be dead for ever. If I had cancer, I would certainly be tempted to start a campaign to blame it all on somebody else.'

'Is that what you think? I thought you liked her.'

'I don't know what to think,' said Giles. 'But I do adore her.'

'I don't think you're really frightened of cancer,' I said. 'If you actually got cancer it would be completely different.'

'You think I'd suddenly turn out to be brave?'

'I just mean it would be completely different. It would have nothing at all to do with what you've said. And I think it's wrong of you to say that she would have started this campaign because of her cancer. We don't know about her attitude to cancer. We don't know how the campaign started.'

'Isn't this great?' he said.

'What do you mean?'

'We've escaped from the noise and the dirt of the city and we're here in Nature and we can talk and relax and examine our lives.'

'Dirt?' I said. 'We've just visited a rubbish dump.'

I looked around me and saw that the garden had now filled up with people.

Giles looked around and smiled. 'It looks like everybody who is anybody in Marston Green is here,' he said.

'I think that's right,' I said. I noticed a familiar face. 'That's a guy from Marshco.'

'Where?'

I pointed him out. 'I had a chat with him where the lorries were loading up the incinerator.'

'Let's go and say hello,' said Giles.

THE MAN was leaning on the fence talking to a friend. He saw us approaching and gave a sign of vague, half recognition.

'Hi,' I said. 'We met up by the incinerator.'

'Yeah, that's right.'

I introduced Giles and myself and the man told us he was called Tony Thorn and introduced the other man as his brother-in-law, Ewan. Giles asked them what they were having.

'A pint each of County, cheers very much,' said Tony.

Giles went off to get it and in the meantime we had that ritualistic conversation I'd got so used to in my very short time in Marston Green. I said that we came from London and they went into an elaborate expression of horror as if it was some combination of Sodom and the Western Front. They couldn't live there. The traffic. The crowds. The crime. A friend of a friend of Ewan's had had his mobile phone pinched in Oxford Street. He was just talking on it and it was whipped off of his ear. Would you believe it?

Giles returned with the beers and the mood became very affable. It turned out that Tony and Ewan were both fishermen in their spare time and, weirdly, it turned out that Giles knew quite a lot about fishing. They had an almost entirely incomprehensible conversation about chub and pike and perch and different ways of catching them.

'By the way,' Tony said. 'Steve Yates'll be in later.'

'That right?' I said.

'Who's that?' Giles asked.

'I've never met him,' I said. 'But he's the father of . . . you know.'

'Oh, really?' said Giles, interested now. 'I'd like to meet him. You all work at Marshco?'

'That's right,' said Tony.

'Five years,' said Ewan.

'You make it sound like a prison sentence,' said Giles and we all laughed, mates together.

'No, it's a good job,' said Ewan. 'I work on maintenance.'

'We work for Marshco as well, in a way,' said Giles. 'We work for their main insurance company. We heard about the problems with illness in the area and that people say it's connected to the plant. Have you heard about that?'

The two men exchanged glances.

Tony gave a shrug as if it didn't matter much. 'Bloody troublemakers,' he said and took a deep gulp of his ale. 'I mean, what do they want? Do they want Marshco to shut up shop and go somewhere else with their jobs? Then this place'll go straight down the toilet.'

'Too right,' said Giles. He was one of the blokes now, railing against the know-nothing, bleeding-heart activists.

Giles nodded at me and I went off and returned with a tray of four more pints of beer and a selection of crisps, peanuts and pork scratchings. We all settled down around one of the tables, which was a relief because I was becoming slightly unsteady.

'Now,' said Giles. 'If you want to find a really toxic substance that is a major threat to the health of humanity, then I offer you the pork scratching.' He tried to open the packet but it resisted his attempts and he had to bite it violently until it split open and scattered on the table. We all helped ourselves.

'It is well known that its basic ingredients are the bits left on the floor of slaughterhouses. These bits are left to harden in the sun, then they are deep-fried in oil recycled from fish and chip shops in the north of England. They are then salted with salt retrieved from popcorn containers under cinema seats.'

There were groans from around the table and then another pint of beer appeared in front of me as if by magic. It didn't seem long enough since the previous glass. I thought I might have drifted drunkenly off to sleep, but then I remembered I'd been telling them in detail about my comparison between swallows and fighter aircraft. Tony and Ewan were quite impressed and actually began to cheer the low-level attack of one particular swallow. 'Send it out to Iraq,' someone shouted. It might have been me, and there were shushing sounds from surrounding tables. Then there were shouts of 'Steve, Steve, over here, mate' and a tall, solid man with freckles and very light brown hair sat down at the table.

'These gents were asking after you,' Tony said.

'We met your daughter,' Giles said.

I took a gulp of beer.

'That right?'

'We're working up at Marshco,' I said.

'They're insurance salesmen,' Ewan said.

'Not exactly . . .' I started to say. I was concentrating on keeping my thought processes very precise and logical so that nobody would think I was drunk and so that I wouldn't say anything stupid, and I was making a very carefully constructed plan on how to deal with Steve Yates. It all depended on what he knew. For all I knew East Anglia might be like Sicily and he would turn up at Clover chalet with a sawn-off shotgun and two huge brothers. I would be led off and have to marry Sandy. I'd settle down in Marston Green and get a job here. Probably at Marshco. Maybe he didn't know, however. Therefore my immediate plan would be not to drink any more, and to stay almost entirely silent. I kept a firm hold on my half-full glass. Nobody would be allowed to get hold of it and swap it for a full one. I felt mellow and in control.

There was a slight lull in the conversation and people were staring reflectively into their beers. It was one of those moments when somebody needs to break the silence and start a new topic of conversation. But it wasn't going to be me. They couldn't catch me out.

The first to speak was Giles. 'I work for insurance now but the reason I'm on this job is that I've got a bit of a background in waste management.'

There was a slightly surprised murmur around the table. I was completely stunned but on the other hand I was deeply grateful that Giles hadn't started a discussion about sex.

'It was after I left college and I spent some time just trying to earn money. I got a job with a guy in the Black Country, a right old cowboy. He had a few lorries and some contracts. It was a laugh what those guys got up to. We'd clear out a site, and then we'd strip off anything you could trace, and then we'd dump the stuff any old place. In people's skips, on other building sites—we'd tip loads over bridges into canals, onto other loads of rubbish that were ready for collection.'

There were chuckles around the table.

'I know what you mean,' said Tony. 'We've all been there and done that. Sometimes there's so many bloody rules and regulations from Brussels that in the end you think, just fuck it, and you tip it off the side of the road.'

'I guess that Marshco aren't like that?'

'You'd be bloody surprised,' said Ewan.

'But they've got all that space,' said Giles.

'Yeah,' said Ewan. 'The question is: what do you take and where do you shove it? If you're starting up a new waste-disposal operation, you're not going to grow like Marshco if you start saying, oh, I'm not sure if we can take that, and have you separated that one out. It's all about speed, growth, throughput, so and so much money per cube. Us lot, we work for the company, but a load of the driving is contracted out. Who knows where half their stuff comes from? Then there was the bloody foot and mouth.'

This roused me briefly. 'I saw that on TV. They weren't put in rubbish dumps. They dug big pits and burned them.'

'I wasn't talking about the pits,' said Tony. 'I was talking about the lorries. The ministry were hiring hundreds of them, paying anything the companies asked. Unbelievable, it was. So there was a knock-on effect up at Marshco. We were working double shifts. It was absolute chaos up there. One manager totally lost it. What was his name?'

'Preece,' said Steve.

'He was under so much pressure that he'd been sending everything, industrial, medical, contaminates and other stuff, all with the general waste. By the time they discovered it, it was all bloody mixed up like a Christmas pudding. What a shambles.'

There was a pause. More beer staring.

'Preece,' said Giles.

Suddenly there was a chill in the atmosphere. People seemed to have sobered up, except for me.

'It wasn't that big a deal,' said Ewan. 'He was booted out, end of story. I think they got most of it sorted anyway.'

'There's always one, isn't there?' said Giles, and sounding drunk once more, he told a long and entirely untrue story about his time in the Black Country. I looked at Steve. He looked quite like his daughter, which was a bit strange. I tried not to think about it. When the story was finished, Steve and Ewan laughed, but the spark had gone. They muttered their thanks and drifted away.

6

We were sitting in Paul Creek's office at ten past ten the following morning. Creek stirred his coffee and gave a sniff. 'His name was James Preece. He was dismissed fourteen months ago because he wasn't up to the job and this has absolutely nothing to do with what you're here to deal with.'

Giles took a sip of coffee. 'Nothing?'

'This is an issue of environmental cancer. Cancer that must have developed over ten, fifteen or more years. Preece was involved in a dumping incident that happened last year.'

'That's why you didn't tell me about it, when I asked?'

Creek took a deep huffy breath. 'I didn't decide not to tell you about it, Mr Buckland. The fact is that we're a company like other companies. We have good employees and bad employees. When you asked me about problems, I'm afraid I didn't come up with every single example of incompetence in our history.'

'Mr Creek, you're handling dangerous materials. The claim that you have some incompetent employees and bad practices would, for a jury, be an explanation of *how* you poisoned the good people of Marston Green rather than a defence. Imagine you've gone for a restaurant meal and been up all night with food poisoning. You return to the restaurant next morning to complain. You go into the kitchen and find a piece of beef crawling with maggots. That's not relevant, the manager says. That meat only arrived this morning. And anyway, you ate fish, not meat, so there's no connection.'

Paul Creek had gone very pale. He had stopped stirring his coffee and was now holding his pen in his left hand, flicking the cap off and clicking it on, again and again. 'Where did you hear about Preece?'

'What?' said Giles.

Giles had a very good way of saying one-syllable words like 'what' when he was angry.

'I just wanted to say that there are some disaffected people in this company. Let me be clear. Four years ago, when I arrived here, this was not a well-run operation. What I've done is introduce a modern management structure, invest, upgrade the machinery and processes and also import new flexibility. If it's cheaper to buy in a service than to provide it ourselves, that's what I've done. If it's more effective to employ people on short-term contracts than to have them as full-time employees, I've altered their terms of employment. There are a couple of dozen people I've fired face to face. There's at least another fifty who know that they may be made redundant or reassigned. Are you sure it wasn't one of them? Do you know what it's like to run a business, Mr Buckland?'

'No,' said Giles. 'I don't.'

Creek stood up and walked over to the window. He looked assertive again. He clearly felt back in control. We were in his office now, not the meeting room we had been in before, but the view was much the same, over the reeking piles of rubbish.

'One day, in five or ten years, when I or my successor looks out of this window, it will be over a landscape that will be as beautiful as the view from the other side. There will be recycling and reclamation facilities on a level you can hardly imagine.' He turned and smiled at us. 'But do you think I can bring that about just by being kind to people? Do you think I could have managed the transformation of Marshco overnight? This is waste, for God's sake. Rubbish, trash. Let's be grown up here. People send the stuff they think is too dangerous or disgusting to keep in their own homes and factories and we do the best we can. And finally, Mr Buckland, I suspect that you were going to ask if you could see the files concerning James Preece. And the answer to that request is no, because there are no such files. We dealt with the situation in the way that we have dealt with other awkward situations. Namely by clearing them up and moving on. This is a waste-disposal business, not the Public Record Office. If the name of James Preece is mentioned, we will deny that the matter has any importance and that will be the end of it. Now, is there anything more I can do for you?'

Giles walked over to a side table where a coffee pot stood. He gestured towards Paul Creek with it and Creek shook his head.

'Yes, please,' I said.

Giles filled my mug and then filled his own. 'We could sit here all day,' he said, 'and talk about the future of waste management. At the moment—Mr Creek—I don't think you seem to realise the seriousness of the situation you're in. This isn't a question of just not having files. You're facing the very clear possibility of having this entire facility closed. There is no point in scoring this or that point if you lose the company in the process.'

Creek was silent for a time. He leaned back, flexing his hands on the sharp edge of his desk. 'There are one or two things you do not understand. You are not my adviser or my conscience. You are a very lowly member of the insurance company to which we give our business. When I heard you were coming in to see me I talked to your boss, Walt Broberg. He told me your remit, which is not to come in here wasting my time. And it's not to go stirring things up. Your job is to come here, find out what's happening, which is nothing, and then go back to the office. Well, you can go back to London now and I will tell you one thing, my friend. If your meddling does result in anything being stirred up, I will fuck you. Do you understand?'

With a calmness I had to admire, Giles drained his coffee and placed the mug on the side table. 'I think you missed my point,' he said. 'But perhaps I wasn't clear enough in putting it across. Thank you for the coffee.'

'This is the last time I expect to see you here,' said Creek. 'I'll deal with London from now on.'

IN THE CAR on the way back, Giles was as cheerful as he'd been after our last meeting with Creek. You'd think the meeting had gone well.

'Quite a character, don't you think?'

'Wasn't that a total disaster?' I asked.

'What do you mean? It's not as if we were caught climbing over the wire with trowels.'

'So what do we do next?' I asked.

'I don't know,' said Giles. 'Probably we should hang around for another day or so and then leave. I don't think anything's going to top that, do you?'

I HAD ACTUALLY got around to making a shopping list and I suggested to Giles that I go to the supermarket and do a shop. He said there was no point now in going and buying packets of butter and sugar that we'd leave behind. And so, at twelve-thirty, we were back in the Four Feathers, where Jan had fixed a delicious lasagne and we each had a pint of Abbot ale.

Giles finished his lasagne with much scraping out of the dish. 'It's at moments like this,' he said, 'that what you really need is a cigar or a pipe. When we get back to England . . . I mean London, although it's much the same thing . . . we should find a pub with a table close to a phone connection where we could plug in a laptop and we'll move out of Wortley altogether.'

'Giles?'

'Yes?'

'Last night you started on that complicated business of getting those guys from Marshco drunk and coming up with that load of crap about "dodgy adventures I had in the Black Country" and getting them to talk about this guy Preece. And then we go in to see Paul Creek, and he shouts at us. We sit through that rubbish about what it takes to run a business. After all that, you just say, oh, well, it's time we went back to London. What was the point of going to all that trouble last night?'

Giles pulled a face. 'I don't know,' he said. 'Fun, partly. Sometimes it's interesting to lead people on and see what they'll tell you if they think you're on their side.'

'But you found out stuff. It may be really damaging. Why are you just letting it go?'

'You know, Mark, Creek wasn't entirely wrong. They're a waste company. What do you expect from them? They don't employ Nobel prize winners to move the crap around, so I'm not surprised that it sometimes gets tipped into the wrong place.'

'If that's your attitude, then why did you do this in the first place? Last night may have been quite fun, if you weren't me, but the result is you've had a massive row with Paul Creek and he's phoned our boss to complain. I could just about understand this if you were going to take Marshco on, but from what you've said, the plan is to just slink back to London and tell Donna that everything is fine.'

'I wouldn't say "slink" exactly. And I'm not going to say that everything is fine.'

'But we're not going to take a position.'

Giles took a sip of beer. 'What position would you suggest?'

'I wouldn't suggest any position. We don't have enough information.'

'That's roughly the position I'm going to take in my report, which will cover one side of a sheet of A4. Which is the maximum that Walt Broberg's famously limited attention span will tolerate.'

'We could gather some more information.'

'We could take blood samples from the population of Marston Green and compare them with our own blood. We could climb over the fence at Marshco with a Geiger counter and search for illegal dumping. We could break into their office and search for incriminating files. We could hack into their computer system and read their emails. Is that what you want?'

'I don't want to sound like I'm not seeing the funny side of this,' I said. 'But I don't think there really is a funny side.'

'Oh, come on,' said Giles. 'There was Paul Creek ranting at us this morning. That was pretty funny. And from certain angles, Kevin Seeger and his amazing collection of filing cabinets has its amusing side. Which reminds me.' Giles's smile faded and he looked serious. 'We can leave our phone number with Hannah Mahoney and she can get in touch. There's nothing else I can think of that's realistic.'

We fell silent for a time. I wasn't sure what I'd expected of the visit to Marston Green but I was starting to realise that there was a real possibility that it wasn't going to amount to anything. I also felt that I didn't have the capacity to enjoy that as much as Giles did.

Geoff brought coffee over to us and we chatted for a while. Just as Geoff went back to work, Hannah Mahoney walked through the door. She saw us and came over.

'Don't you teach at the school?' Giles said.

'It's the lunch hour,' said Hannah. 'I thought I'd find you here.'

'This is our new office,' I said. 'For the time being. Giles has decided it's time to return to London.'

'I didn't know you were going,' said Hannah. 'This may not matter, then. I came to say that there are a couple of people you could come and see, if you wanted.'

'You mean people with cancer?'

'Yes.'

'Mark can go,' Giles said. 'If that's all right.'

Hannah looked at me, surprised. 'All right. I'll pick you up at six.'

When Hannah had gone, I said: 'Now what was that about?'

'I felt the same. I wonder why she's suddenly giving us access. She may be worried she's losing us.'

'I didn't mean that. I mean, why aren't you coming?'

'Because I believe that it is almost certainly pointless,' said Giles. 'I can't think that there is anything that could possibly be learned from visiting one or two or three sad cancer sufferers.'

'What if you're wrong?'

'That's why you're going.'

'Second question, why didn't you tell Hannah about Preece? That would be a great help to their campaign.'

'We're not here to be a great help to their campaign. And our clients might not be very happy if we were reporting private conversations to their opponents. I suspect that Paul Creek would, in his words, fuck me.'

'The campaign group might be able to defeat Marshco if they had the information we had.'

'Maybe,' said Giles. 'But anybody should be able to beat Marshco, if they're not hopeless amateurs. Honestly, I sometimes think I should retire from insurance and offer myself out as a professional activist. Like those ambulance chasers in America who fight cases for a mere forty per cent of the damages, just to cover expenses.'

'What are you going to do when I'm out working?'

'That's none of your business,' said Giles. 'I'm the boss, you are the exploited worker. In fact I'm going to write emails and go through some papers that Kevin Seeger lent me. Is that acceptable?'

'Maybe we can meet for steak and kidney pudding later?'

'I'll talk to Jan about it.'

LIZA BARRY was a friend of Hannah's. She was forty-eight years old, with dark-brown reddish hair, streaked with grey. She was thin, so thin that her cheeks were caved in, her clothes flapping on her. She would have been a striking woman, but it almost looked as if all that radiation had made the colours run out of her. Hannah told me on the way over that Liza had been one of the pioneers of the campaign and that she had a lymphoma in an advanced stage. Hannah explained to Liza who I was and that I worked for Marshco's insurance company.

'So you've been there?' Liza said.

'I was there this morning.'

'They'll never meet us,' she said. 'We've been trying to talk to them for years.'

'You don't mind me being here?' I said. 'It's an intrusion.'

'At the moment, I haven't got much to do except tell my story.'

She made us tea and then led us out into her small back garden where she had herbs growing by the door: rosemary, tarragon, different shades of thyme. At the back, there was a small vegetable plot.

'I've lived here all my life,' Liza said. 'About twenty years ago, when the wind was in the right direction, down from the sea, it was like wispy snow. You'd come out in the morning and it looked as if the world had gone grey. You left footprints on the lawn and you had to do your washing all over again. We brushed it out of our hair. We used to joke about it. And the funny thing is that I've been a vegetarian for twenty-five years. I do yoga. I go on long walks. I've never smoked. I went to great lengths to keep toxic substances out of my body. What was the point?' She gave a sad smile. 'It seems a little unfair. But then I suppose it always does.'

I didn't ask questions. I felt it wasn't my right. I just waited for her to say what she needed to say.

'I hardly ever used to get ill,' she said. 'Two years ago I got a swelling in my neck and I went to the doctor. I felt silly doing it, but it was quite big. I had had swollen glands before, when I had colds. I remember telling him that this one couldn't be a problem, because it wasn't even sore, the way the others were. And that was almost the moment I knew. His eyes just gave a flicker of interest. They did some tests and they found that I had an intermediate-grade lymphoma. They were pretty buoyant about it. They told me that aggressive treatment was very often successful. Do you want to hear this?'

'If you want to tell me,' I said.

'I had the aggressive treatment but the lumps came back and so they gave me an even more aggressive treatment. I was so, so sick. And now there are symptoms that the doctors are concerned about. What I'm now being offered is a form of radical bone-marrow transplantation. The odds are one in three that the treatment will kill me, one in three that it will do nothing, and one in three that it will cause a remission. They sound like good odds. The only problem is that I've been having rather bad luck with odds. When they first diagnosed me, the odds were very good. They told me they had a ninety-five per cent cure rate. Unfortunately I was in the five per cent and I've been in it all the way along.' She paused. She seemed to have finished.

'Liza,' I said. 'What is it you want?'

'If you're giving out wishes, I'd like to be cured. More realistically I would like to be listened to, I would like all of this to make sense.'

I shook her long, thin hand. I could feel the bone under the skin. 'Thank you.'

'Do something,' she said.

IT WAS A SHORT DRIVE to our second destination. This was a smarter house with a curved gravel drive. The sort of place you expected horse-drawn carriages to pull up in front of. Hannah's Fiat looked definitely shabby beside the gleaming Range Rover and BMW saloon that were already parked there. We crunched over to the front door and Hannah rapped the heavy knocker. The door opened and it was Charles Deane, the chairman of the campaign. Hannah introduced me and we shook hands.

'I feel awkward about this,' Deane said. 'I don't want to display Ella like a freak show. Perhaps we can just say hello and then we can talk somewhere else.'

At that moment I felt in a cold rage against Giles who had sent me to go through this. As we walked up the large staircase to Ella's bedroom, I felt that inviting me here was just a sign of their desperation and sadness. I knew, and Charles Deane knew, that I was low, low down on the list of people who could do anything for his daughter. Did he maybe think that I would tell someone who would do something? And what was it that they could do?

We knocked on the door and there was a grumpy 'come in'. We all walked in, three adults looking awkward in a fourteen-year-old girl's bedroom with its posters and piles of books and funny, cheap little bottles arranged on bookshelves. Ella Deane was sitting at her desk, wearing a merry little skullcap made out of silk triangles, gold and black. It didn't conceal that she had almost no hair.

'Ella, this is Mark Foll. He's from an insurance company.'

'Hi.' She looked around.

'Hi,' I said, hoping that she would see that I was young like her and not just another man in a suit.

'How are you feeling?' Charles Deane asked.

'All right.'

'No, really, Ella.'

She pulled a sulky face. 'I'm just a bit tired, all right?'

'Have you been sick today?'

'Oh, for God's sake, Dad.'

I felt my cheeks burning with the embarrassment of this. We backed out of her room, leaving her to her homework.

Charles led us into a large sitting room with big sofas and a chandelier. He asked if we would like a drink. I said yes. Charles took a decanter from the shelf and poured us each a whisky in a cut-glass tumbler. We sat on the sofa. Charles said he was sorry that his wife wasn't here but he was trying to encourage her to get out of the house. Ella was their only daughter, so sometimes things got a bit . . . you know.

He described how Ella had become lethargic and how they'd thought she was becoming a problem child. She used to sulk in her room, lie in bed all evening. She used to get sudden nosebleeds. They thought it was all part of her hysteria. Then she got a throat infection, and when she hadn't shaken it off after a fortnight they took her to the doctor. He took a blood test. Acute lymphocytic leukaemia. The doctors were very positive, he said. A better than half chance of a cure. He and his wife had spent the past year accompanying her to treatment. And they had sat with her while she was injected in her spine and while she vomited and while she cried.

As Charles talked I gradually had the feeling of sinking into blackness and thinking: what is real apart from fear and pain?

'What are the doctors saying at the moment?' I asked.

Charles started to say something, coughed, shook his head, looked away. I could see that there were tears running down his face. He wiped them away clumsily. Hannah put her hand on his knee.

'I'm sorry about that,' he said. 'What you probably want to know about is the campaign, how it got started. We met another child at the hospital. She came from Marston Green as well. That made us think. And it started from there.' He drained his glass and stood up. I placed my own untasted drink next to his. He led us to the front door. As he opened it, I felt he was searching for something appropriate to say.

'What we feel, Mary and I, is that something good must come out of this.'

I shook his hand. Hannah gave him a hug and he shut the door.

When we got back in the car, Hannah said she was in a hurry. A friend was baby-sitting Bruce, but she had to get back. She'd drop me off at the Four Feathers on the way. We were moving through Marston Green quite quickly and I suddenly had the feeling that this was it, and if I didn't do anything I would leave Marston Green as I had everywhere else, without touching the sides, without a trace.

'Hannah, there's something I've got to tell you.'

'What?'

'I know about your cancer.'

When we were outside her house, she stopped the car instead of driving across the village to the Four Feathers. She was looking out of the windscreen, away from me, so I couldn't see her expression. I could see her face very much more closely than I had before. I could see the soft down on the edge of her firm jaw. 'I'd better take over from Gina. Do you want to come in for a moment?'

I followed her to the door. She introduced me to Gina as a man from an insurance company.

'I need to check on Bruce,' Hannah said when Gina had left. 'Pour yourself something, if you want.'

I wasn't at all clear what I should be pouring or where I'd find it, so I stood and waited.

When she came down, she said, 'What was it? Was it the map?'

'What?'

'My cancer.'

'Oh,' I said. 'No. I'm really sorry about this. When Giles went to your lavatory, he noticed some sort of pill that you've been taking because of, you know . . .'

'Breast cancer,' said Hannah. 'You're allowed to say it out loud. I won't faint.'

'I might,' I said.

'Sit down over there,' she said. 'On the sofa.'

She walked over to a cupboard and took a bottle and two glasses. She gave each glass a good splash of Scotch, then came over and sat by me on the sofa and handed me one of the glasses.

'So I suppose Giles saw me as a hysterical woman who had started a campaign because she was angry about getting cancer.'

I felt an odd pang of disappointment that she was focused on Giles. 'That's not what he said. He was impressed that you'd done all this without putting your illness at the centre of it.'

Hannah took a sip of her drink, almost a gulp. 'It was two years ago,' she said. 'A lump in my right breast.' She pushed a strand of hair behind her ear. 'I didn't find it. It was found by my boyfriend, Don.'

'I didn't know that you had a boyfriend.'

'We broke up. He found it difficult. He was very apologetic. He couldn't touch me. He tried, but it was impossible. He said he couldn't think of me in that way any more.'

As Hannah spoke, it felt all the time as if she was putting something strange and unexpected on the table in front of us and seeing how I reacted, seeing if I was shocked.

'I find that hard to believe,' I said.

'I had a biopsy, which showed I had breast cancer. The doctor told me that it would almost certainly need nothing more than a small operation. There would just be some scans, X-rays, blood tests. But these showed I had invasive breast cancer, so I needed a quite big operation, modified radical mastectomy. They removed the whole breast and some of the lymph nodes in my armpit. That was a big deal.'

Yes, I thought. Too much detail. I took a gulp of whisky and coughed. She continued.

'My mother came down and lived here on and off for a year. You see, it wasn't just the operation. I had a few courses of chemotherapy and I spent days throwing up. I thought I was going to be so strong, for Bruce, and for other reasons. But I wasn't. I spent days lying in bed with a bucket on the floor. And then of course my hair fell out. So the fact that I had cancer wasn't exactly the best-kept secret in Marston Green. I think that over the next few days someone would have mentioned it to you.'

I looked at Hannah. She was wearing a brown cardigan with small square buttons. You couldn't tell. There, apparently, were her two medium-sized breasts.

'How are you now?' I said.

'Waiting,' said Hannah. 'If I wait five years and there's nothing, then that's good. And in the meantime I'm looking after Bruce and doing my job and I've got involved in this campaign.'

There was a long embarrassing silence.

Hannah finished the last of her whisky. She stood up. Maybe it was time for me to go.

'What I want, what we all want is some sort of acknowledgement. I've got about a fifty–fifty chance of being alive in five years. I don't want it all to mean nothing. I want Marshco to face up to what they have been doing. The alternative is that we'll all just disappear and the world will continue.'

'But the world *will* continue.'

She gave a sad smile. 'Sometimes I forget which side you're on.'

I stood up as well, which brought me quite close against her, almost awkwardly.

'I'm not sure I'm on any side,' I said. 'Not anymore.'

'It doesn't matter. I'm not expecting anything from you. I don't want some huge expression of sympathy. I've had enough of people's sympathy.'

I felt confused by the situation. I didn't know what I was doing here. I could hardly think of what to say or do. She had been open with me and I don't think I'd ever felt so awkward.

'I'd better go,' I said.

'Yes.'

I walked to the door and she walked with me. I felt her shoulder brushing on mine. I turned to her. 'I'm sorry.' I put out my hand and touched her shoulder, as if I were brushing a piece of dust.

She moved away just a step. 'I've told you. I don't need that.'

'I mean sorry just generally.'

I walked out and I heard the door close softly behind me. It was colder than I expected. It was a cloudless night with more stars than I could ever remember seeing before. I looked up and there was nothing but sky in my field of vision. Suddenly I had the feeling that I was falling upwards into them. I felt dizzy and almost stumbled. I put my hand out and I steadied myself on the wall by the garden gate. Then, suddenly, I clenched my right hand into a fist and brought it down hard on the wall two times, three times, four times.

I turned and looked at Hannah's cottage. I could feel the pulse in my neck, my chest, my head. There was no point in thinking. I walked back up the path and knocked on the door. It opened almost immediately. Hannah had a questioning look.

There was nothing I could say that wouldn't be another disaster so I just stepped forward and put my hands on either side of her face, and paused just for a moment to think properly for the first time how lovely it was, and then kissed her, first softly and then deeply. I stopped and pulled back to look at her. Her lips were half open, glistening. She gave a release of breath which could almost have been an expression of pain. She leaned forward towards me. It was about a millimetre but I saw I hadn't been wrong and we kissed again. I moved my arms around her back and felt her arms holding me. When we stopped we were both gasping as if the air was thin in the room.

I stroked her cheek and then kissed her and undid the top button of her cardigan. She pulled her head away from me.

'No,' she said.

I gulped. I could hardly speak. 'Is it too early?'

'Not my sweater,' she said. 'The rest.'

I was surprised by how intensely relieved I was by that. 'Shall we go upstairs?'

She shook her head. 'Bruce comes into my bed sometimes. Down here.'

Entangled in each other, we hobbled across the room and fell onto the sofa. It was all very fast and flailing and desperate in a way I wasn't used to. I felt her come, and then I came and we lay there, entangled.

'I can't believe this. I thought you liked Giles,' I said.

She smiled drowsily. 'Giles?'

'He's the clever, interesting one. He's married, but he thinks you're wonderful. He keeps talking about you.'

She stroked my hair. 'Do you remember when we met in the High Street? I said that awful thing about you being the *pretty* face of your company, instead of the public face.'

'I thought you despised me.'

'Well,' said Hannah. 'There was the problem that you were part of the enemy. Are part of the enemy.'

'I keep saying that's not true.'

She looked at me with a tired, lovely smile. 'If you could go back to London with a killer fact that let Marshco off the hook, you'd be a hero, wouldn't you?'

'Giles says it's not like that. It's all too messy and hard to make connections that really stick. That's your problem.'

'Is it?' she said. She kissed me. 'I'd like you to stay the night.' I was about to say 'yes' when she added, 'But you can't. Because of Bruce.'

I stood up and put my clothes on while Hannah lay sprawled on the sofa and looked at me, with a smile. She walked over to the door with me and we kissed again.

'That was . . .' I said and then the sentence trailed away.

'Yes,' she said. 'And please don't say something like I'll call you.'

'What do you mean?'

'I don't know. I don't know what I mean. My life's a mess and I don't want to make it any worse. And I'm probably going to start crying in a moment, so you'd better go.'

AS I WALKED back under the stars, I felt confused. It was as if I had been on my way somewhere and had had my pocket picked. Except that it was sort of the opposite. Someone had brushed against me and I'd felt something strange happen; something had been put in my pocket without my knowledge.

There was also the further question of what I was going to say to Giles. What I was going to say to anyone.

It was a short walk back to the Four Feathers and I had made sense of nothing by the time I arrived at my room. I opened the door and something fell to my feet. I switched on the light and saw that it was a note that had been wedged in the door. It said: 'Come and see me. However late you get in. Geoff.'

I walked over to the back door of the pub and rang the bell. There were footsteps on the stairs then Geoff appeared in a dressing gown, looking awful. I started to apologise and then he told me that Giles was in hospital.

7

I managed to get Giles's car keys from his room and I drove myself to the hospital in Melwarth along winding dark lanes.

A man in a uniform at the front desk gave me the name of a ward and I walked down an immensely long corridor, through a wing that looked as if it was left over from the war. I arrived at Giles's ward and a nurse directed me. I padded along, looking left and right at people in various stages of damage until Giles came into sight.

I would hardly have recognised him if his name hadn't been on a label at the end of the bed. There was a plastic tube inserted into his nose and a cord leading to a machine. His face looked as if it had been inflated with a bicycle pump and it was livid and raw with purple bruises. I could see that his right hand was bandaged and two fingers were attached to strips of plastic like miniature rulers.

I pulled a chair over and sat down. 'Giles,' I said. 'It's me, Mark.'

'Ark.'

'That's right. Are you all right?'

'Up.'

'What?'

'Cup,' he said, as if the word had several syllables.

I looked around and there was a small plastic cup by the bed.

'You want a drink?' I said.

'Spit,' he said.

I held the cup under his mouth and he spat in a splattery way, saliva streaked with yellow and red. I wiped his mouth.

'They've given me stuff,' he said. 'Strong stuff. I'm speaking from somewhere far away.'

He did indeed sound as if he was speaking from somewhere distant, but his voice was becoming stronger and clearer.

'What happened?' I said. 'Geoff said you were attacked along from the pub.'

'Got hit,' said Giles. 'Didn't see anything. Heard something from behind, started to turn, things went bright, lots of flashes. Fell on the ground. Stamped on my hand. Which hand is it?'

'Your right hand.'

'Fuck.'

'I'm so sorry, Giles.'

'Does it look bad?'

'Pretty bad.'

'So how was your evening?' he said. 'Depressing?'

'Sort of mixed.'

'Did you tell her that we knew?'

'Yes, I did.'

'What she say?'

'It didn't matter. She said it wasn't a secret.'

There was a silence. Looking at the dismal figure in the bed, I could see that they hadn't just set out to rough him up a little. He was really smashed up.

'I'm so sorry,' I said. 'I should have been there.'

Another snuffle. 'Yes,' said Giles. 'Should have been you.'

I leaned over him. 'Giles, we'll talk about this tomorrow, but do you have any idea who they were?'

'Didn't see.'

'People who thought we were going to close the plant down, maybe?'

'Dunno.'

'I'll be back tomorrow morning. Can I get you anything?'

'Call Donna.'

'All right.'

His face tipped and then I saw that he was asleep.

THE NEXT MORNING I woke up in a fog of tiredness. First I phoned Hannah, who was in the middle of breakfast with Bruce. I told her about Giles and at first she sounded more intrigued than sympathetic. She started asking questions about what had happened and I wondered if she saw some sort of campaigning opportunity.

'What do the police say?'

'I don't know,' I said. 'They weren't there by the time I arrived. I'd like to see you.'

'I'd like to see you as well. Come at nine, when Bruce is in bed. If you want. It's not compulsory.'

'I want to.'

THEN I PHONED Donna Kiely and was given her mobile number. When she answered, she sounded as if she was in the car.

'It's Mark Foll,' I said. 'Giles is in hospital.'

'I'm very sorry to hear that. What happened?'

'He was beaten up. Badly beaten up.'

Even over a bad mobile-phone line I could hear that her tone had changed from dutiful concern to alarm. 'What? Who by?'

'I don't know. From what he said, he was attacked from behind. He didn't see anything.'

'Jesus. Has this anything to do with Marshco?'

'Probably.'

'Is it quicker to drive or go by train?'

'I'm not sure. About the same.'

'I'll drive. I'll head out of London straight away. I'll see you at the hospital when I arrive.'

'Somebody should tell Giles's wife. Have you got the number?'

'I'll get on to it. I'll see you when I get there.'

That was going to be fun.

I WASN'T SURE what I could take Giles. I looked in at the village shop but the only fruit they had were some very green bananas and the only newspapers they had were a couple of weird tabloids. So I did what I had been meaning to do over the past few days, which was to go to the massive supermarket, which was almost identical to the one in Camden I sometimes dropped into on my way home from work. I bought some grapes and nectarines, and an armful of newspapers.

When I arrived at the hospital, Giles was fast asleep. In the morning light I could see more clearly the bruises, swellings and stitches. There was a bruise on his forehead that was so swollen and purple that it looked like a boil caused by bubonic plague.

He seemed peaceful so I sat on the chair by the bed and read a paper and ate some of the grapes.

'Mark,' said Giles in his distant-sounding voice.

'Hi. I brought you some stuff. Would you like a nectarine?'

'Can't. Might be operated on.'

'I'll go ask the nurse.'

I found a nurse and learned that as of this morning and the doctor's visit there were now no plans to operate on Giles. There were going to be further investigations for suspected ligament injury and a few other things. But he could eat and drink. So I cut one nectarine into chunks and fed them to him chunk by chunk. It was a slow process.

'Been thinking,' he said when we were done. 'Maybe they thought I was you. That girl. One you seduced. Abandoned.'

'Sandy? You don't think she could have . . .?'

'Her father. Him and friends taking revenge.'

'Giles, this isn't Sicily.'

'They don't like it. Men coming from London, violating their women.'

'It might be a mistake but you're about three inches shorter than me. Maybe this is what they do for fun in Marston Green when the pub closes.'

There was a low mooing groan from Giles. 'No,' he said. 'It's to do with Marshco. It was me they were after. People thought we could shut it down.'

'Do you think they did it to warn you off?'

I could hear Giles breathing deeply, long slow breaths. 'Hurting a bit more,' he said. 'Reduced the good drugs. Don't need to warn me off. Don't give a fuck. Have I lost teeth?'

'I think a couple maybe.'

He groaned. 'The plan was . . . What was the plan?'

'To get in and out very quickly. Do a quick report.'

'Yes. We were about to go. Oh, bother.'

'I'm sorry, Giles, but I don't understand you. You were the one who found out about Marshco dumping things in the wrong places. You were the one who threatened Paul Creek. I don't see how you want to just walk away from it.'

A coughing sound from Giles. I leaned over and decided it was a gloomy laugh.

'Can't fucking walk. That's one. Two—doesn't matter.'

I SPENT twenty minutes sitting on the front steps of the hospital with my mobile and a map on my knees, guiding Donna Kiely towards Melwarth until her blue BMW glided into the car park. She saw me without the tiniest flicker of greeting. She behaved as if she was in the office, as if I had just come back from the coffee machine.

'What have you clowns been up to?' she asked.

I was going to say nothing, and then I thought this wasn't strictly accurate. I gave a noncommittal shrug.

As Donna entered the ward and caught sight of Giles, she visibly flinched. Then she gave a warm smile and stepped forward. She sat at the bedside and took Giles's good hand between hers.

'It's Donna. How are you, Giles?'

'Crap,' said Giles.

'We're driving Susan here and she should be here by lunchtime. The plan is to transfer you to the Middleton in London as soon as possible.' She paused, but Giles said nothing. 'Are you in pain?'

'OK,' he said. 'Not that bad.'

'I am so sorry this happened.' She stroked his hand absently. 'Giles,' she said, 'Can we have a brief talk about Marshco? If you feel you can't, it can wait.'

'I can talk,' he said. 'Bit slow.'

'Have you any idea why this may have happened?'

Giles proceeded to give a halting, wheezy précis of our activities in Marston Green. I realised that he was giving a judiciously edited version. He talked about certain concerns about Marshco's dumping practices and he said he had raised them with the management. But he didn't describe Creek's response and made no mention at all of our encounter with Tony, Ewan and Steve at the Four Feathers.

'What precise concerns were these?' Donna said.

Giles described the problem of Marshco not being straight with him and the effect of the information coming too late if Wortley weren't prepared.

Donna was silent for a long time. 'Of course,' she said, 'it could arguably be said that your job was just to garner information about the status of the protest and the implications the campaign might have on any policy with which we are associated. Forgive me for being stupid, but I'm not quite sure why you were confronting Marshco's management over questions of practice.' Giles didn't reply. 'Did you have a next step?'

Now Giles spoke slowly and clearly. 'The next step, if any, would be a full assessment of the evidence on dioxin contamination. You would need to take scientific advice on this.' He paused, as if he needed to control the pain. 'My view is that such evidence is not compelling enough to be a risk in itself. That was why I considered other factors that might be used to muddy the waters in a legal case.'

'I see,' said Donna. She gave his hand a stroke. 'Take all the time you need to make a full recovery, Giles. I'll talk to you later.'

She gave me a look, signalling me to follow her. We walked out of the ward. Then she turned to me. 'What have you two been up to?'

'I don't know what you mean.'

I immediately regretted that I hadn't just said sorry, so that she wouldn't have that scary expression on her face.

'The idea was for you to come up here and assess the situation without creating any waves. You've already been involved in a major argument with the company we're supposed to be representing—yes, I heard about the call he made to my boss. And now you have become so embroiled in this dispute that somebody has decided that you two are a part of the problem and has done something about it. Are the police involved?'

'Of course.'

'Oh, shit.'

'They might think it was just a couple of drunks having fun.'

'No, they won't. They'll know it's something to do with Marshco and they'll have to investigate. We need to make this go away.'

I looked thoughtful. I was thinking about what would happen if

Donna learned about the meeting in the pub with the Marshco workers. Then there was Sandy, which was irrelevant but which could possibly be made to sound relevant in the context of what happened. And Hannah. I remembered her, lying on her sofa with a peaceful smile on her face, looking at me. It occurred to me, in the midst of everything that was happening, that I wanted to be with her again.

'Make it go away . . .' I repeated.

'That's right,' she said. 'I'm driving straight back to London. Is there anything that needs sorting out here?'

'I'll finish a couple of things off,' I said. 'Say goodbye to people.'

'Fine,' she said. 'But no more trouble, OK?'

I THOUGHT THAT Hannah might be feeling awkward about what had happened, regretful even. I would need to tell her about going back to London and that we would need to talk about things. This was something that we had both stumbled into. I was still surprised by it.

But when she opened the door to me, we didn't talk at all. We didn't manage to get more than a few feet away from the front door.

'I thought about you all day,' Hannah said, when we were lying in each other's arms.

My clothes were half off and I stood up and took them off. I kneeled, looking down on her. I kissed her on the lips and on her neck. Then I started to undo the buttons of her sweater.

'No,' she said.

'Shut up.'

'Mark, I've told you . . .'

'I'm stronger than you are.'

Her jaw was set, her eyes shining. I undid the last button and pushed the sweater off. She could have fought it but she didn't. She looked straight at me as if she was daring me. Then she unclipped her bra and let it slide down her arms and off.

I'd thought that I was going to be all cool and casual about it but it didn't work out like that at all because I wasn't the same person anymore. Something had happened to me. There was one quite normal breast. On the other side of her chest it wasn't just absence. There was a long scar that began just above her armpit and crossed her chest to the centre.

'So if you're going to say I look beautiful anyway,' said Hannah, 'you needn't bother.'

Sex that time was slower, more gentle, better really. Eventually we took a shower together. We helped each other dress and then Hannah cooked a very basic pasta meal. We ate hungrily, drinking red wine.

I didn't say anything about going back to London. There was no discussion about where we were going to go from here. There was no need. I felt as if I'd dropped off a cliff and I knew exactly where I was going. I was going to keep falling and falling. Eventually, no doubt, I would hit the ground. What was the point of talking about it?

Instead we talked about Giles. I told her about my day at the hospital. She asked me why I thought it had happened. I gave her a detailed account of what had happened on our evening in the Four Feathers with Tony and Ewan and, yes, Steve Yates.

'That's the father of Sandy,' Hannah said.

'I didn't mean to bring it up,' I said. 'I'm just telling you what happened that night.'

'I don't mind,' she said. 'I quite like the idea of sex with someone who picks up nineteen-year-old girls in pubs.'

'You shouldn't say that. You make it sound like I'm doing you some kind of a favour. It's not like that.'

'It certainly isn't,' she said. 'You're lucky to get me.'

'Don't joke,' I said. 'I *am* lucky.'

'Did Steve know about you and Sandy?'

'No idea,' I said.

Then I told her about the row at Marshco.

'So what do you think happened?'

'I reckon there's about a one per cent chance that some mad drunk attacked Giles at random. There's about an eight per cent chance that Paul Creek got a couple of heavies to teach Giles a lesson. But I reckon it's about a seventy-five per cent chance that Tony and Ewan realised that Giles had tricked them and they panicked. They may have thought that would discourage him from taking it any further.'

'I think you've got a few per cent left over.'

'I was never any good at arithmetic.'

'So what are you going to do?'

'Not much. I guess the police will investigate. I doubt they'll find anything.' Hannah looked thoughtful. 'I know what you're going to say,' I said.

'What?'

'That I have to leave. But I'd like to stay the night.'

'No,' she said. 'Definitely not. Bruce isn't ready.'

We argued for several minutes over this. Hannah yielded a bit and said that maybe I could sleep in the spare room. I said I would only do that if she would sleep there with me. We compromised by saying that she would spend a bit of the night with me.

'I'm not sure it's a good idea,' she said. 'It's Saturday morning tomorrow. Bruce is going to his football.'

'That's fine,' I said. 'I'll take him.'

She looked as if I had slapped her. 'You're not serious?'

'Why not? I'm an expert on football.'

It was the first time I'd seen her look baffled and indecisive. When she spoke it was as if she had just tossed a coin.

'All right.'

'WHAT'S YOUR favourite team?' asked Bruce sternly.

'You mean football team?' I said, playing for time.

'Course *football team*,' he said.

I was a man. There was meant to be a football team that I was emotionally attached to. I'd never in my life watched sport. It seemed as much use as watching people eat. I tried to think of the name of a team that I could be sure really existed. 'Manchester United.' I said. 'Who's *your* favourite team?'

And Bruce was away. His favourite team was Arsenal and he had an encyclopedic knowledge of all of the players.

It was a short walk to the football pitch and Bruce was barely halfway through the team by the time we arrived.

As soon as we had left the house I had become very nervous. It was as if Hannah had suddenly said: here's this priceless Ming vase. Carry it around the park and bring it back safely. It seemed too intimate a thing for me to be doing. But Bruce was apparently untroubled.

Around the football pitch there were various groups of small boys and fathers. I was carrying a black bag. From it I removed shin pads, football boots, juice bottle. I helped Bruce tie the laces.

'Under or behind?' I said.

'Under, course,' he said, as if he was starting to have suspicions about this person disguised as a man.

It was curious that Bruce was so passionate about football, because he wasn't very good at it. He was incredibly agile, throwing himself at even the most feeble, bobbling shot. But he seemed to have very little sense of where the ball really was. It would sail past him into the goal and he didn't seem to see it, or dived in an odd direction which suggested he was only guessing.

On the other hand, he wasn't particularly outshone by his fellow players. None of them ever passed the ball. They just ran blindly for the opposition's goal, wherever they were on the pitch. Because they knew that they were never going to get the ball unless they won it for themselves, the players all gathered around it, like a very tight, slow-moving swarm of bees.

At half time Bruce came over to me. I gave him his juice.

'It's five–six,' he said.

'Is that right?' I said. 'You had a good first half. Well done.'

'Did you see my save?'

'Excellent,' I said.

'He tried to bend it round the wall.'

'Fantastic. One thing, Bruce . . .'

Bruce wasn't paying attention. 'I've gotta go. Team talk.'

I walked up and down the touchline and a man in a track suit engaged me in conversation.

'Which is yours?' he said.

'Bruce. He's in goal.'

'Mine's Tom. He's up front.' Suddenly he shouted so loud that I jumped. 'Get stuck in, Tom!' He turned back to me and spoke again in a normal tone. 'The ref's a father from the other team. He's blatantly biased. It's a bloody scandal.'

Fortunately my phone rang and I excused myself. It was Giles. His voice sounded stronger.

'They've got me in this private ward,' he said. 'I've got colour TV, my own phone, incredible food. I don't want to go home. Susan's out of the room at the moment. This afternoon they're going to give me a brain scan. But in the meantime I've been thinking. You know why I gave up working in genetics?'

'It was something to do with your aunt, wasn't it?'

'Do you know how many people in the world today are descendants of Genghis Khan?'

'No, I don't.'

'Sixteen million. One in every two hundred men in the world.'

'When's your scan?'

'Because he was Genghis Khan, he could have sex with anyone he wanted, the pick of every captured citadel and castle. And you can see the result by sticking a cotton bud in the mouth of almost any man in Central Asia. When you study Darwinian genetics you realise that nothing matters except transmission of genes. What I realised was that we're all the descendants of rapists and pillagers and murderers and I decided I wanted to get into another line of business so I wouldn't have to think about that on a daily basis.' Giles sounded very down.

'I'm sorry,' I said. And then an idea came to me. 'Giles? That aunt of yours. The one you said was the cleverest person you'd ever met.'

'Aunt Frankie, yes.'

'Is she still alive?'

'Yes. She's pretty old, though.'

'I've been thinking,' I said. 'I wondered if someone who knew about this sort of thing might be able to look at Hannah Mahoney's map and Kevin Seeger's information and, well, you know . . . come to a conclusion.'

There was a long silence. 'Interesting idea,' he said finally. 'Do you think that there's any way you could get a copy of her map? I know that Hannah's pretty scary.'

'I'll talk to her. But do you think that aunt of yours might be a help?'

'She might,' he said. 'I'll get her number. And I'll phone her, tell her to expect your call. Would it be better if I came and saw Hannah Mahoney myself? I'm not too well, though. Tell her you're speaking on behalf of me, if there's a problem. You need to make it clear to her that this will benefit the campaign.'

I looked over at Bruce, who was flying through the air, totally missing a long-range shot. 'I'll try to convince her.'

When we got back, Hannah had made lunch. She asked if I wanted to stay and I said yes, I needed to talk to her about something. She gave me a suspicious look and we ate mainly in silence while Bruce maintained a monologue which was almost a minute-by-minute account of the match. He only stopped when Hannah gave him an ice lolly.

'I've arranged for you to go round and see Nicky this afternoon.'

Bruce gave a loud slurp on his lolly. 'I can't,' he said. 'I want to stay here.'

'Sorry, love, I've arranged it. I'll pick you up later.'

In a pre-emptive strike, Hannah told me to make coffee and she scooped him up and led him out of the house, still protesting. I'd only just poured it into the pot when she came back.

'We've got about two hours. I thought you might like to try my bed. It's better.'

SHE WAS SUSPICIOUS when I told her about my conversation with Giles. 'He asked for my data before. I was dubious then and I'm dubious now. You say that he wants to revenge himself on Wortley. There's another possibility. From what you say, he feels he's in trouble. He might be going along with your suggestion because he thinks it will bring him back into favour with his employer.'

'He didn't sound like that,' I said. 'He sounded like he was happy to go down in flames.'

Hannah leaned over and kissed me. 'And you may go down with him,' she said.

'I'm just interested,' I said. 'I want to know. Don't you?'

'Who is this aunt? What can she do?'

'I don't know. I'm meant to phone her. But there's no point in talking to her if I don't have your maps.'

'Maps? Not just the Marston Green map?'

'The others as well.'

'The others aren't ready yet. I've got the responses but the maps aren't finished.'

'I'll help you with the maps.'

'I don't need your help,' she muttered. 'I haven't said I'll let you have them.' She was frowning with concentration, but it is hard to look grim and businesslike lying naked on a bed in the middle of the afternoon. 'Phone this woman,' she said eventually. 'It may be a dead end anyway.'

The number was on a piece of paper in my trouser pocket. I dialled it and it rang for a long time. When it was finally answered it sounded as if the phone had been pushed off a table onto a hard floor.

'Hello?' I said.

There was no answer but I could hear the sound of someone making a fumbling attempt to pick the receiver up.

'Hello?' said a voice. 'Is that Gerald? Would two o'clock be all right?'

'Is that Frankie McDonald?'

'Gerald?'

It took a long time to make my identity clear. I had to explain things slowly. I managed to convey to Frances McDonald that I knew Giles Buckland.

'My nephew,' she said.

That was a start. I started to explain about Marston Green and the cluster of illnesses.

'Giles told me about that,' she said. 'He said you're coming to see me. Would you like to come for lunch?'

'Mrs McDonald . . .'

'Call me Frankie. You have maps, don't you?'

'I've got a map of the affected village. There are two or three others of adjacent villages that are being prepared. They were done as a sort of control.'

'Excellent. They're essential. Would you like to come tomorrow?'

'They aren't ready just yet. Excuse me for just one moment.' I covered up the receiver and looked down at Hannah. 'She wants to know when I can come.'

'I haven't agreed,' said Hannah.

'Hannah, I've seen your map. It's dynamite. And anyway, what have you got to lose?'

She looked hesitant. 'What's she going to do?'

'I don't know. Why not try it?'

She looked doubtful but she nodded. 'All right.'

'When?'

'A couple of days.'

'Hello? Are you still there, Frankie? I'll have the finished maps by Tuesday. Is that all right?'

'What do the maps look like?'

'They're just maps of the villages with the addresses of people suffering from cancer marked on it as dots.'

'You need to draw a grid over them. These should be a quarter of a square kilometre each. And cross out squares that are mainly playing fields or woodland or farmland. Can you do that?'

'I guess so.'

'I'll expect you for lunch on Tuesday.'

WE HAD TO START almost straight away. Hannah started to unpack her files and I went down to the Four Feathers to buy a bottle of wine. I noticed Ewan further along the bar, having a drink with someone. I thought, fuck it, and walked over.

'How are you doing?' I said.

'All right,' he said. 'How's your friend? Heard he got banged up.'

'Yes,' I said. 'He was badly beaten up. He's in hospital.'

I looked at Ewan's florid face, the face of a pale, red-haired man who had spent too long in the sun. I just couldn't tell whether he was hostile or just showing the basic indifference we feel when something bad happens to someone we don't much care for. I pushed it a bit. 'Why do you reckon someone in Marston Green would do something like that?'

'Maybe he'd scared people,' Ewan said, taking a sip of his pint. 'People don't like people coming in from outside, interfering. So what about you? Going back to London?'

WHEN I GOT BACK to Hannah's house, there were files and filled-out forms spread out across the floor. I poured us each a glass of wine.

'You know what worries me,' I said. 'Giles always says that it's always about the quality of the data. Isn't it a problem relying on people who just happen to fill in a form?'

Hannah gave her slow smile. She walked over to me and took my wine glass from my hand and put it on the table. Then she gave me a long slow deep kiss. I could taste the wine, cold, sharp, on her tongue. She stepped back and looked at me. 'One of my best friends works as a GP,' she said. 'She also has a young son who has been treated for leukaemia. She's played no public part in the campaign but she has obtained for me the epidemiological details I needed. Completely off the record. Now, I've told you that, and I haven't insulted you by asking you not to tell anyone else.'

I kissed Hannah on her face and neck. 'I just talked to Ewan,' I said. 'One of the guys I think beat up Giles. He said that some people didn't like people coming in from outside and interfering.'

'Do you think he was threatening you?'

'He was being fairly unambiguous,' I said. 'And then he asked me when I was going back to London.'

'That's a good question.'

'I'll have to check in at Wortley soon,' I said. 'They'll be wondering what I'm up to. Which I'm wondering myself.'

IT DIDN'T TAKE two days. It took one very long Sunday, and quite a lot of the Saturday evening before. Hannah carefully drew the map of Heiston, Lingham and Chapel Willow that formed a mass stretching north-east from Marston Green. I used street plans to plot the incidences onto the map. It was laborious and fiddly. Meanwhile Bruce lay beside us on the floor with a large sheet of paper, drawing.

At six o'clock we ate pizza and beer, and then Hannah got Bruce into a bath while I worked and then I read to him while she worked and then Hannah lured him into bed and we worked together. After the map was finished, we made a tracing of the whole thing and then Hannah of the steady hand drew the quarter-kilometre squares over it. Just before nine it was all finished. We propped the map against the wall and proudly surveyed it. There were dark, nasty clumps of speckles, one in Chapel Willow and a few in Heiston and Lingham, but there were clearly more specks in Marston Green.

'So what does that say to you?' Hannah said.

'It's devastating,' I said.

'Are you won over?'

'In all sorts of ways.'

There was a new exhilaration in our sex that evening, as if we were flying together high up in thin air and bright sunlight. Later we lay exhausted, but I couldn't stop caressing her warm, damp skin.

'I think I'm going to leave Wortley,' I said.

'I thought you loved it.'

'I do. I did. I'm not sure if it's right.'

'Why? Maybe we'll get them to pay out lots of money to people who deserve it.'

'Maybe,' I said.

All of a sudden I felt distant from my own life, as if I could hide from it in Hannah's bed. I kissed her breast and then stroked it. Suddenly I wanted to stop the moment. Stop it and go back. Not go through what I was going to have to say. 'Hannah?'

'What?'

I touched her breast slightly more firmly, at the point where it met her chest.

'I think I can feel something.'

8

It was a long and tiresome journey via London, by train, to Frankie McDonald's cottage in High Shapland in Oxfordshire. The village was almost directly a hundred miles west of Marston Green, and by the time I got out of a taxi outside Frankie McDonald's cottage, I had been travelling for five and a half hours.

High Shapland was a more beautiful village than Marston Green. Marston Green had been messed up by new houses built for people who didn't want old cottages with thatched roofs and honeysuckle round the door. They wanted driveways, garages, gravel paths, picture windows with double glazing, conservatories. In High Shapland the houses were made out of the rough, biscuity local stone, the windows were tiny, the walls bulged and curved.

Frankie McDonald's house was right on the High Street, I knocked on the door, but there was no answer and I walked up an alley that led along the side of the house to the garden. A woman was on her knees by the side of a flower bed. I called over the gate but she didn't look round. Finally I had to let myself in through the gate and tap her on the shoulder. I helped her to her feet. She was white-haired with a leathery wrinkled face and was incredibly shabbily dressed in brown paint- and mud-spattered trousers and a navy-blue smock.

'Frankie McDonald?' I said.

'Lunch is cooking away. Are you hungry?' she asked.

'Quite. I brought you this,' I said, handing her a bottle of red wine.

'Oh, goody,' she said. 'Excellent. Come inside.'

She lived in a real old-fashioned cottage with floorboards that were almost black with age, except for the kitchen, which had a floor of smooth stone flagging. It was full of nice bits of furniture, but there was a basic sense of a grip having been lost, of faded paint and dust.

'Now, what have you brought me?'

I unrolled the map on the floor and placed a book on each corner to keep it flat.

She looked down at it. 'These are the four villages?'

'That's right.'

'Excellent. Have you heard of the Texas sharpshooter problem, Mark?'

'No. What is it?'

'Someone empties their gun into a barn door and draws a target carefully around the bullet holes.'

'I don't understand.'

'Hmm,' she said. 'It suggests that people are doing things the wrong way round. You ought to define an area and then look for the incidence of disease inside it. Instead, they sometimes find a number of cases in an area and then draw a line around those cases and it can look alarming. But this doesn't apply in this case. This is excellent. Shall we open your bottle of wine, Mark? There's a corkscrew somewhere around.'

I found the corkscrew after a search through several drawers and opened the wine. I poured two glasses and passed one to Frankie.

'Your good health, Mark,' she said and took a large gulp and then another, so that her glass was already half empty. 'So you've been visiting cancer sufferers?'

'I've seen a couple,' I said. 'A few.'

'Very sad,' she said. 'I never did any of that.'

'You worked in insurance, didn't you?'

'Yes. I was an actuary.'

'Doesn't that deal with illness and death?'

'Oh, absolutely. But just with figures, you know. I think I would have found it terribly off-putting if I had actually gone and met people with dreadful illnesses.'

Frankie drained her glass and I filled it again.

'I'll prepare lunch for us, Mark, and in the meantime if you would be so kind, I should like you to count up the number of squares on your map.'

'There are five hundred and seventy-six,' I said.

'Jolly good. Then I should like you to count up the number of squares with no dots, the number with one, two, three, four and lastly five or more. It will be frightfully boring, I'm afraid.'

It was, but at least it took my mind off lunch, which I had already glimpsed. In an old saucepan there were a couple of carrots, a couple of potatoes and a strange and very fatty cut of meat boiling away in some water. I was finished in twenty minutes and Frankie spooned her strange casserole out onto plates.

'I think we're going to need some more wine,' she said. I had barely touched my glass but the bottle was finished when Frankie helped herself to another glass. 'You'll find some in the cupboard.'

I opened another bottle of red wine.

'The Texas sharpshooter problem. Did I tell you about that?'

'Yes,' I said.

'But that map's not a problem. It's excellent. Was it done by your girlfriend?'

I was stunned. Did Giles know something?

'She's not exactly my girlfriend.'

'Are you sexually involved?'

I took a deep breath. 'Well, yes.'

'You see, it's all about figures. What you have to see is that disasters have to be seen as deviations from a baseline of routine, background tragedy. Do you know what I mean?'

'No, I don't.'

'The truth isn't something that you can just go and look at. The truth is a product of the statistical analysis of trained professionals. Do you want some gravy?'

'Yes, please.'

Unfortunately the gravy turned out to be nothing more than the water that the meat and vegetables had been cooked in.

'The war,' she said, taking another sip of wine. 'Was I talking about the war?'

'No.'

She looked puzzled. 'Did I say I worked in insurance?'

'Yes.'

'I was a statistician.' The word 'statistician' was now rather hard for her to say. 'But in the war, I worked for an intelligence division that was connected with Bomber Command. Oh, now I remember, sex. You were talking about sex.'

'Not really.'

'There was a lot of sex. Do you know, people talk about the sixties, but there was a lot more in the war. It's to do with death. It's a well-known psychological phenomenon.' 'Phenomenon' was also a challenge. 'When people think they are going to die next week, then why not have sex now? My husband was already my fiancé but he was in the army. I slept with pilots and soldiers and all sorts of people.'

Frankie caught my eye and just for a second I had a glimpse of the beautiful, brilliant, naughty, young woman she had been fifty-five years earlier.

'It sounds amazing,' I said. 'But I wanted to talk about these figures. What are you going to do with them?'

'I'm going to apply the Poisson frequency distribution to them.'

'Obviously that means nothing at all to me,' I said.

'The war,' she said. 'Did I mention Bomber Command?'

Conversation with Frankie moved in the shape of a spiral. She would circle back to a previous subject, but just a little further along.

'Yes, you did.'

'We did the maths,' she said. 'We did the calculations for trajectories and flight paths and whether one big bang was better than two small bangs. Once we worked on the flying bombs. Wonderful things. Brilliant German invention. They were unmanned rockets that flew to London. Then the engine would cut out and they would fall. The bombs were falling on London in quite large numbers and people started to claim that the bombs were falling in clusters. Now this might have meant that they were tending to cut out at certain points. But there were even rumours that particular areas were being targeted. So some of us were asked if we could test this mathematically. And we did what you did. We selected an area of South London and we divided it into squares and counted the impacts.'

'Won't you need a computer or something?'

'Just a calculator,' she said.

JUST UNDER an hour later, the cab arrived to take me back to the station. We stood on her front step while the driver waited in the car.

'That was great fun,' Frankie said. 'Let me know what happens.'

'All right.'

'Quite like the old days.'

'I'm glad,' I said. 'Thank you very much.'

'You know, the world is so complicated with all the things in it, sunsets and forests and people making decisions, falling in love, making jokes. It's all noise, fluff on the surface. It can all be reduced to figures. As long as you get the right figures.'

I pretended that I was in a desperate hurry to catch my train and didn't reply.

THINGS SEEM CLEARER when I'm thinking about them in the middle of the night. It's in the daytime, with all the noise and distraction, that it gets complicated. I guess you make about three basic decisions in your life. Where you work, where you live, who you live with and who you love. That's more than three but they're not exactly separate. I felt like I had Kevin Seeger's filing cabinets in my head. Kevin had everything you could possibly get hold of about dioxins and furans, and he sort of knew where everything was, but if you asked him the basic question about whether he could show that Marshco were responsible for the cancer, this funny look came on his face. And I felt like that about almost everything.

When I saw Hannah again, late that evening, I told her about Frankie. We were sitting in Hannah's living room. I was on the sofa and she was in the easy chair, facing me.

'She was an actuary. And in the Second World War she was attached to Bomber Command.'

'Bomber Command? What's that got to do with anything?'

So I told Hannah the flying bomb story. 'She showed me a report on it. There was a map with the impacts marked on it. It really looked as if somebody had tried to hit particular areas and avoid others.'

'And had they?'

'No,' I said. 'It was an illusion. The impacts were entirely random.'

There was a very long silence.

'How could they be sure?'

'It's some incredibly complicated theorem. It made my head ache just looking at it. But if you have a certain number of squares and a certain number of, well, in this case bombs, it tells you, how many squares you would expect with no hits, how many with one, how many with two, and so on if the hits were random. And then they compared that with the distribution of actual hits. It was an amazingly close fit. There was no pattern, except for the pattern you get from randomness.'

'So does it prove that the cancer in Marston Green doesn't come from an environmental cause?'

'No,' I said. 'It just proves that there is a random spread across Marston Green, Heiston, Lingham and Chapel Willow. What is certain is that there is no special cluster in Marston Green.'

There was a long silence and Hannah looked so alone.

'I assume this woman is right,' she said finally, hopelessly. 'You said she was drunk and mad.'

'I didn't understand the formula, but the agreement between the expected figures and the ones on your chart is amazing. I've got them here.' I took a piece of paper from my jacket pocket and unfolded it. 'She said the figures indicated . . . "perfect randomness and homogeneity of the area". I've faxed a copy to Giles and he's going to get someone to check the figures. But they're right.'

'You gave it to Giles?'

'Yes.'

'I guess he would have got the report from his aunt anyway.'

'I suppose so. Did you go to the doctor?'

'I called him. I'm going in for a scan tomorrow.'

'There's a possibility that it might be nothing.'

'That's true.'

At that moment, I had a stinging sensation in my cheeks. It was something I last felt when I was eight years old and about to start sobbing, not because I was sad or in pain but because I was confused and it was all too complicated. I didn't cry. That was the one good thing. I went to the cupboard and got the whisky and two glasses and filled them both. I handed her one and took a deep gulp from my own. I sat next to her. I wasn't going to defend myself. I had nothing to be ashamed about. I hadn't betrayed her. I'd done nothing wrong.

'Were you trying to prove something?' she said.

'Giles thought it was the only way you could win.'

'I don't care what Giles thought. What did *you* think?'

'It didn't work out the way I wanted.'

'You found the killer blow,' she said. 'They'll be very pleased with you.'

'That's not what I've been thinking about,' I said.

'What have you been thinking about?'

I took another burning gulp of whisky. 'The plan was that I was going to come back with these findings and that would make up for the bad things that are happening. But on the train back I was thinking about being afraid.'

'I'm not so afraid,' Hannah said. 'I'm angry.'

'You'll beat it,' I said.

She looked at me sharply. 'Are you an oncologist?' she said. 'Oh no. I forgot. You're making yourself feel better.' I put my hand on her arm but she shook it away. 'Do you want to have sex? Is that what you want? You'll excuse me for having other things on my mind. I'm thinking of Liz and Ella and the others and how it looks as if it's all been for nothing.'

I started to say something and gulped and stopped myself and then didn't stop myself and said it anyway: 'It wouldn't have cured them. If the campaign had worked, some of them would have died anyway.'

Hannah leaned towards me. I thought she was going to kiss me, but she took my glass and placed it on the table.

'I think it's time you went back to London,' she said.

EVEN THOUGH it looked as if we had achieved what Wortley wanted, I just wanted to sneak in unnoticed and get back to work. Giles was even more paranoid than I was and he made elaborate arrangements to prepare the report without attracting the attention of anybody from the office. He summoned me to his house on a day when Wortley assumed I was still in Marston Green.

He still looked rough. His face was discoloured and his movements were generally slow and accompanied by much groaning.

'What do they need to know?' he asked.

'Frankie's analysis of the cluster will have to go in the report.'

'Obviously,' said Giles. 'In fact they already know about it. I sent her figures to Ross Cowan to check. How did you persuade Hannah to give you the figures, by the way?'

'I asked her for them.'

An expression of pain slowly spread across Giles's face. 'Say it isn't true,' he said. 'You and Hannah. It's not true.'

'It *is* true.'

'That's not allowed. It's against the rules, it's forbidden.'

'Why?'

'Lots of reasons. One, it's unprofessional. Two, she's a generation older than you.'

'Six years.'

'Three, she was on the other side. Four, she has a disease.'

'What are you talking about?'

'Five, she has a child, who is presumably psychologically vulnerable to strange men appearing on the scene. Six, you were meant to be working. Seven, you have already seduced and abandoned one Marston Green girl . . . I could go on. And there is certainly going to be no mention of this in the report.'

'Obviously,' I said. 'And you don't know what you're talking about.'

'I'm wondering if we need to mention my business.'

'You mean the assault? Of course you do.'

'I could probably make it work for us. Ill-feeling in the town against anything that could impact on employment prospects, even to the point of violence. Poor old Kevin Seeger probably isn't worth mentioning at all. There should be a mention of our meetings with Marshco. Cooperative and helpful briefings from the management and technical staff, blah blah blah. Anything else?'

'What about the allegations of illegal dumping?'

Giles frowned. 'You're right. We'll need to cover ourselves with a reference. How shall we put it? Allegations of undocumented disposal. No corroborating documents or testimony found. That should do it.' Giles wrote something illegible on his notepad. 'I'll type it up tomorrow morning, send a copy to Donna copied to Broberg, Cowan and Vicki Hargest and it will go into a file, never to be seen again.'

'Is that it?' I said.

'If we're lucky,' said Giles.

'Don't you think it's a bit ironic? Marshco's an awful company and you were badly beaten up by someone connected with them. And you're writing a report letting them off the hook. I won't even mention the people with cancer that we're cutting adrift.'

'I know what you want me to say. You want me to say that I'm worried about my mortgage and my children and I can't afford to take a stand. But I'm not going to. You know what I think about the people with cancer? The truth is, they're ill. And some of them couldn't just accept it. It needed to be someone's fault. They needed to be compensated for being ill by being given money.'

'Is that what you think of Hannah?'

'Do you want my approval of Hannah?' Giles said. 'Do you want me to tell you she's all right?'

'She's not all right,' I said. 'There's another lump.'

Giles started at that. 'I'm sorry,' he said. 'Are you . . .? I don't know how to say it? Are you really involved?'

'I don't know,' I said. 'It feels too hard for me.'

I'D PHONED HANNAH during the day but there was no answer, so I tried her again when I got back to my flat and this time she answered. It felt wrong on the phone, like talking through a narrow crack in a fence. I asked meaningless questions about how she was and how Bruce was and all the notes seemed wrong because there was only one thing to talk about.

'Did it go all right today? At the hospital.'

'What do you think?'

I wasn't sure if she was playing some ridiculous game because I hadn't been there for her.

'Is it back?' I asked.

'Yes,' she said. 'They're doing some further tests. On Monday I go into hospital to have more bits of me cut out, including my other breast. And then I have another course of chemo.'

'I'm so sorry, Hannah.'

'So what are you going to do?'

'I don't know.'

'To prove to me that you care.'

'That's not fair.'

'Not fair? Oh, I'm so sorry. I'm going to have another breast cut off. Am I not being sufficiently sensitive to your needs? I'm so sorry. How's work? Are they pleased with you? I bet they are.'

'I haven't talked to them yet.'

'They will be. I'm sorry, Mark, I've got to go. I'm tired. I'm sorry.'

'We'll talk soon.'

'Sure.'

She put the phone down. I found myself looking at my own reflection in the window. At first I had a puzzled expression and then I smiled at myself. What was there to smile about? I'd known absolutely for sure that the cancer was back, so there was no shock about that. I think that what would have depressed me would have been if she had been all friendly and civilised. It hadn't been like that at all. She was scratching at me like we were two people horribly entangled and she didn't know what to do.

GILES WAS WRONG about everything being forgotten. Within an hour of his delivering the report we were both back in the conference room at Wortley. The circumstances were not exactly the same. We were ordered up with no notice. Nielsen wasn't present and there was no coffee in silver pots. Donna hustled us into the room and Broberg, Cowan and Hargest were huddled in a group at the end. I saw copies of the report on the table. They looked up when we came in. There were odd smiles on their faces but it wasn't exactly a friendly welcome. It was more as if the circus had come to town. Giles limped along the table like Quasimodo, which must have been a feeble bid for sympathy.

'Guys,' said Broberg. 'Welcome back.' We murmured something. Broberg continued. 'We thought you were going to sit in the back of a village hall and take some notes, just a quiet sniffing around. But this, this was quiet like the Vietnam War.'

'I know there was the odd incident,' said Giles.

'Incident? You mean a possible attempted murder? A stand-up row with the boss of the company we represent? Have I missed anything?'

Yes, he had. I stayed silent and looked at the floor.

'I don't see the point of this,' said Giles. 'As our report clearly states, the issue of the alleged cluster in Marston Green is now settled. I don't know what else there is to talk about.'

'Do you two gentlemen know the name Simon Tierney?' asked Broberg.

Giles and I looked at each other. I had never heard the name.

'Mr Tierney is the solicitor representing the Marston Green campaign,' said Broberg. 'He contacted us earlier today. He claims that Marshco made physical threats against you, Giles Buckland, and that the men who assaulted you were employees of Marshco who then made further threats against Mr Foll here. And Tierney tells us that they intend to call Mr Buckland and Mr Foll as witnesses. Do you gentlemen have any comment on that?'

I almost laughed. Fucking Hannah. Shafted. Utterly shafted. I was like a beetle that had had a needle pushed through it and was being displayed on a card. But didn't they kill them first? My legs were still waggling . . . I looked at Giles, who had gone a curious colour.

'It's not relevant,' he said. 'The issue of my severe injuries is utterly marginal to this case.'

'We'll leave that question to our legal department,' said Broberg. 'But I'm intrigued. These alleged threats. This was in a private meeting with the three of you, correct?' Giles nodded. 'Mr Foll, if you were cross-examined on this question, would you testify that threats were made against Giles Buckland by Paul Creek?'

'Yes,' I said.

'And were threats made to you by the people you believe to have assaulted Mr Buckland?'

'That's the way it seemed to me.'

Broberg seemed slightly at a loss for anything to say. He looked at his colleagues. 'Ross? Vicki? Any questions?'

They shook their heads. They seemed in a state of shock.

'I think we can resume this at another time,' Broberg said. 'I believe that we're in a poker game, gentlemen. You can go now.'

WE WERE TOLD to stay in the office until further notice. I hardly dared to catch Giles's eye. As he had limped down from Broberg's office, he had looked the way that people in films look like when they have suffered a trauma. He had stary eyes and was almost unable to speak. We spent a grim day and a half completing paperwork.

I tried to stay out of Giles's way but he came and found me.

'We need to go out,' he said.

He led me out of the office and along the road to an upmarket snack bar. He looked at the list of coffees on the wall.

'Do you just have coffee?' he asked the woman behind the bar.

'Caffé Americano,' she said.

'Can't they speak English?' he complained, as he led me to a table.

It wasn't something I could get worked up about at a time like that.

Giles looked at me warily. 'I'm not sure it was such a good idea to be so clear about the way you'd testify.'

'What else could I have done?'

'You could have lied. That's always a good tactic. If you can't lie, just be vague or boring or unintelligible.'

'Sorry,' I said.

'I suppose there's no point in my even asking you how this lawyer heard about a conversation that took place in an office with only three of us present.'

'I told Hannah,' I said. 'She trusted us with her research. I felt I owed it to her to be frank with her.'

'And she shopped you.'

Suddenly I felt light-headed. I didn't care. 'Didn't we shop *her*? We took her data and used it to destroy her campaign.'

'I don't suppose there's any point in my saying that you let me down?'

'I was trying to do the right thing.'

He took a sip of coffee. 'Let me tell you, Mark. These guys play a tough game. We need a plan. One possibility is that we should get a lawyer. Or lawyers.' He looked thoughtful. 'But that might just make them angry.'

'Stop,' I said. 'I'm not interested in any of this. If you want, I'll walk into Donna's office this minute and resign.'

Giles didn't seem to hear me. 'The question is whether Wortley might sue us.'

'I don't care.'

'I admit, there's a funny side to this,' said Giles. 'But I wish it was happening to somebody else. It was all going to be so simple. And now we're going to court in order to extract damages from our own company. I think firing us is down on the list of the things they're going to do with us.'

I only gave a sort of shrug in response.

'You see,' said Giles. 'This is the problem I have with you. I get this impression that you are planning to immolate yourself as a matter of principle. But you're doing it on behalf of a wrong cause. You saw the figures. You saw the chart. There is no cluster. It's not there.'

There didn't seem anything left to say. We stood up. I told Giles that I couldn't face going back to the office.

Giles looked concerned. 'Don't destroy yourself,' he said. 'Leave that to Donna and Broberg.'

'They know where to find me.'

When I got back to my flat I phoned Hannah and a woman I didn't know answered. She told me that Hannah was in hospital. I wondered if it was Hannah's mother, looking after Bruce. I said something feeble about calling back later.

I had a shower. I put on some jeans and a T-shirt. It was only mid-afternoon and now I regretted coming home. I didn't have anything to do. My mind was buzzing. I should read a book or go shopping or make a decision about my life or do something. Then I found something. That picture, the boat in the sunset that looked as if it had been knitted. I pushed the sofa over and stood on the arm and finally, after all this time, I straightened it.

Afterwards I pushed the sofa back and sat on it. There was a buzz of traffic from outside but inside the flat it was quiet. I felt for just a moment that I could sit here for ever, but I knew it was an illusion. Soon the world would come to get me.

THE NEXT MORNING I went to work but it wasn't like real work. I was like a robot that had been brilliantly designed to imitate work. I arranged files and moved papers around and took some calls and noticed people looking at me in a funny way.

I was an object of curiosity. Look, that's Mark Foll. He's the one who's going to be appearing in court.

I knew it was only a matter of time, and that afternoon, Donna Kiely appeared in the door of our office.

'Both of us?' asked Giles.

'Just Mr Foll,' said Donna. 'Mr Broberg wants him on the seventh floor.'

All these misters. We all knew each other but suddenly it had become formal. It sounded like a bad sign.

'Come on, Donna,' said Giles. 'What's up? If there's any trouble, I was in charge. It's down to me.'

'Write a memo,' said Donna. 'Except I wouldn't, if I were you.'

I followed Donna along the corridor and into the lift. She didn't speak to me, or even look at me.

I tried to think of something I could say in my own defence but my brain wouldn't work properly. My perceptions were hyper-sharp. Everything around me seemed clear and brightly coloured. But I couldn't think. I made myself some quick promises. I wasn't going to beg. I wasn't going to say sorry.

When Donna led me into Broberg's office, he was sitting at his desk, his jacket on, like a king in his throne room. He didn't seem to be doing anything except waiting for me. He spoke first to Donna.

'Donna, will you step outside and set up the call?'

She gave me a curious look and backed out of the office closing the door. I was still a long way from Broberg's desk, so I padded over towards him on the thick carpet. Broberg stood up and walked towards one of the great windows.

I took a deep breath and suddenly felt calm.

'I'm happy to resign,' I said.

'What?' said Broberg.

'If there's some problem, then it's probably best if I just leave.'

Broberg looked thoughtful. 'You like football, Mark?' he said.

'I don't know much about it,' I said.

'Did you know that we have an executive box at Highbury?'

'No.'

'It's a major asset. Like with our modern art. Football's not really my game but it's something we guys are meant to do. You know it's funny, the kind of men that we entertain on match days, chief executives, finance directors, actuaries. They weren't captain of the first eleven when they were at school. They were the boys with thick glasses who sat at the front and paid attention, the ones who joined the electronics club. Now they come to our box and shout like hooligans and pretend that they're all guys together.'

'It's part of being a man, I guess,' I said.

'So the beautiful game doesn't interest you, Mark?'

What was this about? 'I never really saw the point,' I said.

'The phone lines have been burning over the last twenty-four hours.'

'Are we still talking about football?'

Broberg greeted that with a forced smile. 'No, Mark, I'm talking about Marston Green now. We've been exploring the various legal implications.' I didn't reply. 'Now, none of us believe that senior executives at Marshco directly ordered the attack on Giles Buckland, do we?'

'I'm out of this now,' I said. 'I've tried not to speculate.'

Broberg looked at me closely as if he was trying to assess which side I was on. 'Be that as it may,' he said, 'Marshco has been conducting an unofficial enquiry into what happened. One issue that arose was that Giles and you were considered hostile to the company and its activities.'

'Why should that be?'

Broberg gave an impatient gesture. 'Comments you made, questions you raised. Oh, and one other thing. It's the reason I asked you about football. One of the employees allegedly involved takes his son to football on Saturday mornings. He claims that last Saturday you were accompanying the young son of one of the leaders of the protest campaign there. Is that true?'

'Yes.'

Broberg took his jacket off and draped it over his chair. It had a beautiful silky rose-coloured lining.

'I was staggered,' he said. 'Marshco is a significant client. We send two representatives to investigate an issue that threatens their entire existence and one of them forms a liaison with Marshco's leading opponent. Is that what happened?'

'I've been seeing her. It was from her that I got the map which we used to disprove the cluster hypothesis.'

'There's another thing, Mark. When you got possession of this crucial data, which incidentally was a damn good piece of work, why the hell did you take it to an eighty-five-year-old woman in Oxfordshire? I'm paying six-figure salaries to a bunch of actuaries two floors down. Why didn't you give it to them?'

'The only way of getting Hannah's data from her was to promise that it would be looked at independently.'

'I almost don't want to ask you what would have happened if this woman had found that the cluster was genuine.'

'As you said at the beginning, Mr Broberg: if the cluster was genuine, it would be good if we were the first to know.'

Broberg put his hand across his forehead as if he could feel a migraine coming on. 'I take it that you gave her the information which she then passed on to her lawyer.'

'I didn't mean her to make use of the information. She was being open with me, I wanted to be open with her.'

'You realise, I assume, that you have been guilty of gross negligence in your behaviour at Marston Green.'

'I don't know,' I said. 'It was a complicated situation.'

'It's complicated *now*,' said Broberg. 'Jesus.'

The phone rang and Broberg picked it up as if he was expecting it.

'Yeah,' he said. 'Good.'

He pressed a button and replaced the receiver. Immediately a booming voice came out of a speaker. 'Hello?'

'Fergus, good to hear you. I have Mark Foll here with me.'

'Mark. I heard about the old lady. Good job.'

'Thank you, sir.' Suddenly I'd forgotten the second name of the head of Wortley's parent company. 'Sir' would have to do. I was bemused. Did this mean that for some bizarre reason they weren't going to let me resign?

'So where are we, Walt?' Fergus asked.

'What do you say to five million?'

'What does that buy us?'

'The whole deal. Any other claims against Wortley are forfeited.'

'So we have closure?'

'It's a done deal, Fergus.'

'Fantastic. I owe you guys. See you.'

There was a click and the line went dead. Broberg looked at me as if he had just produced a rabbit from his hat and an ace of spades from his ear simultaneously.

'Mark,' he said. 'You are one lucky fellow.'

'I don't understand,' I said. 'Have the people on the campaign agreed to this?'

'Through their legal representative, yes. They'd lost anyway. If you're sitting there with a couple of deuces and someone offers you a few chips, you'd better take them. These cancer sufferers will receive their money now. And five million is a small price to pay for ruling out any nasty surprises in the future.'

'What about the attack on Giles?'

'It's our view that nothing more will come of that investigation. We realise that Giles has undergone a traumatic experience and we will offer an ex-gratia payment to reflect our concern.'

'Ex gratia,' I said. 'Is that Latin for "bribe"?'

'Hey, Mark, let's not be prim about this. I'm sorry for bringing you up here and scaring you but you've got to realise that fucking the opponents of our clients isn't always going to be an appropriate way of working. However, on this occasion, it's all worked out.' He held his hand out. With some hesitation I shook it. 'You did good, Mark. Congratulations. You're an insurance man.'

HANNAH HAD NOTHING to do but wait and I had nothing to do but wait with her, so we had time to talk properly.

'Do you know how much you're getting?' I said.

'That's all being hammered out,' she said. 'There's some very technical sliding scale based on age, dependants, that sort of thing. I'll probably get about sixty grand because of Bruce.'

'Who gets it?'

'It's limited to the original list we drew up for the campaign group.'

'That's a bit tough on the cancer sufferers in Heiston, Lingham and Chapel Willow.'

Hannah swallowed hard. I knew she was already feeling nauseous and the treatment hadn't even started. I felt so sorry for her. 'I'm not going to argue about the justice of this. I didn't achieve anything I wanted. I didn't stop Marshco.' Another deep breath. 'In the end—thanks to my own figures—we had nothing to bargain with. So I just did what I could. Sorry. Hang on.' She clutched my hand, the nails hard in my palm. I found the sensation intensely pleasurable—that it was me she was reaching for out of her fog of sickness. 'We got all we could. It was something.'

A nurse came over and told Hannah they were ready for her.

A LITTLE BIT MORE than two hours later I was sitting next to her in her bathroom. Her head was over the bowl.

'I'm feeling a bit . . .' she started to say and then a shudder gripped her body, a spasm and it was as if she was trying to turn her mouth inside out. All that came out was some slime. It just hung from her lips. I wiped it with my hand and then rinsed my fingers under the tap. I dried my hand and then stroked her naked back.

'The amusing thing,' she said, 'is that Dr Leonard told me that the two chemos I got today rarely cause nausea. That's a comfort.' Even her voice seemed to move in sickening lurches.

I led her to her bedroom. I fetched a bucket from downstairs. She lay naked on top of the covers. She couldn't bear to have anything weighing down on her. The other breast had been removed now and she should have looked like a man but she didn't. She might not have been able to feel the breasts that weren't there, but I could. I ran my fingers over her stomach and chest. Sometimes she flinched and sometimes she gave a slight groan that signalled it made her feel just a bit better.

'Dr Leonard is upbeat,' she said. 'The odds are surprisingly good. No distant spread. There's a fifty per cent chance I'll be alive in five years. Are you going to London tomorrow?'

'I'll be back in the evening.'

'There are other good things,' she said. 'Do you want to marry me?'

'I was the one who asked you,' I said.

'I was asking whether you really want to. I'm not much of a catch. I'm probably dying. I've got no breasts. I'm probably sterile. I throw up all the time.'

'It's your money,' I said. 'I'm after your money.'

'I'm putting it in a trust fund for Bruce. You won't be able to get your hands on it.' She was getting drowsy now. 'I never thought I could fall in love with someone who worked in an insurance company. Can you say it?'

'What?'

'Can you say that you love me? It makes me feel better. Just a little bit.'

'I love you,' I said. But she was already asleep. I looked at her gaunt body that had taken so much punishment, and I saw her chest rising and falling in sleep. The heart was still pumping, the lungs filling and emptying, struggling against it all.

I switched the light off and walked to the window. It was a full moon and the outline of the trees was hard against the sky. There was a squeaking sound from outside, loud and insistent. Was that an owl? Was I gradually going to learn things like that? Was it possible that I might end up living in Marston Green? Was that what growing up might mean? It was a sobering thought.

I turned and looked at Hannah's body, dimly illuminated in the moonlight. I thought of what it would be like if her body was dead. I thought of being dead. Being dead is not being here, but even when we're alive we're still equally absent from almost everywhere. It was a thought that confused me. I couldn't think if it was a comfort at all.

Hannah was one of the dots on her own map. She was one of the figures who, in Frankie McDonald's application of the Poisson distribution, had not formed a pattern. She was part of the noise, the fluff on the surface of reality, the mess, the non-digital part of existence.

I walked across the room and lay down next to her.

SEAN FRENCH

Sean French is one half of the successful husband-and-wife writing partnership that has produced a string of best sellers, such as *The Memory Game, Beneath the Skin* and *Secret Smile* under the Nicci French pseudonym.

We asked Sean, who has written two other books under his own name, and who produces a popular column for the *New Statesman*, what triggered the idea for *Start From Here*. 'I was inspired by all sorts of things. My grandfather was born into a very poor family in Liverpool and left school when he was thirteen. He got a job at an insurance company and worked his way up. I've always wondered what it was like for him—he died before I was old enough to ask. Maybe the rise of Mark Foll in the insurance company is a fairy-tale version of my grandfather!

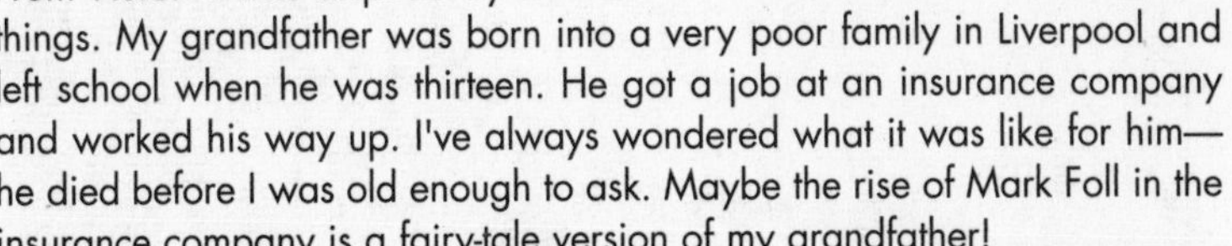

'The germ of the novel was a story I heard about the Second World War (it features in the book). During the bombing of London some areas suffered more damage than others and rumours spread that certain groups were being targeted. These rumours were disposed of not by bombing experts but by actuaries from an insurance company, who were able to demonstrate that the bombs were falling entirely randomly. I was haunted by this story—by the contrast between the suffering and violence of the war and these insurance men with their pens and paper; and how we see patterns where none exist. I wanted to write a story about facing up to the mess and randomness that makes up most of our lives.'

The book also explores the contrast between the careful logic of the world of the claims adjuster and the wonderful illogicality of falling in love. It led us to wonder whether Sean makes most of his decisions based on logic or impulse. 'I am half-Swedish and I am a cautious person; I don't know if the two are connected. But I think that you should make the really big decisions in your life entirely on instinct. Don't be too rational. Virtually everything important you'll achieve in your life will be against the odds—and any rational person will advise you not to attempt it.'

AT RISK
STELLA RIMINGTON

'Our concern is that the opposition may be about to deploy an "invisible".'

An 'invisible' is intelligence-speak for a terrorist who is a native of the target nation; someone who can cross its borders unchecked, move around the country with ease and penetrate to the heart of its institutions.

For Britain's security services an 'invisible' is always very bad news.

ONE

With quiet finality, the tube train drew to a stop. A long hydraulic gasp, and then silence.

For several moments no one in the crowded carriage moved. And then, as the stillness and silence deepened, eyes began to flicker. Passengers peered worriedly through the windows into the blackness.

They were halfway between Mornington Crescent and Euston, Liz Carlyle calculated. It was five past eight, it was Monday, and she was almost certainly going to be late for work.

Liz leaned back into her seat and cautiously extended her feet in front of her. She shouldn't have worn the pointed plum-coloured shoes. She'd bought them a couple of weeks earlier on a light-hearted shopping trip, but now the toes were beginning to curl up from the soaking they'd received on the way to the station. From experience she knew that the rain would leave nasty indelible marks on the leather. Equally infuriatingly, the kitten heels had turned out to be just the right size to get wedged in the cracks between paving stones.

After ten years of employment at Thames House, Liz had never satisfactorily resolved the clothes issue. The accepted look, which most people seemed to fall into, lay somewhere between sombre and invisible. Dark trouser suits, neat skirts and jackets, sensible shoes. While some of her colleagues took this to extremes, cultivating an almost Soviet drabness, Liz instinctively subverted it. She often spent Saturday afternoons combing the antique clothing stalls in Camden Market for quixotically stylish bargains which, while they infringed no Service rules, certainly raised a few eyebrows. At thirty-four, she still resisted being submerged by the gravity and secrecy of her work.

Inclining her head, Liz once again touched her cheek to the silky scarlet nap of her scarf, enveloping herself in a faint scented miasma that brought Mark's physical presence—his eyes and his mouth and his hair—rushing home to her. He had bought her the scent from Guerlain on the Champs Elysées and the scarf from Dior on the Avenue Montaigne. He had paid cash, he later told her, so that there would be no paper trail. He had always had an unerring instinct for the tradecraft of adultery.

She remembered every detail of the evening. On the way back from Paris, where he had been interviewing an actress, he had arrived without warning at Liz's basement flat in Kentish Town. She'd been in the bath, listening to *La Bohème,* and suddenly there he was, and the floor was strewn with expensive white tissue paper and the place was reeking—gorgeously and poignantly—of Vol de Nuit.

Afterwards they had opened a bottle of duty-free Moët and climbed back into the bath together. 'Isn't Shauna expecting you?' Liz had asked guiltily.

'She's probably asleep,' Mark answered cheerfully. 'She's had her sister's kids all weekend.'

'And you, meanwhile . . .'

'I know. It's a cruel world, isn't it?'

The thing that had baffled Liz at first was why he had married Shauna in the first place. From his descriptions of her, they seemed to have nothing in common whatever. Mark Callendar was feckless and pleasure-loving and possessed of an almost feline perceptiveness—a quality that made him one of the most sought-after profilists in print journalism—while his wife was an earnest feminist academic. She was forever hounding him for his unreliability; he was forever evading her humourless wrath. There seemed no purpose to any of it.

But Shauna was not Liz's problem. Mark was Liz's problem. The relationship was complete madness and, if she didn't do something about it soon, could well cost her her job. She didn't love Mark and she dreaded to think of what would happen if the whole thing was forced out into the open. She really had to end it. She hadn't told her mother about him, needless to say, and in consequence, whenever she stayed the weekend with her in Wiltshire, she had to endure a well-intentioned homily about Meeting Someone Nice.

'I know it's difficult when you can't talk about your job,' her mother had begun the night before, 'but I read in the paper the other day that over two thousand people work in that building with you, and that there are all sorts of social activities you can do. Why don't you take up amateur dramatics or Latin American dancing or something?'

'Mum, please!' She imagined a group of Northern Ireland desk officers and A4 surveillance men descending on her with eyes blazing, maracas shaking, and ruffles pinned to their shirts.

'Just a suggestion,' said her mother mildly.

Extricating herself from the maternal web last night had meant that Liz hadn't got on to the motorway until 10 p.m., and hadn't reached the Kentish Town flat until midnight. When she let herself in she found that the washing that she'd put on on Saturday morning was lying in six inches of cloudy water in the machine, which had stopped mid-cycle. It was now far too late to start it again without annoying the neighbours, so she rooted through the dry-cleaning pile for her least crumpled work outfit, hung it over the bath, and took a shower in the hope that the steam would restore a little of its élan. It had been almost 1 a.m. when she finally made it to bed and now she felt puffy-eyed, adrift on a tide of fatigue.

With a gasp and a long, flatulent shudder, the tube train restarted. She was definitely going to be late.

THAMES HOUSE, the headquarters of MI5, is on Millbank. A vast and imposing edifice of Portland stone, eight storeys in height, it crouches like a great pale ghost a few hundred yards south of the Palace of Westminster.

Clutching her coat around her against the rain-charged wind, Liz hurried up the entrance steps and pushed open one of the doors into the lobby. She raised a quick hand in greeting to the security guards at the desk, slotted her smart pass into the barrier, and stepped into one of the security capsules. Briefly she was enclosed. Then, as if she'd travelled light years in an instant, the rear door slid open and she stepped out into another dimension. Thames House was a hive, a city of steel and frosted glass, and Liz felt a subtle shift inside herself as she crossed its security threshold and was borne noiselessly upwards to the fifth floor.

The lift doors opened and she turned left and moved at speed towards 5/AX, the agent-runners' section. This was a large open-plan office lit by strip lights and lent a faintly seedy character by the clothes stands that stood by each desk. These were hung with the agent-runners' work clothes—in Liz's case a worn pair of jeans, a black Karrimor fleece and a zip-up leather jacket.

'And, coming into the home straight . . .' murmured Dave Armstrong from the next desk, his eyes on his computer screen.

'Courtesy of the bloody Northern Line,' gasped Liz, extracting a blue file from the locked cupboard beside her desk. 'The train just *stopped*. For at least ten minutes. In the middle of nowhere.'

'Well, the driver could hardly sit and smoke a joint in the station, could he?' asked Armstrong reasonably.

But Liz, folder in hand and minus coat and scarf, was already halfway to the exit. En route to Room 6/40, one flight up, she hurried into a washroom to check her appearance. The mirror returned an image of unexpected composure. Her fine, mid-brown hair fell more or less evenly about the pale oval of her face. The skin beneath the sage-green eyes was a little bruised by fatigue, perhaps, but the overall result would serve. Encouraged, she pressed on upwards.

The joint counterterrorist group, of which she had been a member for the best part of a year, met at 8.30 a.m. every Monday morning. The purpose of the meetings was to coordinate operations relating to terror networks and to set weekly intelligence targets. The group was run by Liz's forty-five-year-old head of section, Charles Wetherby, and made up of MI5 investigators and agent-runners and liaison officers from MI6, GCHQ and Metropolitan Police Special Branch, with Home Office and Foreign Office attending as required. It had been created immediately after the World Trade Center atrocity, following the Prime Minister's insistence that there must be no question of terror-related intelligence being compromised by lack of communication or turf wars of any kind.

To her relief, Liz saw that the doors to the conference room were open and no one had yet sat down. *Thank you, God!* She would not have to endure all those patient male glances as she took her place at the long oval table. Just inside the doors, a bullish duo from Special Branch were regaling one of Liz's colleagues with the inside track on the *Daily Mirror*'s cover story—a lurid tale involving a children's TV presenter and crack-fuelled orgies at a Manchester hotel.

Charles Wetherby had assumed an expectant attitude by the window, his pressed suit a mute reproach to Liz's clothes, on which the vaporous bathroom air had failed to work any significant magic. The ghost of a smile, however, touched his uneven features.

'We're waiting for Six,' he murmured. 'They're bringing over someone new—one of their Pakistan people. Bruno Mackay.'

'And what's the whisper on Mr Mackay?'

'He's an old Harrovian.'

'As in the story of the woman who walks into a room where there are three former public schoolboys. The Etonian asks her if she'd like to sit down, the Wykehamist pulls up a chair, and the Harrovian . . .'

'. . . sits on it,' said Wetherby with a pale smile. 'Exactly.'

Liz looked out at the rain-slicked expanse of Lambeth Bridge. She was grateful that she had a superior officer with whom she could enjoy such exchanges.

'I think we finally have a full house,' he murmured, glancing over her shoulder.

MI6 were represented by Geoffrey Fane, their coordinator of counterterrorist operations, and by the newcomer, Bruno Mackay. Hands were shaken and Wetherby moved smartly across the room to close the doors. A summary of weekend reports from overseas security services lay beside each place.

Mackay was welcomed to Thames House and introduced to the team. The MI6 officer had just returned from Islamabad, Wetherby said, where he had been a much-valued deputy head of station.

Mackay raised his hands in modest demurral. Tanned and grey-eyed, his flannel suit murmuring unmistakably of Savile Row, he cut a glamorous figure in this generally nondescript gathering. But to Liz, imbued as she was with the restrained culture of Thames House, he appeared much too expensively got up, and his good looks—the deep tan, the sculpted nose and mouth—were far too emphatic. This was an individual—and every ounce of her professional being rebelled against the idea—who people would remember.

With the courtesies done, the group began to work their way through the overseas reports. Geoffrey Fane started the ball rolling. A tall, aquiline figure, Fane had built his career on MI6's Middle Eastern desk, where he had acquired a reputation for unswerving ruthlessness. His subject was the ITS—the Islamic Terror Syndicate—the generic title for groups like Al Qaeda, Islamic Jihad, Hamas, and the myriad others like them.

When Fane had finished speaking he darted his patrician gaze leftwards at his younger colleague. Leaning forward, Bruno Mackay shot his cuffs and addressed his notes. 'Pakistan liaison,' he began, 'has reported a sighting of Dawood al Safa. Their report suggests that al Safa has visited a training camp near Takht-i-Suleiman in the tribal northwest of the country, and may have made contact with a group known as the Children of Heaven.'

To Liz's acute irritation Mackay pronounced the Islamic names in such a way as to make it abundantly clear that he was an Arabic speaker. Just what was it with these people? she wondered. Why did they all think they were T. E. Lawrence?

'Our feeling at Vauxhall is that this activity is significant,' continued Mackay. 'Two reasons. One: al Safa's principal role is as a bag man, moving cash between Riyadh and the Asian terror groups. If he's on the move, then something nasty's in the pipeline. Two: the Children of Heaven are one of the few ITS groups thought to have included Caucasians in their ranks.'

He extended sun-browned fingers on the table in front of him. 'Our concern is that the opposition may be about to deploy an invisible.'

He let the remark hang for a moment. An 'invisible' was CIA-speak for the ultimate intelligence nightmare: the terrorist who, because he or she is an ethnic native of the target country, can cross its borders unchecked, move around that country unquestioned, and infiltrate its institutions with ease.

'That being the case,' Mackay continued smoothly, 'we would suggest that Immigration be brought into the loop.'

The Home Office man frowned. 'What's your view on likely targets and the timing of all this? We should probably up the security status of all government buildings from black to red, but I don't want to move on it too soon.'

Mackay glanced at his notes. 'Pakistan are already on the case. They're checking all passenger lists out of the country. No idea of targets yet, but we'll keep our ears very close to the ground.' He looked across at Wetherby, and then at Liz. 'And we need to stay in constant touch with our agents this end, too.'

'That's already happening,' said Wetherby, glancing interrogatively at the GCHQ rep. He pursed his lips noncommittally then said, 'We've had a bit more background noise than usual. Nothing approaching the traffic you'd associate with a major operation, though.'

Liz looked covertly around the room until her eyes met Mackay's. He didn't smile or look away but stared straight back. Wetherby, in turn was watching Mackay. The circuit held for a long, taut moment and then Fane cut in with a question about MI5 agents in the UK's militant Islamic communities. 'Just how close to the action are these people of yours?' he demanded. 'Would they be amongst the need-to-knows if a major ITS operation was being mounted against this country?'

Wetherby let Liz field it. 'In most cases probably not,' she said, knowing that optimism cut no ice with Fane. 'But we've got people in the right orbits. Time will see them move closer to the centre.'

'Time?'

'We're not in a position to accelerate the process.'

She had decided not to mention Marzipan. The agent would have been a strong card to play but at this early stage in his career she wasn't prepared to reveal him. Wetherby, inscrutable, was tapping his lips with a pencil, but Liz could tell from his posture that he considered her decision the correct one.

And Mackay, she realised with a faint sinking sensation, was still watching her. Was she unknowingly transmitting some kind of bat-like sexual sonar? She felt more irritated than flattered.

Above their heads one of the tube lights began to flicker. It seemed to signal the meeting's end.

ON THE OTHER SIDE of the river, a mile to the east, a Eurostar train from Paris was pulling in to the terminus at Waterloo station. Halfway along its length, a young woman stepped from the soporific warmth of a second-class carriage into the bracing chill of the platform, and was borne on a hurrying crowd towards the terminus building.

The woman was wearing a parka jacket over jeans and Nike trainers. On her head, a brown corduroy Beatles cap from a stall on the Quai des Celestins, its peak pulled low over her face, and—despite the overcast day—a pair of aviator sunglasses. She looked somewhere in her early twenties, she was carrying a holdall and a large rucksack, and there was nothing to distinguish her from the other long-weekenders who spilled from the train that Monday morning.

At the Avis rent-a-car counter, the woman joined a four-strong queue, and if she was conscious of the CCTV camera mounted on the wall above her she gave no sign of it. Instead, opening the morning's edition of the *International Herald Tribune*, she appeared to bury herself in a fashion article.

When she arrived at the front of the queue, the assistant processed her with due courtesy, but he could tell from her cracked nails, poorly kept hands and choice of car—an economy hatchback—that she was not worthy of the full beam of his attention. Her driving licence and passport, in consequence, received no more than a glance.

Slinging her luggage onto the passenger seat, the woman eased the black Vauxhall Astra into the stream of traffic crossing Waterloo Bridge. Accelerating into the underpass, she felt her heart race. Breathe, she told herself. Be cool.

Five minutes later, she pulled into a parking bay. Taking the passport, driving licence and rental documents from her coat pocket, she zipped them into the holdall with her other passport, the one she had shown at the immigration desk in the terminal. Then, checking her mirror, she pulled out slowly into the traffic stream.

READING THROUGH the Marzipan file at her desk in 5/AX, Liz Carlyle felt the familiar sick unease. As an agent-runner, anxiety was her constant companion. The truth was grimly simple: if an agent was to be effective, then he or she had to be placed at risk.

But at just twenty, she asked herself, was Marzipan truly aware of the risks he ran? Had he taken on board the fact that, if blown, he might have a life expectancy of no more than a few hours?

Marzipan's name was Sohail Din, and he had been a walk-in. An exceptionally bright young man of Pakistani origin, whose father was the proprietor of several Tottenham newsagents, he had been accepted to read law at Durham University. A devout Muslim, he had decided to spend his gap year working in a small Islamic bookshop near his home in Haringey, in the hope that it would provide an opportunity for religious discussion with other serious-minded young men like himself.

It had rapidly become clear, however, that the tone of the place was rather less moderate than the compassionate creed that Sohail had absorbed at home and at his local mosque. Extremist views were aired as a matter of course, young men openly discussed their intentions of training as mujahidin and taking up the sword of jihad against the West, and there was jubilation every time the press reported that an American or Israeli target had been hit by terrorists.

Unwilling to voice his dissent, but clear in his own mind that a world view which celebrated the murder of civilians was abhorrent before God, Sohail kept a low profile. Unlike his fellow employees, he saw no reason to hate the country of his birth. The crunch came one late summer afternoon when three Arabic-speaking men had entered the shop from an elderly Mercedes. One of Sohail's colleagues had nudged him, indicating a nondescript figure with thinning hair and a scruffy beard. This, Sohail learned, when the three men had been taken to the rooms above the shop, was Rahman al Masri, an important fighter against the Satanic ally, the United States.

This was the point at which Sohail decided to act. At the day's end he had not caught his customary bus home but instead, after consulting an *A to Z*, had made his way to Bethnal Green police station.

Special Branch had acted fast; Rahman al Masri was a known player. MI5 had been notified, an observation post had been set up near the bookshop, and, when al Masri left the following day, it was with a discreet surveillance escort. Intelligence allies had been informed and al Masri was allowed to run. He was eventually picked up at Dubai Airport and taken into custody by that country's secret police. After a week of what was officially described as 'intensive questioning', al Masri admitted that he had visited London to deliver instructions to terrorist cells there. Attacks were to be unleashed against targets in the City.

Forewarned, the police were able to identify and arrest those involved. One of the prime objectives throughout the operation had been to preserve the original source of the information, because it had been agreed between a senior Special Branch officer and Charles Wetherby that the young Asian might be suitable for development as a long-term agent. Wetherby had handed the file to Liz, who drove up to Tottenham a couple of days later. Their first meeting took place in a disused classroom at the evening institute where Sohail took a weekly computer course.

She had been shocked by how young he was. Physically slight and neatly dressed in a jacket and tie, he still looked like a schoolboy. But, talking to him, she was struck by the unswerving rigour of his moral code. Nothing justified murder, he told her, and if informing on his co-religionists helped to prevent it, and to protect the good name of Islam from those who sought the nihilist Apocalypse, then he was happy to do so. She had asked him if he would consider putting off university for a further year in order to remain in place at the bookshop for another twelve months—twelve months in which, for all she knew, anything could happen. And, at the very least, the delay would seriously threaten his dream of becoming a lawyer.

His distress had been almost invisible—a momentary shudder behind his eyes. And then, with a quiet smile, as if to reassure Liz that all would be well, he had agreed to continue.

His bravery had wrung Liz's heart. She prayed that she would never have to meet Sarfraz and Rukhsana Din, never have to tell them that their son had died for his faith and his country.

'Bad one?' asked Dave Armstrong from the next desk.

'You know how it is,' said Liz, exiting the Marzipan file on screen. 'Sometimes this job can be really shitty.'

'I know. And that supposed goulash I saw you tackling in the canteen can't have improved your mood either.'

Liz laughed. 'It was kind of a wild choice. What did you have?'

'A sort of chicken thing, glazed with Ronseal.'

'And?'

'It did exactly what it said on the tin.' His hands flickered briefly over his keyboard. 'How was the meeting this morning?'

'Oh . . . hang on a sec.' Liz leaned forward towards her screen again, where an icon had appeared. She clicked her mouse.

'Trouble?'

'Flash from German liaison. UK driving licence ordered from one of the fake documents guys in Bremerhaven. Four hundred marks paid. Name requested, Faraj Mansoor. Ring any bells?'

'No,' said Armstrong. 'Probably just some illegal migrant who wants to rent a car. You can't shout terrorist every time.'

'Six reckons there could be an ITS invisible on the move.'

'Where from?'

'One of the Northwest Frontier Province camps.'

'Definitely?'

'No. Just smoke.' She saved the message.

The office door swung open and a hard-faced young man in an Aryan Resistance T-shirt strolled in.

'Yo, Barney!' said Dave. 'How's the world of the Far Right? I take it from the haircut that you've got a social engagement later on?'

'Yeah. A lecture, on the European Pagan Tradition, or should I say New Age Hitler-worship.'

'Excellent!'

Barney grinned. 'Can I show you guys something?'

'You sound like a flasher. Quickly—I've got a full in-box here.'

Barney reached beneath his desk, bringing out a limp rubber mask and a scrap of red felt. 'It's for the Christmas party. I've found this place that makes them. I've had fifty done.'

Liz stared incredulously at the mask. 'That's brilliant! It's so like him,' she said.

'I know, but don't say anything. I want it to be a surprise for Wetherby. No one in this department can keep a secret for five minutes, so I'm not going to hand them out until the actual day.'

Liz laughed out loud, the plight of Sohail Din temporarily displaced by the thought of their section leader faced with fifty beaming David Shaylers in Santa hats.

WHEN LIZ arrived back at her basement flat in Kentish Town, the place had a reproachful air about it. It wasn't so much untidy as neglected; most of her possessions still lay where she had left them at the beginning of the weekend. The remote control in the centre of the carpet. The Saturday papers strewn about. On the answering machine, a tiny pulsing red light.

For the next half-hour she tidied up. When the place was well enough ordered for her to be able to relax, she took a cook-from-frozen lasagne from the stack in the freezer, slid the package into the oven, and poured herself a large vodka-tonic.

There was just one message on the answering machine. It was from Mark. He had rung at 12.46 that afternoon from Nobu in Park Lane, where he was waiting to give an American actress an expense-account lunch. The actress was late, however, and Mark's thoughts had turned to the flat in Inkerman Road, NW5, and the possibility of spending the night there with the flat's owner. Following a bite to eat, perhaps, at the Eagle in Farringdon Road.

Liz deleted the message. The idea of meeting in the Eagle, a favourite hang-out of *Guardian* journalists, was insane. Had he told people at the paper about her? It was clear that the game had moved beyond the realm of acceptable risk. He was playing with her, drawing her inch by inch towards self-destruction.

Taking a deep swallow of her drink, Liz called up his mobile. She was going to do it right now—finish it once and for all. It would hurt like hell, but she wanted her life back under her own control.

She got his voicemail, which probably meant that he was at home with Shauna. Where he bloody well should be, she mused sourly.

ANNE LAKEBY woke to see her husband Perry standing in front of the open bedroom window, looking out over the garden towards the sea. The day was a clear one, sharpened by the suggestion of a salt breeze, and her husband looked almost priestly in his long Chinese dressing gown. His hair was damp, and had been smoothed to a dull gleam by the twin ivory-backed hairbrushes in the dressing room. He also appeared to have shaved.

The old bugger certainly brushed up well, she thought, but it was unlike him to take quite this much trouble so early in the day. Squinting at the alarm clock she saw that it was barely 7 a.m.

As Perry pulled the window shut, Anne closed her eyes, feigning sleep. The door closed, and five minutes later her husband reappeared with two coffee cups and saucers on a tray. This was truly alarming. The breezier his demeanour, in her experience, the closer to the wind he was sailing.

At the faint rattle of crockery Anne mimed her own awakening. 'This is a . . . nice surprise.' She blinked drowsily, reaching for the glass of water on the bedside table. 'To what do I owe . . .'

'I was expecting a titanic hangover after last night,' Perry said, 'but a benign deity has stayed his hand. The sun, moreover, is shining. It is a day for gratitude.'

Anne pulled herself into a sitting position against the pillows, not quite believing in this considerate, coffee-making version of her spouse. He was definitely up to something.

'They really are the bloody end though, aren't they?' Perry continued, referring to last night's dinner guests.

'Who? Dorgie and Diane?' Dorgie was Anne's nickname for Sir Ralph Munday, whose snouty features reminded her of one of the Queen's corgi-dachshund crosses. Inasmuch as the Lakebys and the Mundays owned the two largest and most consequential properties in Marsh Creake, they considered themselves 'neighbours', although their houses were a good half-mile apart.

'Who else? All that awful shooting talk. High cocks . . . full choke at fifty yards . . . he sounds as if he's learned the whole thing from a book. And she's worse, with her—'

'Where does he shoot?'

'Some pop-star syndicate near Houghton. One of the members, Dorgs was telling me, made his money out of Internet porn.'

'Well, you shoot with an arms dealer,' said Anne mildly.

'True, but that's all very ethical these days. You can't just flog the stuff to African dictators off the back of a lorry.'

They drank their coffee in silence for a few moments.

'You know Ray?' said Anne, her tone exploratory.

Perry looked at her. Ray Gunter was a fisherman who lived in the village and who kept a couple of boats and a tangle of lobster-nets on the private beach at the end of the Hall's grounds. 'What about him?'

'Do we absolutely have to keep up this business of him coming and going through the grounds? He gives me the creeps.'

Perry frowned. 'The Gunters have had boats there since my grandfather's time, at least. Ray's father—'

'I know, but Ray's father is dead. And where Ben Gunter was the nicest old boy you could hope to meet, Ray is frankly sinister. The dogs don't like him either.'

'He may not be the world's most sparkling conversationalist, and he probably niffs a bit, but that's fishing for you. I think we might get into all sorts of trouble if we tried to run him off the place.'

'At least let's find out what our legal position is.'

'Why go to the expense?'

'Why not? Why are you so . . . ' She placed her coffee cup on the bedside table. 'I'll tell you something else Sophie told me. You know the sister, Kayleigh? Apparently she works a couple of nights a week in a club in King's Lynn as a stripper.'

'Really?' Perry raised his eyebrows. 'I didn't know King's Lynn offered such lurid temptations. Did she mention the club's name?'

'Perry, stop it. The point I'm making is that the present generation of Gunters are not quite the simple fisherfolk their parents were.'

Perry shrugged. '*Tempus mutantur, et nos mutamur in illis*.'

'And what's that supposed to mean?'

He walked back to the window. Looked out over the shining expanse of Norfolk coastline to the east and west of them. 'Times change,' he murmured, 'and we change with them. Ray Gunter's doing us no harm at all.'

Anne sighed. Perry could be wilfully obtuse when he wanted to be. She was worried, too. She could always tell when he was up to something—and he was up to something now.

TWO

Nu-Celeb Publications of Chelmsford, Essex, occupied a low modular building on the Writtle Industrial Estate to the south-west of the town. The premises were spare and utilitarian, but they were warm, even at nine in the morning. Melvin Eastman hated to be cold and he was still wearing the camel-hair overcoat in which he had arrived ten minutes earlier. A smallish man with neatly dressed hair of a slightly unnatural blackness, Eastman's features remained expressionless as he sat at his desk examining the front page of his newspaper. Finally, leaning forward, he reached for one of the telephones on the desk.

'Ken, how many Mink Parfait calendars have we had printed up?'

On the floor below, his foreman looked up at him. ''Bout forty thou, boss. Should be the big Christmas seller. Why?'

'Because, Ken, according to the *Sun*, Mink Parfait are splitting up. We're not going to be able to give those calendars away.'

'I'm sorry, boss. I dunno what to say.'

Eastman replaced the phone and frowned. Nu-Celeb was not the only iron that he had in the fire—the celebrity calendar business had been created as cover for a raft of other, less legal activities that had made him a millionaire many times over. But it still irked him that he could take a bath to the tune of twenty large on the whim of a bunch of scrubbers like Mink Parfait.

A key player in one of Eastman's other business activities, a narrow-featured man in a black bomber jacket named Frankie Ferris, was sitting against the wall. He had a mug of tea in one hand and was smoking, tapping the ash into the bin with nervous frequency.

Folding the newspaper away, Eastman turned to Ferris. Noted the pallor of his lips and the shake of the cigarette between his fingers.

'So, Frankie,' he said. 'How's it going? Everyone paying their way?'

'Yeah. No problem.'

'Any special requests?'

'Yeah, the Ecstasy. Everyone suddenly wants the butterflies. Word is they're stronger than the doves.'

'That's bollocks, Frankie. They're identical. As you know.'

Frankie shrugged. 'Just telling you.'

Melvin Eastman nodded and turned away. From his desk drawer he took a plastic bank envelope and handed it to Frankie.

Frankie frowned. Turned the envelope over incomprehendingly.

'I'm only giving you three fifty this week,' said Eastman, 'because it's clear that I've been overpaying you. You did six fifty at the blackjack table in the Brentwood Sporting Club last Friday, Frankie, and that kind of behaviour attracts attention. I don't put a grand a week in your pocket for you to piss it away in public, understand?'

Eastman's tone and expression were unchanged, but the edge of threat was very close to the surface. The last man to seriously displease his employer, Frankie knew, had washed up on the mudflats.

'I understand, Mr Eastman.'

'You sure?'

'Yes, Mr Eastman. I'm sure.'

'Good. Then let's get to work.'

Handing Frankie a Stanley knife from his desk, Eastman indicated four sealed cardboard boxes that were stacked against one wall. The boxes' stencilled sides indicated that they contained Korean-built document scanners.

Cutting across the seal, Frankie opened the first box, revealing the advertised hardware. With care he removed the scanner and its Styrofoam mould. Beneath were three tightly filled, sealed polythene bags. He cut a small incision in the first bag, drew out a wrap of paper and passed it to Eastman.

Unwrapping the paper, Eastman touched the tip of his tongue to the off-white crystal, nodded, and returned it to Frankie.

'Let's just see if Amsterdam's sent us doves or butterflies.'

'Looks like doves in this one,' said Frankie nervously, peering at a bag of Ecstasy tablets. 'Must be using up old stock.'

The same operation was applied to the other three boxes. Carefully, Frankie packed a rucksack with the bags of Ecstasy, temazepam, and methamphetamine crystal, topping the load off with a dingy T-shirt.

'The butterflies go to Basildon, Chelmsford and Southend,' said Eastman. 'The doves to Harlow, Braintree, Colchester—'

His phone rang and he held up a hand, indicating that Frankie should wait. As the conversation progressed he glanced at him once or twice, but Frankie was staring out over the shop floor.

Was he using? Eastman wondered. Or was it just the gambling? Should he offset the morning's stick with a bit of carrot—push a couple of fifties into his back pocket on the way out?

In the end he decided not to. The lesson had to be learned.

'FARAJ MANSOOR,' said Charles Wetherby, returning his tortoiseshell reading glasses to his top pocket. 'Name mean anything to you?'

Liz nodded. 'Yes. German liaison flashed him to us yesterday. He bought a fake UK driving licence last weekend in Bremerhaven. I ran him through the database and there's a Faraj Mansoor on the list logged by Pakistan liaison of all those contacted by Dawood al Safa during his visit to Peshawar earlier this year.'

'Al Safa the ITS bagman? The one Mackay was telling us about?'

'Yes, that one. This Mansoor—and it's got to be a common name—

is identified as one of half a dozen employees of an auto repair shop on the Kabul road. Apparently al Safa stopped there and looked at some second-hand vehicles.'

'And that's it?'

'That's it.'

Wetherby nodded pensively. 'The reason I'm asking is that for some reason I can't presently fathom, Geoffrey Fane's just called me with a request to be kept in the loop.'

'About Mansoor?' asked Liz, surprised.

'Yes. I told him that, as things stood, there was no loop. And that was it. He thanked me and hung up.'

Liz allowed her eyes to wander round the bare walls. Wondered why Wetherby had called her to his office for a conversation that could easily have taken place over the phone.

'Before you go, Liz, is everything all right? I mean, are you OK?'

She met his gaze. As always, a subtle irony seemed to pervade their professional relationship, as if they met at other times and on some different basis. But they never had, and outside the context of their work Liz knew very little about him. There was a wife who was supposed to have some sort of chronic health problem, and there were a couple of boys at school, but that was the limit of her knowledge.

'Do I look as if I'm not OK?'

'You look fine. But I know this Marzipan business hasn't been easy. He's very young, isn't he?'

'Yes. He is.'

Wetherby nodded obliquely. 'He also promises to be one of our key assets, which is why I gave him to you. You debrief him and let me see the product—I don't want him declared for the time being.'

Liz nodded. 'I don't think he's registered on Fane's radar yet.'

'Let's keep it that way. We have to play a long game with this young man. Just concentrate on getting him solidly dug in. If he's as good as you say he is, the product will follow.'

'As long as you're prepared to wait.'

'For as long as it takes.'

SHE RETURNED to her desk to find the message light on her land line flashing. To her surprise, there was an invitation to lunch from Bruno Mackay.

'I know it's hideously short notice,' came the languid voice, 'but there's something I'd like to . . . *mull over* with you, if I may.'

She shook her head in disbelief. That was so Six, the suggestion that the day—and the business of counterterrorism—was really one long cocktail party. *Mull?* She never mulled. But why not? At the very least it would be an opportunity to examine Mackay at close quarters. For all the supposed new spirit of cooperation, Five and Six would never be serene bedfellows. The better she knew her opposite number, the less likely he was to outmanoeuvre her. She called the number he had left her and he picked it up on the first ring.

'Liz!' he said, before she had opened her mouth. 'Tell me you can come.'

'All right.'

'Fantastic! I'll pick you up. Can you be on Lambeth Bridge, your end, at twelve forty-five?'

'OK.'

She hung up. This could be very interesting, but she was going to have to stay on her toes. Swivelling round to her computer screen, she turned her thoughts to Faraj Mansoor. Fane's anxiety, she supposed, sprang from his uncertainty as to whether the buyer of the fake driving licence in Bremerhaven was the same person as the al Safa contact in Peshawar. He'd probably have someone in Pakistan checking the auto repair shop right now. Odds were that they *were* two different people, and that the Mansoor in Bremerhaven was an economic migrant who was looking to make his way across the Channel. Odds were the whole thing was an Immigration issue, not an Intelligence one. She posted it to the back of her mind.

By 12.30 she was feeling a curious anticipation. As luck would have it—or maybe not—she was smartly dressed. With all her work clothes either damp from the washing machine or languishing in the dry-cleaning pile, she had been forced back to the Ronit Zilkha dress she had bought for a wedding. It had cost a fortune and looked wildly inappropriate for a day's intelligence-gathering. To make matters more extreme, the only shoes that went with the dress were ribbed silk.

At twenty to the hour she left the office with the Zilkha dress partly covered by her coat.

Lambeth Bridge, she discovered, was not an ideal rendezvous in December. After a fine morning the sky had darkened. A fretful east wind now whipped down the river.

She had been standing there for five minutes, her eyes streaming, when a silver BMW came to an abrupt stop at the kerb and the passenger door swung open. To the blaring of car horns she bustled herself into the seat, then Mackay pulled back out into the traffic stream.

As they slotted into the traffic-crawl on Albert Embankment, Mackay said, 'So, Liz, how are you?'

'I'm . . . fine,' she answered. 'Thank you very much.'

'Good.'

She looked sideways at him. He was wearing a pale blue shirt, open at the neck and with the sleeves rolled halfway up so as to provide a generous expanse of tanned forearm. The watch, which looked as if it weighed at least half a kilo, was a Breitling Navitimer.

'So!' she said. 'To what do I owe the honour . . .'

He shrugged. 'We're opposite numbers, you and I. I thought we might have a bite of lunch and a glass of wine and compare notes.'

'I'm afraid I don't drink at lunchtime,' Liz rejoined, and then regretted it. She sounded shrewish and there was no reason to suppose that Mackay was trying to be more than friendly.

'I'm sorry about the short notice,' said Mackay, glancing at her.

'No problem. I'm not exactly a lady who lunches, unless you count a sandwich and a batch of surveillance reports at my desk.'

'Don't take this the wrong way,' said Mackay, glancing at her again, 'but you do actually look quite like someone who lunches.'

'I'll take that as a compliment. In fact, I'm dressed like this because I've got a meeting this afternoon.'

'Ah. You're running an agent in Harvey Nichols?'

She smiled and looked away. The vast and intolerant bulk of the MI6 building rose above them, and then Mackay swung left-handed into the convolutions of Vauxhall's one-way system. Two minutes later he was parking the BMW in a narrow cul de sac off the South Lambeth Road.

Mackay jumped out and opened Liz's door for her. 'Are you hungry? he asked.

'I think I am,' said Liz.

'Excellent.' Taking an indigo tie and a dark blue jacket from the back seat, he rolled down his sleeves and put them on, before locking the car with a quick squawk of the remote. 'Do you think those shoes will carry you a couple of hundred yards?' he asked.

'With a bit of luck.'

They turned back towards the river, and made their way to a new luxury development on the south side of Vauxhall Bridge. Greeting the security staff, Mackay led Liz through the atrium into a busy and attractive restaurant. The tablecloths were white linen, the silver and glassware shone, and the dark panorama of the Thames was framed by a curtained sweep of plate glass. Most of the tables were occupied. The muted buzz of conversation dipped for a moment as they entered. Leaving her coat at the desk, Liz followed Mackay to a table overlooking the river.

'This is all very nice and unexpected,' she said sincerely. 'Thank you for inviting me.'

'Thank you for accepting.'

'I'm assuming a fair few of these people are your lot?'

'One or two of them are, and when you walked across the room just then, you enhanced my standing by several hundred per cent. You will note that we're being discreetly observed.'

She smiled. 'I do note it. You should send your colleagues down-river for one of our surveillance courses.'

They examined the menus. Leaning forward confidentially, Mackay told Liz that he could predict what she was going to order. Taking a pen from his pocket he handed it to her and told her to tick what she had chosen.

Taking care not to let him see, holding the menu beneath the table, Liz marked a salad of smoked duck breast. It was a starter, but she wrote the words "as main course" next to it.

'OK. Now fold the menu up. Put it in your pocket.'

She did so. She was certain that he hadn't seen what she'd written.

When the waiter came Mackay ordered a venison steak and a glass of Italian Barolo. 'And for my colleague,' he added with a faint smile, nodding at Liz, 'the duck breast salad. As a main course.'

'Very clever,' said Liz, frowning. 'How did you do that?'

'Classified. Have some wine.'

She would have liked some, but felt that she had to stick with her not-at-lunchtime statement. 'I won't, thanks.'

'Just a glass. Keep me company.'

'OK, just one then. Tell me how you . . .'

'You don't have the security clearance.'

Liz looked around her. No one could possibly have seen what she'd written. Nor were there any reflective surfaces in sight.

'Funny guy. Just tell me,' she said, overcome by irritation.

'OK, I will. We've developed contact lenses that enable us to see through documents. I'm wearing a pair now.'

She narrowed her eyes at him, beginning to feel distinctly angry.

'And you know something,' he continued, 'they work on fabric too.'

Before Liz could respond, a shadow fell across the tablecloth, and she looked up to see Geoffrey Fane standing over her.

'Elizabeth. What a pleasure to see you on our side of the river. I hope Bruno's looking after you properly?'

'Indeed,' she said, and fell silent. There was something chilling about Fane's efforts to be friendly.

He gave a slight bow. 'Please give my regards to Charles. As you know, we hold your department in the highest esteem.'

'Thank you,' said Liz. 'I will.'

At that moment the food arrived. As Fane moved away, Liz glanced at Mackay and was in time to see a look of complicity pass between them. Was there an element of the put-up job about the occasion?

'Tell me,' she said. 'How is it, being back here?'

Mackay ran a hand through his sun-faded hair. 'It's good,' he said. 'Islamabad was fascinating, but hard core. I was undeclared there rather than part of the accredited diplomatic team, and while that meant I could get a lot more done in agent-running terms, it was also a lot more stressful.'

'You lived off base?'

'Yes, in the suburbs. Nominally I was employed by one of the banks, so I turned up every day in a suit and then did the social circuit in the evening. After that I'd usually be up all night either debriefing agents or encrypting and flashing reports back to London. So it was pretty knackering.'

'What drew you into the business in the first place?'

A smile touched the curve of his mouth. 'Probably the same as you. The chance to practise the deceit that has always come naturally.'

'Has it? Always come naturally, I mean?'

'I'm told that I lied very early. And I never went into exams at school without a crib. I'd write it all up the night before with a mapping pen on air-mail paper, and then roll it up inside a Biro tube.'

'What was the reason you gave for wanting to join Six?'

'Patriotism. It seemed the right line to take at the time.'

'And is that the true reason?'

'Well, you know what they say. Last refuge of the scoundrel, and so on. Really, of course, it was the women. All those glamorous Foreign Office secretaries. I've always had a Moneypenny complex.'

'I don't see many Moneypennys in here.'

The grey eyes flickered amusedly around the room. 'It does rather look as if I got it wrong, doesn't it? How about you?'

'I never had a secret agent complex, I'm afraid. I was one of the first intake that answered that "Waiting for Godot?" advert.'

'Like the chatty Mr Shayler.'

'Exactly.'

The waiter approached, and before Liz could protest Mackay had pointed at their glasses to indicate a refill. Liz took advantage of the brief hiatus to take stock of the situation. Bruno Mackay was an outrageous flirt but he was undeniably good company.

'So what about you?' she asked. 'Did you join the Service straight out of university?'

'No. I read Arabic at Cambridge and went into the City as a Middle East analyst for one of the investment banks. Banking lost its shine after a bit, so I sat the Foreign Office exam. Do you want some pud?'

'No, I don't want any, thanks, and I really don't want that second glass of wine either. I should be thinking about getting back.'

'I'm sure our bosses won't object to a little . . . inter-Service liaison work,' protested Mackay. 'At least have some coffee.'

She agreed, and he signalled to the waiter.

'So tell me,' she said, when the coffee had been brought. 'How *did* you see what I'd written on the menu?'

He laughed. 'I didn't. But every woman I've eaten with here has ordered the same thing.'

Liz stared at him. 'We're that predictable, are we?'

'Actually, I've only been here once before, and that was with half a dozen people. Three of them were women and they all ordered what you ordered. End of story.'

She looked at him levelly. Breathed deeply. 'How old were you, again, when you started lying?'

'I can't win, can I?'

'Probably not,' said Liz. She drank her thimbleful of espresso in a single swallow. 'But then who you have lunch with is no business whatsoever of mine.'

He looked at her with a knowing half-smile. 'It could be.'

'I have to go,' she said.

He raised his hands in surrender and summoned the waiter.

Outside the sky was sheet steel. The wind dragged at their hair and clothes. 'It's been fun,' he said, taking her hands.

'Yes,' she agreed, carefully retrieving them. 'See you on Monday.'

He nodded, the half-smile still in place. To Liz's relief, someone was getting out of a taxi.

THREE

Dersthorpe Strand was a melancholy place at the best of times, and in December, it seemed to Diane Munday, it was the end of the world. Despite the goose-down skiing jacket, she shivered as she descended from the Cherokee four-wheel drive.

Diane did not live in Dersthorpe. A handsome woman in her early fifties, with expensively streaked blonde hair and a Barbados tan, she lived with her husband Ralph in a Georgian manor house on the eastern edge of Marsh Creake. There was a good golf links outside Marsh Creake, a little sailing club and the Trafalgar pub. Carry on along the coast and you got to Brancaster and the yacht club proper.

There was evidence of none of these benefits in Dersthorpe, however. Dersthorpe had a country-and-western theme pub, a Londis mini-mart and a wind-scoured council estate. West of the village was the desolate strip of coastline known to locals as the Strand. A mile or so along its length stood five 1950s-built bungalows.

Diane Munday had bought the Strand bungalows a year earlier as an investment. A surprising number of people, strange though it seemed to Diane, craved the near-nothingness that the Strand offered. The unceasing slap of tide on shingle, the wind in the salt marshes, the empty junction of sea and sky, these seemed to be more than enough.

Hopefully they would satisfy the young woman now standing with her back to the westernmost of the bungalows. A postgraduate student apparently, completing a thesis. Dressed in a parka, jeans and walking boots, and holding the Tourist Board directory in which Diane advertised, she was staring expectantly towards the horizon as the wind blew her hair about her face. She could probably look quite presentable if she could be bothered to make the effort, Diane thought.

'It's such a lovely spot, isn't it?' she said, proprietorially.

The woman frowned absently. 'How much for the week, including deposit?'

Diane hiked the price as high as she dared. The woman didn't look particularly wealthy but nor did she look as if she could be bothered to continue her search. Parental money, almost certainly.

'Can I pay cash?'

'Certainly you can,' said Diane, and smiled. 'That's settled then. I'm Diane Munday, as you know, and you're . . .'

'Lucy. Lucy Wharmby.'

They shook hands, and Diane noticed that the other woman's grip was surprisingly hard. With the deal concluded, she drove off eastwards, towards Marsh Creake.

The woman who called herself Lucy Wharmby watched until the Cherokee had finally disappeared into Dersthorpe. Then, opening the passenger door of her Astra, she reached for her holdall and rucksack and carried them through the front door of the bungalow and into the white-emulsioned front room. On the table in front of the seaward window she placed her wallet, her binoculars, her quartz diver's watch, a Pfleuger clasp knife, a small NATO survival compass and her Nokia mobile phone. It was almost 15.00 hours GMT. Seating herself cross-legged on a low divan against the wall, half closing her eyes against the thin light, she began the steady process of voiding her mind of all that was irrelevant to her task.

THE CALL REACHED Liz's desk shortly after 3.30. It had come through the central switchboard, because the caller had dialled the publicly advertised MI5 number and asked for Liz by an alias she'd once used. The caller, who had identified himself as Zander, had been placed on hold while Liz was asked if she wanted to speak to him.

As soon as Liz heard the code name she asked for him to be put through, demanded his number, and called him back. It was a long time since she had heard from Frankie Ferris and she was far from sure that she wanted to hear from him again. She had first encountered him when, as an agent-runner for the organised crime team, she had been part of a move against an Essex syndicate boss named Melvin Eastman, who was suspected of moving heroin between Amsterdam and Harwich. Surveillance had identified Ferris as one of Eastman's drivers, and, when gently pressured by Special Branch, he had agreed to provide information on the syndicate's activities. Essex Special Branch had passed him to MI5.

From her earliest days with the service Liz had had an instinctive understanding of the dynamics of agent-running. At one end of the scale there were agents like Marzipan, who informed on their colleagues out of patriotism or moral conviction, and at the other end there were those who worked strictly out of self-interest, or for cash. Zander was halfway between the two. With him, the issue was essentially an emotional one. He wanted her to value him, to sit and listen to his catalogue of the world's unfairnesses.

Discerning this, Liz had found the necessary time and, gradually, the information had come in. Some of this was of dubious value, but much added substantially to MI5's knowledge of Eastman's operations. Ferris was never admitted to Eastman's inner circle, however, so in the end it had proved impossible to build a satisfactory case against the security-conscious crook. Nevertheless, Essex Special Branch had remained on the case, and when Liz moved to Wetherby's counterterrorism section, the running of Zander was taken over by one of their officers, a hard-bitten Ulsterman named Bob Morrison.

'You should be talking to Bob Morrison, Frankie,' she said.

'I'm not telling Morrison—this is for you. There's a big drop-off Friday, at the headland. Twenty, plus a special, from Germany.'

'I don't know what that means, Frankie. I'm out of that game and you shouldn't be ringing me. I can't act on this.'

'Friday, at the headland,' repeated Frankie urgently. 'Twenty plus a special. From Germany. Have you got that?'

'I've written it down. What's the source?'

'Eastman. Took a call when I was there a couple of days ago.'

'You in a phone box?'

'Yeah.'

'Make another call before you leave. Don't leave this as the last number dialled.'

They both hung up, and for several minutes Liz stared at the scraps of phrases on the notepad in front of her. Then she dialled the Essex Special Branch number and asked for Bob Morrison. Minutes later he called her back from a motorway payphone.

'Did Ferris say why he called you?' the Special Branch officer asked her, his voice echoing indistinctly in her earpiece.

'No,' said Liz. 'But he was adamant he wasn't talking to you.'

'As a source,' said Morrison, 'Frankie Ferris is a total write-off. Ninety per cent of the money Eastman pays him goes straight over the betting-shop counter, and I wouldn't be surprised if he's using, too. He's probably made the whole thing up.'

'That's possible,' said Liz carefully.

There was a long moment of crackle, the whine of car horns.

'. . . going to get anything useful while Eastman's putting money his way. And if he isn't, I wouldn't give much for his . . .'

'You think Eastman would get rid of him?'

'I think he'd consider it. Frankie knows enough to bury him. But I don't think it would come to that. Eastman's a businessman. Probably sees him as a business overhead. They're joined at the hip, basically.'

'OK. Do you want me to send you what Frankie told me?'

'Yeah, why not?'

They rang off. Liz had covered herself; as for the information being acted on, that was something else.

Once again she stared at the fragmentary phrases. A drop-off of what? Drugs? Weapons? People? If it was a sea landing, and the word 'headland' suggested that it was, then perhaps she should have a look at the northern ports.

Just to be on the safe side—it could be hours before Morrison got back to his office—she decided to have a word with a contact in Customs and Excise. Where was the nearest UK landfall from the German ports? Had to be East Anglia, Eastman's patch. No small craft bringing a dodgy cargo was going to run the gauntlet of the Channel; they'd go for the 100-odd miles of unguarded coastline between Felixstowe and the Wash.

THE *SUSANNE HANKE* was a twenty-two-metre Krabbenkutter stern-trawler, and after more than thirty hours at sea Faraj Mansoor loathed every rust-streaked inch of her. He was a proud man, but he did not look like one as he crouched in the vomit-slicked fish-hold with his twenty fellow passengers. Most of these, like Faraj, were Afghans, but there were also Pakistanis, Iranians and a couple of Iraqi Kurds.

All were identically dressed in used blue mechanics' overalls. In a warehouse near Bremerhaven docks they had been stripped of the rancid garments in which they had travelled from their countries of origin and fitted out with secondhand jeans, sweaters and wind-cheaters. They were also handed the overalls and looked, to the casual eye, like a team of guest workers. Before embarking, they had been given coffee, bread rolls and hot mutton stew—a meal that, over the course of the eighteen months that the Caravan had been up and running, had proved acceptable to the bulk of its clients.

The Caravan had been set up to provide what its organisers described as 'Grade 1 covert trans-shipment' of economic migrants from Asia to Northern Europe. For US$20,000, customers were promised safe travel, appropriate EU documentation (including passports), and twenty-four hours of hostel accommodation on arrival.

While the *Susanne Hanke* was equal in terms of stability to anything the North Sea might throw at it, the vessel pitched and rolled like a pig in bad weather. And the weather, from the moment the *Susanne Hanke* made open sea, was very bad, blowing an unremitting December gale.

This did not worry the cutter's bearded German master or his two-man crew, as they held a steady westwards course in the heated wheelhouse. But it had a disastrous effect on the passengers, who were soon retching in misery as the hull reared and fell, and they were thrown, hour after hour, around the steel-ribbed hold.

Faraj Mansoor concentrated on survival. The cold he could deal with; he was a mountain man. But the nausea was something else, and he worried that it would weaken him beyond the point where he could defend himself.

Bracing himself in his seat, Faraj rode out the *Susanne Hanke*'s rise and fall. Was it his imagination, or were those hellish peaks and troughs finally beginning to subside? He pressed the Indiglo light button on his watch. It was a little past 2 a.m., UK time. In the watch's tiny glow he could see the pale, fearful faces of his fellow travellers. To rally them, he suggested prayers.

AT 2.30 A.M., Ray Gunter finally saw it. The light that the *Susanne Hanke* was showing was too muted to register to the naked eye, but through the image intensifiers it showed up as a clear green bloom.

'Gotcha,' he muttered, flipping his cigarette butt to the shingle.

'We on?' asked Kieran Mitchell.

'Yeah. Let's go.'

Together they pushed the boats into the water, felt the spray at their faces and the icy water at their calves. Gunter took the lead vessel, and the two men began to row through the choppy offshore swell. Both were wearing heavyweight waterproofs and life jackets. A hundred yards out they shipped their oars and pull-started the Evinrude outboards. These burbled into life, their sound carried away on the wind. Ten minutes later they were alongside the *Susanne Hanke*.

Clutching their meagre baggage items, and divested of the fouled overalls, the passengers were helped down a ladder to the boats. This was a slow and dangerous process to undertake in near darkness and high seas, but half an hour later all twenty-one of them were seated with their baggage stowed at their feet. All except one, that is. One of them insisted on carrying his heavy rucksack on his back. And if you go over the side, mate, thought Mitchell, it's your bloody lookout.

The return journey to shore was the part Kieran Mitchell dreaded. The old wooden fishing boats could only just manage a complement of twelve, and sat terrifyingly low in the water as the waves broke over their bows. It was a shivering and bedraggled group that helped him drag the boat up the beach and—as every consignment did—fell to its collective knees on the wet shingle to give thanks for its safe arrival. All except one, that is. All except the man with the black rucksack, who just stood there, looking around him.

Once the boats were in place Gunter and Mitchell removed their life jackets and waterproofs. As Gunter unlocked a small wooden shed at the beach's edge and hung the gear inside, Mitchell led the men in single file away from the sea.

The shingle gave way to a turf path, which in turn led up to an open ironwork gate that Mitchell closed behind them. They marched upwards, and the shapes of formal hedges and the flat plane of a lawn were just visible before the path led them to the left. A high wall appeared in front of them, and a door. Gunter opened this with a key, and Mitchell pulled it shut behind the last man. Some fifty yards up the narrow road was the dim outline of an articulated truck.

Unpadlocking the back entrance of the truck, Mitchell led the migrants inside. When they were all in position at the front of the container, Mitchell pulled an alloy barrier across which, draped as it was with ropes and sacking, effectively formed a false front to the container. To the casual observer—a policeman with a torch, for example, looking in from the back—the artic would appear empty.

Mitchell drove, and Gunter took the passenger seat next to him. Gunter reached into his pocket for his lighter and his cigarettes. He usually went home to bed at this stage of the game, but this morning he was taking a ride off Mitchell as far as King's Lynn.

Twenty minutes later they pulled into the lorry park of a transport café on the A148 outside Fakenham. This was where, according to instructions, the 'Special' was to be let out.

As the lorry's hydraulics gassily exhaled, Gunter took a heavy fourteen-inch Maglite torch from the passenger-side locker and jumped down from the cab. Unlocking the rear doors he clambered inside, switched on the torch and opened the forward compartment.

The man with the rucksack presented himself. He was of medium height, lightly built, with unruly black hair and a studious half-smile. He lowered himself to the ground, and hitched the heavy rucksack higher up his back. What did he have in there that had to be so carefully guarded? Gunter wondered. Something valuable, that was for sure. Maybe even gold—he wouldn't be the first illegal to carry in a slab of the shiny stuff.

Following Mansoor to the ground, Gunter locked up the truck. Mansoor held out his hand. 'Thank you,' he said.

'Pleasure,' said Gunter brusquely.

The Afghan nodded, his half-smile still in place. Rucksack on back, he began to walk the fifty-odd yards to the toilet block.

Gunter came to a snap decision, and when the door of the block had opened and closed, he followed in Mansoor's footsteps. Extinguishing the Maglite, he reversed it in his hand so that he was holding it by the knurled grip. Stepping into the toilet block he saw that only one of the stalls was occupied. Genuflecting, he saw the base of Mansoor's rucksack through the gap beneath the door. It was shaking slightly, as if its contents were being repacked. I was right, Gunter thought, the sneaky bastard *has* got something in there.

When Mansoor stepped out of the stall a couple of minutes later Gunter rushed him, swinging the big torch like a steel-jacketed nightstick. The improvised weapon smashed into Mansoor's upper arm, sending him staggering and the rucksack sliding to the floor.

Gasping with pain, Mansoor made a desperate grab for the rucksack with his good arm, but the fisherman got there first, clubbing at Mansoor's head with the Maglite so that the Afghan had to throw himself backwards to avoid having his skull shattered.

Skidding the rucksack out of reach, Gunter kicked Mansoor hard in the guts and crotch. As his victim writhed and clawed for breath, he grabbed for his spoils. The rucksack's weight, however, slowed him down. The couple of seconds' hesitation as he swung it over his shoulder was long enough for Mansoor to reach agonisedly inside his windcheater. He would have shouted if he could have—attracted the stupid English lout's attention to the silenced weapon—but there wasn't the breath in his body. And he couldn't lose sight of the rucksack; that would be the end of everything.

Faraj Mansoor's choices raced to the vanishing point.

The detonation was no louder than the snapping of a stick. It was the impact of the heavy calibre round that made the noise, such as it was.

SECATEURS in her gloved hand, Anne Lakeby moved purposefully along the bank of ornamental sedges and grasses at the foot of the front lawn, cutting back the dead stems. It was a fine morning, cold and clear, and her Wellington boots left crisp imprints in the frosted turf. The shoulder-high grasses prevented any sight of the beach below, but the brownish glitter of the sea showed beyond them.

Robust and unfussy, Anne was a popular figure in the community, and there were few events in and around Marsh Creake at which her loud neighing laugh was not to be heard. Like the Hall itself, she had become something of a landmark.

In thirty-five years of marriage she had never developed much of a fondness for the grey late-Victorian sprawl that her husband had inherited. The gardens, however, were her pride and joy. She worked hard to maintain them, and opened the grounds to the public several times a year.

Perry had brought the house to their marriage, but it was all that he had brought. Born to a local landowning family, Anne had inherited on the grand scale when her parents had died, and had made it her business to keep her personal accounts separate from her husband's. Many couples would have found such a relationship unsustainable, but Anne and Perry managed to rub along together without too much friction. She was fond of him, and within limits was prepared to indulge him in the little things that made him happy. But she liked to know what was going on in his life, and right now she didn't. Something was up.

Pocketing the secateurs, Anne proceeded towards the path that led to the beach. This, like the lawn, was still frosted hard, but Anne noticed that it had recently been considerably churned up. That bloody man Gunter, she supposed. Why Perry put up with him tramping backwards and forwards through their property, night and day, she would never know.

Her thoughts were interrupted by the crackling roar of fighter jets. She looked up as three US Air Force fighters drew cursive trails across the hard blue of the sky. Lakenheath, she supposed vaguely. Or Mildenhall. Which reminded her that police cars had been whizzing backwards and forwards in front of the house since well before breakfast. The place was like Piccadilly Circus at times.

Anne walked down the path towards the sea. The Hall and its gardens occupied an elevated spit of land flanked to east and west by open mudflats. At high tide these were covered by the sea but at low tide they lay shining and exposed, the domain of cormorants, terns and oystercatchers. At the far point of the spit was the seventy-yard bank of shingle known as Hall Beach. This was the only navigable landfall for a couple of miles in either direction, and as such afforded Anne and Perry Lakeby considerable privacy. Or would have done, mused Anne grumpily, had it not also been the place where Gunter kept his boats and nets.

LIZ ARRIVED at her desk at 8.30 a.m. to discover a message to contact Zander as a matter of urgency. She flicked on her computer and pulled down Frankie Ferris's encrypted file. The number he had left for her was that of a public call box in Chelmsford, and he had asked her to ring on the hour until he answered.

She rang at 9.00. He picked up on the first ring.

'Can you talk?' Liz asked, lining up a pencil and pad.

'For the moment, yeah. I'm in a multistorey. But if I hang up, you'll . . . The thing of it is, someone got done on the pick-up.'

'Someone got killed?'

'Yeah. Last night. I don't know where, and I don't know the details, but I think it was a shooting. Eastman's gone completely off his head, ranting on about raghead this and Paki that . . .'

'Just keep to the point, Frankie. Start at the beginning.'

'Well, I went into the office first thing and I ran into Ken Purkiss, that's Eastman's storeman. He says not to go up, the boss is like totally off his . . .'

'Because someone's been killed on a pick-up?'

'Yeah. What he said, according to Ken, was that he'd told the Krauts they were overloading the network. Something about when their problems ended, his began.'

'So did you speak to Eastman yourself?'

'No, I took Ken's advice and slung it.'

'Why are you telling me all this, Frankie?' Liz asked, although she knew the answer. Frankie was covering his back. If Eastman was going down, as well he might if there was a murder hunt, Frankie didn't want to go down with him. He wanted to be in a position to make a deal while he still had a few cards in his hands.

'I want to help you,' said Frankie, his tone injured.

'Have you spoken to Morrison?'

'I'm not speaking to that bastard. It's you and me or nothing.'

Liz considered her options. She didn't want to step on Essex Special Branch's toes, but Frankie did seem adamant about not speaking to Morrison. And she would bounce the information straight back to them. 'How do I contact you?' she asked eventually.

'Give me a number. I'll call you.'

Liz did so, and the phone went dead. She stared at her scribbled notes. Germans. Arabs. Pakistanis. The network overloaded. Was this a drugs story? It certainly sounded like one. Drugs were Melvin Eastman's game. But then a lot of the drugs people had moved into people-smuggling. Hard to resist when you'd got your border guards bribed and a good shipment line up and running.

Liz picked up her phone and rang the Special Branch office in Chelmsford. Identifying herself by her counterterrorism team code, she asked if any reports of a homicide had come in that morning.

There was a short silence, the faint clicking of a keyboard, and she was put through to the duty officer.

'Nothing here,' the officer said. 'But apparently Norfolk had a shooting early this morning. Toilet block of the Fairmile transport café near Fakenham. Crime are on the case but we've sent a man down there because there was a query on the weapon used.'

'What sort of query?'

'Ballistics identified the round as . . .' there was the sound of papers being shuffled, '7.62 millimetre armour-piercing.'

'Thanks,' said Liz, noting down the calibre. 'What's the name of your bloke down there?'

'Steve Goss. Want his number?'

'Please.'

He gave it to her and she broke the connection. For some minutes she stared at her notes. She was no expert, but she knew that 7.62 calibre weapons were usually military or ex-military rifles. Perfect for the battlefield, but a pretty unwieldy choice for close-quarter murder. And an armour-piercing round? What was that all about?

She turned the facts round in her mind. Whichever way she combined them they looked bad. Dutifully she rang Bob Morrison. Once again the Special Branch officer rang her back from a public phone, but this time the reception was better. He had heard about the killing at the transport café, he said, but not in any detail.

Liz repeated what Ferris had told her. Morrison's responses were curt, and she sensed his acute resentment that his source, however supposedly useless, had cut him out of the loop.

'Zander says that Eastman was livid,' she told him.

'I'd be livid if I was Eastman. The last thing he wants is trouble on his patch.'

'I'm sending you the details of Zander's call, OK?'

'Yeah, sure. Like I said, I don't believe a word the little toerag says, but do by all means nod the stuff over if you like.'

'On its way,' said Liz, and hung up.

Would he forward the conversation to the Norfolk Special Branch? she wondered. He certainly ought to. But he might just sit on it out of sheer bloody-mindedness. It would be a way of putting her—Liz—in her place, and if anyone asked questions afterwards he could claim that Zander was an unreliable source.

Reaching for her keyboard she called up an Ordnance Survey map with Fakenham at its centre. The town was about ten miles due south of Wells-next-the-Sea, which was on Norfolk's long north coast, most of which seemed to be salt marshes and inlets, with a sprinkling of villages and large private estates. Lonely, sea-girt countryside, it looked. A perfect smuggler's coast. And less than 300 miles from the German ports. Slip out of Bremerhaven when the light began to fade, and you could be lying off one of those creeks under cover of the early-morning darkness thirty-six hours later.

Bremerhaven again. The place where the fake UK driver's licence had been issued to Faraj Mansoor. Was there a connection? At the back of her mind was Bruno Mackay's report that one of the terrorist organisations was about to run an invisible against the UK.

Could Faraj Mansoor be the invisible? Unlikely—it would almost certainly be an Anglo-Saxon type. So who was Faraj Mansoor and what was he doing in Bremerhaven buying a forged driver's licence? The fact that he wasn't after a passport suggested that he didn't need one, was he already a UK citizen?

Mansoor, she wrote, then underlined the name. *UK citizen?*

Because if he wasn't a UK citizen, then two things were possible. That he was coming into the UK on a fake passport that he had acquired from some other source. Or, more seriously, that he was someone whose entry had to remain unknown to the authorities. A senior ITS player, perhaps. A contact of Dawood al Safa, whose job in a Peshawar auto repair shop was a cover for terrorist activities. Someone who couldn't risk passing a Customs' point.

Every instinct that Liz possessed—every sensibility that she had fine-tuned in a decade of security intelligence work—whispered to her of threat. Pressed, she would have had difficulty in defining these feelings, but she had, however, learned to trust them. Five minutes later she was sitting in Wetherby's office and Wetherby was smiling his uneven smile.

'What exactly do you think you would establish by going up there?' he asked her.

'At the very least I'd like to eliminate the possibility that there's a terrorism angle,' said Liz. 'The calibre of the weapon worries me, as it obviously does the Norfolk Special Branch, given that they've got a man sitting in on the investigation. My gut instinct is that Eastman's had his organisation hijacked in some way.'

Wetherby rolled a dark green pencil thoughtfully between his fingers. 'Do the Special Branch know about Zander's call?'

'I passed the information on to Bob Morrison in Essex, but there's a good chance he's going to sit on it.'

Wetherby nodded. 'From our point of view, that wouldn't necessarily be a bad thing,' he said finally. 'I think you should go up there, have a quiet word with the local Special Branch man, see what's what. If you're not happy I'll speak to Fane and we'll move on it straight away. You're sure Zander isn't just making the whole thing up?'

'No,' said Liz truthfully. 'I'm not sure. He's the attention-seeking type, and according to Bob Morrison is now gambling, so almost certainly has financial problems. But that doesn't mean he isn't speaking the truth on this occasion.' She hesitated. 'It didn't sound made up to me. He sounded scared stiff.'

'If that's your judgment,' said Wetherby, returning the pencil to a stoneware jar that had once held Fortnum and Mason marmalade, 'then I agree that you should go. Keep me informed.'

'Don't I always?'

He looked at her, smiled faintly, and turned away.

FOUR

In the tiny bedroom at the east end of the bungalow, Faraj Mansoor slept in unmoving silence. Was this something he had learned to do? the woman wondered. Slung over the bedhead was the black rucksack that he had been carrying when she met him. Would he trust its contents to her? Treat her as a partner? Or would he expect her, as a woman, to walk behind him? To behave as his subordinate?

In truth, she didn't care. The essential thing was that the task should be executed. The woman prided herself on her chameleon nature, her preparedness to be whatever she was required to be at any given moment. At Takht-i-Suleiman she had listened, she had learned, and she had obeyed. She had become a cipher, a selfless instrument of vengeance, a Child of Heaven.

She smiled. Only those who had experienced initiation knew the fierce joy of self-nullification. Perhaps—*inshallah*—she would survive this task. Perhaps she would not. God was great.

And in the mean time there were things to do. When he woke Mansoor would want to wash and he would want to eat. After her landlady's departure the day before she had driven into King's Lynn and stocked up with oven-ready curries from Tesco.

Her name was not Lucy Wharmby, as she had told Diane Munday. But what she was called no longer mattered to her, any more than where she lived. Movement and change were in her blood now.

It hadn't always been so. In the distant past there had been a place called home, a tiny house in South London. A place to which, with the simplicity of a child, she had thought she would always return.

But then the shadows had begun to fall. There was a move from the cosy London house to a Midlands university town. Her father's new teaching job was a prestigious one, but for the bookish seven-year-old it meant permanent separation from her London friends and a hellish new school in which bullying was rife.

She was desperately lonely, but said nothing to her parents, because by then she knew from the tense silences and the slammed doors that they had their own problems. When she was eleven her parents divorced. On the surface the arrangement was amicable. She moved between the two households, but kept herself to herself. She developed mysterious stomach pains, which kept her at home but which refused to yield to any treatment.

When she was thirteen, her parents took the decision to send her away to a progressive boarding school in the country. Classroom attendance was optional and pupils were encouraged to undertake free-form art and theatre projects. In her second year her father's new girlfriend sent her a book for her birthday. One night, unable to sleep, she had finally reached for it and begun to read.

AS LIZ DROVE into the village of Marsh Creake, where the dead man had lived and where the incident room had been set up, she passed the outlying greens of a golf course. No one seemed to be playing but a few hardy souls were gathered outside a small clubhouse roofed in green-painted corrugated iron. She continued past rain-swept bunkers of pale sand on one side of the road and 1960s villas on the other, and found herself facing the sea. The tide was out, and beyond a low sea wall an uneven expanse of grey-green mudflat lay exposed.

Liz nosed her Audi Quattro into the main body of the village. Marsh Creake consisted of a handful of houses strung unevenly along the coast road. There was a garage with three pumps and an oily-floored workshop, and next to it the Trafalgar pub, whose brick-and-beam exterior suggested that it had been built after the Second World War. Alongside the pub stood a gabled village hall, the village stores and a ship's chandler. Behind the shops were several streets of red-brick houses and a low council block.

Parking the Audi on the seafront, Liz stepped out into a stiff east wind, causing a line of herring gulls to lift from the back of a concrete bench and wheel complainingly away.

The words *In Memorium* were inscribed above the entrance to the village hall. Inside, it had the cold, slightly damp feel of a building that was not in regular use. At one end was a small stage, and at the other a laptop computer and a printer had been set up on a trestle table. In front of the table a female constable and a male plain-clothes officer were setting up a VCR and a monitor.

As Liz looked around, a wiry ginger-haired man in a waxed jacket stepped enquiringly towards her. 'Can I help you?'

'I'm looking for Steve Goss.'

'That's me. You must be . . .'

'Liz Carlyle. We spoke.'

'We did indeed.' He glanced at the rain-spattered window. 'Welcome to Norfolk!'

They exchanged smiles and shook hands.

'The DS is still winding things up at the transport café where the shooting took place, but the photographer's just emailed us the pictures. Why don't I take you through them, and then we can wander up to the pub for a sandwich and a chat?'

'Suits me,' said Liz. She nodded to the police personnel, who watched her warily. Stepping over a trail of electronic cables, she followed Goss to the trestle table. The Special Branch officer pulled up a chair for her, sat himself in another, and flicked his fingers over the laptop's touchpad.

'OK, Gunter, Raymond . . . here we are.'

Columns of thumbnail images flickered into view. 'I'll just give you the key shots,' murmured Goss. 'Or we'll be here all day.'

The first image that Goss enlarged was a wide shot of the vehicle park. Along the far boundary of this muddied expanse the heavy goods vehicles crouched like sullen prehistoric beasts. To the left was a low, prefabricated building with a sign reading *Fairmile Café*. Strip lights shone dimly inside it, and the coloured loops of Christmas decorations were visible. To the right stood a concrete toilet block, beyond which a line of policemen in fluorescent yellow foul-weather jackets were conducting a ground search.

The shots that followed showed the toilet block. First the exterior, with the forensics people milling around in their pale blue protective overalls, and then the interior. This was empty—at least of the living. It was dressed in glazed white tiles and contained a hand basin, two wall-mounted urinals and a toilet stall.

The final sequence showed Ray Gunter lying on the floor beneath a starburst of blood and brain tissue. At the centre of this was a black hole where the bullet had passed through a ceramic tile. The round had entered through the left eyebrow, leaving the face more or less intact. The back of the head, however, sagged away from the skull.

'Who found him?' asked Liz, narrowing her eyes against the photograph's bloody horror.

'An HGV driver. Just after six a.m. The pathologist reckons he died between four fifteen and four forty-five.'

'And the round?'

'We were lucky. It went right through the toilet block and lodged in the boundary wall.'

'Any forensic from the gunman?'

'No, and we've been over every inch of the floor and walls. Whoever did this knew what he was doing.'

'What makes you say that?'

'He went for the head shot. The chest shot would have been much easier, but our killer wanted his man down in one. Gunter would have been dead before his knees started to bend.'

Liz nodded thoughtfully. 'And no one heard anything?'

'No one will admit to hearing anything. But then there would have been lorries coming and going and all sorts of incidental noise.'

'How many people were there around?'

'A good dozen drivers sleeping in their cabs. The café shut at midnight and opened at six a.m.' He switched off the laptop and leaned back in his chair. 'We'll know a lot more when the CCTV footage comes in, which will be in about an hour. How about that drink?'

'The drink that started off life as a sandwich?'

'That's the one.'

THE WARMTH of the Trafalgar was welcome after the cheerless cold of the village hall. The saloon bar was panelled in oak and decorated with portraits of Nelson, knotted ropes, ships in bottles, and other naval paraphernalia. A handful of middle-aged customers were nodding and murmuring over ploughman's lunches and pints of beer.

Goss ordered a pint of bitter for himself, a cup of coffee for Liz, and a plate of toasted sandwiches.

'So,' she began, when they had settled themselves at a quiet corner table with their drinks, 'this 7.62 round.'

Goss nodded. 'That's why I'm up here. It looks like a military-spec rifle was involved. An AK or an SLR.'

'Have you ever come across a weapon like that used in an organised crime context?'

'Not in this country. Far too bulky. Your average UK gangster tends to go the handgun route—preferably tooling up with a status weapon like a 9mm Beretta or a Glock. Professional hitmen prefer revolvers because they don't spray used cartridge cases around the place for forensics to pick up.'

'So what's your take on the whole thing? Unofficially?'

He shrugged. 'My first thought, given that Gunter was a fisherman, was that he was involved in drugs- or people-smuggling and had a falling-out with someone. My second was that he stumbled into someone else's operation—some heavy-duty Eastern European mob's, perhaps—and had to be silenced.'

'If that was the case, though, why do it ten miles inland at Fakenham, in a busy place like a transport café?'

'Well, that's the question, isn't it?' He looked at her assessingly. 'Does your presence here mean that your people think there's a terrorist connection?'

'We don't know anything your people don't,' said Liz.

Technically, given that she had reported Zander's call to Bob Morrison, this was true. Goss glanced over at her, but any suspicions that he might have been about to voice were silenced by the arrival of the toasted sandwiches.

'Has the murder caused a big stir?' she asked, when the barmaid, a heavy girl of about eighteen had withdrawn.

'Yeah. Major chaos. A driver called Dennis Atkins actually found the body. He drove down from Glasgow last night and parked up at the Fairmile about midnight. The café had just opened and he was going for a pre-breakfast wash.'

'And all that checks out?'

Goss nodded. 'It looks kosher enough.'

'Much press interest?'

'The locals were there within the hour, and the nationals weren't long after.'

'What did the DS tell them?'

Goss shrugged. 'Man discovered dead as a result of a shooting. Statement as soon as we know more.'

'Have they named Gunter?'

'They have now. They spent several hours trying to locate his only relative, a sister who lives in King's Lynn. Apparently she was working last night—she works at a membership club called PJs—and has only just got home.'

'And the dead man—do we know what he was doing last night?'

'Not yet.'

'And none of the vehicles in the car park were his?'

'No—the police have identified all of them as driven there by other people.'

'So we've got him ten miles from home in a transport café without any transport.'

'That's about the shape and size of it, yes.'

'Was Gunter known to the CID? Did he have any form?'

'Not really. He was involved in an affray after a pub lock-in in Dersthorpe a couple of years back, that's all. Just a bit mouthy and free with his fists when he'd been drinking.'

'I take it he was single,' said Liz drily.

'Yes,' said Goss, 'but not gay, which is what occurred to me when he was discovered in the toilets at the Fairmile.'

'Is it a gay pick-up place, then, the café?'

'It's every kind of pick-up place.'

'Could Gunter have been there to pick up a woman?' Liz asked.

'He could have been, and there were certainly a few toms who worked the place, but that still leaves the question of how he got there without a car? Who brought him? If we can answer that I suspect we might get somewhere.'

Liz nodded. 'So what do we know about the shooting?'

'Not a lot, frankly. No one heard anything, no one saw anything. Unless we get a forensic break I'd say our best hope is the CCTV.'

'Fingers crossed, then.'

'Fingers crossed,' agreed Goss.

DETECTIVE Superintendent Don Whitten had just arrived back from the Fairmile Café when they walked into the village hall. A bulky, moustached figure, he shook Liz's hand briskly and apologised for the spartan conditions in which they found themselves.

'Can we sort out some sort of heating for this place?' he demanded, looking around the bare walls. 'It's brass monkeys in here.'

The constable, who was crouched in front of the VCR, got uncertainly to her feet. The DS turned to her. 'Ring the station and ask someone to bring over one of those hot-air blowers. And a kettle, and some tea bags and the rest of it. Jolly the place up a bit.'

The constable nodded and thumbed a number on her mobile. A plain-clothes officer held up a video cassette. 'Norwich have run us off a copy of the Fairmile CCTV tape,' he announced. 'The quality's terrible. They're working on an enhanced version, but we won't see it before tomorrow.'

'Can we have a look at what we've got?' said Whitten, lowering himself into a chair.

The plain-clothes officer nodded. As he had said, the CCTV footage was pretty much unwatchable. The time code, however, flickered strong and clear. 'We've basically got two bursts of movement between four and five a.m.,' he said. 'The first is this.'

Two shuddering white lines scribbled across the blackness as a vehicle arrived in the park, slowly reversed out of shot, and extinguished its lights, returning the screen to blackness.

'From the distance between the head- and taillights we reckon that's an HGV of some sort, and probably nothing to do with our case. As you can see, that sequence is time-coded 04.05. At 04.23 things get a bit more interesting. Watch this.'

A second vehicle, clearly shorter than the earlier one, came to a halt and extinguished its lights in the centre of the parking area. As before, the screen returned to blackness.

'Now we wait,' said the officer.

They did so. After approximately three minutes, a lower, smaller vehicle—a saloon car, Liz guessed—suddenly switched on its lights, reversed at speed from its position at the left-hand edge of the parking area, swung round the parked truck or van, and disappeared out of the front gates. More time passed—at least another five minutes— and then the truck followed it out.

'And that's it until five a.m. So, given that the pathologist has given us four thirty as the time of death, give or take fifteen either way . . .'

'Well, it's certainly not going to win any Oscars for best camerawork,' said Whitten. 'What's your reading of it, Steve?'

Goss frowned. 'I'd say the first vehicle is just a regular commercial rig. It's the second one I'd like to see more of. It doesn't park up, so is obviously expecting to be on the move sharpish . . .'

Unobtrusively, Liz removed her laptop from its carrying case. There were a couple of queries that she had emailed to Investigations at Thames House, and with a bit of luck the answers might have come through. Logging on, she saw that there were two messages, with numbers in the place of sender names.

Liz recognised these as Investigations sender codes. The messages took a couple of minutes to decrypt, but they were short and to the point. They could only trace one UK citizen named Faraj Mansoor, and he was a sixty-five-year-old retired tobacconist living in Southampton. And Pakistan liaison had confirmed that Faraj Mansoor was no longer working at the Sher Babar auto repair shop in Peshawar. He had left six weeks earlier, leaving no forwarding address. His present whereabouts were unknown.

Switching off her laptop and replacing it in its case, Liz pulled her coat tightly around her and allowed her mind to wander through the incoherent mass of loose ends that the case had so far thrown up.

FARAJ MANSOOR woke thinking that he was still at sea. He could hear the crash of waves, feel the sucking undertow as the *Susanne Hanke* reared up the side of the next peak to come crashing down into the trough. And then the noise and the sea seemed to recede, and he realised that the waves were some distance away, dragging at a beach of stones, and that he was lying fully clothed in a bed, unmoving.

With this realisation came the knowledge of where he was, and the surreal memory of the landing on the beach and the attack in the café toilet. He was not greatly troubled by the fact of having taken another man's life. But the killing would attract attention to the area, and that was bad. He had said nothing to the girl about the killing of the boatman—the knowledge that a murder hunt would soon be under way would have agitated her. For himself, he felt detached, a spectator of his own behaviour. How strange it was to find himself on this cold and lonely shore, in a land in which he would almost certainly die. If it was to be, however, it was to be.

He could remember very little about the drive back to the coast from the service station. He had tried his best to stay awake, but fatigue had blurred his senses.

He had barely registered the girl. She had been pushed hard at Takht-i-Suleiman, the man who had trained her had told him, but she had not broken. She was intelligent, a prerequisite in civilian warfare, and she had courage. Faraj preferred to reserve his judgment. Anyone could be brave in the bullish, sloganeering atmosphere of a mujahidin training camp. The important questions were answered only at the moment of action. The moment at which the fighter gazes into his or her soul and asks: Can I do what has to be done?

He looked around him. Beside his bed was a chair, on which was folded a red towelling dressing gown. On the end of the bed was a towel. Accepting the invitation that these items seemed to offer, he stripped off his dirty clothes and put on the dressing gown.

Tentatively, weapon in hand, he pushed open the door to the main area of the bungalow and stepped through, barefoot. The girl was facing away from him, filling a kettle from the tap. When she turned round and saw him she jumped, and her hand went to her heart.

'I'm sorry, you gave me such a . . .' She shook her head apologetically and collected herself. '*Salaam aleikum*.'

'*Aleikum salaam*,' he returned gravely.

They stared at each other for a moment. Her eyes, he saw, were hazel, and her hair was brown and hung straight to her shoulders. Her features, while pleasant enough, were utterly unmemorable. She was someone you would pass in the street without noticing.

'Bathroom?' she hazarded.

He nodded. The stench of the *Susanne Hanke*'s hold—vomit, bilge and sweat—still hung about him. The woman handed him a sponge bag and showed him to the bathroom. Laying the gun on the floor, he turned on the bath's hot tap.

He unzipped the sponge bag. In addition to the usual washing equipment there was an extensive first-aid kit and a diver's watch like her own. Nodding approvingly, Faraj set to work with the razor.

When he finally emerged, she had cooked. There were places set, covered dishes on the table and a smell of spiced chicken. In the tiny bedroom he dressed in the clothes she had bought for him in King's

Lynn the afternoon before. These were of good quality: a pale blue twill shirt, a navy-blue sweater, chinos, buckskin walking boots. A little hesitantly, he returned to the central room, where the woman was scanning the horizon with a pair of binoculars. Hearing him, she turned round and looked him up and down.

'Are the clothes comfortable? I used the measurements they sent.'

'The fit is good, but the clothes seem . . . too fine? People will look.' He pulled out one of the chairs at the table and sat down.

'Let them look. They will see a respectable professional man taking his Christmas break. A lawyer, perhaps, or a doctor. Someone whose clothes say that he is one of them.'

'I look like such a person?'

'You will do when I've given you the right haircut. But first you must eat.'

His eyebrows rose for a moment, and then, seeing the seriousness of her expression, he nodded his acceptance. This was what she was here to do. To make these decisions. To render him invisible. He took a knife and fork and began to eat. The rice had a flaccid, overboiled texture but the chicken was good.

He ate in silence, chewing with the thoroughness of a man who is used to making a little go a long way. When he had finished he looked up at her and spoke. 'I killed a man last night,' he said.

'SO WHAT DO we know about Peregrine and Anne Lakeby?' asked Liz. 'They sound rather exotic.'

'I suppose they are, in their own way,' said Whitten. 'I've met them a few times, and she's quite a laugh, actually. He's more your standard bow-your-head-and-tug-your-forelock aristocrat.'

'So what's their connection with Gunter again?' asked Liz.

'He kept his fishing boats on their strip of waterfront,' said Whitten. 'That's as much as I know.'

The three of them were standing beneath a vaulted stone porch outside Headland Hall.

Goss reached for the bell-push. There was a ringing sound within.

The door was opened by a tall, thin-faced woman in a tweed skirt and a quilted waistcoat that looked as if it had lost an argument with a rosebush. On seeing them, she exposed a mouthful of long teeth.

'Superintendent Whitten, isn't it?'

'Detective Superintendent, ma'am, yes. And this is Detective Sergeant Goss and a colleague from London.'

The toothy smile switched directions. Behind the upper-class good manners a shrewd concern was apparent. She knows I'm not police, thought Liz. She knows our presence means trouble.

'You've come about this awful business with Ray Gunter.'

'I'm afraid so,' said Whitten. 'We're speaking to everyone who knew him and might have had an idea of his movements.'

'Of course. Why don't you all come in and sit down?'

They followed her along a long corridor floored with patterned tiles. The walls were hung with foxes' masks, sporting prints and unprepossessing ancestral portraits.

Peregrine Lakeby was reading the *Financial Times* before a log fire in a tall room furnished with books. He stood up as the others came into the room and were seated by his wife, and then, sitting down again, said, 'You're here, I assume, about poor Mr Gunter?'

He was a good-looking man for his age, Liz thought, but from the mocking, faintly supercilious quality to the grey-blue gaze he was very much aware of the fact.

Whitten fielded the question. 'Yes, sir. As I explained to Mrs Lakeby, we're speaking to everyone who knew Gunter.'

Anne Lakeby's brow knitted. 'We didn't actually *know* him terribly well. He came and went, one saw him around, but . . .'

Her husband stood, moved to the fire, and stabbed at it languidly with an ancient steel bayonet. 'Anne, why don't you go and make us all coffee.' He turned to Whitten and Goss. 'Or would you prefer tea?'

'That's quite all right, Mr Lakeby,' said Whitten. 'I'll do without.'

'Me too,' said Goss.

'Miss . . .'

'Nothing for me, thanks, either.'

'Just for me then,' said Peregrine airily. 'And if we've got some Jaffa Cakes, you might sling a few on to a plate.'

Anne Lakeby's smile tightened for a moment, then she was gone. Peregrine leaned back in his chair. 'So what actually happened? I heard the poor bugger had been shot. Is that true?'

'It looks like it, sir, yes,' said Whitten.

'Do you have any idea why?'

'That's what we're trying to ascertain right now. Can you tell me how you knew Mr Gunter?'

'Well, basically, like his father and grandfather did before him, he kept a couple of boats on our beach. Paid us a peppercorn sum in return and offered us first refusal on his catches.'

'Do you know when Gunter last went out fishing? Or out to sea for any other purpose?'

The smile remained in place but the gaze sharpened. 'What d'you mean, exactly? What other purpose could there be?'

Whitten smiled benignly. 'I've no idea, sir. I'm not a boating man.'

'The answer is no, I have no idea when he last went out to sea, or why. He had his own key to the grounds, and came and went as he pleased.'

'When he went fishing, what time did he usually go out?'

Peregrine inflated his cheeks and exhaled thoughtfully. You're lying, thought Liz. Hiding something. Why?

'That depended on the tide, but usually at first light. Then he'd run the catch into Brancaster during the morning.'

'Did you buy fish off him?'

'Occasionally. He had a permit for half a dozen lobster pots, and if we were having people for dinner we might take a couple of lobsters off him. Or bass, if he had any big enough—which wasn't often.'

'So fishing was the only way he made his money?'

'As far as I know. He certainly didn't have any other job.'

'So why do you think someone found it necessary to shoot him?'

Lakeby extended his arms proprietorially along the back of the sofa. 'I think the whole thing was a horrible mistake. Ray Gunter was a bit of a rough diamond. He probably had one too many at the Trafalgar and . . . who knows? Picked a fight with the wrong man.'

'Any idea why he might have been at the Fairmile Café in the early hours of the morning?'

'None whatsoever. As you probably know, it's got a reputation as a queers' pick-up joint.'

'Might Gunter have been looking for a male pick-up there?'

'Well, I suppose he might have been. I must confess I'd never thought of him in that light . . . Anne, what would you have said?'

With a faint rattle, his wife lowered the oriental-patterned tray to a table in front of the fire. 'I wouldn't have said so, personally—especially since he's been seeing Cherisse Hogan.'

'For God's sake—who on earth is Cherisse Hogan?'

'Elsie Hogan's daughter. You remember Elsie? Our cleaner?'

'I didn't know her name was Hogan.'

'So where might I find this young lady?' enquired Whitten.

'She's behind the bar at the Trafalgar most days.'

Lakeby leaned forward in surprise. 'The fat girl?' he asked.

Anne raised her eyebrows. 'Peregrine! That's not very gallant.'

'How long had she and Gunter been an item?' Whitten cut in.

'Well,' Anne replied, 'it wasn't the untroubled romance he'd have liked it to be. According to Elsie, Cherisse had her sights fixed on bigger game. Namely Clive Badger, the publican.'

Peregrine stared. 'You didn't tell me any of this.'

'You didn't ask,' smiled Anne. 'It's Gomorrah-on-Sea up here if you keep your ear to the ground. Much better than television.'

Peregrine drained his coffee with an air of finality. 'Well, all I can say is: I hope Badger's got life insurance. I believe he's got a heart condition.' He looked meaningfully at his watch. 'Was there anything else? Because if not I might just . . . press on with various things.'

'Nothing,' said Whitten, remaining resolutely seated. 'Thank you very much for your time.' He turned to Anne. 'I wonder if, before we go, I might just ask Mrs Lakeby a few questions?'

Anne Lakeby smiled again. 'Certainly. Perry, off you push.'

Lakeby hesitated, rose to his feet, and, with the air of one unreasonably evicted, left the room.

'To be quite frank with you,' she said when he'd gone, 'I couldn't stand Ray Gunter and I couldn't stand having him around. Just last week I told Perry that I wanted him off the estate for good, but Perry's got some incomprehensible attachment to him. Partly loyalty to old Ben Gunter, I suppose, and partly . . . Put it this way: if there was a court case, and we lost . . .'

'Things would have been much worse?'

'Quite. In every sense of the word. But that said, Ray Gunter was certainly up to something. I'd hear things in the night. Trucks, moving about on the side road. People talking.'

'Surely that's what you'd expect to hear, given that he had a sack of fish to get into town?'

'At three a.m.?' She shook her head and fell silent.

'Could we possibly have a look at the garden and the place Gunter kept his boats?'

'Certainly. It's a bit blowy today, but if you don't mind that . . .'

The four of them proceeded through the house to the garden entrance. This was a stone-floored area housing a rack of Wellington boots and hung with gardening clothes. The garden itself, Liz saw, was much more attractive than the house's austere Victorian front suggested. A long rectangular lawn flanked by flowerbeds and trees unrolled towards a stand of grasses and, presumably, some sort of descent to the sea. Through the trees to either side she could see the mudflats, now half submerged by the incoming tide.

'As you probably know, the thing about the Hall is that it's got the only halfway decent landing place for a couple of miles in either direction,' Anne Lakeby said as they walked across the lawn. 'The sailing club's got a tidal inlet, but it's not much good for anything bigger or heavier than a dinghy.'

A couple of minutes later they were looking down at the shingle and the sea. 'It's really very private, isn't it?' said Liz.

'The trees and the walls are there as a windbreak as much as anything else,' said Anne. 'But yes, you're right. It is very private.'

'Has anyone been on the beach today?'

'Only me. This morning.'

'Did you notice anything out of the ordinary?'

Anne frowned. 'Not that I can remember,' she said.

'Which way did Gunter come and go?'

Anne pointed to a low door set into the garden's right-hand wall. 'Through there. It leads out to the lane. He had a key.'

Whitten nodded. 'I might get a couple of our blokes to give the place a quick look, if that's all right.'

Anne nodded. 'Mr Whitten, do you think Ray Gunter was involved in anything illegal? I mean, drugs or anything?'

'It's too early to say,' said Whitten. 'It's not impossible.'

Anne looked thoughtful. Worried, even.

It was her husband that she was worried about, thought Liz, not the late Ray Gunter. And she had every reason to worry, because Peregrine was undoubtedly lying.

As they left the Headland Hall driveway Liz glanced at her watch. It was 3 p.m. 'I've got to get back to London,' she told Whitten. 'But before I go, I'll try to speak to Cherisse Hogan.'

'Sure. I'll get one of my people to give you her address.' He turned up his collar against the returning rain. 'What did you think of the Lakebys?'

'I think I preferred her to him,' said Liz. 'You were right.'

He nodded. 'Never underestimate the upper classes. They can be much nicer—and much nastier—than you'd think possible.'

IT DIDN'T TAKE Liz long to find the council block where Cherisse Hogan lived. Outside it, in the rubbish-strewn car park, two youths were desultorily booting a punctured football around. Dersthorpe might have been just a couple of miles down the road from Marsh Creake, Liz reflected, but culturally it was another world.

Cherisse lived on the third floor. She had changed from her work clothes into a crumpled black sweater and jeans. A tattoo of a baby devil was visible in the sweater's deep V-front.

'Yeah?' she asked, flicking her cigarette ash out of the doorway.

'I was in the pub this morning,' said Liz.

Cherisse nodded warily. 'I remember.'

'I want to talk about Ray Gunter. I'm working with the police.'

'What's that mean, working with the police?'

Liz reached inside her coat and found her Civil Service identity card. 'I report back to the Home Office.'

Cherisse stared blankly at the card. Then she nodded and took the door off the chain.

'Is this your place?' Liz asked, squeezing through the gap.

'No. My mum's. She's out at work.'

Liz looked around. The air in the flat was close, but the place was comfortable. An electric fire blazed beneath a mantelpiece decorated with glass ornaments and photographs. The TV was wide-screen.

Cherisse knew Gunter, she told Liz—she knew pretty much everyone in Marsh Creake—but denied that there had ever been anything between them. Having said that, she admitted, it was perfectly possible that Gunter had gone round telling people that there had been.

'Why?'

'He was that sort,' said Cherisse blithely, stubbing her cigarette out in a tin ashtray. 'Basically, Ray Gunter thought that if he wanted to impress someone all he had to do was start on me. He liked to give the impression that I was his for the asking.'

'So who was Ray Gunter wanting to impress?'

'Oh, various odds and sods. And there was one guy . . . Mitch. I used to call him Staffy, because he looked like a bull terrier. When he came in Ray never sat at the bar like he usually did.'

'Where did they sit?'

'Off in a corner. I asked Ray once who he was, because he'd been having, like, a good stare at me, and Ray said he was someone who bought from him. Lobsters and that.'

'Did you believe that?'

Cherisse shrugged. 'It wasn't a nice stare.'

'Do you have any idea what Ray would have been doing at the Fairmile Café last night?' Liz asked.

'No idea.'

'Do you know if he was into anything illegal? Anything to do with his boats?'

She shook her head again, her expression vague.

Liz thanked her and made her way back to the front door.

After the heat of the Hogans' flat, the seafront was bracingly cold. The phone box smelt of urine and Liz was grateful when Wetherby picked up on the first ring.

'Tell me,' he said.

'Things look bad,' said Liz. 'I'm coming back now.'

'I'll be here,' said Wetherby.

FIVE

With each click of her scissors, another rat's tail of black hair fell to the floor. Faraj Mansoor was seated on a wooden chair in front of her, a white bath towel round his shoulders. He didn't look like a murderer, but by his own account that was exactly what he had become—and within an hour of entering the United Kingdom.

That made her . . . what? A conspirator to murder? It didn't matter. All that mattered was the operation and its security. She had been told enough about Faraj Mansoor to know that he was a consummately professional operative. If he had shot and killed the boatman last night, then that would have been the best course of action at that particular moment. If it didn't worry him that he had ended the man's life, then it shouldn't worry her.

He was, she supposed, quite a good-looking man. She had preferred him as he had been when he'd woken up—still the wild-haired fighter. Now, beardless and neatly cropped, he looked like a successful website designer or advertising copywriter. Handing him the scissors, she took the binoculars, stepped out onto the shingle, and scanned the horizon. Nothing. No one.

The book that she had read shortly after her fifteenth birthday was a life of Saladin, the twelfth-century leader of the Saracens who had fought the Crusaders for possession of Jerusalem. At first the events she was reading about had seemed distant and obscure. Unexpectedly, however, she had found herself engaged by the book's subject. She pictured Saladin as a spare, hawk-faced figure, black-bearded and spike-helmeted. She learned how to write the name of his wife, Asimat, in Arabic script, and imagined her rather like herself. And when she read of the final surrender of Jerusalem to the Saracen prince in 1187, she was in no doubt that this was the outcome she would have wished.

The book represented the first step of what she would later describe as her orientalist phase. She read indiscriminately about the Muhammadan world, from love stories set in Cairo and Samarkand to *The Arabian Nights*. Within a couple of years, however, the romantic novels had given way to dense volumes of Islamic doctrine and history, and she had begun to teach herself Arabic.

Essentially, she longed for transformation. For years she had dreamed of leaving her unhappy and unremarkable background behind her, and of entering a new world where she would, for the first time, find total and joyous acceptance. Islam, it seemed, offered precisely the transformation she sought.

She took to visiting the local Islamic centre, and, without telling her parents or teachers, started receiving instruction in the Koran. Soon she was regularly visiting the mosque and shortly after her eighteenth birthday she was received into the Islamic faith. Later that year, already speaking fluent Arabic, she became proficient in Urdu. When she was twenty, she was accepted as an undergraduate at the Department of Oriental Languages at the Sorbonne in Paris.

It was at the beginning of her second year at the university that she began to feel trapped within an utterly alien culture. Islam prohibited the belief in any god but Allah, and this prohibition included the false gods of money, status or commercial power. But everywhere she looked, among Muslims as well as unbelievers, she saw a crass materialism, and the worshipping of these very gods.

In response, she stripped her life to the bone and sought out the mosques that preached the most austere forms of Islam. Here, the imams preached the need to reject all that was not of Islam, and especially all that pertained to the great Satan—America. Her faith became her armour, and her abhorrence of the profit-motivated culture that she saw around her grew to a silent, all-consuming fury.

One day she was sitting on a Métro station bench, returning from the mosque, when she was joined by a young North African with a straggly beard. His face seemed vaguely familiar.

'*Salaam aleikum*,' he murmured, glancing at her.

'*Aleikum salaam*.'

'I have seen you at prayers.'

She half closed the book she was reading but said nothing.

The young man leaned forward over his knees. 'Sheik Ruhallah is preaching at the mosque this afternoon. You must come.'

She looked at him, surprised. Despite his unkempt appearance, there was a quiet authority about him.

'So what is it that this Sheik Ruhallah preaches?' she asked.

'He preaches jihad,' the young man said. 'He preaches war.'

LIZ SAT DOWN opposite Wetherby shortly after eight. She had arrived at her desk to find a two-word telephone message: Marzipan Fivestar. This, Liz knew, meant that Sohail Din wanted to be rung at home as a matter of urgency. She dialled his number, and to her relief it was Sohail himself who picked up the phone. In the background she could hear canned laughter from a television.

'Is Dave there?' she asked.

'I'm sorry,' said Sohail. 'Wrong number.'

'That's strange,' said Liz. 'Do you know Dave?'

'I know six or seven Daves,' said Sohail, 'and none of them lives here. Goodbye.'

In six or seven minutes, then, he would call her back from a public phone. She had instructed him never to use the nearest one to his house. In the interim, she called up her firearms instructor at Fort Monkton, the MI6 training school, and by the time Sohail called back, her laser printer was disgorging the relevant information.

Wetherby, she thought, looked tired. His manner, though, was fastidiously courteous, and as she spoke she was conscious of his absolute attention.

'I agree with you about Eastman,' he said. 'He's being used in some way, and it looks as if the situation's spiralled out of his control. It sounds certain that there's a German connection of some kind, and that the connection points east. More specifically there's a probability that some sort of hand-over was made in the truck park.'

Liz nodded. 'The police seem to be proceeding on the basis of the weapon in question being some sort of military assault rifle.'

The faintest of smiles. 'You clearly think otherwise.'

'I remembered something we were told at Fort Monkton. How the KGB had developed a new generation of handguns with massive payloads. Things like the Gyurza that weighed more than a kilo and fired armour-piercing rounds. I contacted Barry Holland down there and he told me the FBI have test-firing results on a 7.62 calibre pistol that so far doesn't even have a name. It's just known as the PSS.' She glanced at the print-out. '*Pistolet Samozaryadne Specialny*.'

'Special Silenced Pistol,' translated Wetherby.

'Exactly. It's an ugly-looking thing, but technically it's way out in front. It's got the lowest sound signature of any existing firearm. You could fire it through a coat pocket and the person standing next to you wouldn't hear a thing.'

Wetherby's left eyebrow rose a millimetre or two.

'It has silent ammunition. It's called SP-4. The way it works is that the explosion is completely contained in the cartridge case in the body of the gun. None of the gases escape, so there's no noise and no flash.'

Wetherby didn't smile, but regarded her thoughtfully for a moment. 'So why has our man gone to the trouble of acquiring a specialist weapon like this?' he said.

'Because he is expecting to find himself up against armoured or flak-jacketed opposition. Police. Security guards. Special forces.'

'Any other conclusions we can draw?'

'That he, or more likely his organisation, has access to the best. This is a limited-edition weapon. So far they've only been issued to a handful of Russian Special Forces personnel, most of whom are currently engaged in undercover operations against Chechen militants. It's reasonable to suppose that one or two of these weapons have somehow passed into rebel hands.'

'And from there into the hands of the mujahidin armourers . . . Yes, I see where you're going.' Wetherby glanced bleakly at the window. He seemed to be listening to the beat of the rain. 'Anything else?'

'I'm afraid it gets worse,' said Liz. 'When I came in this evening I returned a Fivestar call from Marzipan.'

'Go on.'

'There's some kind of online Arabic newsletter that his colleagues read. He thinks it's written by ITS militants in Saudi—possibly al Safa's crowd—who are in on the planning stages of some kind of symbolic event here in the UK. No clue as to the what, when or where, but the reported wording is that "a man has arrived whose name is Vengeance before God".'

Wetherby sat unblinking for a moment. 'And you think that the man they're talking about could be our silent gunman from Norfolk,' he said carefully.

Liz said nothing. Wetherby reached downwards to one of the lower drawers of his desk. Opening it, he took out a bottle of Laphroaig whisky and two tumblers, and poured a shot into each. Pushing one of the tumblers towards Liz, and raising a hand to indicate that she should stay where she was, he lifted the receiver of one of the telephones on his desk and dialled a number.

The call, Liz swiftly realised, was to his wife.

'How did it go today?' Wetherby murmured. 'Was it awful?'

The answer seemed to take some time. Liz concentrated on the smoky taste of the whisky, on the beating of the rain at the window.

'I have to stay late,' Wetherby was saying. 'Yes, I'm afraid there's a bit of a crisis and . . . No, I wouldn't unless it was absolutely unavoidable, I know that you've had the most hellish day . . . I'll call as soon as I'm in the car. No, don't wait up.'

Replacing the receiver, he took a long swallow of the whisky, and then reversed one of the photo frames on his desk so that Liz could see it. The photograph showed a woman in a striped navy blue and white T-shirt sitting at a café table, holding a coffee cup. She had dark hair and delicate, fine-boned features and was looking into the camera with an amused tilt of the head.

The thing that struck Liz most forcibly about the woman, however, was her complexion. Although she couldn't have been more than thirty-five years old, her skin was the colour of ivory, so pale and bloodless as to appear almost transparent.

'It's called red blood-cell aplasia,' said Wetherby quietly. 'It's a disorder of the bone marrow. She has to have a blood transfusion every month and she went into hospital today.'

'I'm sorry to be the bringer of news that keeps you here,' said Liz.

A minute shake of the head. 'You've done exceptionally well.' He swirled the Laphroaig and raised his tumbler with an oblique smile. 'Apart from anything else, you've provided me with the wherewithal to ruin Geoffrey Fane's evening.'

'Well, that's something.'

For a minute or two, as they finished their drinks, they sat in complicit silence. The distant sound of a Hoover told Liz that the cleaners had arrived.

'Go home,' he told her. 'I'll get started on telling everyone who needs to know.'

'OK. First, though, I'm going back to my desk to run a few checks on Peregrine Lakeby.'

'You're going back to Norfolk tomorrow?'

'I think I should.'

Wetherby nodded. 'Keep me informed, then.'

Liz stood. A barge sounded a long mournful note out on the river.

AFTER A WET NIGHT the day dawned clear, and as Liz drove northwards towards the M11 the roads hissed beneath the Audi's tyres. She had slept badly. The amorphous mass of worry that the investigation represented had taken on a crushing weight, and the more desperately she had sought oblivion between the crumpled sheets, the faster her heart had raced in her chest. People's lives were threatened, she knew that much, and the image of Ray Gunter's broken head endlessly replicated itself in her mind.

She had aimed for an early start and a fast exit from London, but unfortunately a sizable proportion of the city's inhabitants seemed to have had the same idea. By eleven o'clock she was still half a dozen miles from Marsh Creake, trapped on a narrow road behind a low-bed truck loaded with sugar beet.

Eventually, her shoulders aching with tension, she pulled up outside the Trafalgar, and on venturing inside found Cherisse Hogan polishing glasses in the empty lounge.

'You again!' said Cherisse, darting Liz a lazy-eyed smile. She was wearing a tight lavender sweater and looking, in a gypsyish way, rather spectacular.

'I was wondering if you had a room?' Liz enquired.

Cherisse's eyebrows rose, and she moved unhurriedly into the shadowed fastness of the kitchen area—there presumably to consult her employer.

She returned a couple of minutes later holding a key suspended from a miniature brass anchor, and led Liz up a narrow carpeted stair to a door bearing the legend 'Temeraire'.

'Temeraire' was low-ceilinged and warm, with a plum carpet, a tiled fireplace and a divan with a candlewick bedspread. It took Liz no more than a couple of minutes to unpack her clothes. When she went downstairs again Cherisse was still alone in the lounge bar, and beckoned Liz over with an inclination of the head.

'You know I told you about Mitch? The one that drunk with Ray? Well, he was on the tobacco game.'

'Importing cigarettes for cash, you mean? Without paying duty?'

'Yeah.'

'How do you know? Did he offer you some?'

'No, Ray did. He said Mitch could get as many as I wanted. He said I could have them for cost and then mark them up and flog them on to the punters at bar prices.'

'Hang on. You're saying that Ray told you this on Mitch's behalf?'

'Yeah—he obviously thought he was doing him a favour. But Mitch went completely off his head. Told Ray to button it.'

'And have you ever bought any?'

'Me? No! I'd lose my job.'

'So Mr Badger doesn't buy from them either?'

Cherisse shook her head and continued with her desultory processing of the glasses. 'I thought I'd mention it, though,' she said. 'He's a nasty piece of work, that Mitch.'

'He certainly sounds it,' said Liz. 'Thanks.'

She stared out into the empty bar. Pale winter sunshine streamed through the leaded windows, illuminating the dust motes and gilding the accessories on the wood-panelled walls. If Mitch was involved in the selling of cut-price tobacco, why was he so angry when Gunter had mentioned it to Cherisse? The only reason that Liz could fathom was that Mitch had graduated from tobacco-smuggling to more dangerous games. Games in which loose talk could be fatal. She called Frankie Ferris from the payphone in the pub's entrance hall. Ferris, as usual, seemed to be in a state of advanced agitation.

'It's really come on top with this murder,' he whispered. 'Eastman's been locked in his office since yesterday morning. Last night he was there till—'

'Was the dead man anything to do with Eastman?'

'I don't know, and I wouldn't ask. I just want to keep my head down, and if the law comes knocking I want some serious protection, OK? I'm taking a risk just making this call.'

'Mitch,' said Liz. 'I need to know about a man called Mitch.'

A short, charged silence.

'Braintree,' said Ferris. 'Eight o'clock this evening on the top level of the station multistorey. Come alone.' The phone went dead.

He smells trouble, thought Liz, replacing the handset.

She wondered briefly about going to the village hall, to find out if Whitten had moved the case forward. After a moment's thought, however, she decided to drive down to Headland Hall and speak to Peregrine Lakeby first. Once she had linked up with the others it would be harder to keep information to herself.

WITH A QUIET popping of gravel, the Audi came to a halt outside Headland Hall. This time the doorbell was answered by Lakeby himself. He was wearing a long Chinese dressing gown and a cravat.

He looked surprised to see Liz, but swiftly recovered himself and led her along the tiled corridor into the kitchen. Here, at a broad work table of scrubbed pine, a woman was drying wine glasses with an unhurried action that Liz immediately recognised. This must be Elsie Hogan, mother to Cherisse.

'Anne will be back from King's Lynn in an hour,' he said. 'Coffee?'

'I'm fine, thanks,' said Liz, reflecting ruefully that you couldn't say to a man what she was about to say to Peregrine Lakeby and be drinking his coffee at the same time. So she watched as he poured the steaming liquid into a bone-china cup.

'Now,' said Peregrine, when they had left the kitchen and were comfortably disposed in the drawing room, 'tell me how I can help you.'

Liz met his enquiring, faintly amused gaze. 'I'd like to know about the arrangement you had with Ray Gunter,' she said quietly.

Peregrine's head tilted thoughtfully. 'If you mean the arrangement by which he kept his boats on the beach, I was under the impression that we had discussed that in some detail last time you were here.'

'No,' she said. 'I mean the arrangement by which you agreed to turn a blind eye when Ray Gunter brought illicit consignments ashore by night. How much was he paying you?'

Peregrine's smile tightened. 'I don't know where you've got your information from, Miss . . . er, but the idea that I might have had a criminal relationship with a man like Ray Gunter is quite frankly preposterous. What led you to such a bizarre conclusion?'

Liz reached into her briefcase and removed two printed sheets. 'May I tell you a story, Mr Lakeby? About a woman known in certain circles as the Marquise, real name Dorcas Gibb?'

Peregrine said nothing. His expression remained unaltered, but the colour began to ebb from his face.

'For several years now, the Marquise has been the proprietor of a discreet establishment in Shepherd Market, Mayfair, where she and her employees specialise in . . .' she consulted the printed sheets, 'discipline, domination and corporal punishment.'

Again, Peregrine said nothing.

'Three years ago, the Vice Squad raided the place, and guess who they found strapped to a flogging-horse with his trousers down round his ankles?'

Peregrine's gaze turned to ice. 'My private life is my own business, and I will not be blackmailed in my own house.' He rose from the sofa. 'You will kindly leave, and leave now.'

Liz didn't move. 'I'm not blackmailing you, Mr Lakeby, I'm just asking you for details of your commercial relationship with Ray Gunter. We can do this the easy way, or we can do it the hard way. The easy way involves you giving me all of the facts in confidence; the hard way involves a police arrest on suspicion of involvement in organised crime.'

His eyes narrowed warily, and the arrogance seemed momentarily to drain out of him.

'I'm not suggesting you did anything worse than take Gunter's money,' said Liz quietly. 'But there's an issue of national security at stake here.' She paused. 'What was the deal with Gunter?'

He stared bleakly out of the window. 'The idea was that I turned a blind eye to his comings and goings at night.'

'How much did they pay you?'

'Five hundred a month. Cash. He left it inside the locker on the beach. The place where he kept his fishing gear. I had a key.'

'And what did those comings and goings consist of?'

Peregrine gave a strained smile. 'The same as they've consisted of for hundreds of years. This is a smuggler's coastline. Always has been. Tea, brandy from France, tobacco from the Low Countries . . .'

'That's what they were landing, was it? Booze and tobacco?'

'That's what I was told.'

'By who? By Gunter?'

'No. I didn't actually deal with Gunter. There was another man, whose name I never found out.'

'Mitch? Something like Mitch?'

'I've no idea. Like I said . . .'

'Can you describe the second man?'

'He looked . . . violent. Pale face and a skinhead haircut.'

'Is there anything else you can tell me? About their vehicles? About the vessels they picked up from?'

'Nothing, I'm afraid. I honoured my side of the bargain, and kept my eyes and my ears closed.'

Honoured, thought Liz. There's a word.

'And your wife's never suspected anything?'

'Anne?' he asked, almost bullish again. 'No, why on earth should she? She heard the odd bump in the night, but . . .'

Liz nodded. The second man had to be Mitch, whoever Mitch was. And the reason he had been so furious with Gunter for talking about tobacco-smuggling to Cherisse was that the two of them had something much more serious to hide.

She looked at Peregrine. The urbane façade was almost back in place. She had given him a brief scare, but no more. On the way out she passed Elsie Hogan, who was standing with a calculatedly blank expression in the kitchen doorway. Had Elsie, she wondered, been listening at the door? Would there soon be lurid tales of upper-class spanking orgies circulating in the local bus queues and supermarkets?

IN THE THIRTY-SIX hours since his arrival, Faraj Mansoor had spoken very little after describing the circumstances surrounding the death of the fisherman. Now, however, he seemed disposed for conversation. He called the woman Lucy, since this was the name on her driving licence and other documents, and for the first time he seemed to look at her closely, to fully acknowledge her presence. The two of them were bent over the bungalow's dining table examining an Ordnance Survey map. As a security precaution they were using stalks of dry grass as pointers. Road by road, intersection by intersection, they planned their route.

'I suggest we park here,' she said, 'and walk up the rest of the way.'

He nodded. 'Four miles?'

'Five, perhaps. If we push ourselves we should be able to do it in a couple of hours.'

He nodded, and stared intently at the undulating countryside. 'How good are the security people? What will they be looking out for?'

'We would be foolish to assume that they are not very good. They'll be looking for anyone who doesn't fit.'

'Will we fit?'

She glanced sideways at him. His light-skinned Afghan features marked him out as non-European in origin, but his English was flawless and his accent was classic BBC World Service.

'Yes.' She nodded. 'We'll fit.'

'Good.' He pulled on the dark blue New York Yankees baseball cap that she'd bought him. 'And you know the location well?'

'Yes. I haven't been there for several years, but it can't have changed much. This map is new, and it's exactly as I remember it.'

'And you will have no hesitation in doing what has to be done? You have no doubts?' he asked.

'I will have no hesitation. I have no doubts.'

He nodded again and carefully folded up the map. 'They spoke highly of you at Takht-i-Suleiman.' He reached into his pocket. 'I have something for you.'

It was a gun. A miniature automatic, the size of her hand. Curious, she picked it up, ejected the five-round magazine, ratcheted back the slide and tried the action. 'Nine millimetre?'

He nodded. 'It's Russian. A Malyah.'

She hefted it in her hand, slapped back the magazine and thumbed the safety catch on and off. 'They decided that I should be armed?'

'Yes.'

Fetching her waterproof mountain jacket, she unzipped the collar section, pulled out the hood and zipped it up again with the Malyah inside. The hood effectively hid the slight bulge.

'Can I ask you something?' she said tentatively.

'Ask.'

'What are we waiting for? Now that the boatman is dead, every day makes it more likely that . . .'

'That they'll find us?' he smiled.

'People don't get shot here every day,' she persisted. 'The security people here aren't stupid, Faraj. If they smell a rat when they find that round of yours they'll come looking. They'll send their best people. And you can forget any idea you might have about British fair play; if they have the faintest suspicion of what we are planning to do they will kill us outright, proof or no proof.'

'You're angry,' he said, amused. Both of them were conscious that it was the first time she had used his name.

She closed her eyes. 'I'm saying that we can accomplish nothing if we are dead. And that with every day that passes it becomes more likely that . . . that they will find and kill us.'

He looked at her dispassionately. 'There are things that you don't know,' he said. 'There are reasons for waiting.'

She met the pale green gaze for a moment—the gaze that at times made him look fifty rather than a score of months short of thirty—and bowed her head in acceptance. 'I ask only that you don't underestimate the people we are up against.'

Faraj shook his head. 'I don't underestimate them, believe me.'

Taking the binoculars, she opened the door, stepped outside on to the shingle, and scanned the horizon to east and west.

'Anything?' he asked, when she returned.

'Nothing,' she said.

He watched her. 'What is it?' he asked.

'They are looking for us,' she replied. 'I can feel it.'

He nodded slowly. 'So be it.'

LIZ WALKED into the village hall just as the enhanced CCTV tape arrived from Norwich. The female constable loaded it into the VCR.

A good fug had been got up in the hall. Ashtrays had been distributed, a kettle installed, and a hot-air blower roared quietly beneath the stage. Liz and Goss found themselves chairs, while Whitten and three plainclothes officers milled purposefully in front of the monitor. There was a faint smell of conflicting aftershaves.

'Tell me something, Steve,' she said. 'How obvious was it that there was a CCTV set-up at the Fairmile Café?'

'Not obvious at all. It was wired up in a tree. You wouldn't have seen it if you didn't know it was there.'

'A good place for a drop-off, then?'

'It would have looked like one if you weren't in the know, yes.' He looked sombrely up at the darkening sky. 'Let's hope that we've finally got something. We badly need to move this thing forward.'

'Let's hope,' said Liz.

'They eliminated the first vehicle we saw on the tape yesterday,' he murmured. 'It was just some bloke parking up his rig for the night.'

'OK.'

As the police retreated to their chairs a frozen wide-shot of the vehicle park filled the screen and the time code began to flicker at 04.22. Soon the silvery image of a truck wobbled into the picture. The truck turned so that it was facing the exit and the headlights were extinguished. Stillness for several seconds, and then a bulky figure jumped down from the cab. Was that Gunter? wondered Liz. As the figure made for the truck's rear doors and disappeared, a light flared briefly in the cab, illuminating a second figure on the driver's side.

'Lighting a cigarette,' murmured Goss.

Two shapes climbed from the back of the truck. One was the original figure from the cab, the other an anonymous blob, possibly carrying a coat or rucksack. The two seemed to drift together for a moment, and then separate. A pause, and then the darker figure began to walk in a straight line out of frame. Twenty-five seconds passed, and then the other followed.

The image cut to black and then restarted. The time code now read

04.26. The truck was still in place, but no light showed inside the cab. After sixty seconds the darker of the two figures returned from the direction in which it had gone and disappeared behind the truck. Forty seconds later a parked car switched on its headlights and reversed at speed out of its parking space. Inside the car, the pale figures of a driver and a passenger were briefly visible, but the vehicle itself was no more than a black blur and there was clearly no question of recovering its registration number. Swinging round the truck it drove at speed towards the road and exited the frame.

When it was over there was a long silence.

'Thoughts, anyone?' asked Whitten eventually.

THE FENLAND village of West Ford, some thirty miles southeast of Marsh Creake and the coast, offered little in the way of entertainment. There was a panel-beating and exhaust repairs business, a small village stores incorporating a sub-post office, and a pub, the George and Dragon. But precious little, reflected Denzil Parrish, to engage the imagination of a sexually frustrated nineteen-year-old with time on his hands. And Denzil, over the next fortnight, would have quite a lot of time on his hands.

The evening before, he had arrived home from Newcastle, where he was at university. He had considered staying there until Christmas Eve, but he hadn't seen much of his mother in the last year—since her remarriage, in fact—and had felt that he should try to spend some time with her. He hadn't arrived at Downham Market station until well after dark. With no prospect of a bus to West Ford, he had walked over four miles through the rain, jerking out his thumb at every passing car, before an American airman from one of the bases had stopped for him. He had known the village of West Ford, and had joined Denzil for a beer at the George and Dragon before speeding on southwards to the US Air Force base at Lakenheath.

After he had gone Denzil had scanned the pub. Typically, there wasn't an unattached girl in the place, so he had trudged home, only to find the place empty except for a gormless creature who had identified herself as the night's baby sitter. His mum, she had explained without taking her eyes off the TV, had gone to a dinner-dance with his stepfather. And no, no one had said anything about anyone arriving from Newcastle. Denzil had dug out a frozen pizza and with sinking spirits joined the baby sitter in front of the TV.

At least the sun was shining today. That was a plus. His mother had apologised for being out when he arrived home, given him a quick kiss and hurried off to mix up a bottle of formula. What was the woman thinking of, wondered Denzil vaguely. Having a second baby at this time of her life. It was just undignified, surely? But what the hell. Her money. Her life.

Denzil had decided to get out his wet suit and do some canoeing. He had had a vague project in mind of exploring the area's interconnecting grid of drainage channels. The Methwold Fen relief drain was only ten minutes' drive away, and promised many miles of deserted but navigable water. Denzil was a keen birdwatcher, and his silent glides between the fenland channels had brought him into rewardingly close contact with bitterns, reed warblers, marsh harriers and other rare species.

Throwing his wet suit into the back of his mother's old Honda Accord, Denzil manoeuvred the glass-fibre kayak out of the garage and onto the car's roof rack, where he secured it with bungee cords.

On the way out of the village he was forced to brake behind a tractor and trailer that were blocking the road. The tractor's driver was attempting to back the trailer, which was loaded with fertiliser sacks, into a field. Realising that the operation was going to take some time, Denzil switched off the ignition and settled back in his seat. As he waited, he noticed a young couple in hiking clothes crossing the field purposefully towards him. Or at least the woman's step was purposeful. The man, an Asian-looking guy, looked more laid back. Neither was smiling, neither gave the impression of being on holiday. Perhaps they were a couple who could never fully unwind, even away from work.

Up close, he saw that the woman was attractive in a no-nonsense, no-make-up sort of way. All that was missing was a smile on her face.

The car behind him beeped, and Denzil saw that the road ahead was clear. Engaging the Honda's ignition, he moved forward in a shudder of exhaust.

'TWO HADDOCK and chips,' said Cherisse Hogan breezily, depositing large oval plates on the table in front of Liz and Detective Sergeant Steve Goss as they sat in the saloon bar of the Trafalgar. She returned a minute later with a bowlful of sauce sachets.

'I hate these bloody things,' said Goss, tearing at one of the sachets with his large fingers until it exploded in his hand. Liz watched him for a moment, and then, taking a pair of scissors from her bag, neatly decapitated a tartare sauce sachet and squeezed it onto her plate.

'No brain versus brawn gags,' warned Goss, wiping his fingers.

'I wouldn't dream of it,' promised Liz, passing him the scissors.

They ate in companionable silence, though Liz couldn't help feeling slightly guilty for keeping the Special Branch officer in the dark about 'Mitch', Peregrine Lakeby, and the Zander calls. Until she had spoken to Frankie Ferris, however, she could see no sense in sharing what she had discovered. 'Beats the Norwich canteen,' said Goss after a few minutes. 'How's your fish?'

'Good,' said Liz. 'I wonder if it was one of Ray Gunter's.'

'It's had its revenge if it was,' said a familiar voice.

She looked up. Bruno Mackay stood at her elbow.

'Liz,' he said, extending his hand.

She took it, forcing a smile. Did his presence mean what she thought it meant? Belatedly, she glanced at Goss, frozen opposite her in an attitude of enquiry. 'Er . . . Bruno Mackay,' she said, 'this is Steve Goss. Norfolk Special Branch.'

Goss nodded, lowered his fork and guardedly extended his hand.

Bruno shook it. 'I've been asked to come up and share the strain,' he explained with a broad smile. 'Lend a helping hand.'

Liz forced a smile of her own. 'Well, as you can see, the strain's not too unbearable yet. Have you had anything to eat?'

'No. I'm ravenous. I might just go and have a quick word with Truly Scrumptious over there. Would you mind . . .'

Dropping his keys proprietorially on the table he marched off to the bar, where he was soon locked in consultation with Cherisse.

'Something tells me you've been stitched up,' murmured Goss, as he watched Mackay march off to the bar.

Liz emptied her face of her feelings. 'No, I've just had my phone switched off. I obviously missed the message that he was on his way.'

'Get you anything?' Bruno called out cheerfully from the bar.

Liz and Goss both shook their heads.

The rest of the meal was distinctly unrelaxing. There were too many listeners-in at nearby tables for any discussion of the case to be possible. Instead, Mackay quizzed Goss about the area's competing attractions. Treating him, thought Liz, like a Norfolk Tourist Board representative. Then, as they finished eating, with cavalier nonchalance, Mackay paid the bill for the three of them.

Steve Goss stood up. 'I'd better make a move,' he said. 'I'm due back to Norwich at two o'clock.' He gave Liz the ghost of a wink and raised a hand to Mackay. 'Thanks for lunch. Next one's on me.'

'Cheers,' said Mackay.

'Will you just excuse me a minute?' Liz murmured to Mackay when Goss had left the bar. 'I'll be right back.'

She called Wetherby from the public phone outside on the seafront. He picked up on the second ring, and sounded tired.

'Please,' she said.

'I'm sorry,' he answered. 'You have to have Mackay with you. Fane is insisting on him being there, as indeed he has every right to insist.'

'Full disclosure? Full data-sharing?'

The briefest of pauses. 'That was the agreement between our respective services. But make him work,' suggested Wetherby. 'Make him earn his keep.'

'I certainly will. I have a meet with Zander tonight that I'm hopeful about. I'll call you afterwards.'

'Do that. And take our mutual friend to the meet.'

The phone went dead and Liz stared for a moment at the receiver in her hand. Conventionally, agent rendezvous were only ever conducted by one officer at a time. Shrugging, she returned to the bar.

'Do you want to walk while I brief you, or sit upstairs?' she asked.

'Let's walk. I suspect that today's lunch wasn't the first outing for that chip oil. I could use some air,' Mackay replied, grinning.

Liz filled him in. Zander's calls. The conclusions she had drawn from the armour-piercing round. Her questioning of Cherisse Hogan and Lakeby. Her belief that the man in the front of the truck with Ray Gunter was 'Mitch'. Her hope that Mitch was an associate of Melvin Eastman and that Zander would be able to help identify him.

'And if you do get an ID on this Mitch?' asked Mackay.

'Give him to the police to pick up,' said Liz.

Mackay nodded. 'You've done well,' he said without condescension. 'What's the score on Lakeby? Are you going to have him lifted too?'

'Not much point, I'd say—he's just one of the links to Mitch. I don't think he knew what was going on on his beach. He preferred to hide behind the idea that they were honest smugglers just bringing in a few cartons of booze and fags. He may be a snob and a bully, but I don't think he's any kind of traitor.'

'So what do you think our shooter's here to do? Why do you think he's gone to so much trouble to get himself here in particular?'

'Some sort of spectacular, perhaps?' she hazarded. 'There are the USAF bases at Marwell, Mildenhall and Lakenheath, but they're on a high state of alert and would represent very difficult targets for a single individual or even a small team. There's the Sizewell nuclear plant, I suppose, but again, a very tall order. More likely, to my mind, is the assassination possibility: the Lord Chancellor's got a house in Aldeburgh, the Treasury Chief Secretary's got a place at Thorpeness . . . not the most high-profile of targets but you'd certainly make headlines if you put a bullet through one of them.'

'Have their people been warned?' asked Mackay.

'In general terms, yes, they've been told to step things up.'

'And the Queen's at Sandringham for Christmas, I suppose.'

'That's right, but security's as tight as a drum.'

'I guess we'd better go and see what the plods have uncovered. What time do you want to make a move for Braintree?'

'Not later than five?'

'OK. Let's go back to the Trafalgar, order up a pot of coffee from the lovely Cherisse, spread out a few Ordnance Survey maps, and try and think ourselves into this man's mind.'

SIX

'This is a strange country,' said Faraj Mansoor, ejecting the five-round magazine of the PSS into his hand and placing it carefully on the table. 'It is very different from the place of my imagination.'

The woman who had borrowed the name of Lucy Wharmby was peeling potatoes at the sink. 'It's not all like this,' she said. 'It's not all so exposed and bleak . . .'

He waited for her to finish. Outside, the sun still cast its pale glaze over the sea, but the wind was whipping at the wave caps, lifting them into a fine spray.

'I think the country makes the people,' he said eventually, checking the action of the PSS before slapping back the magazine. 'And I think that I understand the British better for seeing their country.'

'It's a cold country,' she said. 'My childhood was spent in a cold flat with thin walls, listening to my parents arguing.'

Pocketing the handgun, he said. 'What were they arguing about?'

'I was never quite sure at the time. My father was a university lecturer at a place called Keele. It was a good job for him, but my mother had never wanted to move there from London. She didn't like the place and she didn't make any effort to get to know the people. She ended up having treatment for depression.'

Faraj frowned. 'What were her beliefs?'

'She believed in . . . books and films and holidays in Italy and having her friends round to dinner.'

'And your father? What did he believe in?'

'He believed in himself. He believed in his career, and in the importance of his work.' She reached for a kitchen knife and began quartering the potatoes with short, angry strokes of the blade. 'Later, when my mother's depression became serious, he believed that he had the right to sleep with his students.'

Faraj looked up. 'Did your mother know?'

'She found out soon enough. She wasn't stupid.'

'And you? Did you know?'

'I guessed. They sent me away to school in Wales.' She wiped her hair from her eyes with the back of her hand. 'There are hills there, and even one or two you might call mountains.'

He looked at her, his head inclined. 'You're smiling. That's the first time I've seen you smile. Were you happy there?'

She shrugged. 'I suppose so. I've never thought of it in those terms.'

Unbidden, a memory rose before her, a memory she had not revisited for some years. It had been her friend Megan who had discovered the magic mushrooms growing in the pine woods behind the school. They had downed half a dozen each, spread out a groundsheet and settled themselves down to wait. For half an hour nothing had happened, and then she had begun to feel nauseous and fearful. Control of her reactions seemed to be sliding away from her, and then suddenly the fear lifted and it was as if she were drowning in heightened sensations, which, after a time, had begun to shape themselves into a kind of sublime architecture. She seemed to be wandering through a vast and constantly evolving vista of cloud-topped ziggurats, hanging gardens and dizzying colonnades.

'Yes,' she said, 'I was happy there.'

'So how did it end?' he asked. 'Your parents' tale?'

'Divorce. The family smashed. Nothing unusual.' Lifting the handle of the kitchen knife between two fingers, she dropped it so that its point stuck into the wet chopping board. 'And your parents?'

'My parents were Tajiks, from Dushanbe. My father was a fighter, a lieutenant of Ahmed Shah Massoud.'

'The Lion of Panjshir.'

'Just so. May he live for ever. As a young man my father had been a teacher. He spoke French and a little English, which he learned from the British and American soldiers who came to fight with the mujahidin. When I was fourteen, we moved to Afghanistan, following Massoud, and I went to one of the English-language schools in Kabul. My father hoped that I would not have to live the life that he had lived, he saw education as the means of my betterment.'

'What happened?'

'In '96 the Taliban came and laid siege to Kabul. We managed to escape and my father went north to rejoin Massoud. I wanted to go with him but he sent me south with my mother and my younger sister towards the border country. We had hoped to enter Pakistan from there, to escape the Taliban altogether, but after months of wandering we finally settled with other displaced Tajiks and Pathans opposed to the Taliban in a village named Daranj, east of Kandahar.'

Falling silent, he appeared to sink into a reverie. Finally he roused himself. 'My father returned after years of fighting. He had been wounded, and he could no longer fight. With him, though, was a man. A man whom my father had persuaded to guide me across the border into Pakistan. A man of influence, who would enrol me in one of the *madrassahs*—the Islamic colleges—in Peshawar. I bade goodbye to my parents and my sister, and together with this man I crossed the border at Chaman and journeyed north to Mardan, and was taken to the *madrassah*.'

'So who was this man? This man of such influence?'

He smiled and shook his head. 'So many questions. What would you have done with your life, had things been otherwise?'

'They were never otherwise,' she replied. 'For me, there was never any other path.'

LIZ INSISTED that she and Mackay travel in her car. The meeting with Zander was her operation and she wanted Mackay to realise that he was a passenger, there strictly on sufferance.

Mackay did not argue. Instead he made a point of deferring to her.

'Tell me why Zander should exert himself on our behalf,' he said. 'What's in it for him, apart from your approval?'

'I'm his insurance policy. He knows that if he comes across with good product then I'll stir myself on his behalf if the drugs squad or the CID march in and scoop him up on a charge. That's why he wouldn't talk to Bob Morrison. Morrison's the kind of hard-nosed officer who despises the Zanders of this world, and Zander knows it.'

'Seems a bit shortsighted of Morrison. And it strikes me that if the police pick up Melvin Eastman they're going to need someone like Zander to go into the witness box and testify against him.'

They arrived in Braintree with forty minutes to spare.

'Can we just run through again how you want to play this?' asked Mackay, as they followed the signs to the railway station.

'Sure. He's expecting me to arrive alone on the top level of the multistorey car park, so I'm going to drop you off outside. I'll drive up to the top storey and park; you follow on foot, install yourself near the staircase and start logging incoming cars. When I see Zander I'll call you and describe his car. As soon as you're sure that he wasn't followed in you call me back, and I'll approach him.'

Mackay nodded. This was standard tradecraft. It was just possible that Eastman might have put a tail on Ferris.

Liz pulled up outside the station, and Mackay slipped off into the shadows, while Liz drove up to the top floor of the car park.

In the course of the next half-hour, three cars left the top level. Several others entered the car park, but all occupied vacant bays on the lower levels. Finally, at five to eight, a silver Nissan Almeira climbed to the top level, with Frankie Ferris at the wheel. Quickly, she thumbed the speed-dial button on her phone.

'Give me a couple of minutes,' came Mackay's voice, muted. Frankie parked in the corner furthest from her, and turned off the Nissan's engine and lights.

At three minutes past eight her phone rang.

'He was followed,' said Mackay.

'I'm aborting, then,' said Liz immediately.

'No need. Zander's tail met with a problem. He's immobilised in the stairwell. Go ahead with the meet.'

'What have you done?' hissed Liz.

'Secured the situation. Now go for it. You've got three minutes.'

Liz looked around her. There was no sign of any movement. Deeply apprehensive, she climbed out of the Audi and crossed the concrete floor. As she approached the silver Almeira she saw the driver's window slide down. Inside, Frankie looked thin and scared.

'Take these,' he said, his voice shaky. 'And make like you're paying me.' He handed her a small paper bag, and Liz reached into her pocket and pretended to pass him money.

'Mitch,' she said urgently. 'Tell me.'

'Kieran Mitchell. Transport man, fixer, enforcer, whatever. He's got a big place outside Chelmsford on one of those gated estates.'

'Works for Eastman?'

'With him. Got his own people.'

'Do you know him?'

'Seen him. He drinks with Eastman. Nasty-looking bastard. White eyelashes like a pig. Oh, and he carries. Now get out of here, please.'

Liz walked quickly back to the Audi and drove to the ramp. A level down, she picked up Mackay, who was leaning against a barrier. 'What the hell is going on?' she asked angrily.

'Zander was followed. Eastman obviously suspects something's up. The tail parked on this level. He arrived a minute after your man.'

'How do you know he was a tail?'

'I followed him to the stairwell, and he went up, not down. So I zapped him.'

'What do you mean, you zapped him?'

Reaching into his pocket, Mackay extracted a slim black plastic object resembling a mobile phone. 'The Oregon Industries C6 stun-gun, aka the Little Friend. Delivers six hundred thousand volts straight into the central nervous system. Result: target incapacitated for three to six minutes, depending on physical constitution.'

'And completely unlicensed for use in the United Kingdom,' retorted Liz, furious.

'Undergoing trials with the Met as we speak, actually. The point is that zappers are established criminal accessories, which is why I relieved our man of his watch and wallet. These things do no lasting damage. My guess is he'll keep quiet about the whole thing. He'd look pretty stupid admitting to Eastman that he failed to do his job because he was mugged.'

'You hope.'

'Look, Zander was blown,' said Mackay. 'The fact that there was a tail tells us that. The essential thing was to identify Mitch. Now, I suggest that we get out of here before our zappee finds his feet again.'

Letting out the clutch with deliberate force, Liz spun the Audi forward. 'And what do you propose to do with the watch and wallet?'

'Run a check on the owner and see if they belong to one of Eastman's people,' said Mackay. 'Then, if you like, we can post them back to him with an anonymous note saying they were found in the car park. How's that?'

She said nothing, keeping her eyes on the road.

'Look, Liz, I know that you're pissed off that I've come busting into your case. But in the end we both want the same thing, which is to nail this bastard before he takes any more lives, agreed?'

She took a deep breath. 'If we're going to work together we fix the ground rules now, and the first is that there will be no freelancing, no cowboy weaponry. You risked the life of my agent back there, and with it the whole operation.'

Mackay began to answer but she overrode him. 'If this case ends up with an arrest, and we've broken the law, the defence will have a field day. This is the UK, not Islamabad, OK?'

He shrugged. 'Zander's a dead man, and you know it.' He turned to face her. 'You think Bob Morrison's on the take from Eastman, don't you? That's why you agreed to this meet, isn't it? To keep Morrison out of the loop?'

'I thought there was an outside chance,' admitted Liz, 'although I've got no proof of any kind against Morrison. It's purely instinct.'

'In future, can we share your instincts?'

'Let's see how we go, shall we?'

BY THE TIME Kieran Mitchell reached the Brentwood Sporting Club, he knew that he was enjoying his last evening of freedom for a long time. His wife Debbie, frantic with worry, had rung to say that the police had called at the house, and voicemail messages had piled in from contacts in at least half a dozen pubs and clubs. They were looking for him in all his usual haunts. It was only a matter of time.

Looking around him at the familiar surroundings—the punters crowding the oxblood-red leather banquettes, the croupiers in their tight red dresses—he tried to impress its details on to his memory. He would need something to draw on in the months ahead.

He was fucked, basically.

From the moment he'd walked into the toilet at the Fairmile and seen Ray Gunter's body lolling against the tiles, he'd known that the people-smuggling racket had been blown to the four winds. The police wouldn't have a choice; they'd have to follow this as far as the trail led. And the short answer, of course, was that it led to him.

What the hell had Eastman been thinking of, getting into bed with those Krauts? Before they'd come calling he'd had a sweet little franchise running, bringing in illegals for the Caravan. Asians, Africans, working girls from Albania and Kosovo, all of them properly cowed and respectful. No trouble, no argument. The moment he'd clocked that Paki he'd known he was going to be trouble. A real hard nut.

Ray Gunter, of course—idiot that he was—had spotted the rucksack and decided to take it off the Paki. And so the Paki—psycho nutcase that he was—had taken him out.

All of these events leading him, Kieran Mitchell, in his slate-grey silk suit and his midnight-blue Versace shirt, to this moment. Not for the first time, he considered cutting and running. But if he ran, and they found him, it would go worse for him. It would cancel out the one card that he held. The card that, if he played it properly . . .

In the mirror he saw movement near the entrance. Purposeful men in inexpensive suits. The crowd parting. Downing his Scotch in three measured draughts, he felt in his trouser pocket for the coat-check disc. It was cold out, so he'd brought the dark blue cashmere.

LIZ SENSED the quiet excitement in the place as soon as she walked into the operations room at Norwich Police Station. The Gunter murder investigation had been going nowhere fast and suddenly here was a solid lead in the shape of one of Melvin Eastman's senior associates.

Seeing Liz, Steve Goss waved and extracted himself from a group of bullish-looking officers. 'They think I lined up Mitchell's arrest,' he murmured, running a hand through his scrubby ginger hair. 'I feel a total bloody fraud.'

'Enjoy it,' suggested Mackay.

'And let's pray it's not a dead end,' agreed Liz.

She had called Goss with Kieran Mitchell's details as soon as she and Mackay were clear of Braintree. Then they had driven north to Norwich, stopping on the way to pick up a pizza and a bottle of beer each. For the time being, perhaps as a way of acknowledging Liz's earlier fury, Mackay had shrugged off his romantic seducer's skin, and without it he proved a surprisingly entertaining companion. He had a near inexhaustible fund of stories, most of them concerning the extreme behaviour—or misbehaviour—of his service colleagues. At the same time, Liz noticed, he never actually fingered anyone directly.

He's on to me, thought Liz, enjoying the game. He's aware that I'm waiting for him to make a mistake. And he's playing up to my expectations of him as a reckless freelancer, because if he can convince me that's what he is, then I'll stop taking him seriously. And the moment I do that he'll find some way of stitching me up. There was even a certain elegance to it.

She had briefed Goss over the phone about the conversations with Cherisse Hogan and Peregrine Lakeby that had led her to Kieran Mitchell's name, and suggested that he set up the arrest. She had considered sharing her concerns about Bob Morrison with him, too, but had decided to let the matter lie. She had no evidence that he might be in Eastman's pocket. Besides which, Eastman would know, with or without Morrison, that Kieran Mitchell had been arrested, and would make his arrangements accordingly. And if Mitchell came up with solid information and was prepared to go the distance in court, then Eastman would be out of the game anyway.

Don Whitten, coffee cup in hand, was presiding over the melee in the operations room. Mitchell's solicitor had been petitioning for immunity for his client in return for giving the police everything he knew in relation to Gunter's murder. Whitten had given him nothing.

'Nice one,' said Bob Morrison, who had been sent over as an observer by the Essex force.

Whitten shrugged. 'They all try it on. They know it's a loss leader, we know it's a loss leader . . . Anyway, Mitchell's on his way to the interview room now.'

Five minutes later, Mitchell, accompanied by the duty sergeant and his lawyer, took his place at the white laminate table in the interview room. It was midnight.

'TELL US AGAIN about the Germans,' said DS Don Whitten, smoothing down his moustache. Bob Morrison was sitting next to him in the interview suite. Both Whitten and Kieran Mitchell had chain-smoked their way steadily through the last hour's interrogation and now a blue-brown pall hung in the air over the interview table.

Mitchell glanced at his lawyer, who nodded. Mitchell's eyelids drooped, and against the dour backdrop of the brightly lit interview room he looked cheap and gangsterish in his designer clothes. To Liz, watching through the one-way glass screen, it was clear that he was desperately trying to hold things together, to display a helpful patience rather than the snappish exhaustion that he felt.

'Like I said, I know nothing about the Germans. I only know that the organisation was called the Caravan. I think that Germans organised the runners' transit from mainland Europe to the point when me and Gunter picked them up off the Norfolk coast.'

'The runners being the migrants?' asked Whitten.

'The runners being the migrants,' Mitchell confirmed.

'And the boat's point of origin?'

'I never asked. There were two boats, both converted fishing cutters. I think one was called *Albertina Q*, registered port Cuxhaven, and the other *Susanne* something, registered Bremen . . . Breminger . . .'

'Bremerhaven,' murmured Liz. Beside her, in the observation suite, Steve Goss was opening a greaseproof-paper-wrapped clutch of cheese sandwiches. He nudged the packet in her direction and she took one. Was there a Mrs Goss? she wondered.

'To be honest,' Mitchell was saying, 'the name of the boat was the last thing on my mind. But I do know that the organisation was known as the Caravan.'

'And the Caravan paid Eastman?' asked Whitten.

'I assume so. He was responsible from the pick-up at sea to the delivery point in Ilford. There'd be another crew waiting there with documents, and they'd take them on to . . . wherever.'

'And there would be how many again in each consignment?'

Whitten was repeating earlier questions, checking the answers for inconsistencies. So far, Mitchell's answers seemed steady.

'If it was girls, it went up to twenty-eight. Ordinary runners twenty-five, tops. Gunter's boats couldn't take more than that, especially if there was a heavy sea.'

'And Eastman paid you, and you paid Gunter?'

'Yeah.'

'Tell me how much again.'

Mitchell's head seemed to slump. 'I got a grand per head for girls, one-five for runners, two for specials.'

'So on a good night you might be pulling down forty grand?'

'Thereabouts.'

'And how much did you pay Gunter?'

'Flat rate. Five grand per pick-up.'

'Nice profit margin there!'

Mitchell shrugged. 'It was risky work. Can I take a piss?'

Whitten nodded, spoke the time into the tape recorder, clicked it off, and called for the duty sergeant. When Mitchell had left the room, accompanied by his solicitor, there was a moment's silence.

'Do we believe him?' asked Mackay, rubbing his eyes.

'Why would he lie to us?' asked Goss. 'He'd just be defending the person who murdered his partner, wrote off a nice forty-K-a-month earner, and basically got him nicked.'

'Eastman could have asked him to feed us disinformation as part of a damage-limitation exercise,' said Mackay. 'Mitchell wouldn't be the first criminal to take the drop for his boss.'

Mitchell came back into the room and Whitten began asking about the Fairmile Café again. 'Tell us about the special.'

'Eastman told me he was some Asian fixer who was being brought in from Europe. He wasn't a migrant, like the others; he'd paid to be brought in and then, in a month's time, to be taken out again.'

'Had this happened before?' Whitten asked.

'No. The whole special idea was new on me.'

'Go on,' said Whitten.

'Well, when we got to the Fairmile Café, Ray let the Special out of the back of the truck and followed him into the toilet.'

'Do you know why Gunter followed him?' asked Whitten. 'Had he said anything to you about needing to use the toilet?'

'No. But the Paki guy, the special, had a heavy rucksack. The guy wouldn't be separated from it.'

'So you saw him close up, this Pakistani guy?'

'Yeah. I mean, it was pretty dark on the beach but he looked different to the others. Like he wasn't going to let anyone grind him down. Not a big guy, by any means, but hard. You could tell that about him.'

'And what did he look like . . . physically? Did you see his face?'

'Yeah. He was quite pale-skinned. Sharp features. Bit of a beard.'

'So you'd recognise him again?'

'I reckon so, yeah. I wouldn't want to swear to anything, but if you showed me a photo, I'd . . . I'd probably be able to say if it wasn't him, put it like that.'

Behind the glass, Liz felt the steady drip-feed of adrenaline. Glancing at Goss and Mackay, she could see the same rapt attention.

'So why do you think Gunter followed him?' Whitten repeated.

'My guess is that he thought he had something valuable in the rucksack—the rich ones bring in gold, bullion, all sorts—and wanted to . . . well, take it off him, basically.'

'OK. So Gunter follows the guy into the toilets. You hear nothing. No shot . . .'

'No. Nothing at all. A few minutes later I saw the Paki walk across to a car and get in. The car then drove off.'

'And you saw the car?'

'Yeah. It was a black Vauxhall Astra 1.4 LS. Couldn't see if it was a man or a woman at the wheel. I took its reg number, though.'

'Which was?'

Consulting a scrap of crumpled paper handed to him by his lawyer, Mitchell told them.

'Why did you take the number?'

'Because I hadn't got any form of receipt for the guy. He was worth two grand to me, remember.'

'Go on,' said Whitten.

'Well, I waited ten minutes and Ray didn't show. So I got out of the cab and walked over to the toilets and found Ray dead. Shot, with his brains all over the wall.'

'So what did you think?'

'I thought . . . it's illogical, because I'd seen the guy drive off, but I thought I was next. That the Paki had done Ray because he'd seen his face in the light and was going to do me too. I was crapping it, frankly. I just wanted to get out of there.'

'So you drove away.'

'Bloody right I did. Straight to Ilford, no stops, and dropped off the other runners.'

'So when did you ring Eastman?'

'When I'd finished in Ilford.'

'Why didn't you ring him as soon as you found the body?'

'Like I said, I just wanted to get out of there.'

'What was Eastman's reaction when you rang?'

'He went totally spare, like I knew he would . . . totally off his head.'

'And since then? What have you been doing with yourself?'

'Waiting for you blokes. I knew it was just a matter of time.'

There was a pause, then Whitten nodded. As he walked to the door to call the custody sergeant, Mitchell's solicitor touched his client's elbow and the pair got to their feet. Opposite them, Bob Morrison glanced at his watch. Frowning, he hurried from the room.

'Off to ring Eastman, do you think?' Mackay murmured, touching his forehead to the one-way glass.

Liz shrugged. 'It's not impossible, is it?'

Don Whitten swung heavily through the door of the observation suite. 'Well?' he asked. 'Do we buy the story?'

Goss looked up from the notes he'd been studying. 'It's logical, and it's certainly consistent with the facts we know.'

'I'm the newcomer here,' said Mackay. 'But I'd have said the guy was telling the truth. I'd like to spend a few hours with him tomorrow going through photographs of known ITS players. See if we can get a provisional make on the gunman.'

'I agree,' said Liz. 'And I'd say that we need to get onto that black Astra as a matter of urgency.'

'Agreed, but what do we tell people?' asked Whitten. 'Do we link the search for the car to the Fairmile murder?'

'Yes. Put out a nationwide alert that the car has to be found and placed under observation, but that the driver and passengers must not be approached. Instead, Norfolk police should be contacted immediately.' She raised an eyebrow at Steve Goss, who nodded, and turned back to Whitten. 'Do you know where Bob Morrison went?'

Whitten shook his head uninterestedly. 'My guess is that our shooter's still on our doorstep. Otherwise why did he have himself dropped off outside that transport café rather than going on to London?'

'The car could have taken him anywhere,' said Goss. 'Perhaps he was heading north.'

Mackay leaned forward. 'More than anything else, we need details of this Caravan organisation. These Germans that Mitchell told us about. Is there any reason why we can't just haul Eastman in right now and sweat him for twenty-four hours?'

'He'd laugh at us,' said Liz. 'Mr Eastman is very switched on indeed, legally speaking. Once we've got enough information to put him away we can bring him in and break him, really give him a bad time but until then . . .'

Mackay looked at her speculatively. 'I love it when you talk dirty,' he murmured.

Whitten sniggered, but Goss stared at Mackay disbelievingly.

'Thank you,' said Liz, forcing a smile. 'A suitable note to end up on, I think.'

SHE KEPT THE SMILE going until she and Mackay were in the Audi. Then, as they pulled their seat belts over their shoulders, she rounded on him, pale with fury.

'If you ever—*ever*—undermine my authority in that way again, I will have you moved off this case. You're here on sufferance—*my* sufferance, Mackay, and don't you forget it.'

He stretched his legs in front of him, unperturbed. 'Liz, relax. It was just a joke. Not a very good joke, I admit, but . . .'

Gunning the throttle and snapping her foot off the clutch so that he was thrown backwards against his seat, she swung out of the police-station car park. 'But *nothing*, Mackay. This is my operation, and you take your lead from me, understand?'

'As a matter of fact,' he said mildly, 'that's not strictly true. This is a joint service operation and with all due respect to your achievements to date, it's actually a fact that I outrank you. So can we please loosen things up a notch? That was a red light, by the way.'

'It was still yellow. And I don't give a toss about your rank. The point I'm making is that if we're going to have one tenth of a chance of catching our shooter, then we're going to need to keep the local force onside. That involves getting and keeping their respect, which in its turn involves your not treating me like some bimbo.'

He raised his hands in surrender. 'Like I said, Liz, I'm sorry, OK? It was meant to be a joke.'

Without warning, the Audi screeched hard leftwards off the road, jolted over two puddle craters, and came to an abrupt halt.

'Bloody hell!' gasped Mackay, straining against the taut lock of his seat belt. 'What are you doing?'

'I'm sorry,' Liz said breezily. 'It was meant to be a joke. Actually, I'm pulling into this lay-by to make a couple of calls. I want to find out who hired that black Astra.'

SEVEN

Liz's phone woke her at 7.45. She rolled over unwillingly and pressed the answer button.

'We've got a fix on the Astra,' someone on the investigation team was saying. 'It was hired by an English-speaking woman at the Avis car-hire outlet at Waterloo Eurostar station last Monday. She paid cash in advance and showed a British driving licence. The manager, who's French, like most of his customers, handled the transaction himself and vaguely remembers her, because she insisted on a black car and did not use a credit card.'

'Tell me about the driving licence,' said Liz, reaching for the pen and notebook on her bedside table.

'Name of Lucy Wharmby, aged twenty-three, born in the United Kingdom, address 17A Avisford Road, Yapton, West Sussex. Photograph shows brown-haired Caucasian woman, oval features, no distinguishing marks.'

'Go on,' said Liz fatalistically, certain of what was to follow.

'The driving licence, along with credit cards, cash, a passport and other documents, was reported stolen to the British consulate in Karachi, Pakistan, in August. Lucy Wharmby is a student at the West Sussex College of Art and Design in Worthing, and was provided with a replacement licence, which is still currently in her possession.'

'You contacted her?'

'I rang her. She was at home in Yapton where she lives with her parents. She claims never to have visited Norfolk.'

'And the Avis CCTV?' asked Liz.

'Well, it's taken us a bit of time, but we found the right person eventually. I've emailed the images to you. The customer's a woman, about the right age as far as I can see, and definitely dressed to beat the cameras. She's got sunglasses on and a peaked cap pulled down over her face, so you can't see her features, and she's wearing a long parka-style coat, so you can't see her figure.'

'The invisible,' murmured Liz.

'I beg your pardon?'

'Nothing . . . Just thinking aloud. We need to keep a whole team on this—can you clear that with Wetherby?'

'Sure. Go on.'

'I want you to get the passenger list for that Monday morning's Eurostar arrival—the one immediately preceding the woman's visit to the Avis counter. Check if the name Lucy Wharmby's on the list, and if not, find out what name she came in on. My guess is that the person we're looking for is a UK citizen and passport holder aged between seventeen and thirty and will have used her own passport to enter England. Get everyone you can onto it straight away.'

'Understood. I'll keep you posted.'

She fell back against the pillows, fighting the fatigue that was dragging at her. A session beneath Temeraire's unreliable-looking shower, a cup of coffee downstairs, and things might seem clearer.

LESS THAN HALF a mile from the cell in which Kieran Mitchell spent the night, a black Vauxhall Astra pulled into a parking bay in Bishopsgate, Norwich. Climbing from the passenger seat, Faraj Mansoor glanced around him and took a handwritten shopping list from the inside pocket of his coat. Remote-locking the Astra, the driver sauntered across to the pay-and-display ticket machine.

At Faraj's side a man in a green and yellow Norwich City scarf was extracting a child from a battered Volvo estate car and harnessing her into a Maclaren buggy. 'Saturday mornings,' he grinned, nodding at Faraj's shopping list. 'Don't you hate them?'

Faraj forced a smile, not understanding.

'The weekend shopping,' explained the man, slamming the Volvo's door and releasing the buggy's brake with his toe. 'Still, it's the Villa game this afternoon, so . . .'

'Absolutely,' said Farat. 'Tell me,' he added. 'Do you know where there's a good toy shop here?'

The other man frowned. 'There's a good one in St Benedict's Street, about five minutes' walk away.' He gave elaborate directions.

Returning, the woman slipped her arm through Faraj's, took the shopping list from him, and listened to the tail end of the directions. 'That's very helpful.' She smiled at the man, then turned away.

'Excuse me, you've dropped your . . .'

Her heart lurched. The man with the scarf was waving the shopping list. Apologetically she took it from him. On it were visible the words *clear gelatin, isopropol, candles*; his fingers covered up the rest.

Clutching the list she took Faraj's arm and walked away. He looked at her with controlled anger.

'I'm sorry,' she said, her eyes watering in the cold. Her chest was still pounding. The list looked harmless, but to anyone with a certain sort of military experience it would send an unmistakable message.

'Remember who you are,' he told her quietly, speaking in Urdu. 'Remember why we're here.'

'I know who I am,' she snapped in the same language. 'And we need to find this toy shop.'

LIZ STARED DESPAIRINGLY at the image on her laptop. Lifted from the Avis car-hire CCTV at Waterloo, it showed the woman who had hired the Astra. Hair, eyes, body shape, all were obscured.

She glanced at her watch—ten to eleven—and snapped the laptop shut. For the moment, there was nothing that she could do. The description and registration number of the Astra had gone out to all forces nationwide that morning and Whitten's team was checking with all garages within fifty miles of Marsh Creake.

Liz herself had rung Investigations to check on the Eurostar passenger-list search. The Investigations team was being led by Judith Spratt, who had been in the same intake as Liz a decade before.

'It's going to take time,' Judith had told her. 'There were at least two hundred British women passengers on that train.'

'OK. The Avis manager specifically remembered an English woman in her early twenties, and Lucy Wharmby, the woman whose stolen driving licence our target used, is twenty-three and British. Can you concentrate on British females between the ages of seventeen and thirty?'

'Sure. That brings the number down to, let's see . . . fifty-one, which is a bit more manageable.'

'And can you also get onto Lucy Wharmby and have her email you a recent photograph; there's a good chance that she looks like our target and that the driving licence was stolen to order in Pakistan.'

When the photographs came in an hour later, Investigations forwarded Liz a set. They confirmed the evidence of the driving licence, and showed an attractive but not especially memorable-looking young woman with brown eyes and shoulder-length hair.

The team wasted no time. Of the fifty-one female passengers to be checked, thirty had addresses in the Metropolitan Police area; the rest were spread countrywide. To help the police eliminate those who were clearly not their target, the Avis CCTV stills were emailed to all the relevant forces, and officers sent out to check alibis.

Mackay, meanwhile, was in the village hall with Steve Goss and the police team, making personal calls to the heads of all the major civilian and military establishments in East Anglia that might possibly constitute Islamic Terror Syndicate targets.

At midday Judith Spratt rang Liz to request a call-back, and Liz walked to the public phone box on the seafront. Out of the fifty-one women on the police check-list, she learned, twenty-eight had been interviewed and cleared, five were black, and seven were 'of a body size not compatible with existing subject-data'.

That left eleven of the women uninterviewed, of whom five lived alone and six lived in multi-person households. Nine had been out all morning and were uncontactable by mobile phone, one had not returned from a party in Runcorn, and one was on the way to Chertsey.

'The Runcorn one,' said Liz.

'Stephanie Patch, nineteen. Catering apprentice employed by the Crown and Thistle Hotel, Warrington. Lives at home. We've spoken to the mother, who says that she was working at the hotel on the night of the murder and returned home before midnight.'

'What was Stephanie doing in Paris?'

'Pop concert,' said Judith. 'The Foo Fighters. She went with a friend from work.'

'Does that check out?'

'The Foo Fighters were playing at the Palais de Bercy on the night in question, yes.'

'Has anyone spoken to the friend?'

'She apparently went to the same party in Runcorn and hasn't come home either. Stephanie's mother thinks they've stayed away because one or both of them has gone out and got a tattoo, which they were apparently threatening to do. And she can't drive.'

'Which rules her out. Any of the others look even faintly possible?'

'There's an art student from Bath. Sally Madden, twenty-six, single. Lives in a studio flat in the South Stoke area. Holds a driving licence, but according to a neighbour doesn't own a car.'

'What was she doing in Paris?'

'We don't know. She's been out all morning.'

'She sounds like a possible.'

'I agree. Somerset police's tactical firearms group is standing by.'

'Thanks, Jude. Call me when you have more.'

'Will do.'

AT 12.30, following a call from Steve Goss, Liz made her way to the village hall, where half a dozen computer screens now cast their pale glow over the intent faces of officers that Liz didn't recognise and an air of unhurried urgency prevailed. Goss beckoned her over. 'Small garage outside a place called Hawfield, north of King's Lynn.'

'Go on.'

'Just after six p.m. on the evening before the shooting at the Fairmile Café, a young woman pays with two fifty-pound notes for a full tank of unleaded fuel, plus several litres which she takes away in a plastic screw-top container. The assistant particularly remembers her spilling fuel on her hands and coat—he remembers a green hiking-type jacket—presumably while filling the container. He makes some friendly remark to her about this but she blanks him and hands him the notes as if she hasn't heard him. She also buys—get this—an *A to Z* of Norfolk.'

'That's her. It's *got* to be her. Any CCTV?'

'No, which is presumably why she chose the place. But the guy has good recall of her appearance. Early twenties, wide-set eyes, mid-brown hair held in some sort of elastic band. Quite attractive, he says, and with what he describes as a "mid-posh accent".'

'Have the garage still got the fifty-pound notes?'

'No. Banked them a couple of days ago. But Whitten's got an Identifit artist working with the garage guy right now. We should have the portrait on our screens within the hour.'

'She's right under our noses, Steve. I can practically smell her.'

'Yeah, me too, petrol and all. Have London come up with anything?'

'They're down to a dozen or so possibles. No sighting of the Astra, I assume?'

'No. We've circulated the details but you need a hell of a lot of luck with cars. We usually only find them once they're dumped.'

'OK. Can we have spotters in unmarked cars lying up on the approach roads to the American air bases?'

'Mr Mackay's already suggested that, and Whitten's onto it.'

Liz looked around her. 'Where is Mackay?'

'He's driven to Lakenheath, to liaise with the station commander.'

'OK,' said Liz. Good of him to keep me in the picture, she thought.

'I've heard they do a very nice hamburger there,' said Goss.

Liz glanced at her watch. 'Would you settle for a ploughman's at the Trafalgar?'

'Reckon so,' he nodded.

THEY SAW A POLICE car on the way back from Norwich. They were approaching the village of Bawdeswell and she saw the distant blue light of a patrol car at the roundabout a quarter of a mile ahead. Briefly engaging its siren, the police vehicle took a westbound exit lane and disappeared. She felt a sick lump of fear and breathed deeply in an attempt to control it.

'I think it's time to get rid of this car,' she said. 'It was in the car park when you killed the thief. Someone could have made a connection.'

He thought for a moment and nodded. She knew he had seen and heard the police car. 'We'll need another.'

'That was allowed for,' she said. 'I hire it in my own name.'

'So what do we do with this one?'

'Disappear it. I know a place.'

He nodded and they drove on in silence.

At the bungalow, when they had eaten, and she had spent several minutes searching the coastline east to west with the binoculars, he laid the morning's purchases on the kitchen table. In silence, they rolled up their sleeves. She knew the routine well—the urban warfare cadre had been made to memorise it at Takht-i-Suleiman. It was curious, though, seeing it done here.

They worked in silence. It was tiresome and messy work, but finally the mixture assumed the requisite melted-fudge consistency and the hydrometer showed the correct reading. Both of them knew that the next stage, in which the two highly unstable mixtures had to be folded together, was the most dangerous. Expressionless, Faraj laid the hydrometer on the table.

'I'll finish it,' she said quietly, laying a hand on his wrist.

He stared down at her hand.

'Take the weapons, the documents and the money,' she continued, 'and drive a few hundred yards up the road. If . . . if it goes wrong, get out fast. Fight on without me.'

He looked up from her hand to her eyes.

'You must live,' she said. She tightened her hold on his wrist, which somehow required more courage than anything that had yet been required of her. 'Go. As soon as I've finished you'll see me walk down to the sea.'

Briskly, he moved away. It took him no more than a minute to assemble all that he needed. At the front door, he hesitated and turned back to her. 'Asimat?'

She met his flat, expressionless gaze.

'They chose well at Takht-i-Suleiman.'

'Go,' she said.

She waited until she could no longer hear the gravel beneath the Astra's tyres, and moved to the fridge. Lifting the chilled box care-from the freezer, she retrieved the gelatin mix Faraj had prepared and added it to the contents of the bowl. Gently but surely, murmuring a prayer to steady her hands, she worked the two compounds together.

C4, she murmured to herself. The north, south, east and west winds of jihad. Composition Four explosive. Taking a knife from the cutlery drawer, continuing her prayer, she cut the creamy paste into three equal-sized lumps. With the help of a teaspoon, she smoothed each lump into a sphere the size of a tennis ball. Spherical charges, they had told her, guaranteed the highest detonation velocity.

As she melted a couple of candles in a scratched Teflon saucepan, she allowed herself to draw breath. The worst was over, but one more test remained. 'Too hot the wax,' she remembered the instructor telling them at Takht-i-Suleiman, his eyes merry, 'and *poo-o-o-o-f!*' He had shaken his head at the sheer hilarity of the idea.

Taking the saucepan off the flame, and waiting until a pale film had formed over the wax, she laid the three balls of compound in the pan with the teaspoon, and gently rolled them around. When they were evenly coated she nudged them together so that they fused in a three-tiered line. Gradually the wax hardened, became opaque. The charges now looked like giant white chocolates, perhaps Belgian, like the ones that her mother . . .

Don't go there, she told herself. That life is dead.

But it wasn't quite dead, and the prayer that she was murmuring had somehow mutated into the Queen song 'Bohemian Rhapsody', which, before the split-up, her parents had liked to play in the car. And there they were, their hazy figures drifting casually through the bungalow kitchen, laughing together and calling her by her old name, the name that they had given her. Furious, she stepped back from the table, closed her eyes hard for a second or two and murmured her Islamic name. 'Asimat. My name is Asimat. *My name is Asimat.*'

The intense pleasure that had accompanied Faraj's approval had evaporated now. She turned her attention back to the explosive. Taking three pipe cleaners, she pushed them through the cooling wax of the central sphere and out the other side, and then twisted the ends together for connection to the detonator hook-ups.

Feeling more balanced, she carried the explosive over to the fridge and laid it reverently on the top shelf. That done, she walked out of the back door and down the shingle to the sea's edge, the wind lashing her hair about her face.

IN HER ROOM at the Trafalgar, Liz scrolled through the list of passengers on her laptop. It was just 2.30 p.m. They had drawn a blank.

What have we missed? she asked herself, staring at the screen. *What have we missed?* Somewhere on that neat black and white list was the invisible's name. Think. Analyse. Why did she come into the country under her own name?

Because whoever she was working for insisted on it. They would never have risked using false documentation and compromising their operation if they didn't absolutely have to.

Why use a stolen licence to hire the car? Because once she was past Immigration and in the country there was nothing to connect her to the transaction. Even if the car was spotted its hirer would be untraceable, leaving the woman free to use her own identification. But for Ray Gunter, however, the plan would have been perfect. Gunter had got himself killed, and from then on things had started to unravel.

But not quite fast enough. Were the terror cell planning an assault on one of the American air bases? If so, what kind of attack could two people mount? You couldn't get near the bases for security. A bomb, perhaps? But how delivered? Every incoming consignment of baseballs, auto parts or hamburger buns was being X-rayed or hand-searched. No vehicle venturing outside a base was now left unattended or out in the open so that a device could be attached. Loose off a rocket-propelled grenade at a gatehouse? Only with enormous difficulty, she suspected. And you'd never live to tell the tale.

No, Liz told herself. Her best bet was to go at the problem from the other end. Find the woman. Catch her. Stop her. Scrolling back to the top of the screen, a thought occurred to her. Had the Avis manager been wrong? Was the woman in fact French, but fluent in English?

Instinct said no. You couldn't see the details on the blurry Avis CCTV footage, but in a strange sort of way you could see the person. Something in the diffident carriage of the upper body spoke to Liz of a particularly English coupling of intellectual arrogance and muted physical awkwardness.

By 5 p.m. the light had faded and afternoon had become evening. The Identifit portrait had come in, but had proved disappointingly generic and unrevealing. The woman was wearing a blue-black baseball cap and olive-coloured aviator sunglasses and looked vaguely like Lucy Wharmby, although the eyes were a little wider set.

The portrait was quickly emailed to Investigations, and to all the police forces involved. In response Judith Spratt requested a call-back, and, when Liz had once again made her way to the phone box, told her that the police had drawn a blank on all the seventeen to thirties British and non-EU women.

Eighty-odd women checked. And none of them the target.

'How can you tell if a woman is French, Jude? By passport?'

'No. Both Brits and French hold EU passports. I do it by name, mostly. So what do you want me to do now?' asked Judith. 'Do you want me to go with the French women?'

'I just don't believe she's French. Instinctively, I *know* she's English. Still, I guess it's got to be done.'

'Go for it, then, Liz?'

'Yup. Go for it.'

WHEN LIZ got back to the Trafalgar, Mackay had returned and was holding a Scotch up to the light in the bar.

'Liz. What can I get you?'

'Same as you.'

'I'm having a malt. Talisker.'

'Sounds good.' And maybe it'll help nudge the answer into place about our phantom Eurostar passenger, she thought tiredly.

'So what kind of day have you had?' he asked, when they were installed at a quiet corner table.

'Mostly, a bad one. Wasting the time of half a dozen police forces. And failing to identify our invisible. On the credit side, I had a nice toasted sandwich with Steve Goss at lunchtime.'

He smiled. 'Are you trying to make me jealous?'

She tilted her chin at him. 'It's no contest. Steve's a considerate guy. He's not arrogant. He keeps me in the picture.'

'Ah, so *that's* the trouble.' He sipped his whisky. 'I thought I left a message.'

'Yeah, and the cheque's in the post. Ring me, Bruno. Keep me in the loop. Don't just bugger off.'

He looked at her steadily, which she guessed was the nearest thing she was going to get to an apology.

'Let me fill you in now,' he said. 'I've had a word with our friends at Lakenheath, all of whom seem very switched-on and generally *prepared* . . . and I've stressed the need for them to continue so to be. When you see the size of those places you do begin to wonder what a single bloke and a girl could achieve in the way of damage.'

'I've seen those bases, and I was thinking much the same thing. My instinct says that they're after a softer target.'

'Like?'

'Like I don't know. Something.' She shook her head. '*Damn it!*'

'Look, Liz, for the moment there's nothing we can do. Relax. Why don't we see what sort of a dinner Bethany can rustle up for us . . .'

'Who on earth's Bethany? That sullen adolescent behind the bar?'

'She's twenty-three, in fact. Come on, lunch was a long time ago.'

Why not? thought Liz. He was right; until the French women had been checked there really was nothing they could do. And she really ought to try and unwind a few notches.

'OK, then,' she smiled. 'Let's see what Mr Badger and his catering team can do.'

'HOW'S YOUR FISH?' asked Bruno Mackay.

'Long on bones and short on taste,' said Liz. 'This wine, on the other hand, is seriously fabulous.'

'These out-of-the-way places sometimes do have good things in their cellars. No one ever orders them so they lie there for years.'

'Waiting for a discriminating chap like yourself?' said Liz archly.

'Basically, yes. Ah, here's Bethany with the tartare sauce.'

'Who, like the wine, has been quietly maturing downstairs . . .'

'You know something, you're a very judgmental woman.'

Liz was searching for a reply when her phone rang. It was Goss.

'Just calling to say that we might have a name for our shooter. Mitchell's been looking at photographs all day, and he's made a provisional identification. Shall I email you the data?'

'Definitely. Send a copy to Mackay too.'

She handed the phone to Mackay. 'Tell Steve Goss your email address. He's got an ident on the shooter.'

It was ten minutes before the pictures came through. They were sitting in Mackay's room. He had saved the wine and their glasses, but the smell of cheap air freshener put Liz off drinking any more.

She nodded at the computer on the dressing table. 'You know who this is going to be, don't you?'

He frowned. 'No, do you?'

'I've got a pretty good idea,' she said, as a dust-coloured portrait of a man in a mujahidin cap materialised on the screen.

'Faraj Mansoor,' he read. 'So who the hell's Faraj Mansoor?'

'Former garage worker from Peshawar. Known contact of Dawood al Safa and holder of a forged UK driving licence made in Bremerhaven.'

He stared at the image on the screen. 'How do you know? What haven't you been telling me?'

'What hasn't Geoffrey Fane been telling you? He's the one who picked up on this guy after German liaison flashed us about the driving licence. Are you really telling me you don't know anything about this man? You're Mr Pakistan, after all.'

'That's exactly what I'm telling you. Who is he?'

She told him the little she knew.

'So ultimately all we've got is a name and a face,' said Mackay. 'Nothing else. No known contacts, no—'

'Nothing else that I know about, no.'

'Damn!' He sank down onto the bed. '*Damn!*'

'At least we know what he looks like,' said Liz. 'Quite handsome, I'd say. I wonder what's going on between him and the girl?'

'I wonder,' said Mackay drily.

'How about the Eurostar passenger list? Any inspiration on that?'

'Only a confirmation of life's unfairness.'

'What on earth do you mean?' she asked.

'Can you imagine the start in life it would give you to have a name like Adrienne Fantoni-Brizeart or Jean D'Alvéydre?' asked Mackay. 'Every introduction would be a declaration of love.'

'Were those two names on the list?' asked Liz. *Something, some urgent thread of an idea* . . .

'As far as I can remember, yes? Why?'

'I don't know. Something . . .' She squeezed her eyes shut. 'Yes.' *Damn*. 'No. Lost it.'

'I know that feeling,' Bruno said sympathetically. 'Best to file and forget. The memory'll throw it up when it's ready.'

She nodded. 'I know you went to Lakenheath today; did you go to either of the others, Mildenhall or Marwell?'

'No. I'd hoped to get to Mildenhall but the station commander was away. I'm due there tomorrow morning. Want to come?'

'No, I'll stay here. Sooner or later someone is going to spot that hire car. Whitten's had people looking for it all over the—' Liz stood up suddenly. 'Wait here,' she said. 'I want to look at that list on the laptop. I'll be back in a sec.'

Leaving Mackay's room, she crossed the corridor to Temeraire. Switching on her laptop she called up her incoming email list. It took her less than a minute to find what she wanted.

'You were right,' she told Mackay, back in his room. 'There is a Jean D'Alvéydre. She consulted a handwritten list. 'And a Jean Boissevin, a Jean Béhar, a Jean Fauvet, a Jean D'Aubigny and a Jean Soustelle.'

'Right.'

'And I bet you anything you like that one of them isn't a Jean, rhyming with *con*, but a *Jean*, rhyming with *teen*.'

Mackay frowned. 'Who's been put with the French men because she's got a French-sounding surname, you mean?'

'Exactly.'

'My God,' he murmured. 'You could be damn well *right*.'

She reached for her bag. 'Wait here. Give me five minutes.'

The cement floor of the phone box was covered with cigarette ends and the receiver stank of beery breath.

'Jud—' Liz began.

'I'm afraid the answer's no so far,' said Judith Spratt. 'About sixty per cent of the French names are in, and they're all negative.'

Liz quickly asked her to check all the Jeans on the list, and explained why.

There was a pause. 'Oh my *Lord*. Yes. I see what you mean. That could easily be an old English name. I'll call you back.'

She and Mackay had time to finish the wine and drink a cup of coffee each. When Judith Spratt finally called back, Liz knew from her tone that she'd been right. In the phone box her back ended up pressed against Mackay's chest but she couldn't have cared less.

'Jean D'Aubigny, twenty-four,' said Spratt. 'Nationality, British, current address, Seventeen Passage de l'Ouled Naïl, Corentin-Cariou, Paris. Registered as a student at the Dauphine department of the Sorbonne, reading Urdu literature. Congratulations!'

'Thanks,' said Liz, twisting round to nod at Mackay, who gave her a wide grin and a clenched fist salute. *Got you*! she thought.

'Parents are separated and neither was expecting Jean for Christmas as she had told them she was staying in Paris with university friends. We've just finished speaking to her tutor at Dauphine. He told us that he has not seen Jean since the end of the term before last and assumed that she had withdrawn from the course.'

'Can the parents get us pictures? We're going to need everything,' said Liz. 'Friends, contacts, people she was at school with . . .'

'We're on to all that,' said Judith. 'Just keep checking your email. Are you going to stay up there in Norfolk?'

'I am. She's in this area somewhere, I'm sure of it.'

'Talk later, then.'

Liz cut the connection and hesitated, finger poised over the dial. Steve Goss first, she decided, and then Whitten. *Yes!*

EIGHT

What people saw in the Strand bungalows, mused Elsie Hogan, was more than she could fathom. They were poky and cold, you had to drive to Dersthorpe if you wanted so much as a box of tea bags, and there wasn't a telly or a phone in any of them! Still, Diane Munday had to know what she was doing. She wouldn't hang on to them if they weren't turning her a profit.

Elsie 'did' for the Mundays on the days that she wasn't 'doing' for the Lakebys. She wasn't particularly fond of Diane Munday, who was liable to argue when it came to totting up the hours. But cash was cash, and she couldn't survive on what the Lakebys paid her.

Sunday was Elsie's morning to look in on the bungalows. As she lurched slowly up the uneven track in her ten-year-old Ford Fiesta, windscreen-wipers thonking back and forth against the steady rain, she could just see the nose of the black car belonging to the woman staying in number one.

From the front seat of the Astra, Jean D'Aubigny watched the Fiesta's slow approach through her binoculars. She had driven up to within a couple of feet of the track to give herself a clear field of vision in either direction, and for the last hour's watch had been listening to the local BBC station on the car radio, hoping for news of the Gunter murder, attempting to subdue her mounting agitation. The last time-check, a couple of minutes ago, had been 10.20 a.m.

Slowly, like a mirage, the clapped-out Fiesta crept towards her. It was old, Jean could now see, to be carrying plainclothes policemen. But to be on the safe side she drew the Malyah and laid it in her lap.

The Fiesta was almost on her now, and Jean could see the driver—a solid-looking middle-aged woman. Putting the car into gear, she accelerated, intending to reverse out of the other car's way. But the car was not in reverse. Somehow she had put it into first, and as the gears engaged the car leapt forwards and hammered into the wing of the oncoming Fiesta. There was a crunch, a lurching cough as the Astra stalled, and a cascade of headlight glass.

Shit, thought Jean. *Shit!* Shoving the Malyah into the waistband of her jeans, she jumped from the car, heart thumping. The Astra's bumper was dented and it had lost a headlight. The Fiesta's entire passenger-side wing, however, was a write-off and the car's driver was sitting motionless, staring in front of her.

'Are you all right?' shouted Jean through the Fiesta's closed window. Rain sluiced down, drenching her hair.

The window opened a couple of inches, but the middle-aged driver continued to face ahead of her. 'I've hurt my neck,' she whimpered plaintively. 'Whiplash.'

Like hell you have, thought Jean savagely. 'Look, we really didn't hit each other very hard,' she pleaded. 'Why don't . . .'

'I didn't hit anyone,' said the woman. 'You hit me.'

'OK, fine. I hit you. I'm sorry. Why don't I just give you a hundred and fifty pounds right now—cash, right—and we can . . .'

But to her horror, Jean saw that a phone had appeared in the woman's hand and that the two-inch gap in the window was closing. She grabbed at the Fiesta's door handle but it was locked solid, and through the rain-blurred glass she saw the woman stabbing at her phone.

No time to think. Wrenching the Malyah from her waistband and releasing the safety catch, Jean screamed, '*Drop the phone!*'

The two plinks at the windscreen were barely louder than the beating of the rain, and the woman seemed to sink in her seat belt. For a moment Jean thought that she had somehow fired the Malyah without knowing, and then Faraj ran forward with the PSS, shouldered her out of the way and put two more rounds through the driver's-side window. The woman's body sagged further forward.

Reaching down to the ground for a large stone, Faraj heaved it through the bullet-crazed side window, reached inside, unlocked and opened the door, and rummaged beneath the woman's body. His arm came out bloodied to the elbow, and wiping the phone on the woman's blouse he glanced at the display and cut the connection.

'Load the car,' he said, rainwater streaming down his face. 'Go.'

Hurrying to the water's edge, he hurled Elsie Hogan's phone and the four 7.62 shell cases out to sea. Inside the bungalow, desperately trying to ignore the shrieking panic that was expanding within her, Jean made up two bin-liners of clothes and bundled them into her rucksack with the Malyah ammunition, the map book, the compass, the clasp knife, the phone, the two washbags, and the wallet containing the money. Faraj, meanwhile, carefully took the C4 device from the fridge, placed it in a biscuit tin that he had packed with a hand towel, and took it out to the car.

Everything else that might assist a forensic investigation—their clothes, sheets and blankets, the spare food—was bundled into the centre of the sitting room and sprinkled with petrol from the container Jean had filled at the Hawfield garage. Further fuel-soaked combustibles were packed round Elsie Hogan's body in the Fiesta.

'Ready?' asked Faraj, surveying the disordered front room.

'Ready,' said Jean, flicking a plastic briquet lighter at the fuel-soaked sleeve of one of the shirts she had bought Faraj in King's Lynn. They left the house at a run, heads down into the rain. As she leaned through the Fiesta window with the lighter, he swung the rucksacks into the back seat of the Astra.

Then she drove. They had planned for a fast exit, thanks be to God. She knew exactly where she was going.

IT TOOK DIANE MUNDAY several minutes to come to a decision. She hadn't picked up Elsie Hogan's call, she'd let the answering machine do the work, as she always did.

When the call had come in—'Mrs M? *Mrs M . . .*'—something had stayed her hand. 'It's Elsie, Mrs M,' the voice had shakily continued. 'I'm at the bungalows, and I've—'

Then a shout of some kind. Not Elsie's voice, but stifled and indistinct. Two plinks, like a teaspoon on bone china, and a long gasping groan. The plinking sound repeated, a thump, and silence.

Diane tried calling Elsie back, but got the engaged tone. She knew that she ought to react in some way. Drive over there, perhaps. But she decided against this. Her fear was that some sort of tiresome medical episode had occurred, which could well entail driving Elsie to hospital, hanging around in King's Lynn and having her Sunday morning well and truly ruined.

Really, she thought. I'm not the woman's keeper. She sipped her coffee, telling herself that she should sit tight until Elsie rang back.

After five minutes, during which the phone remained resolutely silent, Diane reluctantly punched out Elsie's number again. An electronic voice informed her that the mobile phone was out of service.

Staff, Diane mused irritably, wondering where she'd left the keys to the four-wheel drive. One couldn't survive without them, but my *God* they could take it out of you.

On the way out she glanced at the kitchen clock. It was 10.30.

THEY LET the first car pass. It was a Fiat Uno covered in unpainted patches of filler, and didn't look as if it had much life left in it. Parking the Astra in a lay-by at the side of the road between Dersthorpe and Marsh Creake had been a calculated risk. If a police car had passed, that would probably have been the end of it.

But no police car came. The Fiat was followed by a Nissan, in equally poor shape, and as it disappeared a mushroom of flame-red smoke leapt into the sky beyond Dersthorpe. The Fiesta's petrol tank, thought Jean, as the smoke joined the thickening grey coil from the house. The fire service would almost certainly be on their way already—someone would have seen the bungalow go up—but they probably had to come from Fakenham. With a bit of luck it would be a good five minutes or so before the police were on the case.

A sporty-looking silver car swung into view and she stepped into the road, arms waving.

The driver was in his late twenties, with an earring and a greasy centre-parting. 'Want to get yourself bloody killed?' he shouted angrily, half opening the door. 'What's your problem?'

Wrenching the Malyah from her jeans, she pointed it at his face. 'Get out,' she ordered. '*Now!* Or I'll shoot you.'

He hesitated, slack-jawed, and dropping her aim for a second she put a 9mm round into the seat between his track-suited legs.

'*Out!*'

He half fell, half climbed out of the car, bug-eyed with shock, leaving the key in the ignition and the engine running.

'Into the passenger seat, now. *Move!*'

He scrambled unsteadily inside.

'Seat belt. Hands on your knees.'

He nodded mutely, and she kept him covered as Faraj exited the Astra, loaded the rucksacks into the boot of the silver car, and took his place in the back seat with the map book and the biscuit tin on his lap. The baseball cap concealed his face.

'OK,' she said, reversing sharply into the lay-by and swinging the nose back towards Marsh Creake. 'Like I said, you just sit there, understand? Try anything and he'll shoot you in the head.'

From his pocket Faraj drew the blunt-nosed PSS, reloaded with SP-4 rounds, and slapped back the magazine, which engaged with a businesslike click. The man, very pale, gave the ghost of a nod. Jean let out the clutch. As she drove off, they passed Diane Munday's Cherokee speeding in the opposite direction.

'Navigate for me,' she said to Faraj in Urdu.

DIANE MUNDAY'S CALL was logged at 10.39. It was taken by PC Wendy Clissold, and Liz saw the police constable's face freeze at the significance of what she was hearing. Clapping her hand over the mouthpiece she turned and shouted across the village hall. '*Guvnor!* House and vehicle alight at Dersthorpe Strand. Unidentified dead female in the vehicle.'

Within a couple of minutes an investigative team had been dispatched to Dersthorpe Strand. Forensic officers were making their way from Norwich and the local fire crew, it turned out, had just left the Burnham Market station. The burning car had been identified as Elsie Hogan's by a near-hysterical Diane Munday, who had been pretty certain that its occupant was Elsie too.

At 10.45 a call came through from one of the investigative team to say that, while en route to the Strand bungalows, they had discovered a black Vauxhall Astra matching the description of the vehicle sought in connection with the Gunter murder. Its engine was still warm.

As Whitten reported the situation to the chief constable in Norwich, Liz called Wetherby at his desk. Wetherby listened to Liz in silence as she summarised the events on Dersthorpe Strand. 'I'm calling a COBRA meeting,' he said quietly when she had finished. 'Can I give them any clue as to a probable target for our terrorists?'

'Guesswork at this stage,' replied Liz, 'but one of the USAF bases would have to be most probable. Bruno Mackay's over at Mildenhall now, liaising with the station chief.'

'OK, I'll go with that. Keep me up to speed and be careful.'

'I will.'

Smiling, she replaced the phone. In anyone else she might have objected to this note of concern, but Wetherby was not anyone else.

She glanced over at Whitten. If a COBRA meeting was being convened, it was almost certainly only a question of time before the case was taken out of his hands. The acronym referred to the Cabinet Office Briefing Room in Whitehall. The meeting would probably be chaired by a representative of the Home Office, with liaison officers from the Ministry of Defence, the police, and the SAS in attendance. Geoffrey Fane would be there too, she guessed, poised crane-like over the discussion. If the situation was considered acute enough, the case would then be nudged up to ministerial level.

Liz had sat up for most of the night in the village hall with Whitten, Goss and Mackay, monitoring the incoming information about Jean D'Aubigny, of which there had been quite a volume, and about Faraj Mansoor, of which there had been almost nothing, beyond the information from Pakistan liaison that someone of that name had attended one of the more radical *madrassahs*.

Around 5 a.m. Liz had returned to the Trafalgar and tried to sleep. But her mind was flying and as she had lain there, a grey and unwilling dawn slowly illuminated the gap between the curtains. In the end she had drifted off, only to be dragged back to consciousness almost immediately by a call from Judith Spratt's deputy to alert her to an incoming message.

Blearily, Liz had switched on her laptop, and scanned and decoded the report. After several hours of questioning during the night, it seemed, the D'Aubigny parents, having begun to realise that their daughter was less a potential victim of terrorism than a wanted suspect, had become more circumspect. Finally, they had refused to cooperate any further, and enlisted the services of Julian Ledward, a well-known radical lawyer.

Urgently need D'Aubigny's connection w E Anglia, if any, Liz typed in return. *Job? Holiday? Boyfriend? Schoolfriend? (Was D'Aubigny @ boarding school or UK university?)*

She had encrypted and sent the reply, and hoped for the best. After a shower and breakfast in the Trafalgar dining room, she had been back in the village hall by 7.30. Mackay, as planned, had driven off to Mildenhall USAF base, armed with a sheaf of print-out portraits of Faraj Mansoor and Jean D'Aubigny.

In the village hall she had discovered Don Whitten, alone. The brimming ashtray at his elbow suggested that he hadn't gone home since she had taken her leave at 5 a.m. They had sat and stared together at a big print-out of Jean D'Aubigny. Taken four years earlier, it was an interior shot, and showed a surly-looking young woman. Short brown hair framed a pale, oval face with intense, wide-set eyes.

'It'd be good to get her alive,' Liz murmured.

'You think we won't?'

She met Jean D'Aubigny's twenty-year-old gaze. 'I don't think she'll come out with her hands up, put it like that. I think she'll want to be a martyr.'

Whitten pursed his lips. The steel-grey of his moustache, Liz noticed, was yellowed with nicotine. He looked exhausted.

Now, three hours later, she watched as, with measured grimness, he stuck an arc of pins into a 1:10,000 Ordnance Survey map. Each pin, and there were twelve of them, marked a roadblock. 'I've requested helicopters and a Tactical Firearms Unit, too,' he told her. 'The TFU are going to be on standby within the hour—but we're getting Deputy Chief Constable Jim Dunstan too. I've been bumped to second-in-command.'

'What's he like?' asked Liz sympathetically.

'Good enough bloke, I suppose,' said Whitten. 'Not over-keen on your lot, though, from what I've heard.'

'OK, thanks for the warning.' She looked again at Jean D'Aubigny's portrait. This was their quarry, the enemy. These people were prepared to murder a harmless creature like Elsie Hogan just because she had found herself in the wrong place at the wrong time.

They had to be stopped. Stopped before they destroyed more lives, and caused more desperate and needless grief.

JEAN HAD BEEN driving for twenty minutes when they saw the roadblock. They were travelling southwards at a careful twenty-five miles an hour along a rutted single-lane track enclosed by high hedges.

Beside her, the young man whose car she was driving had subsided into a silent, sulking torpor. Jean saw the blue light at the same moment that he did, through a gap in the hedge; a gap which revealed momentarily the junction with the Birdhoe road, half a mile ahead.

'Police,' the greasy-haired young man murmured fearfully.

'*Shut up!*' Jean ordered him tersely. Her heart was pounding. Had they been seen? There was a good chance that they hadn't.

'Reverse,' ordered Faraj.

Jean hesitated. To drive back past the gap would give the waiting police a second chance to see them.

'*Reverse*,' repeated Faraj angrily.

She came to a decision. A short way in front of them, to their right, was a narrow track leading to a motley collection of barns and farm outbuildings. No actual dwelling was visible. Ignoring Faraj's protests, she swung the Toyota up the track. As far as the roadblock was concerned, they were invisible. Thirty yards on the ground opened out into a walled yard. A rusted tractor and a silage heap covered by a plastic sheet and old tyres stood in the centre of the yard.

Driving round the far side of the silage heap so that the car was hidden by the road, she came to a stop. She turned to Faraj and he nodded, seeing belatedly that the idea was a good one.

'Out,' Jean said to the youth, into whose fearful eyes a faint spark of hope had crept. 'Get into the boot.'

He nodded, and did so, tucking himself deep and fearful into the carpeted space. The rain lanced down, cold against Jean's face after the warmth of the car. For a moment his eyes met hers, frankly imploring, and then she felt Faraj press the butt of the PSS into her hand and knew that the moment had come. 'To kill an enemy of Islam is to be reborn,' her instructor at Takht-i-Suleiman had told her. 'You will know the moment when it comes.'

Behind her back the PSS was heavy in her hand. She smiled at the young man. His knees were drawn up to his face, covering his chest. 'Could you just shut your eyes a moment?' she asked him.

The discharge was soundless and the recoil negligible. The youth twitched once, and was dead. It was the simplest thing in the world. The boot closed with a faint whisper, and when she turned to Faraj to return the weapon, she knew that nothing now stood between them.

They grabbed a corner each of the plastic sheet and dragged it off the silage heap and over the car. Half a dozen tyres came rolling with it, and they heaved three of these on top of the sheet. It was the sort of scene you drove straight past.

SHE WAS LEADING Faraj now, across the yard and down to the narrow drainage cut. Their rucksacks were on their backs and their waterproofs zipped to the chin. The biscuit tin containing the moulded and wax-sealed C4 explosive was at the top of Faraj's pack.

The water in the cut was agonisingly cold as it crept up past her crotch to her waist, but Jean's heart was still racing with the relief that killing, when all was said and done, had proved to be such a simple thing.

Reborn, remade.

After 100 yards they stopped, and peered through the dead foliage bordering the cut. Faraj passed her the binoculars. A policeman was clambering over blue fertiliser bags on top of a truck at the roadblock.

'We will be seen if we go across country,' murmured Faraj, scanning the open fields before them.

'They're local police, not soldiers,' said Jean, glancing at her watch. 'My guess'd be that we've got another twenty minutes to half an hour. After that it'll be helicopters, dogs, the army, everything.'

'*Go*, then.'

They pressed forward through the waist-deep water, the mud sucking at their feet and rain slashing at their faces. The lower half of Jean's body was completely numb now, and at intervals the scene in the boot of the car replayed itself in her mind. That quarter-second glance had been enough. The image was imprinted on her memory.

NINE

The repair hangar at the Swanley Heath Army Air Corps base was impressively vast, and considering its size, impressively warm. At 11 a.m. the Deputy Chief Constable of Norfolk, Jim Dunstan, took over what was now officially an antiterrorist operation. Dunstan's first act had been to request that the Swanley Heath base, halfway between Brancaster to the north and the Marwell, Mildenhall and

Lakenheath USAF bases to the south, act as host to the inter-service operational team. The operations team was now, hopefully, at the centre of the area through which their quarry was moving.

By midday, the fifteen-strong police team, headed by Dunstan, occupied an area dominated by a ten-yard-square electronic map of the region, showing the deployment of roadblocks, helicopters and search teams. In front of each member of the team was an assortment of laptop computers, land lines and mobiles, most of them in use. In the case of Don Whitten there was also an ashtray.

Beyond them, parked in a ready-to-go line, were the three unmarked Range Rovers of the Norfolk Constabulary's SO19 Tactical Firearms Unit. Its nine members, all men, lounged on benches in their dark blue overalls and boots, passing round a copy of the *Sun*, rechecking their Glock 17 pistols and MP5 carbines. From outside came the distant beat of rotors as Army Air Corps Gazelle and Lynx helicopters lifted away from the tarmac.

The official estimate, by default, was that the target of the two terrorists was either one of the USAF bases or the royal residence at Sandringham, where the Queen was now staying—as she did every Christmas. The worst had been assumed concerning the weaponry that the two were carrying. Neither chemical nor biological weapons, nor a so-called 'dirty bomb' had been ruled out.

Whitten was confident that D'Aubigny and Mansoor were still confined to the seventy-mile square whose northern boundary was Brancaster Bay and whose western boundary was the Wash. But Liz was not so sure. Apart from their predilection for murder, the two hadn't done too badly so far when it came to concealing themselves and moving across hostile terrain. The D'Aubigny woman clearly knew the lie of the land.

What was her connection with the area? Liz asked herself for the hundredth time. Why had Jean been chosen? Investigations were checking every one of her known contacts, but the parents' silence was desperately unhelpful. Couldn't they see that the one chance of saving their daughter was to catch her before it came to the final reckoning?

From the other side of the room she saw Don Whitten pointing in her direction. A neatly dressed young man in a green Barbour coat was walking towards the trestle table on which she had her own laptop set up. 'Excuse me,' he said, holding out his hand. 'I'm Jamie Kersley, Captain, 22 SAS. I'm looking for Bruno Mackay.'

She shook the proffered hand. 'He's due any time. Why don't you take a seat and I'll steer him in your direction when he shows up.'

'Er . . . thanks. I've got two four-man teams unloading a Puma outside. Let me get them squared away and I'll be back.'

She watched him march away, then turned to her laptop. *SAS here mob-handed*, she typed out. *But ITS target still unknown. Unusual, surely. Something I shd know???*

Encoding the message with a couple of swift keystrokes, she dispatched it to Wetherby. The reply came back less than a minute later.

Agree unusual. Regiment present at request of G Fane. Essential ready deploy at short notice he told COBRA. Yr guess good as mine.

As she watched, the eight SAS soldiers passed the entrance to the hangar carrying a wide assortment of weapons including carbines and snipers' rifles. Altogether, a hellish volume of firepower was being brought to bear. Against what exactly? Liz wondered.

BY 12.30 the car park of the Plough public house in Birdhoe was almost full; Sunday lunch was a popular fixture, and there wasn't another pub for three or four miles.

Exiting the ladies' toilet in the corner of the car park, where she had been waiting until the coast was clear, Jean D'Aubigny looked about her. Luckily, it was still raining. No one was hanging around in the car park to chat. The car she had identified as the easiest to steal, if not necessarily the most suitable, was an old racing green MGB. Its great advantage was that due to its age it had no steering lock that had to be disabled, a hard operation to perform unobtrusively.

She walked purposefully to the MGB, deftly slashed the wet vinyl top with her clasp knife, dipped in her hand, slipped the lock, and climbed into the driver's seat. Glancing around her to make sure that she was not being observed, she wrenched the four wires out of the bottom of the ignition barrel and stripped them back with the knife. Taking the red wire—the main ignition lead—she quickly touched it to the others in turn. With the third, a green wire, there was a brief lurch as the starter turned over. Isolating the green wire, she quickly connected the other two to the red one. The dashboard was now live.

OK, she told herself. Here we go—*Inshallah!*

Touching the green starter wire to the other three she depressed the accelerator an inch or two. The MGB howled, terrifyingly loud, but no furious owner appeared out of the pub. Jean put the MGB into reverse, let off the handbrake and backed out of the parking space. Even the gentlest manoeuvre seemed to engender an outraged snarl from the old car, and Jean's heart was thumping painfully in her chest as she shifted to first gear and nosed towards the car park exit.

On the open road she felt no less self-conscious. This, surely, was a vehicle that local people would know and recognise. But the area seemed deserted. A mile beyond the village she came to the spot they had located on the map, where the cut they had walked along disappeared into a culvert under the road. She pulled up just beyond it, leaving the engine running. Within moments, Faraj was climbing into the passenger seat and arranging the rucksacks beneath his knees.

'*Shabash!*' he murmured. 'Congratulations!'

'It's not perfect,' she admitted, 'but it was the easiest to steal.'

She pulled back onto the road. The petrol gauge read a quarter full, and her brief elation faded as she realised that they weren't going to be able to refill the tank, which almost certainly only ran on leaded fuel. Right now, though, she couldn't face explaining this. Her senses felt simultaneously taut-wired and dulled to a kind of slow motion. She was running on empty herself.

'Let's get out of here,' she said.

'BUT WHY *this* man?' asked Liz. 'Why send this particular man? He's never been here, he's got no family here . . . As far as we know he's got no connection to Britain whatsoever.'

'I can't answer that question,' said Mackay. 'I genuinely have no idea. He certainly never came to our attention in Pakistan. If he was a player out there, it was at too low a level to show up on our radar.'

'But the Pakistanis had him on file.'

'So it turns out. But I'd guess that that's more coincidence than inside knowledge.'

They were driving in Mackay's BMW to the Marwell USAF base. The MI6 man had returned from Mildenhall to Swanley Heath shortly after midday, and after swapping phone numbers with Jamie Kersley, the SAS captain, and sitting down for a sandwich lunch with Liz and the police team, had prepared to leave for the last, and nearest, of the three USAF bases. Mackay had asked Liz if she felt like coming too, and with no other positive leads it had seemed a constructive course of action. Thanks in part to the atrocious weather, the search for D'Aubigny and Mansoor had stalled, despite the arrival of teams from the regular and Territorial Army.

'They'll make a mistake,' said Mackay confidently. 'They always do. Someone up there will spot them.'

'You think they're still contained in the search area?'

'I think they've got to be. I'd back Mansoor to make it through alone, but not the two of them.'

'Don't underestimate D'Aubigny,' said Liz, obscurely irritated. 'This is not some thrill-seeking teenage bimbo, but a graduate of the Northwest Frontier camps. If either of the two has made mistakes so far, it's Mansoor. He got himself jumped by Ray Gunter and ended up leaving us vital ballistic evidence.'

'Do I detect a note of empathy there? Admiration, even?'

'No, not an ounce. I think that she's a killer too, almost certainly. But I'm beginning to get a sense of who she is and how she operates. What I want is for her to start feeling twenty-four-hour pressure—the sense that she can't afford to rest, can't afford to stop, can't even afford to think. I want it on top of the pressure that's already there, the sense of being torn between two utterly opposing worlds.'

'She doesn't seem very torn to me.'

'Outside, maybe not. Inside, believe me, she's being pulled apart, and that's what makes her so dangerous. The need to prove to herself, through violent action, that she's committed to this militant path.'

He permitted himself an oblique smile. 'So, would you rather the rest of us withdrew, and left you to get on with it?'

'Funny guy. In any campaign, the first stronghold that you have to occupy is your enemy's consciousness.'

'That sounds like a quote.'

'It is a quote. Feliks Dzerzhinsky.'

'Founder of the KGB. A suitable mentor.'

'I like to think so.'

Mackay put his foot down to pass a green MGB. They had just driven through the village of Narborough. 'I had a car a bit like that once,' he said. 'An old '74 MG Midget. God, but that was a beautiful car. Teal blue, tan interior, chrome bumpers . . .'

'And a real babe magnet, I'm sure,' said Liz.

'Well, it didn't put them off, that's for sure.' He looked pensive for a moment. 'The guy we're going to see, to put you in the picture, is a man named Delves. He's a Brit, because Marwell is nominally an RAF station. The American commander is a USAF colonel called Greeley.'

'So is this more than just a courtesy call?'

'Not just. We have to look at the station and the security set-up through terrorist eyes. Put ourselves in their place. Decide what the weak spots are. Decide what we'd go for.'

'Did you come to any conclusions from the other two stations?'

'Only that the security was damn near impassable. Those bases, from what I've seen, are sewn up tighter than a rat's proverbial.'

'All security can be beaten,' said Liz.

'Agreed. And the people we're after wouldn't be in play if there wasn't a weak spot somewhere. All I'm saying is that I haven't found it yet.'

FIFTEEN MINUTES later, at a road bridge over the river Wissey, they were being flagged down by three uniformed policemen, one of them carrying a Heckler & Koch carbine, another holding a dog. A Range Rover containing other uniformed men was parked at an angle at the roadside. The base was over a mile away, and not yet even visible.

Liz and Mackay showed their passes, and stood outside the BMW while a radio clearance was made. The officer with the dog, meanwhile, carefully searched the car.

'I see what you mean about the security,' said Liz.

Two minutes later Marwell's outer perimeter came into view. Mackay halted the car at the steel gates. 'Smile!' he said as a CCTV camera mounted above the razor-wire fence nosed towards them.

Soon they were sitting in a large, well-heated office. The furniture was worn but comfortable. A portrait of the Queen shared the walls with squadron insignia and photographs of men and aircraft taken in Diego Garcia, Saudi Arabia and Afghanistan.

Wing-Commander Colin Delves, a pink-faced man in RAF blue battledress trousers and pullover, was the British station commander, while Colonel Clyde Greeley, solid and tanned in civilian golfing clothes, was his USAF opposite number.

'We're damned pleased to see you guys,' Greeley was saying, as he sipped at his coffee. 'And we appreciate the lengths you've gone to, but it's hard to know what more we can do.'

'I'd defy the pair of them to get within a mile of our perimeter,' said Delves. 'Really, not a blade of grass moves without our registering it.'

'Do you think you're a terrorist target, Colonel?' asked Mackay.

'Hell, yes!' said Greeley. 'I have no doubts in my mind that we are *the* terrorist target.'

Greeley spread his arms expansively. 'The facts are on the record. Of the three East Anglian bases we're the only one to have deployed in the Central Asian theatre.'

'Where exactly?' asked Liz.

'Well now, until a couple of months ago we had a squadron of A-10 Thunderbolts stationed at Uzgen in Kyrgyzstan, three AC-130 gunships at Bagram, and rather less publicly, a couple more AC-130s supporting Special Operations out of Fergana, Uzbekistan. Police work, you might say.'

'Did you deploy in Pakistan?' asked Liz.

'We deployed on the Afghan border,' said Greeley.

'So did you make any new enemies out there?' asked Liz mildly. 'If that's not a naive question?'

'It's certainly not a naive question,' said Greeley. 'But I can honestly say that with the possible exception of certain diehard bad boys whom we tickled out of their caves with our Sidewinder missiles, we made only new friends.'

'So why would this particular man have crossed the world from Pakistan to attack this particular airfield?' she persisted.

'I guess we're a symbolic target,' said Greeley. 'We're American military and we're on British soil, symbolising the alliance that overthrew the Taliban.'

'But nothing . . . *specific*?' asked Liz.

'With respect, who the hell knows? There were people who were mightily pissed at our presence there and there were people—rather more people—who were mightily glad to have us.' He gestured at the portraits of D'Aubigny and Mansoor. 'Concerning this trigger-happy duo and their grievance, I have to say that I have every confidence in our base security measures.'

'Can you tell us about the USAF personnel who live off-base?' asked Mackay. 'Surely they're vulnerable to attack? Everyone must know where they live.'

Delves fielded this question. 'If you were an outsider round here,' he said, smiling pinkly, 'you'd find it pretty damn hard to get information like that. We have a very close relationship with the local community, and anyone asking questions of that sort would very quickly find themselves face to face with a military policeman.'

'But your people have to let their hair down from time to time, surely?' persisted Mackay.

'Sure they do,' said Greeley, his rangy smile belying the grimness of his tone. 'But things have changed since Nine Eleven. The days of our young men and women belonging to the local darts teams, stuff like that, that's way in the past.'

'Do they get specific training in security and countersurveillance?'

asked Liz. 'I mean, supposing I decided to follow a couple of them back from the pub to wherever they lived . . .'

'You'd last about five minutes, I'd guess, before encountering a hostile response involving security vehicles and quite possibly helicopters. If our people want to have a few beers, they go somewhere that's at least seven or eight miles away, so that they've got plenty of time to spot any vehicle that might be following them home.'

'And what about yourself, Colonel?' asked Liz.

'I live on base.'

'Wing Commander?'

Colin Delves frowned. 'I live with my family more than a dozen miles away, in one of the villages. I never leave this establishment in uniform, and I doubt there are half a dozen people in the village who have the first idea what I do. The house I live in is a Grade II listed property, owned by the MOD. It's the last place you'd expect to find a serving RAF officer.'

'And is it under police surveillance?'

'Broadly speaking, yes. But not in such a way that would draw attention to the place.'

He fell silent and Greeley took over again, his broad smile fading. 'We can protect our people and we can protect our aircraft. I took three hundred and seventy-six people and twenty-four aircraft out to the Central Asian theatre, we worked our tour, and I brought them all back. Every person, every aircraft. I'm proud of that record and I'm not going to see it tarnished by a pair of psychos who like shooting up old women. Trust us, OK?' He indicated Delves, who nodded confidently. 'We're on top of this thing.'

TWENTY MINUTES LATER Liz and Mackay were driving back towards Swanley Heath in the BMW. They were sitting in silence. Mackay had started to play a CD, but Liz had asked him to turn it off again. Something was worrying at her subconscious.

'What did Greeley mean when he was talking about Mansoor and D'Aubigny's "grievance"?' she said eventually.

'How do you mean?'

'He said something about "this trigger-happy duo and their grievance". Why did he say that? What grievance?'

'I'm assuming he meant the same grievance that's led the ITS to bomb and shoot innocent civilians all over the world.'

'No, I don't buy that. You wouldn't use that word about members of a professional terror cell. They didn't kill Ray Gunter and Elsie Hogan out of a sense of grievance. Why did he use that word, Bruno?'

'Grievance *schmievance*, how do I know? I never met the guy before in my life.'

'I didn't say you had.'

'Look Liz, I'm genuinely in awe of the way you've moved this thing forward, *but you have to cool it*. You can't carry the entire case on your shoulders or it will break you, OK? I'm sure you think me the worst kind of cowboy operator, but please—*I am not the enemy here*.'

She blinked. The sky was steel-grey over the long, level horizon. 'I'm sorry,' she said. 'You're right. I'm letting it all get to me.'

But he might well have met Greeley, she thought. *We deployed on the Afghan border* . . . Why did she feel as if she was in free fall? Exhaustion? Lack of sleep? *What didn't she know?*

They proceeded in silence towards Swanley Heath, and were only five minutes away when a squawk from her mobile alerted Liz to a text message. It read *Call Jude*. They pulled up at a roadside telephone box, Mackay tipped his seat into the recline position and Liz climbed out onto the wet verge and rang Investigations.

'OK,' began Judith Spratt, 'here's where we are. We've got from the parents that from the age of thirteen Jean D'Aubigny attended a boarding school near Tregaron in Wales named Garth House. Small co-ed establishment, progressive in character, run by a former Jesuit priest named Anthony Price-Lascelles. School has a reputation for accommodating troubled children. We've had people visit the school but it's locked up for the Christmas holidays and Price-Lascelles is in Morocco, at a place called Azemmour, where he has a flat. Six sent a man round to the flat this morning but learned from the houseboy that Price-Lascelles has gone into Casablanca for the day. They've got a bloke sitting outside the flat waiting for him.'

'Isn't there anyone else we can ask about the school? No former teachers you can talk to?'

'We haven't been able to track down any that remember anything significant about her. The impression we're getting is that the establishment is very small and there were fairly severe money problems. Staff came and went pretty fast.'

'Can't the police just unlock the place and go through the records? The Prevention of Terrorism Act makes that possible, surely?'

'It does, and that's in hand right now. As soon as we've got anything I'll let you know.'

'Anything from the Paris end?'

'Again, nothing significant. One fellow student named Hamidullah Souad knew her quite well. They went to the cinema once or twice, but they stopped seeing each other when she told him that she disapproved of his lifestyle.'

'So we've still got no connection with East Anglia?'

'None at all. Does she need to have one?'

'No, she could just be Mansoor's cover, in which case all she has to be is English. But if she's ever been here before it might just point us to where she's gone to ground, or even what the target is. So don't let up, Jude, please.'

'We won't.'

Liz hung up, deeply frustrated. What they needed was a bloody great slice of luck. Right now, it was the best they could hope for.

'OUT!' SAID FARAJ urgently. 'Put the bags under the tree and then help me with the car.'

Jean arranged the rucksacks at the base of the willow. It had begun to rain again, the light was fading and the place was deserted.

Jean D'Aubigny knew this place, where the Lesser Ouse and the Methwold Fen relief drain intersected. She knew that the water was deep here and that visitors were few. Remembered in a rush of memory almost painful in its intensity what it was like to be sixteen years old, to smell the green, muddy aroma of the river and feel the dizzying rush of vodka and cigarettes on an empty stomach.

It had taken them some time to find the place but they were now a clear twenty-five miles south of the village from where they had stolen the MGB, and since the roadblock they had not encountered any police, apart from the glimpse of a military helicopter far to the north. Given that they had to assume that the theft of the MGB had been swiftly reported, they were grateful.

Faraj wound down the MGB's windows and pulled back the vinyl top. The car stood beside the old bridge across the river. In front of it a flight of cracked concrete steps led down to a narrow towpath. From the far side of the river the narrower drainage channel led off northwards. The river was deep here, but slow, and a scum of foliage, cigarette ends and fast-food containers circled at the foot of the steps.

Turning, she looked around her. Nothing. Then Faraj caught her wrist hard and she froze, backing away from the bridge. There was movement in the relief drain. Something was silently displacing the bullrushes and reeds. An animal? she wondered. A police dog? Nothing was visible, just that slow, terrifying bending of the reeds.

They were well back from the bank now, crouching behind the car with their weapons in their hands.

The reeds in the relief drain parted, and the pointed nose of a kayak moved silently into view. Sitting inside it was an unmoving figure in hooded olive waterproofs. Jean's first, paralysing assumption was that this was a Special Forces soldier, and when the figure slowly raised a pair of binoculars to its face this seemed to be confirmed.

But the figure was scanning the bankside vegetation and completely ignoring the MGB standing by the bridge. Suddenly a small, nondescript bird flew from under the bridge and alighted on the broken stem of a bullrush. Smoothly and unhurriedly the binoculars swivelled to focus on the bird, and now an appreciative smile was visible on the face of the hooded figure in the kayak.

Her heart thumping with the sick, dragging ebb of tension, Jean thumbed on the Malyah's safety and glanced sideways to see if Faraj had registered that the young man was not a threat. The bird must have caught her slight movement, because it swung quickly away from its perch and darted back beneath the bridge. The young man looked after it for a moment, then reversed his kayak and disappeared the way he had come.

'We've got to get rid of the car,' Jean said when they were sure he would not return. 'Those were military helicopters we saw earlier and it'll show up through the trees on their thermal imaging cameras.'

Faraj nodded. 'Let's do it.'

Leaning into the car, he checked that it was in neutral and released the handbrake. They pushed from the rear. The old MGB was heavier than it looked and took several seconds to budge in the rain-slick mud. Then it nosed as if unwillingly to the top of the steps, lurched over the first of them, and with a loud grating noise stuck fast. 'Axle's caught,' muttered Faraj. 'Bastard thing. We have to keep pushing.'

They pushed, their shoulders to the MGB's chrome back-bumper, the cleated soles of their boots digging deep. At first nothing happened, then the cement facing of the brickwork steps cracked, the rear of the MGB swung upwards, flipping Jean off balance so that Faraj had to grab her to prevent her skidding into the river, and the car commenced a slow-motion descent of the steps. At the bottom, with something close to stateliness, it somersaulted onto its roof with a crashing displacement of water and began to sink into the deep water below the bridge. Gasping for breath, Jean and Faraj watched from the bottom of the steps as the chrome of the bumpers faded, became invisible.

They climbed the steps again and Faraj checked the biscuit tin containing the C4 charge.

'OK?'

Faraj shrugged. 'It's still there. And we're still here.'

Jean took stock. She was cold, filthy, hungry and soaked to the skin. On top of this, the day's terrors—the repeated jolt and ebb of adrenaline—had shocked her into an almost hallucinatory exhaustion. She sensed, as she had for some days now, an implacable pursuing figure. A figure that dragged at her like a shadow, whispering hell and confusion in her ear. Perhaps, she thought, it was her former self, trying to reclaim her soul. Faraj, by contrast, appeared untouched. He gave the impression that his physical state had at some point been unharnessed from his will. There was neither pain nor fear nor tiredness, just the mission and the strategy required for its execution.

Jean watched him, and insofar as she was capable of a response at that moment, the austerity of his self-control impressed her. It also profoundly frightened her. There had been a time when she had been certain that faith and determination had empowered her in the same way. Now, she was sure of nothing. She had been reborn, certainly, but into a place of utter pitilessness. Faraj, she realised, had occupied that place for a long time.

Distantly, perhaps five miles away, the pulse of a helicopter. For a moment neither of them moved.

'*Quick!*' said Jean. 'Under the bridge.'

They scrambled down the steps to the narrow towpath, and hurled themselves at the sodden canopy of brambles. Thorns tore at Jean's face and hands and then they were through, crouching in darkness beneath the arch.

After about a minute the sound of the helicopter returned, louder this time, perhaps three or four miles away, and even though she knew herself invisible she shrank against the bridge. Close to tears of exhaustion, shaking with cold, she said tonelessly, 'I think we should get the bags down and lie up here for the night. The helicopters' infrared cameras can't read a heat signature through brick.'

He glanced at her suspiciously, detecting the defeat in her voice.

'If we're caught in the open,' she pleaded, 'we're dead, Faraj.'

He was silent, considering. Eventually he nodded.

Liz was about to go online and decode an incoming email when, from the corner of her eye, she saw Don Whitten fold forward and bury his head in his hands. He held the position for perhaps a second before, his face contorted and his fists clenched, silently swearing.

There were now eighteen men and three women in the hangar. Six of the men were army officers, and all of these except Kersley, the SAS captain, were in combat dress. As one, they all fell silent and stared at Whitten.

'Tell us,' said Dunstan, levelly.

'Young man named James Martindale has just reported a twenty-five-year-old racing green MGB stolen from outside the Plough pub in Birdhoe. Could have happened any time after twelve fifteen this lunchtime when he arrived at the pub. He's been watching the rugby on TV all afternoon.'

There was a collective exhalation—a sound of extreme frustration. It was too much to hope for that the theft of the car was unrelated to D'Aubigny and Mansoor. Whitten reached glumly for his cigarettes.

'Birdhoe is half a mile the wrong side of the roadblock. They must have outrun us across country while we were setting things up. And now they've got four hours' bloody start on us.'

The army officers looked at each other, tight-lipped. Two battalions of regular and TA soldiers and half a dozen Lynx and Gazelle helicopters were still in deployment in the northwestern sector.

'Wait,' said Mackay, craning his head to where Liz was sitting. 'A racing green MGB? We *passed* one! I told you I used to—'

'Teal blue? The babe-magnet?'

'Yeah, that's the one—where were we? Let's look at that screen. We'd driven southwest from here, been going what, fifteen minutes? Must have been somewhere near Castle Acre or Narborough. So if our appointment at Marwell was for two p.m., and that was the right car we saw, then it puts our two terrorists near Narborough at approximately one forty-five. Two and a quarter hours ago. You're right,' he addressed Whitten, 'they could be anywhere.'

'But why steal such a recognisable car?' asked Liz.

The police looked at each other. 'Because they're easy to hot-wire, love,' said Whitten. 'Most cars less than twenty years old have an automatic steering lock.'

'OK. Point taken. Surely, though, that makes it a bit of a last resort? A desperate dash to get the hell away from the roadblock. They wouldn't have risked driving into a city in an immediately recognisable car that, for all they knew, had been reported stolen.'

Dunstan nodded. 'I agree. They'd allow themselves an hour's drive at most, sticking to minor roads, then they'd ditch the vehicle.'

'An hour's drive on minor roads takes them to RAF Marwell,' said Mackay quietly.

'OK, let's suppose that Marwell is their target,' said Dunstan, looking around him. 'It's a fair guess that (a) they're not going to drive too close to a secure government establishment in a stolen car, and (b) they ditched the car within an hour of passing through Narborough. That puts them right now either to the east of a five-mile circle surrounding Marwell, or to the west of it. Lying up out of sight, I should think—they've had a pretty stressful day. Either that or preparing to walk up to the target.'

Whitten crushed out his cigarette. 'So what do you suggest?'

'That we draw two rings around Marwell. Establish an inner circle, radius five miles, which we saturate with police, army and TA personnel right now. Give them night-vision goggles, searchlights, whatever they need . . . Basically, no one gets past.'

A balding man in the crown and star insignia of a lieutenant colonel made a swift calculation with a pencil. 'That's about eighty square miles in total. If we pull in all the search parties from the northwest sector, bring up another battalion . . .'

'And outside that,' Dunstan continued, 'a further ring, five miles wide—that's a two hundred square mile area—which we overfly all night using thermal-imaging . . .' He looked around for approval. 'Anyone got a better idea?'

There was silence.

'Good enough,' said the lieutenant colonel.

'DS Goss,' Dunstan continued, 'I'd like you to get yourself over to Marwell and act as our liaison with Colonel Greeley. I'm going to call him right now and put him in the picture.'

Goss nodded and left the hangar at a run, raising a farewell hand to Liz as he passed her. In some way that she couldn't quite define, events seemed to be spinning out of control. There were too many people involved and too many services represented.

With a start, she realised that she had not yet read her message, and without further ado flipped up the screen of her laptop and logged on. The message, when she had decoded it, was a long one, marked for the urgent attention of herself, Mackay and Dunstan only. She opened the attachment.

TOP SECRET—BEARER EYES ONLY
RE: MANSOOR, FARAJ

At midnight on Dec 17 2002, following reports of ITS activity on Pak–Afghan border near Chaman, an AC-130 transporter gunship departed a USAF base in Uzbekistan (believed to be Fergana), on a search and destroy mission. On board was the AC-130's crew plus 12 Special Operations personnel . . .

As she read the activity around her seemed to fall away, and the ambient buzz of the hangar to fade to silence.

'HOW MUCH do you think they know?' asked Faraj, when they had changed out of their wet clothes into the dry ones that Jean had stuffed into the rucksacks that morning.

'I think we have to assume that they know who we are,' said Jean after a moment's thought. 'The weak links in the chain are the driver of the truck, who saw you, and the woman who rented me the house, who would recognise me. They know who we are, take it from me. These are the British we're dealing with, and they are a vengeful people. And the officers who are directing this operation against us will be the best that they have.'

'We shall see. Let them send their best man. They won't stop us.'

Jean frowned. 'They've sent their best man. Their best man is a woman.'

Faraj shifted on the narrow flagstoned towpath beneath the bridge. 'What do you mean, a woman?'

'They've sent a woman. I can feel her shadow.'

'You're crazy! What kind of stupid talk is that?'

She shrugged. 'It doesn't matter,' she said.

She heard his faint, irritated outbreath. They were lying head to head, wrapped in the blankets that Diane Munday had provided for her tenants. Now that she was dry, the cold didn't seem quite so agonising. She had known worse in camp.

'We killed two people today,' she said, the boy's head cracking open once again before her half-closed eyes.

'It was necessary. It was not a matter for consideration.'

'I'm not the person that I was when I woke up this morning.'

'You are a stronger person.'

Was this strength? she wondered. This waking sleep. This frozen distance from events? Perhaps it was.

'Paradise waits for us,' said Faraj. 'But not yet.'

Did he believe that? she wondered. Something in his voice—an oblique, faintly ironic note—made her unsure.

'Who waits for you in this world?' she asked. He had spoken of parents and a sister. Was there a wife?

'No one waits.'

'So you never married?'

He was silent. Through the darkness, she sensed a sinewy resistance to her questions.

'Tomorrow we may be dead,' she said. 'Tonight, surely, we can talk?'

'I never married,' he said, but she knew from his tone that there had been someone.

'She died,' he added eventually.

'I'm sorry.'

'She was twenty years old. Her name was Farzana, and she was a seamstress. My parents had wanted someone well educated for me, and a Tajik, and she was neither of these things, but they . . . they liked her very much.' He fell silent.

'Tell me about her,' she prompted, sensing that at some level, and despite his protestations, he wanted to talk.

He shifted in his blanket, and for almost a minute said nothing.

'I was at Mardan,' he began. 'At the *madrassah*. I was older than most of the other students—I was already twenty-three when I went there—and in religious terms I was very much less extreme. I had been there for almost two years when a letter came from Daranj in Afghanistan saying that my sister Laila was about to become betrothed and there was to be a celebration to mark the occasion.

'I travelled back to Daranj in the back of a truck headed for Kandahar. I arrived on the day of the betrothal, I met Khalid, who my sister was to marry, and that night the celebrations began. There was the usual feasting and the usual high spirits. You have to remember that there was precious little opportunity for joy in these people's lives, and so the chance to dance and sing and let off *fatakars*—home-made fireworks—was not to be missed.

'I was the first to see the American plane. These were not such an uncommon sight in the area—there were regular operations around Kandahar and on the border—but what was unusual was that the plane was so low. It was a huge thing—an AC-130 transporter gunship, I discovered later. The betrothal ceremony had taken place at a small encampment outside the town, and I had wandered away from the celebrations to a nearby hill to gather my thoughts. I was happier than I had ever been in my life. I had proposed marriage to Farzana, she had accepted me. Below me the celebrations surrounding Laila and Khalid, her betrothed, were in full swing, with fireworks exploding, music playing and rifles being fired in the air.

'When the searchlights came on I thought, stupidly, that they were sending some sort of signal. Responding to the fireworks and the musical instruments with a friendly display of their own. The war against the Taliban, after all, was over. So I stood there, staring, as the gunship opened fire on the encampment.

'Within seconds, of course, I understood what was happening. I ran towards the encampment waving my arms, yelling at the plane—as if anyone up there could hear me—that the people were just letting off fireworks. And all the while the plane was moving in these slow, methodical circles, drilling every inch of the place with cannon-fire. The dead and dying were everywhere, with the wounded writhing on the ground screaming. I ran through the firing as if it was rain, untouched, but I couldn't find anyone I knew. And I couldn't find Farzana. I screamed her name until I had no voice left, and then I felt myself lifted off my feet and thrown down on the rock. I had been hit.

'The next thing I knew was that Khalid, my future brother-in-law, was dragging me to my feet and yelling at me to run. Somehow he got me out of the killing zone and back up the hill I had been standing on earlier. I had been hit in the side with shrapnel but I managed to drag myself beneath a fold of the rock. After that, I passed out.

'When I came to, I was in hospital in Kandahar. Khalid had loaded eight of us into a truck and driven us there during the night. My sister Laila was alive, but had lost an arm, and my mother had suffered severe burns. She died a week later. My father, Farzana and a dozen others had been killed in the attack.

'That night the television carried a CNN report of a "firefight" near Daranj. Elements loyal to Al Qaeda, the reporter said, had attempted to bring down a US transport aircraft with a surface-to-air missile. The attempt had failed, and the terrorists had been engaged and several of their number killed. Twenty-four hours later Al Jazeera ran a counter-story. A US aircraft, they said, appeared to have launched an unprovoked attack on a betrothal party in an Afghan village, in the course of which fourteen Afghan civilians had been killed and eight critically wounded. Of the dead, six were women and three were children. None of those involved had any connection to any terrorist organisation.

'After refusing to comment on the incident for almost a week, a USAF spokesman conceded that it had taken place more or less as reported by Al Jazeera, and described the loss of life as "tragic". In mitigation, he said, the aircrew maintained that they had come under sustained small-arms fire and the pilot stated that a surface-to-air missile had been fired at them. Pictures were published of the unit's commander, Colonel Greeley, pointing to what he claimed was bullet damage to the fuselage of an AC-130 transporter gunship. The subsequent military inquiry totally exonerated the gunship's crew.'

'That was two years ago?'

'That was almost exactly two years ago. As soon as my wounds were healed I returned to Mardan, but inside myself I was a dead man. All that remained was the necessity of vengeance. The matter of *izzat*—honour. At the *madrassah* they were sympathetic. They sent me to one of the Northwest Frontier camps for a few months, and then sent me back across the border into Afghanistan. I took up work at a truck stop which operated as a cover for one of the *jihadi* organisations, and there, a few months later, I was introduced to a man named al Safa.'

'Dawood al Safa?'

The same. Al Safa had been considering revenge against those responsible for the Daranj massacre for some time. Not a general action, but a specific, targeted reprisal. He had just met a young Englishwoman, he told me, who had dared to take the name of Asimat—bride of Salah-ud-din. This woman had specialised knowledge that would enable us to take revenge of exquisite appropriateness.'

'I didn't know any of this,' she said. 'Why wasn't I told?'

'For your own safety, and that of our mission.'

'Do I know everything now?'

'Not yet. When the time comes, you will know everything.'

'It's tomorrow, isn't it?'

'Trust me, Asimat.'

She stared out into the darkness. At that moment, the rain-dripping chamber beneath the bridge was the whole world. If this was to be her last night on earth, then so be it. She reached out her hand, and found the roughness of his cheek. 'I am not Farzana,' she said quietly, 'but I am yours.'

Silence, and from beyond the stillness surrounding them, the long sigh of the fenland wind.

'Come here, then,' he said.

TEN

'Well, at least we now know what the target is,' said Jim Dunstan.

'It's certain that the AC-130 involved in the Daranj incident was one of the ones based at Marwell, then?' asked Whitten.

'No doubt at all, according to the report,' said Liz.

'What's the provenance of the report?' asked Mackay, a little testily.

'Everything in it except the involvement of Faraj Mansoor is public domain,' said Liz evasively. She turned to Mackay. 'I'm surprised the reports didn't cross your desk.'

'They did,' said Mackay. 'And as far as I remember the Islamabad Stars and Stripes burners made quite a meal of the incident. I was just curious as to the Mansoor link. That's not mentioned in any file we've ever received from Pakistan liaison.'

'I'm assured that the source is reliable,' said Liz, watching Mackay's discomfiture with some pleasure.

'And tomorrow's the anniversary,' said Jim Dunstan. 'Do we think they'll try to stick to that?'

'Symbolism and anniversaries are hugely important to the ITS,' said Mackay. 'September the eleventh was the anniversary of the British mandate in Palestine. October the twelfth, when the Bali nightclub bombing took place, was the anniversary of the opening of the Camp David peace talks between Egypt and Israel. I think we can count on them moving heaven and earth to stick to it.'

'Do we discount all possibility of a dirty bomb?' asked Jim Dunstan.

'We've not found any radioactive material near the Dersthorpe bungalow or in the Vauxhall Astra they were using,' said Whitten.

'I'd put money on them using C4,' said Mackay. 'It's the ITS's signature explosive and you can buy most of the ingredients in the high street. The question is: How are they planning to deliver it?'

'Jean D'Aubigny,' said Liz. 'She's the key.'

'Go on,' said Jim Dunstan.

'Mansoor's controllers wouldn't waste an asset like her on a pointless assault on a high-security installation. She must have privileged information of some kind.'

'Have your people got through the door of that Welsh school yet?' asked Mackay pointedly.

'Yes, they have. They're emailing me a list of D'Aubigny's contemporaries as soon as they can.'

'Quite frankly,' said Jim Dunstan, 'I can't see how the hell an investigation of this young woman's school career is going to move things forward. We know who we're after and we know what they look like. We have a target, we have a motive, and we have a date. We have a counter-strategy and we have people in place to implement it. All we have to do now is wait, so why don't you get some sleep, young lady?'

Not over-keen on your lot, Whitten had said about Jim Dunstan, and to begin with she had thought him mistaken in that respect. But the DS had been right. The old resentment lingered. Senior policemen, with their public face and their accountability, had long distrusted the state's secret servants.

Liz looked around her. The faces were friendly enough but the message from each of them was the same. This was the endgame, the point at which theory was translated into action. The cerebral stuff—the intelligence-gathering and analysis—was over.

And she sensed something else. A muted but definite anticipation. The army people, in particular, were like sharks smelling blood. They wanted Mansoor and D'Aubigny to try to hit Marwell, she realised. They wanted the pair to dash themselves against its impenetrable wall of armed manpower. They wanted them dead.

DENZIL PARRISH arrived back in West Ford well after sunset, knowing that an unpromising evening lay ahead. His mother had warned him well in advance that her new in-laws were not the easiest-going people she'd ever met, but the fact that his stepfather's parents were digging in for a whole week had only been sprung on him once he had arrived home from Tyneside, and the subterfuge rankled. Deep down, however, he understood his mother's predicament, and was forced to admit that since her remarriage she'd been happier than he could remember her, and for that Denzil was grateful.

He backed the Accord into the driveway. Halfway down the incline he braked, and got out of the car to unlock the garage and remove the kayak from the roof rack. It had been, in its way, a fantastic day. On the Methwold relief drain he'd seen a marsh harrier, a very rare bird indeed these days. He'd heard the call first—the shrill *kwee*, *kwee* and then a moment later he'd seen the hawk itself, hanging almost casually on a wing before plummeting into the reeds and rising an instant later with a screaming moorhen between its talons. Nature red in tooth and claw. The sort of moment you remembered for ever.

A moment not at odds, in a weird sort of way, with the helicopters that, at intervals, he'd seen hovering and whispering in the northern distance. What had that been about? Some sort of exercise?

Rolling up the garage door, he hauled the kayak inside and shoved it up into the rafters. Then, parking the car and closing the garage door, he returned up the ramp and climbed the stone steps to the front door. Having pulled off his wet waterproofs and hung them to drip in the front hall, he found his mother in the kitchen opening a jar of prune-based sludge for the baby's dessert. With his mother stood a uniformed police officer.

The officer was smiling, and Denzil recognised him as Jack Hobhouse. A solid middle-aged man holding a peaked cap bearing the insignia of the Norfolk Constabulary, he had been to the house several times before when Denzil had been at home.

'Denzil, love, Sergeant Hobhouse has been warning us that there are a couple of terrorist-type people on the loose. Not near here, but they're armed, and they've apparently . . .' Reaching down in response to a sudden sharp cry from Jessica, who was lying on a rug on the floor, she gathered up the child, arranged her over her left shoulder and started patting her back.

'Apparently . . . ?' prompted Denzil.

'They've killed a couple of people up on the north coast,' she said as Jessica, burping, released a milky posset down the back of her mother's expensive black cardigan.

'Fakenham,' said Denzil, regarding his mother's back with fastidious horror. 'I saw something about it in the local paper. They're looking for a British woman and a Pakistani man, aren't they?'

'That's what they think,' said Hobhouse. 'Now, as your mum said, there's no reason to suppose they're anywhere near here, but . . .'

He was interrupted by the ringing of the phone. His mother snatched it up, listened for a moment, and then replaced the receiver. At the same moment the baby started to cry.

'Traffic backed up for a mile because of roadblocks,' she said. 'Thinks he's going to be at least an hour late back. And I've got his bloody parents arriving at any minute. Which reminds me, we're going to need some wine . . . My *God*, Denzil, is that them?'

'I'll, er . . . I'll leave these,' murmured Hobhouse, handing Denzil two photocopied A4 sheets and replacing his cap, 'and be on my way. Obviously, if you spot anyone . . .'

Denzil took the sheets, gave the officer a distracted thumbs-up, and glanced out of the window. Judging by the Jaguar and the intolerant bearing of the couple stepping out of it, it was indeed 'them'.

'Mum, you've got sick on your back.' He took a deep breath and made the supreme sacrifice. 'Give me Jessica. Go upstairs and change. I'll hold the fort.'

FARAJ WATCHED dispassionately as Jean, kneeling on the flagstoned towpath beneath the bridge, bent forward to rinse her hair in the river. Beyond the arches of the bridge lay a grey, baleful dawn.

It was the day.

Pressing her flattened hands into her armpits to warm them for a moment, she searched in the washbag, found a pair of steel hairdressing scissors, and handed these and a comb to Faraj. 'My turn for a haircut,' she said, a little self-consciously.

He nodded. Frowning, he flickered the scissors experimentally.

'It's simple,' she said. 'You work from the back to the front, cutting so that every strand'—she held up her index finger—'is this long.'

The frown still in place, Faraj seated himself behind her and began to cut, carefully dropping the severed locks into the river as he went. Fifteen minutes later he laid down the scissors.

'Done.'

'How does it look?' she asked. 'Do I look different?'

A word of tenderness. A single word would do.

'You look different,' he said brusquely. 'Are you ready?'

'I just want to take a last look at the map,' she said, glancing sideways at him. She reached for the book. As the crow flew, they were just three miles from the target.

'I'm still worried about the helicopters,' she confessed. 'If we go across country and they spot us, we're finished.'

'It's less risky than taking another car,' he said. 'And if they're as clever as you say they are, they won't be searching round here anyway. They'll be concentrating on the approaches to the US bases.'

'We're probably fifteen miles from Marwell here,' she admitted.

But fifteen miles still didn't seem very far. 'I think we should walk to West Ford along the towpath,' she said, levelling her voice with a conscious effort. 'That way, if we hear any helicopters, we've . . . we've got a chance of hiding under the next bridge.'

He looked expressionlessly down at her hands, which had begun to shake again. 'All right,' he said. 'The path, then. Pack the bags.'

In the Swanley Heath mess hall, Liz sat in front of an untouched slice of buttered toast and a cup of black coffee. Investigations had finally got hold of the Garth House school list, but it had failed to turn up anything of interest. Several of the pupils lived in Norfolk or Suffolk, or had done so at some point in the past, but while most remembered Jean D'Aubigny, none had any significant connection with her. A loner, had been the universal judgment.

The D'Aubigny parents were still refusing to assist the police in any way, most probably, Liz suspected, at the lawyer's prompting.

And despite an extensive search operation involving several units of the Moroccan police, MI6 had still not located Price-Lascelles, who, it was now thought, had driven up to the Atlas Mountains.

Liz looked around the room. The police and firearms officers were in one group, the army officers in another, the SAS team in a third. Bruno Mackay, she saw, was standing with the SAS team, and laughing uproariously at something that Jamie Kersley had just said.

Liz had taken a seat next to PC Wendy Clissold, who had spent much of the meal giggling on her phone, obviously to a boyfriend.

'They reckon today's the day, then,' said Clissold, 'that they're going to have a bash at that Yank base.'

'That's what they reckon,' said Liz.

'It's not what I reckon,' said a familiar voice at her shoulder.

Liz looked round. It was Don Whitten, and judging from the bloodshot eyes he had clearly had a bad night.

'Remind me never to join the army, Clissold. The beds don't suit me. You're not allowed to smoke in them, for a kick-off.'

'Isn't that a violation of your civil rights, Guv'nor?'

'You'd have thought so, wouldn't you?' said Whitten mournfully. 'Have you heard from Brian Mudie this morning Clissold?'

'What d'you mean, Guv?'

He looked at her wearily. 'When he rings you, tell him I'm waiting for the inventory on the forensic from the bungalow fire. I particularly want to know about packaging.'

Clissold looked at her fingers. 'As it happens, I have just been speaking to Sergeant Mudie. They're still making up the inventory . . .'

'Go on.'

'There was one thing he said, and that was they found more than a dozen melted containers of Silly Putty. All empty, Guv.'

Whitten's eyes met Liz's. 'How much would that make?' he demanded tonelessly.

'Enough to flatten this building.'

Wendy looked from one to the other of them, mystified.

'C4 explosive,' explained Liz. 'Putty's one of the principal ingredients. The toy shop sort is best.'

'So what's the target?' Whitten demanded.

'RAF Marwell seems to be the popular favourite right now.'

Whitten shook his head. 'That lot over there'—he nodded at the army officers—'think that Mansoor and D'Aubigny are just going to walk into one of our search teams. They're crediting them with no intelligence whatsoever.' He shrugged. 'Perhaps they're right. Perhaps the two of them are just going to find the largest concentration of people that they can, and . . .' He made a starburst with his hands.

Liz took an exploratory bite of her toast, but she seemed to have lost all sense of taste. She wanted to walk out to her car and leave. Draw a line under the case. Leave it to the police and the army. She had done all that she could do.

Except that she knew she hadn't, quite. There was still a single thread, tenuous but nevertheless logical, to be followed. If the D'Aubigny parents thought that their daughter had no connection of any kind with East Anglia, then they would unquestionably have said so, whatever Julian Ledward said. And given that they didn't have much clue about their daughter's life after she left home, the chances were that it was a connection established *before* she left home. Which took her—and Liz—back to school, and Garth House.

THEY PASSED SEVERAL people on the riverbank. There were walkers hunched into jackets and coats, there was a pair of elderly fishermen keeping a chilly vigil beneath their umbrellas, and there was a woman in a turquoise windcheater chivvying an elderly labrador along the towpath. None of them paid Faraj or Jean any attention.

Finally, the edge of the village of West Ford came into view. The first dozen or so houses along the towpath were newish pseudo-Georgian boxes. Beyond these, the river narrowed and passed between, on the north side, a stand of mature yews marking the boundary of the churchyard, and on the south side a coppice of rough evergreen woodland bisected by a public footpath.

Jean and Faraj were on the south bank of the Lesser Ouse, and a flight of stone steps led them onto this patch of woodland. It was all just as Jean remembered it that summer ten years ago—a place of slanting green light and curling hash smoke. In December, however, there was little magic about it. The path was boggy and littered with bottles and fast-food wrappers, and the trees had a dank, sodden look about them.

Beyond the trees stood the village cricket ground. By following the path through the woodland it was possible to approach the back door of the cricket pavilion.

The lock on the rear door was a cheap one, they had noted on their recce three days earlier, and unlikely to give any trouble.

In the event it quickly yielded to Jean's credit card and, scrambling into the dimness with the rucksacks, they closed the door behind them and slumped down onto a bench.

Jean looked around her. They were in some sort of changing area, lit by two small, high, cobwebbed windows. A line of hooks ran along the wall above the wooden bench and a heavy stoneware sink stood in one corner. Beside the sink a door led into a toilet stall.

Cautiously, she opened the door to the forward part of the pavilion. This was an open area, wooden-floored, fronted by a locked door and two sets of green-painted shutters covering windows through which players could watch the game. On the long wall a pair of umpires' coats were hanging beside several dusty team photos.

'Play up, play up and play the game!' murmured Faraj.

'I'm sorry?'

'Just a poem I learned at school.'

Jean stared at him blankly. 'We need to make a lookout position. Maybe cut a hole in these shutters.'

He shook his head. 'Too risky. And we haven't got the tools to do it with.' Climbing onto a pile of deck chairs, he peered through the small side window. 'Try this.'

He climbed down and she took his place. Through the small opening she could see right across the northwest quadrant of the cricket ground, to the rain-darkened sweep of The Terrace and the George and Dragon. Disappearing into the back room, Faraj returned with the binoculars, which he passed to her. Outside Number One, The Terrace, stood a dark red Jaguar. On the ground floor, through the windows, she could see a tall, unmoving figure. Was that him? she wondered. The man who, on the other side of the world, had been selected to die. To die with his family around him, as so many innocent citizens of Iraq, Afghanistan and other states had died.

The tall figure moved away from the window, and Jean was about to lower the binoculars when a figure in the road caught her eye. A man in a pale raincoat had just exited a black car in order to stretch his arms and legs.

'There's security there,' she whispered urgently. 'A man in a car, and . . . yes, another inside the car.'

Faraj nodded. 'It was to be expected. We'll have to approach the house from the garden at the back.'

'When it's dark I'll find my way in there from the alley that runs between two of the houses. I should be able to lower the device over the wall.'

'We might not kill them all.'

'It's the only option we've got, Faraj.'

'Let me think about it. And you get changed. You have to buy us some food.'

She nodded and went into the back room. There she washed her face and hands, using a cracked rind of soap that she found in a saucer by the sink. Then, locating her washbag, she took out her small stock of make-up, and went through the half-forgotten ritual. A faint skim of foundation, a touch of shadow on the eyelids, and a pale dab of lipstick. From her rucksack she took one of the bin-liners of clothes. There was a soft lilac cashmere sweater, grey combat pants and a fitted denim jacket, all bought in a Parisian department store. When she was ready, she looked at herself in the changing room mirror. The transformation was startling. Hesitantly, she went through and showed herself to Faraj. He nodded, and said nothing, but some unreadable emotion touched his gaze.

'I'll wire up the weapon,' he said. 'Don't be seen on the way out.'

'When I knock six times, let me in. Any other number of knocks, it's not me, or they've taken me.'

'I understand. Go.'

WEST FORD'S village stores were at the near end of The Terrace, and as Jean crossed the road she saw a fair-haired young man saunter down the steps of Number One. Like her he seemed to be heading for the shops. This must be the man's son, she thought with a crawl of foreboding.

She steadied herself. In the long term, the action that she was taking today would save lives. The cascading triple detonation in which the British family would die would make the West think twice before raining bombs on those they considered of no consequence. The young man would have to give up his life with the rest.

The two of them reached the village stores at the same time, and he stood aside politely as she pushed the door open. Inside, as she crammed a basket with bread, mineral water, fruit, cheese, chocolate, and for good measure a couple of Christmas cards, she felt the young man's eyes on her. Covertly glancing between the aisles, she saw that he was grinning amiably at her and she looked away. She was prepared to kill him, but she couldn't bring herself to smile at him. And why—*why*—did she think that she recognised him?

Near the counter, and with a heart-thumping shock, she saw a photograph of herself on the front of the *Daily Telegraph*. It was an unsympathetic portrait that her mother had taken three or four years ago. *WOMAN, 23, SOUGHT* . . . Taking a copy, forcing herself not to read further, she refolded it so that the images were on the inside.

'Rain's stopped, anyway!' It was the young man by now in front of her in the queue.

'That's true,' she said flatly. 'How long for, though?'

The question, as she had intended, was unanswerable, and he did not reply, just shuffled forward. When the till girl had scanned his Cheerios and his six-pack of Newcastle Brown Ale cans, he asked for the total to be put on Mrs Delves's account.

Jean suddenly had an idea. Dumping her basket on the counter and letting the girl scan and bag the items, she reached out and touched the boy's arm as he left. He looked round at her, surprised.

'Can I just ask you something?' she whispered. 'Outside?'

'Er, sure,' he murmured.

Engrossed in the business of the till, and giving Jean her change, Beverley had not registered the exchange.

Outside the shop Jean assumed her friendliest expression. It was not easy. Smiling was almost painful. 'Sorry to sort of . . . grab you like this,' she said. 'But I was wondering, do you know of any good pubs round here? I'm staying nearby . . .' she nodded vaguely westwards, 'and I don't know the area, so . . .'

He scratched his head cheerfully. 'Well, let's see . . . there's the George,' he jerked a thumb left-handed, 'but it's a bit Ye Olde, if you know what I mean. I usually go to the Green Man, which is a mile or so up the Downham Road. I'd say it's the best round here.'

'Right,' said Jean, meeting his self-conscious gaze with a warm smile. 'That's . . . can you tell me how to get there on foot? Because I'm not sure that I can borrow my parents' car.'

She was amazed at how easy she found this close-up deception.

Just as killing, when it had come to it, had been so easy.

'Well, you want to cross the cricket ground, and . . .' He took a deep breath. 'Look . . . I can . . . take you if you want. I was going up there myself tonight, so if you, er . . .' He shrugged.

She touched his forearm. 'That sounds *really* great. What time?'

'Oh, er . . . eightish?' He looked at her with a kind of dazed disbelief. 'Say eight thirty? Here? How would that be?'

'That would be lovely!' She gave his arm a quick squeeze, then walked away.

ON THE TARMAC outside the hangar, the SAS were taking on the Tactical Firearms Unit at football, and losing. Without doubt, the players were having a considerably better time than their immediate superiors, who were sitting inside waiting for news.

All morning, as the negative results came in from each sector, Liz had had an increasing sense of her own uselessness, and only a terrible fascination with the endgame process prevented her from slipping away and driving back to London.

At 3.30 p.m. one of the army officers voiced the thought that no one else had dared put into words. Was it possible, he ventured, that they had been sold a dummy? Led by a false process of deduction to guard the wrong institution? Could Lakenheath or Mildenhall be the real target?

The question was greeted with silence, and all present turned to Jim Dunstan. 'We continue as we are,' he said. 'Mr Mackay assures me that the Islamic regard for anniversaries is absolute, and we have several hours until midnight. My suspicion is that Mansoor and D'Aubigny are lying up waiting to run the cordon under cover of darkness. We continue.'

Shortly after 4 p.m. the rain came, lashing the hangar roof and dimming the outlines of the waiting Gazelle helicopters.

'All we bloody well need,' winced Don Whitten, forcing his hands frustratedly into his jacket pockets. 'They say rain's the policeman's friend, but it's our enemy now, and no mistake.'

Liz was about to answer when her phone bleeped. The text message indicated a waiting email from Investigations.

Price-Lascelles still n/a in Morocco but have identified and contacted one Maureen Cahill, formerly matron at Garth Hse School. MC claims D'Aubigny's closest friend Megan Davies, expelled from GH at age 16 after various drug-related incidents. According to school records Davies family lived near Gedney Hill, Lincs. There's no current record of Davies family whereabouts. Do we follow up?

Liz stared at the screen for a moment. She was clutching at straws, but in truth it was all she had to go on. If there was any chance, however slim, of saving lives by ordering an investigation into the whereabouts of the Davies family, then she had to take it.

Go for it, Liz typed out. Use everything. Find them.

She looked outside. The rain was pounding remorselessly down. Dark was falling.

'AGAIN,' SAID FARAJ.

'When we get to the pub I ask to leave my coat in the car. I leave the bag, too—under the coat. I persuade him to stay at the pub for as long as possible, preferably till closing time, and then take me back to the house. When it's time to leave the pub, I set the timer to one hour. In the car I drop some coins and squeeze round to the back seat to retrieve them. While I'm down there, I stuff the backpack under the passenger seat. When we get back to his house, I stay for ten minutes maximum, perhaps arranging to meet him tomorrow, and then I leave. I walk back to the cricket pavilion and knock six times on the door. We then have an estimated thirty-five minutes to get away.'

'Good. Remember that he must not take the car out of the garage once he has returned there. That's why I want you to return as late as possible. If there seems to be any possibility of him or any other member of the family taking the car out again, you must prevent him. Either steal his car keys or disable the car. If you cannot do these things, then take the backpack into the house with you and hide the bomb somewhere there.'

'Got it.'

'Good. Put the backpack on.'

Faraj had wired up the C4 device earlier and together with its digital timer and electronic detonator this was now enclosed in an aluminium casing. At one end of the casing was the red timer-activator button, and protruding from the other a stubby inch-long aerial. If necessary, the timer could be over-ridden and the device remotely detonated by a matchbox-sized transmitter that was zipped into the inside breast pocket of Faraj's mountain jacket. The maximum range for remote detonation was 400 yards, however, and it went without saying that if either of them was that close when the device went off, things would have gone badly wrong.

Rolling up the casing in the muddy jeans she had taken off that morning, Jean had tucked it at the bottom of the backpack. She had stuffed her make-up bag on top of the jeans, and zipped up. Now she folded her waterproof jacket through the backpack's strap, so that it hung in front of her.

He squinted at her. 'Are you ready to do this thing, Asimat?'

'I'm ready,' she said calmly.

He took her hand. 'We will succeed, and we will escape.'

She smiled. An impossible calm seemed to have settled over her. 'I know that, Faraj,' she said.

He nodded, holding on to her hand in the darkness. Outside, the wind scoured the pavilion and the dark, wet trees.

'It is time,' he said.

DENZIL PARRISH had no desire to conform to the unhygienic science student stereotype. He had bathed, shampooed and shaved himself, and was dressed from head to foot in clean clothing. Encounters like today's were once-in-a-lifetime opportunities and he was not going to squander this one. The woman had appeared as if from outer space—cool, chic and confident. He didn't know her name, he didn't know where she was staying . . . He knew nothing about her.

'You look very smart,' said his stepfather, carrying an early-evening beer from the kitchen into the sitting room. For security reasons Colin Delves changed into and out of his RAF uniform at Marwell, and now he was wearing jeans, loafers and the tan leather jacket he habitually wore to drive to and from the base. Despite his casual clothes, however, a palpable air of tension surrounded him.

'And you look a bit knackered,' said Denzil.

'It's been a long day,' said Delves. 'There's been another big security alert. This time they think terrorists might have targeted the base because of the Fighter Wing's involvement in Afghanistan. So Clyde Greeley and I decided all off-base personnel should clear off home, me included, and let the security people lock the place down.'

'Is that for my ears only?' asked Denzil.

His stepfather shrugged. 'Hard to keep it completely quiet, given that they've leafleted the locals, erected roadblocks around the base and moved three battalions of troops into the area.'

'So what'll happen to them? The terrorists, I mean.'

'Well, they won't get anywhere near the base, put it like that. What are you up to this p.m.?'

'Pub,' said Denzil, lowering himself on to the sofa. 'Green Man.'

Colin Delves's parents came into the room and looked about them with the bright, enquiring air of people requiring alcoholic drinks. Buoyed with the secret knowledge of the evening ahead of him, Denzil took their orders himself.

'Lord!' said Charlotte Delves several minutes later. 'There's enough gin in here to tranquillise a horse.'

'Aren't you going to have one?' Royston Delves, who had made his money in commodities, was a pinker, fleshier version of his son.

'I'm driving,' said Denzil piously.

'Yes, straight to the pub,' said Colin.

They were still laughing when Denzil's mother came in with Jessica. The baby had been bathed, fed, and dressed in a clean white babygro. Now, sleepy-eyed and talcum-scented, she was ready to be shown off before being tucked up for the night.

It was the moment Denzil had been waiting for. Amid the cooing and clucking, he slipped away. The woman was waiting outside the shop, as she had said she would be.

'Sorry,' he said, as she buckled herself in to the Honda. 'It's a bit of a tip. Try and pretend it's a Porsche.'

'I'm not sure I like Porsches very much,' she said. 'A bit flash, don't you think?'

He turned to look at her. She was dressed as she had been earlier, and was carrying a green waterproof jacket. 'Well, I'm glad you see it that way,' he grinned. 'Have you had an OK day?'

'A quiet day. How about you? I'm Lucy, by the way.'

'I'm Denzil. So what do you do, Lucy?'

'Very boring, I'm afraid. I work for a company that produces economic reports.'

'Wow, that . . . that really *does* sound quite boring!'

'I have dreams,' she said.

'What dreams?'

'I'd like to travel. Asia, the Far East. Hot places. How about you?'

'I'm studying geology at Newcastle.'

'Interesting?'

'I wouldn't go that far. But it can take you to some interesting places. There's a Greenland trip next year.'

'Cool.'

'Yeah—icy, even. But I'm a cold places person, if you know what I mean. Like you're obviously a hot places person.'

'That's too bad.'

'Well, perhaps we could meet in the middle. In some temperate zone. Like the pub.'

Denzil pulled in to a car park. 'This is it. The Green Man.'

'It looks nice,' she murmured. 'Do you mind if I leave my jacket and bag in the boot?'

ELEVEN

Bruno Mackay covered the receiver and beckoned to Liz. 'Price-Lascelles. That headmaster. Our bloke's found him. Bad line.'

Liz's eyes widened. 'OK. Don't transfer it.'

She walked over to his desk. The headmaster's voice was very faint '. . . do you do. I understand you . . . speak to me.'

'I need to know about one of your ex-pupils. Jean D'Aubigny . . .'

'. . . remember her very well. What can I . . . ?'

'Did she have any particular friends? People she might have stayed in touch with?'

'. . . difficult young woman, who didn't make friends easily. Her closest, as I recall, was a rather troubled . . . named Megan Davies. Her people . . . up in Lincoln, I think. Her father was in the forces. RAF.'

'You're sure about that?'

'Nice couple. John and Dawn, I think their . . . pillar to post . . . Megan very wild in consequence.'

'Did Jean D'Aubigny go and stay with the Davies family?'

'. . . to my knowledge. She may have done so after Megan left Garth House.'

'Where did the Davies family go after Gedney Hill?'

'Sorry, can't help you there.'

'Do you know where Megan went on to? Which school? Mr Price-Lascelles? *Hello?*' But the line was dead. Everyone in the room was staring at her. Mackay wore a particularly indulgent smile.

Was she way off beam here? Was this complete whimsy?

Replacing the receiver, meeting none of the eyes that followed her, Liz returned to her desk. Pulling down the contacts file on her laptop, she rang the Ministry of Defence. Identifying herself to the duty officer, she had herself put through to Files.

'I'm actually just shutting up shop. It'll have to be quick.'

'It'll take as long as it takes,' said Liz levelly. 'This is a matter of national security, so if you don't wish to find yourself outside a Job Centre this time next week, I suggest that you remain exactly where you are until we are finished, is that clear?'

'I hear you,' said the young man petulantly.

'RAF records,' said Liz. 'John Davies, D-A-V-I-E-S, senior officer of some kind, probably admin, wife's name is Dawn.'

There was the sound of keyboard strokes. 'John Davies, you say . . . Yes, here we are. Married to Dawn, née Letherby. He's over at Strategic Air Command.'

'Did he ever have a posting in Lincolnshire?'

'Yes. He spent, let's see, two and a half years running RAF Gedney Hill. Then . . . Six months' attachment in Cyprus, and, after that he was given command of RAF Marwell in East Anglia.'

Liz felt her hand tighten on the receiver. Forced her voice to remain level. 'Where did he and his family live when he was there?'

'In a place called West Ford. Do you want the address?'

'In a minute. First I want you to look up a man called Delves, Colin Delves, D-E-L-V-E-S, who holds that post at Marwell today. Find out if he lives at the same address.'

Another muted flurry of keyboard strokes. A brief silence. 'Same address. Number One, The Terrace, West Ford.'

'Thank you,' said Liz.

Replacing the phone, she looked around her. 'We're guarding the wrong target,' she said.

A frozen silence, utterly hostile.

'Jean D'Aubigny's dowry. The reason she was fast-tracked to operational status. She knew classified information vital to the ITS—namely, where the RAF Marwell CO was billeted. She stayed there with a schoolfriend. They're going to take out Colin Delves's family.'

Jim Dunstan's eyelids fluttered. The blood drained from his face.

The SAS captain was the first to move, punching out an internal number. 'Sabre teams scramble for immediate action, please. Repeat—*Sabre teams scramble to go*.'

'West Ford,' said Liz. 'The village is called West Ford.'

A dozen voices at the level edge of urgency. Running feet, the slash of rotors, and the spotlit hangar falling away beneath them.

THE GREEN MAN was large and beery, with a long oak bar and an impressive array of pumps. The clientele was young and boisterous and noise levels were high. After a brief search, Jean and Denzil found a table against the wall and Denzil went to buy the first round.

He returned with a pint of Suffolk bitter for each of them. As a Muslim, Jean hadn't drunk alcohol for some years, but Faraj had suggested that she have at least one drink to show willing. The beer had a sour, soapy texture but was not altogether unpleasant. It gave her something to do with her hands and, equally important, something to look at as they talked. Earlier in the evening she had made the mistake of looking Denzil in the eye—of meeting his open, inquisitive gaze—and it had been almost unbearable.

Don't look at him, look *through* him, she told herself, but it didn't do any good. She was sharing a small and intimate space with a young man who was sensitive, self-deprecating and kind, a young man whom she found herself liking very much. And planning to kill.

When it was her turn to buy the drinks, she returned with a pint in each hand and gave them to him. Her first pint was only half drunk.

'To save time,' she explained. 'It's a bit jam-packed up there.'

'It gets a lot more crowded when the Americans are here,' he told her. 'Not to mention making things a lot harder with the girls for us local boyos.'

'So why aren't the Americans here tonight?'

'Grounded, probably. Apparently there's been a terrorist scare. There've been a couple of murders up towards Brancaster and they think it might be something to do with Marwell.'

'What's Marwell?'

'One of the RAF bases that the US Air Force use.'

'So what have they got to do with Brancaster? I thought that's where people went sailing.'

'To be honest, I haven't followed the whole thing very closely. I think they reckon the people who committed the murders on the coast might be about to launch some sort of attack on Marwell.'

'Is it near here?'

'Marwell? About thirteen miles.' He raised his glass as if to check the steadiness of his hand. 'And given that there are three battalions of troops between us and it, I'd say we're probably pretty . . .'

She turned to him. She could feel the faint, dizzying effects of the alcohol hitting her system. 'Suppose we weren't? Suppose it all ended tonight? Would you feel you'd lived . . . enough?'

'Wow! That's a bit of a heavy . . . Are you serious?'

She shrugged. 'Yeah.'

'Well, OK. My mum got remarried a couple of years ago and is happy for the first time that I can remember, and I've now got a baby sister, who hasn't really had the chance to get to know me, and so wouldn't be hurt by my death, but who my mum would still have. And I haven't really begun doing anything with my life, careerwise, so, yeah, if I had to go, now would be as good a time as any.'

'What about your father? Your real father?'

'Well . . . He walked out on us years ago, when I was a boy, so he can't ever have really cared for us . . .' He rubbed his eyes. 'Lucy, I really like you, but why are we having this conversation?'

She shook her head, her eyes unfocused. Then, draining her pint glass, she nudged it towards him. 'Could you . . .?'

'Yeah, sure.'

There was a distant roaring in her head, as if she had her ear to a giant sea shell. Yesterday morning she had killed a boy, much the same age as this one. She had smiled at him and squeezed the trigger. Now she was reborn, a Child of Heaven, and at last she understood what the instructor at Takht-i-Suleiman had always found so funny—so funny that it regularly reduced him to shaking incoherence.

She had been reborn dead. The moment had, as promised, changed everything. It had thrown a switch inside her, jamming the circuitry and paralysing the networks. She had feared that she would feel too much; instead, infinitely worse, she felt nothing.

'. . . Another pint for *Mademoiselle* Lucy. You're not married by any chance, are you?'

'Not by any chance, no.' She drank.

'So tell me, unmarried Lucy, just why are you inviting yourself to pubs with strangers?'

Familiarity, she saw, had emboldened and calmed him. 'That's a good question,' she said. 'But a hard one to answer.'

He leaned forward. 'Try.'

She was silent. Took a deep swallow of the beer.

'Or not, of course,' he murmured, looking away.

The alcohol raced round her system. In the old days, with Megan, it had never taken much. A couple of glasses and she was flying. 'If I told you that the conversation we've just had was the most important of your life . . .'

'I'd . . .' He shrugged. 'I'd guess that's possible.'

In his eyes she could see the dawning of the knowledge that she was just one more flaky, difficult woman who was not for him.

She took his hand and, holding it by the fingers, she examined his palm. As she did so, something—everything—became blindingly obvious. She laughed out loud. 'See,' she said. 'Long life!'

'We're a long-living family,' he said warily.

She smiled at him and, releasing his hand, drained her glass. 'Lend me your car keys,' she said. 'I need to get something.'

Outside, at the car, she put on the backpack and zipped up her coat over it. When she returned, wearing her waterproof, Denzil looked at her resignedly. 'You're going to disappear, aren't you? And I'm never going to know anything about you.'

'Let's see,' she said. And touching her hand to his cheek for a moment, she walked away.

Outside, the rain blew gently across her face. She couldn't feel her feet on the ground; instead, she seemed to be floating, buoyed by a lightness of spirit that came with knowing she had been cut loose from the need to obey anyone, or any creed, ever again. They couldn't kill her; neither Faraj and his people, nor her pursuer and her people. She was already dead.

How long she walked, she didn't know. Not more than fifteen minutes, probably. The beer had filled her bladder, and as she crouched at the side of the road with her combat trousers round her ankles she saw Denzil sweep past in the Honda Accord. She walked on, smiling, and the tears were coursing down her cheeks with the rain.

The noise of the helicopters was small at first, and then it became a snarling, slashing fury all around her. Before her was the cricket ground, spotlit from the sky—a scene of unearthly theatricality and beauty. At its centre, rocking on its struts, a British Army Puma from which the black-clad chorus ran to take their positions. The SAS. And on the road beyond them the sapphire winking of police vehicles.

Jean D'Aubigny kept walking. She would have liked to stop weeping but the beauty of it all was just too much. Faintly, at the edge of her consciousness, she heard the multiple snicker of rifle bolts drawn back and locked. Police snipers, she thought, but quickly forgot them, for there at the scene's centre, downlit by a police helicopter, was a slight, determined-looking figure who she knew immediately. The woman's dark hair was slicked back from her face and her leather jacket was zipped to the chin.

Jean smiled. Everything was somehow so familiar. It was as if the scene had played itself out an infinity of times before. 'I knew you'd be here,' she called out, but the wind and the updraught from the helicopters plucked her words away.

In the pavilion, Faraj watched as the security forces flooded the area, and knew himself to be a dead man. He saw the soldiers leap from the Puma, the cricket field flooded with light, and the police marksmen pour down the ropes from the hovering Gazelles onto the surrounding roofs. Thanks to the binoculars, he knew one further thing for certain: that the boy had driven the Honda into the garage several minutes before. The bomb had to be in the car. Where the girl was he had no idea, but he had to act before the police evacuated the place and the entire operation was in vain. From his jacket pocket he took the remote detonator, kissed it, bade farewell to the fighter Asimat, and spoke the name of his father and of Farzana, who he had loved.

As the woman walked uncertainly onto the illuminated cricket ground, Liz realised that she was looking at Jean D'Aubigny. The face was much thinner and sharper than that of the teenager in the posters, but it was recognisably her.

As their eyes met the woman smiled, as if in a kind of recognition, and the lips moved in the rain-blurred face. She looked younger than her twenty-four years, Liz thought. Almost childlike.

The connection between them held for an instant, and then the night shivered and tore apart. A tidal wave of darkness roared towards Liz—pure force, pure hate—lifting and pitching her through the air. The ground slammed up to meet her, and for a moment, as the reverberating undertow of the explosion rolled over her, dragging the breath from her lungs, she knew and understood nothing.

There was a long silence during which soil and clothing and body-tissue fragments rained down, and then, by inclining her head, which hurt atrociously, she saw people moving soundlessly around her, ghostlike beneath the wavering spotlights. To one side a policeman was kneeling on all fours with his uniform hanging from his body. To the other, the overcoated figure of Don Whitten was lying face down, shuddering, and beyond him an army officer was sitting blank-eyed on the ground, bleeding from both ears. In her own ears she could hear a high, thread-like scream. Not human, but some kind of an echo.

A police officer ran up to her and shouted but she could hear nothing and waved him away. Then the helicopters and the lights swung away from them to rake the cricket pavilion and the woods at the far side of the cricket ground. They must have found Mansoor. '*Alive*!' she tried to shout, clambering to her knees with the rain in her face. '*Get him alive*!' but she couldn't hear her own voice.

She was running now, running at an oblique angle to one of the SAS Sabre teams, who were working their way purposefully towards the pavilion. Every step that she took was like a hammer-blow behind her eyes, and she could still hear almost nothing beyond the thready scream in her ears and so was unaware of Bruno Mackay until, launching himself at her from behind and wrapping his arms around the wet calves of her jeans, he brought her awkwardly to the ground and held her there.

She groaned, dazed. 'Bruno, we . . . can't you see, we . . .'

'Don't move, Liz,' he ordered her, pinning her down hard by the wrists. 'Please. You're not thinking straight.'

She lay there, immobilised. Watched as the police helicopter's spotlight bleached the pavilion. Day for night. She wasn't even sure what she'd been trying to do.

'I'm fine,' she murmured.

'You're *not* fine,' he hissed. You've got severe blast concussion.And we've *got* to get away from here.'

'We need Mansoor alive.'

'I know. But move back now, *please*. Let the SAS do their job.'

The four soldiers moved towards the pavilion with their MP5 carbines raised to their shoulders, but as they did so, its front door slowly opened, and a wiry, aquiline figure in jeans and T-shirt stepped on to the spotlit players' terrace. His hands were raised. He was not holding a weapon.

Liz stared at Faraj Mansoor, fascinated. Watched as the first spatters of rain darkened his T-shirt. Mackay, however, barely glanced at him, and in a sudden, terrible rush of comprehension Liz knew exactly what was going to happen, and why.

There was a moment's frozen stand-off, and then one of the SAS men yelled, '*Grenade!*'

From a range of no more than half a dozen yards, the four men each fired a burst of shots into Mansoor's chest. Speechless, Liz watched as his body kicked and bucked and twisted to the ground.

She stared at the spotlit tableau, almost weeping with fury. 'Do you realise—*do you fucking realise*—what you've done?'

Mackay's voice was patient. 'Liz,' he said. 'Get real.'

FOOTSTEPS, which she disregarded. Someone else's problem. She began to drift away again, but heard—as if from a great distance—someone speak her name. Then the footsteps again.

Unwillingly, Liz opened her eyes. The room she was in was spacious and between her bed and the window stood a stainless-steel drip apparatus and an oxygen canister on a trolley. There was a breathing tube in her nostrils and her bed was banked with pillows.

Slowly, the sedative fog cleared. It was over, and Faraj Mansoor and Jean D'Aubigny were dead. But parts of the previous evening, Liz knew, were lost to her for ever. The bomb blast and her subsequent concussion had ensured that.

She pulled the breathing tube from her nostrils. Her head ached and there was a thick, stale taste in her mouth.

The door opened. It was a young blonde woman in combat pants and a USAF T-shirt. 'Hi there! How are you this morning?'

'OK, I think.' Liz struggled to an upright position. 'Where am I?'

'Marwell. The Air Force base hospital. I'm Dr Beth Wildor.' She had a brisk manner and dazzling teeth.

Liz nodded. 'Ah, OK. Um . . . Can I get up?'

'I'll just have a quick look at you.'

For the next ten minutes Dr Wildor peered into her eyes and ears, tested her hearing, took her blood pressure and conducted other tests, noting the results on a clipboard.

'You have impressive powers of recovery, Miss Carlyle. You were not a well woman when they brought you in last night.'

'I'm afraid I don't remember much about it.'

'We call it blast trauma. There are elements of the experience you probably won't recover, but perhaps that's no bad thing.'

'Did anyone die?'

'Apart from the bombers, you mean? No. There were injuries, but no loss of life.'

'Thank God. Can I get up now?'

'You know, Miss Carlyle, I'd rather you took it easy. Why don't you receive your visitor, and when I've done my round, we'll talk?'

'I have a visitor?'

'Indeed you do,' she said with a conspiratorial flash of her teeth. 'And Mr Wetherby seems most concerned about you.'

'*Wetherby?*' She felt an inexplicable flutter of surprise. 'He's here?'

'Right outside.' She regarded Liz levelly. 'I take it he's welcome?'

'He's very welcome,' said Liz, smiling.

'Oh-*kay*! Perhaps you'd like a minute or two to freshen up?'

'Perhaps I would.'

'I'll tell him five.'

When Dr Wildor had gone, Liz swung her legs over the edge of the bed and walked to the washbasin. She felt unsteady and was shocked by the face that regarded her from the mirror. She looked pinched and tired, and there was a dark mask of bruising around her eyes from the blast. She did the best job she could with a washing pack that she found at her bedside, and then arranged herself decorously in the bed.

Wetherby came in carrying flowers. She would not have found it easy to imagine such a thing.

'Can I put these somewhere?' he asked, looking around.

'In the sink, perhaps? They're lovely, thank you.'

He busied himself for a moment with his back to her. 'So . . . how do you feel?' he asked.

'Better than I look.'

He sat himself awkwardly on the end of the bed. 'You look . . . Well, I'm glad it's not worse.'

'I gather there were no deaths on our side?' she said.

'Detective Superintendent Whitten's in the room next door. He was hit by shrapnel and lost a fair bit of blood. A couple of the army people were also cut about quite badly, and there are half a dozen blast trauma cases like yours. But as you say, no deaths. For which, in large part, we have you to thank.'

'I assume you were following everything as it happened?'

'I was in COBRA when your call came through saying that you were on your way to West Ford by helicopter. Five minutes later the police were reporting an explosion with at least a dozen feared injured or dead, and then another report came in almost immediately of some sort of SAS firefight. Downing Street were jumping up and down by this time, as you can imagine, but luckily by the time I got there I'd been able to extract some hard facts from Jim Dunstan—including the fact that one of my officers was down.' He smiled drily. 'The Prime Minister was naturally extremely concerned. He informed me that you were in his prayers.'

'That must be what pulled me through. But tell me, was there time to evacuate the Delves family?'

Wetherby nodded. 'Dunstan got a warning to Delves's security people and they took the family to the village hall, I gather.'

'Meanwhile we all land on the cricket pitch. Enter Jean

D'Aubigny. I can remember her walking towards me. What happened? Why was she walking away from the target?'

'We don't know. It looks as though she must have changed her mind. She was carrying the bomb and Mansoor had a transmitter. We think he must have detonated it. There was a big helicopter search for Mansoor. Somebody reported heat traces around the pavilion, and one of the SAS teams moved up to investigate.' He smiled wryly. 'A process of which, I'm informed, you were a close observer.'

'I'll have plenty to say about that in my report,' murmured Liz.

'I look forward to it.' He looked at her quizzically. 'Would you like some breakfast while we talk?'

'Very much. Let's find a canteen or something.'

'Are you allowed out? I wouldn't want to get on the wrong side of that woman with the teeth.'

'I'll risk it.' Liz smiled, conscious of the faint awkwardness of protocol that prevented them from using each other's names. Buoyed by a sudden reckless effervescence, she stepped out of bed in her shapeless hospital gown and twirled round.

Wetherby stood, bowed with ironic chivalry, and made his way to the door.

She watched him go, and then realising that her gown had no back to it, began to laugh. Perhaps she didn't feel completely normal.

In the locker by the bed, some thoughtful hand had placed brand-new underwear, training shoes, a zip-top grey track suit. All fitted perfectly. Thus attired, she opened the door.

'Follow me,' said Wetherby. 'Fetching ensemble, by the way.'

THE COOKHOUSE was huge—a shining ocean of vending machines and wipe-clean tabletops. Mid-morning, the place had little traffic and the two of them were the only customers. Liz secured herself coffee, orange juice and toast. Wetherby contented himself with coffee.

'I suppose you know who Faraj Mansoor really was,' she said, stirring her coffee.

'Yes. Geoffrey Fane told me early this morning. I came up here on a helicopter with him.'

'So where's Fane now?' she asked.

'Debriefing Mackay on the flight home, I'd imagine.'

'Bastards. *Bastards!* They deliberately kept us in the dark. Watched us struggle. Watched people die.'

'It does look that way,' said Wetherby. 'How did you find out?'

'Mackay's behaviour last night. When Mansoor came out of the cricket pavilion with his hands up Mackay kept his head turned away as if he didn't want to be recognised. They knew each other. It was the only possible explanation.'

'Faraj Mansoor was MI6's man, as his father had been before him. By all accounts he was a first-class agent. Very brave and steady.'

'And Mackay ran him?'

'He inherited him. Mackay arrived in Islamabad at about the time of the US intervention in Afghanistan and, reading between the lines, he pushed Mansoor a bit too hard. Mansoor said that he was being watched closely, and insisted that they cease all contact.'

'So Mackay backed off?'

'He didn't have much choice. Mansoor had to be kept happy.'

'And then the USAF shot up his family.'

'That's right. A tragic accident or lethal incompetence, depending on your reading of the facts, but Mansoor read it as revenge. As punishment for breaking off contact with Mackay. So—unsurprisingly, perhaps—he threw in his lot with the *jihadis*. It was a matter of honour, as much as anything else.'

'An eye for an eye.'

'All that, yes.'

'Enter D'Aubigny.'

'Enter D'Aubigny. Somewhere in Paris, at much the same time, she's telling her controllers that she has privileged information: she knows where the Marwell commander's private residence is. The ITS planners realise that several symbolic birds can be killed with one stone. It's just too good a chance to miss.'

Liz shook her head. 'From the way Mansoor behaved, I'd say that, for him, it was almost entirely personal. When he saw that the task of eliminating Delves's family was no longer possible, he gave up.' She shrugged. 'He probably didn't even particularly hate the West.'

Wetherby shrugged. 'You may well be right.'

Liz frowned. 'Tell me something. If our information about Pakistan was coming to us via Six, and they were suppressing information about Mansoor, how did you find out that it was his family who were killed by the USAF?'

Wetherby regarded her with an oblique smile. 'Six's principal liaison in Pakistan, as you know, is with Inter-Services Intelligence, who answer to the Defence Ministry. Six spend rather less time talking to the Intelligence Bureau, who answer to the Interior Ministry, and whose regard for ISI is, shall we say, a little jaundiced.'

'And you've got chums in the IB?' asked Liz.

'I maintain one or two friendships, yes. I fed them the name Faraj Mansoor and their data bank threw up a suspected terrorist whose father and fiancée had been killed at Daranj. What they didn't know was that Mansoor had been a British agent.'

'So why—*why*—didn't Fane and Mackay tell us all this?'

'It's an information-sharing issue,' said Wetherby. 'As Fane sees it, they have to tell everyone—the Americans included—or nobody. And they decided it has to be nobody. Imagine if Mansoor succeeded in blowing up a London nightclub, say, or doing serious damage to some major defence establishment, and then the world discovers that he's a former MI6 agent. The damage would be incalculable. Much better to keep stum, get us to find him, and then eliminate him before he has a chance to speak.'

Liz shook her head. 'I'm sorry. I take the political point but I still consider what happened last night indefensible. There was no grenade. The man was standing there with his hands in the air.'

'It's academic, I'm afraid. Mansoor and D'Aubigny killed several innocent people. Vis-à-vis the SAS action, there will be an inquiry, but you can guess the conclusion.'

She shook her head again. After a moment, she said, 'We lost, didn't we?'

Wetherby reached across the table and took her hands in his. 'We won, Liz. You saved that family's life. No one could have done more.'

'We were always a step behind. I tried to out-think D'Aubigny, but I couldn't do it. I just couldn't get inside her head.'

'You got as close as anyone could have done.'

'At the moment her life ended we were face to face. I think she was even speaking to me. But I couldn't hear what she was saying.'

Wetherby said nothing. He didn't release her hands, nor did she attempt to take them away.

'What are we going to do?' Liz asked eventually.

'I thought we might get someone to take us over to Swanley Heath and pick up your car. Then I thought I might drive you back to London.'

'OK,' said Liz.

STELLA RIMINGTON

Stella Rimington's first foray into print, her autobiography, *Open Secrets,* caused a furore when it was published in 2001. There was a lot of media debate about whether or not it was a good thing for the former Director-General of MI5 to to spill the beans, with a writer in *The Times* even going so far as to call her 'an affront to her country'. It was a view that baffled the very circumspect Stella Rimington. 'I had the book vetted,' she points out. 'I gave it to the right people to have it looked at and they took out anything they wanted to. I have no idea why everyone made such a fuss.'

During her distinguished career, Rimington worked in all the main fields of intelligence—countersubversion, counterespionage, counterterrorism—and became something of a role model for other women. When she first joined MI5 in 1965, in a part-time administrative role, it was, she remembers, 'very much an old boys' club, full of cloak-and-dagger conversations. It was accepted that women could only have a secondary career in a support role, while the men were at the sharp end doing the intelligence work.'

Dame Stella, who was awarded her title in 1996, is not someone who relishes being in the limelight, but she accepts that in her position it is probably unavoidable—especially now that she has published her first novel. 'I've wanted to write a novel for many years,' she says. 'Because of my former profession, I have a whole series of possible plots in my head.'

Her experience also means that she has a unique insight into the world she writes about in *At Risk*. 'Although what I have written is a pure thriller and entirely imaginary, at the bottom of it I am, in a sense, using my life—not only my life in MI5 but other bits of it as well.' She points out, however, that the real world of Intelligence is very different from the image most people have of it, which tends to be based on James Bond and other maverick male heroes. 'I wanted to demonstrate that a successful investigation comes from a collaboration—people have to work together. Everyone has their own piece of the action and, although there are tensions, at the end of the day it all fits together like a machine.'

HF

The No.1
Ladies' Detective
Agency
Alexander McCall Smith

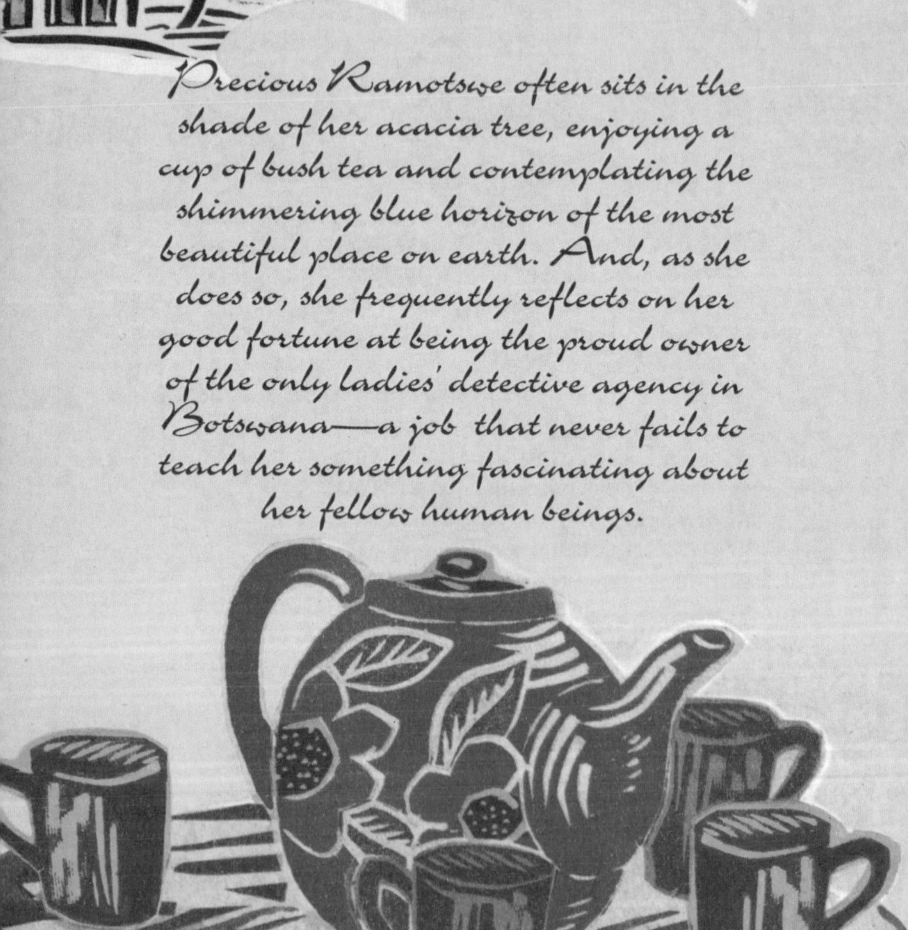

Precious Ramotswe often sits in the shade of her acacia tree, enjoying a cup of bush tea and contemplating the shimmering blue horizon of the most beautiful place on earth. And, as she does so, she frequently reflects on her good fortune at being the proud owner of the only ladies' detective agency in Botswana—a job that never fails to teach her something fascinating about her fellow human beings.

The Daddy

Mma Ramotswe had a detective agency in Africa, at the foot of Kgale Hill. These were its assets: a tiny white van, two desks, two chairs, a telephone and an old typewriter. Then there was a teapot, in which Mma Ramotswe—the only lady private detective in Botswana—brewed redbush tea. And three mugs—one for herself, one for her secretary and one for the client. What else does a detective agency really need? Detective agencies rely on human intuition and intelligence, both of which Mma Ramotswe had in abundance. No inventory would ever include those, of course.

But there was also the view, which again could appear on no inventory. How could any such list describe what one saw when one looked out from Mma Ramotswe's door? To the front, an acacia tree, the thorn tree that dots the wide edges of the Kalahari. And beyond the acacia, over the dusty road, the roofs of the town under a cover of trees and scrub bush; on the horizon, in a blue shimmer of heat, the hills, like improbable, overgrown termite-mounds.

Everybody called her Mma Ramotswe, although if people had wanted to be formal, they would have addressed her as Mme Mma Ramotswe. This is the right thing for a person of stature, but she had never used it of herself. So it was always Mma Ramotswe, rather than Precious Ramotswe, a name that very few people employed.

She was a good detective and a good woman. A good woman in a good country, one might say. She loved her country, Botswana, which is a place of peace, and she loved Africa, for all its trials. I am not ashamed to be called an African patriot, said Mma Ramotswe. I love all the people whom God made, but I especially love the people who live in this place. They are my people. It is my duty to help them to solve the mysteries in their lives. That is what I am called to do.

In idle moments, when there were no pressing matters to be dealt with, she would sit under her acacia tree. It was a dusty place to sit, and the chickens would occasionally come and peck about her feet, but it was a place that seemed to encourage thought.

Mma Ramotswe set up the No.1 Ladies' Detective Agency with the proceeds of the sale of her father's cattle. He had owned a big herd, and had no other children; so every single beast, all one hundred and eighty of them, including the white Brahmin bulls whose grandparents he had bred himself, went to her.

'I want you to have your own business,' he said to her on his death bed. 'You'll get a good price for the cattle now. Sell them and buy a business. A butchery maybe. A bottle store. Whatever you like.'

She held her father's hand and looked into the eyes of the man she loved beyond all others, her Daddy, her wise Daddy, whose lungs had been filled with dust in those mines and who had scrimped and saved to make life good for her.

It was difficult to talk through her tears, but she managed to say, 'I'm going to set up a detective agency. Down in Gaborone. It will be the best one in Botswana. The No.1 Agency.'

For a moment her father's eyes opened wide and it seemed as if he was struggling to speak. 'But . . . but . . .'

But he died before he could say anything more, and Mma Ramotswe fell on his chest and wept for all the dignity, love and suffering that died with him.

SHE HAD A SIGN painted in bright colours, which was then set up just off the Lobatse Road, on the edge of town, pointing to the small building she had purchased:

> The No.1 Ladies' Detective Agency. For all confidential matters and enquiries. Satisfaction guaranteed for all parties. Under personal management.

There was considerable public interest in the setting up of her agency. There was an interview on Radio Botswana, in which she thought she was rather rudely pressed to reveal her qualifications, and a rather more satisfactory article in the *Botswana News*. This article was cut out, copied, and placed prominently on a small board beside the front door of the agency.

After a slow start, her services were in considerable demand. She was consulted about missing husbands, about the creditworthiness of potential business partners, and about suspected fraud by employees. In almost every case, she was able to come up with at least some information for the client; when she could not, she waived her fee, which meant that virtually nobody who consulted her was dissatisfied. People in Botswana liked to talk, she discovered, and the mere mention of the fact that she was a private detective would let loose a positive outpouring of information on all sorts of subjects. This happened with Happy Bapetsi, one of her earlier clients. Poor Happy! To have lost your Daddy and then found him, and then lost him again . . .

'I USED TO HAVE a happy life,' said Happy Bapetsi. 'A very happy life. Then this thing happened, and I can't say that any more.'

Mma Ramotswe watched her client as she sipped her bush tea. Everything you wanted to know about a person was written in the face, she believed. Now Happy Bapetsi was intelligent; that was immediately apparent. She also had few worries: this was shown by the fact that there were no lines on her face, other than smile lines of course. So it was man trouble, thought Mma Ramotswe. Some man has turned up and spoilt everything, destroying her happiness with his bad behaviour.

'Let me tell you a little about myself first,' said Happy Bapetsi. 'I come from Maun, you see, right up on the Okavango. My mother had a small shop and I lived with her in the house at the back. We had lots of chickens and we were very happy.

'My mother told me that my Daddy had left a long time ago, when I was still a baby. He had gone off to work in Bulawayo and he had never come back. Somebody had written to us to say that he thought that my Daddy was dead, but he wasn't sure. He said that he had gone to see somebody at Mpilo Hospital one day, and as he was walking along a corridor he saw them wheeling somebody out on a stretcher, and that the dead person on the stretcher looked like my Daddy. But he couldn't be certain. We decided that he was probably dead. I couldn't even remember him, so it did not make much difference to me.

'I went to school in Maun at a place run by some Catholic missionaries. One of them discovered that I could do arithmetic rather well and he spent a lot of time helping me. He said that he had never met a girl who could count so well. I did very well in my exams and at the end of the day I went off to Gaborone and learned how to be a bookkeeper. I got a job in the bank and I was given promotion after promotion. Now I am the No.1 sub-accountant. I get very good pay and I can finish all my work by three in the afternoon. I go shopping after that. I have a nice house with four rooms and I am very happy. To have all that by the time you are thirty-eight is good enough, I think.'

Mma Ramotswe smiled. 'You're right. You've done well.'

'I'm very lucky,' said Happy Bapetsi. 'But then this thing happened. My Daddy arrived at the house.'

Mma Ramotswe drew in her breath. She had thought it would be a boyfriend problem. Fathers were a different matter altogether.

'He just knocked on the door,' said Happy Bapetsi. 'It was a Saturday afternoon and I was taking a rest on my bed when I heard this knocking. I got up, went to the door, and there was a man, about sixty or so, standing there with his hat in his hands. He told me that he was my Daddy, and that he had been living in Bulawayo for a long time but was now back in Botswana and had come to see me.

'You can understand how shocked I was. He told me my mother's name, which was correct, and he said that he was sorry that he hadn't been in touch before. Then he asked if he could stay in one of the spare rooms, as he had nowhere else to go.

'I said that of course he could. In a way I was very excited to see my Daddy and I thought that it would be good to be able to make up for all those lost years and to have him staying with me, particularly since my poor mother died. So I made a bed for him in one of the rooms and cooked him a large meal of steak and potatoes, which he ate very quickly. Then he asked for more.

'That was about three months ago. Since then, he has been living in that room and I have been doing all the work for him. I make his breakfast, cook him some lunch, which I leave in the kitchen, and then make his supper at night. All he does is sit in his chair outside the front door and tell me what to do for him next.'

'Many men are like that,' interrupted Mma Ramotswe.

Happy Bapetsi nodded. 'This one is specially like that. He has not washed a single cooking pot since he arrived and I have been getting very tired running after him. I would not resent this, you know, except for one thing. I do not think that he is my real Daddy. I think that this man is an impostor and that he heard about our family from my real Daddy before he died and is now just pretending. I think he is a man who has been looking for a good retirement home.'

Mma Ramotswe found herself staring in frank wonderment at Happy Bapetsi. There was no doubt but that she was telling the truth; what astonished her was the effrontery, the sheer, naked effrontery of men. How dare this person come and impose on this helpful, happy person! What a piece of chicanery, of fraud!

'Can you help me find out whether this man is really my Daddy?' asked Happy Bapetsi. 'If he is, then I will be a dutiful daughter and put up with him. If he is not, then I should prefer for him to go.'

Mma Ramotswe did not hesitate. 'I'll find out,' she said. 'It may take me a day or two, but I'll find out!'

Of course it was easier said than done. There were blood tests these days, but she doubted very much whether this person would agree to that. No, she would have to try something more subtle. She stopped in her line of thought. Yes! There was something biblical about this story. What, she thought, would Solomon have done?

MMA RAMOTSWE picked up the nurse's uniform from her friend Sister Gogwe. It was a bit tight, especially round the arms, as Sister Gogwe was slightly more slender than Mma Ramotswe. But once she was in it, and had pinned the nurse's watch to her front, she was a perfect picture of a staff sister at the Princess Marina Hospital.

As she drove to Happy Bapetsi's house in her tiny white van, she reflected on how the African tradition of support for relatives could cripple people. If you believed in the old Setswana morality, you couldn't turn a relative away, and there was a lot to be said for that. But it did mean that charlatans and parasites had an easy time of it.

As she neared the house, she increased her speed. This was an errand of mercy, after all, and if the Daddy were sitting in his chair outside the front door he would have to see her arrive in a cloud of dust. The Daddy was there, of course, enjoying the sun. Mma Ramotswe turned off the engine and ran out of the van up to the house.

'*Dumela, rra,*' she greeted him. 'Are you Happy Bapetsi's Daddy?'

The Daddy rose to his feet. 'Yes,' he said proudly. 'I am the Daddy.'

Mma Ramotswe panted, as if trying to get her breath back.

'I'm sorry to say that there has been an accident. Happy was run over and is very sick at the hospital.'

The Daddy wailed. 'Aiee! My daughter! My little baby Happy!'

A good actor, thought Mma Ramotswe, unless . . . No, she preferred to trust Happy Bapetsi's instinct.

'Yes,' she went on. 'It is very sad. She is very sick, very sick. And they need lots of blood to make up for all the blood she's lost.'

'They must give her that blood. Lots of blood. I can pay.'

'It's not the money,' said Mma Ramotswe. 'Blood is free. We don't have the right sort. We will have to get some from her family, and you are the only one she has. We must ask you for some blood.'

The Daddy sat down heavily. 'I am an old man,' he said.

'That is why we are asking you,' she said. 'Because she needs so much blood, they will have to take about half your blood. And that is very dangerous for you. In fact, you might die.'

The Daddy's mouth fell open. 'Die?'

'Yes,' said Mma Ramotswe. 'But then you are her father and we know that you would do this thing for your daughter. Now could you come quickly, or it will be too late. Dr Moghile is waiting.'

The Daddy opened his mouth, and then closed it.

'Come on,' said Mma Ramotswe, reaching down and taking his wrist. 'I'll help you to the van.'

'No,' he said. 'I don't want to.'

'You must,' said Mma Ramotswe. 'Now come on.'

The Daddy shook his head. 'No,' he said faintly. 'I won't. You see, I'm not really her Daddy. There has been a mistake.'

Mma Ramotswe let go of his wrist. Then, her arms folded, she stood before him and addressed him directly.

'So you are not the Daddy! I see! Then what are you doing sitting in that chair and eating her food? Have you heard of the Botswana Penal Code and what it says about people like you? Have you?'

The Daddy looked down at the ground and shook his head.

'Well,' said Mma Ramotswe. 'You go inside that house and get your things. You have five minutes. Then I am going to take you to the bus station and you are going to get on a bus. Where do you really live?'

'Lobatse,' said the Daddy. 'But I don't like it down there.'

'Well,' said Mma Ramotswe. 'Maybe if you started doing something instead of just sitting in a chair you might like it more. There are lots of melons to grow down there. How about that, for a start?'

The Daddy looked miserable.

'Inside!' she ordered. 'Four minutes left now!'

WHEN HAPPY BAPETSI returned home she found the Daddy gone and his room cleared out. There was a note from Mma Ramotswe on the kitchen table, which she read, and as she did so, her smile returned.

That was not your Daddy. I found out the best way. I got him to tell me himself. Maybe you will find the real Daddy one day. Maybe not. But in the meantime, you can be happy again.

All those Years Ago

We don't forget, thought Mma Ramotswe. Our heads are as full of memories as the sky may sometimes be full of swarming bees; thousands and thousands of memories, of smells, of places, of little things that happened to us and which come back, unexpectedly, to remind us who we are. And who am I? I am Precious Ramotswe, citizen of Botswana, daughter of Obed Ramotswe who died because he had been a miner and could no longer breathe. His life was unrecorded; who is there to write down the lives of ordinary people?

I AM OBED RAMOTSWE, and I was born near Mahalapye in 1930. Mahalapye is halfway between Gaborone and Francistown, on that road that seems to go on and on for ever. I am sixty now, and I do not think God wants me to live much longer. Perhaps there will be a few years more, but I doubt it; I saw Dr Moffat at the Dutch Reformed Hospital in Mochudi who listened to my chest. He could tell that I had been a miner, just by listening, and he shook his head and said that the mines have many different ways of hurting a man.

I did not weep at that news the doctor gave me. I'm not saying that I'm a brave man—I'm not—but I really don't seem to mind this news I have been given. I can look back over my sixty years and think of everything that I have seen and of how I started with nothing and ended up with almost two hundred cattle. And I have Precious, a good daughter, a loyal daughter, who looks after me well and makes me tea while I sit here in the sun and look out to the hills. When you see those hills from a distance, they are blue; as all the distances in this country are. We are far from the sea here, with Angola and Namibia between us and the coast, and yet we have this great empty ocean of blue above us and around us. I love our country, and I am proud to be a Motswana. There's no other country in Africa that can hold its head up as this one can. We have no political prisoners and never have had any. We have democracy. We have been careful. The Bank of Botswana is full of money from our diamonds. We owe nothing.

But things were bad in the past. Before we built our country we had to go off to South Africa to work. We went to the mines, just as people did from Lesotho and Mozambique and Malawi and all those countries. The mines sucked our men in and left the old men and the children at home. We dug for gold and diamonds and made those white men rich. They built their big houses, with their walls and their cars. And we dug down below them and brought out the rock on which they built it all.

I went to the mines when I was eighteen. We were the Bechuanaland Protectorate in those days, and the British ran our country. My family had left Mahalapye and gone to live in Mochudi, where my mother's people lived. I liked Mochudi and would have been happy to stay there, but my father said I should go to the mines, as his lands were not good enough to support me and a wife.

I went off on the truck the next day. I had only one pair of shoes, but I had a spare shirt and some spare trousers. These were all the things I had, apart from some biltong that my mother had made for me. I loaded my case on top of the truck and then all the families who had come to say goodbye started to sing. The women cried and we waved goodbye. Young men always try not to cry or look sad, but I knew that within us all our hearts were cold.

It took twelve hours to reach Johannesburg, as the roads were rough in those days. We travelled through the Western Transvaal, through the heat, cooped up in the truck like cattle. Every hour, the driver would stop and come round to the back and pass out canteens of water, which they filled at each town we went through.

In Johannesburg they spent two weeks training us. They told us how we would be taken down into the mines and about the work we would be expected to do. They talked to us about safety, and how the rock could fall and crush us if we were careless.

Then we went down to the shafts and were shown what to do. They put us in cages, beneath great wheels, and these cages shot down as fast as hawks falling upon their prey. They had trains down there—small trains—and they put us on these and took us to the end of long, dark tunnels, which were filled with green rock and dust. My job was to load rock after it had been blasted, and I did this for seven hours a day. I grew strong, but all the time there was dust, dust, dust.

I worked for years in those mines, and I saved all my money. Other men spent it on town women, and drink, and on fancy clothes. I sent the money home to the Standard Bank and then I bought cattle with it. Each year I bought a few cows, and gave them to my cousin to look after. They had calves, and slowly my herd got bigger.

I would have stayed in the mines, I suppose, had I not witnessed a terrible thing. It happened after I had been there for fifteen years. I had then been given a much better job, as an assistant to a blaster. They would not give us blasting tickets, as that was a job the white men kept for themselves, but I was given the job of carrying explosives for a blaster and helping him with the fuses. This was a good job, and I liked the man I worked for.

He had left something in a tunnel once—his tin can in which he carried his sandwiches—and he had asked me to fetch it. So I went off down the tunnel where he had been working and looked for this can. The tunnel was lit by bulbs which were attached to the roof all the way along, so it was quite safe to walk along it. But you still had to be careful, because here and there were great galleries that had been blasted out of the rock. These could be two hundred feet deep.

I turned a corner in this tunnel and found myself in a round chamber. There was a gallery at the end of this, and there was a warning sign. Four men were standing at the edge of the gallery, and they were holding another man by his arms and legs. As I came round the corner, they lifted him and threw him forwards, over the edge and into the dark. The man screamed, then he was gone.

I stood where I was. The men had not seen me yet, but one turned round and shouted in Zulu. Then they began to run towards me. I ran back along the tunnel. I knew that if they caught me I would follow their victim into the gallery. It was not a race I could let myself lose.

Although I got away, I knew that those men had seen me and that I would be killed. I had seen their murder and could be a witness, and so I knew that I could not stay in the mines.

I spoke to the blaster. He was a good man and he listened to me carefully when I told him that I would have to go. There was no other white man I could have spoken to like that, but he understood.

Still, he tried to persuade me to go to the police.

'Tell them what you saw,' he said in Afrikaans. 'Tell them. They can catch these Zulus and hang them.'

'I don't know who these men are. They'll catch me first. I am going home to my place.'

He looked at me and nodded. Then he shook my hand, which was the first time a white man had done that to me. So I called him my brother, which was the first time I had done that to a white man.

'You go back home to your wife,' he said. 'Go back and give her more children.'

So I left the mines, secretly, like a thief, and came back to Botswana in 1960. I cannot tell you how full my heart was when I crossed the border back into Botswana and left South Africa behind me for ever. In that place I had felt every day that I might die. Danger and sorrow hung over Johannesburg like a cloud, and I could never be happy there. I had left a prison—a great, groaning prison.

When I came home that time, and got off the bus at Mochudi, I just stood and cried. A man came up to me—a man I did not know—and he put his hand on my shoulder and asked me whether I was just back from the mines. I told him that I was, and he just nodded and left his hand there until I had stopped weeping. Then he smiled and walked away. He had seen my wife coming for me, and he did not want to interfere with the homecoming of a husband.

I had taken this wife three years earlier, although we had seen very little of one another since the marriage. I came back from Johannesburg once a year, for one month, and this was all the life we had had together. After my last trip she had become pregnant, and my little girl had been born while I was still away. Now I was to see her, and my wife had brought her to meet me off the bus. She stood there, with the child in her arms, the child who was more valuable to me than all the gold taken out of those mines in Johannesburg. This was my first-born and my only child, my girl, my Precious Ramotswe.

Precious was like her mother, who was a good fat woman. She played in the yard outside the house and laughed when I picked her up. They said she was the most beautiful child in Bechuanaland and women would come from miles away to look at her and hold her.

Then my wife, the mother of Precious, died. We were living just outside Mochudi then, and she used to go from our place to visit an aunt of hers who lived over the railway line near the Francistown Road. I don't know how it happened. Some people said that it was because there was a storm brewing up, and there was lightning, that she may have run without looking where she was going. But she was on the railway line when the train from Bulawayo came down and hit her. The engine driver was very sorry, but he had not seen her at all, which was probably true.

My cousin came to look after Precious. She made her clothes, took her to school and cooked our meals. I was a sad man, and I thought: Now there is nothing left for you in this life but Precious and your cattle. In my sorrow, I went out to the cattle post to see how my cattle were, and to pay the herd boys. I had more cattle now, and I had even thought of buying a store. But I decided to wait, and to let Precious buy a store once I was dead. Besides, the dust from the mines had ruined my chest and I could not walk fast or lift things.

Lessons about Boys and Goats

Obed Ramotswe installed his cousin in a room at the back of the small house he had built for himself at the edge of the village when he had returned from the mines. With the addition of a bed and a small cupboard, and with a coat of whitewash applied to the walls, the room was soon fit for occupation. From the point of view of the cousin, it was luxury almost beyond imagination; after the departure of her husband, six years previously, she had returned to live with her mother and her grandmother, and had been required to sleep in a room that had only three walls, one of which did not quite reach the roof. They had treated her with quiet contempt, believing that a woman who was left by her husband would almost always have deserved her fate. They had to take her in, of course, but it was duty, rather than affection, which opened their door to her.

Her husband had left her because she was barren, a fate that was almost inevitable for the childless woman. Shortly after he left, he wrote to her from Lobatse and told her—proudly—that his new wife was pregnant. Then, a year and a half later, there came a short letter with a photograph of his child. That was the last time she heard from him.

Now, holding Precious in her arms, standing in her own room with its four whitewashed walls, her happiness was complete. She allowed Precious, now four, to sleep with her in her bed, lying awake at night for long hours to listen to the child's breathing. She stroked her skin and held the tiny hand between her fingers. When Precious slept during the afternoon, she would sit beside her, knitting and sewing jackets and socks, and brush flies away from the sleeping child.

Obed, too, was content. He gave his cousin money each week to buy food for the household and a little extra each month for herself. She husbanded resources well, and there was always money left over, which she spent on something for Precious. He never had occasion to find fault in her upbringing of his daughter. Everything was perfect.

The cousin wanted Precious to be clever. She started by teaching her to count. They counted goats and cattle. They counted boys playing in the dust. They counted trees, giving each tree a name: crooked one; one with no leaves; one where mopani worms like to hide; one where no bird will go. They also played a variety of Kim's Game, in which the cousin would load a basketwork tray with familiar objects and a blanket would then be draped over it and one object removed.

'What has been taken from the tray?'

'An old marula pip, all gnarled and chewed up.'

'And what else?'

'Nothing.'

She was never wrong, this child who watched everybody and everything with her wide, solemn eyes. And slowly, without anybody ever having intended this, the qualities of curiosity and awareness were nurtured in the child's mind.

By the time Precious went to school at the age of six, she knew her alphabet, her numbers up to two hundred, and she could recite the entire first chapter of the Book of Genesis in the Setswana translation. The teacher was impressed and complimented the cousin on what she had done. This was virtually the first praise that she had ever received for any task she had performed. Obed had thanked her, and done so often, and generously, but it had not occurred to him to praise her, because in his view she was just doing her duty as a woman and there was nothing special about that.

'We were the ones who first ploughed the earth when Modise [God] made it,' ran an old Setswana poem. 'We are the ones who make the food. We are the ones who look after the men when they are little boys, when they are young men, and when they are old and about to die. We are always there. But we are just women, and nobody sees us.'

Boys

PRECIOUS RAMOTSWE had learned about good and evil at Sunday school. The cousin had taken her there when she was six, and she had gone there every Sunday until she was eleven. That was enough time for her to learn all about right and wrong. She had experienced no difficulty in understanding that it was wrong to lie, and steal, and kill other people.

If people needed clear guidelines, there was nobody better to do this than Mma Mothibi, who had run the Sunday school at Mochudi for over twelve years. She was a short lady, almost entirely round, who spoke with an exceptionally deep voice. She taught the children hymns, in both Setswana and English, and because they learned their singing from her the children's choir all sang an octave below everybody else, as if they were frogs.

The children, dressed in their best clothes, sat in rows at the back of the church when the service had finished and were taught by Mma Mothibi. She read the Bible to them, and made them recite the Ten Commandments over and over again, and told them religious stories from a small blue book which she said came from London.

'These are the rules for being good,' she intoned. 'A boy must always rise early and say his prayers. Then he must clean his shoes and help his mother to prepare the family's breakfast. Then he must go to school and do everything that his teacher tells him. In that way he will learn to be a clever Christian boy who will go to heaven later on. For girls, the rules are the same, but they must also be careful about boys and must be ready to tell boys that they are Christians. Some boys will not understand this . . .'

Yes, thought Precious Ramotswe. Some boys do not understand this, and even there, in that Sunday school there was such a boy, that Josiah, who was a wicked boy, although he was only nine. He insisted on sitting next to Precious in Sunday school. He was always looking at her and smiling encouragingly. He tried also to make sure that his leg touched hers, which angered her. But worst of all, he would undo the buttons of his trousers and point to that thing that boys have, and expect her to look. She did not like this. What was so special about that, anyway? All boys had that thing.

At last she told Mma Mothibi about it, and the teacher listened gravely. 'Boys, men,' she said. 'They're all the same. They think that this thing is something special and they're all so proud of it. They do not know how ridiculous it is.'

She told Precious to tell her next time it happened. She just had to raise her hand a little, and Mma Mothibi would see her. That would be the signal.

It happened the next week. While Mma Mothibi was at the back of the class, looking at the Sunday school books which the children had laid out before them, Josiah undid a button and whispered to Precious that she should look down. She kept her eyes on her book and raised her left hand slightly. He could not see this, of course, but Mma Mothibi did. She crept up behind the boy and raised her

Bible into the air. Then she brought it down on his head with a resounding thud that made the children start.

Josiah buckled under the blow. Mma Mothibi now came round to his front and pointed at his open fly. Then she raised the Bible and struck him on the top of the head again, even harder than before.

That was the last time that Josiah bothered Precious Ramotswe, or any other girl for that matter. For her part, Precious learned an important lesson about how to deal with men, and this lesson stayed with her for many years, and was to prove very useful later on, as were all the lessons of Sunday school.

The Cousin's Departure

THE COUSIN looked after Precious for the first eight years of her life. She might have stayed indefinitely—which would have suited Obed—but he recognised that the cousin might wish to marry again, in spite of what had happened last time. So he readily gave his blessing when the cousin announced that she had been seeing a man, that he had proposed, and that she had accepted.

'I could take Precious with me,' she said. 'I feel that she is my daughter now. But then, there is you . . .'

'Yes,' said Obed. 'There is me. Would you take me too?'

The cousin laughed. 'My new husband is a rich man, but I think that he wants to marry only one person.'

Obed made arrangements for the wedding, as he was the cousin's nearest relative and it fell to him to do this. He did it readily, though, because of all she had done for him. He arranged for the slaughter of two cattle and for the brewing of enough beer for two hundred people. Then, with the cousin on his arm, he entered the church.

After the ceremony, everyone went back to the house, where canvas tarpaulins had been hooked up between thorn trees and chairs set out. The old people sat down while the young moved about and talked to one another, and sniffed the air at the great quantities of meat that were sizzling on the open fires. Then they ate, and Obed made a speech of thanks to the cousin, and the new husband replied that he was grateful to Obed for looking after this woman so well.

The new husband owned two buses, which made him wealthy. One of these, the Molepolole Special Express, had been pressed into service for the wedding and was decked for the occasion with bright blue cloth. In the other, they drove off after the party, with the husband at the wheel and the new bride sitting in the seat behind him.

They set up home ten miles south of Gaborone, in a house that the new husband's brother had built for him. It had a red roof and white walls, and a compound, in the traditional style, with a walled yard to the front. At the back there was a small shack for a servant to live in, and a lean-to latrine made out of galvanised tin. The cousin had a kitchen with a shining new set of pans, two cookers and a large new South African paraffin-powered fridge. Every evening, her husband came home with the day's takings from his buses, and she helped him to count the money. She proved to be an excellent bookkeeper, and was soon running that part of the business with conspicuous success.

She made her new husband happy. As a boy he had been bitten by a jackal, and had scars across his face where a junior doctor at the Scottish Missionary Hospital at Molepolole had ineptly sewn the wounds. No woman had told him that he was handsome before, and he had never dreamed that any would. The cousin said that he was the most good-looking man she had ever met. This was not mere flattery—she was telling the truth, as she saw it, and his heart was filled with the warmth that flows from the well-directed compliment.

Goats

As a girl, Precious Ramotswe liked to draw, an activity that the cousin had encouraged from an early age. She had been given a sketching pad and a set of coloured pencils for her tenth birthday and Obed Ramotswe was proud of her ability to fill the virgin pages of her sketchbook with scenes of everyday Mochudi life.

Her teachers told her that she might one day be a great artist. This encouraged her, and sketch followed sketch. Goats, cattle, hills, pumpkins, houses; there was so much for the artist's eye around Mochudi that there was no danger that she would run out of subjects.

The school got to hear of an art competition for children. The museum in Gaborone had asked every school in the country to submit a picture by one of its pupils, on the theme 'Life in Botswana of Today'. Precious was asked to draw a special picture and then this would be sent down to Gaborone as the entry from Mochudi.

She drew her picture on a Saturday, going out early with her sketchbook and returning some hours later to fill in the details inside the house. It was a very good drawing, she thought, and her teacher was enthusiastic when she showed it to her the following Monday.

'This will win the prize for Mochudi,' she said.

The drawing was sent off to the museum. Then there was a silence for five weeks, during which time everybody forgot about the competition. Only when the letter came to the principal, and he, beaming, read it out to Precious, were they reminded.

'You have won first prize,' he said. 'You are to go to Gaborone, with your teacher and myself, and your father, to get the prize from the Minister of Education at a special ceremony.'

It was too much for her, and she wept, and was allowed to leave school early to run back to give the news to her Daddy.

They travelled down with the principal in his truck, arriving far too early for the ceremony, and spent several hours sitting in the museum yard, waiting for the doors to open. But at last they did, and others came—teachers, people from the newspapers, members of the Legislature. Then the minister arrived and people put down their glasses of orange juice and swallowed the last of their sandwiches.

She saw her painting hanging in a special place, on a room divider, and there was a small card pinned underneath it. She went with her teacher to look at it, and she saw, with leaping heart, her name neatly typed out underneath the picture: 'Precious Ramotswe (10), Mochudi Government Junior School'. And underneath that, the title that the museum itself had provided: CATTLE BESIDE DAM.

She stood rigid, suddenly appalled. This was not true. The picture was of goats, but they had thought it was cattle! She was getting a prize for a cattle picture, by false pretences.

'What is wrong?' asked her father. 'Why are you looking so sad?'

She could not say anything. She was about to become a criminal, a perpetrator of fraud. She could not possibly take a prize for a cattle picture when she simply did not deserve that.

But now the minister was standing beside her, and he was preparing to make a speech. She looked up at him, and he smiled warmly.

'You are a very good artist,' he said. 'Mochudi must be proud of you.'

She looked at the toes of her shoes. She would have to confess.

'It is not a picture of cattle,' she said. 'It is a picture of goats. You cannot give me a prize for a mistake.'

The minister frowned and looked at the label. Then he turned back to her and said, 'They are the ones who have made a mistake. I also think those are goats. I do not think they are cattle.'

He cleared his throat and the museum director asked for silence.

This excellent picture of goats,' said the minister, 'shows how talented are our young people in this country. This young lady will grow up to be a fine citizen and maybe a famous artist. She deserves her prize, and I am now giving it to her.'

She took the wrapped parcel which he gave her, and heard him whisper, 'You are the most truthful child I have met. Well done.'

Then the ceremony was over and they returned to Mochudi in the principal's truck, a heroine returning, a bearer of prizes.

Living with the Cousin and the Cousin's Husband

At the age of sixteen, Mma Ramotswe left school. ('The best girl in this school,' pronounced the principal. 'One of the best girls in Botswana.') Her father had wanted her to stay on, to do her Cambridge School Certificate, and to go even beyond that, but Mma Ramotswe was bored with Mochudi. She wanted to go somewhere. She wanted her life to start.

'You can go to my cousin,' her father said. 'That is a very different place. You will find lots of things happening in that house.'

It cost him a great deal of pain to say this. He wanted her to stay, to look after him, but he knew that it would be selfish to expect her life to revolve around his. She wanted freedom; she wanted to feel that she was doing something with her life. And of course, at the back of his mind, was the thought of marriage. In a very short time, he knew, there would be men wanting to marry her.

THE COUSIN was pleased to have Precious in the house. She decorated a room for her, hanging new curtains of a thick yellow material that she had bought from the OK Bazaars on a shopping trip to Johannesburg. Then she filled a chest of drawers with clothes and put on top of it a framed picture of the Pope. The floor was covered with a simply patterned reed mat. It was a bright, comfortable room.

Precious settled quickly into a new routine. She was given a job in the office of the bus company, where she added invoices and checked the figures in the drivers' records. She was quick at this, and the cousin's husband noticed that she was doing as much work as the two older clerks put together. They sat at their tables and gossiped away the day, occasionally moving invoices about the desk.

It was easy for Precious, with her memory, to remember how to do new things and to apply the knowledge faultlessly. She was also willing to make suggestions, and scarcely a week went by when she did not make some suggestion as to how the office could be more efficient.

'You're working too hard,' one of the clerks said to her. 'You're trying to take our jobs.'

Precious looked at them blankly. She had always worked as hard as she could, at everything she did, and she simply did not understand how anybody could do otherwise.

She did her own checking and although everything usually added up, now and then she found a small discrepancy. These came from the giving of incorrect change, the cousin explained. It was easy enough to do on a crowded bus, and they just ignored it. But then Precious found a discrepancy of over two thousand pula in the fuel bills invoices and she drew this to the attention of her cousin's husband.

'Are you sure?' he asked. 'How could that amount go missing?'

'Stolen?' said Precious.

The cousin's husband shook his head. He regarded himself as a model employer. He could not believe that any of his employees would cheat him.

Precious showed him how the money had been taken, and they jointly pieced together how it had been moved out of the right account into another one, and had then eventually vanished altogether. Only one of the clerks had access to these funds, so it must have been him; there could be no other explanation.

She did not see the confrontation, but heard it from the other room. The clerk was indignant, shouting his denial at the top of his voice. Then there was silence for a moment, and the slamming of a door.

This was her first case. This was the beginning of the career of Mma Ramotswe.

The Arrival of Note Mokoti

THERE WERE four years of working in the bus office. The cousin and her husband became accustomed to her presence and began to call her their daughter. She did not mind this; they were her people, and she loved them. She loved the house, and her room with its yellow curtains. It was a good life that she had made for herself.

Every weekend she travelled up to Mochudi on one of the cousin's husband's buses and visited her father. He would be waiting outside the house, sitting on his stool, and she would curtsy before him, in the old way, and clap her hands.

Then they would eat together, sitting in the shade of the lean-to verandah that he had erected to the side of the house. She would tell him about the week's activity in the bus office and he would take in every detail, asking for names, which he would link into elaborate genealogies. Everybody was related in some way.

It was the same with cattle. Cattle had their families, and after she had finished speaking, he would tell her the cattle news. He said that people were like their cattle. Thin wretched cattle had thin wretched owners. Listless cattle had owners whose lives lacked focus. And dishonest people, he maintained, had dishonest cattle—cattle that would cheat other cattle of food or that would try to insinuate themselves into the herds of others.

Obed Ramotswe was a severe judge—of men and cattle—and she found herself thinking: What will he say when he finds out about Note Mokoti?

SHE HAD MET Note Mokoti on a bus on the way back from Mochudi. He was travelling down from Francistown and was sitting in the front, his trumpet case beside him. She could not help but notice him in his red shirt; nor fail to see the high cheekbones and the arched eyebrows. It was a proud face, the face of a man used to being looked at and appreciated, and she dropped her eyes immediately. She would not want him to think she was looking at him, even if she continued to glance at him from her seat. Who was this man?

The bus stopped in Gaborone before going south on the road to Lobatse. She stayed in her seat, and saw him get up. He stood up, turned and looked down the bus. She felt her heart jump. He had looked at her. No, he had not, he was looking out of the window.

Suddenly, without thinking, she got to her feet and took her bag down from the rack. She would get off because she wanted to see what he did. He had left the bus now and she hurried. Out in the crowd, she looked about her and saw him, standing not far away. He had bought a roast mealy from a hawker, and was eating it now.

He was looking at her, and she turned away flustered. Had he seen her watching him? She looked up again, glancing in his direction, and he smiled at her this time. Then, tossing the mealy cob away, he picked up the trumpet case and walked over towards her. She was frozen, unable to walk away, mesmerised like prey before a snake.

'I saw you on that bus,' he said. 'I thought I had seen you before. But I haven't.'

She looked at the ground. 'I have never seen you,' she said. 'Ever.'

He smiled. He was not frightening, she thought, and some of her awkwardness left her.

'You see most people in this country once or twice,' he said. 'There are no strangers.'

She nodded. 'That is true.'

There was a silence. Then he pointed to the case at his feet.

'This is a trumpet, you know. I am a musician.'

She looked at the case. It had a sticker on it; a picture of a man playing a guitar.

'Do you like music?' he asked. 'Jazz? Quella?'

She looked up, and saw that he was still smiling at her.

'Yes. I like music.'

'I play in a band,' he said. 'We play in the bar at the President Hotel. You could come and listen. I am going there now.'

They walked to the bar, which was only ten minutes or so from the bus-stop. He bought her a drink and sat her at a table at the back, a table with one seat at it to discourage others. Then he played, and she listened, overcome by the sliding, slippery music, and proud that she knew this man, that she was his guest. The drink was strange and bitter; she did not like the taste of alcohol, but drinking was what you did in bars and she was concerned that she would seem out of place or too young and that people would notice her.

Afterwards, when the band had its break, he came to join her, and she saw that his brow was glistening with the effort of playing.

'I'm not playing well today,' he said. 'There are some days when you can and some days when you can't.'

'I thought you were very good. You played well.'

'I don't think so. I can play better. There are days when the trumpet just talks to me. I don't have to do anything then.'

She saw that people were looking at them, and that one or two women were staring at her critically. They wanted to be where she was, she could tell. They wanted to be with Note.

He put her on the late bus after they had left the bar, and stood and waved to her as the bus drew away. She waved back and closed her eyes. She had a boyfriend now, a jazz musician, and she would be seeing him again on Friday night, when the band was playing at the Gaborone Club. Members of the band, he said, always took their girlfriends, and she would meet some interesting people there.

And that is where Note Mokoti proposed to Precious Ramotswe

and where she accepted him, in a curious sort of way, without saying anything. It was after the band had finished and they were sitting outside in the darkness, away from the noise of the drinkers in the bar. He said, 'I want to get married soon and I want to get married to you. You are a nice girl who will do very well for a wife.'

Precious said nothing, because she was uncertain, and her silence was taken as assent.

'I will speak to your father about this,' said Note. 'I hope that he is not an old-fashioned man who will want a lot of cattle for you.'

He was, but she did not say so. She had not agreed yet, she thought, but perhaps it was now too late.

Then Note said, 'Now that you are going to be my wife, I must teach you what wives are for.'

She said nothing. This is what happened, she supposed. This is how men were, just as her friends at school had told her.

He put his arm round her and moved her back against the soft grass. They were in the shadows, and there was nobody nearby, just the noise of the drinkers shouting and laughing. He started to kiss her, on her neck, her cheek, her lips, and all she heard was the thudding of her heart and her shortened breath.

He said, 'Girls must learn this thing. Has anybody taught you?'

She shook her head. She had not learned and now, she felt, it was too late. She would not know what to do.

'I am glad,' he said. 'I knew straight away that you were a virgin, which is a very good thing for a man. But now things will change. Right now. Tonight.'

He hurt her. She asked him to stop, but he put her head back and hit her once across the cheek. Then he immediately kissed her where the blow had struck, and said that he had not meant to do it. All the time he was pushing against her and scratching at her, sometimes across her back, with his fingernails. Then he moved her over, and he hurt her again, and struck her across her back with his belt.

She sat up and gathered her crumpled clothes together. She was concerned that somebody might see them.

She dressed, and as she put on her blouse, she started to weep, quietly, because she was thinking of her father, whom she would see tomorrow on his verandah, who would tell her the cattle news, and who would never imagine what had happened to her that night.

Note Mokoti visited her father three weeks later, by himself, and asked him for Precious. Obed said he would speak to his daughter, which he did when she came to see him next. He sat on his stool and looked up at her and said to her that she would never have to marry anybody she did not want to marry. Those days were over, long ago. Nor should she feel that she had to marry at all; a woman could be by herself these days.

She could have said no at this point, which is what her father wanted her to say. But she did not want to say that. She lived for her meetings with Note Mokoti. She wanted to marry him. He was not a good man, she could tell that, but she might change him. And, when all was said and done, there remained those dark moments of contact, those pleasures he snatched from her, which were addictive. She wanted to be with him, wanted him to possess her. And of course she sensed that she was pregnant. It was too early to tell, but she felt that Note Mokoti's child was within her; a tiny, fluttering bird, deep inside her.

THEY MARRIED on a Saturday afternoon, at three o'clock, in the church at Mochudi. It was late October and the heat was at its worst.

The Reformed Church minister married them, gasping in his clerical black, mopping at his brow with a large red handkerchief.

He said, 'You are being married here in God's sight. God places upon you certain duties. God looks after us and keeps us in this cruel world. God loves His children, but we must remember those duties He asks of us. Do you young people understand what I am saying?'

Note smiled. 'I understand.'

And, turning to Precious, 'And do you understand?' She looked up into the minister's face—the face of her father's friend. She knew that her father had spoken to him about this marriage and about how unhappy he was about it, but the minister had said that he was unable to intervene. Now his tone was gentle, and he pressed her hand as he took it to place in Note's. As he did so, the child moved within her, and she winced because the movement was so sudden and so firm.

AFTER TWO DAYS in Mochudi, where they stayed in the house of a cousin of Note's, they packed their possessions into the back of a truck and went down to Gaborone. Note had found somewhere to stay—two rooms and a kitchen in somebody's house near Tlokweng. It was a luxury to have two rooms: one was their bedroom, furnished with a double mattress and an old wardrobe; the other was a living room and dining room, with a table, two chairs and a sideboard. The yellow curtains from her room at the cousin's house were hung up in this room and they made it bright and cheerful.

Note kept his trumpet there and his collection of tapes. He would practise for twenty minutes at a time, and then, while his lip was resting, he would listen to a tape and pick out the rhythms on a guitar. He knew all about township music—where it came from, who sang what, who played which part with whom. He had heard the greats, too: Hugh Masikela on the trumpet, Dollar Brand on the piano, Spokes Machobane singing; he had heard them in person in Johannesburg, and knew every recording they had ever made.

She watched him take the trumpet from its case and fit the mouthpiece. She watched as he raised it to his lips and then, so suddenly, from that tiny cup of metal against his flesh, the sound would burst out like a glorious, brilliant knife dividing the air. And the little room would reverberate and the flies, jolted out of their torpor, would buzz round and round as if riding the swirling notes.

She went with him to the bars, and he was kind to her, but he seemed to get caught up in his own circle and she felt that he did not really want her there. There were people there who thought of nothing but music; they talked endlessly about music, music, music; how much could one say about music? They didn't want her there either, she thought, and so she stopped going to the bars and stayed at home.

He came home late and he smelt of beer when he returned. It was a sour smell, like rancid milk, and she turned her head away as he pushed her down on the bed and pulled at her clothing.

'You have had a lot of beer. You have had a good evening.'

He looked at her, his eyes slightly out of focus.

'I can drink if I want to. You're one of these women who stays at home and complains. Is that what you are?'

'I am not. I only meant to say that you had a good evening.'

But his indignation would not be assuaged, and he said, 'You are making me punish you, woman. You are making me do this to you.'

She cried out, and tried to struggle, to push him away, but he was too strong for her.

'Don't hurt the baby.'

'Baby! Why do you talk about this baby? It is not mine. I am not the father of any baby.'

MALE HANDS AGAIN, but this time in thin rubber gloves that made the hands pale and unfinished, like a white man's hands.

'Do you feel any pain here? No? And here?'

She shook her head.

'I think that the baby is all right. And up here, where these marks are. Is there pain just on the outside, or is it deeper in?'

'It is just the outside.'

'I see. I am going to have to put in stitches all the way across, because the skin has parted. I'll spray something on to take the pain away but maybe it's better for you not to watch me while I'm sewing! Some people say men can't sew, but we doctors aren't too bad at it!'

She closed her eyes. There was cold spray against her skin and then a numbness as the doctor worked on the wound.

'This was your husband's doing? Am I right?'

She opened her eyes. The doctor had finished the suture and had handed something to the nurse. He was looking at her now as he peeled off the gloves.

'How many times has this happened before?'

'I don't know.'

'I suppose you're going to go back to him?'

She opened her mouth to speak, but he interrupted her.

'Of course you are. It's always the same. The woman goes back for more.' He sighed. 'I'll probably see you again, you know. But I hope I don't. Just be careful.'

SHE WENT BACK home the next day, a scarf tied round her face to hide the bruises and the cuts. She ached in her arms and in her stomach, and the sutured wound stung sharply. They had given her pills at the hospital, and she had taken one just before she left on the bus. This seemed to help the pain, and she took another on the journey.

The door was open. She went in, her heart thumping within her chest, and saw what had happened. The room was empty. He had taken his tapes, and their new trunk, and the yellow curtains too. And in the bedroom, he had slashed the mattress with a knife, and there was kapok lying about, making it look like a shearing room.

She sat down on the bed and was still sitting there, staring at the floor, when the neighbour came in and said that she would get somebody to take her in a truck back to Mochudi, to Obed, to her father.

There she stayed, looking after her father, for the next fourteen years. He died shortly after her thirty-fourth birthday, and that was the point at which Precious Ramotswe, now parentless, veteran of a nightmare marriage, and mother, for a brief and lovely five days, became the first lady private detective in Botswana.

What You Need to Open a Detective Agency

Mma Ramotswe had thought that it would not be easy to open a detective agency. People always made the mistake of thinking that starting a business was simple and then found that there were all sorts of hidden problems and unforeseen demands.

She went to the lawyer at Pilane, who had arranged for her to get her father's money. He had organised the sale of the cattle and had got a good price for them. She took the cheque and the sheet of paper that he handed her. It was more than she had imagined possible. But there it was—all that money, made payable to Precious Ramotswe, on presentation to Barclays Bank of Botswana.

'You can buy a house with that,' said the lawyer. 'And a business.'

'I am going to buy both of those.'

The lawyer looked interested. 'What sort of business? A store? I can give you advice, you know.'

'A detective agency.'

The lawyer looked blank. 'There are none of those for sale.'

'I know that. I am going to have to start from scratch.'

The lawyer winced. 'It's easy to lose money in business,' he said. 'Especially when you don't know anything about what you're doing.' He stared at her hard. 'And, anyway, can women be detectives?'

'Why not?' said Mma Ramotswe. She had heard that people did not like lawyers, and now she thought she could see why. This man was so certain of himself, so utterly convinced. What had it to do with him what she did? It was her money, her future. And how dare he say that about women, when he didn't even know that his zip was half undone! Should she tell him?

'Women are the ones who know what's going on,' she said. 'They are the ones with eyes. Have you not heard of Agatha Christie?'

The lawyer looked taken aback. 'Agatha Christie? Of course I know her. Yes, that is true. A woman sees more than a man sees.'

'So,' said Mma Ramotswe, 'when people see a sign saying "No.1 Ladies' Detective Agency", what will they think? They'll think those ladies will know what's going on. They're the ones.'

The lawyer stroked his chin. 'Maybe.'

'Yes,' said Mma Ramotswe. 'Maybe.' Adding, 'Your zip, rra. I think you may not have noticed . . .'

SHE FOUND THE HOUSE first, on a corner plot in Zebra Drive. It was expensive, and she decided to take out a bond on part of it, so that she could afford to buy somewhere for the business too. That was more difficult, but at last she found a small place near Kgale Hill, on the edge of town, where she could set up. It was a good place, because a lot of people walked down that road every day and would see the sign. Everybody would soon know about her.

The building she bought had originally been a general dealer's shop, but had been converted into a dry-cleaner's and finally a bottle store. For a year or so it had lain empty, and had been lived in by squatters. The owner had eventually returned from Francistown and had driven out the squatters and placed the dejected-looking building on the market. When Mma Ramotswe had offered cash, the seller had leapt at her offer and she received the deeds within days.

There was a lot to do. A builder was called in to replace the damaged plaster and to repair the tin roof. Then Mma Ramotswe set to the task of painting, and she had soon completed the outside in ochre and the inside in white. She bought fresh yellow curtains for the windows and, in an unusual moment of extravagance, splashed out on a brand-new office set of two desks and two chairs. Her friend, Mr J. L. B. Matekoni, proprietor of Tlokweng Road Speedy Motors, brought her an old typewriter that was surplus to his own requirements, and with that the office was ready to open—once she had a secretary.

This was the easiest part of all. A telephone call to the Botswana College of Secretarial and Office Skills brought an immediate response. They had just the woman, they said. Mma Makutsi had just passed their general typing and secretarial examinations with an average grade of ninety-seven per cent; she would be ideal.

Mma Ramotswe liked her immediately. She was a thin woman with a rather long face and braided hair into which she had rubbed copious quantities of henna. She wore oval glasses with wide plastic frames, and she had a fixed, but apparently quite sincere smile.

They opened the office on a Monday. Mma Ramotswe sat at her desk and Mma Makutsi sat at hers, behind the typewriter. She looked at Mma Ramotswe and smiled even more broadly.

'I am ready for work,' she said. 'I am ready to start.'

'Mmm,' said Mma Ramotswe. 'It's early days yet. We've only just opened. We will have to wait for a client to come.'

In her heart of hearts, she knew there would be no clients. The whole idea was a ghastly mistake. Nobody wanted a private detective, and certainly nobody would want her. Who was she, after all? She was just Precious Ramotswe from Mochudi.

At ten o'clock Mma Makutsi got up from her desk and went into the back room to make the tea. She had been asked to make bush tea, which was Mma Ramotswe's favourite, and she soon brought two cups back. She had a tin of condensed milk in her handbag, and she took this out and poured a small amount into each cup. Then they drank their tea, watching a small boy at the edge of the road throwing stones at a skeletal dog.

At eleven o'clock they had another cup of tea, and at twelve Mma Ramotswe rose to her feet and announced that she was going to walk down the road to the shops to buy herself some perfume. Mma Makutsi was to stay behind and welcome any clients who might come. Mma Ramotswe smiled as she said this. There would be no clients, of course, and she would be closed at the end of the month.

Mma Ramotswe was standing at the counter of the shop looking at a bottle of perfume when Mma Makutsi hurtled through the door.

'Mma Ramotswe,' she panted. 'There is a client in the office. It is a big case. A missing man. Come quickly. There is no time to lose.'

THE WIVES of missing men are all the same, thought Mma Ramotswe. At first they feel anxiety, and are convinced that something dreadful has happened. Then doubt begins to creep in, and they wonder whether he's gone off with another woman (which he usually has), and then finally they become angry. At the anger stage, most of them don't want him back any more, even if he's found. They just want to have a good chance to shout at him.

Mma Malatsi is in the second stage, she thought. She has begun to suspect that he is off somewhere having a good time, while she's left at home, and of course it's beginning to rankle.

'Maybe you should tell me a little bit more about your husband,' she said, as Mma Malatsi began to drink the cup of strong bush tea that Mma Makutsi had brewed for her.

'His name is Peter Malatsi,' Mma Malatsi said. 'He's forty and he has—had—has a business selling furniture. It's a good business and he has done well. So he hasn't run away from any creditors.'

Mma Ramotswe nodded. 'There must be another reason,' she began, and then, cautiously, 'You know what men are like, mma. What about another woman? Do you think . . .?'

Mma Malatsi shook her head vigorously.

'I don't think so,' she said. 'Maybe a year ago that would have been possible, but then he became a Christian and took up with some church that was always singing and marching around the place.'

Mma Ramotswe noted this down. *Church. Singing. Got religion badly? Lady preacher lured him away?*

'Who were these people?' she said. 'Maybe they know something?'

Mma Malatsi shrugged. 'I'm not sure,' she said, slightly irritably. 'In fact, I don't know. He asked me to come with him once or twice, but I refused. So he just used to go off by himself on Sundays. In fact, he disappeared on a Sunday. I thought he'd gone off to his church.'

Mma Ramotswe looked at the ceiling. Peter Malatsi had gone off with one of the Christians; that was pretty clear. All she had to do now was find which group it was and she would be on his trail.

BY THE END of the following day, Mma Ramotswe had compiled a list of five Christian groups which could fit the description. Over the next two days she tracked down the leaders of three of them and was satisfied that nothing was known of Peter Malatsi.

When she located the leader of the fourth group, the Reverend Shadreck Mapeli, she knew that the search was over. When she mentioned the Malatsi name, the reverend gave a shudder.

'Are you from the police?' he asked. 'Are you a policeman?'

'Policewoman,' she said.

'Ah!' he said mournfully. 'Aee!'

'I mean, I'm not a policewoman,' she said quickly. 'I'm a private detective.'

The reverend appeared to calm down slightly. 'Who sent you?'

'Mma Malatsi.'

'Ooh,' said the reverend. 'He told us that he had no wife.'

'Well, he does,' said Mma Ramotswe. 'And she's been wondering where he is.'

'He's dead,' said the Reverend. 'He's gone to the Lord.'

Mma Ramotswe sensed that he was telling the truth. Now all that remained to be done was to find out how he had died.

'You must tell me,' she said. 'I won't reveal your name to anybody if you don't want me to. Just tell me how it happened.'

They drove to the river in Mma Ramotswe's tiny white van. It was the rainy season, and there had been several storms, which made the track almost impassable. But at last they reached the river's edge and parked the van under a tree.

'This is where we have our baptisms,' said the reverend, pointing to a pool in the swollen waters of the river. 'This is where I stood, here, and this is where the sinners entered the water.'

'How many sinners did you have?' asked Mma Ramotswe.

'Six sinners altogether, including Peter. They all went in together, while I prepared to follow them with my staff.'

'Yes?' said Mma Ramotswe. 'Then what happened?'

'The sinners were standing in the water up to about here.' The reverend indicated his upper chest. 'I turned round to tell the flock to start singing, and then when I turned back I noticed that there was something wrong. There were only five sinners in the water.'

'One had disappeared?'

'Yes,' he said. 'God had taken one of them to His bosom.'

Mma Ramotswe looked at the water. It was not a big river, and for much of the year it was reduced to a few stagnant pools. But in a good rainy season, such as that year's, it could be quite a torrent. A non-swimmer could easily be swept away, she reflected, and yet, if somebody were to be swept away the body would surely be found downstream. The police would have been called. She thought for a moment. There was another explanation, and it made her shiver.

'You didn't tell the police,' she said. 'Why not?'

The reverend looked down at the ground.

'I know I should have told them. God will punish me for it. But I was worried that I would be blamed for poor Peter's accident and I thought they would take me to court. They might make me pay damages for it and that would drive the church into bankruptcy and put a stop to God's work.' He paused. 'Do you understand why I kept quiet and told all the flock not to say anything?'

Mma Ramotswe nodded and touched the reverend on the arm.

'I do not think that what you did was bad,' she said. 'I'm sure that God wanted you to continue and he will not be angry. It was not your fault.'

The reverend raised his eyes and smiled.

'Those are kind words, my sister. Thank you.'

THAT AFTERNOON, Mma Ramotswe asked her neighbour if she could borrow one of his dogs. He had a pack of five, and she hated every one of them for their incessant barking.

'I need a dog to help me on one of my cases,' she explained. 'I'll bring him back safe and sound.'

The neighbour was flattered to have been asked.

'I'll give you this dog here,' he said. 'It's the senior dog and he has a very good nose. He will make a good detective dog.'

Mma Ramotswe took the dog warily. It was a large yellow creature, with a curious, offensive smell. That night, just after sunset, she put it in the back of her van, tying its neck to a handle with string. Then she set off down the track to the river, her headlights picking out the shapes of the thorn trees in the darkness. In a strange way, she felt glad of the company of the dog, unpleasant though it was.

Now, beside the pool in the river, she took a thick stake from the van and drove it into the soft ground near the water's edge. Then she fetched the dog, led it down to the pool and tied its string firmly to the stake. From a bag she had with her, she took out a large bone and put it in front of the yellow dog's nose. The animal gave a grunt of pleasure and immediately settled down to gnaw the bone.

Mma Ramotswe waited just a few yards away, a blanket tucked round her legs to keep off the mosquitoes, and her old rifle over her knees. Two hours passed. The mosquitoes were bad and her skin itched, but this was work and she never complained when she was working. Then, suddenly, there came a growling noise from the dog. Mma Ramotswe strained her eyes in the darkness. She could just make out the shape of the dog, and she could see that it was standing now, looking towards the water. The dog growled again, and gave a bark. Mma Ramotswe tossed the blanket off her knees and picked up the powerful torch at her side. Just a little bit longer, she thought.

There was a noise from the water's edge, and Mma Ramotswe knew now that it was time to switch on her torch. As the beam came on, she saw, just at the edge of the water, its head turned towards the cowering dog, a large crocodile.

The crocodile's eyes were fixed on the dog and it was edging slowly towards its quarry. Mma Ramotswe raised the rifle to her shoulder and saw the side of the crocodile's head framed perfectly in her sights. She pulled the trigger.

When the bullet struck the crocodile, it gave a great leap and landed on its back, half in the water, half out. For a moment or two it twitched and then was still. It had been a perfectly placed shot.

Mma Ramotswe noticed that she was trembling as she put the rifle down. Her Daddy had taught her to shoot and he had done it well, but she did not like to shoot animals.

She took a knife and slit through the creature's belly. The leather was soft, and the stomach's contents were soon exposed. Inside there were pebbles, which the crocodile used for digesting its food, and several pieces of foul-smelling fish. But she was more interested in the bangles and rings and wristwatch she found, each of them the evidence of the crocodile's sinister appetites.

'IS THIS YOUR husband's property?' she asked Mma Malatsi, handing her the wristwatch she had claimed from the crocodile's stomach.

Mma Malatsi took the watch and looked at it. She was extraordinarily calm. 'Well, at least I know that he's with the Lord,' she said. 'And that's much better than knowing that he's in the arms of some other woman, isn't it?'

Mma Ramotswe nodded. 'I think it is,' she said.

'Were you married, mma?' asked Mma Malatsi. 'Do you know what it is like to be married to a man?'

Mma Ramotswe looked out of the window. There was a thorn tree outside, but beyond that she could see the boulder-strewn hill.

'I had a husband,' she said. 'Once I had a husband. He played the trumpet. He made me unhappy and now I am glad that I no longer have a husband.' She paused. 'I'm sorry. I did not mean to be rude. You've lost your husband and you must be very sorry.'

'A bit,' said Mma Malatsi. 'But then I have lots to do.'

Mma Makutsi Deals with the Mail

The success of the first case heartened Mma Ramotswe. She had now sent off for, and received, a manual on private detection and was going through it chapter by chapter, taking copious notes. She had made no mistakes in that first case, she thought. She had found out what information there was to be had by a simple process of listing the likely sources and seeking them out. Provided that one was methodical, there was hardly any way in which one could go wrong.

Then she had had a hunch about the crocodile and had followed it up. Again, the manual endorsed this as an acceptable practice. 'Don't disregard a hunch,' it advised. 'Hunches are another form of knowledge.' Mma Ramotswe had liked that phrase and had mentioned it to Mma Makutsi. Her secretary had listened carefully, and then typed the sentence out on her typewriter and handed it to Mma Ramotswe.

Mma Makutsi was pleasant company and could type quite well.

She had typed out a report which Mma Ramotswe had dictated on the Malatsi case and also the bill for sending to Mma Malatsi. But apart from that she had not really been called on to do anything else and Mma Ramotswe wondered whether the business could really justify employing a secretary. And yet one had to. What sort of private detective agency had no secretary?

Mma Makutsi had the mail to open, of course. There was no mail for the first three days. On the fourth day, a catalogue was received, and a property tax demand, and on the fifth day a letter that was intended for the previous owner.

Then, at the beginning of the second week, she opened a dirty white envelope and read the letter out to Mma Ramotswe.

Dear Mma Ramotswe

I read about you in the newspaper and about how you have opened this big new agency in town. I am very proud for Botswana that we now have a person like you in this country.

I am the teacher at the small school at Katsana village, thirty miles from Gaborone. My wife and I have two daughters and we have a son of eleven. This boy to whom I am referring has recently vanished and has not been seen for two months.

We went to the police. They made a big search and asked questions everywhere. Nobody knew anything about our son. I took time off from the school and searched the land around our village. He was a boy who liked to wander, because he had a strong interest in nature. He was always collecting rocks and things. He knew a lot about the bush and he would never get into danger from stupidity. There are no leopards in these parts and we are too far away from the Kalahari for lions to come.

I went everywhere, calling, calling, but my son never answered me. I looked in every well of every farmer and village nearby and asked them to check the water. But there was no sign of him. How can a boy vanish off the face of the earth like this? If I were not a Christian, I would say that some evil spirit had lifted him up and carried him off. But I know that things like that do not really happen.

I am not a wealthy man. I cannot afford the services of a private detective, but I ask you, mma, to help me in one small way. When you are making your enquiries about other things, please ask people if they have heard anything about a boy

called Thobiso, aged eleven, who is the son of the teacher at Katsana. Please just ask them, and if you hear anything at all, please address a note to the undersigned, myself, the teacher.
In God's name,
Ernest Molai Pakotati, Dip. Ed.

Mma Makutsi stopped reading and looked at Mma Ramotswe. For a moment, neither spoke. Then Mma Ramotswe broke the silence.

'Do you know anything about this?' she asked. 'Have you heard anything about a boy going missing?'

Mma Makutsi frowned. 'I think so. I think there was something in the newspaper about a search for a boy.'

Mma Ramotswe rose to her feet and took the letter from her secretary. She held it as one might hold an exhibit in court—gingerly, so as not to disturb the evidence. It felt to her as if the letter—a mere scrap of paper, so light in itself—was weighted with pain.

'I don't suppose there's much I can do,' she said quietly. 'Of course I can keep my ears open. I can tell the poor Daddy that, but what else can I do? He will know the bush around Katsana. He will know the people. I can't really do very much for him.'

'No,' Mma Makutsi said. 'We can't help that poor man.'

A letter was dictated by Mma Ramotswe, and Mma Makutsi typed it carefully. Then it was sealed in an envelope, a stamp stuck on the outside, and it was placed in the new red out-tray. It was the second letter to leave the No.1 Ladies' Detective Agency, the first being Mma Malatsi's bill for two hundred and fifty pula.

THAT EVENING, in the house in Zebra Drive, Mma Ramotswe prepared herself a meal of stew and pumpkin. She loved standing in the kitchen, stirring the pot, thinking over the events of the day, sipping at a large mug of bush tea. Several things had happened that day, apart from the arrival of the letter. A man had come in with a query about a bad debt and she had reluctantly agreed to help him recover it. Then there had been a visit from a woman who was concerned about her husband.

'He comes home smelling of perfume,' she said. 'And smiling too. Why would a man come home smelling of perfume and smiling?'

'Perhaps he is seeing another woman,' ventured Mma Ramotswe.

The woman had looked at her aghast.

'Do you think he would do that? My husband?'

They had discussed the situation and it was agreed that the woman would tackle her husband on the subject.

'It's possible that there is another explanation,' said Mma Ramotswe reassuringly.

'Such as?'

'Well . . .'

'Many men wear perfume these days,' offered Mma Makutsi. 'They think it makes them smell good. You know how men smell.'

The client had turned in her chair and stared at Mma Makutsi.

'My husband does not smell,' she said. 'He is a very clean man.'

Mma Ramotswe had thrown Mma Makutsi a warning look. She would have to have a word with her about keeping out of the way when clients were there.

But whatever else had happened that day, her thoughts kept returning to the teacher's letter and the missing boy. How the poor man must have fretted—and the mother, too. What thoughts would have been in their minds as each hour went past with no sign of the boy, and all the time he could be in danger, stuck in an old mine shaft, perhaps, too hoarse to cry out any more while rescuers beat about above him. Or stolen perhaps—whisked away by somebody in the night. What cruel heart could do such a thing to an innocent child? That such things could happen in Botswana made her shiver with dread.

She began to wonder whether this was the right job for her after all. It was all very well thinking that one might help people to sort out their difficulties, but then these difficulties could be heart-rending. The Malatsi case had been an odd one. She had expected Mma Malatsi to be distraught when she showed her the evidence that her husband had been eaten by a crocodile, but she had not seemed at all put out. What had she said? 'But then I have lots to do.' What an extraordinary, unfeeling thing for somebody to say when she had just lost her husband. Did she not value him more than that?

When people were unmoved in that way, Mma Christie expected the reader to be suspicious. What would Mma Christie have thought if she had seen Mma Malatsi's cool reaction? She would have thought: This woman killed her husband! That's why she's unmoved by the news of his death. She knew all along that he was dead!

But what about the crocodile and the baptism, and the other sinners? No, she must be innocent. Perhaps she wanted him dead, and then her prayer was answered by the crocodile.

She stopped. It was time to take the pumpkin out of the pot and eat it. In the final analysis, that was what solved these big problems of life. You could think and think and get nowhere, but you still had to eat your pumpkin. That brought you down to earth. That gave you a reason for going on. Pumpkin.

A Conversation with Mr J. L. B. Matekoni

The books did not look good. At the end of the first month of its existence, the No.1 Ladies' Detective Agency was making a convincing loss. There had been three paying clients and two who came for advice, received it and declined to pay. Mma Malatsi had paid her bill for two hundred and fifty pula; Happy Bapetsi had paid two hundred pula for the exposure of her false father; and a local trader had paid one hundred pula to find out who was using his telephone to make unauthorised long-distance calls to Francistown. If one added this up it came to five hundred and fifty pula; but then Mma Makutsi's wages were five hundred and eighty pula a month. This meant that there was a loss of thirty pula, without even taking into account other overheads, such as the cost of petrol and electricity.

Of course, businesses took some time to get established. But how long could one go on at a loss? She had a certain amount of money left over from her father's estate, but she could not live on that for ever.

She thought of Mr J. L. B. Matekoni, proprietor of Tlokweng Road Speedy Motors. Now there was a business that would be making a profit. There was no shortage of customers, as everybody knew what a fine mechanic he was. That was the difference between them, she thought; he knew what he was doing, whereas she did not.

Mma Ramotswe had known Mr J. L. B. Matekoni for years. He came from Mochudi, and his uncle had been a close friend of her father. Mr J. L. B. Matekoni was forty-five—ten years older than Mma Ramotswe—but he regarded himself as being a contemporary and often said, 'For people of our age . . .'

He was a comfortable man, and she wondered why he had never married. He was not handsome, but he had an easy, reassuring face. He would have been the sort of husband that any woman would have liked to have had about the house. He would fix things and stay in at night and perhaps even help with some of the domestic chores—something that so few men would ever dream of doing. But he had remained single and lived alone in a large house near the old airfield.

She liked to call on him at the garage and talk to him in his office with its piles of receipts and orders for spare parts. She liked to drink tea from one of his mugs with the greasy fingerprints on the outside, while his two assistants raised cars on jacks and clattered and banged about underneath.

Mr J. L. B. Matekoni enjoyed these sessions too. They would talk about Mochudi, or politics, or just exchange the news of the day. But that day, when she went to see him, they talked about finances, and about the problems of running a paying business.

'Staff costs are the biggest item,' said Mr J. L. B. Matekoni. 'You see those two boys out there under that car? You've no idea what they cost me. Their wages, their taxes, the insurance to cover them if that car were to fall on their heads. It all adds up. And at the end of the day there are just one or two pula left for me. Never much more.'

'But at least you aren't making a loss,' said Mma Ramotswe. 'I'm thirty pula down on my first month's trading.'

Mr J. L. B. Matekoni sighed. 'Staff costs,' he said. 'That secretary of yours. That's where the money will be going.'

Mma Ramotswe nodded. 'I know,' she said. 'But you need a secretary if you have an office. If I didn't have a secretary, then I'd be stuck there all day. I couldn't come over here to talk to you.'

Mr J. L. B. Matekoni reached for his mug. 'You need a couple of big cases,' he said. You need somebody rich to give you a case. Somebody like . . . like Mr Patel, for example.'

'Why would he need a private detective?'

'Rich men have their problems,' said Mr J. L. B. Matekoni.

They lapsed into silence, watching the two young mechanics remove a wheel from the car on which they were working.

'I've been thinking,' said Mma Ramotswe. 'I had a letter the other day. It made me very sad, and I wondered whether I should be a detective after all.' She told him of the letter about the missing boy, and she explained how she had felt unable to help the father.

'I couldn't do anything for him,' she said. 'I'm not a miracle worker. But I felt so sorry for him. He thought that his son had fallen in the bush or been taken by some animal. How could a father bear that?'

Mr J. L. B. Matekoni snorted. 'I saw that in the paper,' he said. 'I read about the search and I knew it was hopeless from the beginning.'

'Why?' asked Mma Ramotswe.

'Because that boy's dead,' said Mr J. L. B. Matekoni.

Mma Ramotswe was silent. She imagined the father—the father of the dead boy—and for a moment she remembered that awful afternoon in Mochudi, at the hospital, when the nurse had come up to her, straightening her uniform, and she saw that the woman was crying. To lose a child, like that, was something that could end one's world. The stars went out. The moon disappeared. The birds became silent.

'Why do you say he's dead?' she asked. 'He could have got lost . . .'

Mr J. L. B. Matekoni shook his head. 'No,' he said. 'That boy would have been taken for witchcraft. He's dead now.'

She put her empty mug down on the table. Outside, in the workshop, a wheel brace was dropped with a loud, clanging sound.

She glanced at her friend. This was a subject that one did not talk about. This was the one subject which would bring fear to the most resolute heart. This was the great taboo.

'How can you be sure?'

Mr J. L. B. Matekoni smiled. 'Come on, now, Mma Ramotswe. You know as well as I do what goes on. We don't like to talk about it, do we? It's the thing we Africans are most ashamed of. We know it happens, but we pretend it doesn't. We know all right what happens to children who go missing. We know.'

She looked up at him. Of course he was telling the truth, because he was a truthful, good man. And he was probably right—the boy had been taken by a witch doctor and killed for medicine. Right there, in the midst of all that made Botswana a modern country, this thing had happened. The little boy had been killed because some powerful person somewhere had commissioned the witch doctor to make strengthening medicine for him.

She cast her eyes down. 'You may be right. That poor boy . . .'

'Of course I'm right,' he said. 'And why do you think that poor man had to write that letter to you? It's because the police will be doing nothing to find out how and where it happened. Because they're scared. They're just as scared as I am. Scared, Mma Ramotswe. Frightened for our lives. Every one of us—maybe even you.'

The Boyfriend

There were three quite exceptional houses in the country, and Mma Ramotswe felt some satisfaction that she had been invited to two of them. The best known of these was Mokolodi, a chateau-like building placed in the bush to the south of Gaborone. This house was probably the grandest establishment in the country, and was certainly more impressive than Phakadi House, to the north, which was rather too close to the sewage ponds for Mma Ramotswe's taste.

The third house could only be suspected of being a house of distinction, as very few people were invited to enter it, and Gaborone as a whole had to rely on what could be seen of the house from the outside—which was not much, as it was surrounded by a high white wall—or on reports from those who were summoned into the house for some special purpose.

'Like Buckingham Palace,' said one woman, who had been called to arrange flowers for some family occasion. 'Only rather better. I think that the Queen lives more simply than those people in there.'

The people in question were the family of Mr Paliwalar Sundigar Patel, the owner of eight stores—five in Gaborone and three in Francistown—a hotel in Orapa and a large outfitters in Lobatse. He was undoubtedly one of the wealthiest men in the country.

Mr Paliwalar Patel had come to Botswana in 1967, at the age of twenty-five. He had not had a great deal in his pocket then, but his father, a trader in Zululand, had advanced him the money to buy his first shop in the African Mall. This had been a great success. Trade blossomed and shop was added to shop. By his fiftieth birthday, he had stopped expanding his empire, and was concentrating on the improvement and education of his family.

There were four children—a son, Wallace, twin daughters, Sandri and Pali, and the youngest, a daughter called Nandira. Wallace had been sent to an expensive boarding school in Zimbabwe, in order to satisfy Mr Patel's ambition that he become a gentleman. He had been admitted to dental school, after a large donation by Mr Patel, and had then gone to Durban, where he set up a practice in cosmetic dentistry.

The twins had both been sent back to the Natal to meet husbands, which they had done in the manner expected by their father. Both sons-in-law had been taken into the business and were proving to have a good head for figures and a sound understanding of the importance of tight profit margins.

Then there was Nandira, who was now sixteen and a pupil at Maru-a-Pula School in Gaborone, the best and most expensive school in the country. She was bright academically, was consistently given glowing reports, and was expected to make a good marriage in the fullness of time—probably on her twentieth birthday, which Mr Patel had felt was precisely the right time for a girl to marry.

The entire family, including the sons-in-law, the grandparents and several distant cousins, lived in the Patel mansion which, in fact, was several houses linked together, all forming the family compound.

When the twins married, they were each given their own quarters, the house having been considerably expanded for the purpose. The sons-in-law were also each given a red Mercedes-Benz, with their initials on the driver's door.

MMA RAMOTSWE was delighted when she received the telephone call from Mr Patel asking her whether she could possibly call on him, in his house, some evening in the near future. They agreed upon that very evening, and she went home to change into a more formal dress before presenting herself at the gates of the Patel mansion.

You could not just push open the gate at the Patel house; nor could you park outside and hoot your horn, as everybody did with other houses. At the Patel house you pressed a bell in the wall, and a high-pitched voice issued from a small speaker above your head.

'Yes. Patel place here. What do you want?'

'Mma Ramotswe,' she said. 'Private . . .'

A crackling noise came from the speaker and the gate began to swing open. Mma Ramotswe had left her tiny white van round the corner, to keep up appearances, and so she entered the compound by foot. Inside, she found herself in a courtyard that had been transformed by shade netting into a grove of lush vegetation. At the far end of the courtyard was the entrance to the house itself, a large doorway flanked by tall white pillars and tubs of plants. Mr Patel appeared before the open door and waved to her with his walking stick.

She had seen Mr Patel before, of course, and knew that he had an artificial leg, but she had never seen him at really close quarters and had not expected him to be so small. Mma Ramotswe was not tall—being blessed with generous girth, rather than height—but Mr Patel still found himself looking up at her when he shook her hand and gestured for her to come inside.

'Have you been in my house before?' he asked, knowing, of course, that she had not.

'No,' she said simply. 'You have never asked me.'

'Oh dear,' he said, chuckling. 'I have made a big mistake.'

He led her through an entrance hall.

'We shall go through to my study,' he said.

The study was a large room, dominated by a huge desk on which there were three telephones and an elaborate pen and inkstand.

'Sit down, please,' said Mr Patel, pointing to a leather armchair.

Mma Ramotswe sank into the chair and looked at her host.

'I'll get straight to the point,' said Mr Patel. 'There's no point in beating about the bush, is there? No, there isn't.'

He paused, waiting for Mma Ramotswe's confirmation. She nodded her head slightly.

'I am a family man, Mma Ramotswe,' he said. 'I have a happy family who all live in this house, except for my son, who is a gentleman dentist in Durban. You may have heard of him.'

'I know of him,' said Mma Ramotswe. 'People speak highly of him, even here.'

Mr Patel beamed. 'Well, that's a very pleasing thing to be told. But my other children are also very important to me. I make no distinction between my children. They are all the same. Equal-equal.'

'That's the best way to do it,' said Mma Ramotswe. 'If you favour one, then that leads to a great deal of bitterness.'

'You can say that again, oh yes,' said Mr Patel. 'Children notice when their parents give two sweets to one and one to another.'

Mma Ramotswe nodded again, wondering where the conversation was leading.

'Now,' said Mr Patel. 'My big girls, the twins, are well married to good boys and are living here under this roof. That is all very excellent. And that leaves just one child, my little Nandira. She is sixteen and she is at Maru-a-Pula. She is doing well at school, but . . .'

He paused, looking at Mma Ramotswe through narrowed eyes. 'You know how things are with teenagers in these modern days?'

Mma Ramotswe shrugged. 'They are often trouble for parents.'

'That's what is happening,' Mr Patel said vehemently. 'And I will not have that. Not in my family.'

'What?' asked Mma Ramotswe. 'Teenagers?'

'Boys,' said Mr Patel bitterly. 'My Nandira is seeing some boy in secret. She denies it, but I know that there is a boy. And this cannot be allowed in this family—in this house. I have spoken to her about this,' he said. 'I told her that what other children are doing—that is their parents' business. But I have made it very clear that she is not to go about the town with boys or see boys after school. That is final.' He tapped his artificial leg lightly with his walking stick and then looked at Mma Ramotswe. 'I want you to find out who this boy is, and then I will speak to him.'

Mma Ramotswe stared at Mr Patel. Had he the remotest idea, she wondered, how young people behaved these days? She had heard about Indian fathers trying to arrange marriages, but she had never actually encountered such behaviour. And here was Mr Patel assuming that she would agree with him.

'Wouldn't it be better to speak to your daughter?' she asked gently. 'If you asked her who the young man was, then she might tell you.'

'Not at all,' Mr Patel said sharply, his voice becoming shrill. 'Not at all. I have already been asking her for three weeks, maybe four weeks. And she gives no answer. She is dumb insolent.'

Mma Ramotswe sat and looked down at her feet, aware of Mr Patel's expectant gaze upon her. She had decided to make it a principle of her professional life never to turn anybody away, unless they asked her to do something criminal. This rule appeared to be working; she had already found that her ideas about a request for help, about its moral rights and wrongs, had changed when she had become more aware of all the factors involved. It might be the same with Mr Patel; but even if it were not, who was she to condemn an anxious Indian father when she really knew very little about how these people ran their lives? She felt a natural sympathy for the girl, of course; what a terrible fate to have a father like this one, intent on keeping one in some sort of gilded cage.

She looked up. Mr Patel was watching her with his dark eyes, the tip of his walking stick tapping almost imperceptibly on the floor.

'I'll find out for you,' she said. 'Although I must say I don't really like doing this. I don't like the idea of watching a child.'

'But children must be watched!' expostulated Mr Patel. 'If parents don't watch their children, then what happens? You answer that!'

'There comes a time when they must have their own lives,' said Mma Ramotswe. 'We have to let go.'

'Nonsense!' shouted Mr Patel. 'Modern nonsense.'

Mma Ramotswe rose to her feet.

'I am a modern lady,' she said. 'So perhaps we have different ideas. But that has nothing to do with it. I have agreed to do as you have asked me. Now all that you need to do is to let me see a photograph of this girl, so that I can know who it is I am going to be watching.'

Mr Patel struggled to his feet. 'No need for a photograph,' he said. 'I can produce the girl herself. You can look at her.'

Mma Ramotswe raised her hands in protest. 'But then she will know me,' she said. 'I must be able to be unobserved.'

'Ah!' said Mr Patel. 'A very good idea. You detectives are very clever men.'

'Women,' said Mma Ramotswe.

Mr Patel looked at her sideways, but said nothing. He had no time for modern ideas.

As she left the house, Mma Ramotswe thought: He has four children; I have none. He is not a good father this man, because he loves his children too much—he wants to own them. You have to let go.

And she thought of that moment when, not even supported by Note, who had made some excuse, she had laid the tiny body of their premature baby into the earth and had looked up at the sky and wanted to say something to God, but couldn't because her throat was blocked with sobs and no words, nothing, would come.

ON THE DAY following her interview with Mr Patel, Mma Ramotswe parked the tiny white van in the school car park shortly before the final bell of the day sounded. The children came out in dribs and drabs, and it was not until shortly after twenty past three that Nandira walked out of the school entrance, carrying her school bag in one hand and a book in the other. She was by herself, and Mma Ramotswe was able to get a good look at her from the cab of her van. She was an attractive child, a young woman really; one of those sixteen-year-olds who could pass for nineteen, or even twenty.

She walked down the path and stopped briefly to talk to another girl, who was waiting for her parents to collect her. They chatted for a few minutes, and then Nandira walked off towards the school gates.

Mma Ramotswe waited a few moments, and then got out of the van. Once Nandira was out on the road, Mma Ramotswe followed her slowly. It had become clear to her that Nandira was not going directly home, as the Patel house was in the opposite direction to the route she had chosen. Nor was she going into town, which meant that she must be going to meet somebody at a house somewhere. Mma Ramotswe felt a glow of satisfaction. All she would probably have to do was to find the house and then it would be child's play to get the name of the owner, and the boy. It would be a very easily earned fee.

Nandira turned a corner. Mma Ramotswe held back before following her. It would be easy to become overconfident following a child, and she had to remind herself of the rules of pursuit. The manual on which she relied, *The Principles of Private Investigation* by Clovis Andersen, stressed that one should never crowd one's subject. 'Keep a long rein,' wrote Mr Andersen, 'even if it means losing the subject from time to time. You can pick up the trail later. And a few minutes of non-eye contact is better than an angry confrontation.'

Mma Ramotswe judged that it was now time to go round the corner. She did so, expecting to see Nandira several hundred yards down the road, but when she looked down it, the road was empty—non-eye contact, as Clovis Andersen called it, had set in. She turned round and looked in the other direction. There was a car in the distance, coming out of the driveway of a house, and nothing else.

Mma Ramotswe was puzzled. It was a quiet road, and there were not more than three houses on either side of it—at least in the direction in which Nandira had been going. If she has gone into one of the houses, thought Mma Ramotswe, then it must be one of the first two, as she would certainly not have been able to reach the houses further along the road. She stood still for a moment, then she made up her mind and walked up the driveway towards the front door of the first house on the right-hand side of the road.

When she knocked on the door, a dog started to bark loudly inside the house. Mma Ramotswe knocked again, and there came the sound of somebody silencing the dog. 'Quiet, Bison; quiet!' Then the door opened and a woman looked out at her. She was a West African, probably a Ghanaian, judging by the complexion and the dress.

'Hello, mma,' said Mma Ramotswe. 'I'm sorry to disturb you, but I'm looking for Sipho.'

The woman frowned. 'Sipho? There's no Sipho here.'

Mma Ramotswe shook her head.

'I'm sure it was this house. I'm one of the teachers from the secondary school, you see, and I need to get a message to one of the form-four boys. I thought that this was his house.'

The woman smiled. 'I've got two daughters,' she said. 'But no son.'

'Oh dear,' said Mma Ramotswe, sounding harassed. 'Is it the house over the road then?'

The woman shook her head. 'That's that Ugandan family,' she said. 'They've got a boy, but he's only six or seven, I think.'

Mma Ramotswe made her apologies and walked back down the driveway. She had lost Nandira on the very first afternoon, and she wondered whether the girl had deliberately shrugged her off. Could she possibly have known that she was being followed? This seemed most unlikely. Tomorrow she would be more careful.

At eight o'clock that night she received a telephone call from

Mr Patel. 'You have anything to report to me yet?' he asked.

Mma Ramotswe told him that she unfortunately had not been able to find out where Nandira went after school, but that she hoped that she might be more successful the following day.

'Not very good,' said Mr Patel. 'Not very good. Well, I at least have something to report to you. She came home three hours after school finished and told me that she had just been at a friend's house. I said: "What friend?" and she answered that I did not know her. *Her*. Then my wife found a note on the table, a note which our Nandira must have dropped. It said: "See you tomorrow, Jack." Now who is this Jack, then? Who is this person? Is that a girl's name, I ask you?'

'No,' said Mma Ramotswe. 'It sounds like a boy.'

'There!' said Mr Patel, with the air of one producing the elusive answer to a problem. 'That is the boy, I think. That is the one we must find. Jack who? Where does he live? You must tell me it all.'

Mma Ramotswe prepared herself a cup of bush tea and went to bed early. It had been an unsatisfactory day in more than one respect, and Mr Patel's crowing telephone call merely set the seal on it. So she lay in bed, the bush tea on her bedside table, and read the newspaper until her eyelids began to droop and she drifted off to sleep.

THE NEXT AFTERNOON she was late in reaching the school car park. She was beginning to wonder whether she had lost Nandira again when she saw the girl come out of the school, accompanied by another girl. Mma Ramotswe watched as the two of them walked down the path and stood at the school gate. They seemed deep in conversation with one another, in that exclusive way that teenagers have of talking to their friends, and Mma Ramotswe was sure that if only she could hear what was being said, then she would know the answers to more than one question. Girls talked about their boyfriends in an easy, conspiratorial way, and she was certain that this was the subject of conversation between Nandira and her friend.

Suddenly a blue car drew up opposite the two girls. Mma Ramotswe stiffened and watched as the driver leaned over the passenger seat and opened the front door. Nandira got in, and her friend got into the back. Mma Ramotswe started the engine of the little white van and pulled out of the school car park, just as the blue car drew away from the school. She followed at a safe distance, but ready to close the gap between them if there was any chance of losing them.

They drove past the Sun Hotel and made their way towards the mall. Shops, thought Mma Ramotswe. They're just going shopping; or are they? She had seen teenagers meeting one another after school in places like the Botswana Book Centre. They called it 'hanging around', she believed. Perhaps Nandira was going off to hang around with this Jack.

The blue car nosed into a parking place near the President Hotel. Mma Ramotswe parked several cars away and watched as the two girls got out of the car, accompanied by an older woman, presumably the mother of the other girl. She said something to her daughter, who nodded, and then walked off in the direction of the hardware stores.

Nandira and her friend walked past the steps of the President Hotel and then slowly made their way up to the post office. Mma Ramotswe followed them casually, stopping to look at a rack of African print blouses that a woman was displaying in the square.

'Buy one of these, mma,' said the woman. 'Very good blouses. They never run. Look, this one I'm wearing has been washed ten, twenty times, and hasn't run. Look.'

Mma Ramotswe looked at the woman's blouse—the colours had certainly not run. She glanced out of the corner of her eye at the two girls. They were looking in the shoe-shop window.

'You wouldn't have my size,' said Mma Ramotswe. 'I need a very big blouse.'

The trader checked her rack and then looked at Mma Ramotswe. 'You're right,' she said. 'You are too big for these blouses. Far too big.'

Mma Ramotswe smiled. 'But they are nice blouses, mma, and I hope you sell them to some nice small person.'

She moved on. The girls had finished with the shoe shop and were strolling up towards the book centre. Mma Ramotswe had been right; they were planning to hang about.

There were very few people in the Botswana Book Centre. Three or four men were paging through magazines and one or two people were looking at books.

Mma Ramotswe noticed that the two girls were at the far end of the shop, looking at a shelf of books in the Setswana section. What were they doing there? Nandira could be learning Setswana at school, but she would hardly be likely to be buying any of the schoolbooks or biblical commentaries that dominated that section. No, they must be waiting for somebody.

Mma Ramotswe walked purposefully to the African section and reached for a book. It was *The Snakes of Southern Africa*, and it was well illustrated. She gazed at a picture of a short brown snake and asked herself whether she had seen one of these. Her cousin had been bitten by a snake like that years ago, when they were children, and had come to no harm. Was that the snake? She looked at the text below the picture and read. It could well have been the same snake, because it was described as non-venomous and not at all aggressive.

Mma Ramotswe looked over at the girls. The snake book had so absorbed her that she had not been paying attention to them and now—where were they?—gone. They were gone.

She pushed the book back onto the shelf and rushed out into the square. She looked about her. There were some teenagers a little way away, but they were boys. She looked in the other direction. There was a man parking his bicycle under a tree and she noticed that the bicycle had a car aerial on it.

She set off in the direction of the President Hotel. Perhaps the girls had merely gone back to the car to rejoin the mother, in which case everything would be all right. But when she got to the car park, she saw the blue car going out at the other end, with just the mother in it. So the girls were still around, somewhere in the square.

Mma Ramotswe went back to the steps of the President Hotel and looked out over the square. She moved her gaze systematically—as Clovis Andersen recommended—looking at each group of people, scrutinising each knot of shoppers outside each shop window. There was no sign of the girls. She noticed the woman with the rack of blouses. She had a packet of some sort in her hand and was extracting what looked like a mopani worm from within it.

'Mopani worms?' asked Mma Ramotswe.

The woman turned round and looked at her.

'Yes.' She offered the bag to Mma Ramotswe, who helped herself to one of the dried tree worms and popped it into her mouth. It was a delicacy she simply could not resist.

'You must see everything that goes on, mma,' she said, as she swallowed the worm. 'Standing here like this.'

The woman laughed. 'I see everybody. Everybody.'

'Did you see two girls come out of the book centre?' asked Mma Ramotswe. 'One Indian girl and one African girl?'

The trader popped another worm into her mouth.

'I saw them,' she said. 'They went over to the cinema. Then they went off somewhere else. I didn't notice where they were going.'

Mma Ramotswe smiled. 'You should be a detective,' she said.

'Like you,' said the woman simply.

This surprised Mma Ramotswe. She was quite well known, but she had not necessarily expected a street trader to know who she was. She reached into her handbag and extracted a ten-pula note, which she pressed into the woman's hand.

'Thank you,' she said. 'That's a fee from me. And I hope you will be able to help me again some time.'

The woman seemed delighted.

'I am the eyes of this place,' she said. 'This morning, for example, do you want to know who was talking to who just over there?'

'Some other time,' said Mma Ramotswe. 'I'll be in touch.'

There was no point in trying to find where Nandira had got to now, but there was every point in following up the information that she already had. So she went to the cinema and enquired as to the time of that evening's performance, which is what she concluded the two girls had been doing. Then she returned to the tiny white van and drove home, to prepare herself for an early supper and an outing to the cinema. It had been at least a year since she had been to the cinema and she found that she was looking forward to the prospect.

THERE WERE few people in the cinema when Mma Ramotswe arrived. She chose a seat at the back. This gave her a good view of the door through which anybody entering the auditorium would have to pass.

Mma Ramotswe recognised several of the customers. Her butcher arrived shortly after she did, and he and his wife gave her a friendly wave. Then there was one of the teachers from the school and the woman who ran the aerobics class at the President Hotel. Finally there was the Catholic bishop, who arrived by himself and ate popcorn loudly in the front row.

Nandira arrived five minutes before the programme was about to start. She was by herself, and she stood for a moment in the door, looking around her. Mma Ramotswe felt her eyes rest on her, and she looked down quickly, as if inspecting the floor for something.

Nandira walked purposefully across the auditorium to Mma Ramotswe's row and sat down in the seat next to her.

'Good evening, mma,' she said politely. 'Is this seat taken?'

Mma Ramotswe looked up, as if surprised.

'There is nobody there,' she said. 'It is quite free.'

Nandira sat down. 'I am looking forward to this film,' she said pleasantly. 'I have wanted to see it for a long time.'

'Good,' said Mma Ramotswe. 'It is nice to see a film that you've always wanted to see.'

There was a silence. The girl was looking at her, and Mma Ramotswe felt quite uncomfortable. What would Clovis Andersen have done in such circumstances? This was where the subject crowded you, rather than the other way round.

'I saw you this afternoon,' said Nandira. 'At Maru-a-Pula.'

'Ah, yes,' said Mma Ramotswe. 'I was waiting for somebody.'

'Then I saw you in the book centre,' Nandira continued. 'You were looking at a book.'

'That's right,' said Mma Ramotswe. 'I was thinking of buying a book.'

'Then you asked Mma Bapitse about me,' Nandira said quietly. 'She's that trader. She told me that you were asking about me.'

Mma Ramotswe made a mental note to be careful of Mma Bapitse in the future.

'So, why are you following me?' asked Nandira.

Mma Ramotswe thought quickly. There was no point in denying it, so she told Nandira about her father's anxieties and how he had approached her.

'He wants to find out whether you're seeing boys,' she said. 'He's worried about it.'

Nandira looked pleased. 'Well, if he's worried, he's only got himself to blame if I keep going out with boys.'

'And are you?' asked Mma Ramotswe. 'Are you going out with lots of boys?'

Nandira hesitated. Then, quietly, 'No. Not really.'

'But what about this Jack?' asked Mma Ramotswe. 'Who's he?'

For a moment Nandira was silent. Here was another adult trying to pry into her private life, and yet there was something about Mma Ramotswe that she trusted. Perhaps she could be useful . . .

'Jack doesn't exist,' she said quietly. 'I made him up.'

'Why?'

Nandira shrugged. 'I want them—my family—to think I've got a boyfriend,' she said. 'I want them to think there's somebody I chose, not somebody they thought right for me.' She paused. 'Do you understand that?'

Mma Ramotswe thought for a moment. She felt sorry for this poor, overprotected girl, and imagined just how in such circumstances one might want to pretend to have a boyfriend.

'Yes,' she said, laying a hand on Nandira's arm. 'I understand.'

Nandira fidgeted with her watchstrap. 'Are you going to tell him?' she asked.

'Well, do I have much choice?' asked Mma Ramotswe. 'I can hardly say that I've seen you with a boy called Jack when he doesn't really exist.'

Nandira sighed. 'Well, I suppose I've asked for it. It's been a silly game.' She paused. 'But once he realises that there's nothing in it, do you think that he might let me have a bit more freedom?'

'I could try to persuade him,' said Mma Ramotswe. 'I don't know whether he'll listen to me. But I could try.'

'Please do,' said Nandira. 'Please try.'

They watched the film together, and both enjoyed it. Then Mma Ramotswe drove Nandira back in her tiny white van, and dropped her at the gate in the high white wall. The girl stood and watched as the van drove off, and then she turned and pressed the bell.

'Patel place here. What do you want?'

'Freedom,' she muttered under her breath, and then, more loudly, 'It's me, Papa. I'm home now.'

MMA RAMOTSWE telephoned Mr Patel early the next morning. She explained to him that it would be better for her to speak to him at home, rather than to explain matters over the telephone.

'You've got bad news for me,' he said, his voice rising. 'You are going to be telling me something bad-bad. Oh my God! What is it?'

Mma Ramotswe reassured him that the news was not bad, but she still found him looking anxious when she was shown into his study half an hour later.

'I am very worried,' he said. 'You will not understand a father's worries. A father feels a special sort of worry.'

Mma Ramotswe smiled reassuringly.

'The news is good,' she said. 'There is no boyfriend.'

'And what about this note?' he said. 'What about this Jack person? Is that all imagination?'

'Yes,' said Mma Ramotswe simply. 'Yes, it is.'

Mr Patel looked puzzled. He lifted his walking stick and tapped his artificial leg several times. Then he opened his mouth to speak, but said nothing.

'You see,' said Mma Ramotswe, 'Nandira has been inventing a social life for herself. She made up a boyfriend for herself just to bring a bit of . . . of freedom into her life. The best thing you can do is just to ignore it. Give her a bit more time to lead her own life. Don't keep asking her to account for her time. There's no boyfriend and there may not even be one for some time.'

Mr Patel closed his eyes and appeared deep in thought.

'Why should I do this?' he said after a while. 'Why should I give in to these modern ideas?'

Mma Ramotswe was ready with her answer. 'Because if you don't, then the imaginary boyfriend may turn into a real one. That's why.'

Mma Ramotswe watched him as he wrestled with her advice.

'You are a very clever woman,' he said. 'And I'm going to take your advice. I will leave her to get on with her life, and then I am sure that in two or three years she will agree with us and allow me to arra . . . to help her to find a suitable man to marry.'

'That could easily happen,' said Mma Ramotswe, breathing a sigh of relief.

'Yes,' said Mr Patel warmly. 'And I shall have you to thank for it all!'

MMA RAMOTSWE often thought about Nandira when she drove past the Patel compound. She expected to see her from time to time, but she never did, at least not until a year later, when, while taking her Saturday-morning coffee on the verandah of the President Hotel, she felt somebody tap her shoulder. She turned round in her seat, and there was Nandira, with a young man. The young man was about eighteen, she thought, and he had a pleasant, open expression.

'Mma Ramotswe,' said Nandira in a friendly way. 'I thought it was you.'

Mma Ramotswe shook Nandira's hand. The young man smiled.

'This is my friend,' said Nandira. 'I don't think you've met him.'

The young man held out his hand. 'Jack,' he said.

Big Car Guilt

It was three days after the satisfactory resolution of the Patel case. Mma Ramotswe had put in her bill for two thousand pula, plus expenses, and had been paid by return of post. This astonished her. She could not believe that she would be paid such a sum without protest, and the apparent cheerfulness with which Mr Patel had settled the bill induced pangs of guilt over the sheer size of the fee.

It was curious how some people had a highly developed sense of guilt, she thought, while others had none. Some people would agonise over minor slips or mistakes on their part, while others would feel quite unmoved by their own gross acts of betrayal or dishonesty. Mma Pekwane fell into the former category, thought Mma Ramotswe. Note Mokoti fell into the latter.

Mma Pekwane had seemed anxious when she had come into the office of the No.1 Ladies' Detective Agency. Mma Ramotswe had given her a strong cup of bush tea, as she always did with nervous clients, and had waited for her to be ready to speak.

'I'm worried that my husband has done a dreadful thing,' said Mma Pekwane eventually. 'I feel very ashamed for him.'

Mma Ramotswe nodded her head gently. Masculine bad behaviour.

'Men do terrible things,' she said. 'All wives are worried about their husbands. You are not alone.'

Mma Pekwane sighed. 'But my husband has done a terrible thing,' she said. 'A very terrible thing.'

Mma Ramotswe stiffened. If Rra Pekwane had killed somebody she would have to make it quite clear that the police should be called in. She would never dream of helping anybody conceal a murderer.

'What is this terrible thing?' she asked.

Mma Pekwane lowered her voice. 'He has a stolen car.'

Mma Ramotswe was relieved. Car theft was rife, almost unremarkable, and there must be many women driving around the town in their husbands' stolen cars.

'Did he tell you it's stolen?' she asked. 'Are you sure of it?'

Mma Pekwane shook her head. 'He said a man gave it to him. He said that this man had two Mercedes-Benz and only needed one.'

Mma Ramotswe laughed. 'Do men really think they can fool us that easily?' she said. 'Do they think we're fools?'

'I think they do,' said Mma Pekwane.

Mma Ramotswe looked at Mma Pekwane. 'Do you want me to tell you what to do?' she asked. 'Is that what you want?'

Mma Pekwane looked thoughtful. 'No,' she replied. 'I don't want that. I've decided what I want to do. I want to give the car back. I want to give it back to its owner.'

Mma Ramotswe sat up straight. 'You want to go to the police then?'

'No. I don't want to do that. I just want the car to get back to its owner without the police knowing. I want the Lord to know that the car's back where it belongs.'

Mma Ramotswe stared at her client. If the car were to be returned to the owner, then Mma Pekwane's conscience would be clear, and she would still have her husband. On reflection, it seemed to Mma Ramotswe to be a very good way of dealing with a difficult situation.

'But why come to me about this?' asked Mma Ramotswe. 'How can I help?'

'I want you to find out who owns that car,' Mma Pekwane said. 'Then I want you to steal it from my husband and give it back to the rightful owner. That's all I want you to do.'

LATER THAT EVENING, as she drove home in her tiny white van, Mma Ramotswe thought that she should never have agreed to help Mma Pekwane; but she had, and now she was committed. Yet it was not going to be a simple matter.

That evening, after her supper of chicken and pumpkin, Mma Ramotswe telephoned Mr J. L. B. Matekoni. 'Where do stolen Mercedes-Benz come from?' she asked.

'From over the border,' said Mr J. L. B. Matekoni. 'They steal them in South Africa, bring them over here, respray them, file off the original engine number, and then sell them cheaply or send them up to Zambia. I know who does all this, by the way. We all know.'

'I don't need to know that,' said Mma Ramotswe. 'What I need to know is how you identify them after all this has happened.'

Mr J. L. B. Matekoni paused. 'There's usually another serial number somewhere—on the chassis—or under the bonnet. You can usually find it if you know what you're doing.'

'You know what you're doing,' said Mma Ramotswe. 'Can you help me?'

Mr J. L. B. Matekoni sighed. He did not like stolen cars. He preferred to have nothing to do with them, but this was a request from Mma Ramotswe, and so there was only one answer to give.

'Tell me where and when,' he said.

THEY ENTERED the Pekwane yard the following evening, by arrangement with Mma Pekwane, who had promised that she would make sure that the dogs were inside and her husband would be busy eating a special meal she would prepare for him. So there was nothing to stop Mr J. L. B. Matekoni from wriggling under the Mercedes-Benz parked in the yard and flashing his torch up into the bodywork. Ten minutes later, he had a serial number written on a piece of paper and the two of them slipped out of the Pekwane yard and made their way to the small white van parked down the road.

'Are you sure that's all I'll need?' asked Mma Ramotswe. 'Will they know from that?'

'Yes,' said Mr J. L. B. Matekoni. 'They'll know.'

She dropped him off outside his gate and he waved goodbye in the darkness. She would be able to repay him soon, she knew.

THAT WEEKEND, Mma Ramotswe drove her tiny white van over the border to Mafikeng and went straight to the Railway Café. She bought a copy of the *Johannesburg Star* and sat at a table near the window reading the news. It was all bad, she decided, and so she laid the paper to one side and passed the time by looking at her fellow customers.

'Mma Ramotswe!'

She looked up. There he was, the same old Billy Pilani, older now, of course, but otherwise the same. She could just see him at the Mochudi Government Junior School, sitting at his desk, dreaming.

She bought him a cup of coffee and explained what she needed.

'I want you to find out who owns this car,' she said, passing the slip of paper with the serial number written on it. 'Then, when you've found out, I want you to tell the owner, or the insurance company, or whoever, that they can come up to Gaborone and they will find their car ready for them in an agreed place. All they have to do is to bring South African number plates with the original number on them. Then they can drive the car home.'

Billy Pilani looked surprised.

'All for nothing?' he asked. 'Nothing to be paid?'

'Nothing,' said Mma Ramotswe. 'It's just a question of returning property to its rightful owner. You believe in that, don't you, Billy?'

'Of course,' said Billy Pilani quickly. 'Of course.'

'And, Billy, I want you to forget you're a policeman while all this is going on. There's not going to be any arrest for you.'

'Not even a small one?' asked Billy in a disappointed tone.

'Not even that.'

BILLY PILANI telephoned the following day.

'I've got the details from our list of stolen vehicles,' he said. 'I've spoken to the insurance company, who've already paid out. So they'd be very happy to get the car back. They can send one of their men over the border to pick it up.'

'Good,' said Mma Ramotswe. 'They are to be in the African Mall in Gaborone at seven o'clock in the morning next Tuesday, with the number plates.'

Everything was agreed, and at five o'clock on the Tuesday morning, Mma Ramotswe crept into the yard of the Pekwane house and found the keys of the Mercedes-Benz lying on the ground outside the bedroom window, where Mma Pekwane had tossed them the previous night. She had been assured by Mma Pekwane that her husband was a sound sleeper and that he never woke up until Radio Botswana broadcast the sound of cowbells at six.

He did not hear her start the car and drive out onto the road, and indeed it was not until almost eight o'clock that he noticed that his Mercedes-Benz was stolen.

'Call the police,' shouted Mma Pekwane. 'Quick, call the police!'

She noticed that her husband was hesitating.

'Maybe later,' he said. 'In the meantime, I shall look for it myself.'

She looked him directly in the eye, and for a moment she saw him flinch. He's guilty, she thought. I was right all along. Of course he can't go to the police and tell them that his stolen car has been stolen.

She saw Mma Ramotswe later that day and thanked her.

'You've made me feel much better,' she said. 'I shall now be able to sleep at night without feeling guilty for my husband.'

'I'm very pleased,' said Mma Ramotswe. 'And maybe he's learned a lesson too. That lightning always strikes in the same place twice. Whatever people say to the contrary.'

Mma Ramotswe's House in Zebra Drive

The house had been built in 1968, when the town inched out from the shops and the Government buildings. It was on a corner site and Mma Ramotswe was fiercely proud of it. The yard was a large one, almost two-thirds of an acre, and it was well endowed with trees and shrubs. Then there were the purple bougainvilleas, which had been enthusiastically planted by the previous owners, and which had almost taken over by the time Mma Ramotswe came. She had to cut these back, to give space for her papaws and her pumpkins.

At the front of the house there was a verandah, which was her favourite place, and which was where she liked to sit in the mornings, when the sun rose, or in the evenings, before the mosquitoes came out. She had extended it by erecting an awning of shade netting supported by rough-hewn poles. This filtered out many of the rays of the sun and allowed plants to grow in the green light it created. There she had elephant's-ear and ferns, which she watered daily, and which made a lush patch of green against the brown earth.

Behind the verandah was the living room, the largest room in the house. There was a fireplace here, too large for the room, but a matter of pride for Mma Ramotswe. On the mantelpiece she had placed her special china, her Queen Elizabeth II teacup and her commemoration plate with the picture of Sir Seretse Khama, President, *Kgosi* of the Bangwato people, Statesman. He smiled at her from the plate, and it was as if he gave a blessing, as if he knew. As did the Queen, for she loved Botswana too, and understood.

But in pride of place was the photograph of her Daddy, taken just before his sixtieth birthday. He was wearing the suit that he had bought in Bulawayo on his visit to his cousin there, and he looked happy, although she knew that by then he was in pain. Mma Ramotswe was a realist, who inhabited the present, but one nostalgic thought she allowed herself, one indulgence, was to imagine her Daddy walking through the door and greeting her again, and saying: 'My Precious! You have done well! I am proud of you!' But she could not allow herself to think like this too often, for it ended in tears, for all that was past, and for all the love that she had within her.

The kitchen was cheerful. The cement floor, sealed and polished with red floor paint, was kept shining by Mma Ramotswe's maid, Rose, who had been with her for five years. Rose had four children and lived with her mother at Tlokweng. She worked for Mma Ramotswe, and did knitting for a knitting cooperative, and brought her children up with the little money that there was. Rose sang as she worked, and this was how Mma Ramotswe knew she had arrived in the morning, as snatches of song came drifting in from the kitchen.

HAPPINESS? Mma Ramotswe was happy enough. With her detective agency and her house in Zebra Drive, she had more than most, and was aware of it. She was also aware of how things had changed. When she had been married to Note Mokoti she had been conscious of a deep, overwhelming unhappiness that followed her round like a black dog. That had gone now.

If she had listened to her father she would never have married Note and the years of unhappiness would never have occurred. Obed

Ramotswe had never taken to Note, and had told her that, directly. But she had responded by crying and by saying that Note was the only man she would ever find and that he would make her happy.

'He will not,' said Obed. 'That man will hit you. He thinks only of himself and what he wants.'

She had shaken her head and rushed out of the room, and he had called out after her; a thin, pained, cry. She could hear it now, and it cut and cut at her. She had hurt the man who loved her more than any other. If only one could undo the past . . .

'If we could go back,' said Mr J. L. B. Matekoni, pouring tea into Mma Ramotswe's mug. 'I have often thought that. If we could go back and know then what we know now . . .' He shook his head in wonderment. 'My goodness! I would live my life differently!'

Mma Ramotswe sipped at her tea. She was sitting in the office of Tlokweng Road Speedy Motors, passing the time of day with her friend, as she sometimes did when her own office was quiet.

Mr J. L. B. Matekoni warmed to his theme. 'I have made hundreds of mistakes in my lifetime,' he said, frowning at the recollection.

She looked at him. She had thought that everything had gone rather well in his life. He had served his apprenticeship as a mechanic, saved up his money, and then bought his own garage. He had built a house, married a wife (who had unfortunately died), and become the local chairman of the Botswana Democratic Party. He knew several ministers (very slightly) and was invited to one of the annual garden parties at State House. Everything seemed rosy.

'I can't see what mistakes you've made,' she said. 'Unlike me.'

Mr J. L. B. Matekoni looked surprised. 'I can't imagine you making mistakes,' he said. 'You're too clever for that. You would look at all the possibilities and then choose the right one. Every time.'

Mma Ramotswe snorted. 'I married Note,' she said simply.

Mr J. L. B. Matekoni looked thoughtful.

'Yes,' he said. 'That was a bad mistake.'

They were silent for a moment. Then he rose to his feet. 'I would like you to marry me,' he said. 'That would not be a mistake.'

Mma Ramotswe hid her surprise. She did not give a start or drop her mug of tea. She smiled instead, and stared at her friend.

'You are a good kind man,' she said. 'You are like my Daddy . . . a bit. But I cannot get married again. Ever. I am happy as I am. I have got the agency, and the house. My life is full.'

Mr J. L. B. Matekoni sat down. He looked crestfallen, and Mma

Ramotswe reached out to touch him. He moved away instinctively, as a burnt man will move away from fire.

'I am very sorry,' she said. 'I should like you to know that if I were ever to marry anybody, which I shall not do, I would choose a man like you. I would even choose you. I am sure of this.'

Mr J. L. B. Matekoni took her mug and poured her more tea. He was silent now—not out of anger, or resentment—but because it had cost him all his energy to make his declaration of love and he had no more words for the time being.

Handsome Man

Alice Busang was nervous about consulting Mma Ramotswe, but was soon put at ease by the comfortable, traditionally built figure sitting behind the desk.

'I am suspicious of my husband,' she said. 'I think that he is carrying on with ladies.'

Mma Ramotswe nodded. All men carried on with ladies, in her experience. 'Have you seen him doing this?' she asked.

Alice Busang shook her head. 'I keep watching out but I never see him with other women. I think he is too cunning.'

Mma Ramotswe wrote this down on a piece of paper. 'He goes to bars, does he?'

'Yes.'

'That's where they meet them. They meet these women who hang about in bars waiting for other women's husbands. This city is full of women like that.'

She looked at Alice, and there flowed between them a brief current of understanding. All women in Botswana were the victims of the fecklessness of men.

'Do you want me to follow him?' she asked. 'Do you want me to find out whether he picks up other women?'

Alice Busang nodded. 'Yes,' she said. 'I want proof. Just for myself. I want proof so that I can know what sort of man I married.'

MMA RAMOTSWE was too busy to take on the Busang case until the following week. That Wednesday, she stationed herself in her tiny white van outside the office in the Diamond Sorting Building where Kremlin Busang worked. She had been given a photograph of him by

Alice Busang and she glanced at this on her knee; this was a handsome man, with broad shoulders and a wide smile. He was a ladies' man by the look of him, and she wondered why Alice Busang had married him if she wanted a faithful husband. Hopefulness, of course; a naive hope that he would be unlike other men. Well, you only had to look at him to realise that this would not be so.

She followed him, her white van trailing his old blue car through the traffic to the Go Go Handsome Man's Bar down by the bus station. Then, while he strolled into the bar, she sat in her van and put a little more lipstick on her lips and a dab of cream on her cheeks. In a few minutes she would go in and begin work in earnest.

It was not crowded inside the Go Go Handsome Man's Bar and there were only one or two other women there, both of them she recognised as bad women. They stared at her, but she ignored them and took a seat at the bar, just two stools from Kremlin Busang.

She bought a beer and looked about her, as if taking in the surroundings of the bar for the first time.

'You've not been here before, my sister,' said Kremlin Busang. 'It's a good bar, this one.'

She met his gaze. 'I only come to bars on big occasions,' she said. 'Such as today.'

Kremlin Busang smiled. 'Your birthday?'

'Yes,' she said. 'Let me buy you a drink to celebrate.'

She bought him a beer and he moved over to the stool beside her. She saw that he was a good-looking man and his clothes were well chosen. They drank their beers together, and then she ordered him another one. He began to tell her about his job.

'I sort diamonds,' he said. 'It's a difficult job, you know. You need good eyesight.'

'I like diamonds,' she said. 'I like diamonds a lot.'

She moved her left leg slightly, and it touched his. He noticed this, as she saw him glance down, but he did not move his leg away.

'Are you married?' she asked him quietly.

He did not hesitate. 'No. I've never been married. It's better to be single these days. Freedom, you know.'

She nodded. 'I like to be free too,' she said. 'Then you can decide how to spend your own time.'

'Exactly,' he said. 'Dead right.'

She drained her glass.

'I must go,' she said, and then, after a short pause, 'Maybe you'd like to come back for a drink at my place? I've got some beer there.'

He smiled. 'Yes. That's a good idea.'

He followed her home in his car and together they went into her house and turned on some music. She poured him a beer and he drank half of it in one gulp. Then he put his arm round her waist, and told her that he liked good, fat women. All this business about being thin was nonsense and was quite wrong for Africa.

'Fat women like you are what men really want,' he said.

She giggled. He was charming, she had to admit it, but this was work and she must be quite professional. She must remember that she needed evidence, and that might be more difficult to get.

'Come and sit by me,' she said. 'You must be tired after standing up all day, sorting diamonds.'

SHE HAD HER EXCUSES ready, and he accepted them without protest. She had to be at work early the next morning and he could not stay. But it would be a pity to end such a good evening and have no memento of it.

'I want to take a photograph of us, just for me to keep. So that I can look at it and remember tonight.'

He smiled at her and pinched her gently. 'Good idea.'

So she set up her camera, with its delayed switch, and leapt back on the sofa to join him. He pinched her again and put his arm round her and kissed her passionately as the flash went off.

'If only we could publish that in the newspapers,' he said. 'Mr Handsome with his friend Miss Fatty.'

She laughed. 'You're a ladies' man all right, Kremlin. You're a real ladies' man. I knew it first time I saw you.'

'Well, somebody has to look after the ladies,' he said.

ALICE BUSANG returned to the office that Friday and found Mma Ramotswe waiting for her.

'I'm afraid that I can tell you that your husband is unfaithful,' she said. 'I've got proof.'

Alice closed her eyes. She had expected this, but she had not wanted it. She would kill him, she thought; but no, I still love him. I hate him. No, I love him.

Mma Ramotswe handed her the photograph. 'There's your proof,' she said.

Alice Busang stared at the picture. Surely not! Yes, it was her!

'You . . .' she stuttered. 'You were with my husband?'

'He was with me,' said Mma Ramotswe. 'You wanted proof, didn't you? I got the best proof you could hope for.'

Alice Busang dropped the photograph.

'But you . . . you went with my husband. You . . .'

Mma Ramotswe frowned. 'You asked me to trap him, didn't you?'

Alice Busang's eyes narrowed. 'You bitch!' she screamed. 'You fat bitch! You took my Kremlin! You husband-stealer! Thief!'

Mma Ramotswe looked at her client with dismay. This would be a case, she thought, where she might have to waive the fee.

Mr J. L. B. Matekoni's Discovery

Alice Busang was ushered out of the agency still shouting her insults at Mma Ramotswe.

'You fat tart! You think you're a detective! You're just man hungry, like all those bar girls! Don't be taken in, everyone! This woman isn't a detective. The No.1 Husband Stealing Agency, that's what this is!'

When the row had died away, Mma Ramotswe and Mma Makutsi looked at one another. What could one do but laugh? That woman had known all along what her husband was up to, but had insisted on proof. And when she got the proof, she blamed the messenger.

'Look after the office while I go off to the garage,' said Mma Ramotswe. 'I just have to tell Mr J. L. B. Matekoni about this.'

He was in his glass-fronted office cubicle, tinkering with a distributor cap. 'Sand gets everywhere these days,' he said. 'Look at this.'

He extracted a fragment of silica from a metal duct and showed it triumphantly to his visitor.

'This tiny piece of sand stopped a large truck in its tracks,' he said.

'For want of a nail, the shoe was lost,' said Mma Ramotswe. 'For want of a shoe, the . . .' She stopped. It refused to come back.

'The horse fell down,' volunteered Mr J. L. B. Matekoni.

He put the distributor cap down on his table and went off to fill the kettle. It was a hot afternoon and a cup of tea would make them both feel better.

She told him about Alice Busang and her reaction to the proof of Kremlin's activities.

'You should have seen him,' she said. 'A real ladies' man. Stuff in his hair. Dark glasses. Fancy shoes. He had no idea how funny he looked. I much prefer men with ordinary shoes and honest trousers.'

Mr J. L. B. Matekoni cast an anxious glance down at his shoes—scruffy old suede boots—and at his trousers. Were they honest?

'I couldn't even charge her a fee,' Mma Ramotswe went on. 'Not after that.'

Mr J. L. B. Matekoni nodded. He seemed preoccupied by something. He was staring out of the window.

'You're worried about something?' She wondered whether her refusal of his proposal had upset him more than she imagined. He was not the sort to bear grudges, but did he resent her? She did not want to lose his friendship—he was her best friend in town, in a way, and life without his comforting presence would be distinctly the poorer. Why did love—and sex—complicate life so much?

'What are you thinking about, Mr J. L. B. Matekoni?'

He stood up and closed the door, which had been slightly ajar. There was nobody to overhear them. The two mechanics were at the other end of the garage, drinking their afternoon tea.

'If you hadn't come to see me, I would have come to see you,' said Mr J. L. B. Matekoni. 'I have found something, you see.'

She felt relieved; so he was not upset about her turning him down. She looked at him expectantly.

'There was an accident,' said Mr J. L. B. Matekoni. 'It was not a bad one. Nobody was hurt. A truck coming along from the roundabout didn't stop. It hit a car coming from the village. The car was pushed into the storm ditch and was badly dented.'

'And?'

Mr J. L. B. Matekoni sat down and stared at his hands.

'I was called to pull the car out of the ditch. I took my rescue truck and we winched it up. Then we towed it back here.'

He paused for a moment before continuing.

'I looked it over. It was a panel-beating job but there were one or two other things I would have to do first. I had to get at a fuse box under the dashboard, and while I was doing this I inadvertently opened the glove compartment. I looked inside—I don't know why—and I found something. A little bag.'

Mma Ramotswe's mind was racing ahead. He had stumbled upon illicit diamonds—she was sure of it.

'Diamonds?'

'No,' said Mr J. L. B. Matekoni. 'Worse than that.'

Mma Ramotswe looked at the small bag which he had taken out of his safe and placed on the table. It was made of animal skin—a pouch really—and was similar to the bags that the Basarwa used to store herbs and pastes for their arrows.

'I'll open it,' he said. 'I don't want to make you touch it.'

She watched as he untied the strings that closed the mouth of the bag. His expression was one of distaste, as if he were handling something with an offensive smell.

And there was a smell, a dry, musty odour, as he extracted the three small objects from the bag. Now she understood why he had seemed so distracted and uncomfortable. Mr J. L. B. Matekoni had found muti. He had found medicine.

She said nothing as the objects were laid out on the table. What could one say about these pitiful remnants, about the bone, about the piece of skin, about the little wooden bottle and its awful contents?

Mr J. L. B. Matekoni, reluctant to touch the objects, poked at the bone with a pencil. 'See,' he said simply. 'That's what I found.'

Mma Ramotswe got up from her chair and walked towards the door. She felt her stomach heave, as one does when confronted with a nauseous odour. The feeling passed and she turned round.

'I'm going to take that bone and check,' she said. 'We could be wrong. It could be an animal. A duiker. A hare.'

Mr J. L. B. Matekoni shook his head. 'It won't be,' he said. 'I know what they'll say.'

'Even so,' said Mma Ramotswe. 'Put it in an envelope and I'll take it.'

He opened his mouth to speak, but thought better of it. He was going to warn her, to tell her that it was dangerous to play around with these things, but that would imply that one believed in their power, and he did not. Did he?

She put the envelope in her pocket and smiled.

'Nothing can happen to me now,' she said. 'I'm protected.'

Mr J. L. B. Matekoni tried to laugh at her joke, but found that he could not. It was tempting Providence to use those words and he hoped that she would not have cause to regret them.

'There's one thing I'd like to know,' said Mma Ramotswe, as she left the office. 'That car—who owned it?'

Mr J. L. B. Matekoni glanced at the two mechanics. They were out of earshot, but he lowered his voice nonetheless while he told her.

'Charlie Gotso,' he said. 'Him. That one.'

Mma Ramotswe's eyes widened. 'Gotso? The important one?'

He nodded. Everyone knew Charlie Gotso. He was one of the most influential men in the country. He had the ear of just about everyone who counted. There was no door in the country closed to him, nobody who would turn down a request for a favour. If Charlie Gotso asked you to do something for him, you did it. If you did not, then you might find that life became more difficult later on. It was always very subtly done—you might find that there always seemed to be speed traps on your particular route to work; or your staff grew restless and went to work for somebody else. There was never anything you could put your finger on—but the effect would be very real.

'Oh dear,' said Mma Ramotswe.

'Exactly,' said Mr J. L. B. Matekoni. 'Oh dear.'

The Cutting of Fingers and Snakes

In the beginning, which in Gaborone really means thirty years ago, there were very few factories. In fact, when Princess Marina watched as the Union Jack was hauled down in the stadium on that windy night in 1966 and the Bechuanaland Protectorate ceased to exist, there were none. Mma Ramotswe had been an eight-year-old girl then, a pupil at the Government school at Mochudi, and only vaguely aware that something which people called freedom had arrived. She wondered what this freedom meant. Now she knew of course, and her heart filled with pride when she thought of all they had achieved in thirty short years. The great swath of territory, which the British really had not known what to do with, had prospered to become the best-run state in Africa, by far. Well could people shout 'Pula! Pula! Rain! Rain!' with pride.

Gaborone had grown, changing out of all recognition. When she first went there as a little girl there had been little more than several rings of houses about the mall and the few Government offices—much bigger than Mochudi, of course, and so much more impressive, with the Government buildings and Seretse Khama's house. But it was still quite small, really. And no factories. None at all.

Then, little by little, things had changed. Somebody built a furniture workshop that produced sturdy living-room chairs. Then somebody else decided to set up a small factory to make breeze blocks for building houses. Others followed, and soon there was a block of land on the Lobatse Road that people began to call the Industrial Sites. This caused a great stir of pride; so this is what freedom brought, people thought. There was the Legislative Assembly and the House of Chiefs, of course, and there were also these little factories and the jobs that went with them.

Mma Ramotswe knew one or two factory managers and one factory owner. The factory owner, a Motswana who had come into the country from South Africa, had set up his bolt works with a tiny amount of capital, a few scraps of secondhand machinery, and a work force consisting of his brother-in-law, himself, and a mentally handicapped boy whom he had found sitting under a tree and who had proved to be quite capable of sorting bolts. The business had prospered, largely because the idea behind it was so simple. All that the factory made was a single sort of bolt, of the sort that was needed for fixing galvanised tin roof sheeting onto roof beams. This was a simple process, which required only one sort of machine—a machine that never seemed to break down and rarely needed servicing.

Hector Lepodise's factory grew rapidly, and by the time Mma Ramotswe got to know him, he was employing thirty people and producing bolts that held roofs on to their beams as far north as Malawi. His employment habits were paternalistic—there was always plenty of time off for funerals as well as full pay for those who were genuinely sick—and his workers, as a result, were usually fiercely loyal to him. Yet with a staff of thirty, of whom only twelve were relatives, it was inevitable that there would be some who would attempt to exploit his kindness, and this was where Mma Ramotswe came in.

'I can't put my finger on it,' said Hector, as he drank coffee with Mma Ramotswe on the verandah of the President Hotel, 'but I've never trusted that man. He only came to me about six months ago, and now this.'

'Where had he been working before?' asked Mma Ramotswe. 'What did they say about him?'

Hector shrugged. 'He had a reference from a factory over the border. He came to me just six months ago. He was quite good at working the machinery and I upped his pay by fifty pula a month. Then suddenly he left me and that was that.'

'Any reason?' asked Mma Ramotswe.

Hector frowned. 'None that I could make out. He collected his pay on a Friday and just did not come back. That was about two months ago. Then the next I heard from him was through an attorney in Mahalapye. He wrote me a letter saying that his client, Mr Solomon Moretsi, was starting a legal action against me for four thousand pula for the loss of a finger owing to an industrial accident in my factory.'

Mma Ramotswe poured another cup of coffee for them both while she digested this development. 'And was there an accident?'

'We have an incident book in the works,' said Hector. 'If anybody gets hurt, they have to enter the details in the book. I looked at the date that the attorney mentioned and I saw that Moretsi had entered that he had hurt a finger on his right hand. He wrote that he had put a bandage on it and it seemed all right. I asked around, and somebody said that he had mentioned that he was leaving his machine for a while to fix his finger which he had cut. They thought it had not been a big cut, and nobody had bothered any more about it.'

'Then he left?'

'Yes,' said Hector. 'That was a few days before he left.'

Mma Ramotswe looked at her friend. He was an honest man, she knew, and a good employer. If anybody had been hurt she was sure that he would have done his best for them.

'I don't trust that man,' Hector said. 'I don't think I ever did. I simply don't believe that he lost a finger in my factory. He may have lost a finger somewhere else, but that has nothing to do with me.'

Mma Ramotswe smiled. 'You want me to find this finger for you? Is that why you asked me to the President Hotel?'

Hector laughed. 'Yes. And I also asked you because I enjoy sitting here with you and I would like to ask you to marry me. But I know that the answer will always be the same.'

Mma Ramotswe reached out and patted her friend on the arm.

'Marriage is all very well,' she said. 'But being the No.1 Lady Detective in the country is not an easy life. I couldn't sit at home and cook—you know that.'

Hector shook his head. 'I've always promised you a cook. Two cooks, if you like. You could still be a detective.'

Mma Ramotswe shook her head. 'No,' she said. 'You can carry on asking me, Hector Lepodise, but I'm afraid that the answer is still no. I like you as a friend, but I do not want a husband. I am finished with husbands for good.'

MMA RAMOTSWE examined the papers in the office of Hector's factory. It was a hot and uncomfortable room, unprotected from the noise of the factory, and with barely enough space for the two filing cabinets and two desks that furnished it. Papers lay scattered on the surface of each desk; receipts, bills, technical catalogues.

Mma Ramotswe picked up the grubby exercise book that Hector had placed in front of her and paged through it. This was the incident book, and there, sure enough, was the entry detailing Moretsi's injury, the words spelt out in capitals in a barely literate hand:

> MORETSI CUT HIS FINGER. NO. 2 FINGER COUNTING FROM THUMB. MACHINE DID IT. RIGHT HAND. BANDAGE PUT ON BY SAME. SIGNED: SOLOMON MORETSI. WITNESS: JESUS CHRIST.

She reread the entry and then looked at the attorney's letter. The dates tallied. 'My client says that the accident occurred on 10th May last. He attended the Princess Marina Hospital the following day. The wound was dressed, but osteomyelitis set in. The following week surgery was performed and the damaged finger was amputated at the proximal phalangeal joint (see attached hospital report). My client claims that this accident was due entirely to your negligence in failing adequately to fence working parts of machinery operated in your factory and has instructed me to raise an action for damages on his behalf. It would clearly be in the interests of all concerned if this action were to be settled promptly and my client has accordingly advised that the sum of four thousand pula will be acceptable to him in lieu of court-awarded damages.'

Mma Ramotswe read the remainder of the letter, which as far as she could make out was meaningless jargon that the attorney had been taught at law school. She looked at the copy of the medical report. It was brief and said exactly what the attorney had paraphrased. The date was right; the headed notepaper looked authentic; and there was the doctor's signature at the bottom. It was a name she knew. Mma Ramotswe looked up from the papers to see Hector staring at her expectantly.

'It seems straightforward,' she said. 'He cut his finger and it became infected. What do your insurance people say?'

Hector sighed. 'They say I should pay up. They say that they'll cover me for it and it would be cheaper in the long run. Apparently they'll settle up to ten thousand pula without fighting.'

'Shouldn't you do what they say?' asked Mma Ramotswe. It seemed to her that there was no real point in denying that the man had lost a finger and deserved some compensation; why should Hector make such a fuss about this when he did not even have to pay?

Hector guessed what she was thinking. 'I won't,' he said. 'I just refuse. Why should I pay money to somebody who I think is trying to cheat me? If I pay him this time, then he'll go on to somebody else. I'd rather give that four thousand pula to somebody who deserved it.'

He pointed to the door that linked the office to the factory floor.

'I've got a woman in there,' he said, 'with ten children. She's a good worker too. Think what she could do with four thousand pula—'

'But she hasn't lost a finger,' interrupted Mma Ramotswe. 'He might need that money if he can't work so well any more.'

'Bah! Bah! He's a crook, that man. I knew he was no good. And some of the others didn't like him either.'

'But there's a big difference between entertaining suspicions and being able to prove something,' said Mma Ramotswe. 'You couldn't stand up in court and say that there was something about this man that was not quite right. The judge would just laugh at you.'

Hector was silent.

'Just settle,' said Mma Ramotswe quietly. 'Do what the insurance people tell you to do. Otherwise you'll end up with a bill for far more than four thousand pula.'

Hector shook his head. 'I won't pay for something I didn't do,' he said through clenched teeth. 'I want you to find out what this man is up to. But if you come back to me in a week's time and say that I am wrong, then I will pay without a murmur. Will that do?'

Mma Ramotswe nodded. She could understand his reluctance to pay damages he thought he didn't owe, and her fee for a week's work would not be high. He was a wealthy man and he was entitled to spend his own money in pursuit of a principle. So she agreed to act, and she drove away in her little white van wondering how she could prove that the missing finger had nothing to do with Hector's factory. It had all the appearances of a hopeless case.

THAT NIGHT, as she lay in the bedroom of her house in Zebra Drive, Mma Ramotswe found that sleep eluded her. She got up, put on the pink slippers that she always wore since she had been stung by a scorpion while walking through the house at night, and went to the kitchen to make a pot of bush tea.

She settled down to drink it on her most comfortable chair. She thought of Hector. He was a stubborn man—famously so—but she rather respected him for it. Why should he pay? What was it he had said?— If I pay him this time, then he'll go on to somebody else. She thought for a moment and then put the mug of bush tea down on the table. The idea had come to her suddenly, as all her good ideas seemed to come. Perhaps Hector was the somebody else. Perhaps he had already made claims elsewhere. Perhaps Hector was not the first!

Sleep proved easier after that, and she awoke the next morning confident that a few enquiries, and perhaps a trip up to Mahalapye, would be all that was required to dispose of Moretsi's spurious claim. She breakfasted quickly and then drove to the office. It was getting towards the end of winter, which meant that the temperature of the air was just right, and the sky was bright, pale blue and cloudless. There was a smell of wood smoke in the air, a smell that tugged at her heart because it reminded her of mornings round the fire in Mochudi.

The woman who swept her office was already there when she arrived. She asked after her family, and the woman told her of their latest doings. Mma Ramotswe was always interested to hear of their achievements, but that morning she cut the cleaner short—as politely as she could—and got down to work.

The trade directory gave her the information she needed. There were ten insurance companies doing business in Gaborone; four of these were small, and probably rather specialised; the other six she had heard of and had done work for four of them. She listed them, noted down their telephone numbers, and made a start.

The Botswana Eagle Company was the first she telephoned. They were willing to help, but could not come up with any information. Nor could the Mutual Life Company of Southern Africa, or the Southern Star Insurance Company. But at the fourth, Kalahari Accident and Indemnity, which asked for an hour or so to search the records, she found out what she needed to know.

'We've found one claim under that name,' said the woman on the other end of the line. 'Three years ago we had a claim from a garage in town. One of their petrol attendants claimed to have injured his finger while replacing the petrol pump dispenser in its holder. He lost a finger and they claimed under their employer's policy.'

Mma Ramotswe's heart leapt. 'Four thousand pula?' she asked.

'Close,' said the clerk. 'We settled for three thousand eight hundred.'

'Right hand?' pressed Mma Ramotswe. 'Second finger counting from the thumb?'

The clerk shuffled through some papers. 'Yes,' she said. 'There's a medical report. It says something about . . . I'm not sure how to pronounce it . . . osteomy . . .'

'Elitis,' prompted Mma Ramotswe. 'Requiring amputation of the finger at the proximal phalangeal joint?'

'Yes,' said the clerk. 'Exactly.'

There were one or two details to be obtained, and Mma Ramotswe did that before thanking the clerk and ringing off. For a few moments she sat quite still, savouring the satisfaction of having revealed the fraud so quickly. But there were still several loose ends to be sorted out, and for these she would have to go up to Mahalapye.

The attorney proved to be quite willing to see her that afternoon.

Mma Ramotswe chuckled as she put down the telephone. The attorney and his client were due for an unpleasant surprise.

She left her office in the charge of her secretary and set off to Mahalapye in the tiny white van. The day had heated up, and now, at noon, it was really quite hot. She travelled with her window open and the rushing air cooled the van.

She was half an hour from Mahalapye when the snake shot across the road. The first she saw of it was when its body was about halfway out onto the road—a dart of green against the black tar; and then she was upon it, and the snake was beneath the van. She drew in her breath and slowed the car, looking behind her in the mirror as she did so. Where was the snake? Had it succeeded in crossing the road in time? No, it had not; she had seen it go under the van and she was sure that she had heard something, a dull thump.

She drew to a halt at the edge of the road and looked in the mirror again. There was no sign of the snake. It was in the van somewhere, in the works or under her seat perhaps. She had heard of this happening time and time again. People picked up snakes as passengers and the first thing they knew about it was when the snake bit them. She had heard of people dying at the wheel, as they drove, bitten by snakes that had been caught up in the pipes and rods that ran this way and that under a car.

Mma Ramotswe opened her door, hesitantly at first, but then threw it back and leapt out, to stand, panting, beside the vehicle. There was a snake under the van, she was now sure of that; but how could she possibly get it out? And what sort of snake was it? It had been green, as far as she remembered, which meant at least it wasn't a mamba. It was more likely to be a cobra, she thought, because it was large enough and she could think of no other green snake that long.

Mma Ramotswe stood quite still. The snake could have been watching her at that very moment, ready to strike if she approached any closer. She bent forward and tried to look under the van, but she could not get low enough without going onto her hands and knees. If she did that, and if the snake should choose to move, she was worried that she would be unable to get away quickly enough. She stood up.

The road was quiet, but there was a car or a truck every so often, and now she was aware of a car coming from the Mahalapye direction. The car slowed down as it approached her and then stopped. There was a man in the driver's seat and a young boy beside him.

'Are you in trouble, mma?' the man called out politely. 'Have you broken down?'

Mma Ramotswe crossed the road and spoke to him through his open window. She explained about the snake, and he turned off his engine and got out, instructing the boy to stay where he was.

'They get underneath,' he said. 'It can be dangerous. You were right to stop.'

The man approached the van gingerly. Then, leaning through the open door of the cab, he reached for the lever which released the bonnet and gave it a sharp tug. Satisfied that it had worked, he walked slowly round to the front of the van and very carefully began to open the bonnet. Mma Ramotswe joined him, looking over his shoulder.

The man suddenly froze. 'Don't make any sudden movement,' he said very softly. 'There it is. Look.'

Mma Ramotswe peered into the engine space. For a few moments she could make out nothing unusual, but then the snake moved slightly and she saw it. She was right; it was a cobra, twined about the engine, its head moving slowly to right and left.

The man was quite still. Then he touched Mma Ramotswe on the forearm.

'Walk very carefully back to the door,' he said. 'Get into the van and start the engine. Understand?'

Mma Ramotswe nodded. Then, moving as slowly as she could, she eased herself into the driving seat and reached forward to turn the key. The engine came to life immediately.

'Press the accelerator,' yelled the man. 'Race the engine!'

Mma Ramotswe did as she was told, and the engine roared throatily. There was a noise from the front and a thump, and then the man signalled to her to switch off.

'You can come out,' he called. 'That's the end of the cobra.'

Mma Ramotswe got out of the van and walked round to the front. Looking into the engine, she saw the cobra in two pieces, quite still.

'It had twined itself through the blades of the fan,' said the man. 'Nasty way to go, even for a snake. But it could have crept into the van and bitten you, you know. So there we are. You are still alive.'

Mma Ramotswe thanked him and drove off, leaving the cobra on the side of the road. It would prove to be an eventful day, even if nothing further were to happen during the final half-hour. It did not.

'NOW,' SAID Mr Jameson Mopotswane, the Mahalapye attorney, sitting back in his unprepossessing office. 'My client is going to be a little late, as the message only got to him a short time ago. But you and I can discuss details of the settlement before he arrives.'

Mma Ramotswe savoured the moment. She leaned back in her chair and looked about his poorly furnished room.

'So business is not so good these days,' she said, adding, 'up here.'

Jameson Mopotswane bristled.

'It's not bad,' he said. 'In fact, I'm very busy. I get in here at seven o'clock, you know, and I'm on the go until six.'

'Every day?' asked Mma Ramotswe innocently.

Jameson Mopotswane glared at her. 'Yes,' he said. 'Every day, including Saturdays. Sometimes Sundays.'

'You must have a lot to do,' said Mma Ramotswe.

The attorney took this in a reconciliatory way and smiled, but Mma Ramotswe continued, 'Yes, a lot to do, sorting out the lies your clients tell you from the occasional—occasional—truth.'

Jameson Mopotswane glared at her. Who was this pushy woman, and what right did she have to talk about his clients like that?

'My clients do not lie,' he said slowly. 'Not more than anybody else, anyway. And you have no business, if I may say so, to suggest that they are liars.'

Mma Ramotswe raised an eyebrow.

'Oh no?' she challenged. 'Well, let's just take your Mr Moretsi, for example. How many fingers has he got?'

Jameson Mopotswane looked at her disdainfully.

'It's cheap to make fun of the afflicted,' he sneered. 'You know very well that he's got nine, or nine and a half if you want to split hairs.'

'Very interesting,' said Mma Ramotswe. 'And if that's the case, then how can he possibly have made a successful claim to Kalahari Accident and Indemnity, about three years ago, for the loss of a finger in an accident in a petrol station? Could you explain that?'

He sat quite still. 'Three years ago?' he said faintly. 'A finger?'

'Yes,' said Mma Ramotswe. 'He asked for four thousand—a bit of a coincidence—and settled for three thousand eight hundred. The company have given me the claim number, if you want to check up. They're always very helpful, I find, when there's any question of insurance fraud being uncovered. Remarkably helpful.'

The attorney said nothing, and suddenly Mma Ramotswe felt sorry for him. She did not like lawyers, but he was trying to earn a living, like everybody else, and perhaps she was being too hard on him.

'Show me the medical report,' she said, almost kindly. 'I'd be interested to see it.'

The attorney reached for a file on his desk and took out a report.

'Here,' he said. 'It all seemed quite genuine.'

Mma Ramotswe looked at the piece of headed paper and then nodded. 'There we are,' she said. 'It's just as I thought. Look at the date there. It's been whited out and a new date typed in. Our friend did have a finger removed once, and it may even have been as a result of an accident. But then all that he's done is to get a bottle of correction fluid, change the date and create a new accident, just like that.'

Jameson Mopotswane took the sheet of paper and held it up to the light. He need not even have done that; the correction fluid could be seen clearly enough at first glance.

'I'm surprised that you did not notice that,' said Mma Ramotswe. 'It doesn't exactly need a forensic laboratory to see what he's done.'

It was at this point in the shaming of the attorney that Moretsi arrived. He walked into the office and reached out to shake hands with Mma Ramotswe. She looked at the hand and saw the stub of the finger. She rejected the proffered hand.

'Sit down,' said Jameson Mopotswane coldly.

Moretsi looked surprised, but did as he was told.

'So you're the lady who's come to pay . . .'

The attorney cut him short. 'She has not come to pay anything,' he said. 'This lady has come all the way from Gaborone to ask you why you keep claiming for lost fingers.'

Mma Ramotswe watched Moretsi's expression as the attorney spoke. Even if there had not been the evidence of the changed date on the hospital report, his crestfallen look would have convinced her. People always collapsed when confronted with the truth; very, very few could brave it out.

'Keep claiming . . .?' he said limply.

'Yes,' said Mma Ramotswe. 'You claim, I believe, to have lost three fingers. And yet if I look at your hand today I see that two have miraculously grown back! This is wonderful! Perhaps you have discovered some new drug that enables fingers to grow back once they have been chopped off?'

'Three?' said the attorney, puzzled.

Mma Ramotswe looked at Moretsi.

'Well,' she said. 'There was Kalahari Accident. Then there was . . . Could you refresh my memory? I've got it written down somewhere.'

Moretsi looked to his attorney for support, but saw only anger.

'Star Insurance,' he said quietly.

'Ah!' said Mma Ramotswe. 'Thank you for that.'

The attorney picked up the report and waved it at his client.

'And you expected to be able to fool me with this . . . crude alteration? You expected to get away with that?'

Moretsi said nothing, as did Mma Ramotswe. She was not surprised, of course; these people were utterly slippery, even if they had a law degree to write after their names.

'Anyway,' said Jameson Mopotswane, 'that's the end of your tricks. You'll be facing fraud charges, you know, and you'll have to get somebody else to defend you. You won't get me, my friend.'

Moretsi looked at Mma Ramotswe, who met his gaze directly.

'Why did you do it?' she asked. 'Just tell me why you thought you could get away with it?'

Moretsi took a handkerchief out of his pocket and blew his nose.

'I am looking after my parents,' he said. 'And I have a sister who is sick with a disease that is killing everybody these days. You know what I'm talking about. She has children. I have to support them.'

Mma Ramotswe looked into his eyes. She had always been able to rely on her ability to tell whether a person was speaking the truth or not, and she knew that Moretsi was not lying. She thought quickly. There was no point in sending this man to prison. What would it achieve? It would merely add to the suffering of others—of the parents and of the poor sister. She knew what he was talking about and she understood what it meant.

'Very well,' she said. 'I will not tell the police about any of this. And my client will not either. But, in return, you will promise that there will be no more lost fingers. Do you understand?'

Moretsi nodded rapidly. 'You are a good Christian lady,' he said. 'God is going to make it very easy for you in heaven.'

'I hope so,' said Mma Ramotswe. 'But I am also a very nasty lady sometimes. And if you try any more of this nonsense with insurance people, then you will find that I will become very unpleasant.'

'I understand,' said Moretsi. 'I understand.'

'You see,' said Mma Ramotswe, 'there are some people in this country, some men, who think that women are soft and can be twisted this way and that. Well, I'm not. I can tell you, if you are interested, that I killed a cobra, a big one, on my way here this afternoon.'

'Oh?' said Jameson Mopotswane. 'What did you do?'

'I cut it in two,' said Mma Ramotswe. 'Two pieces.'

The Third Metacarpal

All that was a distraction. It was gratifying to deal with a case like that so quickly, and to the clear satisfaction of the client, but one could not put out of one's mind the fact that there was a small brown envelope in the drawer with contents that could not be ignored.

Mma Ramotswe took it out discreetly, not wanting Mma Makutsi to see it. She thought that she could trust her, but this was a matter that was very much more confidential than any other matter they had encountered so far. This was dangerous.

She left the office, telling Mma Makutsi that she was going to the bank. Several cheques had come in, and needed to be deposited. But she did not go to the bank at once. She drove instead to the Princess Marina Hospital and followed the signs that said PATHOLOGY.

A nurse stopped her. 'Are you here to identify a body, mma?'

Mma Ramotswe shook her head. 'I have come to see Dr Gulubane. He is not expecting me, but he will see me. I am his neighbour.'

The nurse looked at her suspiciously, but told her to wait while she went to fetch the doctor. A few minutes later she returned and said the doctor would be with her shortly.

Dr Gulubane arrived. He was wearing a green apron and he seemed quite pleased to have been disturbed.

'Come with me to my office,' he said. 'We can talk there.'

Mma Ramotswe followed him down a corridor to a small office furnished with a bare table, a telephone and a battered grey filing cabinet. It was like the office of a minor civil servant and it was only the medical books on a shelf that gave away its real purpose.

'As you know,' she began, 'I'm a private detective these days.'

Dr Gulubane beamed a broad smile. 'You won't get me to talk about my patients,' he said. 'Even if they are all dead.'

She shared the joke. 'That's not what I want,' she said. 'All I would like you to do is to identify something for me. I have it with me.' She took out the envelope and spilled its contents on the desk.

Dr Gulubane stopped smiling immediately and picked up the bone. He adjusted his spectacles.

'Third metacarpal,' he muttered. 'Child. Eight. Nine. Something like that.'

Mma Ramotswe could hear her own breathing. 'Human?'

'Of course,' said Dr Gulubane. 'As I said, it's from a child. An adult's bone would be bigger. You can tell at a glance.'

The doctor put the bone down on the table and looked up at Mma Ramotswe. 'Where did you get it?'

Mma Ramotswe shrugged. 'Somebody showed it to me. And you won't get me to talk about my clients either.'

Dr Gulubane made an expression of distaste.

'These things shouldn't be handed round like that,' he said. 'People show no respect.'

Mma Ramotswe nodded her agreement. 'But can you tell me anything more? Can you tell me when the . . . when the child died?'

Dr Gulubane opened a drawer and took out a magnifying glass, with which he examined the bone further, turning it round in the palm of his hand.

'Not all that long ago,' he said. 'There's a small amount of tissue here at the top. It doesn't look entirely desiccated. Maybe a few months, maybe less. You can't be sure.'

Mma Ramotswe shuddered. It was one thing to handle bone, but to handle human tissue was quite a different matter.

'And another thing,' said Dr Gulubane. 'How do you know that the child whose bone this is is dead? I thought you were the detective—surely you would have thought: This is an extremity—people can lose extremities and still live! Did you think that, Mrs Detective? I bet you didn't!'

SHE CONVEYED the information to Mr J. L. B. Matekoni over dinner in her house. He had readily accepted her invitation and she had prepared a large pot of stew and a combination of rice and melons. Halfway through the meal she told him of her visit to Dr Gulubane. Mr J. L. B. Matekoni stopped eating.

'A child?' There was dismay in his voice.

'That's what Dr Gulubane said. He couldn't be certain about the age. But he said it was about eight or nine.'

Mr J. L. B. Matekoni winced. It would have been far better never to have found the bag. These things happened—they all knew that—but one did not want to get mixed up in them.

'What do we do?' asked Mma Ramotswe.

Mr J. L. B. Matekoni closed his eyes and swallowed hard.

'We can go to the police,' he said. 'And if we do that, Charlie Gotso will get to hear about my finding the bag. And that will be me done for, or just about.'

Mma Ramotswe agreed. The police had a limited interest in pursuing crime, and certain sorts of crime interested them not at all. The involvement of the country's most powerful figures in witchcraft would certainly be in the latter category.

'I don't think we should go to the police,' said Mma Ramotswe.

'So we just forget about it?' Mr J. L. B. Matekoni fixed Mma Ramotswe with a look of appeal.

'No. We can't do that,' she said. 'People have been forgetting about this sort of thing for long enough, haven't they? We can't do that.'

Mr J. L. B. Matekoni lowered his eyes. His appetite seemed to have deserted him now, and the stew was congealing on his plate.

'The first thing we do,' she said, 'is to arrange for Charlie Gotso's windscreen to be broken. Then you telephone him and tell him that thieves have broken into his car while it was in the garage. You tell him that there does not appear to have been anything stolen, but that you will pay for a new windscreen yourself. Then you wait and see.'

'To see what?'

'To see if he comes back and tells you something's missing. If he does, you tell him that you will personally undertake to recover this thing, whatever it is. You tell him that you have a contact, a lady private detective, who is very good at recovering stolen property.'

Mr J. L. B. Matekoni's jaw had dropped. One did not simply go up to Charlie Gotso just like that. You had to pull strings to see him.

'And then?'

'Then I take the bag back to him and you leave it up to me. I'll get the name of the witch doctor from him and then, well, we'll think about what to do then.'

She made it sound so simple that he found himself convinced that it would work. That was the wonderful thing about confidence—it was infectious. Mr J. L. B. Matekoni's appetite returned. He finished his food, and then drank a large cup of tea before Mma Ramotswe walked with him to his car and said good night.

A Lot of Lies

One of the young mechanics tapped him on the shoulder, leaving a greasy fingerprint. He was always doing this, that young man, and it annoyed Mr J. L. B. Matekoni intensely.

'There's a man to see you, rra,' he said. 'He's waiting in the office.'

Mr J. L. B. Matekoni put down his spanner and wiped his hands on a cloth. He had been involved in a particularly delicate operation—fine-tuning the engine of Mrs Grace Mapondwe, who was well known for her sporty style of driving.

The visitor was sitting in the office, in Mr J. L. B. Matekoni's chair. He had picked up a tyre brochure and was flipping through it when Mr J. L. B. Matekoni entered the room. Now he tossed it down casually and stood up.

Mr J. L. B. Matekoni rapidly took in the other man's appearance. He was dressed in khaki, as a soldier might be, and he had an expensive snakeskin belt and a fancy watch with multiple dials.

'Mr Gotso sent me,' he said. 'You telephoned him this morning.'

Mr J. L. B. Matekoni nodded. It had been easy to break the windscreen and scatter the fragments of glass about the car. It had been easy to telephone Mr Gotso's house and report that the car had been broken into; but this part was more difficult—this was lying to somebody's face. It's Mma Ramotswe's fault, he thought. I am a simple mechanic. I didn't ask to get involved in these ridiculous detective games. I am just too weak.

And he was—when it came to Mma Ramotswe. She could ask anything of him, and he would comply. He had even had to make a false report to the police, which had really frightened him, even if they had not even bothered to come round to investigate. He was a criminal now, he supposed, and it was all because he was weak.

'Mr Gotso is very angry,' said the visitor. 'You have had that car for ten days. Now you telephone us and tell us that it is broken into. Where's your security? That's what Mr Gotso says.'

Mr J. L. B. Matekoni felt a trickle of sweat run down his back.

'I'm very sorry, rra. I had to get a new part. These expensive cars, you can't put just anything in them . . .'

Mr Gotso's man looked at his watch. 'All right, all right. I know how slow these things are. Just show me the car.'

Mr J. L. B. Matekoni led the way out of the office. They stood before the car. He had already replaced the windscreen, but had propped what remained of the shattered one against a nearby wall. He had also taken the precaution of leaving a few pieces of broken glass on the driver's seat.

The visitor opened the front door and peered inside.

'I have replaced the windscreen free of charge,' said Mr J. L. B. Matekoni. 'I will also make a big reduction in the bill.'

The other man said nothing. He was leaning across now and had opened the glove compartment. Mr J. L. B. Matekoni watched quietly.

The man got out of the car and brushed his hand against his trousers; he had cut himself on one of the small pieces of glass.

'There is something missing from the glove compartment. Do you know anything about that?'

Mr J. L. B. Matekoni shook his head—three times.

The man put his hand to his mouth and sucked at the cut.

'Mr Gotso forgot that he had something there. He only remembered when you told him about the car being broken into. He is not going to be pleased to hear that this item has gone.'

Mr J. L. B. Matekoni passed the man a piece of rag.

'I'm sorry you've cut yourself. Glass gets everywhere when a windscreen goes. Everywhere.'

The man snorted. 'It doesn't matter about me. What matters is that somebody has stolen something belonging to Mr Gotso.'

Mr J. L. B. Matekoni scratched his head. 'The police are useless. They didn't even come. But I know somebody who can look into this.'

'Oh, yes? Who can do that?'

'There's a lady detective these days. She has an office over that way, near Kgale Hill. Have you seen it?'

'Maybe. Maybe not.'

Mr J. L. B. Matekoni smiled. 'She knows everything that's going on. If I ask her, she'll be able to find out who did this thing. She might even be able to get the property back. What was it, by the way?'

'Property. A small thing belonging to Mr Charlie Gotso.'

'I see.'

The man took the rag off his wound and flung it on the floor.

'Can you ask that lady then?' he said grudgingly. 'Ask her to get this thing back to Mr Gotso.'

'I will,' said Mr J. L. B. Matekoni. 'I will speak to her this evening. In the meantime, that car is ready and Mr Gotso can collect it any time. I will clear up the last bits of glass.'

'You'd better,' said the visitor. 'Mr Gotso doesn't like to cut his hand.'

Mr Gotso doesn't like to cut his hand! You're a little boy, thought Mr J. L. B. Matekoni. A truculent little boy. I know your type well enough! I remember you—or somebody very like you—in the playground of Mochudi Government Junior School—bullying other boys, breaking things, pretending to be tough. And this Mr Charlie Gotso, with his expensive car and sinister ways—he's just a little boy too.

HE WAS DETERMINED that Mma Ramotswe should not get away with it. She seemed to assume that he would do whatever she told him to do because he never stood up to her. Well, he would show her this time. He would put an end to all this detective nonsense.

He left the garage, still smarting, busy rehearsing in his mind what he would say to her when he reached the office. He did not want to destroy their friendship, but he could not continue with this posturing and deception.

She met him at the door of the No.1 Ladies' Detective Agency. She was throwing the dregs from a teapot into the yard as he drew up in his garage van.

'Well?' she said. 'Did everything go as planned?'

'Mma Ramotswe, I really think . . .'

'Did he come round himself, or did he send one of his men?'

'One of his men. But, listen . . .'

'And did you tell him that I could get the thing back?'

'I cannot . . . You see, I have never lied. I have never lied before, even when I was a small boy. My tongue would go stiff if I tried to lie, and I couldn't.'

Mma Ramotswe upended the teapot for a final time.

'You've done very well this time. Lies are quite all right if you are lying for a good cause. Is it not a good cause to find out who killed an innocent child? Are lies worse than murder, Mr J. L. B. Matekoni? Do you think that?'

'Murder is worse. But . . .'

'Well, there you are. You didn't think it through, did you?'

She looked at him and smiled, and he thought: I am lucky. She is smiling at me. There is nobody to love me in this world. Here is somebody who likes me and smiles at me. And she's right about murder. It's far worse than lies.

'Come in for tea,' said Mma Ramotswe. 'Mma Makutsi has boiled the kettle and we can drink tea while we decide what to do next.'

Mr Charlie Gotso

Mr Charlie Gotso looked at Mma Ramotswe. 'You are the woman from Matekoni?' he asked.

Mma Ramotswe did not like his voice. It was sandpaper-rough, and he slurred the ends of the words lazily, as if he could not be bothered to make himself clear. This came from contempt, she felt; if you were as powerful as he was, then why bother to communicate properly with your inferiors? As long as they understood what you wanted—that was the essential thing.

'Mr J. L. B. Matekoni asked me to help him, rra. I am a private detective.'

Mr Gotso stared at her, a slight smile playing on his lips.

'I have seen this place of yours. I saw a sign when I was driving past. A private detective agency for ladies, or something like that.'

'Not just for ladies, rra,' said Mma Ramotswe. 'We are lady detectives but we work for men too. Mr Patel, for example, consulted us.'

The smile became broader. 'You think you can tell men things?'

Mma Ramotswe answered calmly. 'It depends. Sometimes men are too proud to listen. We can't tell that sort of man anything.'

He narrowed his eyes. The remark was ambiguous. She could have been suggesting he was proud, or she could be talking about other men.

'So anyway,' said Mr Gotso. 'You know that I lost some property from my car. Matekoni says you might be able to get it back for me?'

'I have done that,' Mma Ramotswe said. 'I found out who broke into your car. They were just boys. A couple of boys.'

Mr Gotso raised an eyebrow. 'Their names? Tell me who they are.'

'I cannot do that,' said Mma Ramotswe.

'I want to smack them. You will tell me who they are.'

Mma Ramotswe looked up at Mr Gotso and met his gaze. For a moment neither said anything. Then she spoke, 'I gave them my word I would not give their names to anybody if they gave me back what they had stolen. It was a bargain.'

'You made a promise on my behalf?'

'Yes, I did. It was the only way I could get the item back.'

Mr Gotso thought for a moment. 'Very well,' he said. 'I suppose that was all you could do. Now, where is this item of property?'

Mma Ramotswe reached into her handbag and took out the small leather pouch.

'This is what they gave me.' She put it on the table and he reached across and took it in his hand.

'This is not mine, of course. This is something that one of my men had. I was looking after it for him. I have no idea what it is.'

'Muti, rra. Medicine from a witch doctor.'

Mr Gotso's look was steely. 'Oh yes? Some little charm for the superstitious?'

Mma Ramotswe shook her head. 'No, I don't think so. I think that is powerful stuff. I think that was probably rather expensive.'

'Powerful?' His head stayed absolutely still as he spoke, she noticed. Only the lips moved as the unfinished words slid out.

'Yes. That is good. I would like to be able to get something like that myself. But I do not know where I can find it.'

Mr Gotso moved slightly now, and the eyes slid down Mma Ramotswe's figure.

'Maybe I could help you, mma.'

She thought quickly, and then gave her answer. 'I would like you to help me. Then maybe I could help you in some way.'

'In what way could you help me? Do you think I'm a lonely man?'

'You are not lonely. I have heard that you are a man with many women friends. You don't need another.'

'Surely I'm the best judge of that.'

'No, I think you are a man who likes information. You need that to keep powerful. You need muti too, don't you?'

'You should be careful about saying things like that,' he said. The words were well articulated now; he could speak clearly when he wanted to. 'People who accuse others of witchcraft can regret it.'

'But I am not accusing you of anything. I told you myself that I used it, didn't I? No, what I was saying was that you are a man who needs to know what's going on in this town.'

'You can tell me things?'

Mma Ramotswe nodded. 'I hear some very interesting things in my business. For example, I can tell you about that man who is trying to build a shop next to your shop in the mall. You know him? Would you like to hear about what he did before he came to Gaborone? He wouldn't like people to know that, I think.'

'You are a very interesting woman, Mma Ramotswe. I think I understand you very well. I will give you the name of the witch doctor if you give me this useful information. Would that suit you?'

'That is very good. I shall be able to get something from this man that will help me get even better information. And if I hear anything else, well, I shall be happy to let you know.'

'You are a very good woman,' said Mr Gotso, picking up a small pad of paper. 'I'm going to draw you a sketch map. This man lives out in the bush not far from Molepolole. It is difficult to find his place, but this will show you just where to go. I warn you, by the way, he's not cheap. But if you say that you are a friend of Mr Charlie Gotso, then you will find that he takes off twenty per cent. Which isn't at all bad, is it?'

Medical Matters

She had the information now. She had a map to find a murderer, and she would find him. But there was still the detective agency to run, and there were cases that needed to be dealt with—including a case that involved a very different sort of doctor and a hospital.

Her old friend, Dr Maketsi, had telephoned her from the hospital and asked if he could call in at her office on his way home that evening. She readily agreed; she and Dr Maketsi were both from Mochudi, and although he was ten years her senior she felt extremely close to him. So she cancelled her hair-braiding appointment in town and stayed at her desk, catching up on some paperwork until Dr Maketsi's familiar voice called out 'Ko! Ko!'

They exchanged family gossip for a while, drinking bush tea and reflecting on how Mochudi had changed since their day. She asked after Dr Maketsi's aunt, a retired teacher to whom half the village still turned for advice. She had not run out of steam, he said, and was now being pressed to stand for Parliament, which she might yet do.

'We need more women in public life,' said Dr Maketsi. 'They are very practical people, women. Unlike us men.'

Mma Ramotswe laughed, then asked, 'Why have you come to see me? Do you want me to find you a new wife, maybe?'

Dr Maketsi clicked his tongue in mock disapproval. 'I have come about a real problem,' he said. 'Not just about the question of wives.'

Mma Ramotswe listened as he explained just how delicate his problem was and she assured him that she believed in confidentiality.

'Not even my secretary will get to hear what you tell me,' she said.

'Good,' said Dr Maketsi. 'Because if I am wrong about this, and if anybody hears about it, I shall be very embarrassed—as will the whole hospital. I don't want the minister coming looking for me.'

'I understand,' said Mma Ramotswe. Her curiosity was thoroughly aroused now, and she was anxious to hear what juicy matter was troubling her friend.

'I am worried about one of our young doctors,' said Dr Maketsi. 'He is called Dr Komoti. He's Nigerian.'

'I see.'

'I know some people are suspicious of Nigerians,' said Dr Maketsi.

'I believe that there are some people like that,' said Mma Ramotswe, catching the doctor's eye and then looking away again quickly, almost guiltily.

Dr Maketsi drank the last of his tea and placed his mug on the table.

'Let me tell you about our Dr Komoti,' he said. 'It was my job to interview him, in fact, although I must admit that it was rather a formality. We were desperately short of people at the time and needed somebody who would be able to lend a hand in casualty. Anyway, he seemed to have a reasonable c.v. and he had brought several references with him. He had been working in Nairobi for a few years, and so I telephoned the hospital he was at and they confirmed that he was perfectly all right. So I took him on.

'He started about six months ago. He was pretty busy in casualty. Everything seemed to be going well, but after Dr Komoti had been there about three weeks the consultant in charge had a word with me. He said that he thought that the new doctor was a bit rusty and that some of the things he did seemed a bit surprising. For example, he had sewed several wounds up badly and the stitching had to be redone.

'But sometimes he was really quite good. For example, a couple of weeks ago we had a woman in with a tension pneumothorax. That's a pretty serious matter. Air gets into the space round the lungs and makes the lung collapse. If this happens, you have to drain the air out as quickly as you can so that the lung can expand again. This is quite a tricky job for an inexperienced doctor.

'Dr Komoti turned out to be pretty good at this, and he undoubtedly saved this woman's life. The consultant was impressed, and mentioned it to me. But at the same time, this is the same doctor who had failed to spot an obvious case of enlarged spleen the day before.'

'He's inconsistent?' said Mma Ramotswe.

'Exactly,' said Dr Maketsi. 'One day he'll be fine, but the next day he'll come close to killing some unfortunate patient.'

Mma Ramotswe thought for a moment, remembering a news item

in the *Star*. 'I was reading the other day about a bogus surgeon in Johannesburg,' she said. 'He practised for almost ten years and nobody knew that he had no qualifications. Then somebody spotted something by chance and they exposed him.'

'It's extraordinary,' said Dr Maketsi. 'These cases crop up from time to time. And the people often get away with it for a long time.'

'Did you check up on his qualifications?' asked Mma Ramotswe. 'It's easy enough to forge documents these days with photocopiers and laser printers—anybody can do it. Maybe he's not a doctor at all.'

Dr Maketsi shook his head. 'We went through all that,' he said. 'We checked with his medical school in Nigeria and we also checked with the General Medical Council in Britain, where he did a registrar's job. We even obtained a photograph from Nairobi, and it's the same man. So I'm pretty sure that he's exactly who he says he is.'

'Couldn't you just test him?' asked Mma Ramotswe. 'Couldn't you try to find out how much he knows about medicine by just asking him some tricky questions?'

Dr Maketsi smiled. 'I've done that already. On the first occasion he coped well and he gave a fairly good answer. But on the second occasion, he seemed evasive. He said that he wanted to think about it. This annoyed me, and so I mentioned something about the case we had discussed before. This took him off his guard and he just mumbled something inconsequential. It was as if he had forgotten what he'd said to me three days before.'

Mma Ramotswe looked up at the ceiling. She knew about forgetfulness. Her poor Daddy had become forgetful at the end and had sometimes barely remembered her. That was understandable in the old, but not in a young doctor. Unless he was ill, of course.

'There's nothing wrong with him mentally,' said Dr Maketsi, as if predicting her question. 'As far as I can tell, that is. What I'm afraid of is drugs. I think that he's possibly abusing drugs and that half the time he's treating patients he's not exactly there.'

Dr Maketsi paused. He had delivered his bombshell. If the minister heard that a doctor was treating patients in the hospital while high on drugs, he might begin to question the closeness of supervision in the hospital.

'I can see why you're worried,' said Mma Ramotswe. 'But I'm not sure whether I can help. I don't really know my way around the drug scene. That's really a police matter.'

Dr Maketsi was dismissive. 'Don't talk to me about the police,' he said. 'They never keep their mouths shut. If I went to them to get this looked into, they'd barge in and search his house and then somebody would talk about it. In no time at all word would be all about town that he was a drug addict. And what if I'm wrong? Then I would have as good as killed his reputation for no reason. He may be incompetent from time to time, but that's no reason for destroying him.'

'But if we did find out that he was using drugs,' said Mma Ramotswe, 'what then? Would you dismiss him?'

Dr Maketsi shook his head vigorously. 'We don't think about drugs in those terms. I'd look on it as a medical problem and I'd try to help him. I'd try to sort out the problem.'

'But you can't "sort out" those people,' said Mma Ramotswe. 'Smoking dagga is one thing, but using pills and all the rest is another. Show me one reformed drug addict. Just one. Maybe they exist; I've just never seen them.'

Dr Maketsi shrugged. 'I know they can be very manipulative people,' he said. 'But some of them get off it. I can show you figures.'

'Well, maybe, maybe not,' said Mma Ramotswe. 'The point is, what do you want me to do?'

'Find out about him,' said Dr Maketsi. 'Follow him for a few days. Find out whether he's involved in the drug scene. If he is, find out whether he's supplying others with drugs while you are about it. Because that will be another problem for us. We keep a tight rein on drugs in the hospital, but things can go missing, and the last thing we want is a doctor who's passing hospital drug supplies to addicts.'

'You'd sack him then?' goaded Mma Ramotswe. 'You wouldn't try to help him?'

Dr Maketsi laughed. 'We'd sack him good and proper.'

'Good,' said Mma Ramotswe. 'And proper too. Now I have to tell you about my fee.'

Dr Maketsi's face fell. 'I was worried about that. This is such a delicate enquiry, I could hardly get the hospital to pay for it.'

Mma Ramotswe nodded. 'You thought that as an old friend . . .'

'Yes,' said Dr Maketsi quietly. 'I thought that as an old friend you might remember how when your Daddy was so ill at the end . . .'

Mma Ramotswe did remember. Dr Maketsi had come to the house every evening for three weeks and eventually had arranged for her Daddy to be put in a private room at the hospital, all for nothing.

'I remember very well,' she said. 'I only mentioned the fee to tell you that there would be none.'

SHE HAD ALL the information she needed to start her investigation of Dr Komoti. She had his address in Kaunda Way; she had a photograph, supplied by Dr Maketsi; and she had a note of the number of the green station wagon that he drove. Now all she had to do was to start to watch Dr Komoti and to learn as much as she could about him in the shortest possible time.

Dr Maketsi had thoughtfully provided her with a copy of the duty rota in the casualty department for the following four months. This meant that Mma Ramotswe would know exactly when he might be expected to leave the hospital to return home and also when he was on night duty.

She started two days later. She was there when Dr Komoti drove out of the staff car park at the hospital that afternoon and she followed him discreetly into town, parking a few cars away from him and waiting until he was well away from the car park before she got out of the van. He visited one or two shops and picked up a newspaper from the book centre. Then he returned to his car, drove home, and stayed there—blamelessly, she assumed—until the lights went out in the house just before ten that evening. It was a dull business sitting in the tiny white van, but Mma Ramotswe was used to it.

Nothing happened that evening, nor the next evening. Mma Ramotswe was beginning to wonder whether there was ever any variety to the routine of Dr Komoti's life when suddenly things changed. It was a Friday afternoon. The doctor was slightly late in leaving the hospital, but eventually he came out of the casualty entrance and climbed into his car.

Mma Ramotswe followed him out of the hospital grounds, satisfied that he was not aware of her presence. This time, instead of turning into town, he turned the other way. Mma Ramotswe was pleased that something at last might be happening, and she concentrated carefully on not losing him as they made their way through the traffic.

Mma Ramotswe was surprised to find that Dr Komoti was heading for the Lobatse Road. This was interesting. If he was dealing in drugs, then to use Lobatse as a base would be a good idea. It was close enough to the border, and he might be passing things into South Africa, or picking things up there.

They drove down, the tiny white van straining to keep Dr Komoti's more powerful car in sight. When they did not stop in Lobatse, Mma Ramotswe began to worry. If he was going to drive straight through Lobatse it was possible that he was heading for the border, some miles down the road. Yes! Dr Komoti was going over the border, she was sure of it. He was going to Mafikeng.

As the realisation dawned that Dr Komoti's destination was out of the country, Mma Ramotswe felt an intense irritation with her own stupidity. She did not have her passport with her; Dr Komoti would go through, but she would have to remain in Botswana. And once he was on the other side, then he could do whatever he liked—and no doubt would—and she would know nothing about it.

She watched him stop at the border post, and then she turned back, like a hunter who has chased his prey to the end of his preserve and must now give up.

When she arrived back in Gaborone, Mma Ramotswe was in a thoroughly bad mood. She had an early night, but the bad mood was still with her the following morning when she went into the mall. As she often did on a Saturday morning, she had a cup of coffee on the verandah of the President Hotel and enjoyed a chat with her friend Grace Gakatsla. Grace, who had a dress shop in Broadhurst, always cheered her up with her stories of the vagaries of her customers. One, a Government minister's wife, had recently bought a dress on a Friday and brought it back the following Monday, saying that it did not really fit. Yet Grace had been at the wedding on Saturday where the dress had been worn, and it had looked perfect.

'Of course I couldn't tell her to her face she was a liar and that I wasn't a dress-hire shop,' said Grace. 'So I asked her if she had enjoyed the wedding. She smiled and said that she had. So I said I enjoyed it too. She obviously hadn't seen me there. She stopped smiling and she said that maybe she'd give the dress another chance.'

'She's just a porcupine, that woman,' said Mma Ramotswe.

'A hyena,' said Grace. 'An anteater, with her long nose.' The laughter had died away, and Grace had gone off, allowing Mma Ramotswe's bad mood to settle back in place. She paid her bill and left, and it was then, as she was walking down the front steps of the hotel, that she saw Dr Komoti in the mall.

For a moment Mma Ramotswe stood quite still. Dr Komoti had crossed the border last night just before seven in the evening. The border closed at eight, which meant that he could not have had time to get down to Mafikeng, which was forty minutes' drive, and back in time to cross again before the border closed. So he had only spent one evening there and had come back first thing that morning.

She recovered from her surprise at seeing him and realised that she should make good use of the opportunity to follow him and see what he did. He was now in the hardware store, and Mma Ramotswe lingered outside, looking idly at the contents of the window until he came out again. Then he walked purposefully back to the car park and she watched him getting into his car.

Dr Komoti stayed in for the rest of the day. At six in the evening he went off to the Sun Hotel where he had a drink with two other men, whom Mma Ramotswe recognised as fellow Nigerians. She knew that one of them worked for a firm of accountants, and the other, she believed, was a primary school teacher somewhere. There was nothing about their meeting which seemed suspicious.

He stayed an hour and then left, and that was the extent of Dr Komoti's social life for the weekend. By Sunday evening, Mma Ramotswe had decided that she would report to Dr Maketsi the following week and tell him that there was no evidence of his moving in drug-abusing circles and that he seemed, by contrast, to be the model of sobriety and respectability. Nobody had arrived at the house while she was watching, and nobody had left, apart from Dr Komoti himself. He was, quite simply, rather a boring man to watch.

But there was still the question of Mafikeng and the Friday-evening dash there and back. If he had been going shopping down there then he would surely have stayed for at least part of Saturday morning, which he clearly did not. He must have done, then, whatever it was he wanted to do on Friday evening. Was there a woman down there? That would be the most likely explanation. But why the hurry back on Saturday morning? There was something that did not seem quite right, and Mma Ramotswe thought that she might follow him down to Mafikeng next weekend, if he went, and see what happened. If there was nothing to be seen, then she could do some shopping and return on Saturday afternoon. She had been meaning to make the trip anyway, and she might as well kill two birds with one stone.

DR KOMOTI proved obliging. The following Friday he left the hospital on time and drove off in the direction of Lobatse, followed at a distance by Mma Ramotswe in her van. Crossing the border proved tricky, as she had to make sure that she did not get too close to him at the border post, and that at the same time she did not lose him on the other side. For a few moments it looked as if she would be delayed, as a ponderous official paged closely through her passport.

'It says here, under occupation, that you are a detective,' he said in a surly tone. 'How can a woman be a detective?'

Mma Ramotswe glared at him. If she prolonged the encounter, she could lose Dr Komoti, whose passport was now being stamped.

'Many women are detectives,' said Mma Ramotswe, with dignity. 'Have you not read Agatha Christie?'

The clerk looked up at her and bristled.

'Are you saying I am not an educated man?' he growled. 'Is that what you are saying? That I have not read this Mr Christie?'

'I am not,' said Mma Ramotswe. 'You people are well educated, and efficient. Only yesterday, when I was in your minister's house, I said to him that I thought his immigration people were very polite and efficient. We had a good talk about it over supper.'

The official froze. For a moment he looked uncertain, but then he reached for his rubber stamp and stamped the passport.

'Thank you, mma,' he said. 'You may go now.'

Mma Ramotswe did not like lying, but sometimes it was necessary. An embroidering of the truth like that—she knew the minister very distantly—sometimes gingered people up a bit, and it was often for their own good. Perhaps that particular official would think twice before he again decided to bully a woman for no good reason.

She climbed back into the van and was waved past the barrier. There was now no sight of Dr Komoti and she had to push the van to its utmost before she caught up with him. They had reached the outskirts of Mafikeng; a suburb of neat, well-laid-out streets and houses with large, well-fenced gardens. It was into the driveway of one of these houses that he turned, requiring Mma Ramotswe to drive past to avoid causing suspicion. She counted the number of houses she passed, though—seven—and then parked the van under a tree.

There was what used to be called a sanitary lane which ran down the back of the houses. Mma Ramotswe left the van and walked to the end of the sanitary lane. The house that Dr Komoti entered would be eight houses up—seven, and the one she had had to walk past to get to the entrance of the lane.

She stood in the sanitary lane at the back of the eighth house and peered through the garden. Somebody had once cared for it, but that must have been years ago. Now it was a tangle of vegetation—mulberry trees, uncontrolled bougainvillea bushes that had grown to giant proportions, papaw trees with rotting fruit on the stem. It would be a paradise for snakes, she thought; there could be mambas lurking in the uncut grass and boomslangs draped over the branches of the trees, all of them lying in wait for somebody like her to be foolish enough to enter.

Mma Ramotswe pushed the gate open gingerly and the hinge squeaked badly. She moved forward, placing each foot carefully and expecting at any moment to hear a hiss from a protesting snake. But nothing moved, and she was soon crouching under a mulberry tree as close as she dared to get to the house. She had a good view of the back door and the open kitchen window; yet she could not see into the house itself, as it was of the old colonial style, with wide eaves, which made the interior cool and dark. Now what should she do?

Suddenly a window at the back of the house opened and a man leaned out. It was Dr Komoti.

'You! You over there! Yes, you, fat lady! What are you doing sitting under our mulberry tree?'

Mma Ramotswe experienced a sudden, absurd urge to look over her shoulder, as if to imply that there was somebody else under the tree. She felt like a schoolgirl caught stealing fruit or doing some other forbidden act. There was nothing one could say; one just had to own up. She stood up and stepped out from the shade.

'It is hot,' she called out. 'Can you give me a drink of water?'

The window closed and a moment or two later the kitchen door opened. Dr Komoti stood on the step wearing, she noticed, quite different clothes from those he had on when he left Gaborone. He had a mug of water in his hand, which he gave to her. Mma Ramotswe drank the water gratefully. She was, in fact, thirsty, and the water was welcome, although she noticed that the mug was dirty.

'What are you doing in our garden?' said Dr Komoti, not unkindly. 'Are you a thief?'

Mma Ramotswe looked pained. 'I am not,' she said.

Dr Komoti looked at her coolly. 'Well, then, if you are not a thief, what do you want? Are you looking for work? If so, we already have a woman who comes to cook in this house. We do not need anybody.'

Mma Ramotswe was about to reply when somebody appeared behind Dr Komoti and looked out over his shoulder. It was Dr Komoti.

'What's going on?' said the second Dr Komoti. 'What does this woman want?'

'I saw her in the garden,' said the first Dr Komoti. 'She tells me she isn't a thief.'

'And I most certainly am not,' she said indignantly. 'I was looking at this house.'

The two men looked puzzled.

'Why?' one of them asked. 'Why would you want to look at this house? There's nothing special about it, and it's not for sale anyway.'

Mma Ramotswe laughed. 'Oh, I'm not here to buy it,' she said. 'It's just that I used to live here when I was a little girl. There were Boers living in it then, a Mr van der Heever and his wife. My mother was their cook, you see, and we lived in the servants' quarters at the end of the garden. My father kept the garden tidy . . .' She broke off, and looked at the two men in reproach. 'It was better in those days,' she said. 'The garden was well looked after.'

'Oh, I'm sure it was,' said one of the two. 'We'd like to get it under control one day. It's just that we're busy men. We're both doctors, you see, and we have to spend all our time in the hospital.'

'Ah!' said Mma Ramotswe, trying to sound reverential. 'You are doctors here at the hospital?'

'No,' said the first Dr Komoti. 'I have a surgery down near the railway station. My brother . . .'

'I work up that way,' said the other Dr Komoti, pointing vaguely to the north. 'Anyway, you can look at the garden as much as you like, mother. You just go ahead. We can make you a mug of tea.'

'Ow!' said Mma Ramotswe. 'You are very kind. Thank you.'

IT WAS A RELIEF to get away from that garden, with its sinister undergrowth and its air of neglect. For a few minutes, Mma Ramotswe pretended to inspect the trees and the shrubs and then, thanking her hosts for the tea, she walked off down the road. Her mind busily turned over the curious information she had obtained. There were two Dr Komotis, which was nothing terribly unusual in itself; yet somehow she felt that this was the essence of the whole matter. There was no reason, of course, why there should not be twins who both went to medical school—twins often led mirrored lives. But there was something significant here, and Mma Ramotswe was sure that it was staring her in the face, if only she could begin to see it.

She got into the tiny white van and drove towards the centre of town. One Dr Komoti had said that he had a surgery in town, near the railway station, and she decided to take a look at this.

She knew the railway station slightly. It reminded her of the old Africa, the days of uncomfortable companionship on crowded trains, of slow journeys across great plains, of the sugar cane you used to eat to while away the time.

She stopped the white van outside the railway station and got out. There were a lot of people about; women selling roasted maize cobs and sweet drinks; men talking loudly to their friends; a family, travelling, with cardboard suitcases and possessions bundled up in a blanket.

She approached one of the women traders and spoke to her in Setswana.

'Are you well today, mma?' she said politely.

'I am well, and you are well too, mma?'

'I am well, and I have slept very well.'

'Good.'

The greeting over, she said, 'People tell me that there is a doctor here who is very good. They call him Dr Komoti. Do you know where his place is?'

The woman nodded. 'His place is over there, do you see, where that white man has just parked his truck. That's where he is.'

Mma Ramotswe thanked her informant and bought a cob of roasted maize. Then, tackling the cob as she walked, she crossed the dusty square to the rather dilapidated tin-roofed building where Dr Komoti's surgery was to be found.

Rather to her surprise, the door was not locked, and when she pushed it open she found a woman standing directly in front of her.

'I am sorry, the doctor isn't here, mma,' said the woman, slightly testily. 'I am the nurse. You can see the doctor on Monday afternoon.'

'Ah!' said Mma Ramotswe. 'It is a sad thing to have to tidy up on a Friday evening, when everybody else is thinking of going out.'

The nurse shrugged her shoulders. 'My boyfriend is taking me out later on. But I like to get everything ready for Monday before the weekend starts. It is better that way.'

'Far better,' Mma Ramotswe answered, thinking quickly. 'I didn't actually want to see the doctor, or not as a patient. I used to work for him, you see, when he was up in Nairobi. I was a nurse on his ward. I wanted just to say hello.'

The nurse's manner became markedly more friendly.

'I'll make you some tea, mma,' she offered. 'It is still hot outside.'

Mma Ramotswe sat down and waited for the nurse to return with the pot of tea.

'Do you know the other Dr Komoti?' she said. 'The brother?'

'Oh, yes,' said the nurse. 'We see a lot of him. He comes in here to help, you see. Two or three times a week.'

Mma Ramotswe lowered her cup, very slowly. Her heart thumped within her; she realised that she was at the heart of the matter now.

'Oh, they did that up in Nairobi too,' she said, waving her hand airily, as if these things were of little consequence. 'One helped the other. And usually the patients didn't know that they were seeing a different doctor.'

The nurse laughed. 'They do it here too,' she said. 'I'm not sure if it's quite fair on the patients, but nobody has realised that there are two of them. So everybody seems quite satisfied.'

Mma Ramotswe picked up her cup again and passed it for refilling. 'And what about you?' she said. 'Can you tell them apart?'

The nurse handed the teacup back to Mma Ramotswe. 'I can tell by one thing,' she said. 'One of them is quite good—the other's hopeless. The hopeless one knows hardly anything about medicine. If you ask me, it's a miracle that he got through medical school.'

Mma Ramotswe thought, but did not say: He didn't.

SHE STAYED IN MAFIKENG that night, at the Station Hotel, which was noisy and uncomfortable, but she slept well nonetheless, as she always did when she had just finished an enquiry. The next morning she shopped at the OK Bazaars and found, to her delight, that there was a rail of size 22 dresses on special offer. She bought three—two more than she really needed—but if you were the owner of the No.1 Ladies' Detective Agency you had to keep up a certain style.

She was home by three o'clock that afternoon and she telephoned Dr Maketsi at his house and invited him to come immediately to her office. He arrived within ten minutes and sat opposite her, fiddling anxiously with the cuffs of his shirt.

'First of all,' announced Mma Ramotswe, 'no drugs.'

Dr Maketsi breathed a sigh of relief. 'Thank goodness for that,' he said. 'That's one thing I was really worried about.'

'Well,' said Mma Ramotswe doubtfully. 'I'm not sure if you're going to like what I'm going to tell you.'

'He's not qualified,' gasped Dr Maketsi. 'Is that it?'

'One of them is qualified,' said Mma Ramotswe.

Dr Maketsi looked blank. 'One of them?'

Mma Ramotswe settled back in her chair with the air of one about to reveal a mystery.

'There were once twins,' she began. 'One went to medical school and became a doctor. The other did not. The one with the qualification got a job as a doctor, but was greedy and thought that two jobs as a doctor would pay better than one. So he took two jobs and did both of them part-time. When he wasn't there, his brother, who was his identical twin, you'll recall, did the job for him. He used such medical knowledge as he had picked up from his qualified brother and no doubt also got advice from the brother as to what to do. And that's it. That's the story of Dr Komoti, and his twin brother in Mafikeng.'

Dr Maketsi sat absolutely silent. As Mma Ramotswe spoke he had sunk his head in his hands.

'So we've had both of them in the hospital,' he said at last. 'Sometimes we've had the qualified one, and sometimes we've had the twin brother.'

'Yes,' said Mma Ramotswe simply. 'For three days a week, say, you've had the qualified twin while the unqualified twin practised as a general practitioner in a surgery near Mafikeng railway station. Then they'd change about, and I assume that the qualified one would pick up any pieces that the unqualified one had left lying around, so to speak.'

'Two jobs for the price of one medical degree,' mused Dr Maketsi. 'It's the most cunning scheme I've come across for a long, long time.' He rubbed his chin. 'I'll have to go to the police about this,' he said. 'There's going to have to be a prosecution. We have to protect the public from people like this.'

'Unless . . .' started Mma Ramotswe.

Dr Maketsi grabbed at the straw he suspected she might be offering.

'Can you think of an alternative?' he asked. 'Once this gets out, people will take fright. Our public health programmes rely on trust—you know how it is.'

'Precisely,' said Mma Ramotswe. 'I suggest that we transfer the heat elsewhere. I agree with you: the public has to be protected and Dr Komoti is going to have to be struck off, or whatever you people do. But why not get this done in somebody else's patch?'

'Do you mean in Mafikeng?'

'Yes,' said Mma Ramotswe. 'After all, an offence is being committed down there and we can let the South Africans deal with it. The papers up here in Gaborone probably won't even pick up on it. All that people here will know is that Dr Komoti resigned suddenly, which people often do—for all sorts of reasons.'

'Well,' said Dr Maketsi, 'I would rather like to keep the minister's nose out of all this. I don't think it would help if he became . . . how shall we put it, upset?'

'Of course it wouldn't help,' said Mma Ramotswe. 'With your permission I shall telephone my friend Billy Pilani, who's a police captain down there. He'd love to be seen to expose a bogus doctor. Billy likes a good, sensational arrest.'

'You do that,' said Dr Maketsi, smiling. This was a tidy solution to a most extraordinary matter, and he was most impressed with the way in which Mma Ramotswe had handled it.

'You know,' he said, 'I don't think that even my aunt in Mochudi could have dealt with this any better than you have.'

Mma Ramotswe smiled at her old friend. You can go through life and make new friends but there was never any substitute for those friendships of childhood that survive into adult years. Those are the ones in which we are bound to one another with hoops of steel.

She reached out and touched Dr Maketsi on the arm, gently, as old friends will sometimes do when they have nothing more to say.

The Witch Doctor's Wife

A dusty track, hardly in use, enough to break the springs; a hill, a tumble of boulders, just as the sketch map drawn by Mr Charlie Gotso had predicted; and above, stretching from horizon to horizon, the empty sky, singing in the heat of noon.

Mma Ramotswe steered the tiny white van cautiously, avoiding the rocks that could tear the sump from the car. This was dead country; no cattle, no goats; only the bush and the stunted thorn trees. That anybody should want to live here, away from a village, away from human contact, seemed inexplicable. Dead country.

Suddenly she saw the house, tucked away behind the trees, almost in the shadow of the hill. It was a bare earth house in the traditional style: brown mud walls, a few glassless windows, with a knee-height wall round the yard.

She parked the van and drew in her breath. She had faced down fraudsters; she had coped with jealous wives; she had even stood up to Mr Gotso; but this meeting would be different. This was evil incarnate, the heart of darkness, the root of shame. This man, for all his mumbo jumbo and his spells, was a murderer.

She opened the door and eased herself out of the van. The sun was riding high and its light prickled at her skin. They were too far west here, too close to the Kalahari, and her unease increased. This was not the comforting land she had grown up with; this was the merciless Africa, the waterless land.

She made her way towards the house, and as she did so she felt that she was being watched. There was no movement, but eyes were upon her, eyes from within the house. At the wall, in accordance with custom, she stopped and called out, announcing herself.

'I am very hot,' she said. 'I need water.'

There was no reply from within the house, but a rustle to her left, among the bushes. She turned round, almost guiltily, and stared. It was a large black beetle, a setotojane, with its horny neck, pushing at a minute trophy, some insect that had died of thirst perhaps. Little disasters, little victories; like ours, she thought. When viewed from above we are no more than setotojane.

'Mma?'

She turned round sharply. A woman was standing in the doorway, wiping her hands on a cloth.

Mma Ramotswe stepped through the gateless break in the wall.

'*Dumela, mma*,' she said. 'I am Mma Ramotswe.'

The woman nodded. 'Eee. I am Mma Notshi.'

Mma Ramotswe studied her. She was a woman in her late fifties, or thereabouts, wearing a long skirt of the sort that the Herero women wore; but she was not Herero—she could tell.

'I have come to see your husband,' she said.

The woman came out from the shadows and stood before Mma Ramotswe, peering at her face in a disconcerting way.

'You want to buy something?'

Mma Ramotswe nodded. 'I have heard that he is a very good doctor. I have trouble with another woman. She is taking my husband from me and I want something that will stop her.'

The older woman smiled. 'He can help you. Maybe he has something. But he is away. He is in Lobatse until Saturday. You will have to come back some time after that.'

Mma Ramotswe sighed. 'This has been a long trip, and I am thirsty. Do you have water, my sister?'

'Yes, I have water. You can sit in the house while you drink it.'

IT WAS A SMALL ROOM, furnished with a rickety table and two chairs. Mma Ramotswe sat on one of the chairs while the woman fetched a white enamel mug of water, which she gave to her visitor. The water was slightly rancid, but Mma Ramotswe drank it gratefully.

Then she put the mug down and looked at the woman.

'I have come for something, as you know. But I have also come to warn you of something.'

The woman lowered herself onto the other chair.

'To warn me?'

'Yes,' said Mma Ramotswe. 'I am a typist. I work for the police and I have typed out something about your husband. They know that he killed that boy, the one from Katsana. They know that he is the man who took him and killed him for muti. They are going to arrest your husband soon and then they will hang him. I came to warn you that they will hang you also, because they say that you are involved in it too. I do not think they should hang women. So I came to tell you that you could stop all this quickly if you came with me to the police and told them what happened. They will believe you and you will be saved. Otherwise, you will die very soon. Next month, I think.'

She stopped. The other woman had dropped the cloth she had been carrying and was staring at her, wide-eyed.

'Do you understand what I have said to you?' she asked.

The witch doctor's wife closed her eyes. 'I did not kill that boy.'

'I know,' said Mma Ramotswe. 'It is never the women who do it. But that doesn't make any difference to the police. They have evidence against you and the Government wants to hang you too. Your husband first; you later. They do not like witchcraft. They are ashamed. They think it's not modern.'

'But the boy is not dead,' blurted out the woman. 'He is at the cattle post where my husband took him. He is working there. He is alive.'

Mma Ramotswe opened the door for the woman and slammed it shut behind her. Then she went round to the driver's door, opened it, and eased herself into the seat. The sun had made it burning hot but pain did not matter now. All that mattered was to make the journey, which the woman said would take four hours. It was now one o'clock. They would be there just before sunset and they could start the journey back immediately. If they had to stop overnight because the track was too bad, well, they could sleep in the back of the van. The important thing was to get to the boy.

The journey was made in silence. The other woman tried to talk, but Mma Ramotswe ignored her. There was nothing she could say to this woman; nothing she wanted to say to her.

'You are not a kind woman,' said the witch doctor's wife finally.

'You are not talking to me. I am trying to talk to you, but you ignore me. You think that you are better than me, don't you?'

Mma Ramotswe half turned to her. 'The only reason why you are showing me where this boy is is because you are afraid. You are not doing it because you want him to go back to his parents. You are a wicked woman and I am warning you that if the police hear that you and your husband practise any more witchcraft, they will come and take you to prison. And if they don't, I have friends in Gaborone who will come and do it for them. Do you understand what I am saying?'

The hours passed. It was a difficult journey, out across open veld, on the barest of tracks, until there, in the distance, they saw cattle stockades and the cluster of trees around a couple of huts.

'This is the cattle post,' said the woman. 'There are two Basarwa there, a man and a woman, and the boy who has been working for them.'

'How did you keep him?' asked Mma Ramotswe. 'How did you know that he would not run away?'

'Look around you,' said the woman. 'You see how lonely this place is. The Basarwa would catch him before he could get far.'

Something else occurred to Mma Ramotswe. The bone—if the boy was still alive, then where did the bone come from?

'There is a man in Gaborone who bought a bone from your husband,' she said. 'Where did you get that?'

The woman looked at her scornfully. 'You can buy bones in Johannesburg. Did you not know that? They are not expensive.'

THE BASARWA were eating a rough porridge, seated on two stones outside one of the huts. They were tiny, wizened people, with the wide eyes of the hunter, and they stared at the intruders. Then the man rose to his feet and saluted the witch doctor's wife.

'Are the cattle all right?' she asked sharply.

The man made a strange, clicking noise with his tongue. 'All right. They are not dead. That cow there is making much milk.'

The words were Setswana words, but one had to strain to understand them. This was a man who spoke in the clicks and whistles of the Kalahari.

'Where is the boy?' snapped the woman.

'That side,' replied the man. 'Look.'

And then they saw the boy, standing beside a bush, watching them uncertainly. A dusty little boy, in torn shorts, with a stick in his hand.

'Come here,' called the witch doctor's wife. 'Come here.'

The boy walked over to them, his eyes fixed on the ground in front of him. He had a scar on his forearm, a thick weal, and Mma Ramotswe knew immediately what had caused it. That was the cut of a whip, a sjambok. She reached forward and laid a hand on his shoulder.

'What is your name?' she asked gently. 'Are you the teacher's son from Katsana village?'

The boy shivered, but he saw the concern in her eyes and he spoke.

'I am that boy. I am working here now. These people are making me look after the cattle.'

'And did this man strike you?' whispered Mma Ramotswe. 'Did he?'

'All the time,' said the boy. 'He said that if I ran away he would find me in the bush and put a sharpened stick through me.'

'You are safe now,' said Mma Ramotswe. 'You are coming with me. Right now. Just walk in front of me. I will look after you.'

The boy glanced at the Basarwa and began to move towards the van.

'Go on,' said Mma Ramotswe. 'I am coming too.'

She put him in the passenger seat and closed the door. The witch doctor's wife called out.

'Wait a few minutes. I want to talk to these people about the cattle. Then we can go.'

Mma Ramotswe walked to the driver's door and let herself in.

'Wait,' called the woman. 'I am not going to be long.'

Mma Ramotswe leaned forward and started the engine. Then, slipping the van into gear, she spun the wheel and pressed her foot on the accelerator. The woman shouted out and began to run after the van, but the dust cloud soon obscured her and she tripped and fell.

Mma Ramotswe turned to the boy, who was looking frightened and confused beside her.

'I am taking you home now,' she said. 'It will be a long journey and I think we shall have to stop for the night quite soon. But we will set off again in the morning and then it should not be too long.'

She stopped the van an hour later, beside a dry riverbed. They were completely alone, with not even a fire from a remote cattle post to break the darkness of the night. Only the starlight fell on them, an attenuated, silver light, falling on the sleeping figure of the boy, wrapped in a sack that she had in the back of the van, his head upon her arm, his breathing regular, his hand resting gently in hers; and Mma Ramotswe herself, whose eyes were open, looked up into the night sky until the sheer immensity of it tipped her gently into sleep.

AT KATSANA village the next day, the schoolmaster looked out of the window of his house and saw a small white van draw up outside. He saw a woman get out and look at his door, and the child—what about the child—was she a parent who was bringing her child to him for some reason? He went outside and found her at the wall of his yard.

'You are the teacher, rra?'

'I am the teacher, mma. Can I do anything for you?'

She turned to the van and signalled to the child within. The door opened and his son came out. And the teacher cried out and ran, almost stumbling, to seize his son, and hold him, while he shouted wildly, incoherently, for the village and the world to hear his joy.

Mma Ramotswe walked back towards her van, not wanting to intrude upon the intimate moments of reunion. She was crying; for her own child, too—remembering the minute hand that had grasped her own, so briefly, while it tried to hold on to a strange world that was slipping away so quickly. There was so much suffering in Africa that it was tempting just to shrug your shoulders and walk away. But you can't do that, she thought. You just can't.

Mr J. L. B. Matekoni

Even a vehicle as reliable as the tiny white van, which did mile after mile without complaint, could find the dust too much. It had been uncomplaining on the trip out to the cattle post, but now, back in town, it was beginning to stutter. It was the dust, she was sure of it.

She telephoned Tlokweng Road Speedy Motors, not intending to bother Mr J. L. B. Matekoni, but the receptionist was out to lunch and he answered. She need not worry, he said. He would come round to look at the little white van the following day, a Saturday, and he might be able to fix it there on the spot, in Zebra Drive.

'I doubt it,' said Mma Ramotswe. 'It is an old van. It is like an old cow, and I will have to sell it, I suppose.'

'You won't,' said Mr J. L. B. Matekoni. 'Anything can be fixed.'

Even a heart that is broken in two pieces? he thought. Can they fix that? Could Professor Barnard down in Cape Town cure a man whose heart was bleeding, bleeding from loneliness?

MMA RAMOTSWE went shopping that morning. Her Saturday mornings had always been important to her; she went to the supermarket in the mall and bought her groceries and her vegetables from the women on the pavement outside the chemist's. After that, she went to the President Hotel and drank coffee with her friends; then home, and half a glass of Lion Beer, taken sitting out on the verandah and reading the newspaper. As a private detective, it was important to scour the newspaper and to put the facts away in one's mind. All of it was useful, down to the last line of the politicians' predictable speeches and the church notices. You never knew when some snippet of local knowledge would come in useful.

HE ARRIVED shortly after four, driving up in his blue garage bakkie with TLOKWENG ROAD SPEEDY MOTORS painted on the side. He was wearing his mechanic's overalls, which were spotlessly clean. She showed him the tiny white van, parked beside the house, and he wheeled out a large jack from the back of his truck.

'I'll make you a cup of tea,' she said. 'You can drink it while you look at the van.'

From the window she watched him as he moved backwards and forwards between his truck and the van. Two cups of tea were taken out, and then a third, as it was a hot afternoon. Then Mma Ramotswe went into her kitchen and put vegetables into a pot and watered the plants that stood on the back windowsill. Dusk was approaching, and the sky was streaked with gold. This was her favourite time of the day, when the birds went dipping and swooping through the air and the insects of the night started to shriek. In this gentle light, the cattle would be walking home and the fires outside the huts would be crackling and glowing for the evening's cooking.

She went out to see whether Mr J. L. B. Matekoni needed more light. He was standing beside the little van, wiping his hands on lint.

'That should be fine now,' he said. 'I've tuned it up and the engine runs sweetly. Like a bee.'

She clapped her hands in pleasure.

'I thought that you would have to scrap it,' she said.

He laughed. 'I told you anything could be fixed. Even an old van.'

He followed her inside. She poured him a beer and they went together to her favourite place to sit, on the verandah, near the bougainvillea. Not far away, in a neighbouring house, music was being played, the insistent traditional rhythms of township music.

The sun went, and it was dark. He sat beside her in the comfortable darkness and they listened, contentedly, to the sounds of Africa settling down for the night. A dog barked somewhere; a car engine raced and then died away; there was a touch of wind, warm dusty wind, redolent of thorn trees.

He looked at her in the darkness, at this woman who was everything to him—mother, Africa, wisdom, understanding, good things to eat, pumpkins, chicken, the smell of sweet cattle breath, the white sky across the endless, endless bush, and the giraffe that cried, giving its tears for women to daub on their baskets; O Botswana, my country, my place.

Those were his thoughts. But how could he say any of that to her? Any time he tried to tell her what was in his heart, the words that came to him seemed so inadequate. A mechanic cannot be a poet, he thought; that is not how things are. So he simply said, 'I am very happy that I fixed your van for you. I would have been sorry if somebody else had lied to you and said it was not worth fixing. There are people like that in the motor trade.'

'I know,' said Mma Ramotswe. 'But you are not like that.'

He said nothing. There were times when you simply had to speak, or you would have your lifetime ahead to regret not speaking. But every time he had tried to speak to her of what was in his heart, he had failed. He had already asked her to marry him and that had not been a great success. He did not have a great deal of confidence, at least with people; cars were different, of course.

'I am very happy sitting here with you . . .'

She turned to him. 'What did you say?'

'I said, please marry me, Mma Ramotswe. I am just Mr J. L. B. Matekoni, that's all, but please marry me and make me happy.'

'Of course I will,' said Mma Ramotswe.

ALEXANDER McCALL SMITH

At the age of fifty-five, Alexander McCall Smith has had his life turned upside-down by the phenomenal success of *The No.1 Ladies' Detective Agency* and its sequels. The hectic round of publicity tours that befalls best-selling authors has meant that he has, for example, made about a hundred flights this year. But he insists that he's not complaining. 'There's not a day that goes by now when I don't think "Heavens, my life has changed and this is amazing."'

Until 2003, when global celebrity forced him to scale down his academic work, McCall Smith was a law professor at Edinburgh University. As an expert in medical law, he has also done work for the *British Medical Journal* and UNESCO. 'My academic career was very important to me,' he reflects. 'But obviously things can happen which one hasn't anticipated.'

McCall Smith was born in Southern Rhodesia (now Zimbabwe), and educated there and in Scotland. He's been a frequent visitor to Botswana and helped to set up a school of law at the university there. 'I chose Botswana as the setting for my stories because it is a particularly interesting country, and I like to portray certain of its features—the politeness, the caution, and so on.'

While the author admits that he didn't set out to write 'an important novel', he says there's a strong moral message in the story of Mma Ramotswe. 'I think one can make very serious points about the world in a light way. If you want to get across the importance of compassion and forgiveness, you can lecture away on the subject and nobody would pay much attention, but if you can embody them in a character and in a light story, then that's much more effective.'

Apart from winning three 'author of the year' awards in 2004, McCall Smith has appeared in a BBC TV documentary and has sold film rights to Anthony Mingella. There are now five published Mma Ramotswe books, with three more still in the pipeline, and the author has just embarked on a new series of books about a divorced forty-year-old Edinburgh detective, Isabel Dalhousie, the first of which is entitled *The Sunday Philosophy Club*.

THE MURDER ARTIST. Original full-length edition © 2004 by John Case. British condensed edition © The Reader's Digest Association Limited, 2004.

START FROM HERE. Original full-length edition © 2004 by Sean French. British condensed edition © The Reader's Digest Association Limited, 2004.

AT RISK. Original full-length edition © 2004 by Stella Rimington. British condensed edition © The Reader's Digest Association Limited, 2004.

THE No.1 LADIES' DETECTIVE AGENCY. Original full-length edition © 1998 by Alexander McCall Smith. British condensed edition © The Reader's Digest Association Limited, 2004.

The right to be identified as authors has been asserted by the following in accordance with sections 77 and 78 of the Copyright, Designs and Patents Act, 1988: John Case, Sean French, Stella Rimington and Alexander McCall Smith.

ACKNOWLEDGMENTS AND PICTURE CREDITS: *The Murder Artist*: pages 6–8: photograph: Conorde Clarke; twins: Getty/Stone. *Start from Here*: pages 162–164: illustrator: Sharon Preston. *At Risk*: pages 292–294: Digital Vision; page 433: Jamie Hughes. *The No.1 Ladies' Detective Agency*: pages 434–436: illustrator: Hannah Firmin; page 539: Graham Clark.

DUSTJACKET CREDITS: Spine from top: Photograph: Conorde Clarke; twins: Getty/Stone; illustrator: Sharon Preston; Digital Vision; illustrator: Hannah Firmin.

Printed by Maury Imprimeur SA, Malesherbes, France
Bound by Reliures Brun SA, Malesherbes, France

232/04